They took the el
unusual for Ma
this. Ella grinned
she never did ar
relationship, hers ... Margot Haigh had given
Ella her first break by lending her sufficient money to
take her initial tentative steps into the property world.
To this day, Ella had wondered at the decision. Eight
years ago she had been so naïve: Margot, older, already
an experienced banker, must have known that. Still,
Margot had backed her hunch, and, thought Ella with
satisfaction, it was a decision which had proved to be
more than justified.

The elevator doors swished open. 'This way, Miss
Kovac.'

Also by Deborah Fowler in Sphere Books:

RIPPLES
REFLECTIONS
SOMETIME . . . NEVER

DEAL

Deborah Fowler

SPHERE BOOKS LIMITED

For Innes,
with love and thanks
from your wicked step-mother

SPHERE BOOKS LTD

First published in Great Britain by Michael Joseph Ltd 1989
Published by Sphere Books Limited 1991

Copyright © Shepherd's Keep Studios Ltd 1989

All characters in this publication are fictitious
and any resemblance to real persons, living or dead
is purely coincidental.

All rights reserved
No part of this publication may be reproduced,
stored in a retrieval system, or transmitted, in any
form or by any means without the prior
permission in writing of the publisher, nor be
otherwise circulated in any form of binding or
cover other than that in which it is published and
without a similar condition including this
condition being imposed on the subsequent
purchaser.

ISBN 0 7474 0473 9

Made and printed in Great Britain by
BPCC Hazell Books
Aylesbury, Bucks, England
Member of BPCC Ltd.

Sphere Books Ltd
A Division of
Macdonald & Co (Publishers) Ltd
Orbit House, 1 New Fetter Lane, London EC4A 1AR
A member of Maxwell Macmillan Pergamon Publishing Corporation

PROLOGUE

SILVER SPRINGS, KENTUCKY
July 1956

To Ella, it seemed that the world had turned upside down. Someone must have tripped her, as she had lunged forward to strike that fat, freckled face with its twisted smile, taunting and cruel. A hot, sharp pain shot up the side of her cheek where it made contact with the dirty, dusty ground. Above her she could see the clear, blue Kentucky sky and a mass of brown arms and legs. She gave a roar of frustrated anger and struck out – kicking, biting, scratching at whatever piece of flesh was within her reach. All reason had left her, she wanted to do damage, to hurt as she had been hurt. The dust cloyed at the back of her throat and made her eyes stream with tears but she felt no pain now although she knew she should. She was in a seething, scarlet world of her own.

'Stop that!' The words rang out high above the chaos around her. 'Stop that and stop it now!' The weight of bodies was suddenly lifted off her, the sunlight burned directly into her eyes, causing her to shut them tight. Strong hands gripped her arms. She struggled to be free of them the moment she was set on her feet, but she could not break away, nor could she open her eyes – they were caked with dust.

'Leave me be, leave me be,' she screamed, twisting this way and that, like a caged animal.

'You kids beat it and next time pick on someone your own size.' The calm authoritative voice was not directed at her, but it quietened Ella also. She made an attempt to rub the dust from her eyes and squinted up into a bronzed, smiling face below a thatch of white-gold hair. She knew who he was, of course, and, momentarily intimidated, she ceased to struggle.

'You're Ella Kovac, aren't you?'

She nodded, dumbly.

'My name's Aaron Connors. My Pa's the doctor,' he added unnecessarily. 'I guess we better take you along to Pa right now, you're a real mess.' He chuckled, apparently amused by the sight of her.

His laughter irritated Ella, snapping her out of her temporary inertia. 'I'm OK, I'm going home.' She tried to wrench herself from his grasp but he retained a firm grip on her arm.

Aaron studied the dirty little wretch before him – she was not badly hurt, only bruised and scratched. He understood, or thought he understood, her reluctance to see his father – there would be no money to pay for any treatment. 'OK,' he said, cheerfully, 'but I'll walk you home.'

'There's no need for that.'

'Yes, there is. I'll walk you home or I'll take you to my Pa – that's the choice.'

Without a word, Ella shrugged her thin shoulders and turning, began walking down the dusty street which led northwards out of town. Aaron walked beside her, unselfconsciously still holding on to her arm.

'How old are you?' he asked, after some minutes' silence.

'Eight,' Ella replied.

'I'm fifteen.' He could not resist the note of pride. 'Why were you fighting?' Ella did not reply. Aaron deliberately slowed his pace, forcing Ella to do the same. 'Tell me why?' he insisted.

'No matter,' Ella replied, stubbornly.

'It matters to me.'

The sincerity of his voice made Ella glance up. Their eyes met and held for a moment, and what Ella saw in his face brought a sudden rush of comfort, so unexpected and so unfamiliar that it shocked her into responding. 'They called my Ma names.'

'What names?' Aaron demanded.

'I can't say, I won't use those words.' She hesitated. 'They say she goes with men, goes to their beds, does things.'

'What do you think?' Aaron asked, gently.

Ella shrugged her shoulders. 'I guess she does some of the bad things they say, but that don't give them no right ...' Ella hesitated. 'I wish she was like other mothers.'

'Have you told her that?' Aaron asked, with interest.

'Hell no, she'd just belt me.'

'Do you have a Pa?' Aaron asked.

'No,' Ella replied, 'and I don't want one neither – Ma's enough trouble.'

Aaron laughed. He liked her, this funny little kid in her torn dirty dress. She had something, a kind of – he searched for the word – dignity. Yes, that was it – despite everything, she was not letting her circumstances drag her down.

They had reached the end of the street which had become now nothing more than a track – dirty and dusty in summer, muddy in winter. At the end of the track stood the Kovacs' wooden shack, with a few pitiful items of clothing hanging limply from a line outside.

'Say, Ella,' Aaron at last released his grip on her arm, 'things must be kind of tough for you. Look, I'll pass the word around that no one is to hurt you, right, or they'll have to answer to me. What do you say?'

Ella raised her head and met his gaze defiantly. Her huge, brown eyes regarded him in silence for a moment, the expression in them unreadable. 'I can take care of myself.'

Aaron laughed. 'Oh, sure, like you were doing just now.'

Anger washed across Ella's face. 'I've got to go.' She pushed past him and ran off on down the track towards her home without another word. Yet before she reached the shack, her pace slowed and she glanced fleetingly over her shoulder. Aaron, watching her, raised an arm in farewell. Ella hesitated, and then did the same.

CHAPTER ONE

PARIS
August 1977

Ella fumbled with the unfamiliar francs and handed the cab driver what seemed an appropriate amount. His hitherto surly face broke into a warm smile which left Ella in no doubt that she had grossly over-paid him. Still, what the hell, it was summer and she was in Paris. It was the first holiday she and Greg had ever spent together and besides which, she could afford it. She turned on her heel and surveyed the building in front of her. JOSHKERS BANK: their trademark of gold lettering on marble was instantly reassuring, a home from home. It would be good to be on familiar ground. For as long as she could remember, Ella had longed for a trip to Europe, to Paris in particular, but she found her inability to cope with the language oddly nerve-racking. Communication had never been a problem for Ella – in fact her ability to establish a good dialogue with just about everyone was probably one of her greatest assets. Now, as she struggled to understand what was being said to her, she felt as though she had lost her right arm. Not for the first time she cursed the fact that her formal education had finished at twelve, and certainly French had been no part of it.

'Good morning, Madam.' The doorman clearly did not mistake her for a French woman for a moment.

With a sigh of relief, Ella stepped into Joshkers' elaborate marbled banking hall, identical in style here in Paris to their branches in New York, Washington and London. She started towards the enquiry desk, when a dark young man in a neat grey suit stepped forward to greet her. 'Miss Kovac?'

'Yes,' said Ella.

'If you'd like to come this way, Miss Kovac, Miss Haigh is expecting you. Did you have a good flight?' The American accent, although slight, was music to her ears.

'Yes, it was fine,' said Ella, 'although I've been in France for over a week now. My son and I have been in Provence.'

'Oh, I'm sorry, I didn't realize. Did you have a good time?'

'Great, thanks,' said Ella.

They took the elevator in silence to the fifth floor. It was unusual for Margot to have someone to greet her like this. Ella grinned. Clearly Margot wanted something for she never did anything without a reason. It was an odd relationship, hers and Margot's. Margot Haigh had given Ella her first break by lending her sufficient money to take her initial tentative steps into the property world. To this day, Ella had wondered at the decision. Eight years ago she had been so naïve: Margot, older, already an experienced banker, must have known that. Still, Margot had backed her hunch, and, thought Ella with satisfaction, it was a decision which had proved to be more than justified.

The elevator doors swished open. 'This way, Miss Kovac.'

For a moment the room, luxurious to a point of ostentation, held all Ella's attention. The main feature was an enormous chandelier, lavish drapes hung at the windows and the conference table, following Joshkers' tradition, was a marble oval of vast dimensions. Her absorption with the room and its splendours, however, was quickly diverted by the two women who rose to their feet as she entered the room. Margot — tall, elegant, with her distinctive sleek auburn hair — came forward to greet her and planted a cool kiss on her cheek.

'Ella, welcome to Paris, how lovely to see you. I'd like you to meet Lady Stephanie Bonham. Stephanie, this is Ella Kovac.'

The two women shook hands warmly enough but immediately Ella felt on edge — wary, almost uneasy. It was not just her title: one look at Stephanie Bonham was enough to see she was a force to be reckoned with. Tall, slim, dressed casually in a cool summer dress, she had a natural confidence, an air of authority – that distinct, very individual prerogative of the English upper classes. Ella noted her pale blonde hair, her perfect English complexion and her small, heart-shaped face. Stephanie Bonham looked as though she had just stepped out of the pages of Harpers & Queen. Only her eyes were different – only her eyes showed she was not some empty-headed debutante living off her parents' wealth and status. They were a deep blue, piercing, calculating and even now, Ella was aware, scrutinizing her thoroughly.

'I'm sorry I'm late,' Ella found herself saying. 'It was difficult to find my son something to do while I was away. His French isn't good enough to get much out of TV.'

'How old is he now, Ella, I've lost track of time?' Extraordinarily, Margot was making small talk. Having no children of her own, she never normally asked Ella about her son.

'He's thirteen, an awkward age for him and me – I never know whether to treat him like a kid or a man. When we are out in the streets, he can't keep his eyes off the girls, particularly here in Paris. Yet back home or in our hotel room, he still wants to play kid's games. It's a tough time.'

'Stephanie has children, too,' Margot said, almost ingratiating.

'Oh, do you?' said Ella. 'How many?'

'Two girls,' said Stephanie, 'but I keep them well away from my business.'

The implied criticism rankled. 'Me, too,' said Ella, defensively, 'but I'm not on business at the moment, I'm here in France for a holiday.'

'At least you thought you were,' said Margot, smiling, 'which brings me to the purpose of this meeting. I suppose you're both wondering why I wanted to see you so urgently.'

'Intrigued certainly, speaking for myself,' said Stephanie. She leaned back in her chair, cool and poised. Ella envied her.

'I should perhaps begin by explaining my role in both your lives,' said Margot, 'and in the process introduce you, in a commercial sense, to one another. Through the offices of

Joshkers bank, I have helped you both with your businesses for approximately the same amount of time. I have known Stephanie slightly longer, nine years to be precise, and you, Ella, for eight. Whereas I was in on the ground floor with Ella, Stephanie was already in business when we were introduced. You are both in property and in many ways your activities are not dissimilar, except in two major respects. Firstly, you operate on different sides of the Atlantic – Ella in the States, Stephanie in Britain – and secondly, while Ella concentrates her interests on apartments and office blocks, Stephanie is into hotels and leisure centres.'

Ella and Stephanie regarded one another with sudden interest. Up to this moment, neither had ever met another woman in property, at least not on the kind of scale they had established for themselves. Whereas a moment before there had been slight antagonism, now there was a mutual quickening of interest, a bond almost. Their areas of interest might be different, but instinctively each knew what the other must have come through to be sitting here, in the boardroom of Joshkers bank, at the invitation of Margot Haigh, Director of Corporate Finance.

'OK,' Margot was saying, 'are you with me so far?' Both women nodded. 'The reason for inviting you here today is because a unique and exciting project has landed up on my desk. I have spent a couple of days searching my mind for someone suitable to handle it, and the conclusion I came to is that it's a venture which needs two talents, not one, for it incorporates both leisure interests and the requirement for offices and apartments.'

Ella frowned slightly. 'You're suggesting that Lady Bonham and I join forces in some way?'

'Hear me out,' said Margot. 'About five years ago, a project began to be put together, here in Paris, to create an enormous complex on the south bank of the Seine, just east of the Eiffel Tower. It was the brainchild of the enfant terrible of the French architectural world, a brilliant young man called Gaston Balois. You may have heard of him, perhaps, Stephanie?'

'Yes, I have,' said Stephanie, 'in fact I've met him once – very charming, very chic.' She raised an eyebrow and laughed, suddenly looking young and girlish. Ella found herself smiling back.

'The idea of the complex – which incidentally is known as the Centre des Arts – is to provide a playground for people of taste, coupled with living and working accommodation for people with both taste and money.' Margot leaned forward in her chair and began doodling earnestly on the pad in front of her. If both women had not known her so well, they might have been surprised by the gesture, but endless discussions over many deals had taught them that this little eccentricity meant Margot was starting to talk serious business. 'Currently the complex has been granted all the necessary permissions and licences. It's a wonderful design, incorporating a yacht basin, parades of shops, cafés, restaurants, a luxury hotel, a theatre, an art gallery, a library and, of course, the offices and apartments. The whole scheme is ready to go, and all that is needed now is for somebody to fire a starting pistol and set the builders to work. The trouble is, it's not going to happen.'

'Why?' Stephanie asked.

'The principal moneybags behind the whole scheme is an Englishman named Ronald Slater. He has a first class reputation for successful investment in all sorts of schemes, not necessarily connected with property, and is much respected in the City generally. Neither of you will have heard of him because he tends to play a low profile, but as far as the banks are concerned, Ronald Slater's good for whatever he needs. The trouble is, in the case of the Centre des Arts, he's made the first mistake of his career.'

'Clever old Ronald,' said Stephanie, sagely. 'Oh, that I could have been so lucky as to have only made one mistake.' She glanced at Ella for sympathy and was rewarded with a smile.

Margot, now totally caught up in the project she was describing, ignored them both. 'The problem is Ronald Slater is gay and so is Gaston Balois. Ronald is in his fifties and has quite literally fallen in love with the young Frenchman, with the result that for once his impeccable judgement has been impaired. It has taken far too long to put the scheme together, Gaston has been given enough rope to hang himself, and although the fundamental design is excellent, the whole project is unworkable.'

'But why?' asked Ella.

'It's simply not commercial enough,' Margot replied. 'Gaston, in his enthusiasm, has provided vast areas of public amenity which produce absolutely no revenue. There is an enormous gallery for unknown artists to display their works, reading rooms, the library, a music room for young artists to serenade the public ... yes, it's all wonderful stuff but the cost of the project is just too great to be that philanthropic.'

'So,' said Stephanie, 'Gaston will just have to change his ideas.'

'That's it,' said Margot, 'he won't. He's thrown a complete artistic fit and Ronald, poor besotted fool, is backing him to the hilt. The situation is further aggravated by the fact that the multi-national corporation, which was going to invest in the majority of the office space, has pulled out. So far as Ronald's bank is concerned, it's the final straw and they're withdrawing their support.'

'Wow', said Ella, 'poor old Ronald.'

'Yes indeed,' Margot agreed.

Stephanie stood up and wandered over to the window. 'So let me get this straight, Margot. You're suggesting that Ella and I take over this project?'

'Yes, I am,' said Margot. 'Your unique experience, in two different fields, makes you the obvious candidates. It's an enormously prestigious job, it would absolutely make your reputations world-wide and it's well within both your capabilities. So far as financing the operation is concerned, it goes without saying that Joshkers would be prepared to back you, or I wouldn't be putting the proposal to you at all.'

'How much?' Ella asked.

Margot side-stepped the question. 'It depends whether we take over the existing mortgages, keep Gaston on the job or fire him, and, of course, how radically you wish to change the design. I have all the existing figures for you, the plans and a positive fleet of lawyers and architects available to discuss the project with you. What's vital is that if the idea appeals to you both, you have to move fast. No one outside these four walls knows as yet that Ronald's support is being withdrawn, and that includes Ronald.'

'Jesus!' said Ella.

'What I am offering you is first bite of the cherry. What you also have on your side is the fact that it's August and there's no self-respecting Frenchman left in Paris. I suspect that the authorities would like the project to go to a French company so by the time everyone returns from their holidays, I would like to have the deal stitched up. To use the vernacular, it will be a *fait accompli*, and the authorities will just have to lump it.' She smiled triumphantly, pushing back her great curtain of auburn hair.

Stephanie looked across the room to Ella. 'Well, I suppose we'd be foolish not to look at it.'

'Guess so,' said Ella, 'though I'm not sure it's really for me.'

'How can you say that,' said Margot, 'it's tailor-made for you, and just imagine what it will do for your prestige in New York. Ella Kovac – developer of the Centre des Arts, Paris. It'll knock them cold.'

'I guess you're right,' said Ella, 'and certainly I would be crazy not to take a look at it, but I do have reservations.'

'Like what?' said Stephanie.

'Logistically,' said Ella, looking at Stephanie. 'You're based in London, right?' Stephanie nodded. 'So, great, an hour's hop and you're here in Paris. For me it's a completely different ball game. Then, of course, there's the question of Laurie, I don't know how he'll feel about it.'

'Laurie, who's Laurie?' Stephanie asked, 'another of your children?' Her voice was heavy with irony.

'No,' Ella said, vehemently. 'Laurie Merman is vice-president of my corporation and has a small stake in the business.'

'How awful,' said Stephanie. 'I couldn't bear to defer to

anyone on a business decision. My husband Tim's a co-director of my company but in name only. I certainly don't have to ask his permission to do anything.'

'Laurie doesn't interfere,' said Ella, defensively.

'Laurie's no problem,' Margot cut in. 'I've already spoken to him about the project – not in detail, of course – but he says it's fine with him. In fact he said he'd be very happy to keep a watching brief on New York so that you can spend more time over here.'

For a highly intelligent woman, Margot had all the sensitivity of a bull elephant, thought Ella, angrily. So, Margot had introduced her to Laurie all those years ago, and without them both she certainly would not be in business today. She was well aware of the debt she owed them, but why did Margot always have to rub her nose in the fact by highlighting her easy access to Laurie, and her apparent right to discuss all Ella's affairs with him, direct?

'Alright,' Ella said, sullenly, 'so where do we go from here?'

'You're both staying at the Meyer hotel, I understand, so I've taken the precaution of booking a boardroom for you and I would suggest you spend the next few days looking at the plans and discussing them together. You're going to have to rework the whole internal design structure if it's to pay, but between you, I would have thought that presented no problem. When you have satisfied yourselves as to the viability of the project – and I'm sure you will – then I suggest the three of us meet and talk again.'

'I'm on holiday,' Ella said, 'and there's no-one to look after Greg. I suppose I can give you to the weekend, but no more.'

'That won't be long enough,' said Margot. 'It's not simply a question of coming to grips with the details of the project, you need to get to know one another. If this scheme is to work, it is imperative that you like and respect one another and feel confident that you can work well together.'

'I tell you what, Ella,' said Stephanie, 'let's spend the next two days here, tramping the site and getting a feel as to the contribution the Centre des Arts could make to Paris. Once we've done that, we don't need to do our thinking in Paris, particularly in August. What I suggest is that you and your son come to England and stay with us in Gloucestershire. I'm sure Greg will get on with my children, they're only a couple of years younger than him, and my husband's marvellous with children. He'll look after them while we discuss business.'

'I hadn't planned to come to England,' said Ella, defensively.

'That is an appalling omission,' said Margot, 'of course you must accept Stephanie's offer. She has the most wonderful house in the depths of the country, you'll love it, and so will Greg. There's a farm and horses – after New York the boy will think he's in paradise.'

She was right, of course, Ella knew. Greg had never really enjoyed city life. 'Alright,' she said, 'why not. We can spend tomorrow and Friday in Paris, and then, if it's really OK, Stephanie, Greg and I would love to accept your invitation.'

'Well,' said Margot, leaping to her feet and striding across the room, 'I think this calls for a celebration, don't you?' A little mahogany cupboard concealed a fridge, from which Margot produced a bottle of champagne. She popped the cork and filled three glasses to the brim. She raised her glass. 'It seems to me the only toast appropriate is the Centre des Arts.'

'And perhaps a new partnership?' Stephanie looked enquiringly at Ella.

'Why not?' said Ella. 'I'll drink to that.'

CHAPTER TWO

PARIS
August 1977

Ella surveyed herself in front of the long mirror in her hotel bedroom. Twenty-nine – her age came as no surprise to her. The long, hard years of her youth had passed slowly and Ella felt every inch of twenty-nine though she knew she did not look it. Her hair was cut very short into tight, dark curls; her face, cherubic, like a choirboy's, was dominated by huge brown eyes which stared back at her now, balefully. She was not beautiful; pretty, yes. Vibrant, intelligent and, despite the circumstances of her life and the passage of years, there was an innocent quality about her looks which had enabled her to conclude many a sharp business deal, leaving behind a trail of bemused victims who had rated her little more than a child. No, her face was alright, it was her height which let her down. At barely five foot it was difficult to be taken seriously, particularly in a man's world. Two days with Stephanie Bonham had only tended to highlight for Ella the advantages of being a tall and elegant woman. Still, the light tan she had acquired suited her and the cream silk suit that she had bought in the Champs-Elysées the day before more than did her justice, as well it might, bearing in mind the cost. The telephone by her bed interrupted her thoughts. She walked over and picked up the receiver, watching her reflection as she did so. At least she was slim – the years of malnutrition had seen to that.

'Ella?'

Ella recognized Laurie Merman's gruff voice and felt the

usual rush of warm affection at the sound. 'Hi, Laurie. How are you?'

'OK, Sweetheart. How's Gay Paris?'

'Fine, fine, though I'm missing you, of course.' She kept her voice neutral, not knowing whether he was at home or in the office.

'Great. And how's the Big Boy?'

'Ogling girls,' Ella said, laughing. 'I don't know where my baby's gone.'

'No man worth his salt can start admiring beautiful women too soon, or stop either until he's nailed in his wooden box,' said Laurie, sagely. He was in the office.

'So,' said Ella, 'is this a social call?'

'Not exactly. I'm interfering.'

'What's new?' said Ella.

'I heard a buzz, a snatch of conversation in the café today. Two guys from ADC Engineering having lunch. Ring any bells with you?'

Ella dragged her tired mind away from Centre des Arts to consider her New York properties. 'ADC Engineering ... aren't they the guys who are taking over the ninth and tenth floors of that new property on Park?'

'Precisely, there's my girl, always got a finger on the pulse.'

'So, what's the problem?' said Ella.

'The lease is drawn up all wrong. There's been a mistake somewhere. The rent's been fixed at less than fifty per cent of what you originally quoted them, and they were out to lunch to celebrate. They've signed up, apparently, so I guess there's nothing you can do except kick Henry's ass all over town. I assume it was Henry's fault.'

'Shit,' said Ella, 'I don't believe this! That lease is for fifteen years!'

'I know, I know, you're going to lose your shirt unless you can wriggle your way out of it.'

'I doubt that,' said Ella. 'If Henry entered the wrong figures and they've signed, it's legal and binding. How could that idiot have made such a mistake? Thanks, Laurie, I'll call him right away.'

'No, you won't,' said Laurie, 'I called because I thought you should know what's going on, but leave me to fix the mess for you. I'll call the lawyers, get Henry over here with a copy of the lease and see if I can't persuade ADC to play the white knight. It's worth a try.'

'Bless you, Laurie. It just goes to show, it doesn't pay to have a holiday.'

'Rubbish. You deserved this holiday, Sweetheart, you and Greg. You have fun now, the business will keep.'

'I love you, Laurie,' said Ella.

'I love you, too, Little Girl. Hey, how's this deal Margot's cooked up, any good?'

'I don't know yet,' said Ella, 'but I rather think so. I gather she's already spoken to you about it.'

'Yeh, and I thought she was a bit pushy. Take the advice of an old sinner, keep a cool head on this one. Margot's real keen to do the deal for some reason, too keen. Either there has to be a catch or there's something in it for her. Oh shit, there's the other phone. Bye, Sweetheart. See you in a couple of weeks.'

Ella put down the phone thoughtfully and as she did so, the door to her suite burst open. 'Hi, Mom. Hey, you look great, real neat. Give us a twirl.'

Ella laughed and obliged, then put her hands up on his broad shoulders and kissed her son. It was hardly surprising that most people mistook them for brother and sister. Greg had inherited his mother's dark brown curly hair but in all other respects he was quite different – tall for his age and powerfully built, with an open, freckled face and a strong jaw. He would be a handsome man, and he already looked older than his years. 'Greg, I'm sorry, this must have been a miserable couple of days for you.'

'It's been OK, Mom, in fact today was great.' While Ella and Stephanie had been pouring over designs and figures, Ella had sent Greg on a series of excursions round Paris. Today had been a river trip.

'I'm glad. So you saw all the sights?'

'Yeh, a few and I got to meet a really neat family. They're

American and they have a son, Stephen, a couple of months older than me. They're staying at the Astoria and they've asked me over for dinner tonight. It's OK, isn't it?' Ella looked sceptical. 'Mom, they're a thoroughly respectable American family from Washington. He's something to do with the Senate. They're obviously stinking rich and they just want me to have dinner with them. Stephen says it's a really great hotel.'

'I don't like you wandering all over Paris on your own,' said Ella.

'Look, I'll take a cab from here to the hotel and one back again, I promise.'

'OK, OK. I'm too protective, right?'

'Yep,' said Greg, without rancour, 'but I guess you could be worse. Hey, what's the time?'

'A little after seven.'

'Jesus, I'm supposed to be there in twenty minutes. I'd better go and change.'

'Have you money for the cab?'

'Yes, Ma'am,' said Greg, with a mock salute at the door. 'Just relax, OK. You have fun with your old drawing board and think of me being wined and dined at the Astoria.'

'I want you back here by ten-thirty,' said Ella.

'Oh, Mom!'

'OK, eleven, but come and see me before you go to bed so I know you're back safe.'

'Mothers!' Greg raised his eyes to heaven, dashed across the room and slammed the door behind him.

Ella was left grinning foolishly. How she loved him and how lucky she was. He was such a friend — kind, loving, clever at school, good at games, popular with his peers — yet with the start he'd had, they'd both had, he could have been such a mess. Still, he would never know the circumstances of his birth and what he didn't know, couldn't hurt him. It was not easy though — the older he became, the more he questioned her about his father. How could she tell him, that she was unable to reveal the identity of his father because she did not know which one he was . . .

*

The bar of the Meyer Hotel, Paris, was a lavish affair. It was built round a little piazza in which fountains played and flowerbeds were awash with colourful blooms twelve months of the year. In winter, a glass roof protected the piazza from the harshness of the weather but tonight it was drawn back and the soft evening air was a relief after the heat of the day. Stephanie and Ella had found much common ground in the last couple of days, not the least of which was mutual enjoyment of Kir Royale. Stephanie was waiting for Ella at a table in a quiet corner of the piazza, two glasses already poured and waiting.

'Hi,' said Ella. 'Boy, I need this. It's been a long day, hasn't it?'

'Yes,' said Stephanie, 'and I'll have to admit this is my second. I came down here sneakily early, to get one ahead of you, but my unnatural honesty has shone through and I feel forced to admit it.' The women raised their glasses in silent toast.

'Talking about natural honesty,' said Ella. 'I was speaking just now to Laurie, the stockholder I mentioned to you. He rang from New York because I've a few problems back there and he made a rather interesting observation about Margot.'

'What did he say?' Stephanie asked.

'That she seems a little over-eager to do this deal. He thinks there must be something in it for her, and he's got me wondering. Hell, I guess I'm imagining it, but . . .'

'Go on,' said Stephanie, 'what's on your mind?'

'Well, if you think about what Margot actually said to us, she gave us the impression that the bank pulling the rug out from under this Ronald Slater guy was some bank other than Joshkers. The kind of thing she said was something like . . . I've been informed that the bankers in question . . . that's not actually saying it's another bank, it's simply inferring it.'

'So!' said Stephanie.

'Well, suppose Joshkers are in dead trouble over this guy, Slater. What do they do? They search through their client list, they come up with a couple of suckers — you and me — and they reckon they can off-load the project, at the full price, to us, which gets Slater and his boyfriend off the hook, but far more important saves the bank losing any money as well.'

'So, you're saying that far from Margot doing us a favour, she may have reckoned that we are a couple of daft women who could just solve the bank's problems for her.' Stephanie's voice was full of indignation.

'Just a thought,' said Ella.

Margot was unnaturally obsequious,' said Stephanie, thoughtfully. 'I don't know what she's like with you normally but she's fairly cool with me. And what about the boardroom and the champagne, have you ever had that treatment before, Ella?'

'Never,' said Ella.

'I tell you what, before we go in to dinner, I'll give Tim a ring, see if he can do some undercover work for us.'

So far, all that Ella had learned about Tim Irvine, Stephanie's husband, was his obsession with farming and his insistence on burying himself in Gloucestershire, which clearly irritated Stephanie.

'How can Tim help?' Ella felt compelled to ask.

'Tim had a friend at Cirencester Agricultural College, called Jeremy Colquhoun. When Jeremy left Cirencester he decided to go into banking instead of farming, not least of which because he had a family firm prepared to take him. He's an awful twit. I'm quite convinced the real reason he went into banking was because nobody else would give him a job. Anyway, he's deputy managing director of Joshkers (UK) now.'

'Family business?' said Ella. 'But Joshkers is an American firm.'

'Yes, but Joshkers bought out Charles Colquhoun & Co., a small English bank, about ten years ago, which formed the basis of their UK operation. Jeremy, I assume, just went with the package.'

'So this Jeremy of yours is, in effect, Margot's boss,' said Ella.

'Yes, more or less. If I get Tim to go to London and take

Jeremy out for lunch, we might learn a thing or two. What do you say?'

'Sounds excellent,' said Ella, 'if Tim won't mind.'

'Tim won't have to,' said Stephanie.

The tables at Langan's Brasserie were filling up. Tim Irvine sat gloomily at a table in the window, waiting for his guest. It was a stifling day, making the unaccustomed restrictions of his suit all the more unbearable. He found himself asking yet again, why he allowed Stephanie to impose her will upon him with such apparent ease. He had promised to take their daughters to a gymkhana today, but the call from their mother had his plans in disarray, and here he was lunching a man with whom he had nothing in common and who, when he came to think about it, he actively disliked. So what drove him to assent to his wife's wishes? Was it because he recognized how much he owed her, or was it a concession to the memory of how much he had once loved her? Loving her was becoming a thing of the past, he recognized that now. You could not love indefinitely someone who was a stranger to you.

'Tim, Old Man, how nice to see you. You seem to be in very earnest thought.'

At the sound of Jeremy Colquhoun's voice, Tim forced his thoughts away from Stephanie and stood up, with a trace of a smile. 'Hello, Jeremy, thanks for coming at such short notice.'

They dealt with the pleasantries, ordered both food and wine and at last Tim was able to turn the conversation to Joshkers. Stephanie could offer no advice as to how Tim should extract the information she wanted, other than to play on the fact that there was no love lost between Jeremy and Margot. Jeremy was a pompous idiot, with a chip on his shoulder; it was easy to see why a bright woman like Margot rankled him. 'The reason for asking you to join me today, Jeremy, is to ask your valuable advice.' Jeremy's appalling susceptibility to flattery was already written all over his stupid face, Tim thought with satisfaction. 'Stephanie is having trouble with Margot Haigh, and we just wondered if you could help.'

There was an instant quickening of interest at the mention of Margot's name. 'What sort of trouble?'

'Stephanie has a feeling that Margot isn't being straight with her. Bearing in mind that our company, I think you will agree, has proved to be a very satisfactory, long-standing customer of the bank, understandably Stephanie feels more than a little affronted at the thought that she can't trust a senior member of Joshkers.'

'I think you'd better explain some more, Tim.'

Got him, thought Tim, gleefully. 'It appears that Margot is trying to persuade Stephanie to go into partnership with an American property dealer, to develop a site in Paris known as the Centre des Arts. Margot has introduced the project to Stephanie as a golden opportunity, yet Stephanie has since discovered that the original project was funded by Joshkers Bank and that they have withdrawn their support from the existing developer. This would suggest the bank is trying to off-load a sticky problem onto Stephanie's shoulders.' He spoke with absolute authority and conviction, praying that Stephanie's hunch was right.

He was well rewarded. As anticipated, Jeremy, in his anxiety to discredit Margot, completely overlooked all banker's discretion and took the bait. 'Stephanie's absolutely right, Old Boy. Margot has really dropped herself in it with the Centre des Arts. She's been messing around with that project for years now, dealing with a little poofter called Ronald Slater. The upshot of it all is the whole thing's gone sour and the bank have told her to get out and get out fast. It's not that easy, of course, and between you and me, I think her job's on the line if she doesn't extract her digit, so to speak. I don't mind admitting, the bank could lose a couple of million on this one, if she can't sort herself out.'

'As much as that?' said Tim, casually. 'How on earth did she get herself in such a mess?'

'Oh I've seen it coming for a long time,' said Jeremy. 'She's a clever girl, with her double first from Oxford. I'm not denying it, but banking is an instinctive thing – either you have it in the blood or you don't. To be frank, at the risk of sounding racist, I just don't trust her origins.'

'You mean the fact that she's half Korean?' said Tim, hardly believing what he was hearing.

'Precisely, Old Boy, about as straight as a bloody corkscrew, that lot – look at the war. Even after all these years in England, blood's thicker than water.'

Hurriedly, in case Jeremy regretted his disclosure and sought some sort of confidentiality, Tim changed the subject and limped through the rest of lunch, trying to show the right degree of interest in Jeremy's long catalogue of amorous conquests.

It was after four before they left Langan's. Tim was exhausted, but oddly triumphant. It was from choice he excluded himself from his wife's business world, but now and again he quite enjoyed a brief foray. It was not the real world, of course – more a game really – but surprisingly easy to play.

Stephanie, Ella and Greg sat in a cab on their way to Joshkers bank. It was late Friday afternoon and the Paris traffic was building up for the weekend exodus. 'The bitch!' said Stephanie. 'To expect us to take on 30,000,000 francs-worth of commitment, just to get her off the hook. It's not only unprofessional, it's positively unethical.'

'The question is,' said Ella, 'do we want to do the deal at her price or not?'

'If she is in as much trouble as Jeremy says she is, I reckon we should offer her 15,000,000 francs and she should think herself lucky. It will halve the bank's losses; what more can she expect.' Stephanie's normally full lips were set in a firm, straight line.

'If she's going to take that sort of drop, wouldn't she do better to put the whole project on the open market?' suggested Ella.

'I doubt it,' said Stephanie. 'As she said herself, the French are going to make a stink about the project going to anyone other than a French company and you know how the French like to drag the last franc out of any deal. They'll smell her desperation and really take her to the cleaners, you can be sure of that. Let's face it, if she's going to be screwed, she might as well be screwed by us, as anyone else.'

Ella laughed, 'I can't argue with that.'

Greg sat mutely in the cab. He had heard enough of the Centre des Arts in the last few days to last him a lifetime, but he already knew better than to interrupt. Stephanie Bonham had made it clear that he was to speak when spoken to, or else keep quiet.

'So, how are you two getting along?' Margot greeted them as they walked into her office, Greg having been left in reception.

'We're getting along just fine,' said Ella, 'what we're not crazy about is being taken for a couple of high school kids.'

Margot frowned. 'You've lost me.'

'We've done some checking,' said Stephanie. 'We find that the bank backing Ronald Slater is none other than Joshkers and that the original deal was set up by none other than Margot Haigh. Given that information, I don't think it unreasonable of us to be just a little suspicious that possibly we may have been set up. What did you do, Margot, go through your address book and look for the two greenest people you knew?'

'Don't be ridiculous,' said Margot. 'It's a wonderful opportunity for you both. I can assure you that was my sole motive for getting you two together.'

'I'm sorry,' said Ella, 'but we just can't buy that. OK, so you made a mess of this deal and now you need to off-load. Being honest and telling us the true position would clearly have affected the price. We understand your thinking right enough but in banking terms, you haven't behaved exactly ethically, have you? If you wanted to shed a difficult deal at the full price, you should have approached somebody who was not a bank customer.'

'The site is worth at least the asking price,' said Margot,

apparently unruffled. 'There's nothing unethical about suggesting you pay a fair price.'

'If that's the case, why didn't you explain the full position to us in the first place?' said Stephanie.

'Because I was protecting a colleague,' said Margot, defensively.

'Within the bank?' said Ella.

Margot nodded.

'Jeremy Colquhoun?' said Stephanie.

'Yes!' said Margot, clearly surprised. 'What on earth prompted you to mention him?'

'You may be interested to know,' said Stephanie, 'that Jeremy Colquhoun informs us that you were in charge of the project, not him, and that the whole mess is your error of judgement, not his.'

'That's outrageous,' said Margot. 'All I'm trying to do is cover his tracks for him.'

'Well, one of you has to be lying,' said Ella, 'and I must say this sure as hell doesn't build customer confidence.'

'I agree,' said Margot. 'I'll put a call through to our Chairman right now. You ask him any question you like about the background to this deal and I'll leave the room so you don't feel embarrassed discussing it frankly.'

Sir Nicholas Goddard, UK Chairman of Joshkers bank, courteously suffered a ten minute telephone interrogation by Stephanie, with whispered asides from Ella. 'Well,' said Stephanie, replacing the receiver, 'it seems Margot told the truth. It's Jeremy's cock-up, right enough, and all she's trying to do is sort out the problem for the bank. To that extent I suppose, she has no personal axe to grind, though obviously she's going to be number one blue-eyed girl if she succeeds in extracting the bank from the mess.'

'I accept all that,' said Ella, slowly, 'but I don't see how it changes anything so far as our attitude to the price is concerned. The bank need out and they need out fast. Whether it was Margot's fault or Jeremy's, is simply not relevant. I don't see why the hell we should pick up their pieces for them, without a substantial incentive, do you?'

'You know something, Ella,' said Stephanie, 'you're a woman after my own heart.'

'15,000,000 francs!' said Margot. 'You have to be joking, that's *half* the asking price.'

'It's a risky project, fraught with complications,' said Ella. 'Clearly, the trap we must not fall into is to delay the development any further. This means we have to develop the site within the confines of the existing building permits. The scheme we have worked out does away with the theatre, the library, the art gallery and recreation area. We have increased the size of the hotel, the number of apartments and the office space, but working within the existing framework is far from ideal and there's a great deal of space to sell. We could fall flat on our faces over this one.'

'Stephanie?' Margot looked enquiringly at her.

'I agree with everything Ella says.'

'I'd agree to a 5,000,000 francs reduction, said Margot, 'for a quick deal.'

'No,' said Stephanie and Ella, in unison.

There was a tense silence in the room. 'Alright,' said Margot, '20,000,000 francs for completion by the end of the month. That really has to be my final offer.'

Stephanie stood up. 'We'll think about it over the weekend. Will you be in London next week?' Margot nodded. 'We'll telephone you.'

Ella and Stephanie swept out of the room, well aware that they were leaving a thundercloud behind them.

'Jesus,' said Ella, 'I hope we haven't made a permanent enemy out of her.'

Stephanie shrugged her shoulders. 'What if we have?'

'Well, hell, I don't know about you, but I'm borrowed up to the hilt with Joshkers,' Ella said, apprehensively.

Stephanie grinned at her across the elevator. 'There are always other banks, besides I have a feeling she will play ball, even yet.'

*

'How did it go?' Greg asked, as they walked through reception.

'Your mother and I have just saved ourselves 10,000,000 francs,' said Stephanie.

'That's great, well done, Mom.' Greg slipped an arm round his mother's shoulders and kissed her.

Stephanie watched them, feeling a brief stab of envy. Ella seemed to have achieved the impossible – a successful career and a close relationship with her son. Stephanie's own daughters were little more than strangers to her. Still it was a question of choices, and Stephanie had made hers long ago.

CHAPTER THREE

The first major choice Lady Stephanie Bonham had to make in her life occurred when she was eleven years old. Her father, the Marquis of Burford, remarried just a few months after the death of Stephanie's mother. His bride was a young model named Pamela Hunt, less than half his age and only four years older than his elder child. The controversial move split the family down the middle. Stephanie's brother, George, who was fifteen, had adored his mother, had watched her take three painful years to die of cancer and could not begin to come to terms with the idea of a nineteen-year-old stepmother. To George his father's remarriage represented utter betrayal of his mother and degraded his father in his eyes. Stephanie was less sure. She had loved her mother, of course, but she could not help being attracted to Pamela, and Pamela for her part, sensing a potential ally in an otherwise hostile world, went out of her way to be charming to the child. Pamela was fun, Pamela was pretty, Pamela helped Stephanie with her hair, took her shopping for clothes which Stephanie's mother would have considered quite unsuitable. In fairness, Stephanie's attitude to Pamela was not entirely selfish. Instinctively, it seemed natural to her that her father would be a happier man with a woman in his life instead of struggling alone. In any event, it was fun to have a 'big sister' and after the melancholy of her mother's slow decline, a relief to have the house cheerful again.

George did his best to recruit his sister's disapproval.

'Surely you can see it's revolting, Steph,' he said. 'Have you seen the newspapers, he's nothing but a dirty old man. Mother would have been appalled at the idea of that . . . that girl sleeping in her bed and pretending to be father's wife.'

'She *is* father's wife,' Stephanie said. 'In any case, George, I like her, she's fun.' It was Stephanie's first experience of openly defying her elder brother on a major issue; it was a heady if terrifying feeling.

'You're hopeless,' said George, angrily. 'All you can think about is enjoying yourself and having fun. As soon as I'm old enough, I'm going to leave Wickham and never come back, not while *she's* here, at any rate.'

'You *can't* leave Wickham!' said Stephanie, genuinely appalled at the suggestion.

'I can and I will,' said George. 'Thank heaven's it's back to school next week.'

Wickham was the one true passion of Stephanie's life. It had been the family seat of the Burfords for nearly four centuries. The land, in rich Gloucestershire countryside, had been gifted by a grateful king to the first Marquis. The original building had been a relatively modest affair – a central dwelling house surrounded by a moat and fortified by a high wall and gatehouse. After the Civil War, the fortifications had been removed and in the early 1700s, the house had been greatly improved and extended. Subsequent generations had made their contribution and by the time George and Stephanie were growing up in the house, it had become an imposing twenty bedroomed mansion, though still retaining many of its eighteenth-century features. Perhaps because of the predominance of honey-coloured Gloucestershire stone the house, despite its size, still managed to be a cosy family home. Stephanie adored it.

The rest of the estate comprised just over a thousand acres of mixed quality land and, unusually, a complete village. The village of Wickham included a church, a vicarage, a rather drab public house and sixteen cottages. There were also two working farms on the estate. The environment in which she grew up ideally suited Stephanie. Every day she went riding on a fat little pony across the much-loved acres and back through the village. She knew everyone, everyone knew her and liked her – for her position, yes, but also for her fair good looks and happy, outgoing disposition. Wickham was her life; she could not imagine anyone wanting to leave it.

When, shortly after his marriage, her father had suggested boarding school Stephanie had been horrified and grateful for Pamela's intervention, which resulted in her receiving a very unspectacular education at a local convent school. The years drifted by happily enough for Stephanie. The early teenage years were no problem to her; she suffered neither from puppy fat nor spots, nor a lack of eager young men wishing to squire her to local dances.

In her safe, secure, self-centred little world, however, she was unaware of the deepening cracks in her family life. She never stopped to ask herself why Pamela actively sought her company so often in preference to her father's. She liked Pamela, admired her, tried to emulate her stylish dressing and easy charm. Stephanie simply saw her father's increasing absences from home as an opportunity to spend a jolly girlish evening with Pamela. George, too, was a comparative stranger at home. He had moved on from school to university and apart from turning up at Wickham for the obligatory festivities – Christmas, Easter and the occasional birthday – he spent his vacations with friends.

When Stephanie was sixteen, she left school with two poor 'O' levels – much to her father's disgust. With no idea of what she wanted to do and an apparent complete lack of ambition, her father insisted that after the summer vacation she should enrol at a local secretarial college and at least acquire some shorthand and typing skills. Stephanie agreed because she could think of no alternative, and settled down to enjoy a carefree summer at Wickham. However, it was not to be. One afternoon in the first week of July, Stephanie returned from a ride to find her step-mother waiting for her in the hall. One look at Pamela's tear-stained face and Stephanie knew something was terribly wrong.

'What is it?' she asked apprehensively.

Pamela took her hand. 'Darling, you're going to have to be very brave, something awful has happened.'

'What?' said Stephanie.

'It . . . it's George. We didn't know it until now but apparently he's been on drugs for some time.'

'Drugs!' said Stephanie. 'I'd never have suspected stuffy old George of taking drugs. I suppose he'll have to go into hospital to be sorted out.'

'I'm afraid it's too late for that,' said Pamela. 'He went to a party with some friends in London last night. He must have drunk quite a lot and then injected himself with too much heroin. I'm terribly sorry, Darling, but I'm afraid he's dead.'

The words had no meaning for Stephanie. She stared at Pamela, trying to imagine her childhood companion robbed of life. It was impossible. 'W-where's father?' she managed.

'In his study.'

'I'd better . . .' Stephanie began.

'I wouldn't go near him, Darling, I really wouldn't. He's in the most terrible state and I don't think you'll do each other any good at the moment. Let's go into the drawing room and have a stiff drink and I'll tell you all I know about it.'

For two days, Robert, Marquis of Burford, locked himself away from the rest of his family. When he emerged, he was in control of himself but completely unable to give any form of comfort to his remaining family. The three of them moved in a dream world, which took them through the inquest, the funeral and the unwelcome but persistent interest of the press. When it was all over, what each of them realized in their different ways was that George's death had exposed two tragedies. The first was the needless loss of a young life. The second, that as a family they had been moving around one another as strangers – they simply did not know each other at all and now, it appeared, it was too late to learn.

Without consulting Stephanie, her father rearranged her future and enrolled her in a Swiss finishing school. Stephanie did not wish to go but this time Pamela did not intervene on her behalf and so two months after her brother's death, she found herself entering the world outside Wickham for the first time.

Robert never recovered from his son's death, and nor did his marriage. With Stephanie in Switzerland and a husband who had suddenly become an old man overnight, Pamela began an affair with a local farmer. Robert was aware of what was happening but rather than make any attempt to win back his wife, he simply took solace in the bottle. When Stephanie returned from Switzerland, it was to a very different household. Pamela had become remote, involved now in a secret life of her own. Her father seemed barely to remember who she was and any intelligent conversation with him after midday was quite impossible.

Switzerland had been good for Stephanie, she had grown up and a new and stimulating environment had jerked her out of her inertia. Rather than live with two unhappy people, apparently hell-bent on self-destruction, she found no difficulty in making the decision to move into a flat in London with a group of friends, from where she embarked on a frivolous but enjoyable lifestyle. A generous allowance from her father needed only the occasional top-up from the odd temporary job, and the rest of the time she concentrated on her social life.

Looking back on her life, Stephanie was often to wonder why she did not marry during this period. There were plenty of proposals and potentially serious relationships but she always shied away. Whether the pattern of her father's life had put her off marriage or whether already she sensed that she was not a person suited to family life, it was hard to tell, but somehow she managed to live in London for three years without committing herself to anyone. It was not until 1965, when she was twenty-one, that the second major choice in Stephanie's life presented itself.

It was a cold day in early January. Robert fortified himself with the best part of a bottle of brandy before taking to the hunting field. He had been out for less than an hour, when taking a jump badly, he lost his seat, fell awkwardly and broke his neck – mercifully relieving him, most of his friends believed, of a life that had become a burden to him.

The will was hopeless, for it had not been altered since George's death. The estate had declined and while undoubtedly it represented an enormous asset, there was virtually no money with which to maintain it. The easy friendship which Pamela and Stephanie had once enjoyed was gone. Pamela, now in her early thirties, felt that the Burfords had taken the best part of her youth and so was determined to get something tangible out of the marriage. Stephanie was equally determined that Wickham should not be sold. The battle raged and undoubtedly Wickham would have been lost had not Stephanie met, quite by chance at a party, a young Cirencester graduate named Tim Irvine, who offered to help her sort out the mess.

'Tell me about your husband,' said Ella. Their flight had been delayed and as soon as they had boarded, Greg had fallen asleep. Ella and Stephanie sat companionably sipping champagne on the British Airways flight to Heathrow.

Stephanie, jolted from her thoughts of the past, looked at Ella surprised. 'Tim! He's a nice, kind man, you'll like him.'

Ella smiled. 'Nice, kind . . . the way you say it almost sounds insulting.'

Stephanie laughed. 'Well, I love him dearly, of course, but to be honest he is just a tiny bit of a bore on occasions. Is that dreadful of me to say so?'

'No . . . but in what way?' Ella began. 'Oh, excuse me, it's none of my business.'

'I don't mind talking about him,' said Stephanie. 'After all, you're going to spend the weekend with us, so you might as well know something about us. Tim helped me sort out Wickham, the family estate, after my father died. We worked very closely together and turned what was an absolute financial disaster into a commercial success. You know what it's like when you're working on a project with somebody, how close you become . . .' she touched Ella's arm, 'as I hope we will. Anyway, it was like that – it took us three years to really get things established and during that time we ... well, sort of drifted into marriage. As far as Tim was concerned, once Wickham was saved that was the end of it. But for me, I'm afraid I was bitten by the property bug,' she grinned engagingly at Ella, 'and you know all about that.'

'Yes,' said Ella, 'but it was different for me. I had to work to support Greg and myself whereas you began with something – a family estate.'

'Are you saying I had it all too easy?' Stephanie asked, defensively.

'No, of course not,' said Ella, hastily, 'hell, I know nothing about you and your life. I suppose I'm just saying that you had choices, still do, and I really don't. Sometimes I think it would be wonderful just to be able to enjoy family life, without the constant pressure, hassle and doubt connected with our kind of business.'

'I don't believe you mean that,' said Stephanie, aggressively, 'you may think you do, but in reality you wouldn't have got where you have without a very steely personal ambition. That's really where Tim and I differ. Tim is totally content with his life. He has his fields and his stock, the seasons come and go and now he has the children. He doesn't want to go onwards or upwards, he's perfectly happy as he is.'

Stephanie's obvious agitation surprised Ella. 'Surely in view of the children, his attitude to life has to be a positive advantage – it leaves you free to pursue your career.'

'Yes, indeed,' said Stephanie, 'but everyone makes me feel so guilty: his parents, the children's school teachers, our friends ... they spend all their time saying how wonderful Tim is, playing the role of both mother and father, and by inference, of course, how useless I am.'

'You could change things,' said Ella.

'Yes, but that's the problem,' said Stephanie. 'I don't want to. I love my life and I adore wheeling and dealing. I'm really not suited to being purely a wife and mother, yet everybody makes me feel so damned guilty.'

'How do your children feel about it all?'

'I don't really know, but alright, I think. They look to Tim for everything and, of course, I go along with all his decisions on their wellbeing. I wouldn't dream of interfering, it wouldn't be fair.'

'How old are the children?' Ella asked.

'Eleven and ten. Millie, the elder one, has much the same temperament as me, God help her. The little one, Belinda, is very much Tim's child, both in looks and attitude.'

'I suppose I have rather an idealistic view of marriage, since I've never been married,' said Ella, 'but it must be kind of tough on you both, seeing so little of one another.'

'We've been married for twelve years now,' said Stephanie. 'It's hardly love's young dream any more. Don't get me wrong, I think we're faithful to one another, at least I am to Tim – I've never had time to be anything else – and Tim, somehow, isn't the type to have affairs. For one thing, he'd give himself away in a moment, he's far too honest and open a person.' It should have been a compliment but to Ella it sounded strangely like a criticism.

'Anyway,' said Stephanie, 'enough of me, what about you? Do you live with Greg's father or is it a thing of the past?'

'A thing of the past,' said Ella, and clearly that was the end of the conversation.

At Heathrow the two women parted. Stephanie was staying overnight in London because the following morning she had a meeting with Lord Rainham, who owned a large manor house and substantial acreage just outside Derby. 'He's hoping I may be able to turn the estate into a paying concern for him,' Stephanie explained. 'I'd like to do the job, it's an interesting place, with a lot of potential. He might even be prepared to sell.'

It was proposed, therefore, that Ella and Greg should travel on to Gloucestershire alone, in the chauffeur-driven Bentley thoughtfully provided by Stephanie to meet the plane.

'Why don't we stay over in London and travel to Gloucestershire with you tomorrow?' Ella suggested, uncharacteristically shy at the thought of meeting Tim Irvine.

'Not a good idea,' said Stephanie. 'For one thing London is hell this time of year and in any event, I'm not sure how long I'll be with Lord Rainham. I've only met him a couple of times but from what I can recall he's a tedious old bore – the meeting just could go on all day.'

It was early evening, the end of a beautiful, sun-drenched day, as Ella and Greg bowled down the M4. The surrounding countryside charmed them but it was nothing compared with their delight in the little Gloucestershire villages through which they passed once they turned off the motorway.

Greg was ecstatic. 'Hey, Mom, why don't we live in England? I love it here.'

'Darling, we've only been in the country an hour.'

'So . . . New York is boring, you know I hate New York.'

'Many people consider it to be the most exciting city in the world,' Ella said, valiantly.

'But there's nothing to do – just look at all this country, Mom, isn't it great?' Despite the splendours of their journey, neither of them was prepared for the beauty of Stephanie's home. They travelled through the village of Wickham first and then turned off the lane, through stone pillars, on to a driveway flanked either side by massive chestnut trees. After about half a mile, the driveway opened out and there stood the house. Bathed in evening light it was almost an apricot colour – long, low, built in the shape of an E with the centre prong missing. The roof was turretted, the windows all had tiny leaded panes, and the great oak front door was thrown open in welcome.

'I just don't know how she can ever leave this place,' Ella said, quietly, and that was before she had even met Tim Irvine.

CHAPTER FOUR

GLOUCESTERSHIRE
August 1977

He was already on the driveway to greet them by the time the chauffeur had opened the door for Ella. The imposing house, the strangeness of having just arrived in a new country, the fatigue of the journey, had Ella suddenly feeling self-conscious and longing for the anonymity of a hotel room, where she and Greg might simply have collapsed. All these feelings of awkwardness vanished, however, at the sight of Tim Irvine. He was not at all as Ella had imagined. He was not particularly tall, probably no taller than Stephanie herself. He had bright blue eyes, light brown hair and an open, humorous face, creased with laughter lines. He wore a check shirt and faded cords, and he stepped forward with outstretched hands, taking hers in both of his, exuding warmth and welcome.

'Miss Kovac, how very nice to meet you. You look wonderful. I thought you'd be frazzled from a journey in all this heat. And this must be Greg – how do you do, Greg. It's lovely to have you both here at Wickham.'

'Hi,' said Greg, awkwardly.

Ella, momentarily stunned, made a valiant effort to pull herself together. 'It's very kind of you to invite us,' she said. 'This is wonderful.' She gestured around her.

'It is rather splendid, isn't it? We love it, at any rate. Come inside, I'll take you straight up to your rooms so that you can wash and relax. Supper's in half an hour. No need to dress, as you can see. Oh, and there have been two phone calls for you – one from a Laurie Merman in New York and the other from the indomitable Margot. She said she was happy to speak to either you or Stephanie, it didn't matter who. She was a little curt with me so I think she must have rumbled my lunch with Jeremy.'

Ella was given a turretted room. It was simply furnished but what made it spectacular was the incredible views across the Gloucestershire countryside. She stood by the window for a long time drinking in the scene – she had never expected England to be so beautiful. At last she remembered her telephone calls.

Laurie was brief and to the point. 'I'm sorry, Ella, but I thought I'd better let you know you're stuck with that lease. Henry should lose his job over this.'

'Are you sure there's no way round it?' Ella asked.

'None,' said Laurie. 'It appears that no letter was exchanged between you and ADC confirming the rental structure. Had there been, it's possible it could have been used as evidence. Henry said it was all very last minute and agreed verbally.'

'Yes, that's right,' said Ella. 'I did the deal just before leaving for Europe. Oh hell, it was a good deal, too. I think ADC have behaved like rats.'

'Not really,' said Laurie, 'they've got prime office space for a snip. It's not their fault that you have inadequate staff in your office to whom you handed out too much responsibility. It's your mess, Honey – you made it.'

'I still think . . .' said Ella.

'Forget it, Sweetheart, it's business and this is one you lost. I guess though we need to have a talk when you get back to the States. The one thing I know about is staff – in the catering business they make or break you. If you're going ahead with this Paris deal, you're going to have to gather some people round you who can keep you out of the shit, not drop you right in it.'

'Yes, yes, alright, Laurie,' said Ella, suddenly feeling very weary. 'I must go now, I have to ring the bank.'

The London number Tim had written down for her was

not Joshkers, so Ella presumed correctly she had been given Margot's home number. Margot was such an enigma – Ella had never spoken to anyone who'd had dealings with Margot Haigh who felt they really knew her personally. Her private life was a closed book and the barrier Margot presented to the world kept any inquisitiveness at bay. Disclosing her home number in this way seemed a chink in the armour and quite out of character. Ella dialled the number and waited.

'Margot Haigh.' The familiar brusque voice echoed down the line.

'Margot, it's Ella. I got a message to call you.'

'Thanks for calling, Ella. Where are you?'

'I'm at Wickham, and Stephanie's still in London.'

'That's fine, but you're going to meet her over the weekend, I trust?'

'Yes, of course, she'll be down during tomorrow.'

'Good.' Margot hesitated for a moment. 'I've had a word with my Chairman about Centre des Arts and he's not unsympathetic to your view.'

'What view?' said Ella, knowing perfectly well, but wanting Margot to spell it out.

'That I should have been more frank with you initially and explained the bank's involvement.'

'Yeh, you should,' said Ella. It was a heady feeling having Margot on the run for once.

'Anyway, we've sat down and done some sums and the result is that while we can't agree to your proposed price of 15,000,000 francs, we would be prepared to split the difference with you at 17,500,000 francs. I thought I'd ring you and mention this because it is bound to affect your thinking. Since this weekend is decision time, it's clearly important that you have all the facts.'

'Thank you,' said Ella, 'I appreciate it.' She tried to sound nonchalant but it was difficult to keep the smile out of her voice – it was one hell of a drop in price, one hell of an about-face – she couldn't wait to tell Stephanie.

'I would like to make one thing clear, however,' said Margot, a trifle tartly. 'There is absolutely no room for any further negotiation. There is no point in you coming back to me to try and screw the price a little lower. This is our final offer and it depends on you completing by the end of August. I should also add that if you have not made a decision by Wednesday, then the project will be offered on the open market.'

'I understand, Margot,' said Ella, meekly. 'I'll pass on the information to Stephanie.'

'Fine, OK, have a good weekend. What do you think of Wickham, by the way?'

'It's wonderful,' said Ella.

'And Tim?'

'Very charming.'

'Yes, he is,' said Margot, 'but he's no match for Stephanie.'

Tim met Ella and Gregory at the bottom of the great mahogany staircase which dominated the central hall of Wickham. 'Come out on to the terrace,' he said. 'We've laid for supper there because it's too good an evening to be inside. I'll pour you a much needed drink and then I'll call the brats.'

Millie and Belinda Irvine came running across the lawn in swimming costumes as Tim was dispensing drinks. They were attractive children, very fair, slim and athletic, with a healthy outdoor tan. Millie was clearly going to be a great beauty, better looking even than her mother, while Belinda had the same, open cheerful face as her father. After remaining quiet just long enough to be introduced, their chatter was incessant. Greg who had been a little shy, opened up immediately. They plagued him with questions about America.

Tim immediately came to his rescue. 'Greg, when you can't stand these two any longer and prefer a little adult conversation, just tell them to belt up and come and join us. Would you like a beer?'

'A beer?' said Millie, scandalised. 'He's not grown up enough to drink beer.'

'He certainly is,' Tim corrected her.

Greg flushed with pleasure. 'Yes, please, Sir.'

'Good lad.' Drinks dispensed, the children wandered off to see the stables, giving Ella and Tim a few minutes' peace. 'You made your phone calls?' said Tim. 'No problems, I hope?'

Ella pulled a face. 'I have a few problems back in New York. I've never left my business before and it seems the moment I do, everything falls apart.'

'Oh, I'm sorry – is it serious?'

'Expensive,' said Ella. 'It was the other call that was interesting, though.'

'To Margot?'

'Yes. Amazingly, she's dropped the price again. I don't know whether Stephanie told you, but as a result of the information you gave us, she immediately came down by 10,000,000 francs.'

Tim shook his head. 'No, I haven't spoken to Stephanie since. I just had a message via our housekeeper that she wouldn't be home tonight, and that you and Greg would be arriving in time for supper.'

Ella tried not to show surprise. Tim's role had been crucial – it seemed extraordinary that Stephanie had not told him so. She felt compelled to explain. 'The original price was set at 30,000,000 francs. As an immediate result of your lunch with Jeremy, Margot dropped to 20,000,000 francs. We rejected the price and that call was to say she has agreed with her chairman a final price of 17,500,000 francs.'

Tim grinned. 'That's great. So do you think in the circumstances I can justify charging my lunch to the business?'

Ella laughed. 'I most certainly think you should.' She hesitated, and then asked the question to which she already knew the answer. 'Are you much involved in the business?'

Tim shook his head. 'No, normally not at all. I was initially with Stephanie's original project here at Wickham. We planned the whole thing together, but all her schemes since have been of her own making. She's a clever girl.'

'Yes, she is,' said Ella.

'People knock her, you know, for spending so little time at home, but we're all different and what's right for some is not for others. I miss her, of course, and so do the children but she has a right to respond to this ambition which seems to drive her on.' He smiled, a little wistfully, Ella thought. 'I can't help hoping though that every deal she does will be the last.'

'You can't be too pleased about Paris, then,' said Ella.

'Certainly it's going to be a long and difficult job I should imagine. It will be far from easy to administer from your point of view, I would have thought.'

Ella nodded. Tim had immediately spotted the predicament, which Margot and Stephanie chose to ignore. 'To be honest I've been thinking a lot about that angle – how I'm going to cope from the other side of the Atlantic. Obviously, now the price has dropped so low, it would seem to be crazy not to go ahead, but I clearly can't afford to neglect my New York business . . . and then, of course, there's Greg.'

'He's a nice boy.'

'Yes, he is,' said Ella, 'but you know what kids are like – they do need stability more than anything else. Although my business is demanding, up to now its all been based in New York. We have a nice roomy apartment there, in the same building as the office and Greg goes to school just round the block. OK, so his Mom works but she's always there for him at the end of each day, I'm reluctant to alter that – it's a funny age, thirteen – such a time of change.'

'I admire your concern very much,' Tim said, with obvious sincerity.

Supper, a simple meal of shepherd's pie and salad, was served on the terrace by a strange little woman with peroxide hair. 'This is Mrs Maggs,' Tim explained. 'She cooks, cleans, looks after us in a most wonderful way and keeps the children in order.'

'Oh no she doesn't,' said Millie. 'We keep Maggs in order.'

'You mind your tongue, Miss Millie, or I'll beat your bum.' Clearly, Mrs Maggs was one of the family.

Greg was full of enthusiasm. 'Mom, they have wonderful horses and a swimming pool. Belinda says I can go riding tomorrow. Is that alright, Sir?' He looked enquiringly at Tim.

'Yes, of course. In fact we must make a good, long day of it. Why don't I give you a call at six o'clock, you can come and watch the milking.'

'I'd really like that,' said Greg.

'You can't,' said Millie, appalled, 'it's much too early.'

'I love the country and farming,' said Greg. 'I don't want to miss a single minute.'

'Then we'll get up, too,' said Belinda.

'Oh no, you don't,' said Tim. 'You're going to be spending all day with Greg, and with you two around I won't get a word in edgeways. I'd like to spend some time with him, too, you know; I don't see why he should be your friend and not mine.'

Again, Tim had hit just the right note with Greg, Ella thought. The only men her son knew well were Laurie who was gentle and kind to him but still treated him as a baby, and Aaron, his godfather, who, because of his work, was rather a remote figure. To be placed on an equal footing with this man, who he clearly already admired, had to be very good for him.

The next day was wonderful. They rode and swam, walked and talked and the easy friendship which developed between the five of them was uncanny in its swiftness. There were no squabbles between the children, a great deal of laughter and both Greg and Ella relaxed and blossomed in the warmth of this happy family – indeed it felt as though they had known Wickham and the Irvines for ever.

Stephanie was bone-weary as she turned her MG into the driveway of Wickham. She had spent a long, restless night chewing over the details of the Paris deal, followed by a long, tiresome day with Lord Rainham. He was an irritating little man who knew nothing about the commercial viability of stately houses but behaved as if he knew everything. If it were not for the magnificence of his property, Stephanie would have abandoned the project. No, that was not true, she thought, as she brought the car to a halt by the front door. She was restless. She'd had no new project for some months and while the Paris deal looked like coming together, she could not rely upon it. She eased herself out of the car and straightened her aching back. Her head thumped and she felt sticky and dirty from the twin effects of London and the heat. She was about to enter the house when she heard the sound of laughter, coming from the direction of the swimming pool. Changing direction, she walked round the side of the house.

Tim and Ella were sitting by the pool, a bottle of champagne between them, while the children floundered about in the water. The scene was so perfect, it looked like something out of *Homes & Gardens*: the happy, laughing children, the relaxed couple enjoying their drinks. Stephanie felt a stab of irritation. It was so easy for Tim – all he had to do was enjoy the fruits of her labour and take all the credit for bringing up the children. No, no, that wasn't fair, he made a considerable contribution to Wickham. Yet her resentment swelled as she dragged herself across the lawn towards them. The swimming pool had been paid for from the proceeds of a project Stephanie had undertaken for Lord Montague several years before; the champagne they were drinking had been a gift from a grateful client; and how was it that she and Ella were about to embark upon the biggest project of their respective careers and yet Ella could sit there like any housewife, relaxed and apparently without a care in the world?

Stephanie strode into their midst. 'Very cosy, I must say.'

'Darling.' Tim leapt to his feet and kissed Stephanie's cheek, which she offered to him coolly. 'You look absolutely exhausted. Let me pour you a glass of champagne.'

'What a greeting,' said Stephanie. 'I would have thought that after all these years of marriage, you'd have learnt that the one thing you must never say to a woman is that she looks tired!'

'Sorry, but it's the truth,' said Tim, gently. 'Did you have a sod of a journey?'

Stephanie ignored his question and turned her venom on Ella. 'I expected to find you hard at work.'

Ella shook her head. 'I've spent most of this week hard at work and I am supposed to be on holiday – I guess I've earned a day off.'

'You're lucky you feel you can afford one,' Stephanie said.

'I don't know about *afford*,' said Ella, mildly, 'but *earned* certainly; besides I have some great news for you which is going to make our sums one hell of a lot easier: Margot's dropped to 17,500,000 francs.'

'Certainly, that's good news,' said Stephanie, 'but it's hardly a reason to abandon our calculations.'

Ella was irritated. 'I'm not suggesting it is, but let's face it, the whole project suddenly looks a deal more attractive than it did.'

Stephanie turned away. 'I'm going to change. What time's dinner?'

'Eight o'clock,' said Tim.

'Eight o'clock! But it's only half past six and I'm absolutely starving.'

'I'll see if Mrs Maggs can move it forward, only I didn't dare make it any earlier because I didn't know what time you'd be back,' said Tim.

'Oh, don't worry,' said Stephanie, striding away, 'I wouldn't want to disrupt the domestic arrangements.' She stepped off the terrace, almost tripping with a combination of anger and fatigue. She knew she had behaved badly but the compulsion to destroy the evident easy happiness around the pool had been too strong an instinct to fight.

It was only as Stephanie opened the front door that she realized her children had not even acknowledged her arrival home.

CHAPTER FIVE

'Bye, Stephanie, see you tomorrow,' Ella called, as she, Tim and the children stood at the front door of Wickham. With an elegant wave of the hand, Stephanie slipped into gear and sent her little MG hurtling down the driveway.

'Boy, does that car shift,' said Greg.

'I know,' said Tim. 'It worries me sick. Stephanie drives as she does everything else in life – flat out. I'm worried she'll have a crash one of these days.'

'Do you really think so, Daddy?' Belinda's eyes were wide with sudden panic.

Tim slipped an arm around her. 'No, Darling, not really. Mummy's a brilliant driver – I'm just jealous, because I can't drive as well as she can.'

Such a kind man, thought Ella for the umpteenth time that weekend. His supply of patience seemed unlimited, as he soothed, cajoled and humoured, acting as peace-maker, judge and jury or whatever was required of him to keep his family as happy and secure as possible. After Stephanie's disgruntled arrival, Ella had feared they were in for a difficult weekend, but by the end of dinner that night Tim had Stephanie laughing and relaxed. A brilliant career in the diplomatic service could have been Tim Irvine's for the asking, Ella thought.

Ella and Stephanie had planned to spend most of Sunday working on figures to see how Margot's new offer affected their budget. However, on Sunday morning Stephanie had received a telephone call from Lord Rainham, asking her to come up to Derbyshire immediately as he had thought through her proposals and wished to put them in hand urgently in order to open to the public in the Spring. Stephanie, anxious to secure the deal, felt it important to respond positively to his request which was why on Sunday evening she was leaving her family again and heading for Derbyshire. 'I'll be back by Monday evening,' she assured Ella. 'We can spend all Tuesday on the project and telephone Margot on Wednesday morning, in order to meet her deadline.'

The little group dispersed as soon as Stephanie had left – the children to play tennis, Tim to inspect the stock before sunset and Ella to do some work. At Tim's insistence, Ella settled herself in his study. It was an elegant room facing due south, with wonderful views over the estate. His desk was made of polished oak – solid and dependable, rather like the owner. There was a photograph of the children on their ponies, another of his sheepdog, yet another of himself and Stephanie, clearly taken some years before: they were leaning over a gate, arms around one another, laughing, and for a reason Ella could not define, the photograph disturbed her.

She had just started going through one of the interminable lists of building costs when the telephone rang. She hesitated and then picked it up. 'Wickham . . .' she glanced at the instrument, '253'.

'Ella?' The voice sounded vaguely incredulous but was nonetheless instantly recognizable. As always, Ella felt her heart flip.

'Aaron! How are you? How lovely to hear from you.'

'I'm OK, Ella. I didn't expect to get through to you this easy. I understand you're staying at some grand stately home and so I guess I thought the butler would answer.'

Ella laughed. 'It's not that kind of stately home – very old, very impressive, but inhabited by nice, simple people. It's great to hear from you. How's Alice, and the kids?'

'Fine, just fine.'

There was a silence on the line and Ella instantly felt a sense of apprehension. 'Aaron, is everything OK?'

'Well, kind of, that's why I'm calling, Ella. It's your mother, she's had a stroke.'

Ella waited to feel something but the news seemed to have no impact on her at all. 'Is she . . . is she dead?'

'No,' said Aaron, carefully, 'but she's in a coma and Pa reckons it's unlikely she'll come out of it; in fact he reckons she's slipping away, which is why he asked me to call you.'

Ella felt a sick feeling in the pit of her stomach. 'He wants me to go to her?' she asked incredulously.

'That's right,' said Aaron. 'Although it's unlikely she will regain consciousness before she goes, it's a possibility, and just because she can't communicate herself, it doesn't mean she doesn't know what's going on. You know Pa, he loves playing the amateur psychiatrist. He reckons you should be with her when she goes, as much for your sake as hers.'

'What makes him say that?' Ella said, angrily.

'He reckons you'll regret it if you're not there.'

'I can't come, Aaron. I'm in the middle of finalising a big deal and I have a deadline set for Wednesday.'

'OK,' said Aaron, 'so you're in the middle of a deal. There are plenty of deals in the world, Ella, but you only have one mother and Pa doesn't reckon she'll be around after Wednesday.'

'I can't come, Aaron, I really can't.'

'Sure you can. Shall I tell Pa you're on your way?'

'I'll never get a flight at such short notice.'

'You'll get a flight,' said Aaron, 'but I must know you're definitely coming. It would be wrong for Pa to tell your Ma you're on your way, if you're not going to show.'

'I thought you said she was in a coma,' said Ella.

'So she is, but as I said, who knows what she can hear. Come on, Sweetheart. Shit, I better than anyone understand how you feel about her and all that's happened, but this is no time to be mean spirited. She's dying, Ella. You're the only good thing that's come out of her rotten life, don't deprive her of that, not now, not at the end.'

'I can't go back, I can't face it,' Ella said, hot tears in her eyes. 'Surely, Aaron Connors, you of all people should understand why I can't ever go back home.'

'Ella, you can do anything; you're the bravest person I've ever met.'

'What about Greg?' Ella said faintly.

'Bring Greg, too.'

'But I couldn't – he'll ask questions. What'll I tell him?'

'Ella, Greg is thirteen years old. So far you've managed to fob him off about where he comes from and why, but not for much longer. This trip back to Silver Springs could be just what you need, both of you. You've been running away from your past ever since you left. Maybe, just maybe, this is the moment you should turn round and face it.'

'I can't, Aaron.' Ella was crying in earnest now.

'You can, my brave girl, you must. You owe it to yourself, to Greg and to your mother.'

'I owe Ma nothing,' Ella almost shouted at him.

'She gave you life, Ella.'

Another silence followed. 'I just don't know what to tell Greg, I just don't know how to handle it.'

'Look,' said Aaron, 'one thing at a time. Call the airline and book a flight as early tomorrow morning as you can make it. Then call me with the flight details and I'll get Pa to arrange for a car to pick you up from Cincinnati. Delay your deal, whatever it is, for a few days and when you have all the arrangements sorted and have had a chance to clear your mind, then if you want to call me back, we'll talk through how you handle things with Greg.'

Slowly, Ella replaced the receiver. Wickham and the balmy English summer's evening had receded. She was back in the steamy, dusty heat of Kentucky, and all the superficial achievements of her life seemed, suddenly, to count for nothing. Only the echo of Aaron's voice sustained her – her rock, her secret love. In a trance, she telephoned the American Airways office and booked two seats on a flight to Cincinnati, leaving Heathrow at eight-thirty the following morning, she arranged for a car to collect her from Wickham at five-thirty and then, taking a deep breath, she dialled Margot's home number.

'Margot Haigh.'

'Margot, it's Ella. I'm sorry to trouble you on your home number again.'

'That's no problem, Ella,' Margot sounded unusually friendly.

'Something's come up,' said Ella. 'I've just had a call from a childhood friend of mine to say that my mother's ill – well, dying. She's had a stroke.'

'Oh, I'm sorry,' said Margot, a little guardedly.

Ella hurried on. 'Clearly, I'm going to have to fly back to Kentucky to be with her. The doctor reckons she probably only has twenty-four hours, thirty-six at the most.'

'Is she in a coma?' Margot asked.

'Yes.'

'Then she's unlikely to know you're even there, I suppose.'

'Possibly not,' said Ella, angry at having to defend a decision which was not of her own making, 'but I have to go anyway.'

'I understand, of course,' said Margot, 'and there's no problem provided you and Stephanie can give me the go-ahead on the Centre des Arts project before you leave.'

'We can't do that,' said Ella. 'We need at least another day on the figures and Stephanie's not here right now, she's in Derbyshire, on business.'

'Well, something will have to give,' said Margot. 'I'm not extending my deadline. Either you'll have to delay going to Kentucky or Stephanie will have to cut short her business in Derbyshire.'

'She can't do that,' said Ella, patiently. 'My flight leaves first thing in the morning; by the time Stephanie got back here it would be time for me to leave for the airport.'

'The decision's yours, of course,' said Margot, her voice steely. 'I'm just telling you the facts. The drop in price I've offered you is withdrawn at seventeen-thirty London time on Wednesday.'

Ella managed, just, to cope with family supper but when the children had gone off to bed, Tim poured two hefty brandies and handed one to her. They were sitting round the kitchen table, over the debris of supper. 'Take a hefty swig,' said Tim, 'and then tell me what's wrong.'

Ella did as she was told. Strangely, his intuition did not surprise her. 'How can you tell anything is wrong?' she tempered.

Tim smiled gently. 'Oh come, come, the effervescent girl we know and love is nowhere to be seen. It's been forced jollity tonight and a real strain by the look of it.'

'I hope the girls didn't notice.' Ella's dark eyes looked huge and haunted in the evening shadows.

'Greg might have done but the girls didn't. You're evading the issue, Ella.'

'I've had a call from Aaron Connors. He's a friend of mine, way back from when I was a kid. We grew up in Kentucky together. He's now a consultant gynaecologist in New York.'

'Go on,' said Tim, encouragingly.

'He called to say my mother's had a stroke and is in a coma.'

'I'm terribly sorry,' said Tim. 'Are you close?'

Ella shook her head, vehemently. 'I should be with her though, Tim, so I've booked a flight to Cincinnati for Greg and me. The car's going to pick us up at five-thirty tomorrow morning.'

'I could have arranged for the chauffeur to take you to the airport,' said Tim.

'No, no, I wouldn't dream of troubling you. It's all fixed but it does leave us with a problem.'

Tim lowered his brandy glass. 'Of course, the Centres des Arts. The deadline's Wednesday, isn't it? Still, in the circumstances, I'm sure Margot will extend it.'

'She won't,' said Ella, 'I've already spoken to her on the phone, and she won't budge.'

'Hell's teeth, that woman's impossible. Look, let's go and say goodnight to the kids, then I'll make some coffee and we'll talk this through.'

It was good to have someone else taking charge for once. They kissed the children goodnight and when they came downstairs, Tim felt in the pocket of his trousers and threw a lighter to Ella. 'The fire's laid in my study, you light it while I make the coffee. I'll be with you in a moment.'

At night, Tim's room came into its own. The lighting from two charming standard lamps gave the room a soft glow. The flames from the fire sent flickering shadows round the wood panelled walls. Ella collapsed on to a battered old sofa which was pulled up in front of the fire. By the time Tim joined her she was starting to relax a little. 'So let me get this straight,' Tim said, sitting down beside her. 'You've spoken to Margot and she won't extend the deadline, but you haven't yet spoken to Stephanie?' Ella shook her head. 'Are you prepared to take the risk of going ahead without spending any more time on the deal?'

'No,' said Ella, quickly.

'Is that because you're unsure as to the viability of the project or because you're still uncertain about your personal standpoint?'

Ella smiled at the shrewdness of the question. 'A little of the former and a great deal of the latter,' she admitted. 'Margot and Stephanie between them seem to have swung me along with their enthusiasm and certainly it is a marvellous opportunity. In my view, though, we need more time, there's a lot of money involved, and a great many implications – both commercial and personal – to consider. For example, we have yet to finalise the terms of the funding: the bank might well try to screw us to make up some of the shortfall on the offer price.'

'It seems to me Margot's being more than a little unreasonable.'

'Possibly, yes, but I've never known her to change her mind and honestly I don't think I can make a decision before I've seen my mother.'

'No, of course you can't,' said Tim. 'Look, leave it to me. I'll talk to Stephanie in the morning and between us we'll see if we can persuade Margot to wait a few days. I know this is a ghastly question to ask but, assuming your doctor's prognosis is right and your mother does die during Wednesday, how long will it be before you can be back in England?'

I won't want to stay,' said Ella, hurriedly, 'but I suppose there's the funeral to consider. I could be back by next weekend, I guess.'

'We'll see if we can get a week's extension, then. Here, let me top up your brandy.'

'I shouldn't, I have a very early start in the morning.'

'Rubbish, it will do you good. Tell me, are there any other arrangements you should be making?'

Ella considered for a moment. 'I have to ring Aaron back and tell him what time I'll be at Cincinnati and then he'll arrange for a car to meet me.'

'Give me Aaron's number and I'll do that for you.'

'You're very kind, Tim,' Ella said. 'You know, it's strange, three days ago I didn't even know you.' She grinned, the tension in her suddenly lifting a little. 'I knew *of* you, of course, but I suppose I imagined some pompous, frightfully British guy, who could talk about nothing but horses and shooting small animals. I couldn't have been more wrong – you're so kind, a true friend.'

Tim laughed. 'You're not a difficult person to be kind to, Ella, and I hope we'll be friends for a long time. I do admire you very much. The way you handle your business and still manage to be a full time mother to Greg – it can't be easy.'

'We muddle through,' said Ella, 'but thank you for the vote of confidence.'

'Talking of friendship...' Tim hesitated, swirling his brandy glass to catch the light from the fire, and carefully not looking at Ella as he spoke, '... if we are to be friends, suppose you tell me what's really worrying you about going back to Kentucky.'

The suddenness of the question astonished Ella. 'W-what makes you think that there is anything worrying me?'

'I'm only guessing, and tell me to mind my own business, but for one thing you've not yet told Greg you're going, have you?' Ella shook her head. 'For a normally prudent, efficient woman it doesn't make much sense. The boy has to be packed up and ready to leave at five-thirty tomorrow morning, and yet he doesn't even know he's leaving. That can only mean you have grave doubts about taking him.' Ella still said nothing. 'Well, let me approach the problem from a different angle,' said Tim. 'If, for whatever reason, you don't want to take him to Kentucky, leave him here with us. The girls would love to have him, you know that, and so would I. I'll make sure he has a good time. Certainly, death beds and fourteen-year-old boys aren't really very compatible.'

Ella felt her spirits soar at the unexpectedly easy solution to her problem. 'Oh Tim, that's so kind of you.'

'Are you saying yes, then?'

Acceptance was on Ella's lips when Aaron's words came back to her. 'I-I don't know, I'll have to think about it.'

Tim got up and threw another log on the fire. The sparks fanned out and the shadows created by the flames leapt onto the ceiling. 'Ella, I'm not much of a student of human nature but something's worrying you a very great deal. There's probably a hell of a lot of other people it would be better to talk to than me but I'm here, now. Tell me what's troubling you and I promise I will never pass it on to a living soul.'

The warmth of the fire, the brandy, the tranquillity of the room and the still quietness of the countryside outside the windows which, as a city dweller, Ella found quite extraordinary, all combined to lull her into a sense of peace and security. This subtle blend of atmosphere combined with her instinctive trust in this man, this comparative stranger, made it suddenly seem possible to let someone for once glimpse the turmoil that seethed beneath her apparently easy-going, good-natured exterior. When she spoke at last, her voice was low, barely above a whisper.

'You're right,' she said, 'I am worrying about taking Greg back to Kentucky.'

'I am guessing here,' said Tim, 'but does your worry concern Greg's father?' Ella nodded. 'You're worried you'll meet him again, is that it? Are you still married, or is he likely to cause trouble?'

'No, and I'm not worried I'll run into him again – well, not exactly,' said Ella. 'You see I-I don't know who he is.'

Tim frowned. 'I don't understand.'

Ella stared at the fire, unable to meet Tim's eyes. 'To say I don't know who he is is wrong. I don't know which one he was – you see, I was gang raped.'

On leaving school at fourteen, of one thing Ella Kovac was certain: she had to find a means of escape – from her life, from her mother, from Silver Springs, from Kentucky – but escape equalled money. Still ostracized from society, the Kovacs had no friends but since the day she had fallen under Aaron Connor's protection, no one had actually abused or fought with Ella – neither, though, had they befriended her. The mothers saw to that. Mollie Kovac was a threat to every woman in Silver Springs. If they had a fight with their man, he would likely go to a bar, get drunk and from there, almost inevitably, he would end up at Mollie Kovac's, where he would do to her all the things he wouldn't dare do to his wife. The backcloth to Ella's nights as a child was a noisy one. The sounds of fornication she blocked out, but the drunken arrivals and departures woke her up regularly, every hour or so right through the night. It was not until she moved out that she experienced the luxury of a full night's sleep for the first time.

Money was the key to escape, how to get it was the question. Work in town did not appeal to her. She could imagine the mean, critical eyes of the inhabitants following her every move; besides which, no storeman would employ her, she would be bad for business. There was work in the fields – cotton, tobacco – but that held no appeal for Ella. The work was hard and the money not enough to buy her food and put some away towards leaving town. In the event, it was Dr Andrew Connors, Aaron's father, who provided the answer. Like most country doctors of the time, he relied heavily on the mixing of his own prescriptions to provide medicines for the community. Silver Springs was expanding. There were a growing number of breeding stables in the area, which in turn brought more work and attracted more people. In return for a nine hour day, during which Ella answered the telephone and prepared Dr Connors' home cures, she received ten dollars a week. It seemed a fortune to the fourteen year old who'd never had a dime of her own, and with great foresight she lied to her mother as to the amount of her earnings. Each week she handed over the bulk of her money to her mother but she still had four dollars of her very own. Ella was terrified that her mother would find the surplus money. Initially she kept it wrapped up in a pair of old socks, buried in a hole in her mattress, but her mother was given to poking around in her room during the day, and each evening Ella came home in fear that the money would have been discovered. Eventually she confided her fears to Mrs Connors, who arranged for Ella's precious savings to be kept in a little cash box in Doc's study.

As well as being an enjoyable job and well paid, it had the added advantage of keeping Ella in touch with Aaron. The bond between them had grown steadily since the day Aaron had become her champion, and for Ella's part had developed into adolescent love. She knew there was no future for them, she was not good enough for him, but no one could take away her dreams.

Doc Connors liked his waiting room to be a welcoming place. There were always fresh flowers on the window sill, the curtains were washed each week, the paintwork kept spick and span, and on the table by the door there was a selection of magazines and a copy of the *Wall Street Journal*. Though nearly a week out of date by the time it reached Silver Springs, the paper was still changed on a daily basis, as though it contained the most up-to-the-minute news. In idle moments, Ella took to reading this worthy publication, thirsting for knowledge of the outside world she had to reach. With an inherent love of figures which the local school had been quite unable to encourage, it was here, among the pages of the *Wall Street Journal*, that she discovered investment. Fascinated, day after day, she plotted the rise and fall of stocks and bonds, watched and fretted over Dow Jones and began to understand the workings of the international money markets.

One evening Andrew Connors caught her pouring over the *Journal*. 'Well, I'll be darned,' he said, 'Aaron told me you'd taken a liking to the stock market but I didn't believe him.'

'It fascinates me,' Ella admitted. 'I hope you don't mind me reading the paper now everyone's gone?'

'Of course not, child – so, are you going to tell me where to place my money?'

'The United Railroad Company,' said Ella, promptly.

Dr Connors laughed. 'Show me.' Ella ran her finger down the column. 'There.'

'But the stock is dropping, Honey.'

'Yes, I know, I know,' said Ella, patiently. 'It's been dropping for three months – in fact it's half the price it was three months ago.'

'So, why do you want me to throw my money away. It sounds like your red hot tip is going bust.'

'I read an article in the *Journal* a month back which said there's going to be a big shake-up on the railroads and a lot of these small companies are going to be bought up. Just think what would happen to the stock if it was.'

'And just think what would happen to the price if it wasn't.'

'I think it's worth a gamble,' said Ella stubbornly.

'Do you now,' said Dr Connors. 'Tell me, how much are your savings worth these days?'

'I-I've nearly 110 dollars.'

'OK, here's what I'll do. When I'm in Cincinnati next week for that medical conference, I'll invest 100 dollars of your money and 200 dollars of mine. If your hunch pays off, then we'll split the profits fifty-fifty. If we lose, well, we lose.'

'That's not fair to you,' Ella protested.

'I'm happy with the deal,' said Doc Connors, laughing. 'You've given me the tip, right, so I'm paying for privileged information.'

Five weeks later, after days of nail-biting, watching the price plummet even further, The United Railroads Company was bought out. After a further three months, Ella and Doc Connors' 300-dollar investment was worth just on 4,000 dollars. They cashed up, split the proceeds and Ella reinvested. At fifteen, she owned one pair of shoes, three frocks, slept in a bug-infested shack with her prostitute mother, but she was launched on to the American Stock Market.

One evening that summer, shortly after Ella's fifteenth birthday, she had been working late at the surgery and decided to take the long way home, by the river. It had been stifling hot all day, threatening a storm which never materialised. The atmosphere was still humid but now, with night coming, there was a gentle breeze and the cool air off the river was infinitely comforting. She was reluctant to go home. Now there were two incomes coming into the family, Mollie Kovac's love affair with the rye bottle had become even more profound and the sessions at the shack less discreet accordingly. She sat down on a tree stump, on the edge of the river, enjoying the peace and solitude.

'Why, if it's not little Miss Kovac, out looking for a man like her Mommy.'

Ella swung round. There were three, no, four boys walking along the bank towards her. They had all been classmates from school. They were an irritant but they did not worry her, she knew how to handle them.

'You hush up, Jim Keeting,' she spat back. 'I just want a little peace and quiet. Some of us have been working hard, instead of lounging around bars all day.'

'Will you listen to that,' Jim said. 'Miss High and Mighty, yet I do hear she works nights as well as days.'

'What's that supposed to mean?' Ella said, and then regretted the challenge, knowing what was to come.

'I do hear,' said Jim, addressing his peers, 'that she and Mamma Mollie are a double act now — two for the price of one and a half. May be we should sample the goods sometime.' The other three sniggered a little self-consciously.

The boys had reached Ella now and automatically she stood up so as not to be at a disadvantage. At Jim's words Ella felt the control on her temper ebb away, she drew back her hand and slapped him viciously across the face. He caught her wrist in his hands. He was surprisingly strong despite his small stature.

'Oh, so we like a bit of rough, do we? Well it so happens I like that too.' Drawing back his free hand he slapped Ella across the face and while she was still staggering under the impact of the blow, his lips crushed on to hers, forcing the breath from her body.

Ella had been in so many fights during her short life that one more seemed of no particular significance ... until Jim Keeting kissed her. Then she recognized the difference.

Panic rose as if to smother her, she fought for control of this, new, terrifying fear, but the trembling weakness of her body betrayed her.

'See that boys, she likes it!' Jim still had hold of her shoulders. She tried to tear herself away but apparently she no longer had the strength.

'Leave me be, just leave me be,' she said. There was a pleading note to her voice which appalled her. Terror was recognizable in the high tremors of her voice and she shuddered with a sudden unexplained chill.

Like every predator, Jim scented her fear and thus his victory. For a moment, common sense prevailed, but the warmth of the night, the feel of Ella's warm flesh and surfeit of beer in his belly proved too much for him. He kissed her again and as he did so, his inexperienced fingers fumbled with the buttons of her dress. She fought him but she was no match for his strength and her very resistance seemed to goad him.

Angry, agitated, driven by lust, he tore away her dress, the well-washed cotton giving easily to expose her bare breasts. The other boys stood rooted to the spot.

'Stop him,' Ella yelled at them. They did nothing.

He threw her to the ground with a cry of triumph and tried to hold her down as he fumbled unsuccessfully with her pants and then with his trouser flies. Ella recognized her chance. With a supreme effort, she made to tear herself from his grasp.

'Hold her down, I said hold her down, dammit.' Jim could barely speak for shortness of breath but they heard him alright.

Silently, and therefore all the more menacingly, the three moved forward, one pinned her arms above her head, the other two her thrashing legs while Jim tore away her pants.

Naked, spreadeagled before him, Ella watched in paralyzing horror as Jim stood up and leisurely began to remove his trousers. His white teeth gleaming in the darkness made her realize he was smiling.

They each took their turn with her. The last one turned her on her front, spread her legs wide and sodomized her. Only he could not be the father of her son, but by then she could not distinguish one from the other for a sea of pain which had entirely engulfed her.

The quiet of his room for once brought Tim no comfort. There was a long silence after Ella had finished speaking, broken only by the occasional shifting of the logs as they burned in the grate. It seemed incredible to Tim that this warm, intelligent, humourous human being, with whom he felt he had so much in common, could have been through such an experience, yet he did not doubt her for a moment. The horror of that night still showed on her face as she spoke, and now, sitting in a corner of the sofa, she seemed to have shrunk. The bold, dazzling exterior she showed to the world was nowhere to be seen. The scars were still very near the surface, he realized. 'What did you do?' he asked, at last.

'It-it took me a long time to gain any sort of control of myself and find what was left of my dress,' Ella said. 'I couldn't go home somehow, so I went back to the Connors. I was lucky, if you can call anything about that night lucky. Aaron was home from college and had been to a party in Lexington. We arrived at his house together and so he led me inside and called his father. Doc Connors patched me up and put me to bed in a spare room. He gave me a shot and I slept. When I woke up crying, he gave me another shot and I slept some more.' Ella grinned faintly. 'It went on like that for some time.'

'At least you knew who the boys were so they didn't go unpunished,' said Tim, confidently.

Ella laughed aloud, a small, brittle laugh, which made Tim wince. 'The law in Kentucky isn't quite as automatic as it is in some places,' she said, 'particularly if your mother's the local whore. The fathers of the boys got together and paid off my mother so she wouldn't press charges, and being only fifteen there was nothing I could do about it.'

'I don't believe I'm hearing this. Your own mother sold your . . . your innocence?'

'If you like, yes,' said Ella. 'I didn't realize it at first. Doc called in the law immediately after he put me to bed. He assumed that the four boys would be picked up because I'd been able to tell him who they were. I don't know how things went from there exactly but every time I asked Doc what was happening, he became more and more tight-lipped and finally he burst out with the news that charges weren't being pressed. It wasn't until some time later I found out that my mother had been paid off, and by then, of course, I realized I was pregnant.'

'You make me feel so . . . so humble,' said Tim.

Ella laughed. 'I can't think why.'

'I've had ups and downs in my life, like everyone else, but for you to have been through this horrendous experience and to have come through it so . . . well, magnificently. You've raised your son and founded a business . . . I have to say, Ella, I think you're a most marvellous person.'

Ella smiled. 'You Englishmen are all the same, too much charm for your own good.'

'I mean it,' said Tim. He sighed, 'I suppose what's worrying you is that you may meet these men again, when you go back to Silver Springs.'

'I don't mind if I do,' said Ella, 'that's not what worries me, it'll be them who won't be able to meet my eye, not the other way round. I haven't forgotten them – Jim Keeting, Gregory Daingerfield, Sam Morgan and Warren Clay.' She spoke the names slowly, deliberately and Tim recognized her hatred for them was burned into her very soul. He shuddered slightly, at the depth of feeling he saw there.

'Then you're worried that Greg will start asking too many questions, is that it?' Ella nodded. 'What have you told him so far?'

'I told him that his Pa took off when he was just a baby,

and that I didn't know where he was. I hinted though that we had been married.' Tim frowned. 'Oh I know what you're thinking, you think I'm doing the wrong thing, bringing him up on a fairy tale.'

'No, I'm not thinking that,' said Tim.

'It's what Aaron thinks. He thinks I have to start telling Greg something.'

'Aaron's right there,' said Tim, 'but the way I see it, Ella, you can't ever tell him the truth either.'

Ella leant forward, elbows on her knees, her face suddenly alert and alive again. 'Oh Tim, do you really believe that?'

'Of course I do, it would destroy the boy.'

'I can't tell you how much it means to me to hear you say that,' said Ella. 'You see it's something I've never discussed with anybody in the world, except Aaron, and he, well, I guess he's rather purist, he believes in dealing with the realities of life.' Ella laughed a little. 'I guess it comes from being a gynaecologist.'

'I do think you should tell Greg the truth about as much of your background as you can,' said Tim, thoughtfully, 'but you're going to have to lie about the circumstances of his birth. I use the word *lie* deliberately, and let's not call it anything else, but you have to lie to him to protect him. There's no risk of anyone telling him the true facts, is there, provided the Connors know what you've said to him?'

Ella shook her head. 'No,' she said, 'it was an odd thing, the town's attitude to me changed completely afterwards. I guess the way I was raped, and then my mother selling me down the line, made them recognize that we were two different people and that I wasn't like her. When I found I was pregnant, Doc offered me an abortion but I wouldn't take it, it didn't seem right somehow. Funnily enough, the town seemed to like that, too. Greg can remember very little of the five years we spent there before moving to New York, but for him it was a very different childhood from my own. We lived with the Connors, I worked for them and Greg mixed with other kids without any problems. All the old sly remarks were a thing of the past – everyone was too ashamed, I guess.'

'Then,' said Tim, suddenly decisive, 'this is what I would do. Take him with you to Kentucky, because you could do with his support and he's old enough now to give it. Tell him about your mother, who and what she was, and about your childhood and how tough it was. I take it that'll be news to him?' Ella nodded. 'Tell him that you and his father weren't married, that you spent one imprudent night together, and that you parted the following day without you knowing where his father was going, and of course without either of you being aware that you were pregnant. Maybe that doesn't put you in the best of all possible lights but it saves Greg from any feeling of rejection. Children can't stand that — I should know to my cost.'

'You mean Stephanie and the girls?' said Ella.

Tim nodded. 'They're better now, they've come to terms with it, but when they were small and their mother no longer had any time for them, we had a lot of problems.'

'I'm sorry,' said Ella, 'there's me going on about my troubles.'

'Ella, I don't have troubles, compared with yours,' said Tim. 'Look it's time I packed you off to bed.' He hesitated, his eyes worried. 'I hope you won't regret our talk.'

Ella stood up and walked to Tim where he stood in front of the fire. She put a hand on his shoulder and kissed his cheek. 'I won't ever forget our talk, Tim, and I'm going to follow your advice precisely. I will take Greg with me tomorrow and I'll tell him every detail of my background, except that one night. I know I've been a little over-protective of him in the past, but, well, now he's older perhaps telling him about my life will help him to understand the "odd ball" that's his mother.'

'Odd, yes,' said Tim. 'Oddly magnificent.' The frank admiration in his eyes startled Ella. She still could not understand why she had chosen this man to confide in when she had told no one, not even Laurie, about her past. Alone in bed later, she realized that if she had tried to anticipate his reaction to her story she would have imagined his rather conventional English mind would have recoiled from the sordid tale. The fact that he actually admired her ability to survive the experience astonished her.

CHAPTER SIX

Greg was unusually quiet on the flight. As an only child he was not particularly boisterous, but despite her own worries and preoccupations, Ella became increasingly aware that his silence was not natural. After a meal, he slept for a while. When he woke, she took a deep breath and asked him what was wrong. He shrugged his shoulders. 'Nothing, really, Mom.'

'Something is,' said Ella. 'Are you sad at leaving Wickham?'

'Yes, very,' said Greg. 'I liked it there.'

'Is that the problem then?' There was silence. 'Come on Greg, tell me what's bugging you.'

'Why aren't we like a normal family?' Greg burst out.

'You mean mother, father and children?' said Ella, with a sinking heart.

'I guess so, and grandparents, too. Millie and Belinda see their grandparents all the time. I don't have a father, so I don't know his parents and you've never talked about your mother, not until now when she's dying.' His voice was full of contempt.

'We didn't get on,' said Ella, aware of the inadequacy of her answer.

Greg appeared not to have heard. 'I've been trying to remember her from when we lived in Kentucky. I can remember Doc Connors and, of course, Aaron, and most of all I remember Mrs Connors, she was so kind. I don't remember my grandma though – did we used to visit her?'

Ella shook her head. 'No, she came to see you once after you were born. We got into a kind of argument and I was very upset. Doc thought it was better if we didn't see each other any more, so we didn't.' Greg said nothing. 'Look,' said Ella, 'there are a lot of things I ought to tell you about my past, about our lives in Kentucky but it seems that right now on the plane just isn't a good time. Trust me, Greg. Once we're in Silver Springs and we have a little time on our own, I'll tell you all about it.'

'OK,' said Greg, affably enough, and with the apparent resilience of youth, he was soon flipping through a magazine, apparently unconcerned.

Their brief conversation, however, had left Ella in a turmoil. There was so much of her past which ashamed her and was so very much at odds with the image of the woman she tried to project herself as to Greg, and indeed to the world. To have to face what she had once been was agony to Ella, and as always she found herself blaming her mother. It was typical that her mother should have fallen into a terminal coma, rather than dying outright, forcing Ella to return to Silver Springs – the one place on earth she never wished to see again.

Dan Chamberlain was a regular visitor to Doc Connors' surgery. As a young man he had taken a tumble from a horse and broken his back; it was a miracle that he had survived at all. He had never ridden again but that had been no loss to the Kentucky racetracks, for he had gone on to become one of the top breeders in the State. The legacy from his injury, however, was appalling back pain. He would take no painkillers on the grounds that it would blunt his senses, and his only relief was a once-a-week session at Doc Connors, where Andrew massaged and manipulated the damaged spine, knocking it back into shape and giving Dan, at worst, a few hours and, at best, several days of relief before the pain began again. Despite it all, he was a cheerful man with a big heart. Now well into his sixties, he still worked a twelve-hour-day. The constant demand of race meetings took him all over the

States which meant that he never knew when he would be able to turn up for what he described as 'his servicing'. However, whenever he arrived at the surgery, Doc Connors always fitted him in. Doc admired Dan tremendously and was fond of saying, 'if all my patients had half as much pain and made twice as much fuss as Dan Chamberlain, they'd still be a whole heap less trouble than they are right now.'

One April evening Dan Chamberlain turned up, as usual, unannounced, to find himself in the midst of a birthday party – Greg Kovac's fifth birthday. He planted a hearty kiss on the little boy's cheek, gave him a five dollar bill and accepted a large piece of birthday cake. Only later, when he was alone in the surgery with Andrew, did he raise the question of Greg and Ella, his interest awakened by the charming pair they had made at the tea table. 'So what's to become of the girl, Andrew?' he asked.

Andrew knew it was important to talk to Dan during these sessions. The pain had to be excruciating and the old man controlled it by letting his mind drift away from his body and become absorbed in something else entirely.

'I wish I knew,' said Andrew. 'Ella's ambition, her dream, has been to get away from Silver Springs. As I am sure you will remember, Greg is the result of her being raped. While she stays here, she can never be free of her past, nor indeed that terrible mother of hers. She nearly made it last year – she was doing real well on the stock market and then she took a tumble. She has a wonderful gambling instinct but she over-stretched herself. Until then she was well on the way to accumulating enough capital for her and the boy to take off someplace.'

'Are you saying the girl plays the stock market?' Dan looked over his shoulder and winced with pain.

Andrew smiled at the incredulity in his voice. 'Sure she does.' He repeated, then, the story of Ella's first investment and a brief résumé of subsequent gains and losses. 'As I say, there was a point last year when I thought it was only a matter of time before we'd lose her, but now she's down to about 7,000 or 8,000 dollars and she doesn't reckon that's enough to start a whole new life for herself and Greg. I guess she's right.'

'Would she accept a loan?' Dan asked.

'I doubt it. In any event, I guess I have some reservations about her leaving.'

'Like what?' said Dan.

'Well . . . she's never been away from Silver Springs. She talks about nothing else but she's never seen the big, bad world outside. She sees Silver Springs as her prison, but it's also her protection. She's an accepted part of this town now — they feel they owe her something and by God they're right.'

'How old is she?' Dan asked.

'Twenty.'

'She's young yet,' said Dan, 'she's plenty of time.'

'Ella Kovac's never been young,' said Andrew, quietly.

There was a silence between the two men. 'I tell you what,' said Dan, 'why doesn't she come with me to the Kentucky Derby, just for Derby Week? I can get her a job, I don't know what as but something, and it will give her a chance to see something of life outside Silver Springs. What do you say?'

'It's a good idea,' said Andrew, 'she could do with a break from the child and from us. She knows we'll look after the boy and certainly it has to be a good idea to broaden her horizons.'

Ella's immediate reaction was to say no to Dan Chamberlain's proposal. She did not trust men, and with good cause. Even Dan who she knew so well, who she was perfectly certain took nothing but an avuncular interest in her, still roused her suspicions. Ungraciously she said she would think about it and it took all Doc and Irene Connors' most cunning persuasion to talk her into eventually accepting.

They travelled by horse-box to Churchill Downs, the legendary race track at Louisville. Dan and his racing manager, Joe, were kindness itself. The grooms and Joe slept in the trailer but Dan had secured a room for Ella, at a farmhouse close to the track. There had been excitement and anticipation in the air from the moment they had begun their journey, and when, at last, the famous twin spires of the grandstand came in sight, Ella's apprehension lifted and she, too, felt a sense of elation. While the horses were being unloaded and stabled, Dan told Ella that he would go and talk to some people and find a job for her. He was back within ten minutes. 'I've got just the job for you, 20 dollars per day, plus tips.' It sounded a fortune.

'That's wonderful,' said Ella. 'Doing what?'

'Attendant in one of the Clubhouse washrooms.'

'A washroom attendant?' Ella was appalled.

Dan was not at all apologetic. 'Don't knock it, Ella. The work's easy, the pay's good, the tips I'm told are great, and it's a fine place to work — very clean and smart. You have a uniform, too.'

'I've come all this way with you to clean washrooms?' Ella couldn't believe he was serious.

'Look, Sweetheart, it's a job, a well paid job. Do it nicely, smile sweetly and you'll make a fortune out of tips. I reckon you could clear 800, maybe 900 dollars by the end of the week. It's a hell of a lot more than I was earning at your age.'

It was clear she didn't have much option. She collected her uniform and checked into the little farmhouse where she was to stay, which was just a quarter of a mile's walk from the track. They were pleasant people, her room clean and sunny. It was a strange feeling, for it was the first time she had ever experienced any real privacy. She found it exhilarating.

The work, as Dan had predicted, was neither arduous nor unpleasant. Dan could have fixed for her to work in one of the bars but he had rightly guessed that she would have found it difficult to handle men, so many men, some drunk, some of whom inevitably would have tried to flirt with her. She was a very pretty girl and because of her past she needed protecting. The ladies' washroom might not be glamorous but it was probably about as much as she could handle.

Derby Day came and went and for Ella, cloistered in the Clubhouse washroom, there was little chance to feel the thrill and excitement of the racing. Her tips mounted up: the more she smiled, handed out clean towels, gave opinions on hair, hats, make-up and straight seams on stockings, the more money they gave her.

It was the last day of Derby Week that changed everything. A woman, who Ella had seen many times during the week and remembered for her singular lack of tips, bustled in and, after relieving herself, started a battery of complaints.

'Here, Girl, this towel's real dirty,' she said. There was not a speck on it so far as Ella could see but she replaced it immediately. 'I don't know what this place is coming to,' the woman muttered. Her voice was slightly slurred, her small eyes over-bright. Ella kept silent, watching the woman as she teased her grey curls, stiff with lacquer. She was plastered with make-up, and her diamonds were so ostentatious that they just had to be real. The woman applied lipstick lavishly to camouflage thin lips. Ella hated her. The woman packed away her make-up, took a final look at her reflection in the mirror and then drew out her wallet, much to Ella's amazement. For a moment it looked as though she was actually going to leave a tip, but then she hesitated and turned steely grey eyes to Ella.

'And don't think I'm leaving you a tip, not when you can't even provide clean towels. This place is a real mess.' She let her eyes wander round the spotless room, clearly hoping to see something out of place. She thrust her wallet back in her bag, turned abruptly and clattered on over-high heels out of the door.

'Old bitch,' Ella said, under her breath. She stepped forward to remove the dirty towel and it was then that she saw it – a bright yellow betting slip had fallen into the wash basin. She picked it up. 'Exacta ticket' she read. The date on the ticket was that day's the race number 9, the last of the day. Without pausing for thought, Ella ran out of the door into a seething mass of people. She looked desperately to right and left but there was no sign of the woman. Ella shrugged her shoulders: she'd be back, no doubt. She thrust the ticket into the top pocket of her blouse and went back to her duties.

It was only at the end of the day, when she was putting on her jacket to leave, that Ella remembered the ticket. Earlier in the week, Dan had tried to persuade her to place some money on a horse but she would have none of it. Gambling on the stock market was one thing – she knew a little about the form – but horses were another matter entirely. She wasn't going to risk her money on something she did not understand. She studied the ticket. What did 'Exacta' mean? Outside the washroom the crowds were thinning fast. On the ground were a number of the day's discarded racecards. Ella picked up one. Inside was a list of the various types of bets, and their descriptions.

'EXACTA: to win in Exacta wagering, you must pick the two horses finishing first and second in exact order.'

Ella looked around. A pleasant looking couple were strolling across the grass towards her. 'Excuse me,' Ella said, 'could you tell me the winners in the last race.'

'Why, certainly.' The man consulted his card. 'Horses Four, Two and Six were first, second and third.' He smiled at Ella. 'Well, Little Lady, did you have any luck?'

With a beating heart, Ella tried to reply casually. 'I guess not,' she said, backing away. 'Thanks anyway.'

Back in the washroom, Ella examined the ticket. Horses Four and Two were clearly printed as being first and second home. She checked again: the race, the date, the horses – it all matched. She was holding a winning ticket. It was then that she noticed the value of the bet: 500 dollars – a high stake. Why had the woman not come back – had she been too drunk to even know she'd picked a winner?

Ella caught sight of herself in the mirror. She stared at her reflection for some moments. Then suddenly she was galvanized into action. Scrambling in her purse, she found hairbrush and lipstick. Make up and hair tidied, she buttoned up her jacket to the neck and studied her full-length image. With just the skirt of her uniform showing, she could pass for an ordinary punter. Squaring her shoulders, she left the washroom and took the underground tunnel to the Totalisator.

The wagering windows of the Totalisator were divided into two sections, SELL and CASH. Hesitantly, Ella walked up to one of the CASH windows. She passed the ticket through the grid. 'I guess I've won,' she said, tremulously.

The cashier studied the ticket and then looked down at her and smiled. 'My, my, you're the lucky girl. You'll have to wait a moment, I haven't enough here.' For a moment, he disappeared from view. What did he mean? Ella felt suddenly very sick. Perhaps the winnings amounted to a lot of money, 5,000, even 10,000 dollars, maybe. 'There we go, Young Lady.' He began counting out the money in 1,000-dollar bills. Ella's mouth went dry and for a moment she thought she was going to faint. He kept on counting.

'Twenty, twenty-five, sorry the stuff's so small, that's how it is at the end of the day, thirty-five, forty, there you go, 52,000 dollars. Would you like a bag for it?'

'Y-yes, please,' said Ella.

He produced a brown paper bag which had clearly held his lunch. 'Bit grubby, sorry, probably just as well though, you don't want anyone grabbing this lot, do you?'

'No,' said Ella.

He handed it over as though it was nothing more than a bag of toffees. 'Have fun with it. Well done.' He turned away, dismissing her, completely unaware that he had just irrevocably changed the life of two people.

'Ladies and Gentlemen, we will be landing at Cincinnati in fifteen minutes. We hope you've enjoyed the flight...'

Ella forced herself back into the present. It all seemed so long ago now, yet it was only eight years. She had used the winnings well, there was no doubt about that, but had she founded her business on a fraud? For weeks afterwards she'd imagined that it was only a matter of time before she would be arrested, yet it never happened. The money, apparently, was hers. Over the years she had taken comfort from the fact that her initial instincts had been good, to return the ticket to the woman. Surely it was not her fault if the woman had not come back to reclaim her ticket? She had never told anyone how she had truly come by the money. Dan and the Connors believed she had placed a single bet and been lucky – after all, she had done well on the stock market, why not on the race track. Quite recently, at a particularly boring business dinner, Ella, seated next to a New York Police Chief, had asked his view on cashing in a lost ticket, making out the incident had happened to a friend. The Police Chief was adamant that no crime had been committed, provided the ticket was not stolen. Certainly, it was not difficult to put up a case for justifying what she had done and yet, like everything else about her past, it worried her, undermined her confidence and was something she would rather forget.

CHAPTER SEVEN

SILVER SPRINGS, KENTUCKY
August 1977

Ella and Greg were soon into the terminal building since they only had hand luggage with them – the rest they had left at Wickham. 'Aaron said he would arrange for a car to meet us,' Ella said to Greg. 'Can you see anyone holding up a card with our name on?'

'No,' said Greg, and then laughed aloud, 'but I can see Uncle Aaron.' He let out a whoop and leaving Ella's side, ran to Aaron, standing head and shoulders above everyone else, his shock of fair hair unmistakable.

'Hi, Greg.' Aaron shook Greg's hand, and Greg turned to Aaron's wife, Alice, who embraced him warmly.

Ella stood for a second watching the scene, a great feeling of relief flooding through her. With Aaron and Alice around, she could cope. Aaron was suddenly beside her. 'Hey, you don't look too pleased to see us.'

'Oh Aaron,' said Ella, and uncharacteristically burst into tears.

The journey from Cincinnati airport to Silver Springs was uneventful, but for Greg it was a complete eye-opener. His passion for country living had him craning out of the window, pointing out the virtues of Kentucky in high summer. It was a sweltering day and by the time they finally reached Silver Springs, they were all wringing wet and exhausted. Aaron drove the car slowly up the main street, giving Ella time to take in her surroundings. 'Nothing's changed,' she said, 'absolutely nothing.'

'You're practically right,' said Aaron. 'There's another bar now, a ladies' hairdressers, my mother tells me, and there's some new housing development out beyond ... beyond your mother's old home. We'll stop off at Pa's first and when you've had a chance to change and rest I'll take you up to the hospital.'

The welcome from Andrew and Irene Connors was equally as warm, although Ella had only seen them twice since she had left Silver Springs. Irene looked at Greg in amazement. 'Is this truly my baby boy?' Greg shifted uneasily and grinned self-consciously.

'Some baby, eh?' said Ella, ruffling his hair.

'My, you've turned into a handsome young man. Come here and give your Aunt Irene a kiss.'

Greg obliged and then looked around him. 'I remember this. I couldn't picture it in my mind before coming here but now I'm here I remember it all – particularly the smell ... he sniffed appreciatively.

Andrew threw back his head and laughed. 'That's iodine and disinfectant, the tools of my trade. It's the first thing Aaron always says when he comes home, that it's good to smell the place again.'

'It's true,' Aaron admitted. 'Come on, let's get Ella upstairs, she's exhausted.'

It was early evening before Ella and Aaron made the pilgrimage to the hospital. In some dark corner of her mind, Ella had almost hoped her mother would be dead by the time she arrived in Silver Springs. She was not proud of the thought but the idea of confronting her mother, even in a coma, appalled her.

'Can I come, too?' Greg asked, as she was leaving.

Ella shook her head. 'Not until I see how she is, Greg, but I promise you, tomorrow.'

'OK,' he said, grudgingly.

They drove in silence for some minutes. 'Tell me what you're thinking,' Aaron said, as they turned up the dusty driveway to the hospital.

'I was counting my blessings,' said Ella. 'I just don't know what I would have done at the various stages of my life, without the love and support of the Connors. You're all so good to me – just imagine you and Alice coming out here to be with us, and leaving your practice and your kids behind.' She was close to tears at this moment, painfully aware of the depths of her feelings for Aaron.

'It's nothing,' said Aaron. 'Actually it was Alice's idea. She didn't think you should go through this alone, and she's right, of course, she always is.'

'You're very lucky with Alice,' Ella forced herself to say. It was true, of course, Alice was just right for him in a way she, Ella, could never have been.

Aaron grinned. 'Don't I know it.' They drew up outside the hospital entrance. 'Shall I drop you off?' he asked.

Ella shook her head. 'I'd like you to come with me, if you would, Aaron.'

Aaron Connors was something of a celebrity at Silver Springs County Hospital. His father was enormously admired and respected of course, but his son was a superstar – a Consultant in New York. The nurses lowered their eyes and spoke in hushed whispers as he passed. In different circumstances Ella would have been amused.

Because of Aaron's status, they were shown into matron's office.

'How is she?' Aaron asked. Ella seemed incapable of speech.

'Much the same, Mr Connors, I'm afraid.' The matron was a thin, scrawny woman in middle years, whose best feature was a pair of warm, brown eyes. 'She's showing no signs of coming out of the coma.'

'D-do you think there's any chance of her regaining consciousness?' Ella asked.

'To be frank, I doubt it, but you never know, we've seen some strange sights here over the years, when people are close to death.' Matron looked suddenly uncomfortable. 'I'm sorry, Miss Kovac, I take it you've been told that there is little chance of your mother surviving this.'

'Yes, yes I understand,' said Ella.

'Would you like to see her now?'

Ella took a deep breath. 'Yes, please.'

'Shall I come with you?' Aaron asked, quietly.

Ella shook her head. Up to that moment, she had needed him. Now, suddenly, she didn't want anyone to witness her seeing her mother. She was so unsure as to how she would react – whether she could even bear to be in the same room.

'Call me if you need me,' said Aaron, 'I'll be in the waiting room.'

On Ella's instructions, her mother had been moved to a private room. A nurse opened the door for her, ushered her in and closed it quietly behind her. It was a sunny room: beams of sunlight played on the walls and there were several bunches of flowers on the window-ledge. The paintwork, white and yellow, made the room bright and airy. For a long time Ella stood staring out of the window, unable to look at the figure in the bed. At last, her heart beating as loudly as a drum, she turned and gazed at her mother.

She was a stranger – a tiny, wizened old woman. Her hair had gone completely white, a pretty colour, brushed back from her face and fanning out on the pillow. Her face was lined but her good bone structure still showed through, and it was possible to see that this old woman had once been very good-looking. Her complexion was very pale. For a moment Ella had the absurd idea that they had shown her into the wrong room. It was the lack of make-up she realized gradually. Mollie Kovac had taken her profession very seriously. Her hair had always been dyed with henna, her face heavily made up, her lips scarlet, her skirts short, her heels high. Since her mother slept late in the mornings, Ella could not remember seeing her except when she was dressed for work. Yet this old lady had rather a sweet face, she was the image of everyone's ideal grandmother. Ella could see her sitting in a rocking chair by the kitchen range, knitting for some beloved grandchild, ready with a fund of stories, advice, a helping hand. Ella shook her head as if trying to re-focus the picture. Unable to do so, she sank down on the chair beside the bed and simply stared.

She could not remember the precise moment when she had realized that her mother sold her body to different men each night and that this was considered to be a wicked thing to do. It seemed to her that the knowledge had always been with her from the cradle, and with it had come an almost schizophrenic attitude to her mother's chosen lifestyle. In conversation with her mother, she always sided with the rest of Silver Springs in their condemnation. As a small child, she had even begged her mother to adopt some other way of life. When it became clear that her mother was indifferent to her daughter's suffering, Ella abandoned hope of any change and simply concentrated on being critical, rude and sullen, treating her mother's occasional attempts to form any sort of relationship with contempt.

Yet, away from the shack they called home, Ella was fiercely loyal to her mother. She fought the battle alone, slamming her small fists into anyone who spoke a word against her mother, until Aaron Connors became her champion and together they silenced the many critics. Staring now at the wizened old face, Ella realized with a shock that she could forgive her mother the barren waste that had been her childhood.

What she could not forgive was that she had allowed her daughter's rapists to go free. In the first few hours following the rape, Ella could still remember wanting her mother's comfort but not being able to find the words to tell Doc of this unexpected need. Her horror at learning that her mother had sold her loss of innocence was all the more intense, therefore, and the dull resentment she had always felt had blazed into hatred. Why had she done it, were her motives purely greed? Putting those boys behind bars was the only possible course of action for any parent, surely? Thinking about it now as she sat beside her mother's inert body, Ella realized it was not the lack of justice which troubled her so much as the total lack of loyalty. It had been her mother's one chance to make up for all the years which had preceded that August night. And there was another factor ... if she had not been Mollie Kovac's daughter, she would not have been raped. Ella was sure of that.

*

More from curiosity's sake than anything else, Ella reached beneath the covers and took one of Mollie's hands in hers. It was a small hand, with short, capable fingers – it was warm, a living thing. There was so much, Ella suddenly realized, that she wanted to ask her mother: the question which had formed a million times in Ella's mind but which she had never had the courage to voice – Why, why had Mollie Kovac chosen her way of life? Did she enjoy it, did she really have no choice, and what had started her on the rocky road to ruin and degradation? What, too, of her father? As a small child, Mollie had told her that her father had run off. He had been a tobacco worker, Mollie had said. They'd had a whirlwind romance and married but he had gone off to another part of the state before the baby was born. As Ella grew older and wiser, she no longer believed the story, imagining her father to have been one of her mother's clients. Not for the first time, Ella thought of the similarity between her own conception and Greg's. Neither her mother nor Greg's could disclose the name of their child's respective fathers, because they did not know themselves.

Time passed and Ella did not hear the discreet knock on the door. She looked up, startled, when Aaron placed a hand on her shoulder. 'Come on, Sweetheart, you've been here long enough now.'

Ella stared at him, vaguely. 'Have I? How long?'

'Nearly two hours.'

'Jesus!' Ella looked confused. She ran a hand through her dark curls, her eyes glazed with fatigue and strain.

'Come on,' said Aaron, 'Doctor's orders. I'm taking you home.'

Ella stood up, stiffly. 'She's not on any sort of drip. I imagined she'd be all wired up to equipment.'

'She isn't, at my request,' said Aaron. 'I hope you approve, but I felt there was no point in prolonging her life. The damage caused by the stroke is profound. She's nearly seventy and it didn't seem right.'

'No, no, of course not,' said Ella. 'So what you are saying is that even if she regains consciousness she wouldn't be able to speak or understand?'

Aaron shook his head. 'I very much doubt it.' Ella felt tears spring into her eyes. 'I know what you're feeling,' Aaron said gently, 'you want to talk to her one last time.' Ella nodded. 'Come on, Honey, you'll feel better once you're back home.'

The warmth and kindness of the Connors did help. Ella could face no supper but she drank the whisky and strong coffee with which Doc Connors plied her. Greg seemed perfectly at home and regaled everyone over supper with details of their stay at Wickham, which suddenly seemed a very long time ago to Ella. After Greg and the old people had gone to bed, Aaron and Ella continued to sit out on the veranda, enjoying the peace and quiet of the Kentucky night. 'You know,' said Ella, 'I sometimes wonder what the hell we're doing living in New York.'

Alice looked up and smiled. 'I know what you mean. There's you and Aaron both Kentucky born and me from Wyoming. We're always complaining about what hell the city is and yet there we stay. Why don't we give it all up and buy ourselves a ranch someplace? Raise the kids as kids should be raised — riding, swimming in the river and good fresh air day after day?'

Ella looked at Alice affectionately and thought, not for the first time, how lucky she had been, as well as Aaron, in his choice of bride. For Alice was without any form of jealousy, recognizing, understanding and even enjoying the extraordinary closeness of Aaron and Ella's relationship. It could have been so different, for while Alice was pretty, with her soft brown hair and light blue eyes, she could not begin to compete with Ella in either looks or personality. Yet here she was making plans for the future and automatically including Ella and Greg as part of them. There could be few such generous-spirited people as Alice Connors, yet how would she react if she knew how his childhood friend really felt about Aaron, Ella wondered? Still, the Connors' marriage was safe with her, she would never do anything to hurt either of them. She loved Aaron, loved them both, too much for that. 'Well, I'm all for it,' Ella said at last, 'but we'd better ask the boss.'

Aaron leant forward and knocked his pipe thoughtfully on the veranda railing. 'I think we need a plan,' he said. 'How about us all retiring in, say, ten years' time? We should have made a few dollars between us, and we could then eke out the rest of our days as Alice suggests, playing farmers.'

'But the kids will all be grown up and gone by then,' protested Alice.

'Then they can bring our grandchildren back to see us.'

'I think we waste too much of our lives pursuing so-called success,' Alice sounded suddenly very forlorn.

'You're serious, aren't you?' said Ella, surprised.

'I guess I am — it's something I've thought about more and more lately. Aaron's so busy he has no time for the kids, the kids think cows and horses belong in story books or zoos, we're all suffering from lead poisoning, tearing around like ants in a nest and for what?'

The question might have been answered, but for the shrill intervention of the telephone. 'I'll get it,' said Aaron. He was back in a moment and even before he spoke, Ella knew what he was going to say. 'That was the hospital, Ella. I'm sorry, Sweetheart, I'm afraid she's gone.'

For a moment the breath seemed to be driven from Ella's body and she gasped at the air to fill her lungs. She felt nothing, so why was she sobbing as though her heart would break.

'Why didn't you let me come with you yesterday, why, why, why?' The normally easy-going Greg was lying face down on the bed, thumping his fists into the pillow. It was the following morning and Ella had just told him of his grandmother's death.

Ella was astounded by the apparent violence of his feelings. She had expected no more than a token reaction.

'Greg, I don't understand why you're so upset. I know it's sad but you never actually knew her.'

'Don't you see,' Greg hiccuped, 'don't you see that's what's wrong. I wanted to meet her so much. I want a family, Mom, a proper family. I wanted to ask her stuff, about my grandpa, things like that.'

In an instance Ella understood she was witnessing a carbon copy of her own feelings of the previous evening – the lack of identity, the need to belong. Without thinking too hard for fear she would falter, she said, 'OK, Sweetheart, this is what we'll do ... I'll ask Aunt Irene if we can borrow the car today and we'll take off with a picnic. There's a resort park just near here, it's beautiful. We'll find a quiet spot and have a good long talk. I guess I owe you a few explanations, right?'

The Jenny Wiley State Resort Park was hugged by mountains and rimmed a huge lake. Its beauty was breathtaking and neither Greg nor Ella felt the need for conversation as they drove along the outer perimeter road, until they found a perfect picnic spot by the lake.

'You make a camp fire,' said Ella, 'I'll unload the stuff from the car.'

Irene had done them proud – there were sausages, chicken, bread, salad, ice-cool beer and great chunks of cold apple pie. Ella poured the beer while Greg took charge of the cooking. They talked of inconsequential things – his school friends back home, his grades, his chances in the various teams come the Fall. The beer made them relaxed and talkative. At last, when the meal was finished, Ella embarked on the conversation which she knew was long overdue. She told Greg quietly and unemotionally all about her life in Silver Springs, about what her mother did for a living and how much she owed the Connors. Only when she came to the story of Greg's birth did she hesitate.

'OK,' said Greg, 'you've told me my father went away just like your father, but you must know who he is, Mom.'

Ella shook her head and took a deep breath. 'That's the awful thing, Greg. Your birth was so very much like my own. I behaved like a very silly girl, though I was only fifteen, as you know. I went to a local party and danced a lot with this one boy. He was tall, dark, good-looking, just like you. We went for a walk by the river after the dance and well ... well, I behaved very stupidly and let him make love to me. I was very young and so was he. I don't think it occurred to either of us that I might get pregnant. The next day, he left town. I was sad because I liked him very much. It wasn't until a month or so later I realized what had happened.'

'You must have known his name, though,' said Greg.

Ella shook her head. 'I know this sounds crazy but I didn't.'

'But why was he in town?' Greg persisted. 'He must have been staying with somebody. Didn't the Connors know who he was?'

Ella shook her head. 'He was just a student on vacation passing through, I guess. But-but the thing is, Greg, never feel you've been abandoned by your father – he simply doesn't know you exist. If he did, he'd be very proud of you, and I'm very sorry that you've never had a father of your own.'

'I wish you'd married Aaron, Mom. You were such good friends as kids. Why didn't you?'

Ella smiled. 'I couldn't do that, Aaron's like a brother,' she said hurriedly, terrified her feelings would betray her. 'Anyway, let me go on with the story, I've not finished yet. We might as well go the whole hog so that you know of all the skeletons in my cupboard.' She smiled to lighten the atmosphere and was rewarded with a smile back. So she continued the story, of her working for Andrew Connors, of her interest in the stock market and finally the Kentucky Derby and finding the winning ticket.

'Was it stealing?' Greg asked, round-eyed.

'I don't know,' said Ella, 'but I don't think so. No one else in the world knows about it except you. I pretended to everyone that I'd bought the ticket myself. I tried to find the woman, Greg, I really did, and I don't believe she had any idea that she'd won. Do you think what I did was wrong?'

Greg poked at the fire distractedly. When at last he spoke, his words cut her to the quick. 'I guess you did the right thing, Mom, except that if you hadn't got all that money, we'd still be living at Silver Springs with Uncle Andrew, and I kind of like that idea.'

'But we'd be poor!' said Ella, horrified. 'You'd have no fancy bike, no private schooling, no summer camp, no trips to Europe . . .'

'But we'd be living in the country,' said Greg.

Holding on to what sanity she could muster, Ella recognized that despite his assumed maturity, Greg was still a child and did not mean to be cruel. Yet when she thought of the years of struggle to give him a life away from Silver Springs, the knowledge that he would actually prefer to be there was almost too much to bear.

Later, when she was alone, she mulled over their conversation. Always anxious to be honest with herself, Ella could not help recognizing that part of that struggle to escape had not been purely for Greg but rather more for herself. The thought brought no comfort.

The crowd at the funeral was extraordinary. Aaron had warned Ella that there was likely to be a good turn out – not so much out of respect for Mollie Kovac but more likely to have a sight of Mollie Kovac's daughter. Ella was apprehensive to the point where she threatened not to attend at all, but the Connors would have none of it and insisted she came. In fact it was not the ordeal she had expected. Flanked by the Connors, with Greg standing tall and solemn beside her, she felt among friends and was surprised not only by the number of people, but by their warm greetings as they lined up to shake her hand and offer their sympathy. It was an altogether friendly congregation and any humiliation the town might have heaped on the Kovacs in the past, today was forgotten. If nothing else, Mollie Kovac had been a notorious and well-known figure. It was the end of an era, the town seemed to recognize it and wanted to be there to witness its passing.

As Ella and Greg followed the coffin down the aisle of the church, all eyes were on them. It suddenly occurred to Ella that both her father and Greg's could be in the congregation, unknowingly watching their son and daughter walk down the aisle. The thought made her raise her eyes and hurriedly search the sea of faces. There was no sign of her tormentors of fourteen years ago, although she was not sure now that she would even recognize them. The thought was unnerving nonetheless.

In keeping with their usual generosity of spirit, the Connors offered open house after the funeral. Irene had spent the previous day baking and there was coffee, lemonade and beer on offer. Ella had survived the funeral but she could not cope with the idea of meeting the town face to face. As soon as the service was over, she ran upstairs to her bedroom and lay down on the bed, trying as far as possible to keep her mind blank. After a while there was a knock on the door and Greg entered. 'Aren't you coming downstairs, Mom?'

She shook her head. 'I'm sorry, Sweetheart, but I just can't face it.'

'Aunt Irene says you should be there but Uncle Andrew says not – he says they've only come to gawp at you. He reckons they'll go home all the quicker once they know you're not coming down. Why do they want to gawp at you, Mom?'

'Well, I expect they've heard I've done well in New York and made some money.' She propped herself up on one elbow and smiled. 'They remember me as a scrawny little kid, you see, not the over-fed, middle-aged woman I've become.'

'That's not true,' Greg said, hotly, 'don't say that, you're not middle-aged and you certainly don't eat much.' He hesitated, something clearly still on his mind. 'I'm sorry,' he said at last.

'For what?' said Ella.

'I'm sorry for what I said yesterday. I do like our life in New York really.'

'I'm glad,' said Ella. 'You know something, Greg,' she said, 'you're growing up fast. I'm so proud of you and I do love you very much.'

'I love you, too, Mom.' He looked at her awkwardly. 'I'd better go downstairs now.'

'OK.'

After Greg had left her, Ella swung her legs over the side of the bed and went to the window. The room looked out over the front of Doc Connors' house and gave a good view of the main street of Silver Springs. Ella stared with interest in both directions. The street was busier than usual, as people left the Connors' house to wander home – talking of what, she wondered. Today they had buried Mollie Kovac, the harlot, and with her mother's death, Ella realized that she, too, was released, freed at last from the squalor of her childhood. She thought back to Greg's words of a moment before. They had journeyed back together, she and Greg, faced the drama of their early lives ... and survived. Now it was time to look forward, to plan the future, hopefully released at last from the long shadow of the past.

CHAPTER EIGHT

NEW YORK
August 1977

It felt good to be back in her office, despite the scene that had just taken place with Henry Moss. It was not a question of choice, so far as Ella was concerned. She had to work with someone she trusted and she knew that she no longer trusted Henry. The mistake over ADC was too grave to brush under the carpet. He had to go and go he had.

Ella's offices could not have been much more convenient for they formed part of the ground floor of Gregory Buildings, the first property she had ever acquired. She and Greg lived in an apartment on the first floor and so commuting to work for Ella meant riding the elevator just one floor down. In addition, the building was on Lexington and 39th – nice and central, prestigious even but without being flashy. Ella pressed the intercom and moments later Jessie Lendle puffed into her office. Jessie had been with Ella since the very start of her business. She was middle-aged, black and very large but she had a heart to match her vast size and to Ella she was quite indispensable. In the early days, when Greg was just a small child, Jessie had mucked in with everything – typed letters, collected Greg from school, cleaned the apartment, baby-sat . . . whatever was needed to keep the business going. She was not, to be fair, a great typist but she was blessed with something far more valuable – good, sound commonsense and an absolute, unquestioning loyalty.

'So you threw him out?' she asked, puffing and wheezing as she sat down by Ella's desk.

'I had no choice, did I, Jess?'

'No,' said Jessie, uncompromizingly, 'though I blame myself.'

'How come?' said Ella, who had already spent most of the morning unravelling the affair. 'You weren't even here, you were off sick.'

'I know that,' said Jessie, 'but I had no business to be off sick when you were away in Europe. If I'd typed up that lease, I'd have noticed the mistake, you know that.'

'Of course I know that, said Ella, 'but your job, Jessie, is to type. His job was to think.'

Jessie grinned. 'I think I resent that, Miss Ella Kovac.'

Ella returned the smile. 'You know perfectly well what I mean.'

'Yeh, I know what you mean. I'm just a crazy old black mama, right?' She put her head on one side and eyed Ella shrewdly. 'I never liked him anyway.'

Ella laughed out loud. As usual Jessie always went straight to the heart of the problem. 'No, I didn't like him, either.'

'Then, Ella, why the hell did you hire him in the first place?'

Ella shrugged her shoulders. 'He was well qualified, young and ambitious — I thought he was what we needed.'

'That's no reason and you know it,' said Jessie.

'OK', said Ella, resignedly, 'give me your version.'

'He had class — Harvard Business School, the right connections, a good family — unlike us he's *always* been somebody.'

Her assessment was entirely accurate and Ella could not help her amusement. 'OK, smartass — so you reckon I got what was coming to me for being a snob. I guess you're right, I guess I deserved to lose out on that lease.'

'Everyone deserves to get value for money. That Henry Moss needs his ass kicking. Still, you're young, you'll learn.'

The door burst open. 'You must be talking about me again, Jessie? Welcome home, Ella.' Laurie Merman crossed the office and bending over, kissed Ella on both cheeks.

'Hi, Laurie.' She was at once pleased and irritated — pleased to see him and irritated by the way, as always, he burst into her office as though he owned it.

'OK, OK,' said Jessie, heaving herself out of the seat. 'I'll leave you two lovebirds alone.' She waddled out, slamming the door behind her.

So far as Ella was aware, Jessie was the only person who knew of their affair and this was by force of circumstances – it simply would not have been possible to keep it from her. The fact worried Ella not at all but Laurie was always irritated by Jessie's references to the relationship – a fact which, no doubt, only encouraged Jessie's lack of discretion. Her words angered him now.

'That woman really gets up my ass,' he said. 'Why the hell don't you find yourself a decent secretary, Ella? She can't type, she can't mind her own business and in the space she takes up, you could have three secretaries, three typewriters, a copying machine, a telex and still have room to spare.'

'Without Jessie, Lexington Kovac Incorporated would grind to a halt,' said Ella firmly. 'Are you going to take me out to lunch, Laurie?'

'Why not, where would you like to go?'

'Somewhere cheerful and quick, I want to be in the apartment by the time Greg comes back from the Connors. We have a lot to organize before tomorrow.'

It had been Alice Connors' suggestion that Ella should return to London alone, for it was less than a week before Greg was due back at school, and the heavy negotiations in which Ella was likely to find herself on her return to Europe, were hardly going to entertain a thirteen-year-old. Ella had agreed and so Greg was moving in with the Connors. It was now Thursday and Stephanie had telexed to say that the deadline had been extended to the following Monday morning. It left very little time, and there were still a lot of arrangements to make at home, before she caught her flight out of New York on Friday morning.

'So, how's this Paris deal coming along?' said Laurie, as they sat over the remains of their wine.

'OK, I guess,' said Ella. 'The price has come down one hell of a lot.' She explained the details. 'Stephanie's pretty confident we can do a good deal on the funding, too – as she says, the bank have to be fairly desperate.'

'She sounds a bright girl, this Lady Stephanie,' said Laurie.

'She is, you'd like her.'

'So, you're going ahead?' he persisted.

'I don't know, I suppose so.'

'Forgive me for saying so, Honey, but you're not exactly radiating enthusiasm.'

'I guess I just don't want to be away from New York too much.'

Laurie looked up at her sharply. 'Not because of us?'

'No,' said Ella, gently, 'not so much because of us, although I will miss you, of course. It's mostly because of Greg. I'm all he's got, it doesn't seem right that I should be half way across the world at this particular stage in his life.'

'He has the Connors,' said Laurie. 'And me,' he added, as an afterthought.

'Bless you for that,' said Ella, 'but it's still not family, not in the same way as he and I.'

'You know I wish it could be,' said Laurie, quietly, his small surprisingly delicate hand covering hers for a brief moment.

'Yes, I know,' said Ella.

There was a time when she, too, would have wished to be a permanent part of Laurie's life, but no longer. She wondered if he sensed the change in their relationship and simply chose to ignore it. She still loved him, of course, and admired him tremendously. Like herself, Laurie Merman had come from nothing. Immediately after the War, he had married a young French girl, Colette, who had been sent to New York with her mother, to escape the Nazi invasion. Together Colette and Laurie had opened a tiny French restaurant in Greenwich Village, named Café Colette. Colette's superb cooking soon became the talk of the town and more Café Colettes followed, each on a grander scale, until the prefix Café was almost laughable. What Laurie had created was a chain of top class French restaurants. When Ella met him, she was twenty-one and he forty-seven. He was not a good-looking man – short, though taller than Ella, balding and a little over-weight, but his dynamism fascinated her. It was not long before what had begun as a business relationship promised to blossom into something more. Laurie had been straight with Ella from the beginning – he loved Colette and would never leave her. They had built an empire together, raised three children and he looked forward to a long and happy retirement with his lifetime's companion. But, Laurie explained, the physical side of their relationship was dead and he was only human after all.

Haltingly, Ella had tried to explain that she, too, was not interested in sex but for some reason, this only enhanced Laurie's interest in her. She never told him that the only other experience she had of men was when she had been raped but he certainly took great time and trouble to help her overcome her apparent frigidity. Gently, with infinite patience, Laurie had eventually coaxed her into allowing him to make love to her and after that first time, Ella found her terror receding. Their relationship had never greatly roused Ella but this did not worry her, for she suspected that her feelings towards men would always be tainted by her early experience. Laurie offered warmth, companionship and love of a sort, and in the early days of their relationship occasionally Ella had fantasized about them being married one day. Now she recognized those early feelings towards Laurie for what they were. She could not have Aaron, the man she truly loved and she had simply used Laurie as a substitute. Up to a point the delusion had been successful.

Thursday afternoon was taken up with shopping for Greg's return to school and Friday morning with putting her office to rights.

'You know, Jessie,' said Ella, 'I can't help feeling that you should find my new assistant for me.'

'Lord, Ella, I could do no such thing. Supposing I pick a dud?'

'Well you can't do worse than me,' said Ella. 'Besides which, I just have a feeling you'll make a better job of it.'

'Well I'll try,' said Jessie. 'What kind of person do you want?'

'Well somebody with a little property experience or at any rate commercial experience of some sort, and . . .'

'No, no,' said Jessie, 'I mean do you want a male, a female, young, old like me, good-looking, ugly, with a sense of humour, with no sense of humour . . .?'

'Jess, I'm not looking for a marriage partner,' Ella said.

'Much the same thing,' retorted Jessie. 'You don't get much closer to someone than when you're working with them day in, day out. Look at you and me – I know what you're going to say even before you say it, before you've even thought of saying it: that saves us a lot of time and trouble, you have to own that.'

'OK,' said Ella, 'let's put it another way. What sort of person do you think we need?'

'Someone just like me, with twice my brains and half my size.'

'Done,' said Ella, 'but that won't be easy.'

The cab which delivered Greg and his luggage to the Connors took Ella on to the airport, so there was little time for a goodbye. 'I wish I was coming with you, Mom.' Greg suddenly looked very young.

'I won't be long,' Ella promised, 'a week at the most. You behave yourself, now.'

'Don't worry,' Aaron promised, 'I'll beat him regularly, on the hour every hour.'

Mother and son embraced. He was too old to cry but Ella could see his distress and she realized, with a shock, that this was the longest that they had ever been apart, except for all those years ago when she had spent a week at the Kentucky Derby. She wept in the cab at the thought of leaving her son, but once clear of Manhattan she pulled herself together. The new vigour which seemed to have come to her on the day of her mother's funeral had persisted. She was going to London to discuss a deal which could change her life. She was twenty-nine-years-old, independent, with a fine, healthy son and a good, profitable business. The future looked bright indeed.

CHAPTER NINE

LONDON
August 1977

'I don't believe this,' said Stephanie, 'I just don't believe what you're saying.'

'It's true, I'm afraid,' said Ella, 'and having made the decision I thought it was important to tell you as quickly as possible.' She glanced at Margot. 'I'm sorry to spoil your Sunday morning.' The three women were sitting in a small conference room at the Meyer Hotel, London. Moments before the atmosphere had been pleasant and friendly, now it was thick with anger and accusation.

Stephanie jumped up and began pacing the room. 'It's unbelievable! After all the work we've put in, you just coolly announce that it's over. I don't understand you, I don't understand you at all.'

Margot's voice was quiet and calm by contrast. 'There's no point in getting agitated, Stephanie. Ella, can you explain to us the reason for your decision. Is it something to do with your mother's death?'

Ella shook her head. 'No, not directly, except that it caused me to go back home and therefore step away from the negotiating table for a moment. I guess my reasons are twofold, one commercial, one personal. While I was in Europe, my assistant, Henry, made a very serious mistake which over the next fifteen years is going to cost me thousands of dollars. It highlighted in my mind the fact that my business is a very personal one.'

'So is mine,' Stephanie burst out.

'I appreciate that, Stephanie,' said Ella, with studied patience, 'but your business is based here, in England. Mine is five thousand miles away. In a practical sense, I cannot see how I can do justice to the Centre des Arts on the one hand and run my New York business efficiently on the other.'

'You don't have to employ idiot staff,' said Stephanie, 'just find yourself a good assistant.'

'I'm aiming to do that,' said Ella, 'but however good my assistant, it's still my business and I need to be around.'

'You mentioned a personal reason,' Margot said, attempting to deflect Stephanie's anger.

'Yes,' said Ella, 'and perhaps in a way it's the most important aspect to consider. My son, Greg, has no father and up until now we have enjoyed a very close relationship. Thirteen is not an easy age and I cannot see it's right to choose this moment to be the other side of the Atlantic on a regular basis, for what we have already calculated will be the best part of three years. By the time Centre des Arts is open, Greg will be all grown up and I will have missed what's left of his childhood.'

Stephanie sat down heavily. 'I think you're looking at this the wrong way, and because you're a single parent, you're in serious danger of stifling the boy. This is just the age when you should be letting go, teaching him to fly. I can see just what's going to happen – you'll give up this opportunity because you think Greg needs you and sometime in the next six to twelve months, you'll find out he doesn't. You'll regret your decision, Greg will be irritated by you over-mothering him and your relationship will develop into disaster.'

'I'm sorry, I don't agree,' said Ella. 'And don't think I'm not aware of the dangers. I'm not going to interfere with his life but I want to be there if he needs me.'

'It's strange,' said Margot, 'but here we are talking about the future of what is to become a multi-million dollar venture and yet what it boils down to is a discussion about bringing up children. If we were three men, the question of our children wouldn't even arise.'

'Exactly,' said Stephanie. 'Either you're seriously in business, Ella, or you're not. Employ a good housekeeper, get your friends to rally round, ensure the time you do spend with Greg is prime time.'

'No,' Ella cut in, 'I'm sorry but my mind is made up. I'm pulling out of the Centre des Arts project, I don't feel it's right for my business and I don't feel it's right for me. I'm very sorry, particularly as I asked for the deadline to be extended, but instinctively I know it's wrong for me.' Ella appealed to Margot. 'Surely you can see it, Margot, you know the extent of my business interests in New York and how much time they involve. Before this project came up I was already fairly well extended, both in workload and a financial sense. There's another thing, too. I know about New York – I know how it works, I know instinctively whether a property is right for me or not. I know nothing about Europe, I'm floundering in an unknown territory. The one thing my years in business have taught me is to deal in what you know.' After this speech Ella was rewarded by a gleam of understanding in Margot's eyes.

No such argument was going to carry any weight with Stephanie, however. She pushed her chair back, ran a hand distractedly through her long, fair hair and flicked it over her shoulder. Her colour was high, her eyes sparkling defiantly.

'I can see we're not going to persuade you to think any differently,' she said, 'so I suggest we give up trying. However, I'm not prepared to let this project go, Margot.'

Margot looked up from where she had been doodling on the pad in front of her. 'You're not proposing to go ahead with it on your own, surely? There's no way you can, Stephanie.'

'You mean you're not prepared to back me?'

'I mean the bank will not be prepared to back you, you're simply not large enough.'

'Then I'll just have to find someone else to help me, won't I? The deadline runs out at five o'clock tomorrow, I still have time.'

Margot shook her head. 'The price I was offering you was an exclusive price aimed at you and Ella. If Ella has pulled out then as far as I'm concerned the deal's off.'

'No,' thundered Stephanie, 'you gave us until five o'clock tomorrow afternoon — us by inference means jointly or severally. There's no way you can try and pull out now, Margot. If I can come up with the necessary backing by tomorrow afternoon, then you have to hold your price.' She smiled slightly. 'Either that or I'll go back to Sir Nicholas Goddard, who can act as arbitrator. I think you'll find he'll be none too happy if you persist in your unethical approach to this project.'

For the first time since the meeting began, Margot lost her composure. 'I resent that remark very strongly,' she said. 'I have not behaved unethically, I was under no obligation to advise you as to who was backing the Slater/Bellois venture.'

'That's not what your Chairman said.'

Ella leaned forward in her chair. 'It's no good you two slanging it away like this.' She looked at Margot. 'Honestly, Margot, I don't see how you can withdraw your offer before the deadline is up. OK, so it was your intention that Stephanie and I should undertake the project together, but if one of us wishes to withdraw, I don't see how you can say the deal is off, if Stephanie can find an alternative and acceptable partner.'

'Well, thanks for something, anyway,' said Stephanie.

'It's madness,' said Margot, 'absolute madness. I don't understand what you're trying to prove, Stephanie. OK, some deals you win, some deals you lose and this is one you've lost. Whatever we think of Ella's decision, it's clearly irreversible, so, forget it. I'll offer Centre des Arts to the marketplace and I'm sure we'll find someone to take it on.'

'No,' said Stephanie, 'I want this project and I'm sure I can find some . . .' she hesitated. She had been twirling a pencil in her fingers. Now she held it still and seemed to be staring at it intently.

'What is it Stephanie?' Ella said.

'Meyer Hotels!' Stephanie said, triumphantly, staring at the name engraved on the pencil, 'now that's the kind of organization who might be interested in Centre des Arts.'

'They already have a Meyer Hotel in Paris,' said Margot.

'Not on the South Bank. If Centre des Arts is going to be the prestige tourist centre you would have us believe, then this should be just up Meyer's street.' She glanced up at Margot. 'The European headquarters is in Geneva, isn't it?'

Margot nodded. 'Yes, I think so but the old man, Joseph Meyer, is normally based in New York. Still, he might be in Europe, I suppose.'

Stephanie's expression was elated. 'If you'll excuse me, Ladies, I'll go and telephone.' She pushed back her chair and walked to the door.

'Stephanie, you're clutching at straws,' said Margot, wearily.

'You concentrate on your business, Margot, and I'll concentrate on mine.' Stephanie swept out of the room extravagantly, slamming the door behind her.

Margot smiled at Ella. 'Coffee?'

Ella glanced at her watch. 'Eleven o'clock. Shall we make it coffee and brandy, given the circumstances?'

'Why not?'

Ella lifted the telephone and ordered. 'So, I suppose, now you're going to give me one hell of a lecture, right?' She stood up and wandered restlessly over to the window.

Margot could not help but smile at the sight of her – she was dressed in jeans, espadrilles and an old cotton T-shirt that looked like it belonged to her son. With her short, curly hair, she could have passed easily for fifteen or sixteen at the most. She was so very different from Stephanie with her stylish designer clothes. Yet beneath the child-like appearance Margot knew Ella's astute business brain was always at work. 'No,' she said, affectionately, 'I thought what you said made a lot of sense. Before offering you the project, I have to admit I indulged in a fair amount of soul-searching on the wisdom of your becoming involved. However, I did decide it would work, provided you sold off some of your New York property, which I naturally assumed you would do.'

'Sell my property!' Ella looked appalled.

'It's your one failing you know, your one blind spot,' said Margot, 'I just can't understand why you hang on to all these properties. You're like a mother hen with her chicks.'

'The bank's not complaining,' Ella said.

'Of course the bank's not complaining, it's making a fortune out of you and a safe fortune at that – your collateral is excellent. Look, let me speak as a friend for a moment. The standard property development operation goes like this: the developer buys a run-down apartment block, does it over, leases it and then sells on to an investment company, a pension fund, or whatever. That way, he puts his money back in the bank and he has no requirement to continue servicing the property. He has gone in, made a tidy profit and come out. By contrast the Lexington Kovac way is like a squirrel collecting nuts for the winter. You've bought some wonderful properties at wonderful prices, I don't deny it. You've also shown great flair and imagination in the way you have renovated them and you've tied up some very fancy leases. So why hang on to them, why not get out and move on?'

'Why sell them?' said Ella. 'The price of property in New York is going up all the time.'

'So's your interest bill, Ella. You're paying out a fortune in interest, not to mention the administrative hassle of looking after so many leases. What you need to do is sell off at least seventy five per cent of your property, put the money in the bank and then start again – borrow, pay back, borrow again, pay back again. Alright, I know you're operating a very profitable business but the real profits are being made by Joshkers Bank.'

'Do you remember Stephanie's parting shot?' Ella asked, icily. Margot shook her head. 'You concentrate on your business and I'll concentrate on mine. At least that's one thing Stephanie and I still agree on.'

Tim Irvine lay back in the large sunken bath, with Sunday newspapers scattered all over the bathroom floor. He heard his wife returning to their suite and knew he should get out of the bath and dress. However, the sound of the slamming door and Stephanie's strident voice on the telephone told him that things were not going well for her and he recoiled from the inevitable dramatics which would ensue. It had been a hard week. The rain which had held off for most of August had decided to threaten this week, of all weeks, while he and his men were trying to get in the harvest. They had worked like dogs, combining twenty-four hours of the day to beat the weather. They had managed it but he was frankly exhausted. He was not sure why Stephanie had insisted that he come to London with her, following Ella's telephone call requesting an urgent Sunday meeting. He sensed immediately something was wrong – perhaps Stephanie had, too – which was why she had wanted him around. He let out a sigh, pulled out the plug with his toe and eased his aching body from the bath, stepping gingerly over the papers as he wrapped a towel round himself. He padded into their sitting room just as Stephanie put down the phone.

'What a bit of luck,' she said triumphantly, 'Joseph Meyer's in Geneva and not only that, he'll see me for a breakfast meeting at eight o'clock tomorrow morning. All I have to do is to get myself there and plan my presentation. I'd better book a flight.'

'Hold on a minute,' said Tim, 'you've lost me. Joseph Meyer, Meyer as in this place?'

'The same,' said Stephanie, 'the grand old man of the hotel business. It's quite an honour to get an interview. I mustn't blow it, I really mustn't.'

'Am I being foolish or is it not immediately apparent why you want to see the great Joseph Meyer?'

'Your friend Ella's pulled out.'

'My friend?' said Tim.

'Well, you seemed to think she was so wonderful. After she'd been staying with us, you talked about nothing else but Ella for days.'

'Did I?' said Tim.

'Anyway, it seems your judgement of human nature went sadly astray in this case. She's let us down, badly, by refusing to go ahead with Centre des Arts.'

'Why?' said Tim, collapsing in a chair before his aching legs gave out.

'Ridiculous reasons – she says she can't manage her New York business and a big project in Paris and then she burbled on about Greg, saying it wasn't fair on him. Honestly, I think her relationship with that boy is positively unhealthy.'

'I don't,' said Tim.

'Well you wouldn't. Anyway enough of Ella, I'm not letting Centre des Arts slip through my fingers. I want that project, Tim. Margot won't back me on my own, so I'm going to see if I can do some sort of deal with Meyer Hotels.'

'Why don't you just let it drop, Stephanie?' Tim said, heavily. 'Goodness knows, you have plenty to keep you occupied over here. There's this new project in Derbyshire...'

'Oh that's nothing,' Stephanie interrupted, 'peanuts, I can do that in my spare time.'

'What spare time?' said Tim. 'You don't have any spare time now. If Centre des Arts goes ahead you'll practically be living in Paris.'

'Yes, I've been thinking about that,' said Stephanie. 'I think the best idea is to actually rent or buy an apartment. Buy I think, it has to be a sound investment.' Tim said nothing. 'Oh for heavens sake, you're not sulking are you?' she said, clearly irritated.

'As a matter of fact I think I am. Don't you consider this should be some sort of joint decision?'

'No, not really,' said Stephanie. 'You're the first to admit you know nothing about my business. I wouldn't dream of telling you how many cattle you should buy in a sale or what day you should start hay-making, so why should you interfere with what I do?'

'But this is not just business, is it?' said Tim. 'This involves the whole family.'

'Why?' said Stephanie.

'Well, if you're going to be away from home even more, the girls will see even less of you.'

'They hardly notice me when I'm there anyway.'

'Maybe not, but are you happy with that situation?' It was a well-worn argument but the idea of Stephanie buying a Paris apartment suddenly seemed a real threat to family life.

'Look, Tim, it's no good trying to make me feel guilty yet again because you're simply not going to succeed. The girls have a wonderful life – they have each other, they have you and they have everything money can buy. Their school reports are excellent which suggests they have no real worries, they are happy, healthy and very, very privileged. I really can't see why I should be expected to sacrifice myself on the altar of my children. I want this deal, Tim, I want it very much. I don't see that either you or the children have any right to stop me.'

It was hopeless. 'Well, if that's how you feel,' said Tim, 'there's really nothing else to be said, is there?'

Ella felt oddly deflated after she and Margot had parted. Despite the altercation, she had tried to persuade Margot to join her for lunch but Margot, always the enigma, had hinted at a social commitment, without being specific. Instead, the two women had agreed to meet in New York the following month. Yesterday had been a day for decisions and having geared herself up for this morning's meeting, she now felt utterly exhausted. Yet there was a strange elation, too. She knew in her bones that she had made the right decision. She had used the long hours on the flight from New York to make up her mind, and she had no regrets, other than the severing of her embryonic relationship with Stephanie and Tim – Tim, particularly, she guardedly admitted to herself.

The second decision of yesterday had been somewhat eccentric. The original reason she and Greg had been visiting Europe was to try and acquire for Laurie Merman a château in Provence. Laurie had long held a pipe dream that one day he would buy a piece of France for Colette. In the last few years, that dream had come within his grasp: the cafés were making huge profits. Property was not his scene, Laurie insisted. Recognizing how badly Ella and Greg needed a holiday, he had suggested that seeking the perfect holiday home for the Mermans provided the excuse for a trip to Europe. Margot's summons to Paris had cut short Ella's search but she had loved Provence and suddenly, realizing that no one was expecting her back in New York for a week the temptation to continue the exploration on Laurie's behalf was overwhelming. It was an irresponsible decision with so many commitments at home, but a call to a travel agent the previous day had secured a flight to Lyons, from where she intended to hire a car and explore the area for a few days. Her flight left Heathrow at eleven o'clock the following morning, so she had a whole afternoon and evening in London for sight-seeing. Somehow, uncharacteristically, she could not summon up the energy to move outside the hotel. She ordered lunch in her room and spent the afternoon drifting in and out of consciousness while trying to read *Country Life* which Stephanie had advised her was *the* property magazine in England. It was after six by the time Ella finally roused herself. She had a bath and decided that a meal in the restaurant downstairs would at least get her out of her room. She was just preparing to dress when there was a knock on the door. She opened it cautiously. 'Tim!'

Tim looked affectionately at the diminutive little figure, swamped in a hotel towelling robe, her hair damp from the bath, her face shiny and well scrubbed – a child-woman, he thought.

'Hello Ella, I hope you don't mind me seeking you out like this, only I thought after this morning's drama you might be feeling a bit down and I wondered whether I could take you out to dinner.'

I'd love that,' said Ella. 'I didn't even know you were in London.'

'I came up with Stephanie last night, after we got your call. She's already left for Geneva and I was planning to return to Wickham when I suddenly thought what the hell, they're not expecting me back until tomorrow.'

'Give me half an hour,' said Ella.

They met in the foyer. 'There's a little restaurant I particularly like in Beauchamp Place,' said Tim, as he helped her into a cab. 'It's very French, wonderful food, peaceful.'

'Beauchamp Place, where's that?' Ella asked.

'Knightsbridge.'

She looked blank.

'Near Harrods,' said Tim, with a laugh.

'Ah, Harrods, now that I have heard of,' said Ella.

'Shall I ask the driver to take us the long way to Beauchamp Place and then I can show you some of the sights.'

'Yes please,' said Ella, her spirits and enthusiasm completely restored.

The rain of the day had cleared away, leaving the pavements glistening and a warm, watery sun lit up the old buildings of London to good effect. Ella was entranced.

'It's so much smaller than I imagined,' Ella said, 'and yet not at all disappointing.'

Tim laughed. 'Everything's small compared with America.'

'Have you been to the States?' Ella asked.

'Only once, years ago with Stephanie – we loved it.'

The restaurant was everything Tim had promised. 'This is such a treat,' said Ella, 'I was feeling a bit bleak.'

'Regretting your decision?'

'Oh no,' said Ella, 'I've made the right decision, I'm sure of that.'

'I'm well aware,' said Tim, 'that sorting out the priorities in your type of business is not easy, but you seem to manage it with such ease.' The implied criticism of Stephanie was there but he was not specific.

'It is difficult,' Ella admitted, 'because our business – mine and Stephanie's – is different from most in that there is no consistency.'

'How do you mean?' said Tim.

'Well, take your business – the seasons come, the seasons go, some harvests are better than others, but the business runs on. Similarly, in manufacturing, they have big orders, small orders, orders that go right, orders that go wrong, but the factory goes on producing the goods and they go on getting sold.'

'Surely that applies to your business, too?' said Tim.

'Not really. our businesses are only as good as the next

deal. We could make a fortune on the last deal and lose it all on the next. Our business is all about making the right decision at the right time.'

'Nerve-racking,' said Tim.

'Very,' Ella agreed. They paused while Tim refilled their glasses. Ella could not help noticing his hands — strong, brown, the hairs at his wrist bleached white.

'Enough of me,' she said abruptly. 'Tell me about you and your business.'

And so he talked about his time at college and then about the early days of Wickham, how he and Stephanie had planned it — the gradual turning of chaos into order.

'It was such a slow process because we had no money to speak of,' he said. 'The first few cottages we sold off, we couldn't even convert them because we hadn't the money to do so. With the money we obtained from those sales, we converted the next batch, for which we charged a much inflated price. That's how we progressed, one step at a time, only moving onto the next stage when we had the money to finance it.' Tim gave a small dry laugh. 'I have to admit I greatly regret the day I introduced Stephanie to Jeremy Colquhoun. He put her on to Margot, of course, and it was Margot who taught her that you don't have to wait until you have the money before you spend it.'

They were well into their bottle of wine by now which made Ella more garrulous. 'How do you feel about Stephanie going ahead with the Centre des Arts, if she can get the backing from Meyer?'

'It appalls me,' Tim admitted. 'As far as I can see, it means effectively we will no longer be a family. Stephanie works a six day week now. If she takes on Centre des Arts, she'll be spending a great deal of time in Paris. Just today she was talking about buying an apartment over there. We'll simply never see her.'

'You can't enjoy the thought of that,' said Ella.

'No, I don't but it's the children I worry about most — they should have a mother. Mrs Maggs is wonderful but she's no substitute, nor am I come to that.'

'You seem to be making a pretty good job of it from what I saw.'

'Thanks, but I suppose if I'm honest, there's also something else . . .' Tim hesitated.

'Go on,' said Ella.

'Well, I think I'm a little jealous. Don't misunderstand me, the last thing I'd want to do is Stephanie's job — I can't think of anything worse — but it should be the man who careers round the world, doing exciting deals, while the little woman sits at home and looks after the children. We're in a complete role-reversal situation. I work hard, God knows. I think I run Wickham as efficiently as the next man and I make a decent profit out of the estate. None the less, I deal in relatively small sums of money, while Stephanie deals in millions — it's an odd situation.'

'You mean she's wearing the pants and you don't like it?' said Ella.

Something like that,' said Tim. 'She never defers to me over anything. She makes her own decisions and I have to fit in accordingly. I'm sounding pathetic, aren't I?'

'Just a little sorry for yourself,' Ella suggested.

'I'm sorry to moan, I suppose what I'm really saying is I get so damn lonely.'

It was a surprising admission.

'Loneliness I know about,' Ella said gently.

'But a woman like you . . . surely there must be men queuing up at the door.' Ella shook her head and Tim hesitated a moment. 'Ella, don't answer this if you don't want to, but did your experience put you off men for good, or . . .?'

Ella laughed. 'Are you asking me whether there's a man in my life?'

'Yes,' said Tim, 'I suppose I am.'

'I've had a long term affair with a married man called Laurie. He's a colleague of mine, in fact he has a stake in my business. He's much older than me, comfortable, safe and undemanding.'

Tim looked crestfallen. 'It can't be very satisfactory.'

'No, it's not – particularly since I like his wife and would do nothing in the world to hurt her, but I guess it's better than being alone night after night.'

Tim raised his glass. 'Down with loneliness.'

'I'll drink to that,' said Ella.

It was after midnight by the time they got back to the hotel. 'I should be tired but I'm not,' said Tim.

'Neither am I,' said Ella.

'Why not come up to my room for a nightcap,' Tim suggested.

'No, come to mine,' said Ella. The instinct to avoid seeing the room Tim had shared with Stephanie was very strong.

Tim searched her fridge and decided on champagne. 'You've told me nothing about going back to Kentucky, how you coped with Greg and how you felt when you saw your mother. Do you want to talk about it?' Tim asked, settling down on the sofa, with bottle and glasses.

'It's extraordinary, isn't it?' said Ella. 'Of all the people I have known it's with you I chose to share my secrets.'

'That's just because I was around when you received the particularly emotive call about your mother.'

'Possibly, yet I've never even told Laurie anything about my past. Yes, I would like to talk about it – it was an odd experience. Do you mind?'

'Come here,' said Tim. She sat down beside him and he slipped an arm around her. 'Put your head on my shoulder, relax, take a deep breath and tell me all about it.'

Ella did as she was asked, dimly aware of the strangeness of the situation yet feeling it to be so natural that it could not be wrong. She began to speak, hesitantly at first, but with growing confidence.

'So what you're saying is that you're free from your past, at last?' Tim said when she had finished.

'Yes, in most respects, though, of course, my legacy is Greg – he in a way always links me back to my roots. Not that I'm complaining,' she added hastily, 'I wouldn't be without him for the world.'

'Of course not,' Tim said. There was a silence between

them and in that moment, they both became aware of their closeness. Tim shifted uneasily putting a little distance between them.

'About men,' he said awkwardly. 'You said your relationship with – what is his name – Laurie, was comfortable but nothing more. Do you feel your experiences may have ... well, put you off the idea of sex permanently? I'm sorry, I shouldn't be asking really, it's only that I've drunk enough to release me from my usual good old British inhibitions.'

'It's OK,' said Ella, 'I guess it does some good to talk about it. I don't know, is the answer. You see I have no other experience of men – only Laurie and the rape. I've always imagined though that I'm frigid, certainly I've never ...' her voice tailed off as she saw the expression on Tim's face.

'You see, I have an ulterior motive for asking,' he began, his voice unsteady, and leaning forward, he kissed her, at first gently, and then as his arms tightened around her with a burning intensity.

Somewhere in the recesses of her mind, Ella knew she must not return his kisses and must pull herself away from his arms. What made her hesitate was the certainty that despite the mounting passion between them, at any time she could ask him to stop and he would. She felt safe in his arms, safe in a new unchartered country, for the passion with which she responded to him was something she had never experienced before.

Lulled by this feeling of security, sometime later, she found herself naked on the bed with Tim beside her. How long they had been like that she had no idea.

'I want you so badly, but I'm frightened of hurting you,' he whispered.

'I'm frightened, too,' said Ella.

'I'll be gentle, trust me.' She did, implicitly.

He took her then, tentatively at first, and was almost shocked by her reaction. She clung to him, urging him on, caught up in her own dark world. He concentrated on her pleasure, terrified of making the wrong move, but he felt his own control seeping away until they came together in a single exquisite moment, their tears mingling together on the pillow, their bodies straining together, completely at one.

When Tim woke, he automatically assumed he was at Wickham. His first sensation was of the stiffness of his limbs and then another feeling: Lethargy, a sense of wellbeing, of fulfillment . . . and suddenly he remembered. He opened his eyes abruptly. Through the closed curtains he could see it was already daylight. He turned to the woman beside him. Ella was still deeply asleep, one cupped hand supporting her head, her dark curls clustered haphazardly round her childlike face. It was incredible to Tim that the dramas of her life appeared to have had so little impact on her looks. No wonder she was so successful in business, she was such a novelty. For some strange reason he could not understand, he found himself free to admire Ella's business achievements in a way he could not admire his wife's. Was that because Ella's business offered no threat? That might have been true yesterday, but not today. After last night, he knew he could not let her go. He could see no easy solution to a future together but somehow they had to find a way. He shifted slightly in the bed to ease his stiffness and his movement disturbed Ella. She began rubbing her eyes and Tim cursed himself for waking her. He had needed more time to plan what happened next. Everything was moving too swiftly and he felt ill-prepared.

Ella eyed him a little ruefully, with warm, sleepy eyes. 'Did what I think happened last night really happen?'

Tim nodded and bending forward, kissed her. Ella's expression clouded.

'It was wrong, Tim. What a terrible way to treat Stephanie, to pull out of a business deal and sleep with her husband, all in the space of a few hours.' Ella's voice trembled. He went to take her in his arms. 'No,' she said, 'I must go to the bathroom.'

While she was gone, Tim's mind ricocheted backwards and forwards, trying to find a solution to their predicament, to offer some form of comfort. He couldn't easily leave

Wickham, he certainly couldn't leave the children. It would have been difficult before, but in view of Stephanie's determination to develop Centre des Arts, he really had no choice but to recognize one hundred per cent responsibility for the girls: they were settled in school and happy in their life. He shook his head, hoping the effect would act like a kaleidoscope, rearranging the pieces into the picture he wanted. Supposing Ella was to give up her business in New York and come and live in England. He and Stephanie could divorce; he hardly imagined his wife would mind. They could make a home together with the three children but not at Wickham, that was Stephanie's home . . .

'Tim,' Ella slipped into the bed beside him. At the sight of her slender, naked body, the hopeless grappling with future plans was forgotten. She came into his arms without protest. He held her close, kissing her, murmuring her name, aware of the warmth rising between them.

This time he was more sure. He teased her, tantalised her until she begged him to take her. She cried out his name again and again, her body taut as a bow string, her nails raking his back. There was no one in the world but the two of them, nothing else mattered, until at last, utterly exhausted, they fell into a deep sleep in each other's arms.

Ella stirred first. Sitting up in bed she stared at the alarm clock and then abruptly shook Tim awake. 'It's after eight,' she said, her face anguished. 'This should never have happened. 'I'll have to get started or I'll miss my flight.'

Tim had completely forgotten about her going to France and it threw him into a panic. 'Surely you don't have to go,' he said, 'not today at any rate. Leave it a couple of days. I can ring Mrs Maggs and arrange that . . .'

'No, Tim.' Ella shifted out of the circle of his arms. 'There's no point in prolonging this, because there can be no future for us. Every moment we stay in each other's company is making things worse.'

'There has to be a future for us,' said Tim, 'there has to be.'

'What are you suggesting then?' said Ella. 'That you

divorce Stephanie, give up the children, your life at Wickham and come and live with me in New York? You might have liked America for a visit but a more English Englishman than you, it would be hard to find. You'd never be happy, particularly not in a city, and especially being away from the kids.'

'You could come to me,' Tim said.

'Give up my business, disrupt Greg's schooling, move to a country I hardly know to live with a married man?'

'I don't think there'd be any problem about Stephanie giving me a divorce.'

'OK, so living with you, married – but where? Surely not in Stephanie's family home, that really would be bizarre. So we set up a home together – you separated from your beloved Wickham, me from my business ... we'd have nothing left of the lives we both love. That's hardly the best basis for starting a life together.'

'But we have each other,' said Tim. 'I love you so much, Ella.'

For a moment her expression softened. She reached out a hand and touched his cheek. 'I love you, too, Tim, but it's not just a question of *who* you meet, is it – it's *when* you meet them. We met at the wrong time.'

'I can't accept that,' said Tim.

'Tim, you're going to have to. Hell, I have to get up, I have a plane to catch.'

'Ella, please, please postpone your French trip, you don't have to go, not today. After ... after last night, we must talk. There has to be a solution but we can't find it in this rushed way.' For a moment it looked as though Ella was going to weaken and Tim pressed home what he thought was his advantage. 'We'll never have a better chance than this to talk, with Stephanie in Geneva.'

Ella leapt from the bed as though she had been stung. 'That just about sums up the situation, doesn't it?' she said. 'We're talking about turning our lives upside down and the only reason we're able to have such a discussion is because Stephanie is in Geneva. Don't forget I have commitments, too. I have a very solid, satisfactory relationship with Laurie. OK, so he's a married man, too. The difference is he lives in New York and he's not talking about walking out on his wife and kids to be with me.' She turned and walked into the bathroom again, slamming the door behind her. If her words had been calculated to hurt, they had succeeded.

Tim was out of the bed in a trice, hammering on the bathroom door. 'So why the hell did you spend last night with me? Being unfaithful to this Laurie is sort of cheating in duplicate, isn't it?' Ella didn't reply. 'What was I then, just an acceptable stud to help you pass the time during an otherwise dull Sunday in London?'

The door flew open. 'How dare you speak to me like that,' said Ella. 'For some reason I can't understand, I've told you more about my life than I've told anyone else, ever. Knowing what you know, I don't know how you can make such a remark.'

'I'm sorry,' said Tim, 'that was unforgiveable.'

An angry silence followed. Ella pulled a sweatshirt over her head and turned to face him. She was fully dressed now. Tim, suddenly conscious of his nakedness, felt stupid. He turned away from her and began to dress, hurriedly, but she must have seen the expression on his face for her anger softened a little.

'Look, if it helps, I'll tell you something, Tim. As I told you, my sexual experience is very limited – being raped at fifteen meant I couldn't bear a man to touch me and I spent the next six or seven years living the life of a nun. When I came to New York and met Laurie, he was kind and understanding and being much older than me, he was not in such a hurry as a younger man might have been. I've never told him why I was so frightened of men but he recognized my fear. Anyway, we've had an affair ever since, but sex – well it's just been something warm between us, a way of expressing our feelings. Until last night, Tim, I didn't know what making love meant. Please believe that, if nothing else.'

Tim did not speak for several moments as he finished pulling on his clothes. Then he turned and with a sigh, took

Ella in his arms, pressing her close to him. 'I believe you, because it was very special for me, too. Don't you see, that's why we simply can't lose one another? However long it takes, we have to find a way to be together.'

'And what do we do in the meantime, live some sort of half-life, five thousand miles apart, growing older?' Ella asked. 'Besides, I'm no marriage breaker and I suspect that without me, it would never have occurred to you to leave Stephanie.'

'I don't know,' said Tim, 'I simply don't know the answer to that.'

'Exactly. One night of loving doesn't justify breaking up years of partnership.' Ella released herself from Tim's arms and began dashing round the room, throwing her belongings into her case as Tim watched helplessly. When she had finished, she straightened up and went to him. 'I'm sorry, Tim, but this is goodbye.'

'Let me at least take you to the airport and see you on to the plane.'

Ella shook her head. 'I couldn't bear it – it would only be prolonging the agony.'

'I'll come down to the foyer and help you find a cab.' He was desperate now to keep sight of her for a few more minutes.

'No, please don't make this more difficult than it already is.' With a swift movement, Ella reached up on tiptoes and kissed him lightly on the lips. Then, almost running, she seized her case and wrenched open the door.

'Don't leave me,' Tim said, 'please don't leave me.'

'I have to,' said Ella, 'for both our sakes.' In an instant she was gone, the door slamming shut behind her.

He went to the door, intending to open it and call after her. Instead he leaned his forehead against it, pounding at it with his fists. 'Dammit. Oh Ella, Ella.' As he stood there, washed with despair, a new sensation came to him, a sudden ringing in his ears, getting louder, louder ... Lights flashed, he closed his eyes to avoid the brightness but it was still there, beneath his eyelids, blinding him. 'Ella,' he croaked as he slid to the floor, and into unconsciousness.

CHAPTER TEN

GENEVA
August 1977

Joseph Meyer leant back in his chair and gazed out of the window. It was a beautiful day, warm and sunny. From his office he had a clear view of the lake, the sun sparkling on the water was so bright he had to shield his eyes. The blue-green mountains at the far side of the lake were hazy, an early promise of the heat to come. He was pleased with his choice of Geneva as the European headquarters for Meyer Hotels. Everything about the city delighted him: its clean efficiency, its stylish good looks, the feeling that one was at the centre of things. He watched with pleasure the progress of a small yacht scudding across the water, for small things pleased Joseph Meyer. Every day was a bonus, every bright summer's day a blessing to be counted.

'Well, don't you agree, Pop?'

His son's impatient voice cut through into his consciousness. He knew he should have been concentrating, but the boy's persistence irritated him. 'Don't call me Pop, you know how I detest it. "Father" is what I have asked you to call me. Is that too much to ask? I am your father after all, I have a right to be called what I am.'

Alex Meyer regarded him in disbelief. 'You haven't been listening to a word I've been saying, have you?'

'Yes,' said Joseph, 'it's the same old argument and I still don't agree.'

'Are you ever going to give me a chance to do anything in this organisation without being tied to your apron strings?'

Joseph regarded his son in silence for a moment. A good-looking boy, well hardly a boy – thirty-one – with the dark wavy hair he'd once had himself and which contrasted so effectively with his light, bright, blue eyes: his mother's eyes. He was tall – well, tall by Joseph Meyer's standards: nearly six foot, with a slightly aquiline nose, high cheekbones and full sensuous lips. No wonder he was such a success with the women, but how Joseph wished he would settle down. His heart ached at the thought of grandchildren yet it appeared his son was not prepared to give him any.

'You'll have control of this business soon enough when I'm dead,' he snapped. 'In the meantime we'll run it my way, at least while you persist in these godamn stupid ideas.'

'Look, *Father*,' Alex put an insulting emphasis on the word, 'the Arabs expect a show, they need wooing. They're so damned spoilt, they take it for granted that everything will be handed to them on gold plate. I don't understand your objection. Our profits are spiralling and it wouldn't matter a damn if the whole thing went off like a damp squib, it wouldn't even be a flea-bite in the side of Meyer Hotels. At least, however, you'd have given me a chance to prove myself.'

'Alex, the problem is that it's not a question of *if* your scheme goes off like a damp squib, it *will* go off like a damp squib. We don't need to woo the Arabs with a great PR razzmatazz. One properly constructed, well-run, luxury Meyer Hotel will provide all the PR necessary. I don't mind spending money on any scheme you care to put to me if it makes sense, but this doesn't. I don't want to appear a laughing stock, and I believe your promotional ideas for the Middle East could actually have a detrimental affect on our launch out there.'

'You're so old-fashioned, Father, you're not in touch any more. Why can't you just bend a little, and give me a chance to prove myself. Jesus Christ, I'm not a child.'

'Then don't behave like one,' said Joseph. Father and son glared at one another. The telephone sounded on Joseph's desk. 'Yes?'

'Lady Stephanie Bonham to see you,' said his secretary.

'Hold on a moment. Alex, you ought to be in on this, it's Lady Stephanie Bonham. God knows what she wants but it's interesting. Remember, I told you about her?'

'You can mess around with the English aristocracy if you wish, Father. I'm going to do some real work.' Alex strode angrily to the door and opened it to find Stephanie standing on the threshold. She wore a pale apple-green silk dress, with a prim little white collar. Her fair hair was simply brushed back from her forehead, hanging lose to her shoulders. Her deep, cornflower blue eyes regarded Alex's angry scowl with just a hint of amusement. 'Er . . . Lady Stephanie?' he said, uncertain how to address her.

'Yes, indeed,' said Stephanie, in her clear English voice.

'Er . . . I'm Alex Meyer and this is my father, Joseph.'

Stephanie turned her attention from the handsome young man beside her and stepped into the room. A short, overweight, elderly man walked across the room towards her with surprising speed, shook her hand enthusiastically and showed her to a chair.

'Lady Bonham. How nice to meet you. Welcome to Geneva. Would you like a coffee?'

She nodded her head. The nervousness she felt was momentarily calmed by the avuncular greeting. Joseph sat down in the chair opposite her and regarded her in silence for a moment. The warmth of his greeting did not blind Stephanie to the power of the man she now faced. She noted the Italian silk suit, the Valentino tie, and through the glass top of his desk she caught sight of slim, elegant shoes, again Italian, and toning silk socks. Despite his small stature and bulky frame, the exquisite cut of his clothing, in muted shades of grey, did a lot for Joseph Meyer — as did the perfect shave, the beautifully cut hair and his manicured hands with their surprisingly long fingers. There was a strangely expressive, artistic quality to his hands which stood out in stark contrast to the rest of the man. All this Stephanie noted and stored away for the future.

Joseph Meyer was saying nothing. He leaned back in his

chair, smiling sweetly, cigar in hand. The silence was in danger of becoming oppressive.

'You may have found my call yesterday rather peculiar,' Stephanie began, 'but I have a project I simply must show you. I have the opportunity to finalise a deal at nearly half the asking price and I have until five o'clock this afternoon to decide whether to commit myself to it.'

'Then my dear Lady Bonham, we had better not waste a moment,' said Joseph Meyer.

On the conference table at the far end of Joseph Meyer's office, Stephanie laid out, carefully, the plans of the Centre des Arts, for father and son to study. Alex, who had been intending to leave the room, had remained, fascinated not so much by Stephanie's project but by the woman herself. He had never come across a woman so good-looking, so self-assured and so obviously bright. With a series of artist's impressions, Stephanie outlined the revised thinking on the Centre des Arts which she and Ella had dreamed up between them. She produced costings, building permits and a schedule indicating the timing of the project as a whole. She told the story of the reduction in price, following the discovery of Joshkers involvement, but carefully left out the contributions made by both Ella and Tim. When she had finished, she was trembling with nervous exhaustion but desperate to appear calm. 'Well, what do you think?'

'I think it's a fascinating scheme,' said Joseph, after a tantalising pause. He looked across at Alex. 'What do you think? We already have a presence in Paris, of course. It's very questionable whether we can justify another, and, of course, we've never been involved in this sort of complex before.'

'I think it's a wonderful idea,' said Alex, decisively.

Joseph looked hard at his son. This uncompromising support for a proposition introduced by his father was quite out of character. Invariably, Alex took the opposite view point from his father as a matter of course. Surprised but pleased, Joseph continued. 'I have the germ of an idea,' he said, with gathering enthusiasm. 'I understand from what you've said,

Lady Bonham, that you own a number of country clubs and small luxury hotels in the UK. How many have you?'

'Eight,' said Stephanie. 'Wickham was my first, the family home in Gloucestershire. I also have one in London, in Wiltshire, in Oxfordshire, in Berkshire at Ascot, one in the Lake District, one in Bath and one on the west coast of Scotland.'

'Mmmm,' said Joseph. 'As you may be aware, I have four hotels in Europe presently – one here in Geneva, one in Paris, one in London and then one in Amsterdam. It is my intention to expand in Europe, particularly in the UK, though first we are endeavouring to conquer the Middle East, which we feel has the biggest immediate growth potential. Supposing we were to buy out your hotels – don't let us worry about price at the moment, I am talking principle here. We could put your hotels together with ours, take on the Centre des Arts project and put you in overall control, as manager of the European operation. Although your country clubs and hotels obviously are not in the same league as Meyer, they could be upgraded, enlarged or sold off, as necessary, and your pool of trained UK staff would be very useful. What do you say?' He smiled at her benevolently, as one would to a child upon whom one had just bestowed an enormous and totally unexpected present.

'You have to be joking!' said Stephanie, her voice thick with anger.

'I'm not joking,' said Joseph, 'I'm perfectly serious, though why I'm not quite sure. I've never made such a generous offer to anyone before.'

'A generous offer! You buy up my business, cash in on this Centre des Arts scheme, put me in overall charge as a *manager* ... what sort of person do you think I am, Mr Meyer? If I wanted to be a manager of a hotel group, do you think I'd have gone through what I have during the last eleven years? I may not run a business on your scale but I do run a highly profitable one. I'm answerable to no one. I run my business my way and it works. Why on earth should I sell out to Meyer Hotels or anyone else? I'm sorry, I can see I've been wasting my time.'

Joseph Meyer chuckled. 'I like your style Lady Bonham.'

Stephanie flushed a brilliant scarlet. 'I can't say I like yours, Mr Meyer,' she replied.

'Look, I have an idea,' said Alex. 'I know why you suggested what you did, Father. It's because we are very stretched in a management sense at the moment, trying to develop both in the Middle East and Europe,' he explained for Stephanie's benefit. 'Supposing we thought this through in a different way. It makes sense that if we are joining forces over Centre des Art we should join forces over everything else as well, but it also makes perfect sense – to me at any rate – that Lady Bonham does not want to lose her independence. Supposing, Father, that we put all the hotels together, as you suggest, including this new Centre des Arts project and then we granted Lady Bonham a franchise on the whole European operation. This would have the joint affect of giving her the independence she requires and us the management back-up we need. We would have to form a new subsidiary to achieve it and I would like to suggest that you consider letting me run this new European operation while you concentrate on the Middle East.' He smiled slightly, 'It would keep us out of each other's hair.'

'Look, wait a minute,' said Stephanie, 'I came here two hours ago to present to you an idea for undertaking a single joint project. It certainly was not my intention that we should join forces altogether. I don't want to lose my independence but I do need help with this scheme, which is why I'm here.'

'The proposal that Alex has just put forward would maintain your independence,' said Joseph. 'It needs thinking about, of course, in great detail, but essentially you would receive the revenue from all the hotels, including ours. You would have total management control and would simply account to us with a franchise fee plus an agreed percentage of the profits. Of course, either Alex or I would have to be on the board and as he suggests, it's probably better for him to handle Europe while I concentrate on the Middle East. I've studied your track record in some detail since your call, and I do think we have a lot in common.'

A germ of excitement was stirring in Stephanie. This was the Big Time, yet her excitement was seriously undermined by a feeling of caution. She had been her own boss for a long time. She enjoyed running her tight little ship her way, yet why was she here at all if not for the chance of expansion? It seemed so improbable that in the space of a two hour meeting, the great Joseph Meyer was offering her an opportunity of a lifetime.

'I just don't know what to say,' she admitted. 'A franchise operation is obviously attractive but we hardly know each other. How can we possibly make this sort of decision about joining forces, between now and five o'clock.' All three of them glanced at the clock on the wall — it was just after half past twelve.

'I have a proposal,' said Joseph. 'I think I should take you to lunch, Lady Bonham, while Alex runs through these Centre des Arts figures of yours with our accountant. Over lunch, you and I need to concentrate on getting to know one another. If we're both satisfied by the end of it, and the figures stack up, then I suggest we go ahead with the Centre des Arts project in any event, with no commitment to the bigger involvement until we see how we all get along.'

Alex was furious. If anyone was taking Stephanie to lunch, it should be him, but a scene in front of Stephanie was bound to look childish. He scooped up the figures and disappeared from the room without a word.

The Hotel Beau Revage stood only a few paces from the head office of Meyer International Hotels. A *maitre d'hotel* positively sprinted across the restaurant to greet Joseph Meyer and led him to what was clearly his usual table, in a quiet corner, with a marvellous view of the lake. They were seated with a minimum of fuss and two glasses of champagne followed almost immediately.

'My Dear,' said Joseph Meyer. 'I'm afraid I have reached the stage in life where I have the same lunch every day — a little caviar, followed by sole meunière, washed down with a glass or two of Pouilly Fumé. Does that appeal or would you care to see the menu?'

Stephanie shook her head. 'That sounds wonderful.'

The *maitre d'hotel* disappeared and Joseph Meyer watched in silence as Stephanie examined her surroundings with obvious pleasure. She was a striking woman, Joseph thought, with an intriguing combination of charms. On the one hand, she was a typical English rose in appearance – with her pale blonde hair, perfect complexion, clear blue eyes and tall, slim figure. Yet he sensed beneath the cool exterior there was a volatile, perhaps even reckless streak to her nature, which fascinated him.

'This is beautiful,' said Stephanie.

So are you, Joseph Meyer thought, though he declined to say so. 'Tell me how you built your business, Lady Bonham. I am fascinated that you have achieved so much, so young.'

Stephanie launched into the story of her achievements and Joseph listened attentively, asking the occasional, but always astute, question. The wine arrived, they raised their glasses in a silent toast and as Stephanie talked on, she began to relax. The meal progressed with elegant ease, during which Stephanie learned that Joseph was a widower and had a son and a daughter.

'Alex has come up the hard way,' he said, 'it's the only way to learn, but he's in such a hurry. Every morning when I come down to breakfast, I expect to find banana skins on the stairs.' He laughed, but there was an edge to his laughter.

'It can't be easy for him – you're a tough act to follow.'

There was a moment's hesitation and then Joseph smiled. They had reached the coffee stage. 'Would you mind if I smoked?' he asked.

'Of course not,' said Stephanie. She watched as he went through the preamble of lighting his cigar. She recognized it as a Monte Cristo No.3 – her father had smoked them on special occasions. Like everything else, it appeared that Joseph Meyer enjoyed nothing but the best. Settled now with his cigar and coffee, she judged it was the right moment to start probing a little deeper, as to what made this fascinating man tick.

'You told me the basic facts about your life as it is now but not how you built Meyer Hotels. My achievement, such as it is, pales into insignificance compared with yours. How on earth did *you* begin?'

Joseph Meyer drew on his cigar in silence for a moment. 'You want the story of my life?' Stephanie nodded. The silence that followed was so long she wondered whether he had understood her. Then, quite suddenly, without preamble he began.

'I was born in Germany, in Bavaria,' he said. 'My father owned an inn, not a smart place, mind – the equivalent of one of your English pubs, a little run down. He did good business, though, and I suppose it's where I formed my interest in catering. When I was twenty, young by modern standards, I married a girl from the village. I had loved her since she was a baby.' His voice was warm. 'Two years later we had a daughter, Freda. They were happy years. My father was semi-retired after my marriage and I ran the inn. I made many improvements, it was a good business. We were happy, had plenty of money and then the war came.' His voice hardened perceptively. 'I don't know whether a child like you knows about such things, but the Nazi movement began in Bavaria. We were Jews. Well, it was a rough time, as history now acknowledges. I formed an underground movement. Looking back, it was a foolish thing to do with a young family to consider, but I was young and impetuous. We used to meet at the inn and make desperate, futile plans to halt the direction of Nazi thinking. One afternoon, the storm troopers burst into the inn. Myself, my wife, Annetta and Freda, we were having a picnic with the family dog. It was a beautiful day, I remember, in Spring. Spring in Bavaria is very beautiful.'

He hesitated and Stephanie almost intervened, to ask him to stop. It was obvious what was coming and a sudden, unexpected feeling of compassion made her wish to spare him, though now he had started, it seemed he wanted to go on.

'They shot my parents but first they tortured my father until he told them where I was. They found us by the riverbank, I was fishing. Annetta and Freda had built a little camp fire. They dragged us away but before they did so, they shot the dog. I will never forget the look of surprise in his eyes and the sound of Freda screaming.'

'Where . . . where did they take you?' said Stephanie, almost in tears.

'They sent us over land, by train mostly, sometimes truck, to Poland, to Treblinka. The American 8th Army liberated us.'

'You all survived?' Stephanie asked.

'After a fashion. Annetta and I, yes, but little Freda, she has been in a mental institution ever since the war. She . . .' he seemed to have to force the words out, 'she was thirteen you see, by the time we were liberated. They did things to little girls. Her mind couldn't cope.' Stephanie reached out a hand and as she took Joseph's in hers, he turned over his wrist and pulled away the silk cuff. Stephanie saw the number printed there, T31027. Joseph smiled, a sad, tight smile. 'The Great Joseph Meyer: that's all I was once – T31027.'

'Why don't you have the number removed?' Stephanie asked. 'A skin graft would do it, surely.'

'I'll never do that,' said Joseph, his voice suddenly rough and angry.

'Why?' Stephanie asked.

'Because it reminds me, always, of the depths to which human beings can stoop.'

In the bright, sunny restaurant, amidst every conceivable luxury, his words chilled Stephanie to the bone. There was nothing to say, no response that she or anyone could have made.

After a moment, Joseph shook his head, 'I'm a foolish old man to worry your head with these stories. It is past, there is no value in dwelling on it.'

'I disagree,' said Stephanie, 'it's so easy for us to forget that our generation owes yours everything, but so often we choose not to remember. We see the scars on our parents but we ignore them, imagining that the same thing can never happen to us. And it won't, so long as we remember what you had to suffer, you and your race in particular.'

Her small speech evidently moved Joseph. Carefully removing a spotless silk handkerchief from his pocket, he blew his nose and made no effort to hide the wiping of his eyes. 'I'm sorry,' he said, 'another failing of old age. I'm becoming over-sentimental these days.'

'So what happened after Treblinka?' Stephanie said, gently, anxious to move him on in the story.

'As for so many others, America beckoned,' he said. 'I'd managed to acquire visas and once in the States, I went to the Cornell Hotel School in Michigan. I spent four years there, working my passage through college, supporting my family and perfecting my English.'

'It must have been incredibly hard work, particularly as you must have been weakened by your experiences in the concentration camp.'

'Yes,' Joseph acknowledged, 'but you see I had an incentive, a reason, the best reason in the world.'

Stephanie frowned. 'What reason?'

'It was a miracle really. There we were – my wife and I, suffering from malnutrition and God knows what else, and yet between us we managed to make a baby, a perfect, whole baby, untainted by war.'

'Alex,' said Stephanie, softly.

'Yes, Alex. It was like – like a whole new beginning, like the world was starting over again. Can you understand that?'

'Yes,' said Stephanie.

'Yes, they were hard years, and there was the care of my daughter to pay for.' He shrugged, 'Anyway, I had some luck. While I was studying at Cornell, I worked in a run-down hotel. It went bankrupt and I managed to persuade some people to back me. I bought it, renovated it, improved it, hired the right people . . .' he laughed. 'I make it sound easy, don't I? It wasn't, but then you know about that. The first hotel is always the hardest. Once you have a successful formula, all you have to do is repeat it: I have twenty-two hotels in America now. Then, four years ago, I said to myself, Joseph, you owe this country a lot but you are a European. So, I came to Europe, stumbled upon Geneva, fell in love with it and decided to make it my base.'

'And Germany?' Stephanie asked.

'I'll never go back to Germany, never,' said Joseph. 'I am German but my country betrayed me. Yet we all see things differently. My Annetta, her life's ambition was to go back home to Bavaria and for her I would have gone, but she died when Alex was five; she never really recovered from Treblinka.' He smiled at Stephanie. 'So there you have it, my life history, and what does Meyer Hotels mean to me – hard grinding work and terrible risks, but after Treblinka, it was so damn good to be alive, I felt I could conquer the world. On good days, I still do.' The other diners had long ago left the restaurant. Without turning in his seat, Joseph shouted, 'two cognac, large ones.' In a moment, the fussy little *maitre d'hotel* delivered them with a flourish. 'Well, Stephanie Bonham,' Joseph said. 'May I call you Stephanie?'

'If I may call you Joseph,' said Stephanie, smiling.

'Well, Stephanie, I know a little of you and you know a little of me. What I see of you I like and admire. You are very young and have plenty of mistakes yet to make. Maybe, just maybe, an old man like me has something to offer you.'

'I'm sure that is true,' said Stephanie, 'but what have I to offer you?'

'Your youth, your beauty . . .' seeing Stephanie's surprised expression he laughed. 'Don't misunderstand me, Stephanie, sadly I am past all that, though once maybe . . .' he let his words trail away. 'You and Alex are the future. Alex told me this morning I am out of touch. Perhaps I am. If I am to go into partnership with anyone in Europe, then it should be someone young and ambitious like you. And why not a woman? Women are so much cleverer than men.' He glanced at his watch, 'Four o'clock. I suggest we go back to my office and telephone Joshkers Bank, but first, let us drink to the future.'

'The future,' Stephanie said, again feeling tears prick her eyelids. This extraordinary little man, with his amazing charisma, moved her in a way she found it difficult to explain and instinctively she knew she would always be a better person for knowing him.

CHAPTER ELEVEN

NEW YORK
October 1977

Laurie Merman liked the Fall. That first snap in the air, the changing colours of the trees in Central Park, a different smell in the air. It invigorated him, put a spring in his step, cleared the cobwebs from his mind. He turned the corner into Lexington. Instead of waiting for the traffic lights to change, he sprinted across the road, causing a barrage of protests from passing cab drivers. He grinned, feeling a kid again.

Laurie visited each of his restaurants for two or three hours every week, but never in the same order and never on the same day. His appearance was always unpredictable and ensured that his staff kept on their toes. His wife, his secretary, even Ella on occasions, chastised him for always being on the move and virtually uncontactable, but as he told them, there is no way you can run a restaurant business from behind a desk – you need to be talking to customers, tasting the soup, watching how the staff perform. He had a notorious reputation in the trade for being a tough boss, but he paid well and as a result, his staff were hard-working and loyal. This morning, it was the turn of Café Colette on the corner of Lexington and 39th. It was no coincidence that Laurie had chosen this particular restaurant this morning for it was part of Gregory Buildings, sharing the ground floor with Ella's office, and Ella would be home from Europe any time now.

Did Ella's return account for his mood, Laurie wondered? He had missed her and the prospect of her spending more time in Europe did not please him. 'Selfish old shit,' he said to himself, under his breath, as he pushed open the door of the restaurant. 'Bonjour, Paul, how are bookings today?' In a moment he was enmeshed in the world of his restaurant and for the time being, Ella was forgotten. By midday, however, he was satisfied that Lexington was running as smoothly as it should and accepting a glass of Kir from the barman, he went and sat at a table in the window, with a view of the main entrance of Gregory Buildings. A call to Jessie had already established that Ella had not yet returned, and from his vantage point, Laurie would be able to see her as she arrived.

It was only with Ella Kovac, Laurie mused, that he had come dangerously near jeopardising his marriage. After the birth of their third child Colette, at only thirty-two, had apparently lost all interest in sex. For a while Laurie had waited patiently but eventually, always a practical man, he had began a discreet affair with a young woman journalist who had come to interview him about the opening of a new restaurant. It had lasted for several months, until one day Christine had announced that she was going back to her boyfriend: clearly Laurie had been used to punish the boyfriend. It did not worry him, he simply transferred his affections to Christine's flatmate and so on and so on, seeking and acquiring sexual gratification with the minimum of fuss.

Everything changed on an October day, much like this one. Laurie smiled at the memory – perhaps it was the season which had so addled his brain and twisted his gut. It had begun with a telephone call. 'Laurie, it's Margot Haigh. How are you?'

Laurie smiled with pleasure at the sound of her voice, it was attractive, a little husky and the clipped efficiency and the economy of words only added to the attraction of this complex woman. Laurie was enormously attracted to Margot but recognized she was out of his league.

'I'm fine, Margot, and how are things with you?'

'Oh great. Listen, I know you've been looking for a

property in Lexington, in the mid-30s. I've found the perfect place and at the right price, too.'

'A woman of many talents,' said Laurie. 'I guess when you get kind of tired of banking, you could always turn to real estate.'

Idle banter did not amuse Margot. 'I'm not prepared to tell you where it is unless you agree to a partnership deal, so far as developing the property is concerned.'

'With you?' Laurie was surprised. Margot had her faults, but she was normally dead straight — there were no deals on the side with Margot, no oiling the wheels, no greasing the palm, you couldn't even take her out to lunch.

'No, of course not with me,' said Margot, 'with an extremely attractive young woman, just sweet twenty-one.'

'Oh come on, Margot,' said Laurie, 'I'm too old to act as nursemaid to some kid.'

'If you're not prepared to deal with her,' said Margot, 'I'm not prepared to disclose to you the identity of the property.'

'I'll find it,' said Laurie.

'You won't,' said Margot, 'because it's not on the market.'

There was a long pause. 'What's so special about this kid?'

For a moment, Margot, normally so decisive, did not reply. Then she laughed, a crystal clear sound, like a mountain stream; it made Laurie's heart skip a beat. 'I don't know, Laurie, that's the strange thing. Why I'm insisting on you cutting her in on the action I'm honestly not quite sure. However, don't think for a moment that I'm weakening. I made up my mind as I lifted the phone — either you give her a break or I'll find someone else who can.'

The property was wonderful, an eight storey apartment block, very run down, owned by a property developer who was in deep trouble. The kid, it appeared, already rented one of the apartments but got wind of the fact that her landlord was in a mess and offered to buy the whole property from him.

'I guess it shows spunk,' Laurie said to Margot, grudgingly.

'She's been very thorough,' said Margot, 'It's no pie-in-the-sky plan. She reckons – and I'm sure she's right – that the apartments are far too big and that the real requirement in this city is for small one or two bedroomed apartments for young, professional people. She's drawn up the plans, got the necessary permits. All she needs is the money.'

'How much?' said Laurie.

'The total project, including conversion, will cost upwards of 500,000 dollars. My scheme is that we should go three ways. She can put up ten per cent of the stake money, I want you to put up twenty-five per cent and the bank will find the balance. Included in that conversion money we've allowed additional costs for converting two thirds of the ground floor into a Café Colette. We'll set her up in a corporation, of which she will have a seventy five per cent stake and you twenty five per cent. You'll pay a commercial rent for the restaurant, just like the other tenants but, of course, you'll have a stake in the holding company.'

'Why do I need the kid, why can't I just do this on my own?'

'Because the kid found the property, the kid wants to go into real estate and you're a restauranteur.'

'OK,' said Laurie, 'suppose I go and look at the property. Where is it?'

'Do we have a deal?' said Margot, suspiciously.

'OK, OK,' said Laurie, 'if the numbers work. Now, where is it?'

'On the corner of Lexington and 39th. For the moment it's called Davidson Plaza but Miss Kovac would like to change the name to Gregory Buildings.'

'Gregory Buildings!' said Laurie, 'Why, in God's name?'

'Gregory is the name of her son.'

'Her son! Jesus, how old is he?'

'Six, I understand.'

'Six! Jesus Christ!'

The future Gregory Buildings was everything Margot had promised, and so indeed was Ella Kovac – that and more. She looked like a child, yet there was a sensuous quality about her which attracted Laurie in a way that no other woman had ever done, not even Colette. When his tentative advances had been met first with a cold rebuff and then when he persisted, with something very close to terror, he was totally hooked. This girl he had to win, and he had succeeded, after many months of patience by which time Laurie Merman was hopelessly and irrevocably in love. He still was today.

A cab drew to a screeching halt and Laurie was snapped out of his daydreaming. Moments later he was rewarded by seeing Ella step out of the vehicle. She was casually dressed, as usual, in jeans, sneakers and an expensive multi-coloured silk shirt. She had a nice tan, Laurie noted, but there was a strained look about her and she seemed to have lost weight she could ill-afford. The cab driver was fussing with her bags. Throwing back the remains of his Kir, Laurie ran out to greet her.

Once inside Ella's apartment, uncharacteristically she collapsed on the sofa and allowed Laurie to fetch her a glass of wine. She glanced at her watch. 'Jesus, jetlag, what a pain. Two hours until Greg comes out of school, I guess I'll go and collect him. How is he, Laurie, have you seen him?'

'Most days,' said Laurie, 'he's fine. Wow, is he getting a big boy – he's almost as tall as me.'

Ella looked at him affectionately, 'Well, that's not awfully difficult, Laurie.'

'No, I guess not.' Laurie laughed and lowered his stocky frame onto the sofa beside Ella. 'Are you going to give your old man a kiss?' She leant forward and kissed his cheek. It was not what he had in mind but she was tired and he let it pass.

'Well, Laurie, I've found you your French château, except that it's not a château, it's a castle. It's inside your price range, with about forty acres of land, a small vineyard, two cottages and a little farmhouse. The only problem is you can't have the little farmhouse.'

'Why not?' said Laurie, smiling at her. It was so good to have her back he was hardly taking in what she was saying.

'Because I'm going to have it. I'll buy it off you at the right price, of course. I just fell in love with it, though heaven knows when I'll get to stay there. It's for Greg, really, I guess – It's just his sort of place.'

'Tell me more,' said Laurie. 'A castle – boy, that sounds interesting.'

'Here, wait, I've got some photographs and a map. The property is in the foothills of the Alps Maritime. The nearest town is Digne and all the hot spots – Antibes, Nice, Cannes – are only a couple of hours drive away. The castle is . . . well it's just out of another time, another world. Look at the photographs – they speak for themselves.'

'What's it called?' Laurie asked.

'Castle de Challese. Look, there's the castle and this is the view looking directly south. There's the vineyard, see, and the river below. It won't take more than a few thousand dollars to make it habitable and the asking price is 360,000 francs. It's a snip!' They poured over the photographs for some time.

'I love it,' said Laurie, 'it's dead right, I just hope nobody else gets it. You'd better call the agent right away and say to go ahead.'

'I already have,' said Ella. They both laughed.

Laurie raised his glass. 'Well, here's to Castle Challese. Jesus, just wait until I show these pictures to Colette, she'll just love it.' There was an uncomfortable silence for a moment between them. 'I'm sorry, Ella, that wasn't very tactful.'

'It's OK,' said Ella, her voice sounded weary.

Laurie scrutinized her in silence for a moment. 'You look peaked, kind of sad. What have you been up to, Sweetheart?'

Expecting a negative response denying anything was wrong, Laurie was surprised when Ella stood up, reached for the wine bottle to refill her glass and said. 'We need to talk, Laurie, and I guess now is as good a time as any.'

'Something's happened,' said Laurie. 'I'm right, aren't I?'

'Yes, something has happened.' Ella collapsed back on the sofa and sipped her wine in silence for a moment. Laurie tried to control a mounting sense of panic. 'While I was in England . . .' Ella struggled with the words, 'well, I guess I fell in love.'

Laurie felt as though his world had collapsed. He recognized, only too well, that he was hardly a young girl's dream. He also recognized, however, that the demands he made upon Ella both sexually and socially were about as much as she could handle. The time she devoted to her business and her son, coupled with her strange frigidity made it easy to understand why, up until now, he had been confident that he was the only man in her life. Indeed, the idea of her falling in love with someone else had simply never occurred to him. He forced himself to be generous – after all he was married, and she was young with her whole life ahead of her and deserved a chance to enjoy the fruits of married life.

'Jesus, Ella, I can't pretend that this hasn't come as a shock, but, well, I guess I'm really pleased for you. It is serious, I assume, for both of you?'

'It's serious, for both of us,' said Ella, 'or rather, it was.'

'Was! What do you mean *was*?' Laurie was becoming dangerously over-excited.

'I mean it's all over, finished.'

'But how can it be?' said Laurie, 'You can have only just met the guy – how come you've had the time to fall in love and out again so fast?'

Ella gave a hollow laugh. 'Because just my luck, yet again, I picked on a married man.'

His confidence ebbed back. A married man had made a play for Ella. She had responded and he had gone back to his wife. She would need him more than ever; everything was alright.

'I'm sorry, Honey, it must have been rough on you. Still, you're home now and you have Uncle Laurie to pick up the pieces.'

'That's just it,' said Ella, 'that's what I'm trying to tell you – I'm afraid it's the end for us. After . . . after, well, this experience, it wouldn't be right for us to continue. I mean, we'll go on being friends, of course, and partners, it's just that I don't want . . . well, you know.'

'No, I don't know,' said Laurie, suddenly angry. 'OK, so you take a tumble with some guy and then you find out that bastard's married. English, is he?' Ella nodded. 'OK, it was a bad experience but it's over, he's the other side of the Atlantic, you're home and I'm still here.'

'It is over and I am home, but I am not the same, or rather I don't feel the same about you.' Ella spoke slowly as if to a child. 'I do love you, Laurie, but more as a friend, a brother, a father – I don't know. This thing with Tim, well, it was different. Feeling as I do, I couldn't make love to anyone else and that includes you.'

'So what are you going to do,' said Laurie, 'turn into a nun, take Holy Orders?'

'Who knows,' said Ella. She looked exhausted, with dark shadows round her eyes.

Laurie suddenly felt defeated, his anger sapped. Already, he thought, the relationship is shifting. I should be fighting for her, but I can't.

'This guy – Tim, you say?' Ella nodded. 'Does he want to leave his wife and set up with you? I don't understand the situation?'

'I think he would like to,' said Ella, 'but it's quite impossible. He has commitments at home and his wife, well, she's not very into kids. He's responsible for the children and he has a business to run from home. His wife . . . she's away working most of the time, so you see he can't simply walk out, just like that.'

'This isn't the guy . . . the people at Wickham, the husband of the woman Margot wants you to partner in the Paris project?' Laurie asked.

'Yes,' said Ella, surprised. 'How did you know?'

'Obvious, I guess. You don't know many people in England. Jesus, this is going to make your Paris deal a little complicated, isn't it?'

'I'm not going ahead with the Paris deal. That's the other thing,' said Ella.

'I can't keep up with all this. Are you saying you're pulling out of Paris because of this guy? This is most unlike you, Ella, you've never let your emotions rule your business decisions before.'

'No, it's not because of Tim. I made the decision before ... well, before I realised how I felt about Tim. I pulled out for a combination of reasons, Laurie, but primarily because I have the feeling that I can't do two jobs properly, look after things here and in Paris.'

'So what happens next?' asked Laurie, heavily.

'Nothing,' said Ella. 'I get on with my job, concentrate on looking after my son and do my best to put Tim out of my mind.'

Laurie brightened a little. 'So, we can still have dinner now and again, and lunch maybe? You're going to need cheering up.'

'We can do all those things,' said Ella, 'provided you understand, Laurie, that this really is the end. I'm sorry, I'm enormously grateful to you, in fact I will always be indebted ...'

'Cut the crap,' said Laurie, 'don't patronize me.'

'I'm not patronizing you.'

There were tears in Ella's eyes, threatening to overbalance and run down her cheeks. She looked younger than ever and it wrenched Laurie's heart but he could not stand her pity.

'Then do we have to go through this routine ... thank you for everything, I'm a better person for knowing you. God dammit, Ella, it's too much.'

'I'm sorry, I'm sorry,' said Ella. 'What would you prefer, that I lied to you? Would you have wanted to make love to me while all the time I was thinking of Tim?'

'There's no need to be cruel,' said Laurie.

'I just want you to understand,' said Ella, 'we can't put the clock back and change things. You mustn't think that after a few weeks or months, I'll forget all about Tim and we can go back to where we were. That will never happen and so long as you understand that, then we can meet as often as you like.'

Laurie stood up and sighed. 'The Fall's normally a good time for me.'

'So perhaps this is the right time to find someone else,' said Ella, relentlessly.

'I don't want anyone else,' said Laurie, suddenly realizing how true the words were.

'You will, in time.'

Laurie left the apartment, rode the elevator although it was for only just one floor, and, avoiding his restaurant, stepped out into the street. The early promise of the day had been fulfilled. The sky was a cloudless blue, the freshness of the air invigorating but it meant nothing to Laurie Merman. He suddenly felt very old.

CHAPTER TWELVE

PARIS
November 1977

Stephanie replaced the receiver and stared out of the window in silence for a moment.

'Anything wrong?' Alex came to stand beside her, not touching but close.

As always, Stephanie could feel his vitality flow through her, as if they were joined by an electric current, but her feeling of guilt at the news she had just heard was by far the strongest emotion. She turned away so he could not see her face. 'No,' she said, 'at least not with the business – the business is doing fine. In fact that new manager I've appointed, is unbelievably efficient. I think my absence is actually beneficial.'

'Don't play the wilting violet,' said Alex, 'it doesn't suit you.'

'I agree,' said Stephanie with a smile, meeting his gaze at last.

Alex studied her in silence, his pale blue eyes penetrating, enquiring. 'Alright, so there's nothing wrong with the business, but something is wrong.'

Stephanie shrugged her shoulders. 'It's just that Tim's not too well.'

Alex raised an eyebrow. 'Life threateningly not too well?'

'Oh no, nothing like that,' said Stephanie, with studied casualness. She was not ready to talk about Tim, especially not to Alex. Indeed she doubted she ever would be.

'What is it then?' he persisted.

'Just a recurring childhood illness. The medics will sort it out.'

'You mean you're not going to tell me?'

'No,' said Stephanie, 'but then I don't really think you want to know.'

'You're right, of course. Why should I want to spend time talking about your husband when here we are in your new Paris flat, with *the* most enormous double bed I've ever seen, entirely unchristened.'

Stephanie felt an instant warmth rush through her. She wanted to think through the news she had just heard via the office but Alex's hands were on the nape of her neck, moving slowly, sensuously over her shoulders. It was extraordinary, the power he had over her. He could arouse her with a single caress, a look even — and he knew it.

Their affair had begun during only their second meeting. At Joseph's suggestion, Alex had taken her out to dinner and they had ended the evening in Alex's bed. It was not Stephanie's style. She enjoyed sex, and during her years in London, before meeting Tim, she'd had several lovers. However, she had never been an easy conquest — at least not before Alex.

The situation worried her for it seemed that her mind no longer had control over her body. Only too aware of Alex's charms and his reputation as an international playboy, she did not want to fall into the trap of simply being another notch on his belt.

Yet every time her body betrayed her, as like now. She wanted to think through the implications of Tim's sudden decline in health and its effect on the children. Instead she lay on the great double bed, her mind floating away while her body arched and tensed in ecstatic response to Alex's lovemaking.

She woke sometime later to find Alex hovering over her, carrying a wine cooler and two glasses. 'Some champagne — yet *another* house-warming gift.'

'What was the first?' Stephanie asked, sleepily.

'Why me, of course.' She watched in silence, as his delicate, artistic fingers, so like his father's, expertly worked off the champagne cork and filled the two glasses. He handed one to Stephanie. 'To the Centre des Arts,' he said. They drank in silence.

'Are you coming back to bed?' said Stephanie, patting the pillows.

'Why not, and then we'll go out to supper.'

'How long will you be staying in Paris?' Stephanie asked, snuggling up against his chest.

'As long as I'm needed,' said Alex. 'Now we have the Centre des Arts up and rolling I think it's time we thought about the franchise.'

'Do you and your father still want to go ahead with that?' Stephanie raised herself on one elbow.

'Yes,' Alex said, smiling. 'I think we work very well together, don't you?'

Stephanie sat upright in bed, tossed back the remains of her champagne and refilled her glass. Alex, seeing her agitation, watched in silence. She was half-way through the second glass before she spoke. 'How do you ... see the future, so far as we are concerned?'

'Once we've agreed the nuts and bolts of this franchise deal – in other words, once we have the structure right – Meyer has plenty of capital to invest in Europe. I see us expanding fairly fast and furious, don't you?'

'That's not what I meant,' said Stephanie. 'I was talking about you and me.'

Alex looked blank. 'We enjoy each other's company,' he grinned, running a hand gently over her shoulder, 'in and out of bed. We're both ambitious, the world is ours for the taking.'

'There is one major difference between us,' said Stephanie, 'you're single and I have a husband and two children.'

Without a word, Alex swung his long legs out of bed and disappeared into the bathroom, leaving Stephanie hurt and bewildered. She sat on in the bed in silence, listening to the sounds of the shower. He was behaving like a spoilt child, not wishing to discuss anything, other than the pursuit of pleasure. She was frightened. Despite her skill and experience, she knew that much of the success or failure of her growing relationship with Meyer Hotels depended upon her relationship with Alex. It was not why she had let herself become involved with him, but it was a factor. Her thoughts turned to Tim. If reports were correct, his condition had taken a serious nose-dive caused, she did not doubt, by stress. He did not yet know officially of her affair with Alex, but he had to guess there was something more than business keeping her away from Wickham. How were the children coping, she wondered, with a sick father and an absent mother? When she thought of her daughters, she always thought of them as the babies she had loved and cherished, not the children they were today, not far from puberty, strangers to her. Lying alone in the elegant but impersonal flat, at the emotional mercy of a man who was little more than a stranger, Stephanie had a sudden surge of longing for her home and family. She imagined them grouped round the fire in the library, tea and crumpets on Sunday afternoon with the newspapers spread out, the girls absorbed in a jigsaw. Was it a figment of her imagination, had there ever been afternoons like that? Yes, of course there had, but not in a long time, not since her business had become the cornerstone to her life, insiduously taking her over like a drug.

As abruptly as he had left, Alex emerged from the bathroom, a tiny towel fastened round his waist. He looked sleek, shiny almost, and very confident. 'Sorry,' he said, 'I needed to think.'

'And having thought?' Stephanie felt suddenly as nervous as she had been on the first occasion she had met the Meyers.

Alex sat down on the bed and took one of Stephanie's hands in his. 'Look, I recognize that I've led a charmed life,' he said, seriously. 'Basically, I've been denied nothing. I have been blessed with reasonable looks, a relatively adequate brain and everything that money and power can buy – with one exception.'

'What's that?' said Stephanie.

'I have no status of my own, no feeling of self-worth, no sense of achievement.'

Stephanie could hardly believe her ears. This was Alex Meyer talking – heir to one of the most successful hotel groups in the world, always assured, always charming. His sudden admission was both disarming and disturbing. 'I don't understand,' she said, 'is this something to do with your father?'

'You admire my father very much, don't you?' said Alex. Stephanie nodded. 'He is a truly remarkable man, I cannot deny that. His commercial achievements are amazing by any standards, particularly in the light of his early life. He has not made it to where he is today without being ruthless, yet there remains within the man – perhaps because of his experiences – a deep well of compassion which people at once find enchanting.' Alex paused, as if to give moment to his words. 'He's a great man, Stephanie, but a lousy father.'

'Why?' Stephanie asked.

'He lets me do nothing, he treats me like a child. I have made no real decision of any note since I joined Meyers from college. Initially he did the right thing. He started me off in the kitchens and had me work my way up through the ranks, learning all the jobs along the way. However, when eventually I made it to headquarters, he simply treated me as an office boy – that is until now.'

'What's changed things?' said Stephanie.

'You, apparently.'

'Me?' I don't see how.'

'He's willing to grant you this franchise. It's a snap decision like all his major decisions and that in itself is not surprising. He took to you, recognizes your talents and he always acts on impulse. However, because he doesn't know you, he's nervous, and for the first time I have a use. I am at least the devil he knows, and by allowing us to work as a team, he feels confident enough at last to delegate a major responsibility, namely Europe. You may think this deal is important to you, Stephanie. It's every bit as important to me.'

'I accept that, Alex, and thank you for explaining it all to me,' said Stephanie, slowly. 'It's helpful in that it makes me feel more in partnership with you and less on the receiving end; it's actually comforting to know we both have a lot at stake.' She smiled at him, radiating more confidence than she felt. 'However, what you have so far skilfully avoided doing is answering my question – where do we go from here?'

'I was coming to that,' said Alex. 'I've never been in love, I guess. What I feel for you is good. I like you, I admire you, enjoy working with you and I adore going to bed with you. If that's love – then great.'

'I feel the same,' said Stephanie, quietly.

'What I don't want,' Alex continued, 'are any complications, not at the moment, not when there's so much riding on Meyer's expansion in Europe. What I need is a simple, straight-forward personal life, with no hassle.'

'You think I'll cause you hassle?'

'Potentially, yes.'

Their eyes met. Alex's were steely with determination, Stephanie noted. 'Because of Tim and the children?' she challenged.

'Of course,' said Alex.

'What are you saying – do you want me to divorce Tim and stop seeing my children?'

'I don't mind what you do,' said Alex, with horrifying candour, 'so long as it doesn't affect me. You can divorce Tim if you wish, or not as the case may be. You can see your children as often as you like so far as I am concerned, as long as you don't expect me to play any role in their lives. I don't like kids, I have nothing to say to them. They make a mess, a noise – I don't want your children to be a part of my life.'

'You're being very frank,' said Stephanie, coolly.

'Yes, I am,' said Alex, 'but is there anything wrong with that? You asked me a straightforward question and I'm giving you a truthful answer. I don't know where we go from here, Stephanie, except that right now, I want no other woman but you. However, I do know that I don't want to marry, I don't want kids of my own and I don't want a part of your husband's kids. Alright, I'm a selfish bastard but at least I'm a consistent one. I want to make Meyer Hotels, Europe, the most successful hotel group there is and I'd like to do it with you at my side. I want you as a business partner, a friend and a lover, but not at a price. In other words, whatever trouble this causes for you back home is your problem.'

He must have seen the dismay on Stephanie's face, for his manner softened a little. 'Look, the last thing I want to do is put pressure on you. If you feel you can't cope, I'm sure we're adult enough to terminate the personal side of our relationship and concentrate on working together. Is that what you would prefer?'

Stephanie hesitated only for a split second. 'No, no, that's not what I want.'

'What do you want then?' said Alex, smiling and relaxed now his point was made.

'You,' said Stephanie, in a small voice.

Alex threw back his head and laughed, his white teeth gleaming against his dark skin. 'And I want you, My Love, so is there any reason why it should be more complicated than that?'

'No,' said Stephanie, 'no, I suppose not.' Yet even as she came into Alex's arms she knew that it was. The ambitious, ruthless streak she recognized in Alex she knew she, herself, possessed — they were two of a kind. While many women would have been completely undermined by Alex's frank exposure of his feelings, Stephanie, by contrast, admired his uncompromising honesty. She recognized that she owed Tim nothing less, but that would not be easy, not easy at all.

It seemed to Stephanie that already she no longer belonged in the master bedroom at Wickham, which she had shared with Tim for so many years. She had arrived home without warning, to find Tim at work and the children at school. After a rather awkward cup of coffee with Mrs Maggs, who clearly smelt trouble in the air, Stephanie decided to use the time before Tim returned for lunch to pack the bulk of her wardrobe to take with her back to Paris. For a moment she sat on the wide window seat looking at their large double bed, trying to understand what had occurred to make her feel so detached. Part of it was physical – the bedside table on her side was bare, it actually had a neglected look. On Tim's side, the floor was littered with farming magazines and the table piled high with books. There was an alarm clock, his pills, a discarded handkerchief, a glass of water. And then there were the pillows – no longer lying side-by-side but piled up in a single column, indicating a double bed for single occupancy.

It was not just the physical changes to the room, however, that made Stephanie feel out of place. The long days with Alex, followed by the ecstatic nights, had somehow alienated her and made her feel a stranger in the one place in all the world which she had always felt was home. This had been her parents' room. She could remember the happy days when as a tiny child, she had bounced on their bed, opening presents on her birthday, on Christmas morning, wrapping-paper everywhere. She could remember the feeling of warmth and security, of being tucked up between them on the odd occasion when she felt ill. There was the day she and George had used the bed as a trampoline and their mother had been furious. It was also the bed in which her mother had died, in which her two children had been conceived and where Belinda, in what had been an unholy rush, had been born. Yet she felt nothing.

When would she be back here again, she wondered. Her mind closed, for contemplation of the future was pointless. In recent days she had come to realize that while Alex's declaration was admirable in its honesty, it was hardly comforting, and already she knew she was out of her depth in the relationship. Alex had laid down the terms and she, Stephanie – poor besotted fool – was so in love she was prepared to accept them without a quibble. She let out a sigh and stood up, wearily opened the first of four large suitcases and began to pack.

'What the hell's going on?' Tim burst through the bedroom door.

Stephanie turned and studied him in silence for a moment before answering. He looked haggard and somehow pale beneath his tan. His eyes, normally so warm, were edged with pain.

'You're back early,' Stephanie said, stupidly.

'Mrs Maggs sent for me. She thought I should be here and it seems she's right. Were you planning to pack and be out of the house before I got home for lunch?'

'No, of course not,' said Stephanie. 'I just thought I'd do this while I was waiting for you.' Tim let out a weary sigh and sank down on the stool by the dressing table. 'Are you alright?' said Stephanie.

'Yes, I'm alright,' said Tim, 'but I'd like an explanation.'

'As you can see, I'm packing up most of my things to take to Paris, to the flat.'

'By the size and quantity of suitcases it would seem you're moving all your things. Are you leaving permanently?'

'More or less,' said Stephanie. 'I think it's probably best.'

'Best for who,' said Tim, 'for the children, for me or perhaps for you?'

'For all of us,' said Stephanie.

'Why?' There was a nervous tick hammering away at the side of Tim's right eye.

She took a deep breath. 'I've become involved with someone else, I'm sorry but it just sort of happened.'

'How long has it been going on?' He grimaced, 'Oh God, why in moments of crisis does one always come out with these terrible clichés?'

'It's only just started,' said Stephanie.

'But it's serious?'

'Yes.' Stephanie could not meet his eye.

'So you're leaving me. Do you want a divorce?'

'I-I don't know,' said Stephanie.

'You mean he hasn't asked you to marry him?' Tim's voice was icily calm.

'No.'

'Will he?'

'I don't know, possibly not. Please don't go on with these questions, Tim.'

'Does that mean he's married?' said Tim, ignoring her.

'No, he's not married.'

'Then the man must be a bastard if he's prepared to take you away from your husband but not marry you himself.'

'He's very different from you,' said Stephanie, defensively. 'Certainly many of the standards which you would consider are essential for decent living, he would not. His upbringing's been so different.'

'What is he, a Frenchman?'

'No, he's an American of sorts.'

'Am I permitted to know his name?'

'I'd rather not tell you.'

'I think you owe it to me, Stephanie, to tell me everything. If you're worried I'll make trouble, forget it. I haven't got the strength, particularly at the moment.'

'It's Alex Meyer,' said Stephanie.

'Is that the old man?' Tim looked appalled.

'No, the son.'

'No wonder you've struck such a good deal with the Meyers if you're taking them to your bed.'

Stephanie stepped forward and slapped him hard across the face. At the very moment she did so, she regretted it.

'Tim, I'm sorry, I'm very sorry.'

He remained where he was seated, seemingly oblivious to the blow. Only the red weal appearing on one cheek indicated that she had not imagined what had happened.

'Look, we're only upsetting each other by talking like this,' she said, shakily.

Still he said nothing, he simply stared at her as if she was a stranger to him. His face was so familiar – the crinkle lines around his eyes, caused by his easy, kindly smile, his rugged features, not strictly speaking handsome, but none the less a pleasing face, above all a good face – honest, caring. Suddenly, the enormity of what she was about to lose made Stephanie catch her breath. In response, she saw hope flare in Tim's face.

'Don't do it, Steph,' he said, quietly. 'Look, I know your business means everything to you and presumably this ... this man, Alex Meyer, can do a lot for your career, but is it really worth throwing up a marriage for?'

'Do we still have a marriage?' Stephanie asked quietly.

'I thought so,' said Tim. He stood up and walked to the window. 'OK, not a conventional marriage, perhaps. We see so little of each other and when we do it's rushed and you're always exhausted, but we should be looking at this stage in our life together as just that – a stage.' He turned to face her, his love for her there for all to see. 'We were so happy in the beginning, and in the years that followed when Millie and Belinda were small. I'm not imagining it, am I? Things were, well ... just about perfect, weren't they?'

Stephanie could not meet his eye. 'They were good, certainly.'

'OK, so there has been a considerable deterioration since then but it's not so much our relationship as the circumstances. Supposing I said to you: look, I won't fight your business aspirations any more, you go your way, I'll go mine – wouldn't that help?'

'That's just what I'm suggesting we do,' said Stephanie.

'Don't try to be so bloody clever,' said Tim, angrily, 'I might be prepared to give and take on how much time you spend on your work but I'm certainly not prepared to tolerate you being away from home in order to conduct an affair with Alex Meyer. You must take me for an absolute sucker. OK, so I usually let you have your own way without argument for the sake of family unity, but there is a limit and this is it.' He made an effort to control himself. 'Look, will it help if I tell you I still love you as much now as the day we first made love?'

Slowly Stephanie raised her eyes to meet his. 'No, I don't think it will, Tim. You see it's ... it's too late.'

The fight died in him and he slumped back on the chair. Compassion welled up in Stephanie. She stepped forward and kneeling down, she slipped her arms around him. 'I really am very sorry,' she whispered against his chest. For a moment he responded to her and she was aware, fleetingly, of a sense of warmth and security in his embrace, which despite all the passion of their relationship, she never felt with Alex.

Almost as the thought came to her, Tim pushed her away abruptly. 'I can stand just about anything except your pity,' he said. 'Let's talk about the practicalities, since clearly you're not going to change your mind.'

She took her lead from him and stood up briskly. 'You must stay on here, of course. It's your home as much as mine, you created it. As far as the children are concerned perhaps I could arrange to see them sometimes?'

'Whenever you like,' said Tim, mechanically. 'At least that's one good thing.'

'What's one good thing?' said Stephanie, frowning.

'At least they won't suffer from our marriage splitting up as most poor little wretches do. Having a full-time mother would come as far more of a shock to their systems than having no mother at all.'

'Do you have to rub it in?'

'Yes, I bloody well do,' said Tim, suddenly standing up. The violence of his reaction made Stephanie step back, stumbling over a suitcase as she did so. 'Look, just clear out, get packed as quickly as you can and please be gone by lunchtime. I don't want to have to sit through a meal, trying to make small talk to you. Leave your address on my desk and if there's anything wrong with the children I'll let you know. No news is good news, alright?'

'Alright,' said Stephanie.

In an instant he was gone, not slamming the door but shutting it quietly behind him, as was his way. To her surprise, Stephanie found herself sitting on the bed with tears pouring down her face. It had been so much easier than she had expected. There had been few recriminations, the very minimum of explanation. So why was she crying? As always, Tim had been reasonable, controlled and with right on his side. As always, she was painfully aware that she had let him down, and their children. It was not the indisputable fact that she was the villain of the situation which caused her pain. No, what hurt most was that he had let her go without a real fight. In some ways, it had been so much easier than she had expected, in others so much more difficult.

CHAPTER THIRTEEN

NEW YORK
December 1977

The bitter cold of early December in New York seemed to have penetrated every bone, Margot thought as she hurried on, head bent against the wind. It had been madness to walk through Central Park. The sky was so blue and the sun so bright, that from the safety of a centrally heated office, the prospect had seemed desirable. Besides, she had wanted time to think and she was early for her appointment. Having spent the first thirteen years of her life in Korea, British weather had been bad enough but she would never get used to the New York winter. She was definitely a hot-house bloom, she thought. She quickened her pace at the sight of the Inn on the Park ahead. She was breaking all her normal personal codes of practice, having lunch with Ella Kovac today. She was not quite sure why she was doing it, except she felt instinctively that Ella needed to broaden the outlook of her business and needed the necessary encouragement to do so. Putting such a view across might be better received over lunch. She understood Ella very well, she felt – the impoverished childhood, followed by the phenomenal success of her venture into property had made her strangely vulnerable. If you have nothing, you have nothing to lose. However, once success has been achieved then every decision you make could in theory throw you back to where you've come from. Ella, she felt, was in danger of becoming a prisoner of her own success.

Ella was already at the table by the time Margot had shed

her coat and tidied herself in the ladies' room. She looked peaky, Margot thought, and seemed to have lost even more weight. Man trouble, Margot wondered, or something wrong with the business? She had checked the balances of Lexington Kovac before leaving the bank and everything had seemed in order. 'Ella, how good to see you.' The two women exchanged a perfunctory kiss.

'It's good to see you, too,' said Ella, 'and don't think I'm unaware of the great honour you are doing me. I know business lunches are not your style.'

'I promised you a lunch when we last met in London, I don't forget my promises.'

'I'm sure you don't,' said Ella, drily.

They ordered salmon en croute and a bottle of Muscadet and then settled down to talk. It wasn't just Ella's appearance that had altered, Margot noted. It seemed she had lost her sparkle, her vitality. By contrast, as always, Ella was fascinated by Margot, as indeed the entire restaurant appeared to be. She was a spectacular sight, with her long, dark auburn hair, her pale, oriental face and eyes so dark that they appeared to be black rather than brown – almond-shaped but large, so that they dominated her face. Tall, slim and dressed in a simple black silk Jean Muir jersey and skirt, she was all the more stunning because her appearance was so understated. Long red fingernails tapped the table, since there was no pen and paper with which to doodle. 'So how's business, Ella?'

'OK,' said Ella, without apparent enthusiasm.

'Any new projects?'

Ella hesitated. 'Yes, one, but it's too early to talk about it as yet.'

'Oh come on – try me,' said Margot.

'It's a big one,' said Ella, 'a block on Fifth Avenue. I don't want to tell you anything about it at the moment, because I'm still in negotiation for it. I've found a major store who will lease virtually the whole property and what slays me is the thought that the store may do a deal direct and cut me out. Result: policy decision, I'm telling no one about it until it's in the bag.'

'Fifth Avenue – it must mean a lot of money.'

'It does,' said Ella, 'but there's more than adequate collatoral.'

'Of course,' said Margot. 'There'll be no problem with the finance, you know that, you can have whatever you need. I just hope this time you get out from under when the project's complete.'

'Sell out, you mean? You're on your favourite subject, again,' said Ella, with a grin.

'Yes, I am,' said Margot, 'and you're on your favourite bandwagon – more borrowing secured against more collateral, making yet more profit for Joshkers Bank but not doing a great deal for Lexington Kovac.'

'I'll be doing a great deal for Lexington Kovac,' Ella protested. 'If this project goes through, I'll have an excellent income which will make vast profits over and above the interest I'll be paying you.'

'I don't doubt it,' said Margot. 'I'd have given up backing you long ago if I thought you couldn't do your sums right. It's just that I think it's time you diversified.'

'You mean move out of property?' said Ella.

'Good grief no, stick to where your talents lie,' said Margot. 'It just worries me that your business depends entirely on all this premium property in New York. Supposing the market went sick on you.'

'It won't,' said Ella, 'not in New York, you know that.'

'OK, maybe not, but what you should be looking at is a fresh location where you can make a real killing for the same amount of effort – a real boom area where you can get in on the ground floor.'

'If I wanted a project outside New York,' said Ella, 'I'd have gone for the Centre des Arts. Surely we don't have to go through all that again.'

'Ella, there are an awful lot of places nearer than Paris,' said Margot, exasperated. 'I was actually thinking North America.'

'Like where?' said Ella.

'I don't know, it's not my job to know – this is your

country, Ella, not mine, and it's your business. I just feel that you're in some kind of rut, sitting around waiting for the same old projects to come up.'

'You make me sound as though I'm under-employed,' said Ella, ruefully. 'I work damned hard, Margot. It's more than a full-time job looking after my properties and I always have a new project on the go. I run a tight ship, with the very minimum of staff, you know that.'

'I'm not suggesting you're being lazy, of course I'm not, I'm just saying you're mentally stuck in a rut and it can't be very stimulating.'

'Thanks a bundle,' said Ella.

'Come on,' said Margot, 'it's not often I see you minus your sense of humour. Is there anything wrong, have you any problems?'

'Nothing I can't handle,' said Ella, anxious to steer the conversation away from herself. 'The business is really running very smoothly at present – I have a new assistant.' She smiled, suddenly, at the thought of Jackie.

'Oh really!' said Margot, 'Male, female, tell me all?,

'Female, English, twenty-five. Jacqueline Partridge, her name is.'

Margot laughed. 'That's a bit of a mouthful.'

'It suits her, though,' said Ella. 'I'm not saying this unkindly but she reminds me a little of a partridge – sort of pear-shaped, definitely on the plump side.'

'What with her and Jessie, there can't be a lot of room for moving around in your place,' said Margot.

'You're right about that.'

They talked on a wide range of topics as the meal progressed until Ella could stand it no more and asked the question which had been foremost in her mind since Margot had joined her. 'Tell me about Stephanie Bonham, how are things going?'

'Very well,' said Margot, 'in fact I have to admire the girl her drive and enthusiasm – it's hard to keep up. Not only did she persuade old man Meyer to do the Centre des Arts project with her, she's sold all her hotels and leisure complexes to the Meyer organisation and then taken up a franchise on them and all the Meyer units in Europe. It's worth an absolute fortune but she acquired the license for a song, comparatively speaking. Mind you, I suppose it's not entirely surprising in the circumstances.'

'What circumstances?' Ella asked.

'Oh, you haven't heard the gossip?'

Ella shook her head. 'I've had no dealings at all with Stephanie since that rather unfortunate meeting, when I pulled out of the Centre des Arts project.'

'She's started a well publicized affair with Alex Meyer, Joseph Meyer's son and heir,' Margot added, with a grin. 'They're seen everywhere together and frequently splashed all over the gossip columns. Stephanie's permanently based in Paris now and Alex spends as much time in Paris as he can. It's all very cosy.'

Ella was amazed by her own physical reaction. She felt at once sick and faint; her heart was beating a wild tattoo. 'What about Tim,' she had to ask. 'How has he reacted?'

'There's nothing much he can do, is there?' said Margot. 'He and Stephanie have been leading separate lives for a long time. I gather he's doing what he always has done – keep the home fires burning at Wickham.'

'Are they getting divorced?' said Ella, aware that she was perhaps displaying too much interest.

Margot shrugged her shoulders. When the topic of conversation strayed away from business or banking, her boredom threshold was very low indeed. 'I don't know,' she said, 'probably, unless Stephanie needs Tim as some sort of security.'

'But he wouldn't stand for that, surely, would he?'

'Who knows,' said Margot, 'he's always struck me as a little weak. On the other hand he's an attractive man. Once the green wellie set know he's up for grabs, I should imagine every unattached female in the country will be pushed in his direction.' She laughed, blissfully unaware of the pain her words caused Ella.

Back at Gregory Buildings, Ella found herself loath to go

back into her office. Instead she took the elevator to the peace and quiet of her apartment – after all, she had Jackie now to fend off calls. Jackie was an odd choice by anyone's standards. Ella collapsed on her sofa, remembering her first meeting with Jackie. Jackie was the fifth would-be assistant Jessie had selected for Ella to inspect. She was also the last, and Ella suspected, Jessie's favourite. She was a large girl with wispy, pale brown hair to her shoulders, which flew untidily in all directions. Her good features were her clear grey eyes and a pale peachy complexion. She had a tendency to flush bright scarlet when she was embarrassed or unsure of herself, which was most of the time.

Ella studied the curriculum vitae in front of her. Jacqueline Partridge had been in New York for nearly two years. She had begun working for a British publishing house and more recently had moved to an advertising agency, where she had been for only eight months. School had been Cheltenham Ladies College, followed by a secretarial college in Oxford.

'I assume you're English?' Ella asked.

'Oh, yes,' said Jacqueline. She played nervously with the handles of her handbag. She was conventionally dressed, in a blue suit which was a little on the tight side for her. Beneath the suit was a pink silk shirt, from which a button was missing.

'What are you doing in New York?' Ella asked, anxious to put the girl at ease.

'Oh, I thought I'd like to see a bit of the world, travel around, you know,' Jackie stammered.

'You must know New York pretty well by now, after two years. Forgive me asking this but if I am to take you on, I need to know what your long term plans may be. In other words, are you intending to go back to England shortly? Whoever I employ, I want to feel will be with me for a while.'

'Oh, I shan't be going back to England,' said Jacqueline emphatically.

'Why?' Ella asked, pointedly.

'Because I like it here and because . . .' she stopped in

mid-sentence, looked flustered. 'Oh drat,' she said, 'it's no good, I'm going to have to tell you the truth.'

'I'd appreciate it,' said Ella, dryly.

'I came over here originally because I was in love with my boss and he was transferred to New York. My parents were furious and said I was being very silly. It was awful – there were terrible scenes, but I came anyway.' There was a note of defiance in her voice.

'I presume he was married,' said Ella, sagely.

'Y-yes, I'm afraid so.' Jackie looked surprised.

'What went wrong?' Ella asked.

'He got fed up with me,' said Jacqueline, with commendable candour. 'You see I knew no one else in New York, I was lonely and I smothered him, I think. With his wife still in England, I expected we would be seeing each other all the time.' She shrugged her shoulders. 'Anyway, he began an affair with an American girl. It was bad enough that he was married but that was the last straw, so eventually I left.'

'And clearly you're not very happy with the advertising agency where you're working now,' said Ella.

'No, another disaster – I do seem to pick them. He was married too, only the difference was he told me he wasn't. When I found out, I felt such a fool. Everyone else in the office knew, they must have been laughing behind my back. Anyway, you can see why I can't go home. My parents would have a field day.'

'Well,' said Ella, 'there's one good thing about Lexington Kovac, there are no men in this organization, except for a shareholder, Laurie Merman, who we see fairly infrequently.' Fleetingly, Ella wondered if Jacqueline Partridge could be Laurie Merman's type but dismissed the thought. Laurie liked his women small and dark.

There was something about the girl that appealed to Ella. She was not sure what it was, whether it was her candour or whether, perhaps, her voice which reminded her of Tim, or yet again perhaps it was Jackie's obvious vulnerability. An English girl in New York, totally out of her depth, in some ways mirrored her own early experiences in New York.

Hiring Jackie was a snap decision and one which Ella did not regret for a moment. If Jackie had a fault, she was over-anxious to please, she worked long hours, took her job very seriously and seemed effortlessly to have won the affection and admiration of Jessie. Even Greg liked her, though he teased her unmercifully which she seemed to adore.

Ella glanced at her watch, Greg would be home in half an hour. There was a desk-full of work downstairs, so what was she doing sitting here in a solitary state? She knew, of course. Tim. Tim alone, without Stephanie. It was nearly four months since their one night together and bitter parting, yet there seemed to have been barely a moment of her waking day when her thoughts had not strayed to Tim Irvine. She understood now, what she had never understood before, the strength of love which could exist between a man and a woman. Her youthful infatuation with Aaron had never had a chance to develop because of Alice and Laurie had never touched her soul. Sitting alone at this moment, the twin considerations of her business and her son seemed of shadowy importance compared with her longing to be with Tim, to love him and comfort him. Any why not? His marriage was at an end ... Yet, he could have contacted her. Had he not done so because he had already forgotten her, or was it pride that stopped him? Fumbling nervously, she opened her briefcase and pulled out an address book. She paused for a moment longer, then lifting the phone she dialled the Wickham number.

'Wickham 253.' The comfortable, homely voice of Mrs Maggs was instantly identifiable.

'Hello,' said Ella, awkwardly. 'Could I speak to Mr Irvine, please.'

'I'm sorry,' said Mrs Maggs. 'He's had his breakfast and he's already up and out. He'll be back at lunchtime, though, twelve-thirty sharp.'

'OK, thanks. I'll leave it until then,' said Ella.

'Should I say who's calling?'

'No, no message.'

'Alright then, goodbye.'

'Bye,' said Ella replacing the receiver with a shaky hand. She had tried and he was out – perhaps it was fate trying to tell her something. She cursed herself for not having left a message so that the decision as to whether to ring again would not exist. Placing the responsibility on Tim to call her back if he wished would have been an immense relief. As it was, he would be none the wiser.

She stood up, a little unsteadily, then snapping shut her briefcase strode purposely towards the flat door. She was a fool. It had been madness to think of contacting him. Nothing had changed, just because Stephanie had left him. Tim could not move to New York, nor could she move to England. Those facts still stood between them. Somehow she had to learn to forget him.

CHAPTER FOURTEEN

'Ella, is that you?'

The practical side of Ella's mind recognized the voice, yet since it represented the impossible she rejected it. 'Yes,' she said, cautiously. 'Who is this?'

'It's Tim, Ella, Tim Irvine. You do still remember me, don't you?'

She wanted to laugh and scream and shout, 'I love you, I love you.' Instead she said, 'Yes, yes, of course. How are you, Tim?'

'I'm fine. Look, tell me to ring off if you like and I'll understand, it's just that Mrs Maggs took a call yesterday morning and she swears it was from you. She says she recognized your voice. When you, or whoever it was, didn't ring back, I tried to resist ringing you, but I just couldn't. Was it you, Ella?'

'Yes,' said Ella, in a quiet voice.

'Oh good. I have to admit I thought I might be making an idiot of myself.'

'No, you weren't doing that, Tim.'

'It's lovely to hear your voice,' said Tim. 'How have you been?'

'A bit low,' Ella said.

'Me, too,' said Tim. 'I don't know whether you've heard . . .'

'Yes,' said Ella, 'that was one of the reasons I was ringing you, the main reason I suppose, to say I'm sorry about Stephanie. You must be very upset.'

'Not as upset as I thought I would be,' said Tim. 'My pride has been hurt, of course. Taking second place to her business interests was one thing – recognizing that she is involved with another man introduces a whole new set of emotions. Strangely, though, I find it an odd relief.'

'Why?' said Ella.

'We've been separated for years really, several years at any rate. We kept pretending we had a normal marriage but of course we didn't, and now at least the position is clarified. Stephanie's free to get on with her life, me with mine, and I think the children are better for it, too. I was quite open with them and told them exactly what had happened, but not in a derogatory way so far as Stephanie was concerned, of course. They seem much more relaxed now everything has settled down. Anyway enough of me, how's Greg?'

'Greg's fine,' said Ella, 'enormous, good grades at school, happy and healthy.'

There was a brief pause while both reflected on how easy it seemed to be to communicate. 'Ella . . .' Tim hesitated, 'you may think this is a ridiculous suggestion but I just wondered . . . well, I wondered if you and Greg were doing anything for Christmas.'

Her spirits soared and then plummetted in a space of a second – she was immediately defensive. 'We always spend Christmas with Aaron and his family.'

'Why not break the rules and spend Christmas with me and the girls? Stephanie's not coming home, she's spending Christmas in New York with the Meyers.'

There was no rancour in his voice, Ella noticed with surprise and admiration. It was simply a statement of fact.

'Oh Tim, I just couldn't come to Stephanie's home and take her place, so to speak – it wouldn't feel right. I know it's your home, too,' she said, hurriedly, 'but I'd feel very uncomfortable and awkward.'

'Then why don't we meet somewhere else – at a hotel? I know Christmas in a hotel isn't the same as at home but the children are at an age when they might quite enjoy it. You could come here with Greg or we could fly out to you.'

As he was speaking a thought flashed into Ella's mind. She tried to reject it but it sat there, persistent, demanding — it had to be the obvious solution.

'Ella, are you still there?'

'Yes.'

'Look I'm sorry if I'm embarrassing you. Does the whole idea appal you?'

'No,' said Ella, 'no, it doesn't appal me at all, it sounds wonderful. I was just thinking Tim, I have this farmhouse in Provence. I've never stayed there, I just bought it on a whim. There are a few sticks of furniture, an old kitchen range, running water and electricity but that's about it. We could go there, I suppose.'

'Ella, could we, can we?' The enthusiasm in Tim's voice made Ella smile.

'Hell, why not,' she said, 'it's crazy but let's do it.'

They made hurried arrangements. Tim insisted that it should be he and his daughters who were the advance party, to stock up with food and the equipment they would need.

'It's not fair,' said Ella, 'you're supposed to be my guests, I should be doing all that.'

'You and Greg have a long way to come. We can get out there . . . hang on, let me see when the kids break up . . . we can be out there on the 17th.'

'Greg and I couldn't make it before the 23rd,' said Ella, leafing through her diary, 'and then we'd need to be back by January 4th — sorry, business commitments.'

'That's OK,' said Tim, 'it still gives us two weeks.' The thought of two weeks in each other's company silenced them both. 'It's so simple,' said Tim, 'I can't believe it — it must be more difficult than this.'

'It isn't,' said Ella, 'in fact there's only one thing left to do.'

'What's that?'

'I just have to mail you the key.'

*

They turned a bend in the road. The village of Challese was laid out before them, the valley sloping away to the left before climbing again to form the foothills of the Alps Maritime. Ella slowed the car on the brow of the hill. 'Look, there's Uncle Laurie's castle.'

'Wow,' said Greg, 'that is impressive. Why aren't we staying there?'

'Because it's Laurie's, not ours. Anyway, who needs a castle, it's kind of over the top, don't you think?'

'Yes,' said Greg, laughing, 'yes, it is but it's typical Uncle Laurie. He hasn't been around so much lately Mom. Why is that?'

Ella hesitated. 'We're good friends, but we just decided not to see so much of each other.'

'But why?' Greg persisted.

'Shut up, Greg. Look, we're nearly there.'

Tim and Ella had been in constant touch since their decision three weeks earlier. As the date grew nearer, there had been some frantic telephone calls concerning the practicalities of such details as bed linen and towels, as slowly the realities of living in a semi-derelict farmhouse began to dawn on them. The culmination of it all had been an ecstatic call which Tim and the girls had made from the local post office, saying they had arrived, had fallen hopelessly in love with the farmhouse and that it was perfect in every way. These various conversations had helped to ease the tension between Tim and Ella but now, as they approached the end of their journey, she felt herself becoming increasingly nervous. After all they barely knew one another, this was only the third time they had met: the whole idea was madness. A knot formed in the base of her stomach as she swung the little Renault round the last few bends. 'Here we are,' she said, in a small, strangled voice.

'It's wonderful, wonderful,' said Greg, leaping out of the car before she had finished parking.

It was indeed perfect. The farmhouse was built in the fold of two hills, in soft grey stone. It was five miles from the village and its isolation had troubled Ella slightly on her first visit. Now, though, it seemed appropriate. A watery sun warmed the stonework, lights blazed from all the windows and a reassuringly thick column of smoke was rising from both chimneys.

'Tim, Millie, Belinda, we're here!' Greg ran ahead of her, pushing open the stable door which led into the kitchen.

Wearily, Ella pressed her hands into the small of her back, trying to straighten up after the hours of travelling, and then self-consciously she followed her son. Tim was out of the back door before she had reached it. She formed no immediate impression of him – they simply reached blindly for one another and embraced fleetingly, aware of the children. 'How are you?' Tim said, huskily.

'Tired,' Ella managed before they were swamped with greetings from the children.

The Irvines had worked hard, very hard indeed. Ella walked into the kitchen and stopped, amazed. It was transformed. A lovely old, scrubbed wooden table dominated the centre of the room, already set for a meal. Two Windsor chairs were pulled up in front of the range, highly coloured rugs were spread over the stone flags of the floor and on the dresser, plates and glasses gleamed in the firelight. She turned to them, spontaneously slipping her arms round the shoulders of the two girls. 'You've done wonders, I can't believe this. You must have worked so hard.'

'Daddy did most of it,' said Belinda, 'but come on through, there's lots more to see.'

In the sitting room, a huge log fire crackled in the grate, there were more rugs and easy chairs but the dominating feature was an enormous Christmas tree, filling a whole corner of the room.

'This is unbelievable,' said Ella. 'Greg, can you believe it?'

'It's great. Can we see upstairs?' Greg's face was bright with excitement.

There were four bedrooms – one the girls already occupied, one for Greg and one each for Tim and Ella, divided from the rest of the house by an intervening bathroom.

'Sort yourselves out and then come down for drinks in the

sitting room,' said Tim. 'You two are not allowed to do anything tonight but to let yourselves be spoilt.'

They had a wonderful evening, they drank carafes of the local wine – the younger children's well watered – and ate a delicious beef casserole prepared by Tim, mopped up with garlic bread and followed by superb cheese from the village. The warmth, the good food and wine made Ella and Greg very drowsy, and when it was time for the girls' bedtime Greg went, too, without protest, leaving Tim and Ella alone for the first time.

'This is the most wonderful place, Ella, it was a brilliant find. I know it's cold outside, but come to the back door for a moment.' Tim took Ella's hand, pulling her from one of the Windsor chairs and leading her to the stable door. He threw open the top part and let the cold night air rush in. 'Listen,' said Tim. They leant over the half door, the cold air reviving Ella, and the silence enveloped them. There was not a sound to be heard, except for the tinkling of the stream which ran through the grounds a few feet from the back door. 'It beats New York,' Tim said.

'It certainly does,' Ella whispered.

Instinctively they turned to one another and a moment later they were in each other's arms, kissing as though they would never stop. Tears sprang into Ella's eyes and began flowing down her cheeks. Normally embarrassed by any show of emotion, she made no effort to brush them away and then realized that the wetness on Tim's face was not from her own tears but from his. Without speaking, they crept upstairs and into Ella's room. They undressed quickly because of the cold and fell into bed. 'I'll set the alarm,' said Tim, 'I'd better be back in my own room before the children wake.'

It was not as good as last time, it was better, much, much better. They'd now had time to adjust to their feelings. Stephanie no longer cast a shadow of guilt, and perhaps, most important of all, they were not in a hurry; two glorious weeks stretched ahead of them.

'It's been awful, the last few months,' Tim whispered, when at last they lay sated in each other's arms.

'Yes, every day was an effort,' Ella admitted.

'If that's how we both feel then there has to be a way to be together ... We'll find it,' Tim murmured, as they drifted off to sleep.

The days followed much the same pattern, which seemed to please them all. They were living a life more suited to a hundred years ago, for everything required manual effort. The heating of the house relied entirely on the range, as did the hot water which was heated by way of a back boiler. This meant a never-ending requirement for logs, which they all took it in turns to saw and barrow back from the copse at the end of the garden. Milk and eggs came from a farm, three miles away by car but only a mile on foot over the fields. Everyone seemed anxious to join in the domesticity, as they gradually transformed the farm from a house into a home. Ella found herself buying rough woven cotton in the village to make curtains. Millie picked long sheaves of grass, dried them and arranged them in earthenware pots, again from the village. Belinda, although only ten, showed an enormous interest in cooking and Greg was in his element, working alongside Tim, logging or clearing the garden, or tramping into the village for stores. They rarely used the car, it somehow seemed at odds with their existence. They were completely fulfilled and entirely happy. At times, both Ella and Tim were aware of being perhaps a little over-demonstrative with one another, and on several occasions, Ella caught Millie watching her with Stephanie's eyes and wondered what was going on in the child's head.

On Christmas Eve, Tim and Ella made stockings for the children and for each other, and on Christmas morning, when they were woken early by Belinda rampaging through the house, it was actually snowing. They ate a huge Christmas lunch and afterwards exchanged presents. Ella had struggled hard trying to think of a suitable present for Tim and in the end had bought a watch from Tiffany's, engraved simply with the date and his initials. For Millie and Belinda, she had spent a fortune on dresses she had found for them in Macy's. She'd had to guess at styles and the sizes, but they seemed appropriate presents as she rightly assumed clothes were never high on their priority list, without a mother to help them choose. Judging by the squeals of delight, her decision had been the right one and they insisted on wearing them for the rest of the day.

Tim had bought Ella an antique pearl necklace which, once it was fixed around her neck, she could never imagine taking off again. For Greg, he had bought an air rifle. 'I hope you don't mind,' he said, looking at Ella apprehensively. 'It's just that since he enjoys country life, I thought he probably would like to learn to shoot and this is the right way to start.'

'It's brilliant, great,' said Greg. 'I can't believe it. When can we try it out?'

'This afternoon, if you like,' said Tim. 'I've brought my gun with me and I have already spoken to Jean Valois at the farm, who says we may shoot over his land.'

Ella stared at Tim in amazement, he seemed to have settled in so easily to life in Provence. She recognized that country living anywhere in the world had certain elements in common, but the ease with which Tim, a typical Englishman, had settled into the French way of life still surprised her.

On Christmas night they went to Mass. It was a beautiful little church, lit entirely by candles and as they stood together in the pew, Tim's hand in her own, it already seemed to Ella that they were one family, had always been and would always be. On Boxing Day it had snowed some more and they went tobogganing on kitchen trays. And so the days passed, each one a new delight, until the New Year had come and gone and time was running out.

On the evening of New Year's Day, when the children were in bed, Tim finally raised the question that they had both been avoiding. 'So, where do we go from here?' he asked, gently.

They were in the sitting room, drinking brandy in front of the fire. 'I don't know,' Ella answered truthfully.

'Let's look at the really important issues,' said Tim. 'We have each other and our relationship, we have the children and theirs. What flaws do you see – not in the practicalities of living together for a moment, but purely in how we get along as people?'

Ella considered the question for a moment. 'We're lucky because you have girls and I have a boy, so there is no direct competition. The children seem to get along incredibly well. I wonder about Millie, though. She is always very polite and helpful but I wouldn't dare be demonstrative with her in the way I am with Belinda.'

'That may be her age. Twelve year olds are very independent, and in Millie's case she's had to be.'

'Yes, I guess so but I think she's more aware of our relationship even than Greg and I don't honestly think she's very pleased about it.'

'If you're right, I'm sure she'll come round,' said Tim, gently. 'How do you think Greg and I are doing?'

'That's an unnecessary question and you know it,' said Ella, grinning, 'He thinks the world of you, it's as simple as that.'

'And us?' They kissed and it was sometime before they drew apart.

'There's really nothing to say about us, is there?' said Ella.

'Other than it's perfect?' Tim suggested. Ella nodded. 'Alright,' he said, his voice anxious despite his efforts to be practical. 'Having looked at our various relationships, would you agree there is nothing to stop us being together and we can't possibly live apart? It would be a crime.' Ella nodded. 'So all we have to do,' said Tim, 'is to decide how and where.' He ruffled Ella's curls, 'but I don't think we should start that tonight, sleepy head. We'll pack the children off to bed early tomorrow night and try and make some plans then. Let's think about it during the day, and tomorrow evening, as they say, we can have an in depth discussion.'

But their in depth discussion was never to take place for the following afternoon something happened which changed everything.

CHAPTER FIFTEEN

SOUTH OF FRANCE
January 1978

The next day, in one of the outhouses of the farmhouse, Greg found an old television. Despite the attractions of farm life, having been raised on a diet of television the children were missing it and being something of an expert on all things electrical, Greg set to work to mend it. By lunchtime he had managed to produce a shaky black and white picture which steadily improved, so that by mid-afternoon, when a cold east wind has set in and a snow-laden sky had already made it nearly dark, the whole family were able to settle down and watch an appallingly sentimental French film. So predictable was the plot that even the children understood it without the benefit of much French.

Belinda and Ella had baked a cake of which they were excessively proud. They made tea and sat round the fire, watching the film in perfect, cosy harmony. Ella had almost drifted off to sleep when suddenly she heard Millie's voice, shrill with alarm. 'Daddy, Daddy, are you alright?' Her eyes snapped open to find Tim lurching to his feet, his teacup going in one direction, his plate in the other. He seemed quite oblivious to both, as they crashed to the floor, and although he had his back to her, Ella saw immediately that his limbs seemed to be twitching spasmodically.

'Tim, Tim, what ever's the matter?' She stood up and went towards him.

'Don't touch him,' Millie shrieked, 'clear some space,' and as she spoke Tim suddenly pitched forward and crashed to the floor.

The noise and vibration of a grown man apparently hurling himself to the floor trapped them all in a paralysed silence for a moment, while the television droned on in the background. Then from the body, there began a low gurgling noise, which grew rapidly in strength.

'Tim!' Ella screamed and dropped to her knees beside him. She reached out for him and then stopped, horrified at what she saw. His face was contorted and twitching, his cheeks flecked with spittle, his top lip drawn back baring his teeth like the snarl of an animal. His eyes were wide open but glazed and unseeing.

'It's alright, he's having an epileptic fit,' said the small, cool voice of Millie above her. 'I know what to do.'

Ella watched helpless as the little girl knelt down by her father and began loosening his tie. How could she touch him like that? Ella turned her face away and caught sight of Greg and Belinda, both white-faced and staring at Tim. 'Go into the kitchen you two and wait for us there,' she managed. They went immediately without argument, for which Ella could not blame them.

Shaking from head to foot she stood up and turned off the television. 'What shall I do,' she asked Millie, helplessly.

The child looked up at her: there was no mistaking the look of triumph in her eyes.

'There's nothing to do. We just have to wait until the fit stops.'

At last it was over. Ella sat numb and hunched in a corner of the sofa, watching stupified as Millie wiped her father's face clean every few minutes as foam gathered at the corners of his mouth. The violent twitching began to ease and then it stopped altogether. His head lolled sideways, exposing a large bruise on his temple. The man was returning, the foaming, grimacing animal had gone, it was Tim lying there once more. He was ill and hurt but Ella could not move towards him. She cleared her throat and tried to speak. Her voice sounded strange even to her. 'I'd better fetch a doctor, Millie.'

'There's no need,' said Millie, 'he'll sleep now for several hours and when he wakes up he won't remember anything that's happened. He'll realize he's had a fit, of course, when he finds he's on the floor, but he never remembers this bit, and he'll be quite well.'

'What . . . what about the bruise on his head, he may have knocked himself out?'

'I don't think so,' said Millie, completely self assured. 'This was one of his more violent fits and I don't think he'd have been able to throw himself about if he was unconscious. Once he knocked himself out in the stable – he hit his head on the corner of a beam as he fell. The fit didn't happen at all that time, he just lay there, twitching a bit.'

'Does it, does it happen often?' Ella managed.

'No, at least, he hadn't had a fit in ages until a few months ago, but just recently he's had quite a lot. It was the television that started him off. It was silly of him to watch it but I suppose he didn't want you and Greg to think there was anything wrong with him.'

'He should have told me,' Ella said more to herself than to the child.

'I think he wants to marry you,' said Millie, her cold little voice very self-important. 'He probably thought you wouldn't want to marry him if you knew he was an epileptic.'

Millie's words galvanized Ella into activity. She and the child put more wood on the fire and Millie put some cushions under Tim's head. To her mounting horror, Ella found she still couldn't touch him. When Millie went in search of blankets, Ella found she had to leave the room, too. She could not stay alone with Tim's inert body. She found Greg and Belinda, sitting huddled together in front of the kitchen range.

'It's alright,' she said, 'Tim's going to be fine.'

'What was it, Mom, what happened? Belinda said he does this sometimes, she says it frightens her. I'm not surprised, it frightened me. He's not going to die, is he?'

At Greg's words Belinda burst into sobs. Ella scooped the child into her arms and sat down beside Greg.

'No, of course he's not going to die. He has epilepsy, you

must have heard of that, Greg? It's when people have fits, something goes wrong with their brain just for a moment. He's sleeping now. Millie's just fetching a blanket for him and she says he will be awake in a little while quite OK. In a few minutes I'll give you all a glass of wine to help the shock you've had and then, we'll have some supper in here and let Daddy sleep.' She hugged Belinda tight to her. 'And by the time you wake up in the morning, he'll be completely his old self.'

Supper was a subdued affair and no one was hungry. Greg and Belinda seemed anxious to go to bed but Millie hovered. 'I'll stay with him if you like,' she said, 'I'm not really tired.'

'No, it's OK,' said Ella, 'you go off to bed.' She hesitated. 'Millie, I thought you were great the way you coped with him. It put me to shame, I'm afraid. I'm sorry I didn't behave better but I've never – well, I've never come across anything like it.'

If she'd hoped for some understanding from the little girl, she was disappointed.

'He won't have any more fits tonight, if that's what you're worried about.'

'No, it wasn't,' Ella lied. 'I just wanted you to know that I think you did wonderfully well.'

'It's no problem,' said Millie, 'it's just a part of our lives.' With that she turned away and began climbing the stairs towards bed.

Ella wanted to go after her, to kiss her goodnight, to comfort her, but the barrier between them seemed insurmountable. This child-woman, bearing now a much greater responsibility than Ella had first realized, was clearly demonstrating the importance of the role she played in her father's life. Wearily, nervous, Ella went into the sitting room and closed the door.

Tim was sleeping deeply. Ella sat down on the sofa, on the furthest corner away from him, tucking her legs up in an effort to make herself warm and comfortable, but there was no comfort in the room. She stared at Tim. This was the face that had lain on her pillow last night. This was the face she loved, she told herself. She tried to identify her emotions. Fear was certainly one – and revulsion, she realized. Tim's epilepsy seemed to have changed her whole view of him, standing between them now as an insuperable barrier. There were questions, too. Why had he not told her of his condition? Why had he allowed her to witness the fit without any preparation? How could he have talked of the future when this fundamental fact remained a secret? Suddenly it seemed to her that they were strangers. What did they really know of one another? Precious little, it seemed. How long had he imagined he could have kept his condition from her? Her thoughts, quite unexpectedly, turned to Aaron. Sometimes she felt she was betraying her love for Aaron by loving Tim. It was ridiculous, Aaron was happily married and would remain so. Yet now the thought returned unbidden: perhaps this was the punishment for her betrayal, perhaps the problem lay in trying to deny her destiny – to love Aaron hopelessly from afar. Her tired mind tried to rationalize, to understand her feelings but gradually her eyelids drooped and she slept.

Tim realized what had happened within seconds of waking. The cold hardness of the floor had stiffened his joints. He sat up, rubbing the sleep from his eyes and looked around him. Ella was asleep, propped up on the sofa. He watched her in silence for a moment wondering, with mounting apprehension, what she had seen. Instincts told him it had been a bad fit. Why the hell had he watched television? It was a stupid thing to do. Yet as always, between fits, he was able to convince himself that he was cured. He simply could not accept his condition and really made little effort to try. He stood up stiffly and crept to the bathroom. When he returned to the room, washed and changed, he felt more confident. He sat down carefully on the sofa beside Ella and gently shook her awake.

As she stretched and came out of sleep, Ella turned her face towards him. Her eyes flicked open and seeing his face above hers, she smiled, the happy, sensual smile of a woman in love. Then, suddenly, memory flooded back and she literally recoiled from him, her face a mask of fear. There was no trace of love or friendship, just hurt and hostility. The change in her was so horrific that it left Tim in no doubt that whatever he said or did, this moment marked the end of their relationship.

CHAPTER SIXTEEN

The seeds which were to change Tim Irvine's life were sown on a cold, crisp night in December 1961, when he was seventeen years old. At home for the holidays from Marlborough where he was at school in his final year, he was presented with an early Christmas present in the form of a motor cycle. The gift was unexpected and absolutely perfect – a Yamaha 250 in silver, with a blue trim. While the gift brought him happiness it had caused a considerable amount of strife in the Irvine household, normally so tranquil. Charles Irvine had been given a motor cycle on his seventeenth birthday and had never forgotten the sense of freedom it afforded him. Christine Irvine took the view that her husband had been at far more risk on his motor cycle as a teenager than he had ever been as a mine-sweeper commander during the war, and was appalled when he decided that their only son should be subjected to a similar hazard.

'He's a damn fine young man,' Charles insisted, 'with a good sense of self-preservation. You can be sure he won't put himself at risk, nor others, by behaving foolishly.'

'Oh Mummy, how can you be so mean, you know it's exactly what Tim would like,' Tim's doting and younger sister, Jenny, insisted.

Christine Irvine gave in under the pressure but her forebodings remained and were proved to be not without foundation on the night of December 21st. Tim had spent the evening at a pub in Cirencester with a group of local friends.

Because he was driving he drank only shandy and although somewhat exhilarated by the twin pleasures of the Christmas holidays and the avid attention of the prettiest girl in their group, he left the pub just before eleven, sober and alone. The lanes back to Monkswell Farm, where the Irvines had farmed for three generations, he knew like the back of his hand. The crisp air invigorated him. He had never felt happier – another two terms at school and then freedom, a child no longer. The recent acquisition of his bike had opened up his mind to the possibility of being responsible for his own destiny. There were so many places to see and people to meet. He was looking forward to going on to Cirencester Agricultural College the following Autumn and promised himself exotic holidays during the summer vacs.

He took the final bend before Monkswell Farm at a perfectly acceptable speed. What he did not know was that the old oak, whose boughs formed a canopy across the lane at this point, had been steadily dripping water on the lane all day, which had now turned to black ice. Tim hit the patch of ice at 30 miles an hour. Instinctively he braked, the bike slewed sideways and mounted the bank. The impact pitched Tim over the handlebars and catapulted him head first into the base of the tree with some force. It was all over in a split second. He felt no sense of fear, there was no time.

At shortly after 1 am, Charles Irvine finally gave in to his wife's increasingly worried pleading and telephoned the Cirencester Police. There was no trace of their son, the police reported, slightly less than an hour later. He was probably staying with friends, they suggested. It was a rough night; the lad had clearly made a sensible decision not to risk the roads.

Embarrassed and annoyed, Charles Irvine telephoned the three or four families Tim might have stayed with, waking them to no purpose for he was not there. Finally, putting a heavy overcoat over his pyjamas, he got in his car and drove the familiar route from the farm to Cirencester and back. There was no sign of Tim or his motor cycle, though he frightened himself on the return journey when he nearly lost control of the car on the final bend before the farm. Frustrated, exhausted and secretly worried, he insisted that he and Christine should go to bed as the boy was bound to ring in the morning. They finally slept, while six hundred yards away their unconscious son lay exposed to the freezing night air, in a pool of blood.

Jimmie Holmes, the postman, was angry. Since the baby had arrived, his wife seemed quite incapable of making him an early breakfast in the morning, which he much needed. While she slept on, he made himself a pot of tea and cut two thick slices of bread which he spread with butter and marmalade. He was running late this morning and his frustration and anger mounted when he found that snow had fallen during the night and he had to dig his van out of his own driveway. The result was he was nearly an hour late by the time he got on his round and then he had to take it more slowly than usual because of the treacherous conditions. It was after nine by the time he took the lane to Monkswell Farm and he was far too busy fighting to stay on the road to look either right or left when he made the final turn into the driveway.

At eleven-fifty Trevor Baines negotiated the narrow lane to Monkswell Farm, cursing the weather conditions. There was no let-up in his job: the milk had to be collected, regardless of how icy the roads. As he made the final turn before straightening out into the driveway of Monkswell Farm, he thought he saw something in the ditch from his high advantage point in the tanker cab. He tried to stop but when he applied the brakes nothing happened and he had to accelerate swiftly to avoid losing control altogether. At the farm he was rewarded with a hot cup of tea while the milk was being loaded.

'A bit of a fuss up at the house,' Nevil, the dairyman informed him. 'Young Tim Irvine has gone missing – on his new motor cycle, too.'

Trevor laughed. 'I expect he found himself a girl last night.'

'That's what I told the boss,' said Nevil. 'He thinks so, too, but Mrs Irvine, she'll have none of it.'

Milk loaded, Trevor began the journey back to the depot. At the bend, he again glanced in the direction of the ditch and this time could see, without doubt, the wheel of what looked like a motor cycle. His tired mind began to race. The missing boy, the motor cycle. Cautiously he applied the brakes and in a few yards managed to pull up the tanker. Cursing the cold and the snow, he ran back up the lane and climbed the bank. It was a bike alright, and there beside it, partially covered by snow, was a body. Frightened now, his heart pounding, he turned the body over on its back. It was the boy without a doubt, but to Trevor there seemed little doubt that he had arrived too late.

Trevor Baines was mercifully wrong. Tim was suffering from concussion and severe hypothermia. In the ambulance, on the way to hospital in Swindon, his heart stopped twice. The consultant later informed his parents that another twenty minutes of exposure would have been twenty minutes too long to have saved him. As it was, Tim remained in a coma on a life support machine for five terrible days, while Christine, Charles and Jenny took it in turns to sit by his bed, making futile conversation to his inert body. On the fifth day, when they had all but given up, he opened his eyes, saw his sister and said, 'Hi, Jen, you look ghastly. What's up?'

The road to recovery was a slow one. The blow to the head had indented Tim's skull. In a very difficult, five-hour operation, the skull had to be lifted clear of the brain. The days of coma had left him weak, but he was young and strong and he healed fast. By half way through the Easter term he was ready to go back to school, and more than happy to do so but for the slight embarrassment of his closely cropped hair, where his head had been shaved for the operation. To be self-conscious about something so trivial was an emotion he would look back on with contempt.

The rest of the term progressed without incident. When term ended he went to stay for a few days with John McKenzie with whom he shared a study at school. John lived in London and staying with him involved one long social riot – dances, parties, balls. On the second night in London, after a particularly heavy evening which had begun with a pub session at five-thirty pm and finished with breakfast at five-thirty am, Tim went to bed and woke several hours later to find himself on the floor. Cold and embarrassed, he climbed back into bed and thought no more about it, assuming that his fairly drunken state had been responsible. When the same thing happened two weeks later, at home, it was again after a heavy night and again he was able to dismiss it. However, on the third occasion, it was the beginning of the summer term, and it was John, coming to wake him up for an early morning game of tennis who found him. 'What the bloody hell are you up to, Irvine,' he said, shaking him awake.

Tim stared around him and sat up feeling cold and stiff. He shook his head, 'I don't know, I must have fallen out of bed.'

'You can't have done,' said John, 'it would have woken you up.'

'Well, I don't know, do I?' said Tim, irritably, 'I must have been sleep-walking or something. What bloody time is it, anyway?'

'OK, OK,' said John, 'don't get angry. Do you still want to play tennis or not?'

Tim felt oddly light-headed and tired. 'I-I'll leave it, if you wouldn't mind, this morning.' John gave him an odd look but said nothing.

The demob atmosphere at the end of term was intensified by the fact that it was their final term at school. There were secret excursions to the pub and a round of parties officially organized by the school. With 'A' levels out of the way, everyone was concentrating on having a good time. Three nights before the end of term a dance had been arranged with a local girls' school. Tim and John were less than enthusiastic, maintaining that the girls were all squares, and the whole affair was thwart with embarrassment. Nonetheless they went along and were rewarded, if by nothing else, with an extremely good disco.

Tim was dancing with an exceptionally plain girl, with pale, thin, mousy hair and a mouth full of vicious-looking braces. The music, though, was great, the disco lights flashed and in three days' time his school days would be over. He threw himself into the dancing, but as he danced he found himself more and more attracted to the flashing lights. Soon he found he was staring fixedly at them and he realized, dimly, that he had stopped dancing.

'Tim, are you alright?' The girl was shaking his arm, he could feel her touch but he could not respond to it.

He tried to speak but no words came out. He tried to step away from her but his movements were jerky and uncontrolled. Moments later, he seemed to be hurling himself to the floor. When he came round, he was being supported by two people, who were half-carrying him, half-dragging him through an open door into the school sanitorium. He tried to speak but he still seemed unable to do so. He felt oddly detached and when seconds later he was laid on the bed, he felt no sense of curiosity as people came and went. He must have slept for the next thing he knew was his mother and father leaning over the bed, and they lived a good hour's drive away from the school.

'What's happening?' he asked.

'You had a . . . a little accident,' said Christine.

'Accident! I didn't, I was dancing and something happened.'

'You sort of fainted,' his father said. 'Don't worry, old son, you're going to be alright. Tomorrow morning we'll get you into hospital so they can have a look at you.'

A consultant spelt it out to the shocked family the following day. 'It seems you had an epileptic seizure, Tim. I don't know if it will happen again, and I'm not absolutely certain why it happened but I suspect it's connected with your motorcycle accident. These days it's possible to control fits very well with the right medication, but first you need to have an ECG and a head X-ray so we can see what's going on in there.'

The tests were done the following day, as a result of which the consultant confirmed the diagnosis and suggested that treatment should start straight away. He advised a course of anti-convulsant drugs.

The next few months for Tim were a nightmare. The drugs made him feel lazy and lethargic, something which was totally out of character with his normal temperament. Not only that, they did not seem to be doing any good. The second fit took place in the pub, on a Sunday morning, surrounded by all his friends. When he came round his parents took him home. He could remember nothing but he could tell by the reaction of his friends that however he'd behaved, it had both embarrassed and shocked them.

The third fit happened just a week later, at a summer charity ball. This time the embarrassment he caused was actually palpable. John McKenzie was staying for the weekend. On the following morning, as they tramped across the fields for a walk before lunch, Tim asked the inevitable question.

'What happens to me, John, what do I do?'

'Oh nothing much, you roll around a bit, grunt and so on. Don't worry about it.'

They stopped at a stile.

'How long have we known each other, John?' Tim asked.

'From prep school onwards, nine, ten years, I suppose, yes ten years. Why?'

'Then you would consider us good friends?'

'What is this, Tim? Of course we are, best of friends.'

'Then I think you owe it to me to tell me exactly what happens to me when I have one of these fits. I have to know, you must see that. I'd do the same for you.'

So John told him, with no details spared. The foaming at the mouth, the grotesque movements of his facial muscles, the frightening way he threw himself about and the gurgling noise he made in his throat. From that day, Tim Irvine became a recluse. At his request, Cirencester Agricultural College was postponed for a year. At the time it seemed sensible for his fits were bad, happening four or five times a month. Experimenting with the anti-convulsant drugs gradually improved his condition, and he began to learn his limitations. He discovered that alcohol, at least in heavy doses, tended to worsen the problem which was why his early fits had happened in such public places. Flashing lights and television also provoked them. Above all, the number one enemy was fatigue. If he went without sleep and became even slightly over-tired, then he was asking for trouble.

His family were marvellous, treating his fits as just a normal part of life, as were the men on the family farm with whom he worked. All had been counselled on what to do and advised to minimise the importance of what had happened. Only Jenny, at sixteen, seemed to find it difficult to cope. Having, under great pressure, attended a dinner party his parents were giving one night and then had a fit over coffee he was aware, as he came round, of his sister's embarrassment and he vowed he would not put her through such an exhibition again. One of the things he learnt about epileptics was that, in his view, the family suffered most.

As the year came to an end, Tim's future became the subject of heated family debate. Both his parents were adamant that he should still go to Cirencester.

'Why do I need to?' said Tim. 'One day, you've said I will inherit the farm and I can learn everything I need to know about farming these acres right here.'

'Farming's changed,' his father insisted, 'the techniques I employ are very different from my father's and hugely different from my grandfather's. Yours, too, will be different – besides which, if you are to spend your life here you need some time away first, with people of your own age.'

'I'm rather a liability to people of my own age, I think you will agree with that,' said Tim.

'And that's another thing, Darling,' said Christine, 'you've simply got to come to terms with your – your illness. It's no good hiding away. People who really care about you, the friends that matter, won't mind about it.'

'Of course they mind, I'm a grotesque, grunting, spitting creature.' He stormed out of the room and slammed the door.

In the end, Charles Irvine took what he knew was an appalling gamble. He called his son to his study one morning and announced there would not be further work for Tim on the farm for the next three years, nor would there be a roof over his head unless he went to agricultural college as planned. If he failed to do so, not only would he have to go into the world and make his own living, but his family would all be deeply ashamed of his cowardice.

Tim went to college. He lived out in digs with a landlady who understood and felt she could cope with the problem. He worked hard and made a few friends, but essentially he kept himself to himself. Girls he found particularly difficult, for while he felt able to explain to his menfriends the nature of his condition, he always side-stepped the issue when it came to women, convinced that it would put them off him instantly. As a result he was always too afraid to make a date with a girl, just in case he might have a seizure without her being forewarned.

The three years at Cirencester passed quickly enough, despite the restrictions on his social life. His seizures had been reduced to two or three a year and while this meant he still could not drive, in all other respects he led a normal life.

Having coped with the obvious difficulties of college life, Charles Irvine was happy to welcome his son into the farm as a partner, having failed to persuade him to take a job elsewhere first. 'I can't drive farm machinery and I can't be relied upon. Who would want me?' said Tim. 'There are more people than jobs, anyway. Why take on a farm manager with epilepsy when there are plenty of able-bodied people to choose from?'

His defeatist attitude to his condition upset his parents but there was little they could do about it. The condition, the consultant was absolutely certain, had been caused by Tim's motor cycle accident. It was not hereditary, so there was no reason why he should not marry and have children, and as drugs became better, doctors were reasonably confident that his condition would improve rather than deteriorate. Yet Tim was changed irrevocably: the outgoing, happy-go-lucky young man had gone for ever. Instead, he was a serious-minded, hesitant, shy individual, old beyond his years.

Towards the end of the summer of 1966, the Irvines held a big party at Monkswell Farm, to celebrate Jenny's 21st birthday. It was a sumptuous affair with a marquee on the lawn. Invitations were issued to 250 guests and it was the one social event that Tim recognized he could not avoid. He went on a regime of early nights and decided not to risk even a drop of alcohol during the evening, so determined was he not to make a fool of himself and spoil Jenny's night. Since he also had to keep away from the disco and his parents had employed catering staff to serve all the food and drink, there was little for him to do, and while he wished Jenny well, he longed for the party to be over.

It was shortly after midnight, when Jenny's health had been drunk, speeches made and the cake cut, that Tim was accosted by an exceptionally pretty fair-haired girl. She wore a long, pale blue dress, exposing her shoulders which were slightly suntanned. The dress was the colour of her eyes. 'Hello, Tim. How are you?'

'Fine, thank you.' He looked at her and frowned, struggling to remember who she was and wondering how on earth he could forget a girl who instantly attracted him so much.

She laughed at his obvious discomfort. 'Stephanie Bonham. You haven't seen me since I was about eleven, probably less, ten maybe. We used to ride together, do you remember?'

He did. Lady Stephanie Bonham, daughter of the Marquis of Burford. They had taken riding lessons for a while and attended the same pony club. She had been pretty and vivacious then and that early promise had been more than fulfilled. His mind struggled. The Marquis of Burford, hadn't he? . . . yes, he'd been killed in a hunting accident last season.

'I–I'm sorry about your father,' he said, somewhat lamely. 'It must have been awful for you. I should have written, I'm sorry.'

'Of course you shouldn't have written,' said Stephanie, 'we barely know each other and yes, it was awful.' Her eyes clouded over for a moment. 'There's only me left, you see.'

'Of course,' said Tim, suddenly remembering, 'your mother died when you were young.'

'Eleven,' said Stephanie.

'Have you no brothers and sisters?'

'I had a brother but he's dead, too.'

'Poor you,' said Tim. 'I'm very sorry, I had no idea.'

Stephanie smiled. 'Well, we all have a cross to bear, don't we, you should know that. I'm really sorry about your epilepsy, Tim, I heard about it quite recently. It must be a frightful bore for you.'

Two things struck Tim instantly. Firstly, Stephanie was the only person who had ever been the first to raise the question of his epilepsy. Secondly, she spoke about it entirely unselfconsciously, and the glorious understatement of describing it as a bore had Tim laughing out loud.

'What have I said?' she said, smiling back, 'did I say something wrong?'

'No, no, you didn't, quite the contrary, no one ever talks about it, you see.'

'Don't they?' said Stephanie, 'How extraordinary! Hey, shall we go and dance?'

'I'd rather not, if you wouldn't mind,' said Tim. 'I'm really sorry but the lights . . . they sometimes give me a fit.'

'OK, I don't mind. Why don't we go for a walk instead, it's a lovely night.'

They spent the rest of the evening together and learnt a great deal about one another. From Stephanie, Tim learnt that following her father's death there had been a tremendous fight over the will, between herself and her stepmother. The result was that Stephanie had been left with the bulk of the estate of Wickham but no money nor means to run it.

'So I'll just have to sell it,' she said. 'It seems awful – the family home and all that. There have been Bonhams at Wickham, you know, for nearly four hundred years. That's pretty much a record, even for Gloucestershire.'

Stephanie learnt a great deal about Tim, too – not so much from what he said as from what he didn't say. She sensed the loneliness and isolation caused by his condition and the feeling of self-revulsion. It was after four by the time they realized the party was all but over.

'I can't even offer to run you home,' said Tim, characteristically frustrated.

'It's OK,' said Stephanie, 'I've got my car anyway. Hey look, I know this is rather a cheek, but I suppose you wouldn't like to hand out some free advice?'

Tim would have handed Stephanie the world by this time, if it had been his to give. 'Of course, what sort of advice?' he asked.

'I was thinking, you must have learned a lot at Cirencester, and then, of course, growing up here on your father's farm. You wouldn't come over to Wickham and give me some advice, would you? Daddy never employed a farm manager, you see, he did it all himself, so apart from a couple of old labourers, no one knows anything about the land. I really would appreciate it.'

'Of course,' said Tim. 'When shall I come?,

'Tomorrow?'

'Yes, alright . . .' he hesitated.

'Oh, don't worry about transport, I'll come and fetch you.'

'I'm sorry,' he said, helplessly.

'It's no problem, we're only quarter of an hour down the road.' She glanced at her watch, 'Well, it's this morning really. What shall we say – eleven o'clock?'

They spent the whole of the following day touring Wickham, which consisted of a beautiful old house, one thousand acres and a village. By evening they were both tired and while Tim sat in the garden with a beer and a set of plans, Stephanie cooked some supper.

'I'm sorry you've no choice over the menu but spaghetti is all I can manage. I had to sack the cook, I couldn't afford to pay her any more.'

'This is an awful responsibility for you,' Tim said. 'Isn't there anybody who can advise you?'

'My father's solicitor,' said Stephanie, 'but he's such an old fuddy-duddy. In any case he lives and works in London and so he's no idea about the country. He just thinks I should put the whole thing on the market and not worry my pretty little head about it. Direct quote,' she said, with a grin. She was dressed in an old T-shirt and jeans, her fair hair lose around her shoulders and not a scrap of make-up. Tim found her even more enchanting than the previous evening.

'I do have an idea,' said Tim, 'the land immediately around the house is by far the best quality. I think you should sell off this piece here and here,' he indicated on plan, 'about four hundred and fifty acres in all of the poorer quality land. I think you might find one or two local landowners interested. Then there are these acres here around this farmhouse. It might well be worthwhile renovating the farmhouse and selling it as a complete farm: one hundred and fifty acres should be enough to make it viable and that still leaves you with four hundred, which bearing in mind the quality of the land could be worked up to be very profitable indeed.'

'I was thinking along the same lines,' said Stephanie, 'but not in such detail. Some of the cottages would convert beautifully. The trouble is, I have no money with which to improve them.'

'One step at a time,' said Tim. 'If we start by selling off this land and some of the cottages as they stand, we can use the money we receive to renovate the farmhouse. Then we can sell the farm and use that money to start on the remaining cottages. If, meanwhile, the home farm is properly managed, then . . .' His voice was full of enthusiasm.

'You said we,' said Stephanie.

'Sorry,' said Tim, 'I'm sorry, it was a slip of the tongue – you, I mean, of course.'

'About the land that's left, you really think it could be turned into a profitable working farm. I think my father had been losing money for years.'

'Absolutely,' said Tim, 'It's wonderful land, the best.'

'And could you do it?'

'Anyone could do it, with a little experience.'

'If I paid you the proper rate for the job, I mean no messing about, no favours, could you help me get this place sorted out, Tim? I can't tell you how much it means to me.

The thought of selling up completely, giving up the house, I just can't bear it.'

'I'll certainly help,' said Tim, 'but there's no need for wages.'

'If you won't enter into a proper commercial relationship, then we won't do it at all,' said Stephanie. There was a stubborn set to her chin and it was clear she meant what she said.

'Alright,' said Tim, 'but you must only pay what you can afford. It would be wonderful to be involved in a project like this, you can hardly call it work.'

'What about your father,' said Stephanie, 'won't he mind? I think you'd need to be full time here for a year or so at any rate.'

Tim shook his head. 'He's been plaguing the life out of me to do something else before taking over Monkswell.'

'So, do we have a deal?'

Tim looked at Stephanie, 'We have a deal,' he said.

Tim's parents were not as delighted as he had imagined. Although the Bonhams were arguably the leading family in a social sense in Gloucestershire, they had a reputation for fast living and there had been a long catalogue of drunkenness and divorce in the family.

'You'll have to live on the job, I suppose,' said Christine.

'Yes, I will,' said Tim, 'Stephanie's fixing me up a wing of the house for me.'

'Is any one else living there besides her?'

'No, not really,' said Tim.

'Well, then, I don't see how you can live in the same house as her,' Christine protested. 'It's not right – think of the gossip.'

'Look, Mother, young people of both sexes live together in flats in London all the time and no one thinks anything is wrong with that.'

'That's different,' said Christine, 'this is on our doorstep.'

Despite the criticism and inuendo, Tim moved into Wickham a week later and surprisingly quickly the condemnation of the young people ceased when it became clear that their intentions were to work hard and make a success of the estate. Their plans went well, although money was very tight, and the gradual success of their enterprise fuelled their ambition. The village pub became a hotel and they obtained planning permission to convert the barns, as well as the farmhouses and cottages. The Cotswolds were becoming a very desirable area in which to live and as Stephanie and Tim worked, they found themselves building a new community, which was both lucrative and satisfying.

The close working relationship with Stephanie and the rewarding nature of his work had a miraculous affect on Tim. Not only did he grow in confidence but his fits ceased altogether. He was building something, something good and useful and his feeling of self-worth was restored. After eleven months' work, on the advice of Stephanie's solicitor, they formed a limited company called Wickham Estates Limited, into which they paid all their proceeds and from which they each drew a salary. Stephanie was the major shareholder but she gifted Tim a small stake and they were both directors. It gave Tim the feeling of being in partnership, which was not lost on Stephanie who encouraged his increasing confidence.

One November evening, when they had been together for over a year, they had returned home late from London, where they had been choosing tiles and bathroom fittings for the stable block which they were converting into four houses. They were both very tired. Tim went out to check the stock while Stephanie made some sandwiches. She piled a tray with fruit and a bottle of wine and heard Tim shuffling around in the study, lighting the fire. She entered the room, tray in hand, just in time to see him stagger back and fall to the ground in what was his first fit for nearly two years. She sat with him while the fit ran its course, put a pillow under his head and cleaned him while he slept. When he woke, she was sitting beside him, holding his hand. 'W-what happened . . . ?' he began. 'Oh my God, I had a fit, didn't I?'

'It's my fault,' said Stephanie, 'I'm so sorry, you've been doing too much recently, you need to take things more slowly.' Tim pulled himself into a sitting position and studied her face carefully. There was no obvious signs of revulsion although he searched for them, certain they must be there. 'Go and have a bath,' she said, gently, 'and then tuck yourself up in bed. I'll bring you a drink in a little while.'

They rarely entered each other's parts of the house. When they were together they used communal rooms, the kitchen, dining room and study. Now they were less tight for money, their rooms were cleaned by a woman from the village, who also coped with their washing and ironing, so that they had established a degree of domesticity. Tim's bedroom was cosy, much cosier than her own, Stephanie realized, as she knocked and entered, carrying a cup of coffee and freshly made sandwiches. He had a desk by the window looking out over the fields he had come to love. He had built bookshelves on two of the walls and a couple of comfortable chairs were pulled up to the fireplace, where a fire burned merrily in a little Victorian grate.

'You self-indulgent old thing,' said Stephanie. 'I didn't know you lit the fire in your bedroom.'

'I don't always,' said Tim, with a grin, 'only when I have company.' He was sitting up in bed. His hair, freshly washed, was brushed back which made him look very young. His pyjama top was casually buttoned and Stephanie could not help but notice his strong, deep chest. Slightly confused, she laid down the tray by his bedside table and retreated to the fire.

'I'm really sorry about what happened,' Tim said, after a moment.

'Sorry about what?' said Stephanie, genuinely bewildered.

'About . . . my seizure,' said Tim.

'Tim, you never have to worry about having an epileptic fit in front of me,' said Stephanie.

'But it's horrible,' said Tim. 'I know what happens, I know how ghastly it is.'

Stephanie came and sat on the side of the bed and took Tim's hand in hers. 'Tim, I've seen cancer slowly eat away my mother and I've watched my father drink himself to death. I was here when they brought my father's body in off the hunting field. He was at the front of the field when he fell and half a dozen horses trampled him before they got him out.' Tim winced. 'I'm no stranger to the unpleasant aspects of life. I'm tough, Tim, and I can honestly look you in the eye and say that, without a shred of doubt, your epilepsy worries me not even slightly. It doesn't disgust me or frighten me. It's simply one aspect of you, something one accepts about you like the fact that you never take off your muddy boots when you come into the kitchen. Do you understand what I am saying?'

Tim stared at her. 'You really mean it, don't you?'

'Of course I mean it. You know me, I never say anything I don't mean.'

'Do you know,' said Tim, hoarsely, 'that is the nicest thing that anybody has ever said to me.'

Moments later, they were in each other's arms and from there it seemed quite natural that Stephanie should end up in his bed. When next morning Tim asked her to marry him, she did not hesitate before saying yes.

CHAPTER SEVENTEEN

NEW YORK
March 1978

It was warm for March, the long, cold winter was at last over and New York seemed determined to show its new season's face. The sky was blue and the sun really warming for the first time. Ella had just finished a breakfast meeting with her architect, Ross Campbell, at his studio – a crazy apartment, on the top of an old brownstone on 71st and Park. Ross had worked more or less full-time for her for some years now. He was a young, imaginative architect and surprisingly commercial, his designs being not only stylish but practical, a rare combination. Ella recognizing his potential, had put him on the payroll to ensure no one else got him.

She decided to walk home. With the smell of spring in the air, for the first time in what seemed like for ever, she felt a slight raising of spirits from the black despair that had gripped her ever since she had left France, and Tim. She had failed him, she knew it, failed him in the worst of all possible ways, by rejecting him – not for anything he had done but for what he was. A thousand times she had asked herself why she had reacted so violently, and when she had not been asking herself the question, Greg had. With the resilience of youth, he could not understand why Tim's fit should have shocked and horrified her so much. The sad, strained parting of the two families which, child though he was, Greg had recognized was for ever, seemed to have hurt him as much as it had hurt her. He adored Tim. In many ways he represented the father Greg had never had, and Ella was only too aware that in rejecting Tim she was causing deep distress not only to him but also to her son as well. She had tried again and again to analyse her feelings. She knew much of her anguish was related to the shock of suddenly being confronted with one of Tim's fits. She tried to pass the blame on to him – if only he had told her from the beginning of their relationship, then she could have coped. There were times though when she was not entirely sure that this was true. She recognized that much of the revulsion was a physical rather than an emotional reaction. The intimacy of her love-making with Tim was without restraint. She had given herself to him completely in a way that she would never have believed herself capable of doing. To then find there was a part of him she knew nothing about made her feel in some way betrayed. She could no longer see him as the same person he had been before the seizure.

What had made the situation so particularly terrible was that Ella did not have to explain to Tim any of these feelings. He had understood them all, without words. He kept saying she must not blame herself for he understood, and that he would feel the same in her position. It was heartbreaking. If he had been angry it would have been easier. She could have retaliated by accusing him of deceiving her. As it was, she was aware only of a deep-seated sense of failure and loss. They'd had so much to offer one another and their children and now their future was in ruins and there was simply no road back.

On a corner ahead of her, Ella spied a new shopping arcade. A window full of bright, new spring clothes attracted her and on an impulse she went in. She emerged, an hour and a half later, nearly 2,000 dollars poorer, with a complete new wardrobe. It was not the end of the world losing Tim Irvine, she told herself firmly – it just felt like it.

She turned the corner into 59th Street and glanced at her watch. Five to twelve already and she had a million things to do in the office. She hurried on, laden down with parcels. A group of men staggered out on to the pavement in front of her from Helen's Bar, a seedy but popular basement haunt for most of the local drunks. Restricted by her piles of parcels, Ella tried to step round them.

'Look, you guys, the little lady's been shopping. Happy St Patrick's Day, Sweetheart. How about a kiss from those cherry red lips?'

St Patrick's Day, of course, she had forgotten. The streets would be full of drunks later in the day, but Helen's Bar never closed — this bunch had probably been celebrating since last night.

'Will you let me through?' she demanded.

'After the kiss, Lady, after the kiss.'

They were all round her and suddenly the familiar sense of panic rose and overtook her. Any group of men, threatening or otherwise, had her reeling back in time to that August night when she was fifteen years old.

'Let me through, let me through.' Her voice was shrill with desperation.

'Oh come on, Lady, it's St Patrick's Day. You wouldn't leave a poor Irish boy without a kiss, now would you?' The spokesman among the group lunged at her, but despite the parcels she managed to side-step him. Then, in her agitation, she tripped and half her parcels went scattering across the pavement. 'Will you look at that now, throwing her shopping around.'

Ella was almost in tears.

'Leave me alone, leave me alone.' She bent down to try to scrabble together the carrier bags.

'We'll help you, won't we, Lads?'

'No, no, leave me,' she shouted at the top of her voice, tears now starting to cascade down her face. The feeling of claustrophobia, of panic was stifling she could barely breath. A conversation began above her, Ella heard the words, but they had no meaning. She was plunged into her own personal world of terror.

'You heard the lady, boys, beat it.'

'Who says so?'

'I say so.'

'You and who else?'

'Just do it, will you? Can't you see you've upset her. Come on now, here, have a drink on me.'

'Hey, thank you, you're a gentleman, Sir. Happy St Patrick's Day.'

'And to you, boys.'

Strong hands helped her to her feet. She hurriedly wiped her eyes, before looking up and confronting one of the most handsome men she had ever seen in her life. He was tall, broad-shouldered with a spectacular suntan, extraordinary jet black hair and bright blue eyes. He looked about forty but he could have been younger or older, it was difficult to tell. He gave a roguish grin.

'Michael Gresham, at your service. Here, let me pick up your parcels for you. They didn't touch you, did they, not harm you in any way?'

'No,' said Ella, 'I feel so stupid.'

'You're not being stupid at all, you must have felt very threatened.'

'I was attacked once, when I was fifteen, by a group of men, and it has left me extra nervous, I guess.' Why on earth had she said that? She never referred to the incident, never – she'd had to put it out of her mind for Greg's sake.

Michael Gresham had collected Ella's parcels together. 'Look,' he said, 'on St Patrick's Day the streets are full of guys like those. Please let me escort you to where you're going.'

'Oh no, it's not far,' Ella protested, 'you can almost see my office from here, on the corner of Lexington.'

'Nevertheless,' said Michael Gresham, 'I'll feel happier if I see you safely there. You're not going to send me away, are you?'

'No,' said Ella, smiling.

In the short walk to her office, Ella learnt that Michael Gresham was a lawyer, his home was in Houston and that he was in New York on business for a week.

'Actually,' said Michael, 'now I have persuaded you to trust me I have to admit to being something of a fraud.'

'Oh?' said Ella.

'I'm an Irishman myself, second generation. My father was born and brought up in County Clare. So you see, Miss Kovac, you find yourself in the dangerous position of being escorted through the streets of New York by an Irishman on St Patrick's Day – very unwise.'

They had reached Gregory Buildings by now. Ella realized she would have to go up to her flat first to unburden herself of her parcels and suddenly, on an impulse quite out of character, she heard herself say, 'I live above my office, would you like to come up to my apartment for a glass of wine, to say thank you for rescuing me?' Michael Gresham didn't need asking twice. While Ella poured the wine, Michael wandered around the sitting room. Within the confines of her apartment, she was aware of what a big man he was – tall, handsome, flamboyant, confident, not the sort of man who appealed to her normally, and certainly very different from Tim. She wondered what on earth had possessed her to invite him into her home.

'I love the apartment and you've done it over real tastefully,' he said. 'It's big, isn't it, by New York standards? It must cost you some in rent.'

'No rent,' said Ella, with a grin.

'No rent!' She watched his face. Clearly he was desperate to ask why not, presumably imagining she was a kept woman, a mistress of some rich man. Curiosity got the better of him, 'How come?' he asked, with studied casualness.

'I own the block.'

'You what!'

It was clearly the last thing he had expected to hear and Ella chuckled with amusement at his obvious surprise. 'I own the block, I'm in real estate, that's my business.

'This I can hardly believe. How come – you don't look old enough?'

'I'm older than I look,' said Ella. The wine must be making her garrulous, she was never normally so talkative. 'I was thirty, last birthday. You know it's a funny thing, most women spend their whole lives trying to look younger than they are. For me it's always been a positive disadvantage.

Bankers, lawyers like yourself, it's very difficult to persuade anyone to take me seriously when I look like a kid.' She laughed, a throaty chuckle, which Michael Gresham found very attractive.

'Jesus, this is amazing. Do you own much else in New York?'

'My whole business is based in New York,' said Ella, 'although my banker is always trying to persuade me to diversify. I currently have about twenty, twenty-five projects all up.'

'A lady tycoon, I am impressed.' It was clear that he was.

They drank their wine in silence for a moment. 'The other apartments in this block are much smaller,' Ella said, encouraged by Michael's admiration. 'When I bought the block, there were just four apartments on each floor. There are seven floors altogether. Initially, we lived in the ground floor apartment which is now the offices, while all the other apartments, except this one, were carved up into three units. It's what people wanted at the time — small, medium priced accommodation. I've got sixty apartments where there had been twenty-eight before, and I've never had any trouble letting them.'

'You said "we",' said Michael. 'Are you married, then?' He was not able to disguise the note of disappointment in his voice.

Ella shook her head. 'No, I live with my son, Greg. He's almost fifteen.'

Michael's eyes widened. 'Greg as in Gregory Buildings?'

'That's right,' said Ella, 'this was my first project, so naturally I named it after him. Do you have any kids?'

Michael grinned. 'No, nor am I married. I've managed to avoid the whole scene to date, but I guess one of these days I should settle down. Time marches on, it'll be the big four-oh for me in a couple of years.' He drained his glass. 'Hey, I mustn't hang around. I expect you have a lot to do and so do I. Why don't I take you out for dinner though later, to celebrate St Patrick's Day.'

Ella hesitated. She had not been out with a man since

leaving Tim in France; even Laurie she had refused to see socially. 'Well, I'm not sure ...' she began. Then she remembered that Greg was staying the night with a school friend. It would be another long, lonely evening she would try and fill with work while her thoughts strayed to Tim. Why not have dinner with this charming, handsome man; what harm could it do?

'Alright,' she said, suddenly, 'thank you, I'd like that.'

'Great,' said Michael, 'cocktails in the Rainbow Room and then I know this great little Italian place ... do you like Italian?'

'Love it,' said Ella.

'Good, I'll pick you up at six.'

From their vantage point in the Rainbow Room, at the top of the RCA Building, they had a wonderful view of sunset over Manhattan. They lingered over their cocktails, reluctant to leave the scene. Michael talked of his life in Houston. 'It's a great city, so fast moving. The average age is no more than thirty — it's a young town and that means there's one hell of a lot going on.'

'I've never been there,' Ella said, 'but I think I have a natural prejudice against Texas — a lot of guys walking around, looking foolish in their stetsons, shooting their mouths off about the millions they have made from their oil wells.'

'It's all those things,' said Michael, 'but so much more. I have a tiny bachelor apartment in Houston, it's near where I work, but my real home is a ranch about thirty miles outside the city and it's there I spend as much time as I can. I breed horses in a small way and aim to make as much money as quickly as I can and then retire to my ranch.'

'It sounds great as ambitions go,' said Ella.

'What's yours?' Michael asked.

Ella thought for a moment. 'You know, I don't have one?'

'That's crazy, you must have.'

Ella shook her head. 'My driving force has been to give Greg a good life. I think I've done that and now, in a few years time, he'll be all grown up and have no need of me any more. What I'll do then, I'm not sure.'

'You need dreams of your own,' said Michael, clearly appalled. 'It's great you want to do the best for your boy, but you need to want to do the best for yourself as well. What do you want out of life? A house in Cape Cod, a yacht, a private jet – what grabs you?'

'None of those things,' said Ella, 'not material things.' She hesitated, 'I had a very tough childhood with no money and no security. My sole ambition, I suppose, has been to ensure that I never have to go back to where I started. Money, for money's sake, holds very little appeal for me.' As she spoke the words, she realized how true they were.

'And power?' Michael asked.

'Power, I don't know,' Ella shrugged her shoulders. 'I enjoy the thrill of the chase, doing the deal. I like to feel I'm on top of the situation. I can't bear wasted money or wasted opportunity. Whatever I do, I like to do well, but power – hell, I certainly don't want to be first woman president. Does that make sense?'

'I guess so,' said Michael, 'but you know something, Ella, you could really take the world by storm if you wanted.'

He left the subject until they were drinking coffee at the end of their meal. The little Italian restaurant in Greenwich Village had been everything he had promised. Ella felt relaxed in a way she did not normally feel with men – at least men she did not know well.

'I've been thinking about you a lot today,' said Michael.

'I'm flattered,' Ella grinned.

'You know what you ought to do, you ought to extend your interests to Houston.'

Ella frowned. 'Oh, no, it's too far away.'

'Of course it's not, the flight's only two and a half hours. It's the ideal location for you to expand your activities.'

'Why?' Ella asked.

'Because, like I said, it's a boom town. With the rise in oil prices, more and more people are crowding into the city – young people requiring bachelor accommodation today and family accommodation tomorrow. They need shopping arcades, they need office blocks. There simply aren't enough property developers in Houston to meet the demand, which way-outstrips what's available at the moment. Honestly, Ella, I'm not kidding you.'

'Is this really true?' Ella, could not conceal her interest.

'You bet your life it is. I spend a hell of a lot of time trying to find my clients suitable accommodation and office space.'

'Well, maybe I should check it out sometime,' said Ella.

'Maybe you should,' said Michael, 'and the sooner the better.'

Over the next few days, Michael Gresham showered Ella with invitations to lunch, to dinner, to the theatre, to a concert, his excuse being that he was soon returning to Houston and wanted to see her as much as possible. He was a difficult man to resist. He had just the right balance of apparently sincere flattery, combined with an enthusiasm and joy for living which was hard to resist, and which made people, men and women, feel good in his company. Ella spent three more evenings with him, against her better judgement, during which she grew increasingly relaxed and confident in his company, loving his jokes and his happy-go-lucky ways. She missed him when he left and although he promised to come and see her next time he was in New York, Ella felt she needed to recognize that she might well never see him again. Michael Gresham was no more than a brief happy interlude.

During the week before Easter it was Greg's fifteenth birthday. In a moment of weakness, Ella had agreed to give him a stereo and by seven o'clock on his birthday morning, the apartment was deafened by his new birthday present. There were presents, too, from the Connors and from Laurie, and when the postman arrived, there was a mountain of mail, including a parcel with a clear Gloucestershire postmark. 'It's from the Irvines!' said Greg.

'That's nice,' said Ella, warily.

'At least they haven't forgotten us,' said Greg, and ignoring all his other presents, he settled down to open the one from England, while Ella sat watching him, filled with remorse. His present was four prints of English hunting scenes, showing a pheasant shoot, fishing for salmon, fox hunting in full cry and beagling. They were clearly very old and Greg was thrilled.

'These are wonderful, just wonderful. I'm so glad they haven't forgotten us, Mom. Look, there are letters.'

There was a letter from Millie and Belinda and a short note from Tim, just wishing Greg a happy birthday and sending his love to Ella. 'See, he still likes us,' Greg said, accusingly. 'I'm going to call him and thank him.'

'Not now,' said Ella, hurriedly, 'you're already late for school.'

'When I get back from school, then.'

Ella hoped that he would forget during the school day, but as soon as he returned home he went straight to the telephone.

'I'm going to call England, Mom. Do you want to speak to them?'

'No, no, it's alright,' said Ella. She tried to busy herself in the kitchen while her son spoke on the phone. There was a lot of talk and laughter and all Ella's instincts cried out to run to the phone and speak to Tim. Instead she sat down shakily at the kitchen table, clasping and unclasping her hands. She heard Greg's footsteps come across the hall. It was over then.

'Mom!' he called, 'Tim would like to speak to you.' His cheerful face appeared round the kitchen door. 'He sounds great – the girls are asleep but Tim and I had a good talk. Come on, quick.'

'I told you I didn't want to speak to him,' said Ella.

'But what could I say? He asked if you were in and when I said yes, he said he'd like to say Hi to you. I couldn't say you wouldn't talk to him. Come on, Mom, don't mess about.'

'Hello,' said Ella, tentatively.

'Hello, Ella,' said Tim, his voice warm, deep, so well remembered. 'How are you?'

'I'm fine,' said Ella, 'and you?'

'Yes, much the same.'

'And the children?'

'They're fine, too. Greg sounds very grown up, his voice has completely broken now.'

'Yes, it has,' said Ella.

There was a moment's silence. 'Would it be in order for me to say I miss you?' said Tim. There was an edge to his voice.

'I miss you, too,' said Ella.

'But you don't think we should meet again,' Tim's voice shook a little.

'No,' said Ella, 'I don't think so.' The moment she spoke she regretted the words but did not know how to retract them.

'Well you never know, perhaps our paths will cross again one day. I'd better go, your telephone bill must be getting horrendous. Give my love to Greg.' The phone went dead and Ella stood poised, the receiver still in her hand.

'What happened, did you get cut off?' said Greg.

'No.' She made an effort to sound cheerful. 'They seem fine, don't they?'

'Yes, they do,' said Greg. 'I just hope we can go and visit them this summer, I really miss them.'

'We'll have to see,' said Ella, with a sinking heart.

Her feeling of depression and unhappiness persisted during the rest of the evening. Greg took himself off to his room to watch television and Ella sat at her desk, pretending to work. It was about nine o'clock when the telephone rang. 'Ella?' she recognized the voice immediately.

'Hello, Michael. Are you back in New York?'

'No, I'm not, I'm calling from Houston. Look, I was wondering whether you and your kid would like to come and stay on my ranch over the Easter break. It would be a nice change for you both, and then I could show you round the Houston real estate scene.'

'It's very kind of you, Michael . . .' Ella began.

'It's not kind, it's what I'd really like, Ella. I don't know why I didn't think of it before. Come on, say yes.'

'I'll have to go and discuss it with Greg,' said Ella. 'I could call you back.'

'Why do you have to discuss it with Greg, he's just a kid? You decide what happens and he can go along with it.'

Ella was vaguely irritated. 'We don't have that sort of relationship,' she said, somewhat tartly. 'I'll call you back.'

Greg was not particularly enthusiastic. 'I've got plans for the Easter break,' he said.

'Like what?' said Ella.

'Oh, meeting people, you know, the usual stuff.'

'Well if it's the usual stuff,' said Ella, 'it won't do you any harm to miss it for once. Some country fresh air will do you good. It's a ranch, with horses, you'll love it.'

'Is this another one of your boyfriends?' Greg asked, with heavy irony.

'Well no, not exactly,' said Ella, a little sheepish.

'Whatever he's like, he won't be as nice as Tim,' said Greg, twisting the knife in the wound.

CHAPTER EIGHTEEN

The journey from Houston Airport to Michael's ranch passed quickly enough, mainly because Michael did not stop talking for an instant. Michael's ranch was to the north west of the city which meant from the airport, they had to drive right across town. Michael pointed out landmarks all the way — and opportunities. 'Look at that piece of scrubland there, made for a condominium and there, too. This is where I work, Post Oak, it's a real up and coming area.'

Ella simply sat back and smiled, letting his enthusiasm wash over her. She was surprised by Houston, by the vast great mirror buildings and its attractive lushness. There was an enormous amount of greenery, whereas she had expected it to be dry and arid.

Greg sat silent and morose in the back of the truck. The initial meeting between him and Michael had not been good, Michael had simply said, 'Hi, Kid,' and then ignored him completely. Greg had given Michael a single look of hostility and remained monosyllabic ever since. They'll settle down, Ella thought.

They took the 290 main freeway out of Houston and then turned onto a country road. Lush grass and trees ran for unspoilt mile after mile either side of the road, there was the odd pond and a continuous creek running beside the road. After about half an hour, Michael suddenly veered off to the left, down what was no more than a dirt track. 'Not far now,' he said, 'what do you think of the countryside?'

'I think it's wonderful,' said Ella, genuinely.

'You've seen nothing yet,' said Michael, 'I have the best piece of land in the county.'

'How big is your ranch?'

'Two thousand acres.'

'It's big,' said Ella, impressed.

'Not for these parts. One of the things Texas does have is plenty of space.'

On the road they passed the odd shack but apart from these, there was little sign of life. 'Isn't it lonely, out here?' Ella asked.

'Hell, no, I always bring a bunch of friends with me. Everyone's crazy to get out of the city at weekends; we ride, fish and hunt.'

'I can shoot,' said Greg, from the back.

'Shooting here is a specialist business, deer mainly. In any case, the season's over,' said Michael, dismissively. 'Look, here we are.'

They turned a corner, the trees either side of the track thinned out and all but disappeared. Ahead of them was a vast meadow, in the centre of which sat a strange, but enormous one storey building. 'It's not a great architectural triumph,' Michael said, laughing, 'but it's homely and it's comfortable.'

'It's very strange,' said Ella, as they drove up in front of the front door.

'It's three mobile homes bolted together, with a deck built round it, but we're properly plumbed in – hot water and electricity. One of these days, I guess I'll build a proper home here, but in the meantime this does very nicely.' It was difficult to find anything favourable to say about the building, so Ella kept quiet.

The door opened at the sound of their car and a young couple emerged. They were an attractive pair, with huge dark eyes and olive skins. 'Hi, boss,' they called.

'Hi to you. Everything OK?' Michael said.

'Yes, fine.'

'That is Jesus and Juanita.' Michael whispered as they

began unloading the back of the truck. 'They're illegal immigrants from Mexico, they live here and look after the place while I'm away. Jesus is a wow with horses and Juanita keeps the place tidy. They have a little shack at the back.'

'What happens if the authorities catch up with them?' Ella asked.

'They won't, not if they behave themselves, and they do. They're a nice couple, I don't see why they shouldn't stay with me for ever. It's only if they get fancy ideas about living in the city that they'll run into trouble and find themselves deported.'

Ella and Greg followed Michael up the steps and through the front door. As they entered the house, both of them gasped aloud. The ugly prefabricated exterior stood out in total contrast to the interior. They went straight into a huge sitting room, traditionally furnished with what looked like English antiques. There were old prints on the walls and a Persian rug on the floor. It was the height of traditional luxury and totally at odds with what either of them had expected.

'What do you think?' said Michael.

'Amazing,' said Ella, 'such a contrast.'

'Yeh, well it's not what the outside of a house looks like that counts, is it? Come, I'll show you to your rooms.'

Ella and Greg's rooms were virtually at opposite ends of the house, which Ella immediately hoped was not significant. Hers was a massive double room, with bathroom en suite, lavishly decorated with heavy slub silk drapes and a carpet with the pile so thick her feet seemed to disappear into it altogether. The overall colour scheme was cream and blue. The effect was cool and restful, but far too ostentatious for Ella's tastes.

Greg's room was a little study with a divan in it. It suited him well enough, particularly since the room included a large TV. Some of his sulkiness seemed to be disappearing; he was clearly impressed and intrigued by Michael's somewhat eccentric home.

'Come out on the deck when you're ready,' said Michael, 'and we'll have drinks and then a barbecue.'

It was a beautiful evening. The back of the house faced west and the setting sun was truly spectacular. An enormous barbecue pit glowed, and Juanita was expertly turning steaks and sausages.

'We just have wine or beer here,' said Michael. 'Wine for you?' he asked Ella.

'Yes, please.'

'And some coke for you?' he asked Greg.

'I'd rather have a beer,' Greg said, assertively.

Michael seemed surprised. 'Is that OK?' he asked Ella.

'Yes, of course, he's fifteen,' said Ella.

'I've been wondering whether I could go and see the horses,' said Greg.

'Yeh, of course,' said Michael. 'Jesus!' The Mexican appeared miraculously from the shadows. 'Can you take the boy to see the horses.' The Mexican nodded silently and beckoned to Greg.

Ella watched in silence as the two of them strode across the paddock towards the stables. Greg had done a lot of growing in the last year. He was head and shoulders taller than his mother and the little Mexican walking beside him. She was enormously proud of him, she realized with a rush of maternal satisfaction. Her thoughts were interrupted by Michael handing her a tumbler of wine.

'It's wonderful to have you here, Ella.' He bent forward and kissed her gently on the lips. 'Welcome to Texas.'

The barbecue was a gargantuan affair – venison, sausages, enormous steaks, corn, beans, potato salad and coleslaw. Greg, with a typical fifteen year old's appetite, tucked in with a vengeance. The atmosphere seemed to have lightened a little between him and Michael, particularly when he showed a very real interest in Michael's horses.

'They're cutting horses,' Michael explained.

'What on earth are they?' asked Greg.

'Cutting horses are trained to cut in amongst the cattle. I own to having one of the finest studs in the area. I have no trouble offloading my stock and it's become a real lucrative business. I bought this place as a holiday retreat but now it's entirely self-supporting, in fact it makes a good profit.' Michael grinned engagingly at Ella. 'Horses are in the blood, you see. It's impossible to be an Irishman and not appreciate horse flesh.'

When the meal was finished, Jaunita served coffee on the deck. It was now quite dark, except for a single beam of pale moonlight cutting a path across the paddock in front of them. 'It's beautiful,' said Ella.

'It is,' said Michael, reaching for her hand and squeezing it. 'Right then, Greg, I reckon it's your bedtime,' he said, firmly.

Greg looked amazed. 'It can't be, it's only ten o'clock.'

'Ten o'clock – that late? Then it's definitely your bedtime.'

'He doesn't normally go to bed this early,' Ella ventured.

'Well here in Texas, kids do as they're told. You run along, boy. I need a little time with your mother on her own.' Greg, clearly very angry, left them without a word.

'Was that necessary?' said Ella, as soon as her son was out of earshot.

'Yes, it was,' said Michael. 'Hell, Ella, the boy's had a fine day. He's here in Texas for the first time, he's seen the horses, had a good meal and he can watch TV if he's not tired. Right now, he's overstayed his welcome. You know, you should be firmer with him.'

'Exactly what experience do you have of children?' Ella asked, her anger mounting.

'You don't have to have kids of your own to know something about them,' said Michael. 'I mix with plenty of my friends' kids and I have to tell you, Ella, that boy is spoilt.'

Michael Gresham had gone too far. Like a lioness protecting her cub, Ella went into the attack. 'I resent that remark very much,' she said. 'I've had to bring him up entirely on my own. He's had to cope without a father, a normal family life, brothers or sisters and as a result we're very close. From a very early age I've had to treat him much more as an adult than a child. From as young as six or seven, he's been the man about the house, fixing the washing machine, mending fuses, that kind of stuff.'

'And has it occurred to you,' said Michael, 'that all this time he might have been holding you back? It seems to me this kid of yours could be playing the little Hitler. He resents me, I can see that and I suspect that he sees me, and probably all men, as a threat to his relationship with you.'

The arrogance of the man took Ella's breath away. For a moment her thoughts strayed to Tim. Never for one moment had Greg resented Tim – quite the reverse.

'If he resents you,' she said, 'it's because of the way you're treating him. If we're going to enjoy this weekend, Michael, it would help a great deal if you treated him as an adult rather than some little brat. I'm sorry but I simply won't take any more criticism of him.'

'OK,' said Michael, clearly already bored with the discussion, 'if that's what you want then I'll do whatever you say.' His handsome face broke into a smile. 'I want you to have a really good weekend, have fun and relax because on Monday I'm going to put you to work.'

'Doing what?'

'Looking at the possibilities of real estate in Houston. I'm deadly serious, it's the most wonderful opportunity for you, just sitting here for the taking.'

'I've thought about what you said,' said Ella, 'and really I don't think it's sensible for me to diversify to this extent.'

'Will you just keep an open mind,' said Michael, 'at any rate until Monday.'

'You're very persuasive,' Ella ventured.

Michael grinned. 'That's what I aim to be.'

Despite having had a very heavy week, Ella did not sleep well that night. For one thing she found the heat very oppressive, compared with Spring in New York, and for another, her thoughts disturbed her. She was very attracted to Michael, there was a distinct physical reaction when he touched her, but far from giving pleasure, her feelings horrified her. How could she love one man and be attracted to another? It made her feel no better than her mother had been. Perhaps that was it, perhaps she had in her the genes of a slut and at last they were showing themselves.

Until this stage in her life, men had played no significant role in Ella's list of priorities. That August night, so many years ago, had made her deeply suspicious of all men – men were dangerous, men hurt, men were cruel. Loving Aaron from a distance had been safe and her affair with Laurie Merman had been not so much a relationship between a man and a woman as Ella's way of repaying Laurie for his support, both commercially and personally. Giving her body, which was what he seemed to want, was a simple act of gratitude. The fact that he was married, and happily so, meant she had to keep her emotions in check and this she found comforting. What to some people might have seemed a rather colourless relationship, for Ella was perfect because there was no danger of her losing control of her feelings. Everything had changed that night in London, with Tim. Ella had experienced a true marriage of both mind and body, and discovering this hidden cache of treasure had been a profound shock to her emotions. Now here she was, ricocheting from the ruins of her relationship with Tim into this new and infinitely more dangerous liaison with Michael. Mercifully, he had not so much as hinted that they should sleep together that night, despite the obvious positioning of their rooms, but sometime he would make his move and what terrified Ella was the uncertainty of not knowing how she would react. She felt tense and out of sorts as she tossed and turned in the great double bed. Michael's views on Greg had disturbed her greatly, and when at last she fell into an exhausted sleep, it was with the fervent hope that the following day would see Michael and Greg more reconciled to one another.

The next day was no better. They spent most of it riding over Michael's ranch, getting a feel of the countryside. It should have been idyllic, but it wasn't. They took lunch with them and picnicked by a secluded pond, surrounded by trees, while the horses grazed contentedly. Greg was sulky and silent, quite out of character, and his morose presence clearly irritated Michael. Ella was soon exhausted, acting as the intermediary, trying to keep the peace and the conversation flowing.

When they returned to the ranch, Greg went straight to his room and Ella followed him. He came out of the shower in response to his mother's call. 'What do you want?' he asked, insolently, standing in the middle of the room, dripping, a towel draped round him.

'I want to know why the hell you're being so rude to Michael.'

'He's a jerk, Mom. He treats me like some sort of snotty-nosed kid.'

'Only because you're behaving like a snotty-nosed kid.'

'That's not fair.' Greg paled, a sure sign that his temper was mounting. 'I tried to be nice to the guy when we arrived, but he's impossible, he's so . . . so sure of himself. I can't see why you like him, Mom, and I sure hope we don't have to come back here again.'

'That depends,' said Ella, coolly. 'Look, Greg, I don't tell you who you should or should not have as friends. Why should you start criticizing my friendships.'

'My friendships don't affect you,' said Greg, practically. 'OK, so I bring friends home sometimes but you're usually working anyway. You forced this Michael on me. I'm missing a ball game this weekend and a party and you know I didn't want to come.'

There was a certain logic in his argument which Ella could not refute. 'None the less, you're here,' she said, a little lamely, 'and while you're in Michael's house, you are to be polite to him. Is that clear?'

'Yes, mother,' Greg said, pointedly. He turned his back and returned to the bathroom, slamming the door behind him.

The spontaneous warmth that she and Greg had always shared, Ella had taken for granted until this moment. Of course she was aware of the difficulties of parents and teenage children but she had always assumed it would never apply to them. They understood one another perfectly and she felt nothing could disturb that, yet here they were scrapping away with new, totally unrecognizable aggression. They had fought before, of course – they were two strong-minded people – but this was different. Shaken by their exchange, Ella returned to her room, showered and then joined Michael on the deck, where he waited for her.

'A glass of champagne?'

'Thank you, that would be lovely.'

Michael removed the bottle from the ice bucket and deftly shot the cork high into the evening sky. 'Best sound in the world, what do you say?' He filled their glasses. 'To you, Ella, and your big, brown eyes.'

Ella laughed and sipped her drink, the bubbles making her nose wrinkle She let out a sigh. 'You have a good life, don't you, Michael?'

'Not bad.'

'Tell me something about yourself, you never really talk about yourself at all. Tell me about your family.' She was not sure that expressing such a personal interest in him was the right tactic but she wanted to turn her weary thoughts away from her son.

'Nothing much to tell,' said Michael. 'My father emigrated to America as a young man – very young, only nineteen. He was one of eleven children and I guess life was pretty tough in Ireland then. He worked his passage here and headed straight for Texas. Horses were his passion and he spent his life with them. He worked on ranches for a while and then did an unforgivable thing.'

'What was that?' Ella asked.

'Married the boss's daughter. He fell in love with the sixteen-year-old daughter of the guy he was working for, on a ranch just north of Galveston. Of course she was way above his station socially, so he fixed that good and proper by getting her pregnant. The story has it that my grandfather horse-whipped my father off his land, but Daddy simply came back in the middle of the night, Ma crept out of the house and together they eloped.'

'Very romantic,' said Ella.

'Yes, I guess it was.'

'And was it a happy, successful marriage?'

'Kind of,' said Michael, 'up and down like most peoples', I

guess. They were very different. My Ma, well, she was very genteel.'

'Was?' said Ella.

'Yes, she died a couple of years back.'

'And your father, is he still alive?'

'The drink got him in the end, about ten years ago now. That was the trouble really. My mother loved the madness in him when she was young but as time passed, she grew up and he didn't.'

'And were you the result of that pregnancy?'

'No,' said Michael, 'that was my elder sister, Betsy. I have two sisters. Betsy is married to a doctor, has put on airs and lives in Washington. She pretends I don't exist, she thinks of me as a country hick.'

'Some hick,' said Ella, laughing.

'Well you know, a bit too like Daddy, I guess.' His eyes twinkled.

'And the other sister?'

'Oh she's great, she's married to a Canadian and lives in Banff in the Rocky Mountains. They run a hotel there. I visit them sometimes. They're a really nice couple, but they keep having kids – five now, or is it six?' He laughed and drained his glass.

'Don't you like children?' said Ella.

Michael hesitated, 'I don't know, really. I guess I'm not mad about other people's. I'd probably be different if I had some of my own. Then again, perhaps not. I'm a selfish bastard at heart. Are you going to tell me about Greg's father?'

The unexpected nature of the question threw her for a moment. 'No,' said Ella, 'no, I don't think so.'

'Were you married to him?' Ella shook her head. 'As I thought,' said Michael, 'I've recognized that in you.'

'Recognized what?'

'The independence – you're a free spirit, Sweetheart, like me. So many people tie themselves up in complicated relationships as a security net, so they don't die alone, I guess.'

'That's a very cynical view of love and life,' said Ella.

'Is it so cynical? How many truly happy marriages do you know?'

'Several,' said Ella.

'Really? Well maybe you're lucky with your friends, but mine ... Jesus, most of their marriages are a living hell. The moment they've got themselves into it, they're trying to find a way out of it again, and along the way they pass the time by cheating. It's not my idea of fun; give me the open road.'

'And will you mind, dying alone?' Ella asked, softly.

Michael looked at her sharply. 'What kind of dumb question is that?'

'I'm only applying your theory to yourself.'

Michael sipped his wine and then grinned. 'Maybe when I'm about seventy and a dirty old man, I'll find myself a young bride to see me out of this world in comfort.'

'If she'll have you,' said Ella.

'Oh, she'll have me.'

Again his arrogance irritated Ella but in spite of it, she found herself laughing. He was a rogue but he did not pretend to be anything else. She liked that in him – his honesty.

'What time's your flight?' Michael asked, over breakfast the following morning.

'Four-thirty,' said Ella.

'Do you have to leave that early?'

'I do, really, there's a lot of work waiting for me at home, and although Greg doesn't have school in the morning, he has all sorts of commitments connected with ball games, parties and ...'

'Girls?' Michael asked, 'Are you into girls yet, Greg?'

Greg was embarrassed, 'Not really,' he said, glancing awkwardly at his mother.

'Then it's time you got a move on, Boy. I laid my first girl at thirteen.' It was a remark calculated to humiliate, and it succeeded. Greg pushed his chair back from the table and left the room without a word.

Ella and Michael watched him in silence as he walked off

across the paddock towards the stables. 'Was that really necessary, Michael?'

'Hell, I'm sorry,' said Michael, 'only the boy really gets to me with his long, sulky silences. I was hoping for some sort of reaction from him. I'd have been happier if he'd bonked me on the nose rather than just walked away.'

'I haven't brought up my son to go around thumping people,' said Ella, tartly. 'He's a gentle, pleasant boy, but for some reason, Michael, you bring out the worst in him, and I have to say I don't think that's entirely his fault.'

'What's with you, Ella, that you need to keep defending him all the time?' said Michael. 'He's an individual in his own right, he should be carving his own place in the world, making his own impressions. He needs to learn that because something doesn't suit him, it's no good sulking about it and that in order to get on, he needs to make people like him. He's not going to get very far in life if he persists in being so . . .' he searched for words, 'so sullen.'

'He's a very charming person normally,' said Ella, hotly, 'but for some reason, he just doesn't find it easy to be charming to you. Look, Michael, I've really enjoyed this weekend and it was kind of you to ask us but it's no good you trying to turn me against my son. He and I get along just fine and if you don't like him, well . . . I guess, perhaps, it's better we don't see each other any more.'

'Why – don't you like me? I thought we were getting along real well.' Michael looked genuinely hurt, and never more attractive.

'I like you very much. What I don't like is this unpleasantness between you and Greg.'

'So you're quite happy to give up an otherwise potentially good friendship because your son is throwing some kind of wobbly?'

'It's not just my son who's causing trouble, you're doing your fair share of stirring yourself. Just look at it from my point of view for a moment. It's hardly pleasant, is it, being the jam in the sandwich between your aggression and Greg's?'

'Jesus!' Michael stood up and began pacing the deck. 'You have to be crazy, Ella, you're making yourself a slave to this boy. It's not only stupid, it's unhealthy. If you don't like me, if you don't want us to develop this thing we've started, fair enough, but I know that's not true.' His blue eyes bored into hers. 'When we touch, something happens to us both, you recognize it, so do I. It's only a spark at present but I reckon it could grow to be a forest fire given a chance. We have a lot in common, you and I, Ella. The boy has no right to stand in our way.'

'He has rights,' said Ella, 'and my first loyalty must be to him.'

'Your first loyalty should be to yourself.'

'You've never had a child to bring up. How could you know what you're talking about? When you bring another human being into the world it is your responsibility to do your very best for him.'

'You've more than done that,' said Michael, 'he's clearly got everything a boy could want. About this so-called responsibility of yours, when do you see it ending, when you're a wizened old woman to whom he pays a courtesy call four times a year?'

'That's cruel,' said Ella.

'Is it? I thought I was acting more like a friend by warning you what will happen if you're not careful. Get on with your own life, Ella, let Greg get on with his and if one of you doesn't like the way the other is developing, well that's just life.'

'I can't believe I'm hearing this . . .' Ella began.

There was a sound of footsteps on the deck. Greg had returned without either of them being aware. 'Are we going riding this morning?' he asked, innocently enough.

Ella looked at his face. It was apparently wiped clean of expression but knowing him as she did, she saw a look of triumph in his eyes and for the first time in her life she doubted her son. Was this all of his doing? Was Michael right? The thought appalled her.

*

The rest of the day was strained and it was a relief when Michael suggested that they left early for the airport, so that he could show Ella some of the new development going on around Houston.

'This really is the place for you,' he said, as they drove, 'it's all here, waiting. Condominiums are what you should concentrate on, small units for working people, one or two bed, luxurious, with plenty of facilities. These guys in the city may be hardly out of diapers, but they've got money to burn. They want swimming pools, workout rooms and spa baths. They want somewhere to park their car, someone to bring in their groceries, someone to empty their garbage and clear up after them.'

'What you're suggesting sounds more like a hotel than an apartment,' said Ella.

'That's it exactly,' said Michael, swerving dangerously with elation as he thumped the wheel. 'When these guys aren't earning bucks, they want to be having fun. They don't want any of the hassle of domestic life.'

Something stirred in Ella. Meeting the requirements for accommodating working people was how she had started out. She had followed her instincts and she had been right. She had the same feeling now. She was listening to what Michael had to say but she felt as though she knew it already, as though he was only confirming her own views. 'I thought Texans liked big, open spaces?' she said, challenging her own as much as Michael's feelings.

'There's no bigger open space than the sky,' said Michael. 'High rise condominiums preserve the Texan's love of space. You can have offices on the ground floors, then the facilities, and not even start on apartments until, say, the sixth floor. If you look at Houston from high up, it looks like jungle, it's so green.'

'So you're suggesting I build from scratch, are you?' said Ella.

'Surely.'

'I've never done that, I only convert existing property.'

'So, are there any rules which state you shouldn't start something new?' Michael challenged.

'No,' said Ella.

'OK, we're coming out into Post Oak now, this is the area I recommend. It's got everything – shops, restaurants, classy bars, but there is not enough accommodation and just look at the space around you. Acquiring a site is no problem. The city will fall over itself to give you a permit, as many permits as you want. They're as aware of the problem as anyone else.'

'And money?'

'You'll have your own sources of course, but money's no problem here in Houston. I can introduce you to any number of bankers, if that's what you want. In fact, I can give you all the contacts – the right contractors, designers, realtors to sell your condominiums when complete, business contacts to take your offices . . .'

Ella gave him a shrewd look. 'And what do you want from all this, Michael?'

They were waiting at the traffic lights. Michael turned and gave her one of his lightning smiles. 'Nothing, Sweetheart. I'll charge you a few legal fees if you'd like me to represent you down here, because that would only be fair to my partners. As for the rest, I'll be delighted to help.'

Ella was astounded. In the world in which she moved, no one did anything for nothing. 'You don't want a piece of the action?' she asked, incredulously.

'Of course not, I'm a lawyer. Real estate, it's not my scene, but I can help you a great deal to establish the right contacts.'

'I still don't see why you should want to help me like this.'

'For a clever lady you can be remarkably stupid. I'll be seeing a lot more of you, won't I? You can't start a business in Houston without visiting the place now and again. That, Honey, will be my just reward.'

They smiled at one another and the exchange that had passed between them was a warm and amused one. The moment would have been very special but for a crushing silence from the back of the car, where Greg sat silently and listened.

CHAPTER NINETEEN

NEW YORK
March 1978

Ella said nothing to Greg until they were back in the privacy of their apartment. They had eaten themselves to a standstill while they were in Texas so she prepared them an omelette and salad and then called him to the table. She watched him as he helped himself to a soda from the fridge. He had grown so much just recently. Her son: tall and broad for his age, almost a man. That was perhaps where the problem lay.

'In all the years of your life, Greg,' she said, 'through all the ups and downs, we've always been able to communicate, you and me. I want you to tell me now what's going on in your mind, what turned you this weekend from being your normal, charming self into a sulky, bad-mannered brat.'

Greg sighed, heavily. 'There's no point in talking about it, Mom. You're not prepared to listen to my point of view and so it's just a waste of time chewing the fat. Let's just drop it, shall we?'

'No, we will not drop it,' Ella thundered. 'You were extremely rude to one of my friends. It's out of character and I want to know what prompted it.'

'I told you, Mom, when we were down there. I don't like the guy and I can't see why you do. I think he's creepy and I don't understand why he wants you to start buying real estate in Houston. What's wrong with your business here in New York? We have a good life, Mom, why have you got to go and wreck it?'

'I'm not going to wreck it,' said Ella, 'and it is time I

diversified. Margot's always telling me I should and this just could be a great opportunity.'

'How do you know it's a great opportunity,' said Greg, 'just because the guy says so? Houston is a long way from New York and it'll mean you'll be away all the time.' He suddenly sounded very young and vulnerable.

'I won't be away all the time, I promise, that is even if I do follow Michael's advice, which I may well not. As you say, I can't accept one man's view of the market. There's a lot of research needed. At the moment I'm purely relying on hearsay, and that's no basis for a decision.'

'Are you going to marry him?' Greg challenged, suddenly.

'He's not the marrying sort,' said Ella, 'he's already made that quite clear.'

'Well then, are you in love with him? Are you going to sleep with him?'

'Greg, I hardly think that's any of your business.'

'Of course it's my business. I'm your son, I have a right to know who's sharing my mother's bed.'

The words were spoken with such venom that Ella gasped. 'What is this, Greg?'

'Oh forget it, forget it.' He pushed his plate across the table and stood up so abruptly that his chair fell backwards onto the floor. He did not seem to notice. 'I just don't understand you,' he said, 'if you must have some guy in your life, why couldn't you have married Tim? Then we could have all settled down like a proper family, instead of messing about with that . . .' Words failed him, he was close to tears. Red-faced, he stormed out of the kitchen, slamming the door as he went.

Ella sat in stunned silence for a moment. Clearly, her discovery that men were part of the human race had been as big a shock to Greg as to herself. Understanding this, she acknowledged for the first time that perhaps there was some truth in Michael's words. Their lives had revolved around Greg and his requirements from the moment of his birth. He was the first person Ella had ever really loved and her whole life had been dedicated to giving him everything which she considered to be of benefit to him. In addition, her entire emotional life had been centred upon him and every spare minute when she wasn't working, she was considering his wellbeing. Now, in the last few months, she had discovered new and dangerous emotions. Greg had obviously recognized the signals and felt threatened. But what to do? To give in to him would be wrong and yet . . .

The following morning she found a hasty note placed underneath a jar of peanut butter, on the kitchen dresser. 'Gone to stay with the Connors for a while,' Greg had written. 'Please leave me alone. Greg.'

Greg had always been very fond of the Connors. Aaron was his godfather and certainly Greg respected him and admired him. However, they were not very close for two reasons. Aaron with his busy practice did not have enough time for his own children, let alone Greg, and in any event, in truth they did not have a great deal in common. Aaron was a thinker, an academic, while Greg was an action man; sport was his passion.

Aaron considered the shameful lack of time he had spent with the boy now, as Greg sat across the deck from him, silent and defensive. 'So, you're telling me you've run away from home, is that it?'

'No, not exactly,' said Greg, 'she knows I'm here and she knows why. I'd just really appreciate it, Uncle Aaron if I could stay with you for a while, at any rate until the end of the Easter vacation. It's only another week.'

'And then you'll go home?'

'I guess, I don't have any place else to go.'

'Are you going to tell me why you and your mother have fallen out? In all the years I've known you, Greg, this has never happened before.'

'It's this man she's messing around with,' said Greg. His face was flushed, his eyes avoiding Aaron's. 'I know it sounds kind of dumb but I just don't like the guy. He treats me like a kid and I'm afraid Mom may marry him. I thought perhaps if I stayed away from home for a while, she'd realize . . . well, that she can't have us both.'

'She's an attractive woman and still very young. You're nearly grown and soon you'll be off leading your own life. Do you think it's reasonable to expect her to spend the rest of her life alone?,'

'No, of course not,' said Greg.

'Then what is this all about? Your Mom's no fool, she won't pick a guy who's no good. Speaking personally, I'm all for her marrying — as you know I've been trying to persuade her to do so for years. I think this is something we should welcome, Greg, and encourage.'

'You haven't met the guy,' said Greg, 'you wouldn't like him, I know. Mom's a real smart lady when it comes to business but she's really dumb about men. There was this man in England, we went to stay with him at Christmas. He's real nice and he loves Mom very much. She won't marry him just because he's an epileptic.'

'Has he asked her to marry him?' Aaron was surprised; he had heard nothing from Ella to suggest she was involved in a serious relationship.

'I don't know,' said Greg, 'but if he hadn't already I'm sure he was going to. We could have lived in England then, on his farm. He's someone you would have liked, Uncle Aaron, you really would. Anyway, she messed it up, and now she seems to have taken up with this guy from Houston . . . I don't know why she needs these relationships. She never has before.' His voice trailed off, plaintively.

So that's it, Aaron thought, he's jealous. He hesitated. 'Look, Greg, there are several things we need to get straight. One, you never have to *ask* to come and stay here — this is a home from home so far as you are concerned. Whatever your troubles, whatever your problems, you must always know that you can come to Alice and me, at any time of the day or night. We look on you as one of our own kids and you and your Ma as extended family. Have you got that hoisted in?'

'Yes,' said Greg, quietly.

'Secondly, my advice to you is to give your mother a little breathing space. She's a good woman, sensible, and she's had a hard life. She's not going to do anything to hurt either you or herself, so just don't ride her too hard.'

'Easier said than done,' said Greg, sullenly.

'OK, maybe, but as you're so anxious to prove that you're not a kid any more, I would remind you that only kids say what they think, mindlessly, without giving consideration to other people's feelings – right?'

'Right,' said Greg.

'Thirdly, I think it's about time we dropped this Uncle stuff, don't you? I can't have a boy who's as tall as me calling me Uncle Aaron. It's Aaron and Alice from now on.'

Greg smiled for the first time. 'OK, Aaron, thanks,' he mumbled.

After two days of uncertainty, Ella invited the Connors out to dinner. They met, as usual, at a little Italian restaurant mid-way between their respective homes. Ella, who had been building herself into a state of hypertension, relaxed a little in the familiar surroundings, with these two people who knew her so well. They sat, now, Aaron and Alice – oddly alike in many ways with their kind blue eyes – regarding her thoughtfully. They were her rock, the background security to her life. For her and Greg the Connors had always been there and always would be. 'Where have I gone wrong?' she asked, as soon as the waiter had poured the wine.

'I don't think you have, Sweetheart,' said Aaron, 'it's just that the boy's growing up. When William gets out of line, it's always *one* of us he's angry with, not both. If he's giving his mother a hard time then I move in and sort things out, and vice versa. Kids are meant to have two parents operating as a team. It's a disconcerting business coping with growing children. You need some emotional backup, someone to keep telling you you're doing the right thing.'

'I suppose what you're saying should be comforting,' said Ella, 'but it's not, because I can't provide Greg with a father.'

'Men are so bad at expressing themselves,' said Alice, impatiently, but none the less smiling at her husband. 'What he's trying to say, Ella, is that you mustn't feel inadequate because you're finding it difficult to communicate with Greg.

Aaron and I often have periods when we can't get through to the kids but it usually only applies to one of us, so the channels of communication are at least fifty per cent open. That's what you were trying to say, wasn't it, Honey?'

'That's what I did say,' said Aaron, without rancour.

'Has Greg talked about what's bugging him?' Ella asked, anxiously.

'A little,' said Aaron. 'I know he doesn't approve of the new man in your life and apparently he did approve of the old one. I had a word with William this evening, to see if he could update me on Greg's feelings, but all Greg has said to him is that he's not prepared to have anything to do with this new boyfriend – Michael, isn't it? Aaron grinned. 'You've been keeping a lot to yourself recently, Ella. I didn't realize you were being beseiged with rampant suitors.'

'Hardly that,' said Ella, hurriedly, 'but it's true he doesn't like Michael.'

'What he's saying, I think, is that you have to choose between him and Michael,' said Aaron.

'But that's ridiculous,' said Ella, 'I've only just met the guy. I had dinner with him a few times when he was on business in New York and then he invited Greg and me to Texas, for Easter.'

'Do you really like him, this Michael? Could it be a serious relationship for you?' Alice asked, and then added, 'Tell me to mind my own business if you don't want to discuss it.'

'I don't mind talking about it to you,' said Ella. 'I do like him, he amuses me, he's also very bright. He has this idea that I should expand my interests to Houston. The oil boom has made it an up and coming area at the moment and my bankers are always hassling me to expand.' Ella shrugged her shoulders. 'I've had so many years on my own, I don't actually need anyone. I also know I don't want to marry Michael and he's already made it clear that marriage isn't what he has in mind. As to the future of our relationship – I don't know, though we do seem to have a lot in common.'

'Greg's jealous,' said Alice, 'and it's very understandable, but he'll get over it. What does Michael think of Greg, by the way?'

'Not much,' said Ella, 'that's another problem. Greg behaved pretty badly at the weekend, although to be fair Michael did provoke him. Michael thinks I pander to him too much, spoil him, you know, because of the circumstances. I think maybe he's right.' Ella, her big brown eyes filled with pain, gazed from one to the other, desperately seeking reassurance.

'There is such a thing, Ella, as loving someone too much,' said Aaron, gently. 'Your whole life to date has been geared to Greg's welfare. Perhaps this is the moment you should search your heart and ask yourself a few straight questions. Is this Michael really the rogue Greg imagines him to be? If not, then what right has Greg to dictate the terms of your friendship? Greg can't have everything his own way, Ella, and you can't ease his passage through life for ever. Sometime, he has to take up the reins and be responsible for himself. That's what good parenting is all about, teaching your children to be independent of you.' Ella nodded dumbly. 'In the meantime, I know I'm speaking for Alice when I say that Greg can stay with us as long as he likes. If he asks us for our views then we'll tell him what we honestly feel – that he's out of line on this occasion. In the meantime, I should concentrate on learning to talk to one another again. You can agree to differ but you must communicate.'

'I'll try,' said Ella.

Four days later, Greg Kovac returned home to his mother. He was tight-lipped, monosyllabic and worst of all, horrifyingly polite. Whenever Michael Gresham rang from Texas, he simply left the room. When Michael again invited them to Texas for the weekend, Greg declined and said he would go and stay with the Connors instead. Ella tried to get through to him, to understand how he felt, but all attempts failed. They were living as polite strangers who just happened to share the same apartment. Judging by his reports, Greg was continuing to work well at school, he had plenty of friends and the Connors seemed to have taken over the role of family in his life. It was as though Ella had become suddenly superfluous to his requirements. She was unspeakably hurt but pride forbade her to show him just how miserable she felt.

In the circumstances, apparently deprived of her son's love, it was almost inevitable that her relationship with Michael Gresham should blossom.

CHAPTER TWENTY

LONDON
March 1981

The last few years had changed Stephanie Bonham, Margot noted, watching her surreptitiously, as she sketched a pattern on the pad in front of her and listened with half an ear to Stephanie's chatter. Formerly very much the typical young Englishwoman, Stephanie had become positively continental. Her long fair hair had gone and had been replaced with a smooth stylish bob which capped her head, bright and glossy. She was much thinner, too thin, Margot thought, but undeniably chic. Her clothes, so obviously Parisian, she wore with a style she had not possessed before. The influence of Alex Meyer, perhaps? Margot wondered, idly. She pulled herself out of her reverie. 'So, Stephanie, how's business?'

'Very good, in fact excellent. We seem to be going from strength to strength. The old man's very pleased.'

'And Alex, how's Alex?'

The question was loaded and Stephanie knew it. She smiled. 'He's fine, or to answer your question more fully, we're fine. People may find our relationship odd, but we don't.'

'I don't find it odd at all,' said Margot.

'Ah yes,' said Stephanie, 'but you're an exception because you're not married yourself. Alex and I have been living together now for nearly four years and most people think its time we settled down into a state of married respectability.'

'Do you miss marriage?' Margot asked.

'No, I don't,' said Stephanie, 'I honestly don't think it suited me.'

Margot shifted in her seat. 'Anyway, you didn't come here to talk about relationships. What can I do for you?'

'There's a warehouse coming up for sale on the Thames. It's a four, may be five acre site in Fulham and it's currently owned by a firm of haulage contractors. They have no intention of selling it at the moment, but a little bird tells me they are in trouble and that their major customer is not going to renew their contract next year. When this customer pulls out, the haulage firm will be forced to sell the site or go bust. I would like it and I'd like to develop it as a small scale Centre des Arts.'

'It sounds a good idea,' said Margot, 'but what's it to do with me? Surely it's Joseph Meyer you should be talking to.'

Stephanie gazed out of the window in silence for a moment. 'I was thinking of not involving Meyer in this one.'

'Why ever not?' said Margot.

'I suppose you could call it a need to establish some sort of independence,' said Stephanie. 'I'm up to my neck in Meyer, one way or another, both commercially and personally. There's nothing wrong, truly,' she said, seeing the query in Margot's eyes. 'I just feel the need to have a little insurance. Up until now I haven't had time to consider any outside interests but I have this job very well buttoned up and we're not expanding any more this year so there are no new units to worry about.'

'Are you allowed to diversify under the terms of your contract with Meyer?'

'Yes, amazingly, I am,' Stephanie grinned. 'I think in the rush to produce the contract it was something that was simply overlooked, and I certainly wasn't going to remind them.'

'How much money is involved?'

'Something up to a million pounds, to acquire the site. Development costs — well, I've got no further than a rough outline at the moment, but it should be possible inside a ten million pound note.'

'And who's going to fund all this?' said Margot.

'Well, I'd rather hoped you might,' said Stephanie.

They spent an hour going through the figures. At last Margot pushed back her chair and stood up. 'I'm sorry, Stephanie, I just can't see this one. I know your Meyer franchise is worth a great deal of money, as are your Meyer shares, but basically you just haven't enough capital. OK, so you can raise a million of your own but you should be thinking of putting two, three or even four million into the pot, in order to attract a loan from the bank. There's a high risk factor attached.'

'Oh come off it,' said Stephanie. 'Look at Centre des Arts – it is a most monumental success.'

'Yes, I agree, but how much of that is due to Meyer?'

'Precious little,' said Stephanie, 'it was my scheme. I master-minded it.'

'With unlimited money,' said Margaret. 'Centre des Arts worked so well because you weren't counting the pennies. Meyer could afford to take a long term view about their investment and were prepared to give you access to a bottomless purse. This project in Fulham you'll have to budget down to the last paperclip. You can't afford any mistakes, there is no provision for anything going wrong, and what is more important than either of those two factors, you can't afford to service a loan of this size. I like the idea, Stephanie, but what you need is a partner.'

'I can't work with partners,' said Stephanie, her pretty face sulky and angry.

'You work with Alex Meyer.'

'That's different,' said Stephanie.

'Maybe, maybe not,' said Margot, 'but either way, I'm not prepared to fund you to this extent.'

'Even with my track record?'

'Even with your track record – you'll have to find someone else if you won't involve Meyer.' There was a moment's silence between the two women. 'There is Ella, of course,' Margot said, suddenly.

'Ella! You mean Ella Kovac?' Margot nodded. Stephanie threw back her head and gave a hollow laugh. 'You have to be joking, Margot. I would never go into partnership with her.'

'Because of how she let you down in Paris?'

'That's reason enough surely and then there's the fact that she used to screw around with Tim.'

'You're joking?' said Margot, genuinely surprised.

'You mean you didn't know?' said Stephanie.

'No, of course not.'

'I assumed you did,' said Stephanie, 'in fact I even wondered whether you'd encouraged it, to make us all one big happy family.'

'Come on,' said Margot, 'I'm not that bizarre.'

'Stephanie grinned at her. 'No, I suppose not.'

'When did all this happen, Ella and Tim?'

Stephanie shrugged her shoulders, 'I don't know exactly. It started sometime around the period when the Paris deal collapsed and it drifted on after that for a year or so.' She was feigning vague disinterest, but Margot could see the hurt in her eyes.

'How do you know all this?' Margot was fascinated.

'Millie told me.' Margot looked blank. 'My eldest daughter, Millie.'

'Of course,' said Margot.

'Tim took the girls on holiday to France. They shared a house with Ella and her son. It was obvious Tim and Ella were having an affair but it all went wrong.'

'How come?' Margot asked.

'Tim had a fit – I don't know whether I've ever mentioned to you that Tim is an epileptic?' Margot shook her head. 'Anyway, apparently Ella couldn't take it. No bottle you see, Margot. I don't know why you deal with her, she's nothing but trouble.'

'She's having enormous success in Houston at the moment. I think you'd be very surprised at the change in her. She's grown up and broadened her horizons. She's no longer so obsessed with that child of hers and she has a man in her life now.'

'Who?' said Stephanie.

'A lawyer from Texas. Nice guy. I've met him a couple of times, very good-looking and oodles of Irish charm.'

225

Stephanie leaned back in her chair. 'Ella's something of a dark horse, isn't she? She is hardly the femme fatale – she looks more like a small boy most of the time than a woman – but she certainly seems to know how to pull the men. To be honest at the time, it never occured to me that Tim would get involved with someone else, he just isn't the type. His affair with Ella came as rather a blow to the ego, between you and me. As for Ella – pulling out of our partnership was bad enough without seducing my husband as well.'

'I don't think you're being very fair,' said Margot. 'You and Tim were all washed up by then – you were even involved with Alex. Anyway, think about it. She's making a lot of money currently and expanding fast, and I'd have thought this project might well be of interest to her.'

'I don't know why you're so anxious to throw us together,' said Stephanie, 'particularly after the last fiasco. I'm sorry, Margot, but honestly, if Ella Kovac was the last person on earth with cash to spare, I think I'd still rather let this deal go.'

Even Margot was forced to admit the statement left little room for compromise.

CHAPTER TWENTY-ONE

HOUSTON
April 1981

'How about iced coffee while you're waiting, Miss Kovac?' Jack Smith's pretty secretary smiled at Ella.

'You know my vices,' Ella admitted. 'I guess you've talked me into it. Will he be long?'

'He's been on the telephone for twenty minutes already.'

They smiled at each other, both aware of their fondness for James N. Smith, III, president and founder of Sunbelt Industrial Bank, Houston. Jack Smith had been a good friend to Ella over the last two years – a good friend and an enthusiastic backer, although not without a degree of initial reluctance.

'You want *what*?' he had said, his heavy frame shaking with laughter.

'Three million dollars, to build a high rise condominium, just round the corner from here.'

'Little Lady, you just have to be joking.' He had three chins which seemed to have an independent life of their own, for they did not move in unison. Ella tried not to stare at them.

'I don't joke about business,' said Ella. 'I've bought the site, I'm putting in over a million dollars of my own capital, my collateral is excellent, I can't see you have any reason not to back me.'

'If I wanted to back a property speculator, which I don't, there are plenty of Texans here about to whom I could lend a helping hand, not a little lady from New York I've never met before.'

'I've already explained to you,' said Ella, impatiently, 'I've banked for many years with Joshkers, who, I understand, own ten per cent of your bank. You may not know me personally but I have no secrets from Joshkers. They'll tell you everything you need to know about me and more.'

'Sorry, Little Lady, it's just not my scene. I run a tight little bank here and I have to protect my investors' money. Property speculators I don't need.'

'I'm not a speculator,' said Ella, 'I'm a developer. This town needs accommodation, you know that . . .' but she had been unable to convince him and had left disappointed. She had been too confident, she realized afterwards, relying too heavily on the Joshkers connection to sell her ideas; she should have taken more trouble to prepare her presentation properly.

It came as an enormous surprise, therefore, that on returning to Michael's apartment, she had been there for less than ten minutes when the phone rang. She recognized instantly Jack Smith's deep voice. 'Meet me at the Houston Yacht Club in half an hour,' he said, 'I've had a change of heart.'

It was only in recent months that Ella had learnt the truth of this U-turn. Within minutes of her leaving his office, Jack Smith had received a telephone call from Sir Nicholas Goddard, Chairman of Joshkers Bank, informing him that Joshkers would consider it a great favour if he could advance funds to a certain Ella Kovac, who had a big future. Sir Nicholas Goddard, a legendary figure in banking circles, was not someone one easily ignored. Margot had instigated the call, of course, and had rightly gauged its impact upon Jack.

'Little Lady, come along in.' Jack Smith had waddled to the door of his office which he flung open, revealing his enormous form, resplendent in an appallingly loud check suit which actually made Ella wince. 'How are you, Sweetheart, and how's that good friend of yours and mine?'

'I'm fine,' said Ella, 'and so's Michael. He has a big case on though at the moment, so I hardly see him.'

'There's no such thing as too much business, you know that. Is this a social visit or have you come to twist my arm on some new project?'

'Business, I'm afraid,' said Ella. 'How does the idea of my building a shopping mall grab you?'

'Where?'

'In Tanglewood.'

'Is there a market for it there?'

'There has to be, Jack,' said Ella, 'the neighbourhood's crying out for it.'

'I guess so. It'll be a big project, Ella. Do you think you can handle it?'

'I reckon so, I feel I'm ready for a challenge.'

She looked like she was ready for a challenge too, Jack Smith thought, watching her over the top of the pince-nez which sat incongruously on the end of his nose, totally out of character with the rest of him. There was a sparkle in her eye, her glossy curls shone, her skin had a light tan. She wore a cool, pretty summer's dress in pale apricot, which enhanced her brown eyes.

'OK, so you're going to sell some property to fund it, is that right?'

'No,' said Ella, 'I'd rather borrow the money.'

Jack eyed her in silence for a moment. 'Is that wise?'

'From your point of view there's no risk. You have my Houston properties as collateral. The net revenue I receive from them, I've calculated, will cover the interest payments on the new money I need to borrow, two and a half times over.'

'I see the logic in what you're saying, Little Lady, but don't you feel you're kind of over-stretching yourself?'

Ella shook her head. 'No, it's too soon to sell my Houston properties. The market's still rising strongly, it would be crazy to pull out now.'

'Alright,' said Jack Smith, after a pause, 'shoot me some figures.'

Two hours later, Ella let herself into Michael's apartment in Tanglewood. As always, Ella looked around fondly at the quaint little place Michael Gresham called home. He loved the village atmosphere of Tanglewood he told Ella, believing it emulated, up to a point, the life his forebears had lived. It was a little haven in a big city, where everyone knew one another, had street parties and put a lot of store by the importance of a friendly neighbourhood. When Ella had offered Michael a luxury condominium two years ago as a thank-you present, he had declined. At the time she had been hurt and surprised, now she understood – this place suited him. In the three years they had known each other, Ella had made no mark on the place; with its book lined walls, heavy leather armchairs and a constant, faint, background smell of Michael's cigars, it was entirely a bachelor's apartment. When Ella was staying in Houston for a few days and spread her clothes and makeup about, she always felt it was an intrusion and suspected Michael did, too. Despite it, though, their relationship was a good one. They made no demands on one another, yet what little time they did have to offer was surprisingly emotionally satisfying, and in bed they seemed to operate as one person. It surprised Ella, this development of the sensual side to her nature, which for so many years she had imagined had been killed off in Silver Springs.

Occasionally, Ella allowed herself to fantasize about the idea of she and Michael marrying, settling down and having children, but she could not quite see it – it was simply not practical, their lives did not allow for domesticity. They were two professional people, who loved their work above everything else, understood this and recognized it in one another. They had a good relationship and there seemed no obvious justification for changing it.

Ella knew she would be eternally grateful to Michael for the introduction to Houston. Business had boomed well beyond expectations. Everything she touched seemed to turn to gold. In the last three years she had put up five condominium blocks. Some she had sold off, others she had let, some a mixture of the two but whatever she did, the demand seemed insatiable. Now, as she had told Jack Smith, she was ready for the ultimate challenge of a shopping mall, which she saw as the show piece of her work in Houston.

Going to the drinks cabinet, Ella helped herself to a whisky and collapsed in one of Michael's big, comfortable armchairs. Whisky was a newly acquired habit for so often at parties, all the Texans seemed to drink was beer or whisky. She sipped her drink and glanced at her watch. Michael should be home any moment and there was a lot to tell him tonight. It was good having someone to talk to at the end of the day. She found she had come to rely on this aspect of their relationship now and missed it hugely when she was in New York. New York made her think of Greg, and with it came the customary stab of guilt. Greg was eighteen now, and the relationship between mother and son had never recovered from the arrival of Michael Gresham in their lives. Ella was beginning to doubt now that it ever would. Somewhere they had taken a wrong turning – the little boy with whom she had shared all her hopes and dreams was gone for ever. This tall, handsome stranger neither seemed to love her nor need her in his life.

The telephone rang abruptly, making Ella jump. It was probably Michael calling to say he'd be late. She picked it up casually, 'Hi.'

There was a moment's pause. 'Mom, is that, Mom?'

She recognized Greg's voice immediately, though his manner startled her. It was a long time since he had called her Mom – it was either Mother or Ella, these days, or more often nothing at all. 'Greg, is that you, is something wrong?'

'Yes. Oh Mom,' his voice broke.

She realized suddenly that he was crying. 'Oh my God, Greg, what's happened, are you alright, are you hurt?'

'No, no, I'm OK.'

'Well, what is it, tell me.'

'Oh Mom, it's Alice, Alice and Joan.' Joan was the Connors' younger child. 'They've ... oh Mom, they've been in a terrible accident, on the freeway. Alice ... Alice is dead and Joan's in hospital but they don't reckon she's going to make it.'

'Alice ... dead!' Ella's voice was barely above a whisper.

'Mom, are you there, did you hear me?'

Ella tried to pull herself together. 'Greg, did you say Alice was dead?'

'Yes,' said Greg, brokenly.

'And Aaron and William?'

'They weren't in the car. Alice had just picked up Joan from a ballet lesson. They were on the way back here. We were all waiting for them, to have some lunch together ...' He seemed unable to go on.

'Where's Aaron now?' Ella asked.

'He's at the hospital, with Joan. William and I are here on our own, and Mom, Mom we need you.'

His words were the trigger, tears began pouring down Ella's face. Alice, dear, good, kind Alice – dead. It was impossible. It was only later, sitting numb and shaken on the first flight she had been able to catch back to New York, that Ella had realized in a single moment of horrifying clarity that Alice Connors' death had given her back her son.

CHAPTER TWENTY-TWO

NEW YORK
April 1981

He knew it was vital to keep a grip on reality. To reject everything that had happened during this long and terrible day, even for a moment, would be very dangerous. Yet to face the truth head-on – there seemed to be no resources within him for doing so. He let his mind drift, just a little, to ask himself the question why he of all people, a practical man, could not simply get up, leave the room and go home to comfort his son. He realized, suddenly, that much of it had to do with the familiarity of the surroundings. He knew every inch of the hospital. This little room was exactly the same as so many others where he had treated patients over the years, in the extraordinary number of diverse situations which occur with the birth of a child. How many children had he delivered, he wondered? How many had he lost? How many had he saved? He had never counted; each new human being was an individual. His job was to ensure that every new baby took its first breath and then it became the responsibility of others to begin its journey through life. Yes, it was the familiarity of the room, the colour of the curtains, the lino on the floor, the bed, the bedside table, the drips, now disconnected.

Only the patient was different. This time the patient was his daughter, Joan, and the patient was dead.

Joan Connors should never really have been born. It had been Aaron and Alice's intention to have a large family. William, their son, was born less than a year after their marriage, without any form of complication. When he was two, much to their delight Alice became pregnant again. She lost the baby at seven weeks, another at nine weeks, another at six weeks. Aaron, as a gynaecologist who specialised in the treatment of miscarriages, found the enemy creeping in the back door of his own family. He sent Alice, in turn, to every one of his eminent colleagues across the length and breadth of America. No one could offer a satisfactory explanation. After the fourth miscarriage, Alice developed an infection, something on which, at last, his colleagues were unanimous — it had rendered her infertile. They coped well with the disappointment. William was an easy, sunny child. Alice resumed the medical training she had given up to marry Aaron and their joint incomes meant they could enjoy exotic holidays and many of the luxuries which just a few years before had seemed well beyond their grasp. They bought the lease on a new apartment, with a glimpse of Central Park, entertained a good deal and enjoyed their life to the full.

When William was ten, they took a holiday in the Greek Islands. They both loved sailing, William swam like a fish and so they hired a yacht for four weeks and simply cruised around. Three or four days into the holiday, Alice began to feel sick. William and Aaron teased her unmercifully about being a bad sailor — Alice's father was a retired naval officer who had brought up Alice with a very strict code of ethics when it came to the handling of boats. She was considered by friends and family to be something of an expert and to have her suddenly being seasick was a source of great mirth. When the sickness had persisted for a week, Aaron began to worry. She was eating very little, the dry Greek wine she normally loved no longer had any appeal and she was tired, lethargic and bad-tempered, despite the beauty of their surroundings.

One evening, lying at anchor in a little bay just round the corner from Aghios Nikolaos in Crete, Aaron sat up on deck after his wife and William had gone to bed, enjoying a pipe and sipping a glass of wine, pondering his wife's apparent malaise. The symptoms were classic but it was impossible. In the morning, he tentatively raised the suggestion that perhaps

Alice was pregnant. He had expected her derision. Instead she admitted that the thought had occurred to her but she was too frightened to take it seriously for fear of disappointment. Two weeks later, on their return to New York, the pregnancy test proved positive. The impossible had happened and Joan was the result.

After a miserable pregnancy for Alice, during which she was ill and constantly under threat of miscarriage, Joan had been the answer to all their prayers — pretty, happy, an outgoing little girl whom they all adored. Having come to terms with the idea, William loved his little sister and in return, she hero-worshipped him. Joan completed their family, made them whole; they could hardly believe how lucky they were to have her. Aaron stared at the little head on the pillow. Her face and the floppy fair fringe were unmarked and from where he was sitting, he could not see the great gash in the back of her skull. He had to be pleased she had died — had she lived, the brain damage would have rendered her little more than a vegetable. Her life had ended the moment the car had somersaulted — that had to be the way to look at it. Eight years old and dead, cut off when her life had barely begun. Despite the evidence lying there before him, he could not believe it.

And Alice . . . Alice he could not think of yet, nor begin to come to terms with her death. He had seen her but she had been such a mess, crushed beneath the front wheel of the jacknifed transporter, the mangled body of the woman he had been shown bore no relation to his wife. Alice was whole, Alice would be back later today. Alice would calm his fears, hold him in her arms, tell him that everything was alright. Yes, that was it. It was awful, seeing Joan lying here, but Alice would make everything OK.

He heard the door open behind him and the sound angered him. He had asked to be left alone. The intrusion suggested the onset of reality and he had to fight that now. He swung round in his chair. 'What the hell . . . ?' He saw the image of a crumpled little face beneath a riot of brown curls, eyes red-ringed from crying, arms outstretched. He knew she wasn't

Alice but equally he knew she was his salvation. He half rose and almost fell into the outstretched arms. 'Ella.' As he said her name, the dam burst and the tears began.

The four of them formed themselves naturally into a disciplined self-help group, without any planning or discussion – it simply happened. Greg and Ella fielded visitors and phone calls, well-wishers, the press, the curious and the devastated patients who looked on Aaron as a personal friend. Mother and son moved into the Connors' apartment and Ella told Jackie she would not be in the office for a fortnight. Aaron was kept mercifully busy. Women went on having babies despite his own personal tragedy; they were his patients and he could not let them down. William proved to be surprisingly domesticated. Ella put him in charge of cooking and shopping. He seemed to enjoy cooking, and Ella encouraged him, feeling that on an immediate basis it was therapeutic, and in the long run it would be an essential skill if he and Aaron were to cope alone. William could not face school, exams were over and so Ella kept both boys at home.

Within a few days of the terrible joint funeral, life took on some semblance of normality and they all had routines and responsibilities. Irene Connors had died suddenly the year before, and Doc was now so frail he could not cope with a journey to New York. With no other close relatives, the full responsibility for Aaron and William rested with Ella. She slept in Joan's room and little by little, each day, she packed the child's possessions into boxes, stowing away everything in the basement store when William and Aaron were out of the house. After a week, the room resembled nothing more than an impersonal little guest room. Of the room which Aaron and Alice had shared, Ella clearly could do nothing that would not be an intrusion. Aaron had to work that out for himself, but it seemed a long way off. Except for the moment when he had first seen Ella by his daughter's bedside, Aaron had shown no visible emotion at all. He had been kind and supportive to his son, efficient at work, but he seemed on some sort of auto-pilot. He could not, or would not, discuss Alice and Joan and while on the one hand his calm manner helped to promote a sense of normality, at the same time it worried Ella greatly. Some time the truth would have to be faced and the longer he pushed it away, the harder it would be to accept.

William cried a great deal, mostly at night in bed. To give him privacy, Greg slept on the sofa in the sitting room, and night after night Ella would creep into the boy's room and hold him in her arms until he slept. William's grief was terrible to watch, but there was something positive about it you could see and touch it and therefore deal with it. He and Greg took to going for long walks in Central Park.

'He talks and talks about it, Mom,' Greg said, one night when he and Ella were sitting alone in the kitchen. 'He says the same things again and again, but it doesn't matter, does it?'

Ella shook her head, 'No, you're doing the best possible thing in the world for him, Greg, being the audience he needs to work through his emotions. Think of it like some horrible great boil; you've helped him prick it, now he has to clean it out, and one day, in the future, the wound that's left will heal.'

'I guess,' said Greg. He shook his head, 'I still can't believe it myself.'

'Nor me,' Ella admitted. 'It's made me realize . . .' she hesitated.

'What?' Greg looked up, eagerly, giving her the courage to go on.

'It's made me realize how very silly you and I have been over the last few years. When I think it could have been you, not Joan, in that car.'

'Don't,' said Greg, 'I've thought the same.' And for the first time in over three years, Greg came spontaneously into his mother's arms and they cried quietly together, finding a comfort they thought they had lost for ever.

Greg and Ella had stayed with the Connors for four and a half weeks. Eventually, uncertain what was best, Ella suggested to Aaron, one night, that perhaps it was time to leave him and William alone.

'You've been wonderful,' said Aaron, 'but, yes it is time you got back to your own life.'

'That's not what I mean at all,' said Ella. 'Greg and I just feel you're probably ready for some privacy now – you and William.'

'I suppose you're right,' said Aaron.

He still had a vacant look and it seemed to Ella that he was barely listening to her. Yet what could she do? At some stage he had to face up to what had happened and while she was there to cope with his son and cocoon him from the practicalities of life, he was never going to come to terms with the tragedy.

'Look, we'll leave you guys alone this weekend, and see how things go. If you feel like some company again next week, then we'll come back. Would that be OK?'

'Yes, thanks,' said Aaron, distractedly.

Jackie had worked wonders in her absence. Ella's desk was virtually clear and everything in New York seemed to be running smoothly, but then she had come to expect nothing less from Jackie. Over the three years she had been establishing the Houston development, Ella had left New York almost entirely to Jackie who had taken up the challenge and made an excellent job of it.

'That's all the good news,' Jackie said, clearing away the last of the papers which had needed Ella's attention. 'The bad news is that there seems to be all sorts of crises brewing down in Houston. Someone's put in a counter-bid for the shopping mall site, which is higher than yours, and there's some trouble with one of your tenants, in the office block in Post Oak. They're behind with the rent and it looks like they're in big trouble. I've chased them in the normal way but I think you're going to have to go down there and see them personally. I'd kick them out if you can, they've been nothing but trouble since they took the lease. It's Rogers International, the computer people.'

Ella smiled, enjoying the advice which Jackie now had the confidence to hand out. They had come a long way in the last few years, she and Jackie.

'I think I might travel down to Houston over the weekend,' said Ella, 'it's kind of hard on Greg since we've only just got home but it can't be helped.' She hesitated. 'Has Michael called?' she asked with studied casualness. Jackie shook her head. 'Oh, it doesn't matter, I'll see him when I'm down there.'

Ella, in fact had not heard from Michael for over a week. He had called regularly immediately after Alice's death, but the calls had become less frequent, and though Ella had tried to contact him, he seemed never to be at home in the evening. The situation did not worry her, Ella told herself. After all, their relationship was a relaxed one. Nonetheless, it was a niggle at the back of her mind during the rest of the day.

'Honey, I've got to go down to Houston over the weekend, do you mind?' Ella asked, as she and Greg sat over supper that evening.

'Nope,' said Greg.

'Truly?'

He shook his head. 'There's a party on Saturday night, I thought I'd try and persuade William to go.'

'Now that is a good idea,' said Ella.

'I thought so, too.' Greg smiled at her, an attractive, crooked smile which split his face in half.

How she loved him. 'You're a good friend to have, Greg Kovac, do you know that? William's a lucky guy.'

'I'd like to think I am – the Connors have been so great to me, particularly over the last year or so.'

'I know,' said Ella, quietly. 'Should we talk about the past, do you think, try and decide why it all happened?'

Greg shook his head. 'No, it happened, it's over.'

'Is it over?' said Ella. 'When I'm down in Houston I'll be staying with Michael as usual. How do you feel about that?'

'It's your life, Mom, you do what you think best.'

'Do you mean that?' said Ella. Greg nodded.

For some reason Ella tried hard not to analyse, she did not call Michael before catching her plane for Houston. He had probably gone to the ranch for the weekend, she told herself.

She would not have time to join him and it would be a shame to wreck his break by putting him under an obligation to stay in the city with her.

It was ten-thirty when she caught the cab from the airport. The apartment, on her arrival, was in complete darkness and Ella felt a stab of disappointment. It would have been good to find him there, she realized suddenly. She let herself in with her key and turned on the sitting room light. The place was a mess: discarded glasses, the remnants of a meal, an empty champagne bottle and clothes, Michael's and ... her eyes followed the trail of discarded clothing leading to the bedroom door. She did not stop to think, she simply walked to the door, threw it open and snapped on the light.

'What the ...?' Michael turned over in bed. His hair flopped attractively over his eyes. He raised himself on one elbow and hurriedly flapped the sheet over the lithe, naked body of a young black girl.

CHAPTER TWENTY-THREE

NEW YORK
April 1981

Aaron looked dreadful. He sat at the kitchen table in an old towelling robe, sipping black coffee and wincing with apparent pain as he swallowed. There were deep, dark circles under his eyes and his face played host to a well-established stubble. It was just after eleven-thirty on Saturday morning. He looked up without interest as Ella burst through the kitchen door.

'Hi,' he said, 'do you want some coffee?'

Ella said nothing and the silence eventually penetrated Aaron's mind sufficiently that he raised his eyes to look at her. She was crying – standing in the middle of his kitchen, crying her eyes out, soundlessly.

'What's up?' he asked. He realized, vaguely, he was sorry she was crying but wasn't particularly interested in why.

'The bastard,' she burst out.

'Bastard! Who, me?'

'No, of course not, Sweetheart.' She bent over him and kissed his forehead, tears splattered on to his face.

'Who, then?' he asked, slowly.

'Michael Gresham, that's who.'

Aaron struggled with the name. 'Michael from Houston?'

'Of course Michael from Houston.'

'OK, so what's he done?'

'I've just found him in bed, with a girl, a black girl.'

Her outrage brought a small smile to Aaron's face. 'Does it make it worse because she's black?'

241

'No, of course not,' said Ella, defensively. 'She was just so . . . so young.'

'And pretty?' Aaron asked.

'And very pretty,' Ella conceded.

'What did you do?'

'I stormed out, caught the next plane home and here I am.' She brushed the tears away with the back of her hand, like a child. 'Did you say something about coffee?'

'On the hob, help yourself, you'd better fill up mine, too.' He made an effort to concentrate. 'Look, I'm sorry, Ella, you must be very upset.'

Ella poured the coffee in silence and then came and sat down at the kitchen table beside Aaron. 'I should be upset, I should be devastated. We've been together now for nearly three years. But all I seem to be is mad. I'm angry as hell he cheated on me like that, but it doesn't seem to have touched me. That . . . that's why I'm crying, I guess.'

Aaron frowned, he was finding everything difficult this morning. 'I don't follow you.'

'Well it goes to show what a waste the last few years have been. Clearly I never loved him which makes our affair squalid, trivial and utterly pointless. In other words, Greg was right all along. To think I put my relationship with my son on the line for that . . . shit.'

'Still,' said Aaron, 'he introduced you to Houston, you owe him for that.'

'Yes, I suppose so. I was thinking about that on the way home. I can't just pull out of Houston, I'm too involved down there. Anyway, why should I, now the difficult part is over? I understand the city now and I have the contacts. I suppose I'll just have to find myself my own apartment.'

'That shouldn't be too difficult,' said Aaron, smiling, 'you must have several hundred you can choose from.'

Ella returned a watery smile. 'There have to be some advantages, being in real estate.'

'So,' said Aaron, 'no bones broken. Drink up your coffee like a good girl.'

Ella made to drink her coffee and then began to cry again.

'Now what?' said Aaron, wearily.

'I just feel so . . . so sordid. To think I've messed about with the guy for so long and now I find I don't give a damn that I've lost him. It's so cheap. When I compare it with you and Alice, it makes me shudder.' The words were out before she could stop them. Alice had been a taboo subject since the funeral.

There was a heavy silence. 'There isn't a me and Alice any longer, so that kind of comparison's pretty pointless, isn't it?' The despair in Aaron's voice was an agony to hear.

Ella studied him properly for the first time that morning. He did look terrible. 'But Alice lived and you made each other very happy,' she said, gently. 'No one can ever take that away from you.'

'But someone did,' said Aaron, anguished and close to tears. 'That damned silly truck driver. I keep thinking about him. He must have got up that morning, like we did, had breakfast, said goodbye to his wife and kids – he has two like we did. Supposing he'd forgotten the key to his truck and had to go back for it. Supposing the telephone had rung and he'd stayed to answer it. Supposing it had taken him ten seconds longer to shave, five seconds longer to respond to his alarm clock . . . anything, anything, and Alice and Joan would be alive.' His head sank forward onto his hands and Ella watched as, from somewhere deep inside him, great heaving sobs began, gaining in strength until they racked his whole body.

She did not touch him or speak to him. From time to time he spoke disjointed sentences. 'How can there be a God to let this happen . . . they nearly didn't go out that morning . . . Joan, she'd cut her knee in the playground the day before . . . there was a big bruise on it. She didn't want to go to ballet, you know that . . . perhaps she sensed something. Little kids are strange, they understand things adults don't sometimes. I think about that a lot, supposing deep down she knew she mustn't go to that ballet lesson . . . we talked her into it, didn't force her but said she was being a big baby, it was only a little bruise. Perhaps she knew, Ella, I can't bear that, perhaps she knew.' The sobs renewed in strength.

Ella left him and went into the sitting room. An empty whisky bottle lay by Aaron's chair — clearly that accounted for how he looked this morning. She hunted in the drinks cabinet and found a bottle of brandy, poured two hefty measures, added ice and soda and carried the drinks back to the kitchen table.

Aaron seemed a little calmer. 'Drink this,' she said.

'I can't, I'll be sick.'

'You won't.'

He tried a tentative sip. 'You're right, it's good.'

'Where's William?'

Aaron's eyes clouded as he struggled to think. 'He stayed over with Greg last night, they were going somewhere — a party.'

'Oh good,' said Ella, 'I'm glad Greg persuaded William to go, it'll do him good.'

'Yeh, I guess,' said Aaron, listlessly.

'Have you two talked yet?' Ella asked. Aaron shook his head. 'No, I can't.'

'But Aaron you have to, you're a family.'

'No, we're not,' he shouted the words aggressively.

'Yes, you are. OK, half the family you were but a family none the less.'

'No, no,' said Aaron, shaking his head, tears starting in his eyes again. 'William's nearly grown, he'll be eighteen next month. He'll be off to college to new friends, a new life. That's what I want for him, I want him to put this tragedy behind him. We'll drift apart, of course, but it doesn't matter — coming back home to see me will only re-awaken the sadness. I've nothing to offer him, Ella, nothing at all.'

'This is ridiculous,' said Ella, 'you must stop thinking like that Aaron, you must. That boy needs you, needs you desperately. He lost his mother and his sister less than a month ago and to all intents and purposes he's lost his father, too. He needs to talk, you need to talk. Between you, you need to plan a future. It's painful but life goes on. What do you think Alice would have wanted you to do?'

'Oh don't start that old line about how Alice would have

wanted me to be happy, how Alice would have wanted me to jump into bed with the first girl who showed any interest. I loved Alice, Alice was my wife and now she's gone, I'm finished. I have nothing to offer William, I have nothing to offer anyone else. I'm just a dried up husk.'

'A selfish, cruel husk who's so self-centred, he can't think of anyone else but himself,' Ella spat out the words.

'How dare you speak to me like that,' said Aaron. 'Who the hell do you think you are, anyway, to preach at me? A fine mess you've made of your life. Look at the men you've chosen to knock around with? That jumped-up street vendor, Laurie Merman, married and old enough to be your father, an epileptic English aristocrat and a . . . a bog Irishman who prefers a piece of black. Jesus, Ella, I'd keep your mouth shut if I were you.'

His words bit deep but she knew the reason for them and was glad. He was fighting her which meant he was coming alive again. She persisted. 'You can abuse me all you like, Aaron Connors, but that won't change the facts. You're enjoying playing the martyr, having everyone at the hospital swooning all over you, the nurses bringing you cups of coffee, colleagues slapping you on the back and making a fuss of you. Back home you have me waiting on you hand and foot, the boys treating you with kid gloves. You've got it made, playing the professional widower. You can keep it up for years, Aaron and why not? To hell with your son, he can sort out his own problems. What are his, anyway, compared with yours? You're clearly more important. You know what I think? I think you resent William. I think you resent that he's just starting out on life and that he has the opportunity to put this terrible tragedy behind him.'

Aaron banged down his glass onto the table and stood up. 'How dare you say that? Get out, get out of my sight. I never want to see you again.'

'If you want me out of this house you'll have to throw me out,' Ella said, quietly. She continued to sit at the kitchen table, not daring to stand up, for fear her trembling knees wouldn't carry her weight. She was taking a terrible gamble with their relationship and the thought of life without Aaron terrified her. When she spoke again, it surprised her that her voice was steady and strong.

'I'm your friend, Aaron, the most loyal friend you'll ever have. For most of the time we've known each other, it's been you looking after me, but now the roles are reversed, it's my turn to help, and you must let me. William is going to get over this tragedy, in a way that you probably never will. On the other hand, you have known what it is to have a happy marriage, to raise kids and to carve a successful career. William hasn't, not yet. If you go to pieces at this point, then he may well follow your example – drop out of college, take to drugs, bum around. If he sees from your example that suddenly all the standards by which you and Alice lived your life are no longer relevant, then he's simply going to play copy-cat. OK, so you've had some good years and if you want to mess up the rest of your life that's fair enough, but what right do you have to louse up your son's? Five weeks ago, two wonderful people died on the freeway out there. A casualty list of two out of a family is enough but the way you're behaving, you're going to make it four.'

The fight went out of Aaron. He looked at Ella helplessly like a small child, 'God help me, Ella, I know you're right but I haven't the strength.'

She went to him then, slipping her arms round his waist, resting her head on his chest for she was a foot smaller than him. They held each other in silence. Fleetingly Ella thought how good it felt in his arms and then thrust the thought away. 'You may not have the strength but I have and so has Greg. Between us we can help you and William through this, but only if you want to be helped. We can give you the strength but we can't give you the will.'

'I think the trouble is I feel kind of disloyal.'

Ella drew away a little. 'Disloyal! How do you mean?'

'I feel it's wrong to try and put the pieces together again. It's as though I'm being unfaithful to Alice by trying to build a life without her.'

'Alright,' said Ella, 'reverse the roles. You're dead, Alice is alive. What do you want her to do – hang around mourning, letting her life slip away?'

'No, of course not.'

'You can't have it both ways, Aaron. Either your relationship with Alice was strong enough, deep enough to feel secure about it or it was not nearly as good as you made out.'

'What do you mean?' Aaron asked.

Ella sighed and leaving him walked over to the window and gazed out across the park. 'As you pointed out earlier, I've never been as lucky as you – in having a really close relationship with someone. By that, I suppose I mean marriage – a true partnership, anyway. Perhaps because of that, I may have a rather romantic and idealistic view of marriage, but it seems to me that if you really love someone, you must know how they would want you to react in every situation.' Aaron nodded. 'Well, that being the case, you must know how Alice would want you to react now. If I was able to hold a conversation with her right now, surely she'd say "Ella, I want Aaron to build a new life for himself, I want him to look out for William and I want him to look forward not backwards. I want him to remember Joan and me always but he must realize the past is finished. He and William must build a future together, they must laugh and be happy and one day, perhaps, love again." You know she'd say that, Aaron, don't you?'

'Yes' Aaron's voice was barely above a whisper. He was crying again and for a long time they held each other in silence.

'OK,' said Ella, after a while, 'that's enough heart searching for one day. The new regime starts as of now. Go shave and shower and get dressed. I'm going to take you out to lunch.'

Aaron looked at her quizzically. 'When did you sleep last?'

Ella shrugged her shoulders. 'I didn't sleep last night, I was travelling, but then neither did you, much, from the look of it.' Aaron nodded. 'Look, I tell you what we'll do. We'll have a long, very alcoholic lunch, followed by an early night and tomorrow we'll take the boys out into the country for the day. What do you say?'

'You're wonderful,' Aaron smiled, tipping his head on one side. 'Will that do?'

'For now,' said Ella.

He walked towards the kitchen door and then stopped. 'You came here to talk about your problems with Michael, instead of which we've spent the whole time talking about me.'

'Michael?' said Ella, with a smile, her big brown eyes wide and innocent, 'Michael who?'

CHAPTER TWENTY-FOUR

NEW YORK
August 1981

The shrill sound of the telephone invaded Margot's consciousness. Squinting through sleep-filled eyes, she grappled with the receiver. 'Yes?'

'Your alarm call, Miss Haigh, it's six-fifteen.'

'Oh, thanks.' She replaced the receiver quietly, and resisting the temptation to lie in a little longer, she slipped quietly out of bed and padded into the bathroom. She ran a deep, hot bath. She could never understand the American devotion to the shower. Functional it might be, but a bath was so much more than simply a method of keeping oneself clean. Most of Margot's major decisions were made in the bath – she read reports, plotted and schemed – there was a solution to everything from the vantage position of a bath tub. Now, she pinned up her long, thick auburn hair, creamed her face and with a deep sigh of satisfaction, climbed into the fragrant foam.

Half an hour later, she emerged from the bathroom sparklingly clean and good-tempered. She walked over to the bed and sat down gently on the edge. 'Nicholas?' All she could see of him was a small patch of grey hair emerging from under the sheets.

'Go away.'

'Nicholas, it's nearly seven. Shall I organize us some breakfast?'

'No.' Relentlessly, she pulled away the sheets exposing the pink, good-humoured face of Sir Nicholas Goddard, Chairman of Joshkers Bank. He was a handsome man, if a little on the chubby side. It was a strong, autocratic face, though his eyes were warm and compassionate. He raised one eyelid. 'Miserable woman. What are you trying to do to me?'

'Get you out of bed.'

'You know what a torture New York is to me and if that isn't enough, you lure me out to dinner, drag me back to your room, seduce me, make me the victim of your insatiable desires, and then expect me to be bright eyed and bushy tailed at some unspeakable hour of the morning.'

'As I recall,' said Margot, 'the seducing was entirely on your part. I suggested that after our flight we could well do with an early night. It was you who insisted that while you would agree with the early night, the condition was we should spend it together, and as I also recall, the fact that our early night together didn't seem to involve much sleep wasn't entirely my fault.'

There was a chuckle. He rolled over in the bed and half sat up, displaying powerful shoulders and a deep muscular chest. Margot felt a stab of desire which she dismissed, firmly. Her first appointment was at half-past-eight and she had some work to do first. Nicholas smiled at her, reached out a hand and took hers. 'You know, My Dear, you really are a cracking girl and sometimes I just can't believe my luck. How long is it now since you first led me astray?'

'Sixteen years, more or less,' said Margot, 'and I must protest – it was me who was the victim. I was young and innocent and you should have known better.'

'Young and innocent!' He smiled at her. 'You changed my life, you know that. I had no idea . . . well,' he blushed slightly, 'you've brought me alive, shown me a side of life I knew nothing about.'

'We're not getting sentimental now, are we?'

'Yes,' said Nicholas, 'decidedly so. You know, it does worry me, sometimes . . .'

'We're not starting on the lecture which runs something like "you should marry and settle down, find yourself a decent chap" and all that, are we?' Margot said.

'Yes, yes I think that was going to be the general theme.'

'Nicholas,' said Margot, 'since I love you so much, I'm going to give you your monthly dose of reassurance. My affair with you would in no way inhibit me from falling in love with what you describe as a decent chap, getting married and having the required number of babies, if I ever came across a man who could persuade me that was what I wanted. Such a man has not presented himself and seems unlikely so to do now, and in the meantime . . .' she leant forward and kissed him gently on the lips.

He slipped his arms round her and held her to him, pushing the towel away gently running his hands up and down her smooth back. 'You know I imagine you, sometimes, in the role of my wife.'

Margot drew away abruptly and stared at him. 'Do you?' she asked, genuinely surprised.

He nodded. 'I can see what you're thinking,' he said, 'silly old fool, and I'm not very proud of myself, to tell you the truth. Margery and I are very happy really, but only thanks to you. If it wasn't for you I think I would be very dissatisfied with my lot. Still, she's been a good and loyal wife and I have her to thank for the children. It's just that sometimes I imagine how wonderful it would be to walk into a room with you on my arm, I'd be so proud. It's childish, isn't it, but every man in the room would want you and you'd be mine and they'd think, lucky old sod, and they'd be right. I shouldn't need that sort of ego boost, should I? Mind you, I don't think its as simple as that. It's not that I want to bathe in your reflected glory, exactly, I suppose I just want to show the world how happy you make me.'

It was an uncharacteristic and surprisingly emotional speech for Nicholas, and Margot was touched. She smoothed the hair back from his face and looked deep into his eyes. 'When I consider the importance of your position,' she said, 'your power, your wealth, your reputation, it takes my breath away that you can be so extraordinarily self-effacing. If I were to walk into a room on your arm, it should be me who felt proud and honoured, not you.'

They kissed. It was supposed to be a kiss to seal their words but it deepened and intensified until Nicholas threw back the bed covers and went to draw Margot down beside him. 'No, Nicholas, there won't be time, I have to get to work early.'

He nuzzled her neck, his hands on her breasts. 'It's not often I pull rank where you're concerned, but today I feel it necessary to point out that I'm the boss, and I want you here, now.'

'Oh Nicholas!' she came into his arms without hesitation. As always, he made love proficiently and considerately, but this time it was as though there was something extra, an added warmth and caring, which seemed to reflect his words of earlier.

Margot made it to Joshkers New York branch on Wall Street, at eight-thirty. She sat down at her desk, ordered coffee and eyed the pile of untouched work. It was not worth trying to tackle it before her first appointment, better simply to sit and compose herself for the day. The coffee arrived, she took a sip and then, taking her cup, went and stood by the window. A couple of minutes later she was rewarded with the sight of a limousine drawing up outside the entrance to the bank. Sir Nicholas Goddard stepped from the car. How he hated New York, she thought, fondly, as she watched him look up and down the sidewalk with obvious distaste, and then stomp through the front door. She wondered, for the umpteenth time, what the world would think if they knew of their affair. It was a strange relationship, and its depth and longevity never failed to surprise her when she had time to consider it.

The affair had begun as a straightforward tactic on her part to further her career. Marooned at an appalling banking conference in Torquay, sixteen years ago, she had allowed Nicholas Goddard to make love to her because she saw it as a possible means of promotion. He had been good to her over the years, nurtured her career and taken a guarded but none the less personal interest in her development. Still, she had no doubt she would have made it without him. So why, two or three times a month, all these years later, did they still spend the night together? The sex was good, yes, but he was not a young man and the course of their lovemaking, though satisfactory, was predictable. He was rich and powerful and Margot recognised that this aspect of him attracted her very much indeed, but there were plenty of rich and powerful men in the world. No — she set down her coffee cup and smiled to herself — it was friendship that bound them together, nothing more complicated than that. They liked one another very much indeed, they had the same sense of humour and they both had bright brains which revelled in argument and discussion.

It was this strength of friendship that had saved Nicholas's marriage. Some years ago, Margot had toyed with the idea of becoming Lady Goddard. She knew she had it within her power to break up Nicholas's marriage and it had been tempting — stateless and without a family, always lurking beneath the surface of her psyche was the feeling that she needed to belong and Nicholas could have provided her with the security she sometimes felt she desperately needed. Yet her great fondness for him had kept the relationship in check. Margery Goddard was the perfect wife for Nicholas. They came from the same background; indeed, as was often the way in the British aristocracy, they were even distantly related. They shared a beautiful home, three children, friends and a lifestyle to which they had been born and bred. The scandal of a marriage break-up would have seriously damaged Nicholas's career, and for what? Margot was not prepared to be the sort of wife he needed, who would abandon all of her interests, to be at his side whenever required. No, they were perfect as they were, it was just that sometimes . . . The door opened as she pushed the thought away; perhaps it was not just Nicholas who was getting sentimental in advancing old age.

'Ella, how nice to see you.' Margot turned from the window and the two women kissed warmly. 'Would you like some coffee?'

'Love some,' said Ella. 'Boy, is it hot out there, even at this hour. I feel frazzled.'

'I was about to say you looked a little frazzled,' said Margot.

'Thanks a bunch. A fine friend you turned out to be, and I was going to say I thought you looked rather ...' Ella searched for the word, 'sleek, contented, pleased with yourself – rather like a cat after a bowl of cream. Business must be good.'

'It is,' said Margot. 'And how are things with you?'

'Well, commercially I don't seem to be able to do anything wrong at present, which terrifies me. Personally though, I've been having something of a rough ride, hence the frazzled look to which you so unkindly refer.'

'Sorry about that,' said Margot. 'What's been happening to you?'

'One of my best friends has died, killed in an automobile accident. Greg and I have been kind of looking after her husband and son. Her little girl was killed in the accident, too.'

'That's really awful,' said Margot, 'I'm sorry.'

'Yes,' said Ella. She sipped her coffee thoughtfully. 'You know, Margot, something happening like that really puts life into perspective. They were such an ideal couple, they had everything. Aaron's a gynaecologist, Alice was a doctor, too. They have a classy apartment overlooking Central Park, two super kids, wonderful holidays – you know, the works. Then a truck driver makes a wrong decision and the dream is shattered in seconds. As it's turned out, their terrible experience sure as hell put my petty problems into perspective.'

'How do you mean?' said Margot.

'I stumbled across Michael in bed with someone else over the weekend. A classic case – I travelled down to Houston unannounced and there he was *in flagrante delicto*. God, what a naïve idiot I've been.'

'Are you very upset?' Margot asked.

'No, that's just the point. Compared with Aaron's loss, it's nothing, is it?'

'Is it going to affect your plans in Houston?'

'No, not at all.' Ella's brown eyes sparkled. She grinned at Margot defiantly. and Margot threw back her head and laughed. 'I get it, you're going to take the city by storm, just to show the bastard what he's missing.'

'Something like that,' Ella admitted. 'Hell no, Margot, business is business, I'd be crazy to pull out. I've got a few problems with the shopping mall, but none that can't be ironed out and in fact, in a crazy kind of way, splitting with Michael has made me feel more settled about Houston.'

'How come?' Margot asked.

'Well, as you know, I've always operated out of his apartment, lived in a suitcase and made use of Jack's secretary or Michael's. Now, I guess I'll take over one of my own apartments and set up a proper office down there. I'll never find another girl like Jackie but I'll get someone to run the day-to-day operation, to give me more flexibility. In other words, I'll stop living like a gypsy.'

'It sounds a great idea,' said Margot. 'You know, Ella, you've come a long way in the last two or three years.'

'Don't I know it,' said Ella, 'I hate to admit it, but you were right to make me diversify out of New York.'

'Well I never,' said Margot, 'an admission. Wonders will never cease. You're still hanging on to too many properties, though but that's a failing of yours I can see we're never going to alter.'

'Jack says the same,' said Ella.

'There you go, then, I'm not a voice in the wilderness.'

'Over that particular issue, you won't change me,' said Ella, 'the business works, right?'

'OK, OK I give in,' said Margot.

Surreptitiously she glanced at her watch, a gesture which Ella spotted. The time allotted to personal chatter was over. Margot, if nothing else, was predictable. Ella forestalled her. 'You wanted to see me – have you a new project in mind?'

'Yes, but you're going to be less than crazy about the idea when I suggest it to you.'

'So why are you suggesting it to me?'

'I don't know, a hunch.' Margot stood up and wandered over to the window to where she had watched Nicholas arrive at the bank earlier. The sidewalk had been deserted then, now it was teeming with people. 'You remember Stephanie Bonham?'

The smile left Ella's face. 'Yes, of course,' she said, coolly.

'There's a new project come up, a big one, in London. She needs a partner and I thought of you.'

'Me!' said Ella. 'You have to be joking!'

'Why?' Margot asked.

'Oh hell, come on, Margot. After the Centre des Arts fiasco, Stephanie would laugh herself stupid at the idea of involving me in any project of hers. In any event, while I'm happy to expand into Houston, I'm still operating in North America, which is a far cry from London. The reasons I didn't want to become involved in the Centre des Arts are still valid today.'

'Are they?' said Margot. 'Are you sure? It's five years ago now, Ella. Greg's grown up, he can't need you as he did, and your ideas and experience have greatly broadened, not to mention your financial standing. You have a highly successful business, Ella, you're a very rich woman and you have a unique experience of the trade. Why rest on your laurels? What you need is a new challenge.'

'I need no such thing,' said Ella, 'we've been through all this before, Margot.'

'Look, I wouldn't be trying to involve you in small fry, but this project really has enormous potential. I had a look round the site before coming to the States.'

'Hey, wait a minute,' said Ella, 'I thought Stephanie was all bound up with Meyer Hotels?'

'She is, but she wants to do something on her own. I can understand the feeling – she's a born entrepreneur. Although her relationship with Meyer is set up so that she owns the franchise and in theory operates as an independent, for most of the time it must feel like she's on the pay roll. She was offered this site and decided she would like to do something in her own right again. Apparently the contract with Meyer does not preclude her from doing her own thing.'

'What sort of project is it?' Ella asked.

'Ironically, it's another riverside site, this time on the banks of the Thames at Fulham. It's just under five acres, absolute prime land and the company which owns it, a big haulage firm, is going under in about six months time.'

'You sound very definite about that,' said Ella, with a laugh. 'How come you know?'

'I'm only working on hearsay but I did some checking.'

'Tell me more.'

'Well,' said Margot, 'it seems that the entire profitability of the firm depends on one large contract. It's this contract which keeps them afloat, the rest of their business is worthless.'

'So?' said Ella.

'According to Stephanie, their major customer is pulling out at the end of the current contract.'

'And how would Stephanie know?' Ella asked.

'Can't you guess?' said Margot.

Ella hesitated. 'The major customer's Meyer, right?'

'That's right,' said Margot.

'Shit, Margot, that's not very nice, is it?'

'I did suggest to Stephanie that perhaps it wasn't playing the white knight to bankrupt a company in order to acquire it's biggest asset. She tells me, though, that old Joseph Meyer made the decision to swap his haulage arrangements without any reference to Stephanie, based on the fact that the firm is inefficient. Stephanie only came to know about it because Joseph asked her to look for an alternative haulage company.'

'Do the firm know they're for the chop as yet?' Ella asked.

'Apparently not, or they'd stop performing.'

'Jesus, it's all a bit cut-throat, isn't it?'

'Come on, Ella,' said Margot. 'Would you like me to start quoting some of your past deals at you?'

Ella smirked. 'OK, point taken. What does Stephanie want to do with the site?'

'Shops, restaurants, offices and luxury apartments.'

'And why does she need a partner?'

'She hasn't enough money nor has she enough time to run the project alone. She doesn't agree with me but I'm not prepared to back her unless she has some help. She's the exact opposite to you, Ella – you're over-cautious but she isn't cautious enough. I think it's why I've always wanted to get you two together. Her ideas tend to be a little extreme and she needs someone to put the brakes on. On the other hand, she has a visionary flair which you lack. You two were meant for one another.'

Ella laughed. 'You make it sound like marriage.'

'Which is how most of the big business partnerships operate, isn't it?'

'I don't know,' said Ella, 'I've never had a partner.'

'What about Laurie?'

Ella's voice was flat. 'Laurie and I get along by not interfering with one another.' Her voice was casual but it was difficult for her to hide the sense of hurt she felt. Since she had stopped being Laurie Merman's mistress, the friendship that she'd assumed would always be there seemed to have vanished. They met from time-to-time, to approve accounts or deal with some matter of business which required his signature. Other than that, he did not even send her so much as a Christmas card. 'Anyway,' she said, 'you can't honestly tell me that Stephanie's mad about the idea of us joining forces, can you?'

'No,' Margot admitted, with a smile, 'she's not, but she's mad to do the development and she won't get the backing from anyone but me, I've seen to that. I've issued her an ultimatum – deal with Ella Kovac or no deal at all.'

'No,' said Ella, firmly.

'Just because the last project went wrong, there's no reason for this one to go the same way.'

'OK, may be not,' said Ella, 'but I still don't want to get involved.'

'Because you had an affair with Tim Irvine?'

Ella stared at Margot. 'How the hell did you know about that?'

'Stephanie told me.'

'Stephanie told you? You mean she knows I had an affair with her husband and yet you're still suggesting we work together?'

'Oh come on, Ella, don't be such a wimp,' said Margot. 'What right has Stephanie to resent you having an affair with her husband, when she's living with another man? I don't know why she and Tim are not divorced but it's not because they have any marriage left. She's Alex Meyer's woman and that's the end of it.'

'Still,' said Ella, 'she can't be too happy about what happened between Tim and me.'

'If that's what's worrying you, I'd forget it. Anyway give the idea some thought. I'm here in New York for another couple of weeks. Give me a call if you'd like to talk about it some more, and don't close your mind to it – alright?'

Ella got up and smiled. 'You're a bossy cow, Margot.'

'On this occasion, I'm also right. So, think on it, Ella Kovac – this could be a big opportunity for you.'

CHAPTER TWENTY-FIVE

NEW YORK
August 1981

'Are you sure you guys have everything?'

'Mom, you're fussing,' said Greg.

'You are,' William confirmed, with a grin. He was a nice-looking boy, tall, fair and slender, like his parents.

Ella regarded them both in silence for a moment. 'I'm not sure it's fair to let you two loose on the female population of Canada.'

'They'll be queuing up, Mom, you can be sure of that,' said Greg. 'Hey, is that the cab?'

William crossed to the window and looked down to the sidewalk below. 'Yep.'

'Come on then, we'd better get going.'

Aaron and Ella went down together, to the waiting cab, to see their sons off on holiday. It had been Greg's idea that the two of them should take off for part of the summer, and both Aaron and Ella agreed it was a good idea.

'Will they be alright?' Ella asked, a little tearfully, as they waved the cab out of sight.

Aaron put an arm round her shoulders. 'Come on, Honey, those boys were raised in New York City – they're streetwise, they can run rings round the average Canadian.'

'I guess so. It's just that . . .'

'Stop it,' said Aaron, 'you're clucking away like an old mother hen. They'll be fine. Now how about me buying you some lunch?'

Ella shook her head. 'I've a hell of a lot of work to do today.'

'But it's Sunday.'

'I know but I've spent the last few days getting the boys' things together and I've been neglecting my work.'

'You're very good to us, William and me,' Aaron said, 'I don't know what we'd have done without you in the last few months.'

'You'd have coped,' said Ella, gently, but she was pleased with the compliment. All during her youth Ella had fantasized about she and Aaron having some sort of future together. With Alice dead, she now recognized she was the most important person in Aaron's life, but her fantasies had died with Alice. Ella's affection for Alice had been deep and genuine; the idea of taking advantage of her tragic death was abhorrent. Nevertheless, Aaron's obvious dependence on her brought a warm glow.

Aaron grinned at her. 'Look, I'll do a deal with you, I'll let you off lunch if you'll have dinner with me.'

Ella hesitated. 'I really do have a lot of work.'

'Look, this is blackmail, I know, but today is Alice's and my wedding anniversary and I could really use the company.'

'I know,' said Ella, gently. 'I was thinking about the date this morning. 'Yes, of course I'll have dinner with you, Aaron.'

They dined in Greenwich Village, in a delightful little French restaurant. The food was excellent but neither of them was terribly hungry for it was a hot night and thoughts of the anniversary hung over them both. They drank a great deal of Chablis in an effort to keep their mood light and the conversation flowing. Inevitably, though, over coffee and brandy, the conversation drifted towards Alice.

'I'll never marry again,' said Aaron. 'Never.'

'You can't say that,' said Ella, 'you're not fifty yet. You've years and years ahead and I know you don't like living alone.'

'I don't, you're right of course, but the thought of another woman quite literally repels me. One or two of my colleagues have come on hot and strong in the last few months and I literally have to stop myself from gagging. The idea of kissing another woman, never mind sleeping with her – I guess that side of my life is finished.'

Ella was shocked. 'I can understand you not being interested in women at the moment, but don't you think you're reacting kind of strong, Aaron.'

'Maybe, maybe not, but whatever the rights and wrongs, I can't help it – it's how I feel.'

'It's early days,' said Ella, 'things will get better.'

'I don't particularly want them to get better,' said Aaron, 'I'm quite reconciled in a strange way to my funny bachelor existence. I'm sure now I was right not to move us out of the apartment – it's home for William and me, but the idea of another woman living there is appalling,' he grinned, 'your good self excepted, of course.' He called for more brandy and coffee. 'Anyway enough of me, what about you, Ella, how's your love life?'

'Non-existent,' said Ella.

'Truly?'

'Yes.'

'Any particular reason?'

'Same as yours, I suppose, I feel I can't cope with anyone in my life at the moment. My work's very fulfilling, I have Greg and after the fiasco with Michael Gresham, my natural inclination is to leave men severely alone.'

'A dreadful waste,' said Aaron, shaking his head, sagely.

'You're a fine one to talk,' said Ella, 'I bet the whole female hospital staff are panting with frustration at not being able to get their hands on you.'

The brandy arrived. 'Perhaps we should raise our glasses to celibacy,' Aaron suggested.

'Perhaps we should,' said Ella.

They drank in silence for a moment. 'Do you remember, Ella, how when we were kids we used to talk about what we would do when we grew up? I guess we'd be surprised if we could see ourselves now,' Aaron gazed thoughtfully into his brandy glass.

'Two corrections to that statement,' said Ella, brusquely. 'We never were kids together. I was the kid, you were all but grown up and we never talked of what *we* would do when we grew up, only what *you* would do.'

'Only because you never said what you wanted. All you would ever say when I asked you what you wanted to do, was that you had to get away from Silver Springs as soon as possible. I used to think it was strange, but now, of course, it makes sense. Still, you never seemed to have dreams like other little girls — being an actress, a ballet dancer or whatever.'

'I only had one dream,' said Ella, quietly, 'and that was not to follow in my Ma's footsteps.'

'Yes,' said Aaron, quietly, 'I can see that now, but then I should have understood you better.'

Ella looked at him, amazed. 'You made my life possible, bearable, Aaron. You were the one bright spot in my whole childhood and then, later, after . . . after Greg was born, your family was my rock, my salvation.'

'Perhaps,' said Aaron, 'but when I look back to those days, I don't particularly admire the way we behaved towards you.'

'What the hell do you mean?' said Ella. 'You were all wonderful.'

'We behaved rather as though we were taking in a stray dog. We fed and watered you and patched up your hurts, but did we ever really make any effort to understand you — no, we didn't. There must have been within you a great well of burning ambition to have achieved what you have in recent years, yet I never remember seeing it, even catching a glimpse of it. We shouldn't have just saved you, we should have given you back faith in yourself and courted opportunities for you. It seems to me that what we did for Ella Kovac smacks of charity, and I don't like that word.'

'I think you're being too hard on yourself, and your family. I certainly never saw it like that. Hell, you did more than most people would have done, more than anybody else did do.'

'You know,' said Aaron, with a grin, 'when you were very young, well I suppose round about the time we first met, I decided I'd marry you when you grew up.'

'Did you?' Ella stared at him with incredulity. It seemed impossible, yet at the same time miraculous, that he should have shared some of the dreams that had dominated her life for so long.

'Yes. You were a pretty little kid, even then, though too skinny of course. I used to think when we both grew up I'd marry you and take care of you but I guess I bargained without the difference in our ages.' He looked at her almost shyly. 'Did you ever think about me like that?'

Ella hesitated and then shook her head, 'No,' she answered unsteadily. There was a strangely tense silence between them. Did he know she was lying, Ella wondered. She tried to justify herself. 'You see, you moved in a completely different world to me.' Still the silence. Ella continued nervously, coming nearer to the truth. 'The only thing I do remember is being very jealous when you first brought Alice home. I was pregnant at the time and I know I behaved badly towards her, yet she was so sweet despite the fact I behaved like a brat. She talked to me a lot that first time she came to Silver Springs and by the end of the weekend I just adored her.'

'She gave us a hard time about you, you know,' Aaron said. The bill arrived and he thrust some notes down on the table.

'How do you mean?' Ella asked, grateful the subject had turned to Alice. Just for a moment she had been tempted to tell Aaron that she had loved him always, despite the other men in her life and the passage of years.

'We told her all about you, naturally,' Aaron said, 'about the rape and everything and she was horrified that we hadn't done more. She felt we should have forced a prosecution on those guys and then found more help for you.'

'What more could you have possibly done to help me?'

'A lot, I guess. Today, if a girl gets raped, there's all sorts of counselling available to her, to help her through her ordeal – particularly if she makes the kind of decision that you made, to keep the baby. In your case, once you had decided what you were going to do, I imagine no one ever spoke to you about it again.'

'That's what I wanted,' said Ella. 'You see, in a funny way, Aaron, things were easier for me after the rape – people were kinder. Before, when I went into a store or walked down the street, no one would speak to me and they'd look at me in a really mean way. It was bad enough when I was a kid but as I grew up it got worse. Everyone was expecting me to end up like my Ma, you see. They were just waiting and I sensed in them not only aggression but, in a way, almost fear, particularly from the women. Can you understand that?'

'Yes,' said Aaron, 'yes I can.'

'After the rape, they were ashamed, ashamed I suppose that there was no conviction. At first I thought everybody would think I got no more than I deserved but I suppose everyone knew by then that I didn't like boys. The older women, particularly, seemed to approve of the fact that I decided to keep the baby – they saw it as the correct thing to do. Once Greg was born, I couldn't take two paces in the street without someone stopping to tell me how lovely he was and how like me he looked. That was a laugh, he never looked like me.'

'Come on,' said Aaron, suddenly standing up, and swaying slightly. 'We're going home – we can talk some more there.'

The fresh air made them realize they were both very drunk indeed. They giggled their way into a cab and out the other end, holding each other unsteadily. In the elevator, they pressed the wrong button and ended up on the wrong floor, which for some reason seemed hilarious. Once inside Aaron's apartment, they stood and surveyed each other.

'Do I look as bad as I feel?' Ella asked.

'A little dishevelled, but very sweet. Now, we have a decision to make: we could be sensible and have some coffee or we could tackle the particularly nice bottle of hock I happen to have in the fridge. Somehow it doesn't feel like a night for being sober – shall I crack open the wine and to hell with it?'

'Definitely,' said Ella.

They sat on the sofa by the window, in silence for a while, sipping their wine and watching the night sky.

'Now Greg's a man, or almost,' said Aaron, 'do you know which of those guys was his father?'

'Yes,' said Ella. She had been certain for some time but until that moment she had not admitted it, even to herself.

'Are you going to tell me which one?' Aaron asked.

'Am I drunk enough?' said Ella.

'I guess so.'

'It was Warren Clay.'

'Are you sure?'

'Quite sure. I thought so even when Greg was a little boy, but now he's grown, he has that height and breadth of shoulders which Warren had, and although he has my eyes, the rest of his face, his nose, that squarish jaw: I'm sure of it.'

'You must hate Warren very much,' said Aaron.

'No,' said Ella, 'it was Jim Keating I hated, the others would never have done it on their own. They were all fired up with booze, but he was the aggressive one. They were only young, younger than Greg himself now. Seeing Jim do those things to me ... well, I guess it was bound to turn them on.'

'I don't know how you can be so forgiving.'

'Oh, I'm not forgiving,' said Ella, 'I'm just grateful Greg's father isn't Jim. When he was a little boy, you know, I was always looking for signs of aggression in him, a streak of cruelty which would pinpoint him as Jim's boy. Jim was always a shit even when he was a tiny kid.'

Aaron slipped an arm round Ella and she settled comfortably against his shoulder. 'It should never have happened to you, Sweetheart, not to anyone, but especially not to you. Still, I wonder where you'd have been today, if it hadn't happened.'

'Silver Springs,' said Ella, without hesitation.

'No, not a chance,' said Aaron, 'without the restrictions of a child and the trauma of the rape itself, you'd have left us long before.'

'Greg was my driving force, my *raison d'etre*. Greg gave me the ambition and the strength. Without him, I'd have just festered away in Silver Springs.'

'You undervalue yourself,' said Aaron.

'I don't think so. Of course, I can't pretend my business is all about Greg. I love it for its own sake, but in the beginning I did it for him.'

'And where do you see yourself going – richer still, more properties?'

'I don't think about the future,' said Ella, defensively.

'Nor me,' said Aaron, 'I just get through one day at a time.'

They sat on in the semi-darkness in companionable silence. 'I suppose I should go home,' said Ella, at last.

'No, not yet.' Aaron shifted slightly, drawing her closer to him. 'If you go, I'll start to think about Alice. This time last year, we had dinner together and took in a show. In some ways it seems like just the other day – in others, it seems for ever since I had Alice beside me.'

'Of course I'll stay for a while,' said Ella, gently. 'I'm not really tired, strangely enough, though heaven knows I should be.'

'Have some more wine.' Still keeping his arm around Ella, Aaron leant forward and refilled their glasses. As he lay back on the sofa, a shaft of moonlight streaming through the window illuminated Ella's upturned face. The short tangle of curls, the huge brown eyes, the over-generous mouth, the turned-up nose – everything about her was at once familiar and comforting, and in the moonlight she was suddenly beautiful.

Aaron stared at her in silence for a moment. Everything was the same, but different. The twist in his stomach told him, suddenly, that here was a woman he greatly desired, but it was crazy – it was just Ella, Ella was his friend, his sister. His tired, confused mind tried to conjure up the picture of the scruffy, undernourished brat she had once been but all he could see and feel, snuggled against his shoulder, was a wholly desirable woman, who he suddenly wanted with a passion he could not remember experiencing in a long time. If he had been sober it might have been different but the drink had blunted his caution. 'Ella,' he murmured and leaning forward, he kissed her on the lips.

At first the kiss held no significance for Ella. They had always been openly demonstrative with one another. Only when his hands moved to the buttons of her shirt, a sense of shock thrilled through her, but she did not attempt to draw away. Ella had drunk a great deal less than Aaron, but still enough to blur her senses, to enable her to believe that what was happening between them was normal. Only when his lips found her bare nipple did she recognize what was happening and by then it was too late. She thrilled to his touch, arching her body towards his. She knew it was Aaron, yet the man who was making violent, desperate love to her was a stranger. He was at once heartbreakingly familiar and yet also completely unknown.

When at last their passion for one another was spent, they slept on the sofa in each other's arms, their discarded clothes scattered around them. At some point during the night they woke again, and murmuring her name, Aaron fell upon her once more, taking them both to dizzy heights and so on to another exhausted slumber.

There was no time to consider the implications of what they were doing, the rights and wrongs. They were acting instinctively, fulfilling a desperate mutual need. Reason had no part to play that particular night. Ella was already in the kitchen when Aaron surfaced the following morning. He was in terrible shape but how he looked paled into insignificance compared with the turmoil in his mind. Ella had her back to him, she was making coffee. 'Are you alright?' he asked. She did not reply.

'Would you like some coffee?' she said after a moment. Her voice sounded small and strained.

'I could certainly use some,' said Aaron. He hesitated, 'Look, Ella, I'm really sorry about last night.'

She turned to face him and he was shocked by what he saw. Her face in the morning light was pale with dark circles under her eyes. The smiling, sunny girl of yesterday had gone. Had he done that to her? His mind recoiled from what had happened between them. He had behaved no better than an animal, he had betrayed Ella and he had betrayed Alice

... Alice, God she had not been in her grave five months before he had allowed himself to make love to another woman. And how he had loved – his desire for Ella had been insatiable. It sickened him to think of it. What would Alice have thought, she was always so protective of Ella.

He tried to put his thoughts into words. 'To have behaved like that, to you of all people, I just can't believe it. I feel so ashamed. You must hate me.'

'No, no of course not.' Ella could hear the desperation in her own voice but Aaron seemed oblivious to it.

He took the coffee she offered him and sat down heavily at the kitchen table. 'I guess it would be sensible if we didn't see each other for a while – at any rate while the boys are away. What do you think?'

'If that's what you want' said Ella, dully.

'Well, hell, I don't know what I want.' Aaron brushed the hair out of his eyes and brought his fist down on the table, making his mug jump and spilling the coffee. 'Oh God, Ella, what a fool. Will I ever be able to look you in the eyes again, will I, will I?'

'I hope so.'

'It's going to take some time to get back to where we were, if ever.' Ella said nothing. 'Hell, look Ella, I'm all jumbled up right now. I think it would be better if you went home. I'll call you sometime. When are the boys due back?'

'In about five weeks,' said Ella, 'in late September.'

'I'll call you when the kids come home, perhaps we'll find it easier with them around. I just can't handle this right now.'

'OK,' Ella managed.

She opened the door to her apartment and realized with astonishment that she had no idea how she had reached it. She remembered leaving Aaron's apartment but nothing in between. She fumbled with the lock, at last opening the door and then slamming it behind her with such force that it seemed to shake the whole building. She ran straight into her bedroom, slamming that door, too, and threw herself onto the bed. Only then did she give way to a storm of tears.

Her sense of isolation was complete, there was no one for her now. Laurie Merman had been a fair weather friend. When she was his mistress he was interested in her, but when she no longer offered him anything he had wanted, he had simply faded away. Tim she had let down, Tim would never forgive her. Michael? He didn't seem to count at all. Greg, who was almost grown, would be off to college in the fall. Her mother – even her mother was dead.

With sickening clarity, she realised that all the peaks and troughs of her life, all the problems with which she had had to cope, the hardships and difficulties, had been possible because somewhere in the shadows, guiding, guarding, picking her up when she fell, had been Aaron Connors. From that first day, when he had hauled her skinny, little body from a pile of fighting children, he had been there for her – until today. Today he had made all her dreams come true and today he had told her to go.

The tears poured down her face, she pounded her fists into the pillow. 'No, no,' she wept. She knew she must try to make sense of the conflict in her mind, yet her thoughts shrank from facing reality. To Ella, Aaron Connors had been a man set apart. she had begun life by hating men, men had made her mother what she was, men had raped and humiliated her. She remembered crying hot, angry tears when she was told her newborn baby was a boy – she had yearned for a daughter. That her subsequent relationships had ended in disaster was of no surprise to Ella, in fact it seemed to her almost inevitable. Men were not destined to make her happy; indeed, it never really occurred to her that they could.

Yet Aaron had been different. Despite her fantasies, she had never really considered Aaron as a possible lover. He was her friend, her brother, sometimes the father she had never known, always her mentor . . . until last night. Last night she had seen a different Aaron, his face a mask as his lips, his body devoured hers. At the thought, she felt the heat of passion rise in her again and the sensation horrified her. She was after all her mother's daughter and perhaps, therefore, no better than her mother. Alice had been dead only a few months, Aaron had needed friendship last night, nothing more and she had betrayed him, betrayed them both by letting her secret desires get the better of her. Yet at the time it had seemed so right, so natural, as though it was always meant to be.

Forcing her mind to concentrate, Ella thought over their conversation of this morning. Clearly, the night before had meant nothing to Aaron. He had momentarily given in to his desires because he was drunk, and now was appalled by what had happened. He must despise her, utterly. How could she throw away a lifetime of friendship for one night of passion, for it seemed likely that there would be no way back into Aaron Connors' heart. Get away, that's what she must do. Living in the same city as Aaron without being able to see him was impossible . . . Still half-blinded by tears, she sat up in bed, reached for the telephone and dialled the number. 'Could I speak to Margot Haigh, please, it's Ella Kovac.'

'Ella. How are you?' Margot's voice sounded warm, cheerful and reassuringly normal in a world gone mad.

'I'm fine. Listen, I've been thinking about that warehouse deal of Stephanie Bonham's.'

'Yes,' said Margot, expectantly.

'Well, I wouldn't mind taking a look at it.'

CHAPTER TWENTY-SIX

LONDON
September 1981

'23a, Flood Street, please – it's at the far end, nearest the river on the right.' Margot sank back in the seat of the taxi with a sigh of relief. It had been a long day and it would be good to be home, particularly as Nicholas would be joining her there. It was strange, his telephone call earlier. They had planned as usual to meet for dinner in Covent Garden – an early dinner, to let the rush hour traffic go, before Nicholas made his weekend trip to the family home in Wiltshire. The purpose of his call had been to suggest a change of plan, that they should meet at her house instead. It had been a particularly taxing day, he said, and he would appreciate a couple of quiet hours with her at home rather than eating in a noisy restaurant. It was an odd departure from their normal habit. He rarely visited her house, as if sensing it was too much of an intrusion into her life. Their affair, over the years, had been conducted almost exclusively in hotels up and down the country and on both sides of the Atlantic, and the anonymity of it seemed to suit them both. Still, it would be good to have him at home – Friday night was one of the few occasions on which Margot occasionally regretted living alone. To have someone to come home to, with whom she could talk through the rigours of the week, to relax with – she sensed this was something lacking in her life which she could have enjoyed given the opportunity.

The taxi started its slow progress down the Kings Road and for a moment Margot forgot Nicholas as she reflected on the meeting she had just attended. It had gone better than she had dared hope. Several times over recent weeks, she had doubted her wisdom in trying to bring together two people in the teeth of such opposition, but it had worked. Margot suspected the reason was mutual need, though why that was she was not quite sure. In Stephanie's case it was perhaps more obvious. As Stephanie herself had explained, she felt it was time to step out from under the Meyer umbrella, though Margot suspected it was not quite that simple. One or two odd remarks Stephanie had made suggested that perhaps she and Alex were not as close as they had been and clearly, while she had a very high regard for old Joseph Meyer, he was not the easiest person to deal with on a day-to-day basis. Certainly, there were rumblings in the camp. As for Ella – something must have happened to Ella to so drastically reverse her thinking on becoming involved in a property in London. She looked pale and strained, yet she had thrown herself into the project with an enthusiasm which had surprised both Margot and, she could tell, Stephanie. Still, whatever their motives, they were two quite extraordinary women whose achievements one had to admire, and bringing them together at last was a triumph – her triumph.

'23a, did you say, Miss?' the taxi driver called out.

'Yes, that's right, thank you,' said Margot.

Her little mews house looked well in the golden autumn evening light. She let herself in the front door and sniffed appreciatively. Her daily help clearly had been heavy handed with the beeswax, and the smell mingled attractively with the fragrance from a huge bowl of roses which sat in the centre of the dining room table. Margot consulted her watch – it was quarter-past-five. Nicholas was not due for half an hour, she had time to bath and change.

By the time his ring on the bell sounded promptly half-an-hour later, Margot was ready for him. She had lit a fire in the grate, his whisky and soda were laid out, she had bathed and put on a black velour jump suit which emphasized her graceful figure. The curtains were drawn, the room cosy and intimate and she had made a plate of smoked salmon sandwiches which he adored. She went to greet him, confident that he would be pleased with his welcome. The smile of greeting died on her lips. Nicholas was leaning heavily against one of the stone pillars which flagged either side of her front door, his face grey with fatigue. 'Nicholas, what on earth's the matter, are you ill?'

'No, no, My Dear, just worn out.'

'Come along in.' She took his arm, fussing over him, and ushered him into the house. She took his jacket and urged him into the armchair by the fire while she poured him a whisky.

He looked around him appreciatively. 'This is splendid, just what I needed. You ought to invite me here more often.' She made a face at him and handed him his whisky. He took a hefty swig. 'Ah, that's better, that's much better.'

'Something's wrong,' Margot said, anxiously. 'You really look ghastly.'

'Nothing's wrong, My Dear, but thanks anyway for the vote of confidence. It's just been a long, difficult day and I suppose it's about time I recognized I'm not as young as I was.'

'Any serious trouble?'

'No, no, just the routine niggles of day-to-day banking. I don't want to talk about it. Tell me about your day.'

Margot poured herself a glass of wine and sat in the chair opposite him. The whisky had brought back some of the colour to his face and he seemed more like his old self. 'Mine was fairly routine until this afternoon, when I became involved in a little match-making which looks like it might pay off handsomely.'

'Match-making! I've never quite thought of you in the role of cupid, My Dear.' He smiled at her, lifting one eyebrow slightly and she returned his smile, suddenly aware of how much they amused one another and of how much she cared for him.

'Commercial match-making as between Stephanie Bonham and Ella Kovac – hands across the ocean, one might say.'

A frown of concentration passed over Nicholas's face.

'Stephanie Bonham of Meyer, of course,' he said, 'and Ella Kovac . . . let me see, she's your little protégée, in New York, who's been having such a success in Houston. Am I right?' He looked at her, triumphantly, knowing very well that he was. His phenomenal memory never ceased to amaze Margot, who always considered her own intellect to be not without merit. In Nicholas, though, she had more than met her match. There were tens of thousands of Joshkers Bank customers around the world but Nicholas seemed to know them all. 'You tried to get them together once before, didn't you,' he said, 'over Centre des Arts?' He was showing off now and they both knew it.

'Yes, that's right, but I'm not going to tell you how clever you are to remember it. Actually, getting them together again has been quite a feat. When Ella Kovac pulled out of Centre des Arts she left a very disgruntled Stephanie, and to make matters worse, Ella then embarked on an ill-starred affair with Stephanie's husband.'

'Good grief, and you're proposing these two women should be partners?'

Margot smiled. 'There's been a lot of water under the bridge since then, Nicholas, besides which, women have a tendency to be far more adult about these things than men – they're less dependant on maintaining an unblemished ego.'

'You know, Margot, if I didn't know you better, I'd be tempted to think you had some decidedly odd views on life, feminist almost.'

Margot smiled at him. 'Would it be so terrible if I was a feminist?'

'Yes I rather think it would. I'm not sure I want a feminist infiltrating the senior ranks of Joshkers Bank, that bastion of male chauvinism.'

Margot laughed. 'Well, at least you admit it. No, I'm not a feminist, at least not in the accepted sense of the word, but I have to admit to getting quite a kick out of the fact that Stephanie and Ella, in their own individual ways, have done so well. I have taken a special interest in them and I suppose it is primarily because they are women that I've nurtured their careers. I also imagine that because they are women I know them better, as people, than I would do in the case of the average male customer.'

'Women's talk, you mean,' said Nicholas, disparagingly.

'Alright, so, women's talk, but important stuff to them – the problems of lovers, children and husbands.'

'I never thought you rated the personal aspects of life very highly in your list of priorities; I thought it was all work and no play.'

'What's right for me, isn't necessarily right for everyone else,' Margot said, defensively. 'For some reason, Ella is particularly vulnerable where men are concerned, and Stephanie certainly needs a permanent man in her life as a sounding board, a foil, whatever – she simply couldn't live alone.'

'Unlike Margot Haigh,' Nicholas said. He set down his empty glass and Margot moved to replenish it. He caught her hand and pulled her down so that she knelt beside his chair. He ran a hand down the long, silky sheen of her hair. 'Lovely Margot,' he said. 'Have I done this to you?'

'Done what?'

'Tied up your young life so that while you can recognize the need for husbands and children in other people, you do not recognize that need in yourself.'

'Nicholas, we've been through this a million times.'

'Alright, alright, sorry.'

'I've made some smoked salmon sandwiches, would you like some?'

He shook his head. 'No, another whisky, My Dear, would be lovely, and then let's go to bed.' He was never normally so direct and Margot's surprise at his words must have shown on her face. 'I don't think I'll put up much of a performance tonight,' he said, awkwardly, 'but it would be very good to get horizontal, with you beside me.'

Their lovemaking was swift, as Nicholas had predicted, but it did not worry Margot. It was comforting to lie in the semi-darkness, in her own home, with Nicholas slumbering on her shoulder. She wondered in the half-state between waking and sleeping, whether this change of routine would become a regular feature. She rather hoped so, for just at this moment, it was possible to pretend that he did not have to leave. The thought snapped her into reality. She glanced at the bedside clock, it was half past seven. Cautiously, so as not to wake him, she set the alarm for half past eight – if he was away by nine, he would not be too late home. Satisfied, she snuggled close to him and drifted off into sleep.

A sound woke Margot which she could not at first identify. She woke slowly, fighting her way through layers of deep sleep. The noise was a low rumble. She tried to push it away but it persisted, forcing its attention upon her. Suddenly, she realized it was a groan, a groan of pain. It was quite dark now. She sat up in bed abruptly and switched on the light.

Nicholas was still lying beside her, but his face was contorted with agony. He was writhing, sweat was standing out on his forehead, his face was ashen, his lips blue. 'Nicholas, Nicholas, what is it?'

'Heart,' he managed, between gritted teeth. 'Ring Charles Ellis, my doctor.'

Margot leapt from the bed and retrieved her dressing gown. She was trembling from head to foot. 'Where-where do I find him?'

'In my address book, in my jacket, hurry,' Nicholas managed.

Margot didn't need telling. She looked wildly round the room. There was no sign of the jacket, but then she remembered he had taken it off in the sitting room. Her heart was racing, her mind trying to grasp what was happening. She fumbled, clumsily, in his inside pocket and drew out a slim leather address book. Ellis, Ellis – Charles. With a shaking hand, she dialled the number. A woman answered the phone. 'Could I speak to Dr Ellis, please?'

'He's just having supper at the moment. Is it urgent, or can he call back?'

'It's terribly, terribly urgent,' said Margot. 'It's Sir Nicholas Goddard – I think he's having a heart attack.'

'Nicholas! Good heavens! Hang on one moment.' Relief flooded through Margot.

In seconds a voice said, 'Where is he?' It was a gruff voice but instantly reassuring.

'At . . . my house.'

'The address, stupid girl, quick.'

'Sorry, sorry,' said Margot. '23a Flood Street. Do you know it?'

'Yes, yes, of course. I should be with you in seven or eight minutes, with luck, depending on the traffic on the Embankment.'

'Thank you,' said Margot. 'What shall I do, while I'm waiting for you?'

'Nothing. Keep him calm and keep him still – lying down if possible, or whatever's most comfortable for him. Loosen any restrictive clothing but give him nothing to eat or drink.'

The phone went dead. Margot replaced the receiver and glanced again at the address book. Charles Ellis lived in Victoria. Yes, at this time at night, with a bit of luck . . . She dropped the book and ran back into the bedroom. 'Nicholas, he's . . .' She stopped at the entrance to the bedroom. The atmosphere in the room alerted her to what had happened, even before she looked at Nicholas. He was simply no longer there. Only his body remained, his mouth slightly open and his arms thrown wide as if in final surrender. His face was a dirty grey colour now and there was no sound or movement from him.

For a second, Margot could not move, then she rushed to the bed. What to do – mouth-to-mouth resuscitation, heart massage . . . She tried to remember the first aid lessons dimly learnt at school. She covered his mouth with hers and began blowing desperately, to fill his lungs, depressing his chest as she did so. She paused after a minute or so but nothing had happened. She began banging his chest. 'Nicholas, Nicholas!' Tears were streaming down her face now, inhibiting her. The calm, efficient woman, always so in charge, had become a helpless, hopeless little girl. 'Nicholas!' she screamed. She tried again, forcing herself to stay calm and trying to put some sort of rhythm into her breathing. She continued until she had no breath left in her body. Straightening up, swaying from tension and lack of air, she saw that her efforts had been wholly ineffectual. Nicholas's eyes stared drunkenly up at the ceiling, lifeless, dead. She put her hand over his eyelids, as she had seen it done in the movies and closed them. Then she simply stood by his side, her chest heaving, her mind reeling hopelessly. Time was running out. What could she do, what else *could* she do?

The doorbell rang. She turned, raced to the door and flung it open. A small, energetic man strode into the room. He wore corduroys and an old guernsey sweater, both scruffy and well-worn. His appearance was deceptive though for he was instantly in charge. 'Where is he?'

'In the bedroom, but I think he's . . .' the words died on her lips.

By the time she followed him into the bedroom, Charles Ellis was already hard at work. 'How long has he been like this?' he barked.

'Since I rang you. He was still breathing, talking . . . he gave me your name. Then I came into the sitting room to . . . to telephone you, and by the time I got back, I . . .'

'More light. Can you get me some more light?'

Margot switched on the overhead lights. 'I tried to resuscitate him – mouth-to-mouth, but I probably wasn't very good at it, I've never done it before.'

'Quiet.' Grim-faced, Charles Ellis worked while Margot watched him, paralysed now by the shock of what had happened. It was ten minutes before he straightened up and met her eye. 'I'm sorry, but I'm afraid there's nothing more I can do. He had already gone too far by the time I arrived – there was just a chance, but . . .'

Margot sank down on to the bed. 'He can't . . . be dead,' she said.

Charles Ellis came round to her side of the bed and put his hand on her shoulder. 'Would you like to sit with him for a few minutes? I'll go and make some tea and then we'll decide what to do.'

Margot nodded dumbly. Hardly aware of what she was

doing, she moved closer to Nicholas's body. She took his hand in hers, it was still warm. It was like a terrible nightmare yet she knew she was awake.

Margot Haigh had seen plenty of dead bodies in her life. As a child in Korea, caught up in the war, death and destruction of the human form in various horrific guises had become a normal part of her every day life. She had suffered from nightmares for years, but mercifully these had faded long ago and she found she could remember nothing about her life in Korea. Even her childhood spent with doting parents now long-dead, had been someone else's life, someone she might have read about, been told about, but certainly not experienced. Her life had begun two days after her fourteenth birthday, when she had set sail for England, and what happened before, she had ruthlessly blotted out. The shock, therefore, of seeing Nicholas dead, was as great for Margot as for anyone unfamiliar with the death and destruction of war. And she had let it happen – she should have done more . . .

Margot had always been a doer, her personal philosophy being that if you wanted to do something badly enough, you could always succeed at it. Yet this particular situation had been beyond her. She had failed Nicholas when he had needed her in the most fundamental of all ways, by being unable to preserve his life. Suddenly, she was on her knees, her head on his chest, her hair fanning out to cover him. She wept as though her heart would break, and eventually it was Charles Ellis who gently prized her away, raised her to her feet and led her through into the sitting room. He eased her into an armchair and handed her a mug of tea, hot and sweet. 'Best thing for shock, honestly.' Margot did not hear him. Nicholas's whisky glass still stood on the table beside her. How long ago had he been sitting there alive?

As if in answer to her question, the alarm clock suddenly began ringing in the bedroom, shattering the silence. 'What's that?' Charles Ellis asked.

'It-it's my alarm clock. I-I set it to . . . wake Nicholas.' The irony of her words silenced her. No one would ever be waking Nicholas again.

'Stay there, I'll turn it off,' the doctor said.

It had been an hour, only an hour, Margot thought, that had changed everything. When she had set the alarm, Nicholas had been slumbering quietly beside her, and she had thought there was nothing wrong with him other than the strain of a long week. Tears began flowing down her cheeks again.

The ringing of the alarm clock stopped and Charles Ellis re-entered the room. 'You're ... Margot Haigh, I take it?' he said, sitting down opposite her.

Margot looked up, surprised. 'Y-yes. How did you know?'

'Nicholas has told me a good deal about you over the years. I'd probably better explain the situation. Nicholas is ... was a very good friend of mine. In fact we were at Eton together, then at Oxford, though he read economics and I read medicine. I'm godfather to his eldest child, he's godfather to my son. The families have known one another for many years. He and I were on a golfing holiday, oh, it must have been twelve, perhaps fifteen years ago now, when one evening he told me about his relationship with you.'

'Oh, I see,' said Margot, clearly taken aback. 'I thought no one knew.'

'Don't worry, I'm sure no one else does.' Charles poked at the fire. 'I'm not even slightly disapproving. I'm very well aware that you could have taken Nicholas away from Margery, if you'd been that sort of woman, and the fact you didn't is all credit to you. I also happen to think you made him very happy. He was immensely proud of you and your achievements.'

'I failed him,' Margot burst out, 'I couldn't save him when he needed me.'

'That is something you have to put right out of your mind because it's simply not true,' said Charles. 'He's suffered from angina for years, I don't know whether you were aware of it.'

Margot looked up surprised. 'No, I had no idea.'

'He had a lot of guts, Nicholas – a wonderful war record. He was absolutely determined that his heart condition wasn't going to affect his lifestyle in any way. I've warned him for years that this sort of thing would happen eventually and his view was that we all have to die, and going out like a light had to be one of the best ways. He was too young, of course, but he died the way he wanted. The heart attack was clearly massive and I honestly believe if I had been here at the time it happened, I would not have been able to save him. I'll admit it is those first few minutes immediately after the attack which are crucial, but in his case I suspect the damage was too profound for anything to have been done.'

'You're saying that to comfort me.'

'It also happens to be true.'

Margot looked properly at Charles Ellis for the first time. He was not unattractive, with a lean, angular face and a mop of dark hair, barely flecked with grey. He looked considerably younger than Nicholas. The eyes observing her now were kind and warm and she realized she had a friend in this man, a thought which brought a degree of comfort.

They were silent for several moments as they sat in front of the fire. Margot gradually became aware of her dishevelled state – the dressing gown hurriedly tied, her hair falling about her shoulders. She thought then of Nicholas, lying naked in the bed next door. After all the years of discretion, it seemed so ironic that with his death, their affair should be forced into the open. At the thought, Margot's logical mind began to function properly again. She looked at Charles, hesitantly. 'If only he hadn't died here. I suppose Lady Goddard will have to know.'

Charles smiled, a smile of obvious relief. 'I'm glad you raised the problem rather than me. I was thinking out a plan while I was making the tea. Nicholas was always of the opinion that Margery never knew about you and him. Do you think he was right?'

'I'm sure of it,' said Margot, 'we were very, very careful over the years. I never wanted to break up his marriage because I knew in most respects, they were ideally suited.' She found she could say the words without feeling any anguish. She wondered, for a moment, whether this was because Nicholas was dead, because the cause of any resentment or jealousy had been taken from her.

'Look,' said Charles Ellis, 'it seems to me that all we need to do is to re-write the last hour. Did he come here with a chauffeur or by taxi?'

'Oh, by taxi. He never met me anywhere with the car and chauffeur, except of course for business meetings.'

'Good. Do you know where he was before he came here?'

'At the bank,' said Margot. 'I'm sure of that, because I spoke to him there shortly after five. We had planned to have a meal in Covent Garden, we normally do, on Fridays. Nicholas said he was feeling very tired and would prefer to come here instead. If only I'd realized what that meant.'

'Stop it,' said Charles, 'it's not helping anyone, honestly.'

'No, no, I'm sorry.' Margot pushed a strand of hair out of her eyes. 'He must have left the bank at about six, perhaps a little before. Certainly he was here by half past six.'

'And when and where was the chauffeur going to pick him up?'

'Oh, he never uses his chauffeur at weekends,' said Margot, 'he keeps . . . kept a car at Hyde Park underground car park. He always liked to drive himself home at weekends.'

'Bloody typical,' said Charles. 'Fighting his way up and down the M4 was the kind of stress he didn't need.'

Margot felt compelled to defend Nicholas. 'He said he always felt as though he was still at work if he was in the bank's car, and in any case, he liked his chauffeur to have the weekend off, except if they had any official engagements.'

'So, if he had not been seeing you, he would have taken a taxi, or possibly the car and chauffeur, from the bank to Hyde Park underground car park and simply driven home from there.'

'Yes,' said Margot.

'Let us suppose for a moment that's what he did. He'd been feeling tired and a bit below par all day, and when he reached the car park he began to have some pain. Let me see, to reach the M4 he'd have driven down Exhibition Road and turned into the Cromwell Road.' Margot nodded. 'Supposing by the time he was in Exhibition Road the pain was severe and he did not feel able to tackle the M4, at that point he would have been only ten minutes drive from your house. Is it reasonable that he would know where your house was?'

Margot nodded. 'Yes, I had a party here just a few months ago, for a member of our staff who was leaving. Nicholas and Margery both came.'

'Splendid. So, supposing he thought his best bet was to drive to your house and to ring me from there, knowing it was also on the way to me.'

'It seems a bit far-fetched,' Margot said doubtfully.

'Alright,' said Charles, 'so, he decided that instead of going down the M4, he'd better drive straight to me and it was only when he reached the Embankment, heading towards Victoria, that he suddenly realized he wasn't going to make it, because he felt too ill. If the traffic was heavy on the Embankment, he might have suddenly thought that ducking down into Chelsea was the best answer.'

'That's a lot better,' said Margot.

'Good,' said Charles, 'here's what we do. I'm going next door to dress him, and when I've done that I want you to get dressed as well. Only then will I call the ambulance. As soon as . . . as Nicholas's body has been collected, I will go to the car park, collect his car, and bring it back here. I know I'm asking rather a lot to expect you to indulge in this cloak and dagger stuff but I think for the sake of Nicholas's family it's best, don't you?'

'Oh, yes,' said Margot, 'definitely.'

They came for Nicholas's body quarter-of-an-hour later. Margot stood in numbed silence as the stretcher bore him away, out of her life for ever. When they had gone, Charles handed her a couple of pills. 'Take these,' he said, 'I suggest another warm drink and then straight to bed. I'll put Nicholas's car keys through the letterbox so as not to disturb you. In the circumstances it won't seem odd they were left behind. Now, don't attempt to do too much for the next few days. If you feel unwell, come and see me – shock can play strange tricks. Don't hesitate, I mean it.'

In a daze, Margot thanked him and saw him out of the door. Ignoring his advice, she poured herself a hefty brandy and washed down the two pills. The brandy warmed her and seemed to anaesthetize her mind sufficiently that she was able to clear away the glasses and mugs, throw the sandwiches in the bin, bank down the fire and put up the fireguard. The routine domestic chores seemed to comfort her.

Not looking at her bed, Margot walked through her bedroom to the bathroom and ran a deep bath. She lay in it for a long time, until the water was tepid, her mind drifting. Charles had promised to telephone Margery Goddard as soon as he got home and she wondered how the other woman in Nicholas's life was feeling. She had probably prepared some supper for him, had been expecting him home at any moment. From the few occasions that Margot had visited Coombe Manor, the Goddards' home, she knew that every visitor, particularly a member of the family, was greeted by a pack of dogs, of all shapes and sizes. Margery told her once that the dogs always seemed to know when it was Friday night and lay clustered in the hall waiting for their master to return. They were doing that now probably, or, perhaps, being so much more instinctive than human beings, they already knew he was dead.

Margot tried to feel sorry for Margery but she could find little compassion in her heart. Margery had enjoyed the best years in Nicholas's life and had borne his children. Even now, while she, Margot, lay here alone, Margery would be comforted by their younger daughter who still lived at home and their two sons would be with her in hours. She, by contrast, had no one now, no one at all. Nicholas had been everything to her, she realized. Her boss yes, her mentor – her respect for him professionally was boundless. He had also been the father she had lost, the husband she'd never had, the lover she cherished. Although their meetings had been so infrequent and often rushed, she had wanted no one else because Nicholas had fulfilled every need in her. They were a perfect match because, like her, he was wedded primarily to his job. Now, suddenly, it was finished, and she could not even publicly mourn him.

Only when she began to shiver, did Margot lever herself out of the bath. She felt like an old woman, her joints stiff, her muscles painful. She dried herself hurriedly, trying to buff some warmth into her aching limbs. In the bedroom, she at last looked at the bed. Charles Ellis had made a half-hearted attempt at making it, but when she drew back the duvet on Nicholas's side, the indentation of his body was still there. It was more than she could bear. Throwing herself down where he had lain, she gave way to the tears that were to last through most of the night.

The funeral of Sir Nicholas Goddard was well attended. Most of the key names in the City were present, plus two cabinet ministers, a brace of dukes and a large gathering of the country's top industrialists, many of whom felt they owed their success to the helping hand Nicholas Goddard had given them at some stage in their commercial life.

The service took place at St Martin-in-the-Fields, and afterwards selected members of the congregation were invited to a private room at the Dorchester, where a light lunch was served. Margot stayed close to her bank colleagues and tried to avoid any contact with the Goddard family. However, after the service she found herself in line, waiting to shake Lady Goddard's hand. When it was her turn, she mumbled her condolences and much to her surprise, Lady Goddard leaned forward and kissed her cheek. 'Charles told me how wonderful you were when Nicholas was taken ill, I am grateful.' She smiled, 'It must have been awful for you, him dying like that in your house, particularly as I know how fond you were of him.'

In sheer astonishment, Margot raised her eyes and met Lady Goddard's serene gaze. To an outsider, there was no hint of any double meaning in her words – she seemed simply to be genuinely grateful – yet in that moment Margot realised that, without a shadow of doubt, Margery knew everything about her and Nicholas, knew and accepted it.

Of the two hundred people attending the reception, only Stephanie Bonham seemed to notice there was anything wrong with Margot. 'What's up?' she asked, 'you look a bit peaky.'

'Oh I'm fine,' said Margot, 'there's nothing wrong with me, I'm just tired. Nicholas dying like this has obviously created a lot of extra work.'

'Cold bitch,' Stephanie thought. It was common knowledge that Nicholas Goddard had taken a personal interest in Margot's career. She might at least make an effort to appear sorry about his premature death, rather than moan about the work-load. Still, Stephanie thought sourly, Margot was probably pleased – without a doubt his death would place her one step higher up the ladder.

CHAPTER TWENTY-SEVEN

HOUSTON
October 1981

'What do you think,' said Ella, 'doesn't it look great?'

Greg lounged in the doorway of the new guest suite and smiled indulgently at his mother. 'I guess so – a little fancy though, isn't it?'

'I wanted to make things nice for her. It's not every day one's banker comes to stay, and for a holiday, too.'

'Yeh, but you haven't done out this room just for Margot Haigh. We'll have other people to stay, and it does seem kind of . . . well, feminine.'

Ella looked disappointed. 'It's too late to change it now. Anyway, *I* like it.'

'Well, that's the main thing then.' Greg slipped an arm round her shoulders and kissed the top of her head.

'Don't patronize me,' said Ella, fondly, looking around one last time. The room was predominately cream and apricot. It was a big room, with a huge picture window looking out over Houston and leading from it was a bathroom and dressing room. It was relaxing and spacious and Ella hoped fervently that Margot would like it.

It had been a scramble to get ready. Greg had returned from Canada just ten days ago and he had barely time had to unpack when Ella had spirited him down to Houston to select an apartment, suitable as both a home and an office. They had chosen an apartment on the fourteenth floor of the first block Ella had built in Post Oak. While perhaps it was not ideal as an office, it had spectacular views over the City.

When looking out of the windows, Ella was always reminded of Michael describing Houston like a jungle when viewed from above. It was true, below them was a sea of green. The apartment was a large one, with four bedrooms with bathrooms en suite, a big reception area, ideal for entertaining, and a separate kitchen and dining room. The largest of the bedrooms Ella had turned into an office. She had already hired a secretary from Dallas, a girl in her early twenties called Tessa Decker, who looked promising, and decorators had been tramping through the apartment all week. Normally Ella would not have been in such a hurry but for Margot's call the previous week. It had been out of character, Ella thought. Margot had said she was going to be in New York for a few days and expressed interest in coming down to see the Houston developments. That was understandable although, as Margot was not directly involved in the financing of the Houston operation, it was perhaps a little surprising. What had been most surprising of all, however, had been Margot's request that Ella find her somewhere to stay in Houston for a few days holiday. Apparently, she had been working very hard since the sudden death of Joshkers' chairman, Sir Nicholas Goddard, and she felt a few days in a city where no one knew her would be an ideal break – could Ella recommend a suitable hotel? Ella, of course, had insisted Margot stay with her and Greg, although there were times over the last week when she had regretted the offer. Certainly all the hassle was starting to irritate Greg. 'You'd think we were receiving a visitation from the Virgin Mary herself,' he grumbled, as they crossed the hall to the kitchen.

'Don't blaspheme,' said Ella, sternly.

'Sorry, Mom, but honestly I don't know what all the fuss is about. So, she's the lady who hands out the dollars, but Jesus, her bank have to be real pleased with you. You're the customer; shouldn't she be rolling out the red carpet for you, not the other way around?'

'Yes, I suppose you're right,' said Ella. 'Coffee?'

'Thanks,' said Greg. 'Anyway, I'm not looking forward to her visit. You're going to spend the whole time talking business, I just know it.'

'You're probably right,' Ella admitted. 'I'm sorry, Greg, dragging you down here, so soon after your return. It's just that I wanted to see something of you before you go off to college. It's been a long, lonely summer without you.'

'You had Aaron,' Greg said.

'That's true,' Ella lied. She and Aaron had not been in contact once during the period their sons had been away. When the boys returned, they had met for a celebration supper, but Greg and William had been so full of their adventures that neither of them had noticed that their parents barely spoke to one another. Following that evening, it was Ella's feeling of despair at losing Aaron which had prompted this dash to Houston during the last two weeks of Greg's vacation.

'I don't mind, coming to Houston, Mom. I quite like the city, now we don't have to spend time with – ' he looked awkward, suddenly very much the child.

'It's OK,' said Ella, laughing, 'you were right, I was wrong. Michael Gresham is a slob where women are concerned – that's official, OK?'

Greg laughed. 'What time's her plane?'

'She should be getting in about an hour from now. I had thought about lunch out but I guess she'll be tired, so I thought I'd fix something here.'

'I tell you what,' said Greg, 'why don't I pick her up from the airport, while you fix us lunch.'

'Would you?' said Ella. 'That would be kind. You'll be careful on those freeways, though, won't you? This is the city of the motor car, remember.'

Greg laughed. 'Come on, Mom.'

'OK, I know,' said Ella, 'it just takes some getting used to, you being old enough to drive.'

'Just think of the advantages. You can lounge around here while I sweat it out to the airport.'

'It's just since Alice and Joan . . .'

'I know, I know.' Greg's expression sobered. 'Look, I may be a teenage tearaway in some respects, but I'm sensible on roads. I did all the driving in Canada, you know that, and some of it was quite hairy – real pioneer stuff.'

'Don't tell me about it,' said Ella.

'I wasn't aiming to. How will I recognize your lady banker – does she have dollar signs for eyeballs?'

'No, she doesn't, Greg. Actually she's an extremely attractive woman.'

'Tell me more,' said Greg, leering.

'She's about five feet ten, she has long auburn hair, which normally she puts up. She usually wears black, but always dark colours, and she has a wonderful face – big brown eyes, high oriental cheekbones: she's half Korean. She'll probably travel light because she's very efficient. Why not hold up a card with her name on it?'

'After a description like that,' said Greg, 'I shouldn't have any problem recognizing her. Why didn't you ask this lady to come and stay before?'

'Oh, where's my little boy gone?' Ella mourned.

'Shut it, Mom. Let's have the car keys.'

With Greg gone, Ella had time to turn her thoughts to Margot's proposed visit. The motive still bothered her but she suspected it might be in some way connected to the Fulham warehouse project. Margot was still unhappy about the financing. It was a big scheme and she and Stephanie would be very stretched to cope. Perhaps that explained the visit, perhaps Margot wanted to check up on her collateral. Ella had fixed for them to have lunch with Jack Smith the following day, and certainly she felt confident that Jack could reassure Margot on the success of Houston. Maybe she was taking on rather a lot, the shopping mall and Fulham running concurrently, yet it was what she needed right now, to sink herself into business as never before. With Aaron apparently out of her life and Greg off to college, she recognized that unless she gave herself completely to her business, her life would be a desert.

The sound of Margot laughing in the hall surprised Ella, as she left the kitchen to greet her. From Margot's own description of her general state, Ella had expected to be greeting a pale and weary creature. Instead, Margot was laughing in response to something Greg had just said and the unaccustomed vivacity lit her face and made her look years younger than her age. Ella was pleased. Margot was always something of an unknown quantity but at least if she was in good spirits she would be easier to handle.

The three of them had a relaxed and friendly lunch, steak and salad washed down with two bottles of Beaujolais. Margot was full of praise for the apartment and what she had seen so far of the city. Like everyone visiting Houston for the first time, its greenness had surprised her. Greg had promised her a guided tour the following day. It was a tremendous relief to Ella to see how well the two of them got along. Ella imagined that the moment Margot arrived, she would begin firing questions at her concerning the business, which was normally her way. Instead, she seemed anxious to talk about almost any subject except real estate.

'Mom says you're half Korean,' Greg said, as they sat over coffee. 'Did you grow up in Korea?'

Ella blanched. It was an unwritten law that one never asked Margot anything about her personal life – a few short rebuffs had seen to that.

'Yes, I did,' said Margot, 'until I was thirteen.'

'And then you came to England?' Margot nodded. 'Why was that?'

Greg's persistence was embarrassing Ella, but Margot did not seem to mind. 'Well, it's a strange story, really,' said Margot, 'though I don't know if you'd be interested.'

'Fascinated,' Ella had to admit.

Well, I'm the product of a Korean woman and an Englishman. My father was managing director of a chemical plant. It was an American company with branches scattered around the Middle and Far East. He married late in life. I suspect he was really a confirmed bachelor but my mother was the daughter of a valued customer of his and marriage was probably a political move. At the time of their marriage, he was forty-seven and she eighteen.'

'Was the marriage happy?' Greg asked.

'I think so, fairly. I was born about a year after they married. We had a nice house in Seoul and we enjoyed the best of both worlds, mixing with both the British families and the Korean. My father's job was very well paid. I went to a British school but was more or less bilingual. They were happy, tranquil years, in fact so much so that I remember very little about them. Falling out of a tree and scraping my knee was about the biggest drama.'

Greg laughed. 'I can't imagine you climbing trees.'

'It was a long time ago,' Margot said, swiftly.

'So what happened?' Ella asked.

'The Korean War.' She took a sip of wine thoughtfully. 'I don't want to go into the details of it, you understand.'

'No, I'm sorry,' said Ella, 'we shouldn't have asked.'

'It's alright,' Margot said, amiably enough. 'When the Communists invaded, our world was turned upside down. I was at school when the bombs hit Seoul. My parents were both killed outright. The whole city was in chaos. I wandered around for some days but I had nowhere to go. Eventually I was taken pity on by the good old British Army – the Duke of Wellington's Regiment. Because I was an orphan, I was sent over to England on a troop ship and adopted by the family of one of the soldiers I met. I spent the rest of my childhood in Reading, Berkshire, and then on to university, of course.'

'It must have been an extraordinary contrast for you,' said Ella.

'In a way, yes,' said Margot, 'although I'd always wanted to come to England. My father, like most ex-patriots, had a rose-tinted view of English life. I expect . . .' she hesitated, 'no I won't say that!'

'What?' Greg asked, intrigued.

Margot looked slightly embarrassed, something Ella had never seen in her before. 'Well, I suspect my father's family came from a rather different social background to the family with whom I lived. It sounds very snobbish to say this, but my father talked a great deal about his upbringing and it bore very little resemblance to the life I lived in Reading.'

'Still,' said Greg, 'you've made up for it since.'

Margot laughed, 'Yes, I suppose I have.'

That evening, the three of them had dinner at one of the top Mexican restaurants in Houston, followed by a ride downtown to show Margot around. The following morning was taken up with business. Greg stayed in the apartment while Ella and Margot had lunch with Jack Smith and spent the rest of the day viewing Ella's various properties.

Over cocktails that evening, Margot gave her verdict. 'I like this town,' she said, 'it's crazy but it's got something, there's a feeling of excitement and dynamism about the place. I can quite see its appeal from your point of view. To find yourself a part of its development, its growth, must be very stimulating.'

'Yes, it is,' said Ella. 'I've been lucky.'

'And clever. You must be proud of your mother, Greg.'

Greg nodded. 'I am, though I guess I take it all for granted – all the deals, all the millions of dollars, it's not kind of like real life, is it?'

'I disagree,' said Margot. 'I think it's very much a part of the real world. There is nothing more tangible than property.'

'Ah,' said Ella, 'now you're talking like a banker.'

'Perhaps, but you're doing something useful, Ella. As well as building a profitable business you're making a contribution to the growth of a city, providing homes and offices. It's all so positive.'

'You sound almost wistful,' said Ella. 'Yet banking is your life, isn't it – at least, I've always imagined it so?'

'Yes, of course, but sometimes I wish I could do something for myself, rather than for Joshkers bank. I think it's why I understood just how Stephanie felt when she explained that she wanted to do this Fulham project outside the Meyer umbrella. As part of a big organisation, it's very easy to lose one's sense of personal identity.'

'Yes, I can imagine,' said Ella.

'You two are going to start talking business again, if I'm not careful,' said Greg. 'What are our plans for tomorrow? Why don't we take Margot down to Galvaston, for a peek at the ocean?'

'That's a good idea,' said Ella. 'Would you like that, Margot?'

'I'd love it,' said Margot, 'but don't feel you have to entertain me, I can look after myself.'

'We'd like to,' said Ella. 'I'm only working part-time at the moment because I want to see something of Greg before he goes off to college.'

'Then I'm intruding,' said Margot.

'No, you're not, you stay as long as you wish.'

A very different Margot was unfolding, Ella thought, as she prepared supper that evening. Greg and Margot had embarked on another round of cocktails and were watching the sunset over Houston. She was softer, altogether less brittle, and while not exactly forthcoming, she was certainly more prepared to talk about her private life than at any time during the years Ella had known her. How long was it now? ... twelve, thirteen years of association: it was extraordinary to have known someone that long and yet to know so little about them.

The fact that Margot and Greg were getting on so well pleased her. She had become used to Greg's boredom and frustration over the years, when she had been forced to entertain colleagues in the school holidays. Still, he was almost grown up now and his apparent interest in Margot made Ella wonder whether perhaps there was still hope for her dearest ambition. While Greg had always maintained he would live and work in the country, Ella had secretly hoped that one day he would take over Lexington Kovac. It seemed only right that he should do so since it had been founded for his benefit. He was studying law at college, by choice, which would clearly be very useful if he was to make a career in real estate. It was just a question of biding her time. Ella had enough sense to recognize that the first move had to come from Greg. To suggest he joined her business too soon, so that he felt compelled to reject the idea, would be a disaster.

Ella was just on the point of serving the seafood pasta she had prepared, when the telephone rang. 'Get it, would you, Greg?' she called. 'I expect it's Jackie, with an up-date on New York. Tell her I'll call back after supper.'

Greg appeared in the kitchen doorway, moments later. 'No, it's not Jackie, it's Stephanie Bonham – she sounds in a state.'

'Stephanie!' Ella glanced anxiously at the dish of pasta – if she left it in the oven it would over-cook. 'Did you say I was in?'

'Yes, I'm afraid I did,' said Greg.

'Oh heck, I'd better take it then.' Ella was aware that her relationship with Stephanie still operated on a knife-edge. They both wanted the Fulham project for different reasons and the price they had to pay for having it was to get along with one another, but there was no good pretending it was easy. 'Hi, Stephanie.'

'Oh, Ella, I'm so glad to get you. I've got a problem, a big one and I need your help.'

Stephanie Bonham never normally needed anyone's help. Ella was astounded. 'How come?' she asked.

'Joseph Meyer has found out about our Fulham deal and he's absolutely furious. He's threatening to throw the book at me and says he doesn't care what it costs him, he'll stop us from going ahead.'

'I don't understand,' said Ella, 'I thought your contract didn't preclude you from doing deals on your own?'

'It doesn't,' said Stephanie, 'but Joseph Meyer says I used privileged information for my own ends, because I knew the haulage company was going bust. He's been ringing me on and off all afternoon, shouting about business ethics and so on. He's already called in his lawyer, he says. I just don't know what to do about it. I can't afford to fall out with him irrevocably, but at the same time, I'm damned if we should be forced to give up this venture. The trouble is, he's big – so big I reckon he really could ruin us. I can just see ourselves having mysterious difficulties with planning permission, and builders not being prepared to work for us, that sort of thing.'

'He has that much power even in the UK?' Ella asked.

'Oh yes,' said Stephanie, 'without a doubt, and he won't be afraid to use it either. There's an awful lot of good in

Joseph Meyer but he's absolutely ruthless when he's crossed.'

'Won't Alex help?' Ella asked.

Stephanie gave a hollow little laugh, 'Alex agrees with his father.'

'You hadn't told him then – about the project, I mean?,'

'Good heavens no,' said Stephanie. 'As I explained to you and Margot, it was something I wanted to do on my own, separately from the Meyers, father and son. They're being so unreasonable, Ella, it's not as though we are including a hotel in the complex and going into competition with Meyer. I tried to play it down, to put the whole scheme across to them as a sort of lucrative hobby, but they just won't have it. Look, what I was wondering is whether you could come over to London and help me persuade them that the project isn't going to hurt them. We could change the story a little – say *you* approached *me* to find a project for us both in London, something like that. It would make it seem less premeditated on my part. I'm sorry to ask you, Ella, but they're only in London for a couple more days and I really am desperate.' She sounded it.

Ella sighed. 'It's difficult to get away at the moment. Greg's just about to go to college for the first time and I have Margot staying with me.'

'Margot! So that's where she is, I've been trying to reach her all day,' said Stephanie. 'They kept telling me at the bank she was on holiday but I didn't believe it – Margot never has a holiday. What's she doing with you?'

'Doing just that – taking a holiday, at last,' said Ella. 'It's part business, of course, being Margot. She's looking at my Houston operation but she's planning a few days off as well. Anyway, I'm sure you appreciate in the circumstances I can't very well walk out and leave her.'

'Quite the reverse,' said Stephanie, 'she's the one person who really will understand. After all, it's her project too, she's funding us. I'm sure she'll see that she just has to spare you for thirty-six hours. It shouldn't be longer, honestly Ella. You can fly straight into London and straight out again. I just need a few hours of your time. I'll fix up a meeting with Joseph for as soon as you arrive.'

'I can't make it this week,' said Ella, 'next week, certainly.'

'Next week will be too late. They're a very excitable family, the Meyers, and they're not prepared to let this drop for an instant. It has to be resolved, now. We can't let it fester, or by next week, we'll be in court.'

'Hang on a moment,' said Ella, 'I'll talk to Margot.'

Ella quickly explained the position and Margot was at once efficient and very much back to her old self. 'I think you have to go, Ella,' she said, 'if you want to save the project, that is. My guess is that Stephanie and Joseph have reached a Mexican stand-off. They're both volatile people and it needs someone to intervene and find a compromise.' She smiled at Ella. 'I can't think of anyone better for the job.'

'But what about your holiday?' said Ella.

'Oh, to hell with my holiday,' said Margot, 'this is much more important. I can always fly back up to New York. God knows, there's a desk full of stuff waiting for me there.'

'Why don't you stay here until Mom gets back?' said Greg. Both women turned to him, surprised. He shrugged his shoulders, looking slightly self-conscious.

'Well, you're not going to be away long, Mom, are you?'

'No,' said Ella, 'no, I suppose not. Hell, we'd better talk about it in a moment, I still have Stephanie waiting on the line.'

'Tell her you'll catch the first flight out,' said Margot, 'and then we'll work out what to do.'

The relief in Stephanie's voice only served to emphasize the seriousness of the situation, as did her gratitude. 'I really don't know how to thank you, Ella.'

'It's no problem,' said Ella. 'I'll try and catch an overnight flight tonight, and I'll ask Greg to ring through the flight details. Could you possibly arrange for someone to pick me up?'

'Of course, and Ella, thanks again.'

When Ella returned to the sitting room, Greg and Margot were deep in conversation. 'I've talked her into it,' Greg said, triumphantly. 'She says if you don't mind, she'll stay on for a couple of days while you're away and then the three of us can take in some day trips on your return. I thought we could go to NASA, and if you hurry back, Mom, who knows, we might have time to go down to Mexico.'

Ella looked at Margot uncertainly. 'Are you sure this is what you want to do, Margot?'

Margot seemed equally unsure herself. 'I'd love to stay but I don't want to be in the way. I needn't take up any of Greg's time. I have a lot of reading to do and to be honest, it's just so nice to be out of a hotel and in an apartment for once.'

'If you're sure you don't mind, I'm sure Greg would welcome the company.'

'I would,' said Greg, emphatically.

'And I can earn my keep by providing him with the odd meal,' Margot suggested.

'You cook?' Ella was astounded.

Margot laughed. 'I think I should be insulted by your incredulity.'

Ella was suitably shamefaced. 'I'm sorry, Margot, I just don't see you as being very domestic somehow.'

'You mean you see me as living permanently behind my desk, with one eye on a VDU screen and the other on a balance sheet?'

'Something like that,' Ella admitted, 'certainly not cooking. Oh my God, supper!' She ran through to the kitchen. 'Oh yuck, it's congealed, completely ruined. I could kill Stephanie, it was going to be so good, too.'

Greg and Margot joined her. 'Can't you simply heat it up?' said Greg.

'No, the pasta's gone all soggy and . . . oh shit.'

'Look,' said Margot, 'I can start making myself useful right away. You go and pack, I'll fix your flight and then Greg and I will run you to the airport via a suitable restaurant. What do you say?'

'It sounds a great idea,' said Ella. 'Oh hell!' She picked up the bowl of pasta and began scraping it into the bin, wondering as she did so whether she would be making the same kind of gesture with the Fulham project in a few hours' time. She wanted that deal, wanted it badly. She was also aware that being able to help Stephanie out of the hole into which she had dug herself boded well for their future relationship. There had to be a way to salvage the project, and if there was, she felt confident she could find it.

CHAPTER TWENTY-EIGHT

LONDON
October 1981

It was one-thirty by the time Ella's car drew to a halt outside the Meyer Hotel in Park Lane. Stephanie was waiting for her at reception, in a state of obvious agitation. She embraced Ella warmly, as though none of the former animosity had ever existed.

'Thank you for coming Ella. They're already up in the boardroom waiting for us, but I lied and said I didn't think you'd be in until two. Come up to my room, it will give us a chance to talk tactics.' In Stephanie's room, a pile of sandwiches was thoughtfully waiting for Ella. 'A glass of wine?' Stephanie asked.

'Coffee, I think,' said Ella. 'A combination of jet-lag and booze could be a little dulling on the wits and it looks like we're going to need all ours about us.'

Stephanie ordered coffee from room service and then came and sat down opposite Ella. She looked chic and sophisticated, very European, Ella thought, but terribly thin and pale. There was a strained look about her face which had not been there before and she plucked nervously at the skirt of her dress as she talked.

'I suppose I should have told Alex about the scheme from the beginning,' she said, 'then at least I would have stood a chance of having him on my side. As it is, he seems to feel as let down as the old man, if not more so. I know this is a dreadful thing to say, Ella having dragged you all the way across the Atlantic, but I honestly think we're going to have to pull out. I just don't see how we can go ahead in the teeth of such opposition.'

'We're not pulling out,' said Ella. 'Joseph Meyer can make as much noise as he likes but if your contract with the Meyers is watertight, and Margot says it is, then there's nothing he can do.'

'Don't be so naïve, Ella,' said Stephanie, desperately. 'There's one hell of a lot he can do. To start with, he can make my life unbearable within the Meyer organization. My franchise comes up for renewal in ten months; that gives him plenty of time to prepare a case as to why he shouldn't renew it. And then, as I said to you on the phone, I'm perfectly certain he can pull strings if he's really feeling vicious, to such an extent that we'll never get Fulham off the ground.'

'I think you're over-reacting,' said Ella. 'These kind of bullying tactics go on all the time in New York and my experience is that most of them amount to no more than bluff.'

'And what about when they don't?' Stephanie asked.

Ella smiled. 'The way I've always handled bully boys is to threaten them with the press. Just imagine how the Meyer organisation would look if it could be proved they were trying to put us out of business. You're English, born and bred – if anybody has a right to develop real estate in this country, it's you. A story detailing how Meyer, a German American, is trying to stop you could ruin his reputation in this country.'

'I suppose so,' said Stephanie, reluctantly, 'though I certainly wouldn't like to be the one to threaten Joseph Meyer along those sort of lines.'

'I don't think we'll have to,' said Ella. 'I'm sure we'll find a compromise, but whatever way we have to play it, just remember, we're not letting him stop us going ahead with this project.'

The telephone rang, making them both jump. Stephanie picked it up. 'I gather Miss Kovac has arrived.' Joseph Meyer's voice was clipped and formal. 'Perhaps you would be good enough to join us in the boardroom right away — we've waited more than long enough for you as it is.'

Stephanie put down the phone, white-faced. 'The old bastard knows you're here. He must have his spies everywhere.'

'Calm down,' said Ella. 'Let me use your bathroom to refresh the warpaint and then you and I will go into battle.'

The boardroom was impressive, a large room with big picture windows looking out over Hyde Park, dominated by a round mahogany table. Ella, who had only ever seen Joseph Meyer in press photographs, was immediately struck by the contrast between his diminutive stature and the power of his presence. There were three men sitting at the table when Ella and Stephanie entered. Joseph, with a courtesy which was obviously inbred regardless of the circumstances, rose and came to greet them. He shook Ella warmly by the hand but made no attempt to greet Stephanie, other than with a curt nod. From the moment Ella took his hand and met the appraising gaze of his deep-set eyes, she recognized for the first time the substance of their adversary. No wonder Stephanie was nervous. This man would make a wonderful friend and a terrible enemy. His grip was firm, his hands dry and soft. Taking Ella by the elbow, he steered her to the table. 'I'd like to introduce you to my son, Alex, and this gentleman is our lawyer, Jacob St. Clare.'

The fact of a lawyer being present was disconcerting, but not enough so to detract Ella from a fascinated appraisal of Alex Meyer. He was not her sort of man — he was too obviously sure of himself, too sophisticated. However, there was no good denying, he was extremely attractive. With his dark curly hair and smooth, aquiline good-looks, he had an almost feline grace. Instantly, though, there was something about him she did not like: there was a petulant curve to his mouth and yes, he was clearly enjoying the situation. The realization appalled Ella. He was supposed to be in love with Stephanie, and in the circumstances, her current predicament should either have had him leaping to her defence, or hurt and angry. Alex Meyer was reacting in neither manner — he looked like he was about to relish watching Stephanie squirm like a rat in a trap.

The situation made Ella very angry. She glanced at Stephanie, who was sitting beside her, pale and nervous, and suddenly felt very protective towards her. It was a strange reversal of a relationship which had begun with Ella most definitely feeling the inferior. Her thoughts were interrupted by Joseph Meyer's deep, melodious voice.

'Thank you for joining us, Ladies. I think I should make it quite clear before this meeting opens that neither my son nor I have any argument with you, Miss Kovac. Clearly, if you wish to extend your business interests into the UK that is up to you, and you are free to bid for any UK property, should you feel it appropriate for your business expansion.'

'Thank you very much indeed,' said Ella, with heavy irony. She met Joseph's eye as she spoke.

'However, I do query your choice of partner. My experience would suggest that Lady Stephanie Bonham,' – he emphasized the title, – 'is far from an ideal partner, since you can be assured she will put her own interests before that of the partnership.'

'That's untrue!' Stephanie's complexion had turned from white to pink, her eyes were over-bright.

'Mr Meyer,' Ella cut in, 'I can see absolutely no point in us having a meeting at all, if all we're going to do is to exchange insults. I've known Stephanie Bonham for longer than you. I consider her to be an honourable and trustworthy person and I have decided to go into partnership with her over this venture as a direct result of the recommendation of our mutual banker.'

'Ah, the indomitable Margot Haigh.' Alex said, with a sneer. 'She's always very keen on promoting women's projects, I notice. I should watch yourself, Steph, she's probably a dyke.' The venom in his voice was shocking in its intensity.

Ella rose to her feet. 'I've just flown in from Houston because you requested a meeting, Mr Meyer, but I can only repeat that I am not prepared to sit at this table in order to bandy insults. If you have anything to say then please say it, otherwise I'm catching the next plane home.'

'Please sit down, Miss Kovac,' said Joseph Meyer. 'I apologize for my son's outburst. It was rude and unnecessary.' Alex glared at his father and Ella returned to her seat. 'If you want me to stick to the facts, Miss Kovac, I'll stick to the facts. If you and Stephanie persist with this Fulham project, I will finish you, it's as simple as that.' He looked directly at Stephanie. 'I suppose you think you've been very clever, Stephanie. Yes, technically, under the terms of the contract, you are free to develop other sites independently from us, but where you went wrong was to use privileged information as a director of Meyer Hotels in order to acquire the site at a knock down price. It was a breach of trust of the most serious kind and you, Miss Kovac, should not be a party to it. I must warn you that Jacob here has instructions to serve an immediate injunction upon you both if you decide to proceed.'

'I cannot see your objection –' Stephanie began.

'Can't you?' Joseph Meyer roared, he was truly terrifying when he was angry. 'The most fundamental requirement of any successful business is that the principals involved trust and respect one another totally. For some reason I can't now understand, from the first moment I met you, I believed you to be a person of integrity. I suppose, mistakenly, I based that assumption on your background. That you deceived not only me but Alex is utterly incomprehensible to me.'

'Meyers don't own me,' Stephanie said.

'That, Stephanie, is where you are wrong,' said Joseph. 'Meyers own you from the pretty shoes you are wearing to those little pearl earings of yours. I made you and I can destroy you.'

'I made myself,' said Stephanie, 'and it's your high-handed attitude which made me feel the need to branch out on my own again. I was my own person, with my own business, when I first approached you. OK, may be my business wasn't on the grand scale of Meyer, but it was successful and I was my own boss. Yes, I've learnt a lot from you and I'm grateful. You put a great deal of trust in me and I'm grateful for that, too, but when all is said and done, I am little more than an overpaid office boy. There is no decision, major or minor, that can be made without your blessing. I feel stifled, claustrophobic and that's why I need to do something on my own.' Stephanie looked directly at Alex. 'Surely you understand that, Alex?'

'What if I do,' he said, coldly, 'there are still ways and ways of doing things. 'My father and I don't always see eye to eye — you better than anyone know that but it doesn't mean to say I'd go behind his back, or he behind mine. Whatever the ups and downs of our personal relationship, to the world we present a united front. It's the only way to survive.'

'That's right,' said Joseph. His voice was slightly choked and Ella realized his son's words had moved him — he was vulnerable after all, a man like other men. It was a question of timing, choosing the right moment and now was as good as any, while tempers were momentarily cool.

Stephanie beat her to it. 'I don't believe you can serve an injunction, it's just a bluff. I've done absolutely nothing wrong,' she burst out. It was the worst thing she could have said.

'Oh, can't I?' roared Joseph. 'Well why don't you just sit back and watch me. Jacob, go prepare the papers. I'm sorry you're being involved in this Miss Kovac, but if you persist in joining Stephanie in this project, my argument is with you as much as with her. You're dealing in privileged information, too.'

'One moment,' said Ella. 'I've sat here, listened to you all screaming at one another like kids in a playground and I find it hard to believe my own ears.' She had their attention. She stood up and wandered over to the window, taking her time. At the window she turned to face them. 'Look, whether we proceed with the deal or not is no skin off my nose. As far as I'm concerned, there are other deals in other towns, in other countries. What does concern me, however, is the apparent tragic breakdown of relationship between you Meyers on the one hand and Stephanie on the other. Your partnership has become legendary in the hotel business, you know that.

You're an unlikely trio, God knows, but together you make sweet music. The flair and imagination which you have brought to the new Meyer hotels around Europe has left the other hotel groups gasping with admiration. Speaking personally, I'd never stay anywhere now but at a Meyer Hotel and I like to flatter myself I'm showing good sense and an appreciation of style.' She had them eating out of her hand now. She was talking about their baby, their creation. All three of them were flattered, seduced by pride in what she was saying, momentarily their differences forgotten. 'So,' said Ella, 'we're talking about one crummy site in Fulham. How can you be serious about letting it be responsible for breaking up a partnership which up to this moment has to have been one of the "greats" in the hotel industry? The tragedy is that if either of you win at this stage, you both lose.' She looked directly at Joseph. 'If you win, Mr Meyer, and force Stephanie to withdraw from this project, you will lose the best franchisee you are ever likely to have. If you win, Stephanie, and proceed with this project against the wishes of Mr Meyer, you will lose out on your relationship with the Meyers. Either you will have to quit or wait for your current franchise agreement to finish when, needless to say, it won't be renewed. Maybe, Stephanie, you were a little imprudent going ahead with this project without discussing it with the Meyers. Maybe, Mr Meyer, you have forgotten what it's like to be young and impetuous. I guess if I could take you back, stage by stage, through your amazing career, we could highlight several occasions where your behaviour would bear some startling similarities to Stephanie's. You are both entrepreneurs, you are both used to, and indeed thrive, on taking risks. You have both done things in your commercial life of which you are not particularly proud, as have I. We didn't get to where we are now by always playing it straight down the line. I can admit it. I wonder if you two can?'

'So, what are you suggesting, Miss Kovac?' Joseph said quietly.

'I'm suggesting a compromise. Let's go ahead with this

Fulham project but let's go ahead with it on a fifty-fifty basis. By that I mean fifty per cent Meyer, fifty per cent Stephanie and me. At the moment the project is not intended to include a hotel. Let's change that, let's build a Meyer hotel as part of the complex. Let's run the whole scheme under the Meyer banner but Stephanie and I will only put up half the capital and receive fifty per cent of the action for seeing the opportunity and masterminding the plan. Working together on this project hopefully will have a conciliatory affect on your relationship, but you have me as the filling in the sandwich, to act as arbitrator if things go wrong.'

There was a long silence. Joseph stood up, too, and came to join Ella by the window. His expression was unreadable. She retained her relaxed pose leaning nonchalantly against the window sill, but her heart was hammering. 'You know something, Miss Kovac, I now understand completely why you are so successful. You're a very sensible, intelligent young woman. I like you and I like your scheme. We'll go with it.' He swung round to Stephanie. 'Do you agree?'

'I suppose so,' said Stephanie.

'You *suppose* so, you *suppose* so!' Joseph strode across the room towards her. 'I've just let you off the hook, dropped proceedings *and* I've given you fifty per cent of the action.'

'Correction: it is us who have given you fifty per cent of the action,' Stephanie said.

For a moment there was a horrible silence, during which Ella was convinced that all the progress she had just made was about to be blown apart. Suddenly, without any warning, Joseph Meyer threw back his head and roared with laughter. 'Women!' God spare me from them, particularly smart arse women in business. OK, OK, so *you'll* give *me* fifty per cent of *your* project. I accept, gratefully, thankfully. Lady Bonham, you are too good to me.' He swept a low, theatrical bow. 'Jesus wept, have you ever heard anything like it, Alex?'

Alex made no reply and none seemed to be required. In that fleeting moment Ella began to understand Alex's predicament. Although, when the meeting had begun, it had seemed that the Meyers were the predators and Stephanie the victim, it was clear that despite all their differences, she and Joseph had a lot in common. They had started with very little and made it through their own drive and initiative. Alex had started with everything and yet he had nothing.

'OK, you guys,' said Ella, 'can we shake hands on it? I have to get some sleep, I'm bushed.'

'You must be,' said Joseph.

The four of them shook hands, formally. Ella noticed that when Stephanie shook hands with Alex, neither looked at one another. They sat together for a few minutes more, talking through the details which were necessary to set the project in motion and Ella agreed to return to London in two weeks' time, when Greg was settled in college, to start work on the site in earnest.

Five minutes later, the two women found themselves outside the boardroom door, only half-an-hour after their meeting had begun. 'Phew!' said Stephanie. She put a hand on Ella's arm and squeezed it. 'I'm grateful, truly. We were really riding for a fall there and without you, the meeting would have collapsed.'

'You and Joseph certainly do seem to have the knack of getting under each other's skin.' Ella grinned. 'Boy, he packs a punch, doesn't he?'

Stephanie nodded. 'I still wish it hadn't been necessary to give him fifty per cent of Fulham. What it means effectively is that I'm still tied to Meyer.'

'I don't think you should lose any sleep over that,' said Ella, as they went into the elevator. 'Margot's been very reticent about the financing of this project, you know. She thinks we're under-capitalized and that we're both stretching our personal resources too far. I happen to think she's right. With Meyer's name and money behind us, the project is assured of success, and that, after all, is what we are both aiming for, isn't it?'

'Yes, but at what price?' said Stephanie. 'Hell, look, I'm sorry, Ella, I'm sounding ungrateful and I'm not, truly. You handled the meeting brilliantly and I won't forget it.'

'Good,' said Ella. She leaned back against the wall of the elevator and closed her eyes for a moment.

'God, I'm a selfish bitch,' said Stephanie. 'You must be dying to get horizontal. I've got the key to your room here, let me take you to it.' Inside Ella's room, without discussion, they poured themselves large brandies from the mini bar. 'To us,' said Stephanie.

'To us,' Ella echoed.

'Have you decided what flight you're catching back to Houston?'

Ella consulted her watch. 'Jesus, it's only three o'clock, that's wonderful. I'm booked on a flight from Heathrow that leaves at eleven o'clock tomorrow morning, so I guess I'll do some catching up on sleep between now and then.'

'I tell you what,' said Stephanie, 'I have an idea. Why don't you and I have dinner together later? You have a good sleep now and I'll come and collect you at what . . . eight o'clock?'

Ella studied Stephanie in silence for a moment. 'I have an even better idea. What's happening to the Meyers tonight, will they be going back to Geneva or Paris?'

'I think they're staying in London.' Stephanie's voice sounded bleak.

'Tell me to mind my own business,' said Ella, 'but if I were you, I'd relax in a hot bath for an hour with another of these brandies and then I'd go and find Alex and sort yourselves out. It's clear there's a lot of ill feeling still running between you two and it needs sorting – for the sake of the project, yes, but much more important, for the sake of your own happiness.'

'I shouldn't think he'll want to see me,' said Stephanie.

'Well try, you've nothing to lose.'

'Except my pride,' said Stephanie.

Ella shrugged her shoulders. 'What's pride? I tell you what, don't decide now. Give me a call at, say, seven if you want us to meet for dinner. If I don't hear from you by then, I'll know you've made other plans. OK?'

'You know you're a very nice person, Ella,' said Stephanie. 'I hadn't realized just how nice until now. At the time of the Centre des Arts project, everything was so rushed I never really had a chance to get to know you. Tim kept telling me what a wonderful person you were but I didn't appreciate it.' At the mention of Tim's name, Ella visibly blanched. Stephanie smiled, 'It's OK,' she said, 'I know about you and Tim and I don't mind. I'm sorry it didn't work out for you both.'

'You *must* mind,' said Ella.

Stephanie shook her head. 'Truly, no. At the time, a little. You must admit pulling out of the project and stealing my husband, all at the same time, was a bit rich.'

'I'm not disagreeing,' said Ella, ruefully.

'Realistically though,' said Stephanie, 'Tim and I were already leading separate lives, as you well knew. I had no right to be resentful.'

'How is he?' Ella felt compelled to ask.

'Oh, Tim's fine. I don't see him very often. The girls are old enough now that they come up to London or over to Paris to see me on their own.' A question still seemed to hang in the air. 'Ah,' said Stephanie, 'you want to know if there's anyone else in his life?' Ella started to protest but Stephanie cut her short. 'As far as I know, there isn't. I wish there was but who knows, perhaps he's still pining for you. I will say this though, Ella. Now you're going to be in England a lot more, if you feel like renewing your friendship with Tim, I'll be genuinely delighted. You need have no fear it will cause any trouble between us.'

The words spoken were warm and apparently genuine, but there was an undercurrent which Ella detected but could not identify. 'What tangled lives we lead,' she said, with a laugh, in an effort to ease the tension.

'Yes, indeed,' Stephanie agreed. 'Hey, I must let you sleep.' She looked slightly embarrassed. 'If I don't see you again tonight, I'd really like to drive you to the airport tomorrow.'

'There's no need,' Ella began.

'Yes, there is. We have a lot to talk about.'

Ella grinned at her. 'OK. Now don't take this wrong, but I hope I don't see you until the morning.' The women exchanged a conspiratorial smile as Stephanie stepped out of the door.

Left alone, Ella undressed wearily. Too tired even for a shower, she slipped between the cool sheets and rested her head on the pillow. She was pleased with herself. The meeting had been a success and not only that, she was a great deal happier about the project now she knew Meyer was contributing to it. Her enthusiasm for Fulham had been a means of escaping from Aaron. She had been desperate to get away from New York, and for that reason she had been prepared to become involved on almost any terms. All along, though, Margot's diffidence about the financing had been an echo of her own doubts but now with Meyer money, the project was a sure-fire winner.

In the last moments before sleep, Stephanie's words about Tim came back to her, and in that instant she recognized what had troubled her about Stephanie's little speech of reassurance. It was insincere ... There was no doubt in Ella's mind about that. Stephanie had simply been testing the water, hoping to illicit a response from Ella as to her true feelings for Tim. What did it mean? That Stephanie still cared for Tim, or simply that she did not like the idea of him finding happiness with someone else? And what of Tim – was it possible he still loved her? She doubted it after the way she had behaved. She must be on her guard, though. She could not afford to upset Stephanie and jeopardise their deal. There was another factor, too. Her involvement in London was all about running away from one man; she had to be very careful not to run straight into the arms of another.

CHAPTER TWENTY-NINE

HOUSTON
October 1981

It was three o'clock Houston time, when Ella thankfully staggered out of the elevator and into her apartment. The wonders of modern air travel were all very well but they certainly took their toll.

'Margot, Greg, I'm home!' There was no reply, so Ella walked into the office to find Tessa hard at work at the typewriter. 'Hi,' Ella collapsed in a chair opposite her.

'Ella! That was quick. We didn't expect you back until tomorrow. How did it go?'

'Fine. How are things here?'

'OK.' Tessa consulted her pad. 'There are a few queries but nothing that can't wait.' She pushed her long, straight, dark hair back behind her ear. She was an attractive girl, of Mexican origin Ella suspected, and she took her job very seriously. 'I have a couple of leases here for you to sign.'

'I'll see to them in the morning.'

'It won't take a minute,' Tessa persisted.

'I like to check them first,' said Ella.

'Oh, but I've checked them,' said Tessa.

The girl was definitely an enthusiast. Ella smiled at her. 'Don't think I'm getting at you personally, Honey, but about four years ago, I employed a guy in New York who prepared leases for me, too. He left a couple of noughts off one of them, and the result is I'm still receiving just a few bucks a year for two floors in one of the best locations in New York City.'

'Jesus, that's awful. What did you do?'

'I sacked him,' said Ella.

Tessa grinned. 'Point taken, we'll do the leases in the morning.'

'Any calls?'

'A few but I'm putting them officially on ice.'

'OK, I give in,' said Ella, stretching. 'Where are Margot and Greg?'

Tessa gave her a slightly strange look. 'They're out to lunch, although I thought they'd be back by now.'

Ella frowned. 'Is something wrong?'

Tessa shook her head. 'No, of course not, why?'

'I mean they're getting on alright?'

'Oh yes, fine – no problems there.'

Ella stood up. 'I think I'll take a shower and lie down for a while. When they get back, tell Greg to come and wake me.'

'OK,' said Tessa, 'have a good sleep.'

Her son sitting down heavily on the end of her bed woke Ella some hours later. With the curtains drawn, the room was in semi-darkness. 'Is that you, Greg?' Ella asked.

'It certainly is, Mom, Why, were you expecting someone else? I didn't mean to disappoint you?'

'No, idiot.'

'How was the trip, did it go OK?'

'It went fine.' Ella struggled up in the bed and switched on the light. Greg was grinning at her, a little foolishly she thought. Something was not quite right with him and her tired mind tried to analyse what it was.

'We've had fun, too. We've just had the most brilliant lunch, you should have been there.' His eyes were over-bright, his cheeks flushed.

'You've been drinking, Greg,' said Ella, sternly. 'In fact if I'm not mistaken, you're pissed out of your mind.'

'Hardly that, Mom, but we did manage a couple of bottles of champagne between us.'

'Shit!' said Ella. 'What were you celebrating?'

'I don't know really,' said Greg, 'just life, I guess.' He giggled a little self-consciously.

'So, if this is the shape you're in, how's Margot doing?'

'Much the same, I guess. She's making us coffee right now. Would you like some?'

Ella consulted her watch. 'Six o'clock,' she said, 'I think I'd do better with a cocktail.'

'Good idea, we'll have one, too.'

'No, you won't,' said Ella, 'you'll stick to the coffee. Tell Margot I'll be up in a moment.'

'OK, Mom.'

The sound of their laughter penetrated even through her closed bedroom door and for a moment Ella was irritated. She tried to consider why this was as she brushed her hair. Establishing any sort of personal relationship with Margot Haigh was extremely difficult. That her son had succeeded so effortlessly should please her. After all, leaving them alone could have been a disaster. She slipped on her towelling robe. Perhaps I'm jealous, she thought. The idea appalled her and she strode out into the hall determined to cover her irritation.

They were in the kitchen. Margot was pouring out mugs of coffee and Greg was attempting, somewhat clumsily, to fix his mother a dry martini. It was Margot, though, who rivetted Ella's attention. She was dressed in a pair of designer jeans, loafers and what was clearly recognizable as an old working shirt of Greg's. Her hair hung down on to her shoulders like a young girl's instead of caught up in the severe chignon she so often wore. At first glance she almost looked a contemporary of Greg's. Ella was dumb-struck.

'Ella! How did it go?'

'OK,' said Ella, a little warily, 'I think you'll be pleased with the outcome.'

'Great, you must tell me all about it. I'm sorry we weren't here when you got back. This wretched son of yours took me out to lunch and got me drunk.'

'So I gather,' said Ella, 'though you do seem to be in slightly better shape than he does.'

'Years of experience,' said Margot, with a smile.

'One dry martini, just as you like it, complete with olive.'

Greg handed the glass to Ella with a flourish, spilling some on the kitchen floor as he did so.

'Oh Greg, you're a wreck.'

'Hey, come on Mom, where's your sense of humour?'

'Somewhere over the Atlantic, I expect,' said Ella, wearily.

'You must be absolutely exhausted,' said Margot, 'let's go and sit down.'

They took their drinks through to the sitting room, to catch the sunset, and Ella explained the deal she had struck with Joseph Meyer. As she had anticipated, Margot appeared to be very pleased but in some strange way, oddly detached. Normally Ella would have expected Margot to fire questions at her — she was a stickler for detail and liked to understand precisely what was involved. But not this evening. She asked a few perfunctory questions, confirmed her approval and then started talking about Galvaston, which she and Greg had visited the day before.

'I had forgotten how much I loved the sea,' Margot said, dreamily. 'My father used to take me sailing every weekend. Greg hired a little sailing boat and I realized I had not been sailing in all those intervening years. Strange really, when it was so much a part of my life.'

'You went sailing!' Ella was surprised. 'I didn't know you could sail, Greg?'

'I learnt when we were in Canada, though Margot's much more experienced than me. She was great.'

'Hardly,' said Margot, laughing.

Ella managed to limp through supper without falling asleep, though she found Margot and Greg's high spirits grating on her tired mind. Shortly after ten, she excused herself and it was a relief to be back in the privacy of her bedroom. What was wrong with her, she wondered? She should be pleased to see Margot so relaxed, yet somehow she found herself resenting it. There was a stack of work waiting for her on her desk, she knew, despite Tessa's reassurances and there was a message to ring Jackie which always spelt trouble. Jackie never troubled her unless something was seriously wrong. Then there was the planning of the Fulham project to consider. Suddenly it all seemed too much and Ella found herself wondering whether she really had taken on too much this time. Jet-lag, she told herself firmly, in the morning you'll feel better.

Initially she slept well but by half past twelve she found herself awake again, restless in mind and body. She decided a drink of milk might help her and was on her way out of the bedroom when she heard the sound of Greg coming out of his room. She was about to go out and greet him when something stopped her and she realized it was the stealth with which he was apparently creeping down the corridor. What was he doing, where was he going, she wondered? And then in an instant, with a terrible sinking feeling, she knew. She waited until she heard the bedroom door click and then carefully opening her own door, crept along the passage to Margot's room. A dim light showed under the door. Pressing her ear to it she could hear the sound of whispered voices, punctuated by Margot's crystal clear laugh.

Ella did not sleep again that night. Her initial reaction was to storm into the bedroom and demand to know what was going on. But she knew what was going on. It had been staring her in the face, and she could not face the embarrassment and humiliation of confronting her son in Margot's bed. As she lay, far from sleep, her mind tried to recoil from the obvious facts, but there was no escape: her eighteen year old son was having an affair with a woman who Ella knew to be well into her forties. It was inconceivable, disgusting and, above all, Ella felt a deep sense of betrayal. Margot had known of Greg since he was five years old and she knew only too well how much the boy meant to Ella. To seduce him in his own home, while Ella looked on was unforgivable. In calmer moments during that long night, Ella tried to reason the other side of the story. Was it such a bad thing, after all? Greg had to learn about women from someone and Margot probably was very experienced. However, there was no way she could reconcile herself to the relationship and by morning, hollow-eyed through lack of sleep, Ella was determined to confront them with her knowledge.

Ella was first in the kitchen the following morning. She made coffee and laid the breakfast table, just like on any other morning. Margot appeared next, her hair newly washed, still wearing the casual clothes of yesterday, belying her age. Ella found it difficult to speak at all without her voice sounding waspish, but Margot seemed oblivious.

'Shall I give Greg a call?' she asked.

'No, I'll do it,' said Ella, sharply.

She had heard Greg return to his bedroom shortly after five o'clock in the morning and therefore she was not at all surprised to find she had quite a job waking him. In the innocence of sleep, his dark curls falling into his eyes and his cheeks flushed, he looked little different from the child he had once been. The image fuelled Ella's anger so that she was only just able to contain herself long enough for Greg to stagger into breakfast in his robe, before she turned on them both. 'I know what's going on,' she burst out. 'You must take me for one hell of a fool to have imagined I wouldn't find out.'

'What do you mean, you know what's going on?' Greg said, defiantly.

Margot said nothing but she paled slightly, Ella noticed. 'Don't be ridiculous, Greg. You and Margot – ' She searched for the right words. 'I heard you go to her bedroom last night and I heard what time you came back. Don't tell me you were reading her a bedtime story.'

The smile vanished from Greg's face. He glanced apprehensively at Margot, clearly seeking her guidance as to what to say next.

'I'm sorry, Ella,' said Margot, 'we should have told you about it last night but you seemed so tired and preoccupied. We weren't going to keep it from you though, were we, Greg?' Greg shook his head.

'Keep what from me?' Ella said.

'Margot and I are in love,' Greg said, defiantly.

'Oh, don't be ridiculous,' said Ella, 'there must be nearly thirty years difference in your ages. It's absolutely revolting.'

'Is it?' said Margot quietly. 'Why?'

Ella turned her full venom on Margot. 'I just don't understand how you could have done this, Margot. I leave you alone with my son for no more than forty-eight hours and I come back to find that in my own home, you have seen fit to seduce him. Jesus, I may have said "make yourself at home" but I didn't mean you to go this far; the thought never occurred to me. It's obscene: you're even older than I am. I want you to leave, to leave now and I don't wish to ever see you again.'

'As you wish,' said Margot. She stood up.

'No, wait,' said Greg. 'How dare you speak to Margot like this, Mom. She didn't seduce me, if anything it was the other way round – not that it's any of your damned business.'

Ella struck Greg across the cheek. 'You're my son and that makes it my business. OK, Romeo, let me ask the question – how many girls have you had before Margot?'

'I don't have to listen to this,' said Greg.

'Come on, how many?'

Ella was oblivious to Greg's humiliation – he was puce with anger and embarrassment. 'Oh for Christ's sake, Mom.'

'I'll tell you how many then – none.' She turned to Margot. 'I don't mind my boy losing his innocence, it's about time he did but not like this, not in the arms of someone like you. I've often wondered about you, as indeed I am sure have all your other customers – how you get your kicks, why you've never married. Now it's obvious. Seducing young boys is clearly your particular fetish, but don't you think an eighteen-year-old virgin is going a little too far? You're in the wrong profession, Margot. You'd have been better suited as a hooker than a banker.'

'Stop it!' Greg burst out. 'What the hell gives you the right to speak to Margot like this. You, of all people, the *daughter* of a hooker yourself! Margot's worth ten of you, and me. She had the most terrible childhood, yet she's risen above it all and really made something of her life. I'm proud to know her, proud to be counted as her friend and I won't have anyone abuse her as you've just done.'

'Get out,' Ella screamed, 'get out of here, both of you.'

Margot moved uncertainly towards the door. 'Go,' Ella spat out. 'Now.'

They went, Greg shutting the kitchen door behind him. For a moment Ella stood in stunned silence and then she collapsed at the kitchen table and burst into tears. How could he have said that, how could he have used the knowledge of what her mother had been as a weapon against her – her own son. She had believed that she could forgive him anything – whatever he did, whatever he said – but not this. It seemed as though her heart had turned to stone. How could he, how could he . . . At the thought of the pain he had inflicted, for a moment she was tempted to run after him and tell him that her childhood competed very favourably in terms of deprivation with anything that Margot could dream up; to tell him that he owed his existence to a gang rape on a fifteen year old body. She half-rose and then sufficient sense returned to make her sink once more into her chair. No, never, never. Whatever the provocation, she would never tell him that. To even consider it must mean she was losing control. She must stay calm and think. Margot was leaving, that was good. When Margot had gone, she would try and explain to Greg a little of what she knew about his first love. It was impossible to say anything truly derogatory about Margot because she knew nothing about her, but clearly, she lived an odd-ball sort of life. Besides, there was no point in pursuing their relationship. Margot spent most of her working life in London and Greg would be off to college in five days. Perhaps she had over-reacted – yet, no, the feeling of outrage was justified. She dried her eyes and poured herself a fresh cup of coffee, with shaking hands.

There was a light tap on the kitchen door. It was Greg. The anger had left him, his face seemed calm and composed. 'I thought I'd better let you know we're just going, Mom.'

'What do you mean, *we're* just going?' Ella said, rising out of her seat.

'Like I said, I'm going with Margot.'

Ella was too stunned to react for a moment. 'Where?' she said, at last when her strength returned.

'New York. Not to Gregory Buildings, I'll be staying with Margot.'

'Margot doesn't have an apartment in New York,' said Ella.

'No matter, I'll be staying with her.'

'Greg, this is madness.'

'Mom, don't start again or we'll both say things we regret.'

'We've already done that, I hope,' said Ella.

'Perhaps,' Greg acknowledged. 'I am sorry for what I said about your Ma but you had no right to speak to Margot like that.'

'I had every right to speak to Margot like that,' said Ella. 'Where is she?'

'She's gone down in the elevator. She felt you and I might want a few moments alone.'

'Then let her go, Greg. The sooner she's out of both our lives, the better.'

'No,' said Greg, 'I've already told you I'm going with her.'

'What about college? You start college next week,' said Ella.

'I can't think about college at the moment or about the future at all. I just know I don't want to stay here with you and I do want to go with Margot. That's as far as my thinking takes me.'

'Greg, three days ago you hadn't even met her.' Ella tried desperately to stay calm.

'So?' said Greg, 'Now I have met her and she's without doubt the most wonderful woman I have ever met and am ever likely to meet.'

'You're talking like a child,' said Ella. 'What can you possibly know about anybody in three days?'

'Exactly,' said Greg, cheerfully, 'that's why I'm aiming to learn a whole lot more. I'll call you.' Before Ella could protest further, he had gone, across the hall and out of the front door of the flat.

Ella was too stunned to follow. She picked up her coffee and went to stand by the kitchen window. Her legs felt weak, almost too weak to hold her. She clung to the window sill for support. Of all the women she knew, it seemed to Ella that Margot Haigh was the most unlikely candidate to be having an affair with her son. She was so cool, so remote, so confident and self-assured as to where she was going, so certain that right was on her side. Throughout their association, it had always seemed to Ella that Margot was her rock, the yardstick against which she judged the right and wrongs of the commercial world. That was a laugh. How could Margot have just walked out of the apartment, taking her teenage son with her, without even a word? That, too, was out of character. Margot always dealt with problems head-on, never shirking responsibility nor dodging the issue. Yet this time she had skulked out of the building and left Greg to do the dirty work.

A key sounded in the lock. Ella ran to the hall, expecting it to be Greg already returned and repentant. Instead it was Tessa, looking hot and flustered, a pile of files under her arm. 'Oh, Tessa, it's you.' Ella was close to tears.

'Of course it's me. Hey, what's wrong, Ella, you look awful?'

'Oh, nothing.'

'Is it something to do with Greg? I've just seen him leave, case in hand. Have you two had a bust up or something?'

'You could say that,' said Ella, turning away, anxious to avoid an explanation.

'Because of Margot?' Tessa asked, tentatively.

Ella swung round and stared at her. 'You knew?'

Tessa shrugged her shoulders. 'Only guessed. Yesterday, the way they were behaving together, I thought there had to be something going on.'

'You might have told me,' Ella burst out.

'I'm sorry but what was there to tell you? Greg and Margot seemed kind of friendly? Anyway, for all I knew you might have known all about it and approved.'

'Approved!' How could I approve? She's old enough to be his grandmother, never mind his mother.'

'Look, I'm really sorry,' said Tessa, 'but it's no good yelling at me.'

'You're right,' said Ella. 'I'm sorry, I guess I'm just so worried. They've gone off to New York together and Greg's due to be at college next week. He says he's in love with her. The whole thing's crazy and I just don't know when and where it will end at the moment. All I do know for sure is that Margot Haigh is a tough lady. She always gets what she wants and at the moment, it seems, she wants my son.'

CHAPTER THIRTY

HOUSTON
October 1981

Ella replaced the receiver and sat down at her desk, glad that Tessa was not there to witness the call she had just received. It had been Greg to tell her the astonishing news that he and Margot were now in London and that he was living at her house in Chelsea.

While Ella had viewed her son's encounter with Margot as likely to have an unsettling affect on him, it had never occured to her that he would go to London with her. For one thing, there was the practical difficulty – he did not have the money so clearly Margot must have paid for his airline ticket. The thought distressed Ella still further. Margot was treating her son quite literally like a 'toy boy', and wrecking his life in the process. She considered what she could say to his college. That he'd been involved in an accident, that he was ill? Yet Greg had been quite clear: he was not now going to college. He would look for a job in London, he had told Ella. He had never really wanted to study law anyway, she had pressured him into it. It was the speed with which her son had walked out of the life they had both mapped out together so carefully which astonished her. Ten days ago, Greg had just been a normal boy like any other, humouring his doting mother with a few days at home before going off to college: confident, happy about his future and generally at peace with the world. Yet now he had thrown it all aside, for what? An affair with a woman older than his own mother. The stupidity and the waste of it was upsetting enough, but in the brief telephone call from Greg just now, Ella felt sure she had sensed his own bewilderment. He did not seem to know what had hit him either. How could Margot have done this? How could she? For a moment Ella considered telephoning her but there seemed little point. Margot was not going to relinquish her hold on Greg in response to an impassioned telephone plea from his mother. It would take more, a lot more, to shake him free of Margot's clutches.

Slowly, as Ella sat there, her mind cleared and a plan emerged. She studied it from all angles and considered the pros and cons with steely detachment. In business, many people had found to their cost that despite her childlike appearance, Ella could be as ruthless as anyone, particularly if she felt threatened. But no one before had threatened her son and she recognized in herself at that moment that there was nothing she would not do, nothing she would stop at, in order to protect him.

'Who?' said an astounded voice.

'Ella, Ella Kovac. Surely you haven't forgotten me already. Jesus, it's not been that long.'

'Ella!' Michael Gresham's voice sounded stunned and totally disbelieving, but he rallied quickly, his Irish charm rising to the occasion. 'I knew this morning when I got out of bed that it was going to be a good day. It's really great to hear from you, Ella. You're doing real well in this town – the mall's taking great shape, isn't it? I pass it every day on the way to work.'

Ella let him ramble on for a few moments. 'Michael, I need a favour. Could you join me for lunch, so we can discuss it?'

He hesitated only a split second. 'I guess I owe you one.'

'I guess you do,' said Ella.

It did not surprise Ella that she was not at all distressed at meeting Michael Gresham again. Whatever feelings she'd had about their relationship seemed to have been blotted out by the horror of Alice's death, followed by the pain of her parting from Aaron. Michael was simply a face from her past – familiar, recognizably attractive, yet moving her not at all. He looked as sleek and contented with life as he always did. He kissed her cheek and they settled down in a corner of the restaurant.

'I never thought to hear from you again,' Michael said, 'and I can't say I have anyone to blame but myself. It was stupid but I was lonely and you'd been away a long time . . .'

'Michael, for heaven's sake,' said Ella, 'there's no need to go over all that. I was hurt at the time, yet being realistic I knew our relationship had no serious, long term future. We're two different kinds of people. It doesn't suit me to have casual relationships, it doesn't suit you to have serious ones. Anyway, I'm not here to talk about the past.'

Michael looked obviously relieved. 'OK, so what can I do for you?'

Having ordered, Ella told him briefly of the affair between Greg and Margot Haigh.

'Jesus!' said Michael, 'the boy was only in short pants five mintues ago. Mind you, I always told you —'

'Shut it, Michael,' said Ella. 'You and I always got along just fine, provided you didn't criticize Greg. Don't start now, *please*.'

The strain in her voice and her pale, anxious face, produced in Michael a sudden, unaccustomed tenderness. He reached out and squeezed her hand. 'I'm sorry, that was tactless of me. Look, whatever may have gone on before between us, I'm always your friend, you can be sure of that. Just tell me what I can do to help.'

'Keep a watching brief on the Houston operation for me while I'm in London for the next few weeks.'

Michael smiled. 'Is that all?'

'It's enough,' said Ella. 'I wouldn't ask you but I don't know who else I can rely upon in Houston. I have a good girl working for me down here called Tessa, who operates from my apartment, but she only has the experience to deal with the more mundane problems at the moment. Jackie is fully occupied keeping New York going and it's just not the kind of responsibility I can hand over to anyone. Do you see my problem?'

'Of course I see your problem,' said Michael. 'How long do you expect to be away?'

'I promised Stephanie I'd spend a week in London in a couple of weeks time. I'd like to allow myself two weeks to try and sort out this problem with Greg and then stay on for the week with Stephanie. It wouldn't be worthwhile coming back to Houston in between unless there's a real crisis.'

'Of course not. Where are we now?' He glanced at his watch. '25th October. What you're really saying is that you'd like me to keep a watching brief for the month of November. Right?'

'That would be wonderful,' said Ella, 'but I'm not intending this to be a favour. I expect you to charge me the right rate for the job.'

Michael considered for a moment. 'If you're going to be involved in this project in Fulham, I guess you'll be spending a good deal of time in London in the next few months, irrespective of your troubles with Greg?'

'Yes, I suppose so,' said Ella.

'If that's the case,' said Michael, 'then I will charge you fees. I'll put one of my clerks quite specifically in charge of your business and we'll set the whole thing up as a proper commercial relationship. If we do that, you won't find it difficult to call on me whenever you need me. What do you say?'

The wisdom of his remark was obvious. 'It's a good idea,' said Ella. 'I am grateful, Michael, truly.'

He grinned. 'It's what friends and lawyers are for.'

They spent the rest of the afternoon running through Ella's various Houston projects with Tessa in the office. Tessa and Michael got along straight away and Ella made a mental note to warn her of the dangers of Michael Gresham's charms. By six o'clock that evening, Ella knew her business was in good hands.

'How about dinner?' Michael suggested. 'Just to seal the agreement?'

Ella shook her head. 'I don't want to start all that again.'

'Look, I said dinner. It isn't a big deal, I'm not saying stay the night with me.'

'I know, I know, Michael. I also know the power of your persuasive charm. Just at the moment I'm worried, lonely and consequently very vulnerable. It would be safer to say, thanks, but no thanks.'

It was an unusual speech for Ella. Michael, not particularly sensitive to other people's feelings, was aware that her admission of loneliness showed just how much the boy had upset her. Not for the first time, the hold Greg Kovac seemed to have over his mother irritated and angered Michael Gresham, but there was no point in worrying about it – it was not his problem any longer. Ella was part of his past. She was right. They were two very different people and attracted though he still was to her, he recognized they did not belong together.

'OK, it was just a thought. You'll call just as soon as you reach London?'

'Yes, of course,' said Ella. 'I'm flying up to New York tomorrow morning, I'll spend a couple of days there and I aim to be in London by the weekend.'

'Bless you, Sweetheart. I hope you have success. How do you intend to handle this wayward son of yours?'

Ella looked at him, with her round brown eyes. 'I'm going to find out all there is to know about Margot Haigh.' She spoke the name with bitterness. 'There's something odd about that woman, about her past, I'm sure of it, I feel it. I'm going to find out what it is and when I find it, I'm going to use it to break her hold on Greg.'

Michael shuddered inwardly. The venom with which Ella spoke made him realize that she would stop at nothing to achieve her goal. 'Are you sure you're doing the right thing, Honey?'

'I don't know what you mean,' said Ella, coolly.

'Why not let the boy have his fling?'

'You have to be joking,' said Ella, 'he's ruining his life.'

'Just make sure that if someone *is* ruining his life, it is

Greg, not you,' said Michael. 'Maybe he's running away with Margot Haigh because he can't take the pressure of your relationship.'

'Pressure! What pressure? Don't be ridiculous,' said Ella, hotly. 'He's been away all summer and he's supposed to be at college now. That's not pressure.'

'You're a tough lady, you are also highly successful. It's not an easy act to follow. This Margot . . . maybe she's less demanding, less difficult to live up to.'

'Margot! You have to be joking!' said Ella. 'I'm the proverbial wilting violet compared with Margot.'

'Jesus!' said Michael, with feeling. 'Then I hope to God I don't meet her on a dark night. Perhaps I underestimated that boy.'

Alone in her apartment, Ella went through the motions of packing up for her return to New York. Michael's words had disturbed her for they had made her question what up to now had been a firm decision. She sat on the edge of her bed, going over and over in her mind the alternative ways of handling the Greg/Margot affair. Yet all her instincts told her it was a relationship she must break and fast, and if that was the case, then she recognized pleading with Greg was pointless. It was Margot she had to get to, Margot she had to destroy if necessary, for the sake of her son.

Sitting there alone, a sudden longing for Aaron swept over her. Last time there had been trouble between herself and Greg, Alice and Aaron had been there to help, to act as the buffer, to give them security and reassurance against which to act out their difficulties. The more she thought about it, the more the idea grew. Why not once again turn to Aaron for help? After all, wasn't he Greg's godfather, wasn't William Greg's best friend? They would be able to counsel and advise her as to whether she was doing the right thing. Indeed, they might well have some influence over Greg in a way she had not. It occurred to Ella that they might already know about Margot. After all, Greg had spent some days with her in New York and it would seem unlikely that he had failed to tell his best friend he would not be going to college after all.

Relief flooded through her. She would ring Aaron now and meet him, perhaps tomorrow, for lunch maybe, in a restaurant – somewhere safe and neutral. Talking about Greg's problems would help them to start communicating again, help them to re-establish their relationship on its old footing, or perhaps ... she hardly dared form the thought ... perhaps there might be a future for them after all. She found herself smiling as she lifted the receiver and dialled the familiar number.

The phone rang for some time, and she was on the point of putting it down when a female voice answered, unmistakably young, girlish almost. 'Hello, Dr Connors' apartment. How may I help you?' The voice was mocking and amused.

Ella stumbled over the words, 'Could I speak to Dr Connors, please?'

'I'm sorry but he's in the bathtub right now. Can I ask him to call you back?' There was definite laughter in her voice.

Ella was stunned. 'No, no, it's alright.'

'Just as you like, bye.' The phone went dead.

Ella replaced the receiver slowly. So, Aaron had a new woman in his life. The thought brought a pain so sharp it momentarily took her breath away. How could he? She forgot all about Alice, all she could think was how Aaron had betrayed her love, her caring over all the long years they had known each other. So ... he did not love her, and clearly saw no future for them. At least she now knew the position and in a way it was a kind of release. She was free to concentrate on Greg now and certainly she could manage without Aaron Connors' help. This fight was a personal one, to save her son. She did not need anybody to tell her she was doing the right thing, she knew she was. It was a battle she had to win, and instinctively she knew she could.

CHAPTER THIRTY-ONE

LONDON
November 1981

It had to be the worst yet. The pain behind his eyes had the strong, steady beat of a tom-tom. His mouth was dry and the after-taste was that of fish on the turn. His stomach, so sorely abused, seemed to be twisting and surging in mute protest, desperate for an opportunity to spill its contents. There had been a thousand hangovers in a hundred different cities, but never one like this, or so it seemed that particular morning.

To Ella, seated with some distaste on the only decent chair in the scruffy, dirty, little office, Toby Paradise, standing by the window, hands in pockets, seemed quite at ease. Yet all his concentration was aimed at avoiding the betrayal of his condition. His hands were screwed into fists and the tick below his right eye danced a jig, out of control. He gazed unseeingly through a patch in the window pane, where he had wiped away the grime on some previous occasion, though why he could not imagine. The view was of a filthy grey brick wall, which separated his office from the main railway line into Paddington Station. At that moment, a train thundered past. Toby winced, uncertain whether the pain of the noise was worth it, just to give him a few more seconds to collect his thoughts, before attempting to deal with this wretched woman and her apparently wayward son.

The noise of the train subsided. 'OK', he said, 'what do you want?' His voice was gravelly and deep, the result of too many cigarettes, too many late nights and too much booze. He stared at Ella aggressively and her heart sank. She had acted on a whim, asking Stephanie's advice as to whether she could recommend a private investigator. Knowing so few people in London, she did not know who else to ask and she had been surprised when Stephanie instantly gave her a name and a recommendation.

'I use him when I need commercial information,' Stephanie had said. 'He's not a particularly savoury character but he's good.' Ella had been anxious not to prolong the conversation, in case Stephanie asked her why she wanted the help of a private investigator, and so this was the extent of the information she had on the unlikely-named Toby Paradise.

Now she cleared her throat, suddenly reluctant to begin. 'M-my eighteen-year-old son was due to start college last week,' she said. 'I left him in my apartment in Houston, while I came over to London on business, briefly. On my return, I found that he was having an affair with a colleague of mine, a merchant banker. She's half English, half Korean and she's in her mid-forties.' Toby Paradise showed no surprise whatsoever, so Ella continued, slightly encouraged. 'When I made an attempt to break up the relationship, my son simply left home. He's now living in London, with the woman. He's lost his chance to go to college this year and I'm worried about him, both on moral grounds and because he's clearly thrown away his future.'

'If he's eighteen,' said Toby, 'I suppose the law can't help you?'

'No,' said Ella, 'that's not the way I want to handle it. I know any tactics I try direct with Greg will fail at the moment – he's in no mood to listen. The only way I can split them up is to get at the woman. Her name is Margot Haigh, she's a director of Joshkers bank, she's single and she's something of an enigma. I've known her for twelve, thirteen years, she handles most of my commercial banking but talking to some of her other customers, it seems that, like me, no one knows her well. It's a shot in the dark, I'll admit, but I have a feeling that the reason she is so private about her personal life is because she has something to hide. I want you to find out what that something is and then I can confront her with it.'

'Blackmail her with it, you mean?' said Toby Paradise.

Ella was instantly on the defensive. 'I'm not asking you to make a moral judgement, Mr Paradise, I'm simply asking whether you want the job or not.'

'Yes, I know.' He flipped open a packet of cigarettes and offered one to Ella. She shook her head. 'I just like to get my facts straight. You want me to dig up some dirt on Miss Haigh, something sufficiently juicy that you can threaten to disclose it unless she gets the hell out of your son's life. Am I right, yes or no?,

'Yes,' said Ella. She looked at him doubtfully. 'You think it's wrong of me?'

'As you say, Mrs Kovac, I'm not here to make a moral judgement. I just like to know how my information is going to be used in order to do the best possible job.'

'So, you'll take the job?' said Ella.

'I didn't say that. Tell me, why the hell don't you just let your boy have his fling? Sounds to me like he's having a great time, shacked up with a lady banker, seeing something of a new city. I take it he's not familiar with London?' Ella shook her head. 'Well, hell, Mrs Kovac, it seems to me that you should let this thing ride. They'll soon be pissed off with one another. Either he'll start eyeing up younger crumpet or she'll get tired of changing his nappies.'

'It's not that simple,' said Ella.

'Isn't it?' Toby Paradise drew heavily on his cigarette. 'Far be it from me to talk myself out of a job, but it seems to me you're getting a little uptight here. Kids grow up, they make their own mistakes – you did, I did. Sometimes over-protection rebounds. It's you who may get hurt. Hell, if he finds out about this, he may never speak to you again.'

'Do you have any children, Mr Paradise?' There was an edge to Ella's voice.

'Yes, I have two. I'm divorced from their mother so I don't see them that much, but I know for sure that when my son's eighteen I'm not going to start telling him who he should be sleeping with.'

Ella stood up brusquely. 'Perhaps I'd better find somebody

else to handle this case, someone who understands what I'm trying to do.'

For a moment, Toby was tempted to let her go but the woman intrigued him. She was his sort of woman, small, petite and absurdly young-looking to have a child of eighteen. 'You can go somewhere else if you wish,' he said, 'but I'll get the information you want and I'm cheap.' He looked around his tiny office despairingly. 'As you can see, my overheads are low.'

For a moment Ella hesitated and then she smiled. There was something oddly appealing about the man — his total honesty, perhaps. He was attractive, too, in a crude way, with dark brown hair, a little too long and a good physique. His dress was appalling, though: ancient, baggy corduroy trousers and an awful tweed jacket in a sort of putty colour which at the moment matched his complexion. As she watched him, he put his hand on the back of the chair in which she had been sitting as if to steady himself. 'Are you feeling OK, Mr Paradise?'

He grinned at her. 'Actually, no, I feel dreadful. I had an affair with a whisky bottle last night. Black coffee and a run round the park is probably what I *need*. What I *want* is some more of the same. How about you and I adjourning to the pub round the corner? You can tell me all you know about this Margot Haigh, while I sort out the demands of my liver. What do you say?'

'It sounds a sensible plan,' said Ella.

St. Annes Road, Reading, depressed Toby Paradise beyond belief. It had seen better days: the Victorian terraced houses must have been attractive once and they could be again but currently they were trapped in lower-middle-class respectability. There was no feeling of community spirit, each family seemed to have barricaded itself against the world. An intriguing variety of lace curtains, designed to keep out not only the prying gaze of others but fresh air and sunlight as well, served to heighten the effect. He was disappointed. Although Ella Kovac had been unable to provide him with a photograph of Margot Haigh, he saw her as an exotic bloom – the anglo-oriental mix was usually a good one. He envisaged a willowy, exotic creature with pale olive skin, an image very much at odds with the environment in which he found himself. Heaving a sigh, he threw a cigarette butt into the gutter and walked up the impossibly neat path to number nine.

The bell, when he rang it, had the chime of an ice-cream van and made him shudder. There was a long pause, followed at last by hurrying footsteps, accompanied by the distant sound of a wailing baby. He squared his shoulders and put on his most affable, avuncular expression. The door opened. He had been expecting an elderly woman. Instead a little, brown, mousy creature of no more than twenty-two or twenty-three, stared up at him with anxious eyes. 'I was looking for Mrs Haigh,' he said reproachfully.

She looked blank for a moment and then her brow cleared. 'Oh, Mrs Haigh. She died a year back. We bought the house from her . . .' she searched for the word.

'Executors?' Toby suggested, helpfully.

'Yes, that's it.' The baby's howls in the background grew to fever-pitch. She glanced over her shoulder.

'Do you know anything about the Haigh family? I'm trying to trace them.

The girl shook her head. 'No,' she said. 'I knew of them, of course, I've lived round here all my life. Mrs Haigh had just the one son, his name's Terry. He lives in London somewhere but I don't have the address.'

'And a daughter?'

The girl shook her head, and then much to Toby's relief, corrected herself. 'Oh, unless you mean the girl from Korea?'

'Yes, that's the one, Margot.'

'Yes, Margot. I don't know anything about her. She was very clever. I think she left these parts a long time ago.'

'And there's no one left in the area who has any close connection with the family?' He could see a wary look creeping into the girl's eyes. Now was the moment for his explanation. He might as well try it out on her for want of anyone else. He liked to give his stories a dummy run. 'Perhaps I'd better explain,' he said. 'I work for Joshkers Bank, that's where Miss Haigh works.' The girl nodded, immediately impressed he could tell. 'Our Chairman has recently died,' Toby continued, warming to his theme, 'and a new Chairman has been appointed. I've been asked, by him, to find out something about Miss Haigh's background, because she's due for fairly major promotion and along with giving her the new position, he also wants to make her a presentation for all her years of service at the bank. He is anxious to get away from the usual stuff – you know, a gold watch, that sort of thing – so he asked me to find out a little bit about her, what her tastes are, so he can decide what to give her.' It was the most implausible story, even given the fact he was wearing his one and only suit for the occasion. It made Toby cringe but much to his relief, the girl seemed completely satisfied.

'I knew she was doing well,' she said. There was a silence between them while Toby turned over in his mind what his next step should be. Tracking down all the Haighs in London seemed to be the only option open. He was about to ask the girl if she had any idea where Terry Haigh lived when suddenly she said, 'Dick, of course! You should have a word with Dick Simpson, he should be able to help.'

'Dick?' Toby queried, his spirits rising slightly.

The baby was screaming again. 'Oh, look, would you mind waiting a moment while I go and fetch her.' The woman disappeared, leaving Toby on the doorstep, trying to guess who Dick might be. She returned moments later, with one of the most unattractive babies Toby had ever seen. It was over-weight, purple in the face from exertion, its nose was running profusely and it was dribbling. He could not get away quick enough. 'Dick Simpson,' he prompted, urgently.

'Oh yes, that's right, he was a friend of Terry's. Well, still is, they were at school together, and then in the Army. They were both stationed in Korea, I'm sure and it was there, you know, that Terry came across Margot and brought her back for his Mum to adopt. I bet Dick will be able to help – well, if you're quick, that is.' She glanced at her watch.

'How do you mean?' Toby asked.

'Well, he's a boozer, he can never keep a job because of the drink. He'll be down the Coach and Horses in quarter of an hour and then you'll have difficulty getting any sense out of him for the rest of the day. That's how I know about him really – my uncle runs the Coach and Horses and says Dick pays for his annual holiday by the amount he drinks during the year.'

Toby brightened visibly. Clearly this Dick Simpson had potential. 'Can you tell me where I can find him then, Love?'

The street in which Dick Simpson lived was depressingly like St Annes Road, except that it was one grade down. The same houses, the same basic architecture but the inhabitants had not the same amount of money to spend. The lace curtains were still there but they were grubby. The little squares of garden at the front were ill-kept and largely used to house dustbins. The gate leading to Dick Simpson's house was hanging off its hinges and there was a broken pane in the window of the front room. When Toby pressed the bell, nothing happened. He attacked a rather dilapidated door knocker instead.

Dick Simpson was a big man, he towered over Toby. He had a hefty frame which once must have been very powerful but had now gone to seed. His paunch lapped well over his belt and his face was an expensive purple and puffy. Nonetheless, the clear blue eyes that gazed out from between the folds of flesh were friendly and amused. This man might be going to seed but he knew what he was doing and was enjoying the process. Toby warmed to him instantly. 'Dick Simpson?'

'Yeh, that's right.'

'My name's Toby Paradise. I . . .' Dick Simpson threw back his head and roared with laughter. The laughter shook his heavy jowls, his paunch, indeed his whole frame. Tears squeezed themselves out of the corners of his eyes. Toby waited patiently until he had gained control of himself again. 'It may be a joke to you, Mate, but I've had to live with it all these years.'

'You're kidding – you mean it was the name you were born with?'

'That's right,' said Toby. 'My father was an American, they go in for strange surnames over there.' Dick Simpson seemed satisfied. 'Look, I was given your name because I need some information on Margot Haigh.'

'Margot, really! Why?' The eyes were shrewd and instantly Toby sensed that his prepared story would be not so easily accepted by this man. He needed to stall for time and blunt Dick's perceptions with a few drinks before he explained the situation. 'Look,' said Toby, 'it's a long, complicated story but I gather you're the man I should be talking to. Is there a local pub round here where we could have a few jars and discuss it?'

Dick's face lit up. 'A man after my own heart. Wait there, I'll fetch my coat.'

Two pints of beer and two rum chasers later, Toby judged it was right to try out his story. Dick swallowed it, hook line and sinker. 'How much money are you planning to spend on this gift?' he asked.

Toby shrugged. 'Five or six hundred pounds, I imagine, maybe more.'

'Jesus, the bank must think a lot of her.'

'They do.'

'Funny to think of that snotty-nosed little brat ending up a banker in the City of London.

'Tell me about the first time you met her,' Toby said. 'No wait, let me get in another round of drinks.'

Settled in a corner of the bar, Dick Simpson began. 'It was a bastard of a war – before your time I should think.'

'I was a kid,' Toby said, 'but I remember reading about it.'

'There were dreadful atrocities. The Commies, they were bastards, worse than the Japanese in the Second World War. The things they did to people. It was our Vietnam, of course. The North Koreans poured into South Korea, and we, that is the United Nations Force, moved in to sort out the mess. Everyone suffered.'

338

'I take it you didn't enjoy your time in Korea?'

'Not bloody likely,' said Dick, 'it's a terrible country. Boiling hot in summer – move so much as a muscle and you broke out in a sweat – and freezing in winter. The water supplies were always short and if you were lucky enough to avoid a Communist bullet, you caught every sort of God-damn awful disease known to man. It was hell.' He took a long draught of beer. 'Terry and I were lucky. We were with the Royal Engineers. We saw plenty of action but a lot of our work involved building bridges and so on – it took some of the heat off us. It was late on in the war when we met Margot. Oh, three months before the end, four perhaps. We found her when we were on patrol one day, four or five miles from Seoul. She was terrified, poor child, starving and in rags. She did not know whether we were friends or enemies. In fact Terry had quite a job catching her, she tried to run away from us.'

'How old was she?'

Dick hesitated. 'Twelve, as it turned out but she looked older. She was tall, unlike the rest of the chinks. That was because she was only half Korean, of course; her father was English, we later discovered.

'How come she was in such a state?'

'Her parents had been killed in a bombing raid on Seoul and she had nowhere to go. There were thousands of kids like that who were lost. Some died, some of the girls ended up in brothels, and then there were the lucky ones who worked for the Army, as houseboys or cooks. Our job was to repair a road that particular day and we hadn't time to mess around with kids, but she was in such a pitiful state we took her along. She stayed with us for nearly a week, eating what we ate, living as we lived. We dressed her in some spare army uniform. One or two of the men showed some interest in her – she had a lovely figure – but Terry wouldn't have it, he was very protective towards her. Of course she was different from the usual run of local girls, because she spoke perfect English. She was actually quite helpful to us with her local knowledge of the area. Well, after about a week, as I say, we went back to base and we handed her over to the WVS, reckoning it was the safest place for her.'

Toby looked blank. 'The WVS?'

'Women's Voluntary Service. In their wisdom, the British Army decided what we needed was a few women about the place to look after our needs.' He saw Toby's surprised expression. 'No, no, nothing like that. They were nice girls, wonderful girls, they were literally responsible for the Army's welfare. They wrote letters home for some of the boys who couldn't write, listened to our problems, advised on girl-friends, ran the canteen and organized entertainment for us. Bloody good they were at it, too. Anyway, Margot stayed on with them. The war ended, Terry and I didn't feel ready to go home and so we spent our leave in Japan, returning to Korea for a few months to join the United Nations Peace-keeping Force.'

'Stop there,' said Toby, 'I'll get another round of drinks.'

'You know something, you're a real gentleman,' Dick insisted.

It took some time to interest Dick in the subject of Margot Haigh again and it worried Toby. As was often the way with severe alcoholics, it did not take much drink for Dick to reach the point where he was badly slurring his words. At last, Toby was able to turn him back to Margot, away from a long, rambling story which was largely incoherent. 'So, when you came back from leave, after the war, you obviously met up with Margot again?' he persisted.

'Who?' Dick Simpson asked.

'Margot, the little Korean kid.'

'Oh, yeh, well when we came back from Japan, the war was over. We had more time on our hands, of course, and so we went to see how she was getting on. She was still with the WVS. They were very busy, helping the poor devils who needed repatriation.'

'How do you mean?' Toby asked.

'The prisoners of war, a lot of them were in a terrible state. Their families back home didn't know what had happened to them. In many cases they were presumed dead and in many cases they were half-dead. The women worked like the very devil to sort them out. They were stationed at Britannia Camp. There must have been, oh, a thousand men who passed through their hands.'

'And Margot, what of Margot?'

Dick Simpson smiled. 'She'd cleaned up real nice. They'd got her a smart little uniform. That little khaki dress certainly did show off her figure. I should think she did more to give the prisoners of war a reason to go on living than anything else. Anyway, we took her out a few times and then she told us her one idea was to go to England. She said Korea was finished for her, now her parents were dead and her father had always told her so much about England, she thought she would like to go there. I thought it was just a kid's pipe dream but Terry took it very seriously. Anyway, eventually he fixed it up and she came over to England in a troop ship and was adopted by his mother. They soon found out at school what a bright kid she was. She had only been in England five years when she went to Oxford University. She had a lot of determination, that one.'

'Do you see her much now?'

'No, I'm not in her league any more. She sees Terry, though, regular enough. She goes to visit his wife and family – takes the kids presents, that sort of thing.'

'You must give me Terry's address, I'd like to go and talk to him.' It took some minutes to extract the address from Dick Simpson. His hand was shaking too badly to write now and his eyes seemed barely to focus. God protect me from such a fate, Toby thought. He loved his booze but it wasn't ruining his life – not yet, at any rate.

It was time to go. There was clearly nothing more he was going to get out of Dick Simpson. The guy was almost asleep, lolling back in his chair. Toby stood up and then hesitated as a thought struck him. 'Dick, there's one thing I don't understand. How come she's called herself Margot Haigh? I would have thought she'd have kept her father's name. After all, she was twelve when he died. It wasn't like she was adopted as a little kid.'

Dick's eyes opened. 'Well, that was her name, wasn't it? Having married Terry, his name became hers.'

'Married Terry!' Toby said, 'when did she do that?'

'While we were still in Korea. She left the WVS and she and Terry married. They lived in a little flat as there weren't enough married quarters to go round, a nice little place on the outskirts of Seoul.'

Toby sat down again. 'But I thought you said she was twelve when you found her; she couldn't have been much more than thirteen when she married at that rate.' Clearly in his drunken state Dick had got his facts wrong.

Dick Simpson's eyes suddenly snapped into focus. 'I'm not supposed to talk about the marriage,' he said, like a small child who's been found out doing something wrong. 'Forget what I said about the marriage.'

Toby put a hand on Dick's arm. 'Look, we're pals, right? I'm not going to tell anybody anything you tell me.'

'No, no, that's right, we're pals.'

'Would you like another drink, Dick?'

'Yeh, I would.'

On Toby's return from the bar, Dick was asleep and it took some time to wake him up. 'About this marriage,' Toby said, carefully. 'How come it happened if she was so young?'

'She lied about her age,' said Dick. 'She had no papers, of course, they'd all been destroyed in the bombing. She said she was seventeen and she looked it, too. It was only when we got back to England that the truth of her age came out. Terry's Mum was a real old battleaxe and she saw through the girl at once, realized how young she was and of course she was terrified her boy would end up in prison for, well, you know ... with an under-age girl. Mrs Haigh kept the girl with her, made her son leave home and legally adopted Margot.'

'So the marriage was never annulled?'

'I don't know,' said Dick, 'I shouldn't think so. No one knew about it in this country you see, except me, and I wasn't telling.'

'Oh no, of course not,' said Toby. Dick was drifting off to

sleep and Toby judged it was time to leave before he was asked to make any promises of silence. 'See you around, Dick,' he said, and then made a fast exit out of the door.

In the car on the M4 on the way back up to London, Toby Paradise's mind was racing. If Terry Haigh had married Margot in Korea, was the marriage valid in England? OK, to protect himself Terry had clearly pretended it had never taken place but the fact remained that it had. If Terry Haigh had not acknowledged the existence of a Korean marriage in Britain and he had subsequently re-married, that marriage might well be bigamous. Margot Haigh had never married so there was no hope of bringing pressure to bear there. However, the fact was Terry Haigh had. This in itself did not give Ella Kovac the ammunition she wanted, unless Margot was particularly fond of Terry and wished to protect him and his wife from any scandal. Yes, there was the possible weakness. Margot might well have a great feeling of affection for Terry. After all, he had saved her life and he had made it possible for her to come to England, and when the truth of her age had come out into the open, he had even left home to give her the benefit of his mother's care. The next stage in his enquiry was clear. First he had to find out the validity of a Korean marriage in England. Secondly, he had to visit Terry Haigh.

CHAPTER THIRTY-TWO

LONDON
November 1981

It took Toby Paradise a week to obtain the information he needed, a week during which Ella rang him daily, sometimes twice daily, for a progress report. His patience began to wear very thin. 'Look, if I try and push the Korean Embassy any more, they'll shut up like a clam, they're already deeply suspicious of me as it is. They wouldn't tell me a damned thing until I'd given them my life story.'

'You mean that didn't put them off?' said Ella. He could hear the amusement in her voice.

That was the trouble, he liked the woman. 'I guess it should have done,' he agreed. 'Please, will you just get off my back for a few days. Why not look on this week as a lesson in sex education for your son, OK?' The ominous silence at the other end of the telephone told him he had said the wrong thing. Shit, women and their kids – it was a wonder anyone grew up normal.

A week to the day from when he had first approached the Korean Embassy, Toby had the information he wanted. A marriage had indeed taken place, between a Terry Haigh and Margot Stephenson, on 15th July, 1954. It was a formal, civil service, properly registered and a marriage certificate had been issued. Margot and Terry, it appeared, had been legally married and were still legally married today.

Terry Haigh's house in Forest Hill was almost a carbon copy of the house in which he had grown up – a little bigger, a little uglier, but the same sense of claustrophobic respectability prevailed. Toby had been sitting in his car since seven o'clock that morning. He had seen what had to be Terry go off to work, dutifully kissed and waved goodbye to by his wife. He had then seen the wife take their two children to school, returning with a basket of shopping shortly before ten: coffee time, he gauged. He allowed her quarter of an hour to unpack her shopping on returning home and then crossed the street and rang at the doorbell.

June Haigh was a pleasant-looking woman with a gentle and homely face. 'I wonder if I could talk to you about Margot Haigh for a few minutes. I'm from Joshkers Bank,' Toby began.

'Margot! Is something wrong? Is she ill? has she been hurt?'

'No, no, nothing like that. As a matter of fact I rather was hoping for your help because we want to make her a presentation.' He then launched into his now well-rehearsed story. It was gratifying to see that June Haigh was completely taken in.

'Why don't you come in and have a coffee,' she said, 'I'm just making some.' They sat comfortably at the kitchen table. 'Of course it's Terry you should be talking to really. Margot's his sister, you know — well, at least, she was adopted by his mother. Terry rescued her from Korea.'

'So I understand,' said Toby. 'I expect they're very close.'

'Oh yes, Terry thinks the world of Margot,' the woman confided, without a trace of jealousy in her voice. 'Actually I'm very proud of what he did for her, rescuing her from that terrible place. Just look what she's become — and you say she's going to be made a partner of the bank?' Toby nodded. 'That's wonderful. Mind you, she's earned it. It's not just that she's clever, she's always worked hard, too.'

'It's a shame she's never married,' said Toby, conversationally.

'Yes, that's what I always say to Terry, that she ought to settle down. He says she's not the marrying kind but I think every woman is underneath, don't you?'

'I wouldn't know,' said Toby.

The woman's conversation drifted along as she racked her brains for a suitable gift for Margot. 'The trouble is, you see, she's got everything. I don't know what she earns at that bank but it must be a lot of money. She's always giving the kids wonderful presents.'

'Does she visit you often?' Toby asked.

'Oh yes, on the first Sunday in every month she comes down for lunch, and at Christmas and on her birthday. I often say to Terry I can't understand why she bothers with us. That always makes him angry. He says it's because she's very fond of us, because we're the only family she's got.'

'Don't you think he's right then?'

'I suppose so' said June Haigh. 'It's just that we're so dull and, well, you know.'

It was clear to Toby that as far as June Haigh was concerned, Margot might just as well be a martian — they moved in totally different worlds. 'Perhaps she'd like some jewellery,' said June at last. 'Of course she doesn't wear much but then I don't know whether that's from choice. She always wears black, you see, or nearly always. Very plain clothes, they suit her though. Most people couldn't get away with it, but Margot can.'

Not for the first time during his investigation, Toby had the overwhelming urge to meet Margot Haigh. 'I'll certainly mention jewellery, that's a good idea,' he said. 'What about something for her home?'

'I don't know about that,' said June Haigh. 'We've never been there.' There was an obvious note of hurt in her voice.

'Really! That's rather surprising, isn't it?' said Toby.

'No, not really. I expect it's all very neat and tidy like she is. She wouldn't want me and Terry and the kids all over the place. I understand really but I'm not sure Terry does. You see ... oh dear, I don't know how to say this without sounding disloyal.'

'Try,' said Toby, encouragingly, aware that he was asking a lot of questions.

'Well, Terry's never made much of his life. He works in

the local branch of Lloyds Bank but he's never got beyond being a clerk. He's slow with figures really but it was the only job available when he came back from Korea. Margot's ...' she searched for words, 'Margot is, well, his one real success in life, Margot and the war, that is. The war was hard but he enjoyed it and then bringing Margot back, rescuing her from that place, and then watching her success, well, it's given him a sense of worth. He doesn't like being excluded from her life, because she is the reason his has any point to it.'

'But surely you and the children provide a point to his life?' Toby asked, genuinely interested now.

'Oh yes, of course,' she said, 'but we're just ordinary, like him, we're not special like Margot. He'll be really thrilled about her promotion. I'm surprised she didn't mention it on her last visit.'

'Nobody's allowed to talk about it at the moment, until it happens.'

'Oh, I see,' said June Haigh, with assumed importance, 'I won't tell a soul, except Terry, of course.' She hesitated. 'She's a nice person, Margot, and I think she realizes how important she is to Terry, which is why she comes to visit us so often, but sometimes I feel it's a bit like ...' she searched for the word.

'Charity?' Toby suggested.

'Yes, yes, I suppose that's it. I don't know why I'm telling you all this. It's not how Terry sees things at all.'

'Well, you've been most helpful,' said Toby.

'I haven't been helpful at all, I haven't given you any ideas, other than the jewellery one. Why don't you give me your telephone number, Mr — er —

'Paradise,' said Toby.

'Mr Paradise, and I'll ask Terry to ring you when he's had a few ideas.'

Toby thought fast. 'Oh no, I won't do that because I don't want you to waste your money on Joshkers' behalf. I'll ring you in a day or two and see if Terry's come up with any ideas.'

'Alright,' she said. 'I've enjoyed our chat. Send our love to Margot when you see her.'

'I will,' Toby assured her.

Toby watched Ella over the rim of his wine glass. They were sitting in a wine bar just off Sloane Street. Ella did not look as pleased with his news as Toby had expected. To him, the case was all wrapped up. She was silent for some time. 'Are you sure this is enough?' she said at last.

'Absolutely,' said Toby. 'In my view Margot will do anything to protect Terry. All you have to say to her is that unless she leaves your son alone, you'll tell June Haigh the true nature of her relationship with Terry. They are a very respectable little family, Mrs Kovac. I know the social structure is different in America but here, in England, there is a class of people to whom being respectable is of the ultimate importance and the Haighs fall into that category. If June Haigh was to find out that not only was her husband's sister his former wife, but also that her own marriage is bigamous and her children illegitimate, it would finish her – and Terry, too, come to that.'

'But he already knows,' Ella protested.

'Yes,' said Toby, 'he knows and it's probably the one guilty secret of his life. I haven't met the guy but he sounds to me to be a pillar of the establishment. He works in a local bank, he's a good husband and father – a rather dull, not very intelligent man, who had just one moment of glory when he married an exotic thirteen-year-old, nearly thirty-odd years ago. I don't have any doubt that it's something that makes him feel quite proud, at any rate it gives him a thrill in private, but at the same time the thought of his wife ever finding out must horrify him. Am I getting through, Mrs Kovac?'

Ella seemed lost in thought and then appeared to come to a decision. 'Look, Mr Paradise, would it help if I told you that calling me Mrs Kovac is a misnomer? I'm Miss Kovac – my son, Greg, is illegitimate and I've never been married. OK, there are a lot of problems associated with not having a husband but as for the status of illegitimacy ... that's nothing these days. Heavens, it's almost fashionable.'

Her words made sense to Toby but none the less he was irritated by her lack of understanding. 'In some circles, maybe, but not in the Haigh's. Look, you're not an ordinary woman, are you?' he said. 'I did some checking with Stephanie Bonham after you'd come to see me. I know you have a high-powered business in the States and from just talking to you, it's obvious you have a confidence, a presence if you like, which is unusual.'

'Is that a compliment?'

'Yes, it is,' he said, 'but what your circumstances seem to have done is to alienate you from the world in which most women live. Most women don't have big businesses to run. Their world revolves round their children and their husband, their home, what they're having for dinner, whether the ironing is done and above all, *what the neighbours think*.'

'That sounds very condescending, male chauvinist stuff to me,' said Ella.

'OK, maybe it does, but I'm not knocking it, I'm just saying that those are the facts. June Haigh's world and that of her husband would be completely destroyed by the knowledge which you now have. While you may not have the imagination to see it, Miss Kovac, I bet my reputation and my fees on the fact that Margot Haigh does.'

CHAPTER THIRTY-THREE

LONDON
November 1981

She recognized she must be very nervous for she never drank at lunchtime. Yet here she was helping herself to a gin and tonic, and the hand that held the glass was none too steady. Margot, drink in hand, walked to the sitting room window and checked, yet again, for a sight of Ella coming up the street. It was stupid, she was not due for another ten minutes, and there were plenty of things she could be doing while she waited.

It had surprised Margot that Ella was willing to come to her home, where she must know Greg was now living. She could not guess what Ella had to say but would have imagined her preference would have been for neutral ground for their talk. As it happened Greg was away for the day. Now her holiday was over, Margot had welcomed his suggestion that he should visit the Irvines for the day, while she was working, which had made it possible to meet Ella here in Flood Street. Perhaps Ella was right, perhaps it was better to talk of Greg in private.

Greg: Margot turned the image of him over in her mind, the dark, curly hair, the strong, square jaw, the youthful, muscular body. She loved the boy for how he looked but also for what he was. He had been a virgin on that crazy night when they had ended up in one another's arms in Ella's Houston apartment. She had taught him everything she knew about making love but there was also a very great deal he had taught her, too. The satisfaction over the years she

350

had found in the arms of Nicholas Goddard, Margot now realized, had been as much spiritual as physical. Greg's youthful demands on her body, which left her weak and shaken, represented an entirely new experience. Indeed, he was already master in the bedroom. Yet outside it, he had a vulnerability that she found almost unbearably touching. It surprised her that. Being a strong person herself, Margot had always respected strength in others, yet she revelled in Greg's dependence upon her. She had been late for work this morning on two counts. Firstly Greg had forced her back to bed from the breakfast table when she had been all ready to leave. Then seconds before she tried to leave for a second time, he had admitted he was nervous about getting lost at Paddington Station – which train should he catch, how would he find out, where would he get his ticket? Margot could not understand why this had not irritated her. Instead it had pleased her to the point where she had taken a taxi with him to Paddington and seen him on to the right train, thus making herself later for work than she had ever been in her life before.

So, what was Greg Kovac in her life, her lover or her son? In an effort to try and bring some sort of realism to the situation, at times she tried to equate the man in whose arms she lay with the little boy who had so dominated Ella Kovac's early working life and who Margot had always thought of as a tiresome waste of Ella's undoubted talents and energies. As hard as she tried, she could not force the two separate personalities to become one in her mind, although she knew they were so. She wondered now, standing by the window, what she should say to his mother. This woman who over the years, if she had not become exactly a friend, was certainly more than just a bank customer. What could she say to Ella – I love your son? No, it was not possible. It was not possible because Margot herself could not yet face the truth of her emotions. Deep down, she recognized that her feelings for Greg Kovac were the first entirely unselfish emotions she had experienced in her whole adult life. She wanted nothing from him, nothing at all. All that mattered to her was his happiness and well-being. The strength of her feelings had already in weak moments made her weep with indecision – they had no future together and yet he seemed to need her. Perhaps, somehow, there would always be a place for her in his life.

The door bell rang, making her jump. Ella must have come up the garden path without her even noticing. She must have seen her standing in the window, drink in hand. It was not a promising start. Taking a hefty swig, Margot went to the door and opened it.

Margot had not known what to expect but certainly Ella's appearance took her by surprise. She seemed neither dragged down nor depressed by the apparent loss of her only child. Indeed it was impossible to look at Ella and envisage her as Greg's mother. She was dressed casually, as usual, in tight jeans, a big baggy sweater and trainers. The curls, framing her face, were shiny and bright. She wore little make-up and apart from a slight tiredness round the eyes, she looked like a healthy college kid. Her appearance only served to heighten in Margot's mind the ludicrousness of the situation. She had lost count of the times, over the years, that she and Ella had met. In the past, she had always enjoyed the upper hand because she had something which Ella wanted. Now, the roles were reversed – or were they?

'Would you like a drink?' Margot asked, 'I was just having one.'

'No, thanks,' said Ella.

Margot looked longingly at the gin, discarded on the mantelpiece. 'Won't you sit down?' she said.

'No,' said Ella, 'this won't take long.'

'I assume you've come about Greg?'

'You bet I've come about Greg,' said Ella. 'I'm here because I want you to give him up. At the moment, he's unlikely to listen to reason from me or anyone else. The only way your relationship is going to end is if you tell him that it's over, that you don't care for him any more, that you've had your fling and that he's about as exciting as yesterday's news.'

'You don't seriously expect me to do that?' said Margot.

'I most certainly do, but not because I'm relying on your sweet nature.' Ella's voice was cold with loathing and Margot shivered involuntarily. 'I know the sort of person you are, Margot. I don't know why you chose to pick on my son, but I recognize that for some reason he has some sort of attraction for you right now, but when that attraction wanes, you'll simply chuck him aside. People think I'm tough but I'm in a different league to you, I suppose, thank God, because I've always had a child to soften the edges and make me put someone else before myself. In your case, if you want something, you take it. Are you aware that you're ruining his life?'

'I don't see it like that,' said Margot. 'You'd mapped out his future for him, as you saw it. He doesn't want to go to college and read law. He loves the country, away from the hype of New York and property deals, only you've never been prepared to listen to him.'

'Since when did you become a nature lover?' Ella said, caustically. 'I don't envisage you rising at dawn to milk the cows. Besides, I don't want to hear all this crap. You're not interested in Greg's welfare and for that reason I'm not going to make any attempt to appeal to you as a mother, because it's pointless. My feelings, Greg's feelings, are not relevant to you. An impassioned plea would be wasted.'

'Then why are you here?'

'To fight you, to fight dirty if I have to in order to get my boy back, and I don't like you any more for making me do what I have to do, making me no better than you.'

'You're talking in riddles, Ella,' said Margot. 'I don't understand what you're saying.'

'Let me spell it out,' said Ella. 'I've had a private investigator working on you and your past, and what he has told me is enough to ensure that in order for me to keep my mouth shut, you're going to have to agree to my demands and kiss goodbye to Greg.'

Nicholas, Margot thought. Surely not, not after all those years of care and discretion. How could Ella have found out? No one, no one knew . . . to let him down now, when he was dead. She felt a tightening in her chest, her mouth went dry. She turned away, so that Ella could not see her expression, and walked over to the window. 'So, I gather we're talking about blackmail, is that right, Ella?'

'I can't think of another word for it,' said Ella.

'Then you'd better tell me what skeleton in my cupboard you wish to parade for public scrutiny.'

'Not public scrutiny, exactly,' said Ella. 'What I have discovered is that Terry Haigh's marriage is bigamous – is bigamous because he married a thirteen-year-old girl in Korea, named Margot Stephenson. I know the marriage was hushed-up as soon as you arrived in this country, when Terry's mother rumbled your true age, but I also know that the marriage was never annulled and that technically you and Terry are still married.'

So that was it. For a moment, all Margot could feel was relief. Nicholas was spared and that was all that really mattered. 'I can't see that your information is of any interest to anyone. Neither Terry nor I are exactly celebrities and I can hardly imagine the *News of the World* getting very worked up about the story.' Her voice was full of contempt.

'I wasn't thinking of the *News of the World*,' said Ella, 'I was thinking about June Haigh, Terry's so-called wife, and of their kids. How do you think June's going to feel when she learns that Terry's sister is not his sister after all, that she is not his wife and that their kids are illegitimate. Think about it for a moment. Margot, put yourself in June's shoes, in her little world. How do you think she's going to feel?'

Margot stared at Ella in astonishment. 'You mean to say that you are prepared to tell June all you know about my past, in order to persuade me to leave your son alone?'

'That's about it,' said Ella.

'I honestly think you've judged this wrong, Ella. OK, so it would come as a shock to June, but she and Terry love one another and they'd soon adjust. After all, my marriage to Terry was only a marriage of convenience to get me into the country, she has no reason to feel threatened by it.'

'That's not what Dick Simpson says,' said Ella, 'he says

you and Terry were shacked up in a little flat on the outskirts of Seoul, all very cosy. June and Terry's daughter is thirteen now, I believe. Try telling June that her husband used to have sex with a girl of the same age his own daughter is now. I think that's pushing her understanding a little far, don't you? In fact, Margot, I'd go further I reckon the truth would destroy their lives.'

For a moment Margot was back there. The sun was beating relentlessly, the air was heavy and humid. Her lungs were almost bursting as she ran, her feet already cut and bleeding were lacerated by the dry, brittle grass over which she stumbled, and all the time she could hear the heavy sound of army boots, pounding closer, closer, a man's rasping breath. At last he had caught her, bringing her down in a rugger tackle so that she ended on her back, with him half on top of her. She had looked up expecting to see the devil himself. Instead she had been confronted with a pair of watery blue eyes and a kind, simple face which despite his heavy breathing was wrinkled with concern. 'It's alright, little one, I'm not going to hurt you, I'm here to help, I'm your friend.' Those were the first words that Terry Haigh had ever spoken to Margot and they transformed her life from a living nightmare into the slow rehabilitation process which had ended in the offices of Joshkers Bank.

Terry Haigh had changed little over the years, his first thought was always for others. He was not a clever nor a successful man but his pride in his little protégée was total. That he had found himself married and making love to a thirteen-year-old girl was entirely her own fault, Margot knew, and his horror at discovering he had been having sex with a child was something she would never forget. Yet they had weathered all the early drama of their relationship and here they were now, both middle-aged people and still firm friends. She knew that the Haighs wondered why she bothered with them. They could not understand that their suburban ordinariness was balm to her soul. Ella was right, of course. If June ever knew the truth . . .

Ella's voice cut through her thoughts. 'What I'm asking for,' said Ella, 'is a straight trade. The facts surrounding your marriage to Terry Haigh are safe with me, if you tell Greg to come home. I must stress, however, he must know nothing of our meeting, nothing at all. You must think up your own reasons for parting from him.'

Margot slowly raised her eyes and met Ella's. They were steely and determined, there was no room for negotiation. 'How will I know that you won't use this information you have again?'

'You have my word,' said Ella. Margot waved her hand dismissively and turned away. 'Come on,' said Ella, 'in all the years we've known one another, I've never let you down, have I? I have never misled you in any way, bullshitted you around, I've always been straight.'

'Yes, that's true,' Margot was forced to concede.

'And there's something else,' said Ella, 'a piece of advice, free.'

'Go on,' said Margot.

'The private dick I used – he mentioned something he discovered during his investigations. There is absolutely no reason why you and Terry shouldn't have the marriage annulled, now, and there's no reason for June ever to know about it. It is just a question of some very simple paperwork.'

'That still doesn't make Terry and June married, because their marriage ceremony occurred long before any annulment,' said Margot, wearily.

'Yeh, but I thought that out, too,' said Ella. 'Terry and June were married in a registry office, right?' Margot nodded. 'I don't know how long they've been married but it must be coming up for twenty-five years. Supposing Terry suggested that they remarried in church, to kind of emphasize their continuing vows. It happens quite often in the States and it would put the record straight.' Margot started to speak. 'I know what your next query is,' said Ella, 'you're going to ask how you can explain to Terry why this step is necessary? The weak link is Dick Simpson – he's turning into a regular drunk. My private dick posed as someone from Joshkers Bank trying to learn a little of your background to find the right gift to give you as a company presentation.'

Margot laughed aloud. 'Nobody could have believed that.'

'But they did. As a result, Dick told him about the marriage, and June swallowed the story, too, and explained just how much you all meant to one another. It occurs to me that you could tell Terry how easy it was for the Joshkers representative to find out the information on your marriage and that you had discovered it was possible to annul it. You put all that in motion, Margot, and you'll be safe from me and anyone else.'

'I'd like to think about your proposal,' said Margot, coldly. 'I'll call you later tonight or tomorrow morning.'

'You've got twenty-four hours,' said Ella. 'If we can wrap this up by the weekend, I can still get Greg back for college. I'll wait for your call. I'm staying at the Meyer Hotel.'

Margot shut the front door and leaned a burning forehead against it. 'Would you understand if I told you I loved your son, if I told you just what you were asking me to give up?' she said to the empty room.

When Greg burst through the front door, the cold night air had whipped colour into his cheeks and he seemed more alive and vibrant than anyone Margot had ever met before. 'Wow, what a great day,' he said, kissing her soundly on the lips, and then walking past her into the kitchen. 'They haven't changed a bit,' he shouted, 'the Irvines I mean. Well, Tim hasn't, he's exactly the same. The girls, they're all grown-up, Millie is incredibly sophisticated and Belinda, she's just as sweet as ever.' He came into the sitting room carrying a beer. 'Tim has done a great deal to the farm, he's even bought back some of the land they sold years ago and . . . is something wrong?'

The carefree expression died on his face and Margot mourned its passing with an almost physical pain. She knew she would not see it again for she was just about to murder his youthful exuberance. 'Yes,' she said.

He put down his beer instantly and tried to slip his arms around her. She pushed him away and instantly he looked hurt and bewildered. 'What's wrong, are you ill?'

'No, I'm not ill, Greg, it's just that I have something rather unpleasant to say and frankly I'm not looking forward to it.'

'What is it?' said Greg.

'You and I are finished.' Margot met his eye. Inside she was screaming but on the outside she was icy cold.

'You're kidding.' He smiled a little tremulously. 'Is this some sort of joke?'

'No joke. It was a mistake, you coming to London. You were so keen on it I didn't want to disappoint you, but you don't fit into my world, Greg – you're too young, too unsophisticated. For example, I should be at a dinner with some customers tonight but I couldn't take you along, it wouldn't be right.'

'Why not?' Greg challenged, 'because of our age difference?'

'It's not as simple as our age difference. Look, I-I don't know how to put this . . .'

'Try me,' said Greg.

'Well, you want to make a career out of life in the country, on a farm, something like that.'

'Yes,' said Greg, 'is that wrong?'

'No, it's not wrong, in fact I think you'd be well suited to it. I suppose what I-I'm really saying, Greg, is that you have rather a country hick mentality already, and I guess, well, I'd be ashamed to have you meet my colleagues. You're so naïve.'

'Ashamed!' Colour suffused his face, 'You weren't ashamed of me last night, in the sack.'

'That's different. You're great in bed, Greg. It's outside of bed that things are not so good.'

Greg stared at her, one hand plucking at the edge of his jacket like a child. 'I don't get this, Margot, I don't understand. Everything was so great between us this morning.'

'Great for you, maybe, but not for me. I want you out of

my life, Greg, and I want you out now. It so happens that your mother's in London. I suggest that you call her and sort out a passage home.'

'My mother! So Mom put you up to this?'

'No, your mother and I aren't speaking at the moment. I only happen to know she's in London because she rang a colleague of mine today about a business matter and he mentioned it in passing. She's staying at the Meyer Hotel.'

'I'm not going to Mom, no way.'

'Greg, you have no choice,' said Margot, with forced weariness, 'you have no money, no means of supporting yourself and no home here in England. Mothers are a pain in the neck but she'll welcome you back with open arms, you know that. She warned you I was a shit. All you have to do is tell her she was right and she'll be happy as larry.'

'I want a full explanation, I want to understand what's made you react like this. Somebody, somewhere must have put pressure on you.'

'Nobody's putting any pressure on me, Greg. I'm forty-two years old, I make my own decisions and I've just made one now.' She got up and walked purposefully into the bedroom. 'I've packed your case.' She picked up his grip and carried it out into the sitting room. 'I'll call you a cab.'

'No.' Greg seized her arm.

'Yes,' she thundered back. 'You go without a fuss or I'll call the police.'

His face went from red to deathly white. 'You mean it,' he said, incredulously.

'I mean it,' said Margot. She shook herself free from him and walked to the telephone. Greg watched in a stunned silence as she dialled the number. When she had finished the call she turned to him. 'It'll be here in two or three minutes.'

'Did I do something stupid,' he asked, 'did I upset you in some way, did I say the wrong thing? For Christ's sake, Margot, tell me – you owe that much to me.'

'You said or did nothing wrong, Greg, it's simply what you are – a kid, straight out of school. We had some fun but the party's over. Call it a holiday romance, that's how you should look on it.'

'But I love you,' said Greg, simply.

Just for a moment, Margot nearly weakened. All her instincts cried out to throw her arms round him and tell him how much she loved him. 'Love!' she scoffed. 'What the hell do you know about love at eighteen years old. I'm the first woman you ever had, remember? All you're suffering from is a severe case of lust.'

'Stop it, stop it,' said Greg, 'I won't have you talk about us like this. It wasn't like that, it wasn't.' There were tears in his eyes now, childish tears and she could not bear to watch them. They stood on opposite sides of the room, each locked in an individual world of misery. They were released by the sound of the taxi outside.

Margot went to the door and opened it. 'She's at the Meyer Hotel,' she repeated. 'Have you enough money for the taxi fare?' It was the final insult as indeed it was intended to be.

'You bitch, you bloody bitch,' Greg said, as he stumbled out into the darkness.

'Miss Kovac, please.'

Ella answered the phone, before it had barely rung: she must have been sitting over it, willing it to ring, Margot thought. 'Your son is on his way over,' she said, her voice completely devoid of emotion.

'Back for good?'

'I don't know about for good, you'll have to sort out your own relationship, but he's finished with me.'

'What did you tell him?' Ella asked.

'It's none of your God-damned business,' said Margot, 'but I didn't mention you, as we agreed. All I said was that I knew you were in London because you rang a colleague of mine at the bank today, about a business matter, but he's not thinking straight at the moment, so I doubt you'll be cross-examined.'

'I don't see that I need to say thank you,' said Ella, 'but thank you anyway.'

'Go easy on him, Ella,' Margot managed, before she slammed down the phone.

Ella stared at the receiver in her hand. Margot had sounded quite choked, but it had to be because she couldn't cope with failing to get her own way, Ella reasoned. Still this was not the time to think about Margot. Greg was coming back, Greg was on his way home.

CHAPTER THIRTY-FOUR

PARIS
Christmas Eve 1984

The scene was the very model of elegance and romance, it could have been lifted straight from a glossy magazine. The table was set for two in the little dining alcove where cut glass glistened, the family silver gleamed, the plates were of Crown Derby and the napkins of pure snowy white damask. In the sitting room area, Stephanie reclined gracefully on the sofa, in pale grey satin pants and evening top, a glass of champagne in her hand. Opposite her sat Alex – handsome, dark, debonair. Candles flickered round the room, a Christmas tree sparkled in one corner, exquisite notes of a Beethoven piano concerto contributed the background music. It should have been perfect but it was far from that. The air was heavy with anger, resentment and suspicion.

'OK,' said Alex, 'Are you going to tell me what's bugging you or have I got to guess? It's been a long, hard week and I could do without the guessing games.'

'You know very well what's wrong,' said Stephanie.

'You mean our arrangements for Christmas Day?'

'Of course I mean our arrangements for Christmas Day.'

'Look,' said Alex, 'I don't see I have to justify to you why I want to spend Christmas Day with the old man. Anyone with even the slightest degree of sensitivity would understand. He's all alone, he's not very well and every Christmas could be his last.'

'Of course I understand that,' said Stephanie, 'I just wish you'd told me earlier.'

'How the hell was I supposed to know you were going to cancel Christmas with your family?'

'Because,' said Stephanie, with studied patience, 'when we discussed it earlier in the year, we agreed that we would spend this Christmas together and I went ahead on that basis.'

'OK,' said Alex, 'I had a change of heart. I'm sorry, but there it is. If you hadn't fallen out with father the three of us could have enjoyed Christmas together.'

'I think that's what I resent most,' said Stephanie, 'the way you always side with your father against me, as though our differences are all my fault.'

'I'm not siding with him against you,' said Alex, 'I just understand why he's never forgiven you for the Fulham business. He has a lot of faults but he always plays things straight, you know that. He felt terribly let down by you and since he's old and intractable, he's not going to change his mind.'

'He would, if you pleaded my case,' said Stephanie. Alex stood up and went to refill his champagne glass. His expression was bored. I'm overdoing this and spoiling the evening, Stephanie thought, but there was nothing she could do to stop herself now.

'I don't think anybody's ever persuaded my father to do anything he didn't want to,' said Alex, after a pause. 'I don't understand your sudden desire to play happy families, we've spent several Christmases apart in the past.'

'I don't want to play happy families,' said Stephanie, irritably, 'it's just that thanks to you, I'm not spending Christmas with my family, I can't spend Christmas with yours and so it means I'm going to be alone.'

Alex sat down, wearily. 'Why don't you tell your family you've changed your mind? I'm sure the long-suffering Tim will be more than happy to welcome you back into the fold for the festive season.'

'I can't do that, Tim's made other plans.'

There was an odd note in her voice which quickened Alex's interest. 'What sort of other plans. Don't tell me Tim has found a woman at last! Wonderful!'

'No, no, not exactly. Ella and her son, Greg, are spending Christmas at Wickham with Tim and the girls.'

'And you're jealous!' said Alex, triumphantly.

'No, I'm not. As a matter of fact, Ella and Tim did have an affair some years ago but I don't think there's anything going on now. It's just that Greg and the girls are such friends and apparently Greg has always admired Tim a very great deal. At least that's the way Ella explained it to me.'

'Oh so she admitted it to you, then?' Alex was at his most irritating.

'It wasn't a question of admitting it to me. She asked me if I would mind them going, as it is, after all, my home, and of course I said I wouldn't because at that time I thought I was spending Christmas with you. Now it seems I've fallen between two stools and have nowhere to go.'

'It's just a day,' said Alex, 'like any other.'

'Not to me,' said Stephanie. 'When I think of Christmas, I always think of childhood Christmases at Wickham, when my mother was still alive and my brother, too. They were wonderful, so full of laughter and happiness.'

'Time warps the memory,' said Alex. 'You were probably bored as hell and surrounded by aged relations.'

'Why are you such a cynic, Alex?' Stephanie asked.

'I'm not a cynic, I'm a realist. For most people, Christmas Day means very little more than the excuse to over-eat and over-drink. I'd have thought it was a heaven-sent opportunity for you to get on with some work. After all, the telephone won't ring all day.'

'You're an absolute brute sometimes, Alex,' said Stephanie. 'Come on, we'd better eat or it will be ruined.'

She placed before them plates of smoked salmon and poured a glass of Muscadet. The setting was wonderful but the evening had lost its sparkle, like so many evenings between them in recent months. In her heart of hearts, Stephanie knew she was losing Alex – it was only a question of time. Nothing had been right between them since her decision to develop Fulham. She regretted it now, particularly since after all the trouble it had caused, she had still been forced to accept the Meyers as partners. Her bid for freedom had failed, apparently she had irrevocably angered Joseph Meyer and it seemed to signify the beginning of the end for her and Alex. All this would have been easier to bear if only ... She glanced up at him. She had to tell him now. Every day during the last week, she had promised herself to raise the subject and then had lost courage at the last moment. It had to be now: he was going skiing in early January and she was not even sure she would see him again before he left.

He glanced up at her, sensing her scrutiny. 'Come on,' he said, 'you're not eating your smoked salmon.'

'Alex, there's something I have to tell you.'

He looked at her, mockingly. 'This sounds serious. Another man is it, am I getting my marching orders?' He grinned, superbly confident that this was not the case.

For a wild moment, Stephanie contemplated telling him how wrong he was, just to see the expression on his face. 'No,' she said, 'nothing like that, as you well know. It is a problem, but one I hope we can sort out between us.'

Alex's face was suddenly serious to match her own. 'Well, go on then, spit it out, what is it?'

'I'm pregnant, Alex.'

'You're what!'

'You heard,' Stephanie said, wearily. 'Seven weeks pregnant.'

'Are you saying the child is mine?' Alex said, his voice suddenly very cold.

Stephanie wanted to hit him. 'How dare you! Of course the child is yours. You know damned well there hasn't been another man in my life since the moment you first made love to me.'

'How come this happened?'

'I changed my method of contraception,' said Stephanie. 'I felt I'd spent too many years on the pill and bearing in mind my age, I changed to a coil. Apparently it didn't work.'

'Why the bloody hell didn't you tell me what you were doing?'

'Because you wouldn't have been interested,' said Stephanie, dully. 'You would have said it was my body and my responsibility to take whatever contraceptive measures I thought fit. So I did.'

Alex was silent for a moment, well aware that Stephanie was right in her assessment of his reaction. For a brief moment he felt remorse, but he pushed the feeling firmly aside. 'It's absolutely bloody ridiculous, a woman of your age getting herself knocked up. I'd understand if you were nineteen years old.'

'I didn't do it on purpose, Alex,' said Stephanie.

'Didn't you? Are you sure it wasn't some kind of plot to ensnare me, to force my hand. Is it marriage you want?'

'You're so bloody sure of yourself, aren't you?' said Stephanie. She pushed back her chair, leaving her meal uneaten, and refilling her wine glass. 'What makes you think I want to marry you, any more than you want to marry me? And why should you automatically assume that my getting pregnant is some sort of contrived act. It's insulting and wholly inaccurate.'

'In which case I assume you're getting rid of it?' He spoke with about as much emotion as if he was discussing the disposal of a rubbish bin.

She had known his reaction to the news would be disturbing, but not this bad. 'Alex, we're talking about a human life, about your son or daughter, your precious father's grandchild. How can you cold-bloodedly talk about murdering it, without even giving it a second thought?'

'Oh, don't start all that,' said Alex. 'You know very well I've never wanted kids, never. Just because you have made a silly mistake, there's no reason why I should change my view. Anyway, you haven't got time for a baby.'

'I could make time,' said Stephanie.

'Not you. You're the woman who abandoned her last family without a qualm, remember?'

His words stung her. More and more recently Stephanie

found she valued the time she spent with her daughters and missed them dreadfully when they were apart. 'I left them to be with you,' she said, defensively.

'So,' said Alex, 'it still doesn't make you the most maternal person in the world. Come on, Stephanie, think straight. Life's tough enough without starting it unwanted and this kid isn't wanted by either of us.'

'It's wanted by me,' said Stephanie.

'Why, because you think you'll get back in favour with father?'

The callousness of his words brought sudden tears to her eyes, but she was damned if she would tell him the truth. The truth was that she loved him so much that even without marriage or any assurance as to her future, she wanted his child. 'I-I don't believe in abortion,' she said, after a while.

'On what grounds – moral, religious, legal?'

'On any grounds. I just don't believe however small or unformed a baby may be, that it's right to terminate its life, once it's been started.'

'That's bullshit and you know it, Stephanie. In the past, you'd never have let a baby get in the way of what you wanted. You've always put business before everything.'

'Well maybe I'm changing,' said Stephanie, 'maybe I'm growing up.'

'Or getting soft in the head. I'm sorry, I just don't believe you. It's no good you looking at me all misty-eyed and trying to put yourself across as mother earth. It doesn't suit you, there's no credibility. If you truly want this baby, you want it for a reason and I suspect it has something to do with father.'

'Of course it hasn't.'

'Maybe, maybe not. Either way, I'll say this, Stephanie: if you go ahead with this pregnancy, you do so without my blessing. I will not acknowledge the child as my own, you may not give it the Meyer name and as far as I'm concerned our relationship will be at an end.'

Anger momentarily rescued Stephanie from the depths of her misery. 'You're talking as though I had leprosy. What's so wrong with having a baby, your baby?'

'If for any reason I ever change my mind and decide I would like children,' said Alex, 'it will be a joint decision between myself and my partner. I will not have a child, any child, thrust upon me.'

In silence, Stephanie cleared away the plates, hers still untouched, and in the kitchen began dishing up the main course. It was pheasant casserole: she had bought a brace of pheasants in the market that morning and the smell reminded her of home. She still thought of Wickham as home. What on earth had brought her to this point, she wondered, living in this luxurious Parisian flat, sharing her life with a man who clearly did not love her and carrying his baby against his wishes? She remembered suddenly Tim's reaction to the news of each of her pregnancies, his joy, his pride in her. Had she really thrown all that away for — for *this*? For the first time in a long while, Stephanie thought of her mother. How different things would have been had she lived. Her father would not have drunk himself to death, her brother would have not taken to drugs and she ... there would have been no need to rescue Wickham and so take the first steps into business. Perhaps she would have settled for a normal married life. Hot tears splashed down her cheeks, some falling into the steaming casserole in front of her. Why was she standing here, serving a meal to a man who did not want either her or their baby? She was a little drunk, she knew. If she was sober she would not have reacted as she did. She tossed back the rest of the wine in her glass and slamming the lid back on the casserole, she walked out into the dining area.

'There doesn't seem to be much point in continuing with this meal, does there, since neither of us is having a good time? I suggest you go.' Her voice was surprisingly steady.

He remained unmoved. 'I was planning to stay the night here, as you know.'

'You'll just have to find yourself a room somewhere else in Paris for the night. This is my flat, if you remember, and I don't want you here.'

'As you wish.' He got to his feet and started towards the door.

Stephanie had expected some sort of show of resistance. She panicked. 'When . . . when are you going skiing?'

He stopped and turned to face her. 'I wouldn't have thought you'd have been interested.'

Her mind raced. 'I need to know for business purposes, if for no other reason.'

'I leave on the 7th and I'll be away for a fortnight.' His manner softened slightly. 'Look, Stephanie, be realistic about this baby. Parenthood is not for us. Why not arrange an abortion for immediately after Christmas and then come skiing with me to recuperate? You haven't had a holiday in a long time.'

His sudden kindness brought tears to her eyes. Just for a moment his suggestion was tempting; it was a long time since they had enjoyed a holiday together. Perhaps a fortnight in Austria was just what they needed. They both loved skiing, they were both good at it.

'No,' she thundered, as much to frighten off her own thoughts as to make the point to Alex. 'I'm going to have this baby, with or without your blessing. I'm not sure being excluded from the Meyer empire isn't the best thing that could happen to the child. Certainly I wouldn't want a child of mine to turn out like you, playing to your father's tune, another Joseph Meyer clone.'

For a moment she thought he was going to hit her. She saw the sudden fury in his eyes, the clenching of his fists but the moment passed. The expression that replaced it, though, was almost more chilling, a cold, dispassionate look which suggested he might just as well be addressing a complete stranger. 'I'll be back on 21st January. Either get rid of the baby by then or we're finished. Have I made myself clear?'

'Perfectly,' said Stephanie.

Her heart was still thudding uncomfortably against her ribs long after he had left the flat. She made no attempt to clear up the discarded debris of supper. Instead she poured herself another glass of wine and then remembered the baby. Tipping the wine down the sink, she walked slowly, deliberately to the fridge and helped herself to a glass of milk instead. It was a deliberate act of defiance and sealed for ever in her mind the decision she had already made: this baby would have a chance at life.

Nursing her glass, Stephanie lay back in the chair by the Christmas tree, gazing up at the lights twinkling in the semi-darkness. She was strangely calm now, although she realized she had lost Alex for ever. Instead of reliving the scene that had just taken place, she found her mind drifting back through the years to the Christmases when the girls were small, when she and Tim were happy. One could never turn back the clock, she knew that of course, yet she realized with a shock that the sadness she felt now was not for the man she had just lost, but for the one she had lost what seemed so long ago now.

CHAPTER THIRTY-FIVE

NEW YORK
Christmas Eve 1984

The tall figure of his son stood framed in the doorway. Aaron smiled with pleasure as he looked up from his desk, where he had been sitting staring into space for some long time.

'You were so quiet in here, Pop, I thought you were out.'

'No, no, not tonight. I've given up the high life, particularly now you're home from college.'

'Don't give it up on my account,' said William.

Aaron grinned ruefully at him. 'It's about time I did at my age. Did you have a good evening?'

'The best. I'm sorry I left you alone, though, on Christmas Eve, I shouldn't have done that.'

'William, I don't need a nursemaid.' Aaron's tone was belligerent.

'OK, OK,' said William, 'keep cool, I was only trying to be friendly.'

Aaron pushed back his chair, stood up and walked over to his son, slipping an arm round him. They were of a height: two tall, lean, fair-haired men. 'Hell, I'm sorry, William. If I go on being this tetchy, you give me a right chewing over, OK?'

'Is something wrong?' William asked, anxiously.

'No, nothing more than usual. I'm just getting to be a morose, old man.'

'And lonely?' William suggested.

'That too.'

'So why don't you stop skulking away in your study and

come and have a drink in the sitting room, before we hit the sack?'

'You're a nice boy,' said Aaron.

'I take after my Pop.' They smiled at one another in mutual appreciation and wandered through to the sitting room.

It was after one when William finally went to bed. For Aaron sleep was still a long way off. Pouring himself another whisky, which he justified on the grounds that it was after all the festive season, he went back into his study and looked down at the piece of notepaper on which were written just two words – 'Dearest Ella'. Although he had sat at the desk for most of the evening, he had got no further than that. He slumped back tiredly into his chair, slopping his whisky as he did so. There was so much he wanted to say to her, so much he should have said before. It was three years since Alice had died. Not only had he behaved badly during that period but he was no nearer coming to terms with the grief of losing his wife, and to cap it all in the process he had lost his best friend.

When he thought of his lifestyle during the last three years, it sickened him. Following that one night he had spent with Ella, he had gone a little crazy and laid pretty much everything in sight. As a handsome, revered consultant working in a hospital full of adoring women, he had behaved like a child let loose in a candy store. Over and over again he tried to analyse why he had behaved so stupidly. Part of it, he knew, was a desperate attempt to drive Alice from his mind, to seek relief from the all-consuming grief. It was not as simple as that, though. In recent years, after a long married life together, the physical side of his relationship with Alice had waned. It had not affected their love for one another but it had meant that Aaron had become increasingly unfamiliar with the joys of physical love. Ella, in a single night, had changed all that, awakening something in him that he had thought long dead, if it had ever existed. He recognized that there was a strong sensual side to his nature which had been neglected and ignored, yet the stream of faceless women who he had used and discarded had brought him no nearer coming to terms with his life as a widower. Now at last he knew why. The key to his future happiness was Ella. Whether as a friend or a lover, he needed her, needed her desperately, and it was this that he had to tell her.

One of Aaron's troubles was that his own feelings on the matters were so undecided. That he wanted Ella back in his life on a permanent basis was without question but in what capacity he did not know. Should they simply strive to regain the friendship which for so many years they had taken for granted, or should they be looking for something more? He did not know the answer, and without being able to tell her what he wanted, what was there to say?

He drained the last of his whisky and pulling open a drawer of his desk, drew out a well-thumbed snapshot. It was of he and Ella as children, sitting on the gate leading to his parents' house. He, already long-limbed and tall, was smiling and relaxed. Ella, small, painfully thin, in a ragged cotton dress, stared at the camera with so much defiance it made his heart ache. It was as though she was saying 'OK, this is me now, as I am, but one day I'll show you what I can do'. And she had: Aaron was immensely proud of Ella's achievements. Although he knew nothing about business and was not particularly interested in it, the pride he took in Ella was almost proprietorial, for he knew, instinctively, that without his quiet support over the years, there were many occasions when she would not have been able to go on alone. He wondered how she was faring without their friendship, whether she thought of him at all and if so with what emotion – anger, hurt, regret? And how had she felt about their night together? The following morning he had been so obsessed by his appalling behaviour towards her of all people, he had not even thought to ask her how she felt herself. She had responded to him, he knew that, responded in a way that had both surprised and delighted him. When he thought of that night, his heart was so full of longing for her, so achingly lonely, he knew that the more he considered what to say to her, the more confused he would become.

At last, his eyes aching with tiredness, Aaron picked up the pen and began to write. Not making any attempt to hide or excuse his behaviour, he simply poured out his soul on to paper and the more he wrote, the more the words flew from his pen.

Across town, in the cramped little apartment Jackie Partridge called home, Michael Gresham stretched with a groan and squinted at the clock beside the bed. 'You know something, Sweetheart, you really ought to get a double bed.'

'I know, I should,' said Jackie, anxiously. She looked up at him adoringly from under a thatch of tousled hair. She knew she must look a mess, yet despite the energy of their lovemaking, Michael appeared as cool and as unruffled as ever.

'I must get up,' he said, reaching out an affectionate hand to tousle her hair some more.

'Get up! Why?'

'I have to catch a flight.'

Jackie sat up in bed and stared at him, round-eyed. 'A flight! When?'

Michael glanced at the bedside table again. 'In about two, two and a half hours time. I'm getting the five-twenty out of New York to Houston.'

'But you didn't tell me,' Jackie wailed.

Michael frowned and slid gracefully from the bed. He stood before her, naked, magnificent. She could not take her eyes off him. 'We made no plans to spend Christmas Day together, Sweetheart and I have to get back to Houston. There's a whole bunch of friends dropping by for a party this evening at my place. I have preparations to make.'

Jackie said nothing but watched with growing misery his retreating figure as he padded across the bedroom towards the shower. She supposed it did not occur to him to invite her to come along to meet some of his friends. No, she was being stupid. There would be a girl, if not several girls in Houston. Her place in his life was here in New York. Goodness knows, there was no point in deluding herself, she knew what he was. This was the man who had two-timed

Ella. Ella, a million times more attractive and desirable than she herself. If Ella had not been able to hold him, how could Jackie expect to do so? She stumbled out of bed and went to the dressing table. Her hair, as she had suspected, looked terrible. How did other people manage to look tousled and yet attractive. Her mascara had run, making deep, dark circles under her eyes, like a panda. Her face looked pale, podgy and uninteresting in the dressing table light, which was she knew a flattering one. Hearing Michael turn off the shower, she hurriedly reached for her dressing gown. She envied him his confidence in walking around her flat naked. She could not do it, aware of her bulging thighs and the flab around her middle. She must try and go on a diet.

She was sitting at the dressing table again, frantically brushing at her hair, when Michael reappeared. It was hard to believe he had managed no more than a couple of hours sleep. Showered and shaved, he looked refreshed, invigorated and ready for anything. Jackie's spirits soared at the sight of him. Did it matter that she was not the only woman in his life? The fact remained she did have a place in it. It was over six months now since he had first taken her out to dinner, on calling at the office and finding Ella was in London. He had made love to her on that very first occasion, in his hotel room. She knew she should have been less available, but he was so completely irresistible and she was lucky that he even gave her a second glance.

He dressed hurriedly, seeming anxious to leave. 'Would you like some coffee, or can I fix you some breakfast?' Jackie fussed.

'No, no, I'm fine.'

'You have plenty of time.'

'I said no . . . thanks.' She sat miserably watching him. 'Now you will remember to call Ella,' he said. 'I don't know where the hell she's gone to this Christmas. I've tried ringing her repeatedly from home but she hasn't even bothered to put on the answer phone.' Jackie looked at him blankly. 'Jackie, you do remember what I said?' He sounded impatient.

'About the oil market?' Jackie said, dully.

'Yes, of course. You are concentrating, I hope. This is important, there's something going wrong, I just feel it in my bones. Everyone knows the oil market is in for a slump but I think it could be very serious and I think it could be long-term. The vibes I'm getting are bad and if I'm right, one of the first things to be hit will be property.'

'I'll tell her.'

Michael sighed. 'I don't think I'm getting across to you the importance of it, am I?'

Jackie pulled herself together. 'Yes, you are. Sorry, it's just that it's rather late and I'm sad you're going.'

'Yes, yes,' Michael dismissed her explanation. 'The problem is, the case I'm working on will be taking me to Toronto after Christmas which means I'll be out of town for three, maybe four weeks. Ella knows this, of course, and there are plenty of people geared up to see that her business runs smoothly while I'm away. However, what I'd like her to do is to come over to Houston as soon as possible and take a look around herself, suss it out, see what she thinks about the market. May be I'm over-reacting but since she's made me custodian of her Houston business, I want to do the right thing by her.'

'I understand,' said Jackie, distractedly.

'Just make sure you tell her.'

Jackie hesitated. 'About your business trip . . . will I see you before you go?'

'Not a chance,' said Michael. He was concentrating on straightening his tie in the mirror.

'Oh, I see.'

'I don't expect I'll be up in New York for a couple of months, probably three. There'll be a pile of work waiting for me when I get back to Houston and if I'm right about the oil market, what's bad business for Ella is good business for me.'

'It's Christmas now,' said Jackie, half to herself, 'so I may not see you again until nearly Easter.'

Michael swung round, smiling, bestowing on her the full

force of his charm. 'Cheer up. There must be plenty of young men in New York pining for your charms. Perhaps it's time you gave them some consideration.'

Jackie looked at him appalled. 'Are you saying you don't want to see me again?'

Michael looked at her, with a smile. 'You're such a serious little thing, aren't you?' He seized her shoulders and kissed her warmly on both cheeks. 'What I'm saying,' he said, keeping an arm round her, 'is that the problems in Houston will require Ella's personal attention for some months, I should think. It's my view that when she knows what's going on, she'll be anxious to stick around. I believe she should start carefully, slowly, putting her properties up for sale – not hurriedly, or that'll start panicking people and bring the price down – just one at a time. There's no one like Ella for shaking out a good deal and if she's to dispose of some of her assets, I reckon she'll want to do it personally.'

'Yes, yes, of course,' said Jackie, looking confused.

'You're not following me, are you Sweetheart?' Jackie shook her head. 'Ella and I well, you know, we had a relationship for some time, right?'

'Yes,' said Jackie in a strangled voice.

'Well, I reckon it would be pretty tactless for me to be seen having an affair with you, her right-hand woman, under her very nose. These last few months have been great while she's been away and no one's got hurt, but I don't want to upset her by rubbing her nose in the fact that she and I are no longer together.'

'I've got feelings, too,' said Jackie, in a small voice.

Michael hugged her some more. 'Yes, I'm sure you have but you and I, well it's just been a casual thing, hasn't it? With Ella it was more serious and I'm aware I upset her a lot at the time. I just don't think it would be very considerate, do you?'

He caught a glimpse of her crestfallen face, at the tears hanging on the end of her eyelids. This was proving more difficult than he had anticipated. He had been a damned fool to get involved with her in the first place. 'Look, Jackie,

Ella's done a lot for you, hasn't she?' Jackie nodded. 'Well, this would be a pretty dumb way to repay her, wouldn't it? I'm not saying we won't ever get back together again, of course we may, but not while Ella is in the States. Who knows, she may find herself a new deal once this Fulham project is launched and that will give us a chance to be together again. In the meantime, you understand, don't you, Honey?' He was rewarded by Jackie nodding, miserably. 'OK, I'd better get going.'

'Your plane's not for an hour and a half. It will only take you half an hour to get to the airport.'

'I know, I know,' said Michael, impatiently, 'but I have some calls to make.'

'On Christmas morning?'

'On Christmas morning,' he said, his voice suddenly hard and determined. Jackie knew better than to argue.

After he had gone, Jackie turned on the television – anything to dispel the sense of isolation and loneliness – and sat down in front of it with unseeing eyes. She was crying again but it didn't matter now. It didn't matter how she looked because no one was going to see her. For a moment, she thought longingly of her parents in their neat little terraced home in Harrow, and then dismissed the thought. She had chosen the life of a career girl in New York, she had to expect some knocks. You win some, you lose some but in her heart of hearts, Jackie Partridge knew that she would always be a loser, at any rate where men were concerned. Why was it? She knew she was not particularly attractive but she was not bad-looking either. She had good skin, the Americans loved her accent and she had so much love to give, she was just longing to make some man happy, to look after him, to give him children. Why in this city full of men, was there not one single man who seemed to want her, want what she had to offer?

On to the television screen flashed a group of cherubic choirboys, singing a Christmas carol. The children in the front row were no more than six or seven, hair plastered into place, their crystal clear voices heart-breakingly beautiful.

She would never have a son of her own, she thought, she would never marry now, she was sure of it. She knew she had been foolish to put so much store by her relationship with Michael Gresham but she had kept remembering her mother saying how attractive men often married plain girls — to boost the ego or some such nonsense. Her mother had cited several examples among her friends and it had seemed true at the time. Now her hopes were shattered and why, because of Ella. Ella wasn't even interested in Michael any more, she had told Jackie as much. They'd enjoyed a rather alcoholic lunch one day, having clinched a major deal, and Ella had told Jackie all about her affair with Michael: how she had found him in bed with a young, black girl and how surprised she had been that she had not been more hurt. So why was it necessary to be so cautious? Ella wouldn't mind: she should have told Michael that, made him see. It wasn't fair, Ella had everything: wealth, good-looks, a child, a jet-setting lifestyle . . .

Jackie buried her head in her hands. At that moment she hated Ella Kovac.

CHAPTER THIRTY-SIX

GLOUCESTERSHIRE
Christmas Eve 1984

'Bye, Tim. Thanks for a wonderful party, as usual.' The crystal clear voice of Babs Cunningham, notorious, ageing libertine and impressive drunk, was accentuated by the cold, hard frost of the night, as her car roared off down the drive.

'Thank God she's gone,' said Tim, wearily. 'She shouldn't be driving in her condition but if I'd said anything along those lines, she'd have taken it as an invitation to stay the night. She's a dear, but the thought of Babs with a crashing hangover on Christmas morning is just too much.'

'You sound tired,' said Ella, standing by his side. She shivered, 'And it's cold out here. Let's go inside.'

Tim let out a sigh, closed and bolted the great front door of Wickham and followed Ella into the study, where Greg and Belinda were sprawled on the sofa finishing off the remains of a bottle of champagne. 'Where's Millie?' Tim asked.

'She's already gone to bed.'

Tim looked surprised. 'Is she alright?'

'I think so, Daddy,' said Belinda, 'but she is suffering from a broken heart yet again, I'm afraid. It's some guy she met at a party, back in the summer. She's been seeing a lot of him and now, suddenly, he doesn't seem to be featuring. I've tried to talk to her about it but she won't tell me anything of course.'

Tim ran a hand distractedly through his hair and frowned. 'I can never get through to her either. I suppose it's understandable she won't talk to me about her men friends, but I just wish she'd talk to someone.' The image of Stephanie flashed through his mind. Millie was so like her mother. If only . . .

'Come on, Tim,' said Ella, lightly, 'falling in and out of love and breaking one's heart is all part of being young. You're making it sound like a major tragedy.'

Ella's dismissal of the situation irritated him. 'It is a major tragedy when one can no longer communicate with one's children,' he snapped.

Belinda got up and slipped her arm through her father's. 'Why the mood, Daddy? It's Christmas Eve remember – I hope you've done our stockings?'

'Yes, of course,' said Tim, relaxing a little. 'Though why, in God's name, I'm still doing stockings for you two great girls I can't think.'

'Tradition, like the party tonight,' said Belinda, 'Christmas wouldn't be Christmas without it.'

'Maybe but in order to qualify for a stocking, you have to be in bed and asleep, my girl.'

'Does Greg get one, too?'

'Of course,' said Tim, with a grin, looking affectionately at Greg.

'Oh really, Tim,' said Greg, 'I haven't had a stocking in years, have I Mom?'

'Perhaps not,' said Tim, 'but in this house you have one, the girls would never forgive me if you were left out. Go on now, off to bed, otherwise Father Christmas will miss you out.' Laughing, Belinda and Greg said their goodnights.

After they had gone, Ella gave Tim a quizzical look. 'There's something going on between those two, isn't there?'

'I don't know,' said Tim, 'they're good friends certainly.'

'More than that,' said Ella, 'I'm sure of it.'

Tim smiled. 'Women's intuition. You could be right. It's a strange thought, though.'

'You mean because of what happened between us?'

'Yes, I suppose so,' said Tim.

'You seem very . . . down, tonight,' Ella probed gently. 'Is there something wrong?'

'No, not really,' said Tim, 'I'm just tired. I'm afraid I'm not very good company. You go off to bed and I promise tomorrow to be full of *joie de vivre*. How will that do?'

'And you don't want to discuss it, whatever it is that's bugging you?' Tim shook his head. 'OK, I guess I'll do as you suggest.'

He could see the look of hurt on her face. He felt sorry for her, suddenly, but all he wanted her to do was to go and leave him alone.

'What about the clearing up?' Ella said.

'I'll stack a few glasses and leave the rest for the morning,' said Tim. 'Mrs Maggs will be in early. She's wonderful, that woman. Even on Christmas Day she insists on working.'

'Then let me help you,' said Ella.

'No,' said Tim, too quickly. 'No ... thanks, I won't do much, honestly.'

'You shouldn't do any when you're tired.'

There was a slight note of alarm in Ella's voice which Tim was quick to spot. 'You mean in case I have a fit?' he asked without compromise.

'I suppose so,' said Ella. She could not meet his eye. Instead she knelt down by the fire and started ineffectually poking at the logs.

'I've come a long way since that time in France,' said Tim. 'The drugs I'm taking now are way better and I'm much more experienced in recognizing the danger signals. I'm tired, yes, but more in spirit than body. There's no danger of me having a fit tonight, if that's worrying you.' There was an edge to his voice.

'It isn't worrying me,' said Ella, 'I just don't want you to make yourself ill.'

'It's not an illness,' said Tim, 'it's a condition.'

'I can't do anything right tonight, can I?' said Ella. 'OK, this condition or whatever – all I'm saying is that it upsets you and I don't want it to happen, that's all.'

'Just take my word for it, it won't,' said Tim. He hesitated. Good manners dictated he should be consolatory. 'I'm sorry I'm not being more sociable,' he said at last, 'it's particularly rude of me, bearing in mind that I've dragged you all the way down here for Christmas.'

'I had nowhere else to go,' said Ella, none too graciously. 'I'll see you in the morning.' She rose and left the room without a backward glance – no goodnight kiss, no warmth in her leave-taking. She knew she should be making more of an effort to get through to Tim, but she just could not cope with his cold English reserve.

Ella hurried across the hall, shivering with cold. What was it with the English that they had to have their houses the same temperature as their freeze boxes. She ran up the stairs, hurried across the landing and with relief opened the door of her bedroom to a blast of warm air. Long ago, a condition of Ella staying at Wickham had been established whereby she had to have a large electric fire in her room, summer and winter alike. The fire had been on ever since she had arrived that morning, yet despite the superficial warmth of the room, there was an underlying damp, a coldness – or was she imagining it? Was it her spirits which were making her feel out of sorts? Hurriedly, she stripped off her clothes, removed her makeup and climbed thankfully into bed, absurdly grateful for the warmth that greeted her there – an electric blanket had been another essential ingredient of staying at Wickham. She turned off the light and lay in the darkness, turning over in her mind her conversation with Tim.

During the last few years they had established a good, solid, platonic friendship, yet underneath it all there was always a tension. They had been lovers once, perhaps they could be again. Tim had never so much as hinted that this was the case, but Ella always felt that even the slightest encouragement from her would bring him back to her bed, if that's what she wanted. Now, suddenly, she was not so sure. He seemed preoccupied and distant. Was there perhaps someone else? Had he got tired of waiting for her, if indeed that's what he had been doing? She tried to marshall her thoughts. After all the years of loving, her relationship with Aaron was clearly over. She supposed this meant she needed a man in her life and if this was the case, what better person could there be than Tim? But as always, she could not think of Tim, without in the same breath thinking of his epilepsy, and her fear of it was not something she could either hide from herself nor, it appeared, from him. He had been quick to spot her apprehension tonight and indeed the thought of him suddenly having a fit when the two of them were alone appalled her. She wondered at Stephanie, how she'd been able to cope all those years. It was difficult, no, impossible to understand why it appeared to worry her not at all. The knowledge that she found his *condition* — she stressed the word in her mind — so abhorrent, made Ella feel very ashamed. It was irrational, too, her fear. It was ridiculous, he would never harm her while having a fit, neither was the condition catching or terminal, yet still the very thought of it horrified her and while it did, she knew there was no hope of a future with Tim. Should she tell him, she wondered? No, for in her heart she felt certain he already knew.

It took Tim less than twenty minutes to clear the glasses from the three main rooms. He worked his way systematically round each room. God, people were messy. Cigarettes, half-eaten sausages, all piled in ash trays; glasses knocked over, peanuts scattered across the carpet. He detested the smell of champagne and cigarettes. What's wrong with me? he thought, as he worked — a regular Scrooge. It had been a successful party, it always was. Anyone who was anyone in Gloucestershire came to the Wickham party on Christmas Eve. It was a tradition which had been begun by Stephanie's father and which Tim felt compelled to continue. Not compelled, that was the wrong word. He wanted to continue, he believed in traditions.

The job finally completed, he turned out the lights in the house but the thought of bed and sleep held no appeal. Instead he drifted back to the study, threw another couple of logs on the fire and poured himself a whisky. He had not drunk during the party, he never did. His doctor allowed him one whisky a night and this evening he made it a little larger than normal and took it to his desk, where he sat down and stared at the papers in front of him with unseeing eyes.

There was no future for him and Ella. In reality, he supposed he had known it ever since France, but somehow seeing her here at Christmas only served to highlight the problems of their relationship. It was not simply a question of her being afraid of his epilepsy, though God knows that was enough. The fact remained she didn't fit. Perhaps he was not being fair. She'd been a good co-hostess at the party and done her best to find something in common with his guests, many of whom she found quite extraordinary, he knew. But then the landed gentry of England were a race apart, he recognized that. How could he expect an American, with Ella's background, to fit into his way of life, indeed why should she? Yet strangely her son did: Greg had been at home in the English countryside from the very first day he had set foot in it. It was like he had come home, Tim thought, fancifully, and with affection. He was inordinately fond of Greg – the son he had never had, perhaps, he thought. There was a warmth about the boy, an instinctive gentleness, whether he was dealing with people or animals. He would make a good farmer, the best – and if Ella was right and there was something between him and Belinda, it would make him very happy, Tim realized. So why the depression? He took a sip of his whisky and as he did so his eyes caught the photograph in front of him. It showed a youthful Stephanie, the girls hanging round her neck – babies almost, two and four perhaps, not more. They were all laughing. It was spring and Stephanie had a piece of apple blossom tucked behind her ear. The picture clutched at his heart, making him draw in his breath sharply. It never failed to surprise him that after everything that had happened, he should still be as much in love with his wife as he had ever been. At last he could admit it to himself, but the knowledge brought him no comfort, just a feeling of emptiness, bitterness and jealousy, too, thinking of her in the arms of Alex Meyer.

'Stephanie', he said the word aloud and raising his glass towards the photograph he whispered, 'Happy Christmas, Darling.' That was what was wrong with tonight, there was no Stephanie. Without her at his side, this party, like all parties, held no joy for him. They had spoken early in the day. Stephanie had rung to wish them all a happy Christmas. Her voice had sounded small, sad and ridiculously far away. It was that which had affected him, he knew. At least when she was happy, even if it was with another man, he could convince himself that their parting had been for the best. But when she sounded as she had done today, vulnerable and forlorn, he could not bear it. He wanted to run to her, wherever she was, and take her in his arms and make whatever the hurt was, better.

He looked again at the photograph. He had been so proud to have her as his wife, so proud and grateful. Perhaps it was this gratitude which had adversely affected their marriage. Her obsession with her business, to the detriment of himself and his children, he had accepted because he felt he owed her so much. A different man, a more confident man, would have stopped her. Yet could anyone stop Stephanie Bonham from pursuing something she definitely wanted? He doubted it. He drained his whisky glass and stood up. A smile suddenly flitted across his face at the irony of the situation. Here he had under his roof a charming, desirable woman who had loved him once and might, with careful wooing, love him again. Yet there was no way he could pursue the relationship with all honesty, because he was still in love with his wife who clearly never gave him a thought.

Tim switched out the light and started up the stairs. Then remembering the stockings, he returned to the study, retrieved them from his cupboard and began climbing the stairs again. The past seemed everywhere to be mocking him. He could remember so many Christmases when the children were tiny. Of he and Stephanie, a little drunk from the party, giggling their way upstairs with brimming stockings. They had prepared stockings for each other, too. He remembered one year Stephanie had delivered his in the bizarre attire of a shaving-cream beard, one of the children's red pom-pom hats and nothing else. He had carefully wiped away the foam and then made love to her. Too many memories . . . He shook his head to clear his mind and continued up the stairs.

CHAPTER THIRTY-SEVEN

LONDON
January 1985

Ella glanced at her watch impatiently. It was almost twelve-twenty and Stephanie had been due at twelve. It was not like her to be late, certainly not this late. She had a light lunch already laid out in the conservatory and, on impulse, a bottle of champagne stood waiting to be opened in the cooler. After all, they were discussing the grand opening of their joint project – they deserved a celebration.

The Fulham project had taken three years to emerge from the drawing-board and become a reality. It was known as the West London Meyer Centre which upset Ella not at all but caused Stephanie a great deal of aggravation. Still, it was finished, it looked good and the opening the following month was tipped to be the event of the season.

Unable to settle down to any more work, Ella wandered through into the conservatory and gazed out on the bare January bleakness to the patch of garden beyond. She loved this little house – her own home in London. It was in a quiet mews off Holland Park, not nearly as fashionable as Stephanie's headquarters, nor as flamboyant, but it suited her well. The house had a cottage atmosphere and Greg loved it as much as she did; indeed, he had helped her choose it. Greg ... they had come a long way since his moment of madness with Margot. He was now in his third year at Cirencester Agricultural College and was having a wonderful time. He had stacks of friends and tended to go to Wickham at weekends, taking loads of Cirencester students with him, which always pleased the Irvine girls. In the holidays, though, he spent most of the time with his mother. All trace of their former difficulties had gone, and Ella recognized the reason for this. At last Greg was leading the sort of life he had always wanted. A childhood spent in the concrete jungle of New York had been all wrong for him, and though he had tried to tell her so repeatedly over the years, she had not been prepared to listen. She knew why. Warren Clay, the boy she was sure was Greg's father, was a farmer's son, as indeed was his father and grandfather before him. The Clays had farmed in Kentucky for as long as anyone could remember. Was it so surprising that farming was in Greg's blood? Her reluctance in accepting this fact, of course, had been part of a general reluctance to accept that Greg could have inherited anything from the boy who had raped her. While not fighting her son's instincts exactly, she had chosen to ignore his desire for a country life, something she now deeply regretted. Still, that was all behind them. Thanks to Tim and his encouragement, Greg was set on the right path. She doubted if she would ever get him back to America, but did it matter? He loved England and the English way of life. Once the Fulham project was launched, she would look for other work in England which would keep her in touch with her son.

The doorbell rang and Ella went swiftly to open it. Stephanie looked decidedly frazzled and quite unlike her normal self. She wore an old duffle coat over a faded tweed skirt, her hair was untidy, almost to the point of being unkempt, and her face was deathly pale with dark circles under her eyes. 'I'm sorry I'm late,' she said, 'it's been one of those mornings.'

'Not to worry,' said Ella, lightly. 'Come on in, I have some champagne on ice.'

'Champagne! What on earth for?'

'To celebrate our opening, since that's what we're here to talk about.'

'Oh that!' said Stephanie. 'It's hardly a cause for celebration.'

'Why ever not?' said Ella. 'We've both making a great deal of money out of the development personally, and wearing your Meyer hat, you're going to continue to reap the rewards into the sunset. Where's the problem?'

Stephanie relented a little. 'You're right, of course. I'm sorry, I'm just being scratchy. Perhaps a glass of your champagne would help.'

Ella began opening the bottle. 'Is anything wrong?' she asked.

'No, no nothing. Did you have a good Christmas?' Her voice was sharp.

So that's it, Ella thought. Even after all this time she still minds me seeing Tim. 'Yes, we did have a good time, the children especially.'

'And I suppose you did the full bit – cocktail party at home on Christmas Eve, church on Christmas Day, followed by Major Cowdrey's drinks party and open house at the Stevensons on Boxing Day.'

'Yes, yes, that's right,' said Ella. She handed Stephanie a glass and looked at her shrewdly. 'It's bugging you, isn't it, Greg and I being at Wickham for Christmas? I'm sorry, but I did ask you first, and I honestly never thought you would mind or I wouldn't have gone at all.'

'No, no, of course it hasn't upset me,' said Stephanie, irritably. 'At least I'm not upset that you were there, but perhaps just a little that I wasn't.'

'There's nothing between Tim and me now,' said Ella, hesitantly.

Stephanie rounded on her. 'Oh, so you think that's what is upsetting me, do you? You think I'm jealous of you, because of your relationship with my ex-husband? I'm sick to death of telling you how wrong you are. Tim and I were washed up years ago and I have no feelings for him at all other than the fact that he is the father of my children. I don't know why you persist in thinking that whatever you and Tim get up to is any concern of mine.'

Her words irritated Ella, but she did not attempt to retaliate. She could see that Stephanie was currently a deeply unhappy woman, and for some reason her denial of still caring for Tim was wholly unconvincing. Not for the first time, Ella thanked God she had not been tempted to become involved with Tim again. Quickly, she turned the conversation towards business and soon they were pouring over their files discussing final arrangements for the opening of the West London Meyer Centre. It was nearly three by the time they sat down to lunch.

'I noticed from the guest list,' said Ella, 'that you've included Margot Haigh. I deliberately excluded her.'

Stephanie hesitated, fork poised in mid-air. 'We have to ask her, Ella, whatever your personal feelings. She put together the finance for this project and through me dealt with it on a day-to-day basis.'

'I simply thought we could ask her chairman instead. I've never met John Shepherd and I thought perhaps it's time we did.'

'By all means ask the chairman,' said Stephanie, 'but we have to ask Margot as well.'

'I don't see why,' said Ella, stubbornly.

'Oh really,' said Stephanie, exasperated. 'It's been quite ridiculous the way I've had to be responsible for all contact with the bank over this project just so that you two did not have to deal with one another personally. OK, so I've bridged the gap pro tem, but you can't keep up this feud for ever. You're two mature women and I have to say that while I agree that Greg was probably better out of the situation, the fact is I think he was a very lucky young man to have Margot as his tutor for his first sexual encounter. For most young boys, it's normally an undignified scuffle in the back of a car with a girl no more experienced than they are. Greg certainly embarked on adult life with some style.'

'It's easy for you to talk like that,' said Ella, 'because he's not your son.'

'Look,' said Stephanie, 'it takes two to tango, remember? Margot didn't drag Greg to her bed unwillingly. I actually happen to believe that she was very fond of him and it was quite a wrench for her parting with him.'

'Oh, don't be ridiculous,' said Ella. 'He may have been a sop to her ego but nothing more.'

'Perhaps you're right,' said Stephanie, 'I don't know. Anyway, either way, Margot has to be there.'

'But Greg's coming, along with Tim and the girls.'

'OK, so Greg and Margot and two or three thousand other people are all going to be at the Meyer Centre together on the same day. Big deal. Are you frightened they might get back together again?'

'I suppose I am,' Ella admitted.

'In which case,' said Stephanie, 'I think your fears are groundless.'

'I just hope you're right,' said Ella.

'Always the mother hen,' said Stephanie, 'you worry too much. Children are much better left to get on with it. How are my two, incidentally? You've seen more of them recently than I have?' Again, there was the sharp note in her voice.

'They're fine, very well, they asked after you, of course.'

'Of course,' said Stephanie, sarcastically.

'Look, I know you may not have a very conventional mother/daughter relationship with either of them,' Ella said, anxious to comfort, 'but they're both enormously proud of you, you know that.'

'I don't need you to tell me what my daughters think of me,' said Stephanie.

'I wasn't,' said Ella, patiently, 'I'm just trying to say you needn't feel bad about how little you see them, because they expect their relationship with you to be like that.'

'I don't need your reassurance, Ella,' said Stephanie.

I should have kept my big mouth shut, Ella thought. Whatever the reason, Tim and the girls are clearly a taboo subject. 'I'm sorry, I wasn't trying to interfere,' she said, gently. 'Would you like some coffee?'

Stephanie glanced at her watch. 'No, I think I'd better be getting back. I said I'd be in the office again at three. We've just about covered everything, haven't we?'

'I guess so,' said Ella. The two women got up and walked to the front door. 'I was thinking,' said Ella, 'I would like to do another project in England, I mean a major project, apart from the odd block of apartments I'm dealing in currently.'

'Flats,' said Stephanie.

'How do you mean?' Ella asked.

'They're called flats in England. What sort of project have you in mind?'

'I don't know really, that's what I wanted to ask you. Would you be interested in our joining forces on something else?'

Stephanie shook her head. 'I don't think I could stand the hassle with the Meyers.'

'But surely,' said Ella, 'if we did another project together you wouldn't have any hassle. The reason Joseph was so uptight last time was because you used what he saw to be confidential information. If we found an interesting site with no Meyer connection, the way property's escalating at the moment, particularly in London –'

'The answer's no,' Stephanie interrupted.

'I thought we worked well together,' Ella persisted.

'Look, can you leave it alone, Ella. I'm late, I don't have time to discuss this now and in any event I've given my decision.'

There was clearly nothing more to say. Whatever was upsetting Stephanie was certainly not likely to enhance their relationship just at the moment. The telephone rang. 'Hold on,' Ella said, 'I'll just answer that.'

'I won't wait,' said Stephanie, 'no doubt we'll meet again before the opening. See you around.'

For a moment, Ella stood rooted on the spot, watching Stephanie cross the street towards her car, both confused and dismayed by her behaviour. At last the persistence of the telephone dragged her away.

'Hello, Miss Kovac?'

'Yes,' said Ella. It was a female voice she did not recognize.

'This is Joseph Meyer's secretary. Is Stephanie Bonham with you by any chance?'

'She's just left,' said Ella.

'Oh, no.' The woman sounded distraught.

'I might be able to catch her,' said Ella, 'hang on.'

'Thank you, it is terribly urgent.'

Ella dropped the telephone and ran out into the street. It was virtually dark. Stephanie was just easing her BMW out of the parking space and Ella ran across the road waving her arms. 'What is it?' said Stephanie, opening the window, clearly annoyed.

'It's Joseph Meyer's secretary on the telephone. She says it's urgent.'

'I'll ring her when I get back to the office.'

'Honestly, Stephanie, I think you ought to take the call. I don't know how to explain – she sounded sort of frantic.'

'Oh drat,' said Stephanie. 'Alright, what does he want now, I wonder.' She re-parked the car and followed Ella across the street.

To be tactful, Ella started to leave the room but the tone of Stephanie's voice stopped her. 'No,' she heard her say, 'no. Are you absolutely sure? Is there really no ... no mistake?' There was a pause. 'I see.' Her voice was barely above a whisper. 'Yes, thank you for letting me know.'

'What is it, what's happened?' said Ella.

Stephanie was standing, receiver in hand, her face ashen. Slowly she sank into the chair beside her and raised a tortured face to Ella. 'Alex ... he's been involved in a skiing accident, an avalanche. He's dead.'

CHAPTER THIRTY-EIGHT

NEW YORK
January 1985

Joseph Meyer stood to attention as they lowered the body of his son into the open grave. The snow fell relentlessly, like tears, but much to his own surprise, he remained dry-eyed. There would be years of tears ahead, as long as he lived, but at this moment he felt a strange numbness, as though he was watching a film of someone else's grief and bereavement. He had chosen to bury his son in New York so that he could be beside his mother. That left just two of them – Joseph, as he felt now, at the end of a long and fruitless life, and his daughter, Freda, warped irrevocably by man's inhumanity to man, eking out a nothing life in a body which would not set her free. It was all over except for ... across the gaping wound in the earth, he could see Stephanie standing head bowed beside Ella Kovac. Both women were sheltering under an umbrella and it was impossible to see the expression on either of their faces. Was she grieving, he wondered? Had she really loved his son or was it his position she loved. For above everything else, Joseph judged that Stephanie was motivated by a desire to succeed.

Try as he may, Joseph could not feel sorry for Stephanie. Her long-standing affair with Alex had stopped him settling down with a nice Jewish girl who could have provided the next generation of Meyers. A great believer in family life, it also pained Joseph considerably to think of Stephanie abandoning her husband, and above all her children, for his son's sake. He might have been able to come to terms with it if their relationship had developed into marriage. As it was, he could only see their affair as useless and fruitless, simply hurting people unnecessarily. At this moment, he could not find it in his heart to blame his son but he could blame Stephanie Bonham.

The group of people around the grave were starting to move away. The rabbi came to his side. 'Are you going home now, Mr Meyer? Would you like me to come with you, to talk?'

Over his shoulder, Joseph could see Stephanie and Ella hurrying away. 'No, no, excuse me, I have to see someone. I'm sorry to be rude.' He caught them, by the line of cars waiting to take the mourners away. 'Stephanie?' She turned. Her appearance shocked him profoundly. She had lost a great deal of weight, her face was very pale and her eyes red-ringed. She looked very different from the golden girl he had met so long ago. 'Stephanie, we need to talk.'

'Not now,' she ventured.

'Yes, now. The car's just here, we'll go back to the hotel.'

'I can't,' she said.

Joseph took her arm. 'You owe me,' he said.

They did not speak at all on the journey to the Meyer Hotel, each locked in a silent world of grief. It occurred to Joseph that they were the two people who knew Alex best in the world, yet somehow he did not feel he would ever be able to discuss his son with this woman.

The flags on top of the Meyer building were flying at half mast. A doorman leapt forward, recognizing the car, and ushered them inside. 'Come up to my apartment,' said Joseph. It was an order rather than an invitation. Stephanie followed numbly to the presidential suite on the top floor.

Once inside the sumptuous apartment, and alone, the silence between them seemed to paralyze them both. They stared at one another helplessly. 'Do you want anything,' Joseph asked, 'a drink?'

'I don't know.'

'I'll fetch us some brandy.'

Stephanie watched as the familiar little figure bustled

about, organizing drinks. She had hated him for a long time now, yet today she could not find it in her heart to do so, but then nor could she forgive him either. But for his father's intervention, she was sure those last years with Alex would have been very different. Maybe, after all, they would have married. Maybe he would not have gone on the skiing holiday in view of her pregnancy. Maybe they would have gone together and died together under the mountain of snow. Anything would have been better than this.

'Here you are.' Joseph handed her a large brandy, his hand trembling as he did so. She took it and sipped silently. 'I'm sorry it's necessary to talk to you at this moment, Stephanie. Whatever our differences, I appreciate it is not an easy time for you.' Joseph avoided her eye. 'I imagine you can guess what I want to talk to you about?'

Stephanie shook her head. 'I have no idea.'

'I want to talk to you about the child you're carrying.'

Stephanie gasped. 'How do you know about that? Nobody knows.'

'Alex told his friend, Peter Barlow, the man who survived the avalanche. Peter came to see me a couple of days ago, to tell me details of – well, how Alex died. He asked me if I knew about the child. I didn't, of course. Alex did not often confide in me, as you know. What horrified me most was that Alex apparently wanted you to get rid of it.' Stephanie nodded, dumbly. 'H-have you done so?' The old man tried to keep the emotion from his voice but it was tremulous and there were tears in his eyes.

'No, I haven't.'

'Thank God. I will do everything, everything I can for you, you know that. Please let me help you, Stephanie, in whatever way I can, and the child, of course the child.'

'No,' said Stephanie, quietly, without any visible emotion.

'You mean, you're going ahead with an abortion?' Joseph Meyer was hunched forward now, quite literally ringing his hands in his anguish.

'No,' said Stephanie, 'I'm totally against abortion. I-I'd already told Alex, even though he didn't want the child, that

I was not prepared to have an abortion for his convenience, but nor am I prepared to have it brought up as a Meyer product either.'

'I understand that,' said Joseph, relaxing a little.

'I don't think you do,' said Stephanie. 'I don't wish to be unkind and critical of you at this moment, but ... look, whether you believe it or not, we both loved Alex – I perhaps not as obsessively as you, but I did love him very, very much. However, it did not blind me to his faults. He was impossibly selfish, arrogant, conceited and believed the world should revolve around him. However, far more damaging than any of these characteristics was the core of his problem – an enormous inferiority complex because he could not compete with you.'

'I will not hear you speak of my son like this,' said Joseph.

'I'm sorry if it hurts you but I need to explain. I realize that this child I am carrying represents your one hope for the future but I have to tell you that, boy or girl, this child will be no Meyer. This child will have a normal childhood – he or she will grow up not under your shadow but a free spirit. If nothing else, I owe that to Alex.'

'Don't you think you also owe to Alex the chance for his son or daughter to benefit from what I am and what I have to give?'

'No,' said Stephanie. 'Alex did not want this child. Alex told me that if I persisted in carrying it, he would disown both me and it. He told me that the child would never bear your name and that he would never acknowledge it as his own. The Meyers have already rejected this child, Joseph.'

'Alex in his foolishness may have rejected it, I haven't.'

'It was Alex's right so to do,' said Stephanie, 'not yours.'

Visibly before her eyes, it seemed to Stephanie that Joseph Meyer was ageing. She knew she was responsible, knew she should feel a sense of compassion, bearing in mind the long, long road this old man had come and knowing that today he had buried his only and much loved son. Yet there was no room for compromise and there was no point in leaving a door ajar which she intended firmly to shut.

'Are you saying I may never see the child?' There was a pleading note in Joseph's voice.

'I think it would be best for you both if that was the case.'

'How can you do this to me?' Joseph burst out. 'To deprive me of my dead son's child. How can you do it?'

'I can do it because I believe it is right.'

'What do you want?' said Joseph. 'You can have anything, the whole damned group for all I care. Anything, anything, however much power, money you want, you can have it all.'

Stephanie shook her head. 'I have the franchise and I will continue to run that as I have always done, efficiently and to your satisfaction.'

'You cannot be a good mother and continue in this business, the child will never see you.'

'That's up to me,' said Stephanie. 'I will make arrangements so that the child is well looked after, you can be sure of that.'

'Is this revenge?' Joseph said, after a pause. 'Is this your way of getting back at me because I would never accept you as Alex's woman? If so, you could not have found a more effective weapon.'

'No,' said Stephanie, 'it's not revenge. I can only repeat, I'm doing what I believe is best for the child.'

'I don't believe you,' said Joseph.

'I can't help that,' said Stephanie. She set down the brandy glass. It was time to go now, quickly while she still had the strength. 'I'll go now, shall I, there was nothing else?'

'No, nothing else.' Joseph Meyer suddenly slumped into his chair, a little old man finally broken by life. Stephanie felt remorse but not enough to change her mind. He would rally in a few days, she reasoned. Joseph Meyer was a survivor, she need not waste her sympathy on him. Yet as she crossed the room to the door, she looked back. He sat, small and almost frail-looking, like a helpless baby, and just for a fleeting moment the desire to run to him, to throw her arms round him, to weep out her misery was almost overwhelming. This man had fathered Alex. Could it be right to tear herself away from the one close tie she had with the man she had just lost? She carried the seed of Alex within her; it was Joseph's too. For a moment she hesitated. Then she turned abruptly and left the room.

Back in her own hotel room, Stephanie could not settle. Again and again, she went over in her mind the meeting with Joseph, justifying to herself the things that she had said and the stand she had taken. Joseph had been given his chance at life, Alex, too. This child needed his — she was already sure it was a boy. It was imperative that he was not sucked into the Meyer empire. For a moment she thought of her own childhood at Wickham, that was the sort of environment her child needed but to provide it was not going to be easy. She would never deprive Tim of his home even for her child. Tim *was* Wickham now, the two were inseparable. She tried to detect a flaw in her feelings. Could Joseph be right, could she be seeking revenge? No, no, and yet ... she had to admit that for once it was good to be able to withhold something from the Meyers, something which they wanted but could not have.

CHAPTER THIRTY-NINE

NEW YORK
January 1985

Something had happened to Jackie. Ella recognized it immediately, despite her preoccupation with the mound of work on her desk. The girl was polite, as efficient as ever, but oddly detached. The morning's work included the need for some leases to be delivered to a publishing company, only two blocks up the road. Using the excuse that Jackie looked peaky and needed a breath of fresh air, Ella managed to get her out of the office and immediately called in Jessie.

'England suits you,' Jessie said, without preamble, 'but I miss you and I miss that boy of yours. Tell me about him, every last detail.'

Wasting precious moments, Ella gave Jessie a quick update on Greg and his life and then turned the conversation to Jackie. 'What's wrong with Jackie do you reckon, Jessie?'

'Man trouble,' said Jessie, promptly.

'Again! That girl doesn't have much luck with men, does she?'

'Nor will she, I guess,' said Jessie philosophically. 'She's a born loser where men are concerned. A man's only got to walk in here off the street, and provided he's wearing pants, old or young, she comes over kind of stupid. Not like you and me – we see them as a necessary evil, don't we?' Jessie grinned at Ella, engagingly.

'I think you're right,' said Ella. 'Have you any idea who's causing the trouble this time?'

'I was hoping you weren't going to ask me that,' said Jessie.

400

'I'm asking,' said Ella, firmly.

'I reckon it must be your Michael Gresham.'

'Michael, surely not! She's not his type at all, Jessie.'

'I agree with you,' said Jessie. 'I don't like the man because he hurt you and anyone who hurts you, hurts me. Still, I will admit he has class and I would have thought he'd have gone for something more exotic than Jackie, so maybe I'm wrong. He took her out to dinner once, oh, six or seven months back, and, of course, they call each other normally two or three times a week, but that's always about business. I don't know, maybe I'm losing my touch.' She grinned, hugely, displaying wonderful white teeth. 'Do you want me to do a little detective work for you?'

'I'd appreciate it,' said Ella. 'I have to get back to London in the next couple of days and I don't really feel I have the time to sort out Jackie's love life. Could you do it for me?'

'Leave it to me, Boss,' said Jessie, with a grin.

It was a decision that Ella was to regret, regret very much indeed.

Ella worked in the office until after nine that evening and then went upstairs to her apartment. It was strange – the apartment had been home for so many years, Greg had grown up there, it was the base from which everything had flowed and yet somehow it no longer seemed like home. The little mews house in London was that now. Home is where Greg is, Ella realized, and she found the thought disturbing. More than once in the last two or three years, she found herself recognizing the danger signals which others had pin-pointed over the years. Greg had been her life, her *raison d'être*, but now he was moving away from her, forming his own life and the void created seemed sometimes unbearable.

Jessie, of course, had stocked both fridge and freezer but Ella did not feel hungry. She helped herself to a whisky, sat down on the sofa and eyed the telephone thoughtfully. It was two weeks since she had received the letter from Aaron. It had come as an extraordinary shock for it was the first proper communication she had received from him in nearly four years. His rambling disjointed epistle had nevertheless made his feelings plain: he wanted her, in what capacity he did not know, but he needed her back in his life. On receiving the letter it had been tempting to abandon everything and take the next flight to New York, but caution had prevailed. There seemed so much at stake with Aaron. Having loved him all her life, their estrangement had been an agony to her, but she knew they could not simply pick up the threads of their old relationship as if nothing had happened. Somehow, she had built a life for herself without Aaron but she knew, instinctively, that if she let him into her life again it would be to make herself vulnerable in a way she had not been before. Up until the night they had spent together she had only fantasized about a romantic encounter with Aaron. Now she knew the reality of it, she also knew that all her childish dreams paled into insignificance compared with how things could be between them. His letter suggested that he felt as uncertain as she, but he had not attempted to disguise his need for her. It was a cry for help and she could not but respond. Aaron ... as much a part of her as Greg, as the air she breathed. She drained her whisky glass and taking a deep breath, lifted the telephone. 'Aaron, it's Ella.'

'Ella!' He at once sounded both pleased and apprehensive. 'You got my letter?'

'Yes, I did,' said Ella.

'I thought may be you were angry about it, since I hadn't heard from you. Were you?'

'Of course I wasn't,' said Ella. 'I'm sorry I haven't been in touch, but I ... well, I needed to think about it.'

'And?' said Aaron.

'We need to talk,' said Ella.

'I agree. I was thinking, I have a chunk of holiday owing – why don't I come over to England for a couple of weeks?'

'There's no need for that,' said Ella. 'I'm here in New York.'

'In New York! Now, at this moment?' The obvious joy in his voice warmed her heart.

'Yes, right now,' said Ella. 'I came over to attend the

funeral of Alex Meyer. You probably saw the press coverage.'

'Yes, I did, poor devil. I didn't know you were friendly with the Meyers.'

'Business,' said Ella, 'I didn't know him well.'

'Oh, I see. Ella, can we meet?'

'That's why I'm ringing,' said Ella. 'We could go out to dinner, perhaps.'

'Are you in your apartment?' Aaron asked.

'Yes.'

'I'll be there in ten minutes and then we can decide what we want to do.'

She just had time to change and fix her makeup before the buzzer rang, impatiently. She forced herself to stay calm and walk slowly and steadily to the apartment door. Aaron stood there, taller, fairer, better-looking than her memories of him and at the same time, so infinitely dear and familiar. She did not think, she did not even wait for him to come into the apartment, she simply hurled herself into his arms. He held her close and then scooping her up, carried her into the apartment, to the sofa, where he held her tight and kissed her – lover's kisses but gentle, controlled. She felt safe in his arms.

At last he drew away a little, his face very serious. 'I didn't realize it, until this moment,' he said, 'but that night, the night we spent together, has changed our relationship irrevocably, hasn't it? We can't ever go back to just being brother and sister.'

Ella's face fell. 'Can't we?' she asked, in a small voice.

'I-I don't think so.' He still held her in the circle of his arms, gently, but he trembled a little as he spoke, his face troubled. 'I just never realized how much I was attracted to you. I-I suppose because of Alice the whole thing was unthinkable and therefore it never crossed my mind. Since that night, I've tried so hard to see you as I used to, as my funny little tomboy friend.' He smiled a little. 'Yet the image I have of you now is of a highly desirable woman, a woman who's made me feel as I haven't felt in years, if ever.'

Ella studied his face in silence for a moment, her heart

beating. 'You mean that night together was . . .' she struggled for words.

'For me . . . it was wonderful,' said Aaron, 'like nothing that has ever been before, like a new experience.'

Ella stared at him. 'But that's how I felt, too.'

'Oh, darling, darling Ella.' He drew her into his arms and kissed her.

It was some moments before they drew apart. 'I thought you'd hated the whole thing,' Ella said, in a shaky voice. 'The next morning you seemed so . . . so angry, so upset about what had happened.'

'Only because I felt I'd betrayed our friendship,' said Aaron. 'We were both drunk and I felt I'd taken advantage of you and our relationship. Then of course, because it was you, and because I know how you've suffered in the hands of men, it was all the worse. I suppose I felt guilty, too, about Alice, it was so soon after her death.'

'Yes, it was,' said Ella.

'I felt sure you must hate me and I thought it was probably best that we parted, because I simply couldn't face you.'

'We've been very stupid,' said Ella, 'very, very stupid. You and I of all people, who have never had a moment's difficulty in communicating with one another, letting this happen. It's crazy.'

'We can put it right,' said Aaron gently. 'How long are you in New York?'

'Only for a couple of days,' said Ella.

'A couple of days, oh hell, I thought you'd be back permanently now.'

Ella shook her head. 'I have to get back to London because the Fulham opening takes place at the beginning of next month. She averted her eyes. 'And then, well, I . . . I think I'll look for another project in London. Property's going crazy over there at the moment.'

'But why?' said Aaron. He moved away from her. 'I don't understand you. You have your Houston business and you have your business here . . . surely they can't run themselves indefinitely? Sooner or later something will go drastically wrong if you continue to spend all your time in London.' A thought struck him. 'Is there . . . someone over there — that guy, the one with epilepsy?'

'I've seen quite a lot of him,' said Ella, 'but our relationship is purely platonic, there's nothing to it now.'

'And is that the way you want it to stay?'

'Yes,' said Ella, 'there's no future for Tim and me.'

'Because of his condition?'

'Partly,' said Ella.

'And what are the other reasons?' Aaron persisted.

'Because . . . because of you,' said Ella, simply.

He moved closer, his arms were tight around her. 'Then why, why do you have to find another project in London?'

'I like London, I feel at home there. The pace is much slower than New York and it suits me. It's old age, I expect.' She tried a bright smile but Aaron did not respond.

'It's Greg, isn't it? he said.

'I suppose so,' Ella admitted. 'I know he's making his own life over there and doing very well, but he's still very young, I like to be around, and also . . .' she hesitated.

'Go on,' said Aaron.

'I guess he's probably going to stay in England permanently. He hasn't said so but I think that's his intention.'

'So you want to stay in England, too?'

'Not all the time,' said Ella, defensively, 'but if I have the odd project going on, I could at least spend part of each year there.'

'During the last few years, you've spent practically all your time in London,' said Aaron. 'Why should the future be any different?' His voice sounded bitter.

'Is it so wrong for me to want to be near my child?'

'No, no, of course not,' said Aaron, 'it's just that I don't see what future there is for us.'

'Is there an *us* then?' Ella asked.

'I want to marry you,' said Aaron, abruptly, as though suddenly making the decision. 'I don't want you as my little sister any more, or my lover, I want you as my wife.'

'Oh Aaron,' Ella whispered, they kissed.

'Let me show you how much I love you,' Aaron said, hoarsely, 'properly this time. I love you so much, Ella.'

He took her hand and led her through to her bedroom. They were both nervous and unsure. Before, drink had blunted their senses, enabling them to take the giant step from lifelong friendship to becoming lovers. Ella drew the curtains, Aaron switched on the bedside light. They undressed quickly, turning away from one another, embarrassed, self-conscious. They slipped between the sheets. Aaron held out his arms, and the moment Ella came into them, the moment their bodies touched, they both let out a great sigh of relief. They clung to one another, skin on skin, savouring each other's warmth.

'I can't begin to tell you how often I've longed for this,' Aaron whispered.

'I tried not to think about us at all – I guess I was afraid,' said Ella.

'Afraid of what?' Aaron asked.

'Of daring to think there might be any future for us because I thought you regretted what had happened between us. What took you so long to write, Aaron?'

'I don't know. Perhaps I felt we weren't ready until now . . .'

He kissed her, they began caressing one another, both aware of the extraordinary contrast between knowing each other so well as people but so little as lovers. They made love swiftly then, both aware of the desperate need in the other. It seemed to Ella, as they climaxed together, shouting out in triumph, that they had attained the impossible – the perfect union of mind and body. The thought made her cry and when she reached up to caress Aaron's cheek, she found his face, too, was wet with tears.

It was two o'clock in the morning when Ella woke to the chimes of the grandfather clock in the hall. Aaron slumbered by her side, she drew closer to him, seeking comfort and reassurance. It was extraordinary – almost as though they were two different people. When she thought of Aaron, she thought of the relationship they had enjoyed all their lives, yet now there was this new Aaron, the Aaron who had just made love to her, who made her feel as no man had ever done. She tried to think of the future: the irony of the situation was not lost to her. Years before, when she had loved Tim and thought she would marry him, the fact that she lived and worked in America had stood between them. Now the reverse applied with Aaron. Of course she did not have to stay in London but until this evening, that had been the course she had set for herself. It would not be easy to change direction.

Although Ella was lying perfectly still, the turmoil in her mind was considerable and perhaps it was this that made Aaron stir beside her. 'What are you thinking about?' he asked, softly.

'About us.'

She could hear him smiling as he spoke. 'You never answered my question, will you marry me? You will, won't you, Ella?'

'I-I don't know,' said Ella.

Aaron propped himself up on one elbow. She could see the silhouette of his angular features in the darkness. 'But how can you hesitate after this, after tonight?' His voice sounded anguished.

'It's not that I don't love you, Aaron, and it's not that I don't want to be with you. It's just that before I received your letter, I'd worked out what was going to happen to me next. I'd decided to base myself in London, I had my whole life mapped out and now, suddenly, you've turned it upside down.'

'I'm sorry, truly,' said Aaron, 'but we have to be together always, surely you can see that? We can't conduct a relationship worth anything from either side of the Atlantic.'

'I know and understand why you want a conventional marriage, but I'm not the same sort of person as Alice was,' Ella said carefully. 'I can't be the sort of wife to you that she was – always being there, attending your medical dinners, being kind to junior doctors . . . I can't be like that, Aaron, I must have a life of my own.'

'I know and it doesn't matter,' said Aaron, promptly. 'I wouldn't want you to be the same as Alice. If you were then I would feel disloyal. What is this anyway, Ella? You don't have to explain a single damned thing about yourself to me, I know it all.'

'Do you, do you really?'

'I know you better than any other person in the world.'

Ella sighed. 'Aaron, you're going to have to give me some time. I'll go back to London, as arranged, see Fulham launched and then have a good, long talk to Greg to see what his plans are.'

'You can't link your whole life to Greg,' said Aaron. 'I love the boy like my own son, you know that, but if William decided he was going to live in Hong Kong, or France, or Canada or wherever, I wouldn't give up my practice here and move to be closer to him.' The logic of what he said was indisputable.

'I know,' said Ella, 'I know what you're saying is right but I still need the time, Aaron. Can I have it?'

'Whatever I have, is yours,' he said, 'and if it's a little time you need, you've got it. Just don't hang around too long. We've wasted so much time already we're half way through our lives and what we have left is precious.'

'I promise,' said Ella.

They kissed and instantly they both forgot the future for nothing was relevant to either of them but that moment in each other's arms.

CHAPTER FORTY

LONDON
February 1985

To the world, the opening of the West London Meyer Centre was a triumph. The Prince of Wales agreed to officiate, and during the lavish luncheon which followed the opening ceremony, he was fulsome in his praise both of the architectural design and the amenities so created. The world's press was there. Already enthusiastic, the royal seal of approval was the icing on the cake. Beneath the surface, however, the people most concerned with the creation of the Meyer Centre were far from united in their triumph. Joseph Meyer was there of course, looking terrible. Never really having the appearance of a fit man, his skin now had a grey tinge and he had lost a great deal of weight. More alarming, however, was the decline of his spirit. Much of his charisma and all of his fighting talk had gone – he seemed little more than a cypher. Margot was there too, as Stephanie had insisted, as were Greg and the Irvines.

Ella and Stephanie had devised a table plan which kept Joseph a good distance from Stephanie, Margot as far away as possible from Ella, Greg at the opposite end of the table from Margot, and Tim strategically placed some distance from them both. It seemed to Ella that the complexities of the various relationships would almost be a joke, if it had been not so sad. Perhaps the saddest of all, in many respects, was the decline of her own relationship with Stephanie. The Meyer Centre was a considerable achievement. For two women who had built their own businesses from scratch, it was the crowning glory of all their activities to date, making Stephanie's country hotels and Ella's apartment blocks pale into insignificance by comparison. Yet the relationship between them was horribly strained, and the reason seemed to be Tim. Several times Ella had tried to broach the subject of Tim with Stephanie, in the last frantic lead-up days to the opening, but each time she had been cut short, until finally in a fury, Stephanie had said, 'Oh, for Christ's sake, Ella, you may be obsessed with my ex-husband but I'm not. Just leave it, would you.' There seemed to be so much misunderstanding, of which the most significant was clearly the tragedy of Stephanie and Joseph, running the Meyer empire in tandem, both grieving for the same man and yet worlds apart.

Margot had aged, Ella noticed, with a degree of satisfaction of which she was not proud. Whereas, in the past, there had been a timeless quality about her, although still extremely attractive, she now looked as though she could well be forty. Greg had greeted her warmly on his arrival and despite Ella's nerves about their reunion, she could not help but admire the way her son handled the meeting. He seemed perfectly at ease and having spent some minutes talking to Margot he turned his attention to the Irvine girls, and to Belinda particularly, Ella could not help noticing. Belinda was still the spitting image of her father: the same kind, open face and soft, brown hair. She had not the startling looks of Millie and Stephanie but Ella could well understand why Greg so evidently preferred her company to that of her elder sister.

Those quite specifically involved in the project managed to keep their distance from one another until after the Prince had left. Then, however, it was the turn of the press and suddenly the main players in this strange game were huddled together and barraged with questions. Having always hated presscalls, Ella let Stephanie and Joseph take centre stage and then at last the questions stopped and the champagne flowed once more. She sat alone and watched the proceedings with weary interest, receiving a number of impressions: of Stephanie and Joseph having a short but violent exchange, in which Joseph seemed to be pleading; of Greg and Belinda, kissing in a doorway; of Tim talking earnestly to Stephanie who looked about to crack; and of Margot in avid conversation with an extremely good-looking man, clearly of Arab extraction. 'Who is he?' Ella whispered to Stephanie.

'He's a colleague of Joseph's,' said Stephanie. 'His name's Prince Ahfaad Rochlieu.'

'He's gorgeous,' said Ella.

Stephanie gave her a sharp look. 'A snake in the grass, I should imagine, though. He's an interesting combination – half Arab, half French. His position with Joseph is not unlike mine, inasmuch as he owns a number of hotels in the Middle East and he and Joseph have become kind of partners. The hotels are still separately owned but they undertake a lot of group activities together, marketing and so on.'

'It's funny,' said Ella, 'he's the first man I've ever seen beside Margot who seems to look right with her. They sort of fit together, do you know what I mean?'

'Wishful thinking?' Stephanie suggested.

Ella shook her head vehemently. 'No, I'm not trying to partner her off in order to protect my son. Just – well, look at them.'

'I don't have your obsessive interest in relationships,' said Stephanie. 'I can't say I can get worked up about it one way or the other.' She turned away dismissively.

Margot was enjoying herself, more than she had enjoyed anything in some long time. Part of the reason was Greg. It was nice to see him again but she could now recognize how totally unsuitable the relationship had been. Ella had been right, she realized, ironically. He had grown up certainly, filled out, matured and he had acquired some polish which was not there before. He had been such a babe and she wondered how on earth she could ever have thought herself in love with him – a reaction to Nicholas, she supposed. The second source of pleasure was the Meyer Centre itself. All along she had known that bringing Stephanie and Ella together was a good idea and the end result had certainly proved her point. It was a triumph, not only for them but also for Joshkers Bank, whom it was well known had sponsored the deal to a large extent. Of course Meyer had played a dominant role, but the Centre had a different feel from Meyer's other locations, an individual stamp. It was clearly the best thing that had happened to London since the revamping of Covent Garden. The third reason for Margot's pleasure that day was meeting Ahfaad Rochlieu. Joseph had introduced them early on in the day, and Margot could not remember having met anyone, man or woman, who fascinated her more. He was startlingly good-looking – tall and dark with large brown eyes and high cheekbones. His mind fascinated her, too. She recognized immediately not only a superb intellect but in all probability, a superior brain to her own, which was a challenge indeed. As the opening celebrations drew to an end and people began to drift away, Margot found herself lingering, reluctant to leave Ahfaad's side. The thought of never seeing him again appalled her.

He seemed to sense her feelings for he said, suddenly, 'We'd better have dinner together, hadn't we?' She nodded, it never occurring to her to disagree. 'Why don't you come back to my house? I have an excellent chef, who can prepare almost anything you'd like.' Margot hesitated. 'Are you afraid my Eastern blood will get the better of me and I'll have you shipped off into white slavery?' Ahfaad raised a mocking eyebrow but his intelligent eyes watched her intently.

She laughed. 'No, and I'd be fascinated to see your home.' It was an unusually candid remark for Margot.

They left soon afterwards, in a powder-blue Rolls-Royce, which appeared from nowhere. Margot had never liked pale coloured Rolls but somehow, with its soft French Navy interior and mahogany fittings, she found herself lulled into an appreciation of this one. Ahfaad's house was in Eaton Square. It had been two houses once since he had bought properties adjoining one another.

'Do you live here all alone?' Margot asked, impressed by the size and grandeur before they had even entered the front door.

'Not always.' He grinned at her.

'I am sorry,' she was embarrassed, 'I didn't mean to pry.'

The spectacular exterior in no way prepared Margot for the opulence inside the house. She had an impression of curving staircases, priceless paintings and a beautiful chandelier, as she was steered through the hall and drawing room, to a smaller room at the back of the house overlooking the garden. It was completely dark outside but floodlights played on the garden, in the centre of which was a magnificent fountain. Ahfaad's obsession seemed to be with silks: the curtains were silk, the sofa and chairs in rough, raw silk, all in muted shades of green and blue. There was an instantly recognizable Picasso in the hall, which Margot had no doubt was genuine. Books lined two of the other walls – beautifully bound leather, volume upon volume, but somehow they were too perfect and Margot suspected no one ever took them down and read them. A butler appeared and poured champagne and Margot stood by the window, gazing out at the garden.

'You're a very beautiful woman, Margot,' said Ahfaad, quietly. 'I'd like to drink to that.' Margot inclined her head in acknowledgement. 'Someone told me – Joseph I suppose – that you are half English, half Korean. Is that right?' Margot nodded. 'A mongrel then, like me. We're always the best, certainly the strongest.'

Margot laughed. 'There I'll agree with you.'

'Are you going to tell me your story?'

Much to her own surprise, for a full half hour, Margot talked of the past, reliving the terrible days in Korea. She had taken Ella's advice and the marriage between herself and Terry had been annulled. This meant that at last she was able to talk about it and, unbidden, the story came pouring out.

'It must have been extraordinary for you,' Ahfaad said, 'one moment a child, the next a married woman, and then a child again.'

'Yes, it was,' said Margot, 'particularly coming to an English school. It was so much more restrictive than I had been used to, and the uniform, oh so terrible! Yet, surprisingly, I settled down, though looking back on it, I don't know how I managed it.'

'And this Mrs Haigh, she was kind to you?'

'In her way, yes,' said Margot. 'She was very austere, not given to any form of emotion and always worried about what the neighbours would think. The ultimate horror in her life was the thought of being seen in curlers.' She laughed. 'I remember I bought some coloured briefs from Marks & Spencers when, I don't know, perhaps when I was fifteen. They were fairly brief briefs, but let's face it, M & S don't exactly go in for kinky underwear, do they?'

Ahfaad laughed and shook his head. 'No, not from my rather limited experience.'

'Well, Mrs Haigh wouldn't wash them.'

'Why ever not?' Ahfaad asked.

'Because then she would have had to put them on the line, the neighbours would see them and they would think that I was a fast and loose woman. I had to wash them myself, by hand, and dry them in the bathroom – it was all most unsatisfactory.'

'Did she love you?'

'In a way, yes, I think she probably did,' said Margot. 'I filled the void created by Terry leaving. He was her only child and her husband was dead – she had no one else but me, I had no one but her and we survived on the basis of mutual need. She was very proud when I got to Oxford and did quite well.'

'That was certainly something to tell the neighbours,' Ahfaad said, with a smile.

'Yes.'

'And Terry?' He asked, gently.

'I shall be grateful to him all my life.'

'Yes, yes, now, but at the time when she split up your marriage, did you miss him?'

Margot shook her head. 'No, it was a relief. I was only just fourteen, remember, and I had found it difficult to cope with the sexual side of our relationship, very difficult indeed. I obviously had no experience and well, I ...' she smiled, '... I would not in the normal course of events have been attracted to him. He was my salvation, literally my lifesaver, but it was some time before I realized that poor old Terry's inexpert grapplings were nothing to do with love as such.'

'Why have you never married?' Ahfaad asked.

He was a strange man. His questions could have been construed as impertinent, yet somehow Margot did not resent them. 'I had an affair with a married man for some years — well, sixteen years to be precise. That and my job I found sufficiently absorbing that I never really thought about marriage, nor missed it.'

'And the affair is over now?'

'He died,' said Margot.

'I'm sorry, and is there no one else at present?'

Margot grinned. 'Is this some sort of interrogation?'

'Most certainly it is. I have it in my mind to woo you, Margot Haigh, but first I must know about the competition.'

'I don't like the thought of making it too easy for you,' said Margot, smiling, 'but it is fair to say I am, how shall I put it, between liaisons at the moment.'

'Excellent.' Ahfaad laughed triumphantly and refilled their glasses.

'I am, too,' he said, 'between liaisons. I think this calls for another toast.' They raised their glasses. They were both a little tipsy but pleasantly so.

'Are you going to tell me about you and your life now?'

Ahfaad grinned, briefly. 'After my inquisition, I can see I'm going to have to, aren't I?'

'I rather think so,' said Margot.

'My life pales into insignificance compared with yours, in terms of achievement. My mother was an Arab princess from a minor principality, my father a wealthy and influential Frenchman: the Rochlieus owned chateaux and vineyards, even a castle or two. My parents met during the war. It was a passionate affair by all accounts. very much a marriage of love, but none the less both families were well pleased and in many respects it was as much a business contract as anything else. I was born in 1943, strangely enough here in London. My father moved my mother from Paris to London for safety, though with bombs dropping everywhere, it was hardly that. He himself escaped the invasion and joined the Free French. They were both here for my birth, I gather. My father insisted on being present which was unusual in those days, but it was as well, really, because it was the only time we ever met.'

'Oh I'm sorry,' said Margot, 'he was killed, then, during the war?'

'Yes, a German ambush went wrong. My mother took me back home to her parents. I remember her, just, a shadowy figure but unlike my father, at least she's there in my mind. She was killed in a helicopter crash, just after my fourth birthday. Sabotage was suspected but never proved – it was the usual sort of in-fighting that goes on in our part of the world.' He smiled but the smile did not reach his eyes.

'Poor little boy,' said Margot, 'an orphan at four.'

'A very rich and privileged orphan. I inherited all my father's money and the estates in France and my Arab grandfather showered on me all his wealth, since I was the eldest grandson. My childhood was not unhappy but there was always a slight threat hanging over it, that the people who had killed my mother would kill me or my grandparents, too. However, I was well cared for, indeed lavishly cared for and loved. It was not such a bad life. My grandmother died when I was fifteen, my grandfather when I was eighteen, so I was a man by the time I had to fend for myself – besides which, I've had the benefit of an English education, here at Eton. Having coped with the early years of that, I was equipped to cope with anything.' Margot laughed. 'Yes,' said Ahfaad, 'from the desert to the most illustrious playing fields in the world – a life of strange contrast, not unlike your own.'

'And now,' said Margot, 'how do you spend your time now?'

'About six months of the year, at my home outside Cairo, the rest of the time in Europe, partly for pleasure, partly business. I do all the fashionable things: ski in the right places, spend the prescribed amount of time in the South of France and do my Christmas shopping in Fortnum & Masons.'

'Is it important for you to do the right thing?' Margot, asked intrigued.

Ahfaad shrugged. 'It's like playing a game, it's what is expected of me – international playboy and all that. It requires me to bed the occasional famous actress and be seen from time-to-time with minor European royalty. It's fun, it's quite hard work, but since I'm stuck with the image, I might as well enjoy it.'

'It's why you're familiar, I suppose,' said Margot. 'I have to admit to rarely having my nose out of the *Financial Times* unless it's at the hairdressers, but I expect you have probably stared at me from the pages of *Harpers & Queen* while my hairdresser goes through her ritual torture.'

'Very probably,' said Ahfaad. 'By contrast, I know quite a lot about you. Do you know Joseph Meyer is a great admirer of yours?'

Margot shook her head. 'No, I didn't, I barely know him. My only contact point really is Stephanie Bonham, and the only project with which we have jointly been involved is the Meyer Centre.'

'Nevertheless,' said Ahfaad, 'he's watched your progress over some years.'

'Spooky,' said Margot.

'No, not at all. The phenomena of truly successful women fascinates him. That's why he tolerates Stephanie. He'd have booted her out years ago if she'd been a man, but he can't resist her novelty value.'

'I don't see how the relationship can last a great deal longer in its current form,' said Margot. 'It worries me because so much of Stephanie's success depends on her relationship with Meyer. Since Alex's death it seems to have hit an all-time low.'

'Yes, I agree,' said Ahfaad. 'Still, it's my belief there's a big shake-up ahead.'

'How do you mean?' Margot asked, eagerly. Ahfaad looked wary. 'My lips are sealed,' Margot insisted.

'I'm only guessing,' said Ahfaad, 'truly. He's said nothing to me but I would suspect that Joseph will sell his Meyer interests quite soon.'

'Sell! Joseph! I can't imagine him parting with everything he's built up.'

'Why ever not,' said Ahfaad, 'there's no one now for him to leave it to. He's a strange man. He can be utterly ruthless if the situation calls for it, but he's also very sentimental. I know his staff mean a great deal to him, not just the top management, but the staff in the field, many of whom have worked for him for years. They are his family now and I know he is very anxious to secure their future. If he can off-load Meyer while he's still young enough and well enough to do a good deal, he can at least safeguard the future for them.'

'It makes sense,' said Margot, intrigued. 'I wish Stephanie was big enough to have a go at it.'

'Maybe she is, with a partner,' Ahfaad suggested.

Margot smiled. 'You know I've always coveted Joseph Meyer's banking business. I've approached him of course, on and off, over the years, but always without success. 'I wonder...'

'Stop scheming,' said Ahfaad, 'remember what I have told you is in confidence and in any case, it's only an opinion.'

Margot studied him in silence for a moment. 'I'm surprised you told me at all. I imagine that Meyer selling up must be of interest to you.'

'Not really,' said Ahfaad, 'it would just mean more responsibilities and more work. I have my own hotel group. It makes me a lot of money, more money than I can sensibly use, but of all my interests it is the most troublesome. That's the problem with the industry, it's so labour intensive and labour always spells hassle. Of course I could bring in someone to run it for me but that would rather destroy the whole point of the exercise. No, it's not for me. Now, are we going to eat? What would you like – French, Italian, Arabic, Greek, Spanish?'

'Don't tell me you have a chef for every nation housed in your basement?,

Ahfaad laughed. 'No, just one man but he is a genius.'

'To tell you the truth,' said Margot, 'I'm not really hungry.'

'Then I will organize some *crudites*, no one can make *crudites* like Henri – his sauces!' Ahfaad rolled his eyes and getting up he crossed the room to ring the bell.

An extraordinary man, Margot thought, watching him. Despite all his money, he seemed oddly untouched by it. Margot had always been attracted to wealth and power, she knew that, but never before had she come across it so understated. It was particularly strange, bearing in mind his origins. The Arabs she had dealt with in the course of business were normally ostentatious to the point of vulgarity, but not Ahfaad. She suspected it must be his French blood which was responsible for his style, his chic. She thought of Nicholas for a moment and realized that beside Ahfaad, he suddenly seemed rather colourless and bombastic. She dismissed the thought, hurriedly, aware of its disloyalty. He refilled their glasses. 'I've had more than enough,' Margot protested.

'Maybe,' Ahfaad smiled, and coming over sat beside her on the sofa, not touching her but close. He looked deep into her eyes. 'There's something about you, Margot, something I can't exactly explain but it's as though I've been looking for you for a long time. You talked about recognizing me when we met. I recognized you, but not because I had seen your face splashed across the gossip columns, but because I think I recognize the person for whom I've been searching.' He hesitated. 'You think I'm crazy?' Margot shook her head, feeling suddenly close to tears. 'We're very much the same,' Ahfaad continued, 'we're both mongrels, as I said, both orphaned early in life. In many respects we're rootless, we belong nowhere. May be, just may be, only with one another will we ever feel truly at home. You think I'm talking like an idiot? Perhaps, but I think we might have quite a future together, you and me.'

Margot said nothing but stared back into his great brown eyes. She could not speak, to confirm or deny – her heart was suddenly too full of emotion she could not express. All she knew was that Ahfaad's words mirrored exactly her own feelings.

CHAPTER FORTY-ONE

GLOUCESTERSHIRE
March 1985

Stephanie sat in the car for some long time, simply staring at the house. It was a beautiful clear day, daffodils sprinkled the lawn, the orchard was in full blossom, the honey-coloured Cotswold stone seemed to be shining with exuberance in the spring sunshine. She wound down the car window and took great breaths of fresh air. She had spent the last two months in either London, Paris or commuting frantically between the two and the smell of carbon dioxide had become a way of life. Just sitting in the car, she found herself already beginning to relax – it was extraordinary the effect Wickham always had upon her. How long had she been away, six, seven years? Too long in any event and yet there had been no reason to come back.

Her natural instinct, on being asked to spend Sunday with Tim, was to turn down his invitation. No, the children would not be there, he had told her. Millie was now living permanently in London and Belinda, though still living at home with her father, was away for the weekend with Greg, staying with college friends of his. So what was the point of the invitation? Stephanie was almost tempted to ask, but she had been immediately attracted by the idea and accepted. A day away from London, away from the solitary misery of her life, was irresistable.

She must have been sitting outside the house for at least ten minutes before Tim came to join her. Middle-age suited him, Stephanie thought, as he walked towards her. The insecurities caused by his illness had made him somewhat hesitant in his youth, something which had irritated Stephanie immensely. Now though, he had become quietly self-assured. He had the same thick, brown hair, only slightly flecked with grey and his face, if anything, was better looking for a few lines. His figure was as trim as ever. He stopped by the open window of the car. 'I left you alone with your thoughts for a few minutes, but I think it's time you came in now. Apart from any other reason, I'm gasping for a drink.' She smiled, accepting his hand as he helped her out of the car. They exchanged kisses lightly, impersonally, on the cheek.

Inside, nothing much had changed. The place had the well-cared-for look achieveable only by Mrs Maggs. There were fires lit everywhere and everything was polished and shining. Her mother or father could have walked in and been instantly at home. The furniture was the same, the paintings hung in the same places, there was the odd new piece of upholstery, a lick of paint here and there but no fundamental differences. Stephanie let out a sigh of pure joy.

'Nice to be back in the old place?' Tim asked.

They had naturally gravitated towards Tim's study, as always the cosiest room in the house. He poured her a sherry, without asking. She took it gratefully and sank onto the sofa in front of the fire. 'It's strange, you know, in dreams I always come here.'

'How do you mean?' Tim asked.

'It doesn't matter what I'm dreaming about or who I'm with in my dreams, the setting is always Wickham. I wonder, perhaps, whether I haunt you sometimes.'

Tim smiled. 'Not noticeably.'

'And out of all the rooms at Wickham, it's always this one I visit. It's odd really because this is the one room which has altered most since my childhood. The others have changed far less. When this was my father's study, it was always so austere and chilly, both in atmosphere and temperature. George and I were only ever invited in here to be shouted at if we had done something wrong.' She smiled up at Tim, appreciatively, as he stood warming the back of his legs in front of the fire. 'It's hard to tell what you've done to the room exactly, but now it's the best in the house.'

'Perhaps it's simply because it's more accessible,' Tim suggested.

Stephanie shook her head. 'No, it's more than that – hell, I rabbit on too much. Cheers.'

'Cheers,' said Tim. 'It's very nice to see you back here.'

They talked for some time about the children. 'Lunch is ready, whenever you are, incidentally,' Tim said, after a while.

'Is Mrs Maggs here?' Stephanie looked up sharply.

'No, I gave her the day off. I know things have been rather awkward between you two and I didn't want any bad vibes today.'

'That was kind of you,' said Stephanie.

'Not at all, though the penalty for no Mrs Maggs is very severe – Irvine's stew is on the menu today.'

Stephanie smirked. 'I didn't know you liked cooking.'

'Neither did I,' said Tim, 'it's something I've become a little interested in during the last few years – purely, good old plain English cooking. Mrs Maggs gives me lessons. I suppose I have this idea that when she's too old to look after me any more I'll probably fend for myself. I don't think I could stand living with anybody but her.'

'You should marry again, Tim,' said Stephanie.

'So I'm always being told. The trouble is I don't have much time for a social life these days, what with the two farms to run and the kids home at weekends.'

'Two farms?' said Stephanie.

'My father died a couple of months ago – I didn't let you know because I realized how busy you were. As you know my mother's been dead for five years now, and in that time the stubborn old devil wouldn't let me help him – he absolutely insisted he could manage on his own. The result is the place is in a frightful pickle: The house is falling apart, the land is a mess. I've been trying to sort it out but it's not easy with the responsibilities of Wickham to consider as well.'

'Why don't you put a manager in here for a few years?' Stephanie suggested.

Tim shook his head. 'No, I'm coping. It just wears me out from time to time.'

'You need to be careful,' said Stephanie.

'Yes, though I haven't had a fit now in nearly four years,' said Tim. 'Better drugs and a calm emotional life is what I attribute my success to. Certainly if I overdo things physically I set off the warning bells but I think it's emotional traumas which are really my undoing.'

'I'm sorry,' said Stephanie, 'I must have caused you a few of those over the years.'

'Past history,' said Tim. 'Anyway, enough about me. At the risk of incurring your wrath, I'm going to tell you you look worn out but I suppose it's not surprising. I assume that as well as having to cope with the loss of Alex in a personal sense, you're also having to cover his work.'

Stephanie liked the way he spoke naturally and readily about Alex – everyone else avoided the subject. 'I am finding it very difficult, being on my own,' she admitted. 'Alex and I didn't get on too well during the last couple of years, but it doesn't make losing him any easier.'

'Of course not,' said Tim. 'It must have been such a terrible shock apart from anything else, such a waste of life.'

'Yes.' They were both silent for a moment but it felt to Stephanie as though Tim was waiting for something. To cover the silence, she found herself saying, 'I don't know what the future holds for me really. Joseph and I aren't speaking to each other, which doesn't make for a very happy working environment, and there are various other complications.'

'Like being pregnant?' said Tim, quietly.

Stephanie stared at him. 'W-what do you mean? How do you know?'

Tim smiled. 'I realized you were pregnant at the opening of the Meyer Centre in February. It was one of the reasons I asked you down today, to see if I could help.'

'But how could you possibly know?' said Stephanie.

'My dear old thing, I've seen you pregnant twice before, remember? You get a look about you.'

'I didn't think I'd put on any weight,' Stephanie protested.

'You haven't, well a little perhaps, but not so as most people would notice, but let's face it, I am more experienced than most on the subject of Stephanie Bonham mother-to-be.'

'It's Alex's child, of course,' she said.

'Of course,' said Tim. There was a moment's silence, broken only by the shifting of a log in the grate. 'Does Joseph know?' Tim asked, at last.

'Yes, and he's putting a lot of pressure on me. He wants the child, of course, but I'm damned if I'm going to let that happen.'

'Why?' said Tim. 'He's just lost his son and I'd have thought you'd be grateful for his help in raising the child. After all, you're not exactly the most maternal of people, are you?'

'That was unnecessary,' said Stephanie.

'I'm sorry,' said Tim, 'I just imagined you would welcome sharing the responsibility with Joseph.'

'I don't want my child, boy or girl, to end up like Alex. Joseph is so suffocating, so demanding. I don't want my child to feel that he has to spend his life in the Meyer organization and that he's being groomed for stardom from birth. I want him to grow up with the benefit of a normal childhood ... like, like I suppose I had before my mother died. I want him to be free to make his own choices. Joseph ruined Alex but he's not going to ruin my baby.'

'Alright, I accept that but how will you manage with a baby and your career?' Tim said.

'A nanny, I suppose,' said Stephanie, defensively.

'With Joseph demanding to be involved, it's not going to be easy. He'll expect you to bring up the child yourself, I shouldn't wonder.'

'I know.' Stephanie stood up and wandered to the window seat. She stared out across the drive. In her mind's eye she could see herself and George, bicycling up the drive as children, faces pink with exertion – laughing, carefree.

'Why didn't you have an abortion?' Tim asked suddenly.

'It wouldn't have been right.' Stephanie turned to him, surprised by the abruptness of the question.

'But if you and Alex weren't getting on particularly well . . .'

'I don't approve of abortion,' Stephanie said, 'and in any event . . .' her voice trailed off.

'Go on,' said Tim.

'. . . in any event, I felt I-I had to have this child, it was sort of destiny. Does that sound stupid?' She regretted her words as soon as she spoke, yet Tim's almost aggressive manner seemed to demand answers.

'No,' said Tim. He appeared genuine.

'It was neither intended nor planned,' Stephanie felt compelled to explain. 'It was an accident, but the moment I knew I was pregnant, I also knew I couldn't possibly get rid of the child.'

Tim stood up and came to join her by the window. 'This is possibly a contentious thing for me to say but I'm going to say it anyway. Perhaps you wanted to have this child because it represented the way back to Wickham – an excuse, if you like.'

Stephanie's head jerked up. She stared at him. 'How do you mean?'

'You don't see the child being raised in a London flat, with a series of nannies. You see it growing up here, having the childhood that you and George had, that Millie and Belinda enjoyed. I've been watching you. Just in the short period you've been back here, it's obvious Wickham still holds the magic for you in a way I suspect nowhere else does, and nowhere else will ever be able to do.'

'Yes, that's true,' Stephanie murmured.

'Then I'll move out,' said Tim, decisively. 'I can still run the estate so that you won't have to bother with that, but the house will be free for you to bring up your child. Once Mrs Maggs knows you're pregnant, she'll relent and help you in every way possible – you know how she adores babies.'

From nowhere great tears began to roll down Stephanie's cheeks. 'Oh Tim, no, no,' she said.

'Don't cry.' He set down his glass and drew her gently to him until her head was resting on his shoulder. 'Look Stephanie,' he began, still holding her close. 'I've always known this is your home and that one day you would want it back. Leaving it will be a wrench, of course, but perhaps a change of scene would do me good — in fact I know damn well it would. I'm appallingly stuck in a rut.'

'Stop it, stop it.' Stephanie thumped ineffectually with small fists against his chest and then burst into a fresh bout of crying.

Tim held her firmly. 'Now what?' His expression was warm, even amused.

Stephanie made a superhuman effort to control herself. '*Of course* I wouldn't let you leave, Tim, not for one moment. You are the most impossibly generous, kind person in the world to suggest it, but you're also an idiot. Wickham is *you*, you are Wickham now — it's me who is the visitor. I wouldn't consider your suggestion even for one moment.' The tears returned and she pressed her damp face against the rough tweed of his jacket. 'Sorry, I'm making you all wet,' she mumbled.

'Come and sit by the fire.' He drew her back to the sofa and sat her down, his arm still tightly round her. 'Then why not let the child be brought up here anyway?' he said, after a pause.

Stephanie raised her eyes to his. 'I left you to bring up our children and that was bad enough, but I can hardly expect you to raise another man's child.'

Abruptly, Tim removed his arm and stood up, his expression unreadable. 'Of course that's not what I'm suggesting. Clearly this baby is your responsibility and nothing to do with me. However, this is a big house and there's no reason why the baby and nanny shouldn't be installed in one part of it and I in another, if this is where you'd like the child to be brought up.'

Stephanie eyed him cautiously. The idea had appeal but

was it fair to Tim? Almost certainly, it was not. She tried to test the water of his feelings. 'But why should you share your home with anyone, Tim, particularly a small baby, with all the resultant noise and clutter, and let's face it, this is not just any baby. This baby is the result of your wife's unfaithfulness, the son or daughter of the man who took me away from you. You could hardly be blamed for not feeling very well-disposed towards the child.'

'I love children,' said Tim. 'I expect I'd get fond of the little devil in time and if not, it doesn't really matter, does it? May be it does seem a generous gesture, but frankly it's no great sacrifice. Indeed, perhaps if you could make the nanny impossibly glamorous, nubile and under twenty-five, it would provide the ultimate incentive.' He smiled but it didn't reach his eyes.

Stephanie felt a stab of anger at his words which both surprised and confused her. 'I expect that could be arranged,' she said, sharply.

Tim stared at her and a slow smile spread across his face. 'You don't like the idea, do you?'

'What idea?' Stephanie said, knowing very well.

'Of my fraternizing with this so-called nanny. How very flattering.'

'Tim, don't let's play games,' said Stephanie, wearily. 'It's a very kind offer but I think it's unworkable.'

'You're wrong,' said Tim, 'it *is* workable and I'm sorry if I was flippant. Let me try and put it right by saying that I would actually welcome the opportunity of seeing a little more of you than I have done in recent years – it would be nice to see you at weekends, which presumably you will spend here with the baby. I honestly think you should accept my offer. Look, put it another way if you like – I owe you one. Does that make you feel better?'

'You don't owe me anything,' said Stephanie, 'it's all the other way round, you know that.'

Tim shook his head and came and sat on the sofa beside her once more. 'I'm not denying you've caused me a great deal of pain over the years – it would be foolish to do so –

but you gave me the greatest gift of all. You gave me life, a proper life, a full, normal life like everyone else. But for you, probably I'd still be mouldering away in my parents' home, a crusty old bachelor, embittered and lonely. What a prospect.'

'If you mean I gave you Wickham,' said Stephanie, 'I think I should remind you that we created it together, and in any event, it's you who have sustained it.'

'Of course I don't mean Wickham,' said Tim, dismissively. 'What you gave me was far more valuable than this.' He gestured around him. 'You gave me a sense of self-worth. You made me realize that I could live like a normal person. My accident robbed me of any concept of normal living, yet marvellously, miraculously you gave it back to me.' Their eyes met and held, memories flashing between them. 'There is no more valuable gift you could have given anyone,' Tim said, softly. 'So is it such a big deal, in the circumstances, to suggest I share this house, which is after all yours, with your child whatever its parentage, whatever the circumstances.'

'You're a very special person, Tim,' Stephanie said. On impulse, she leaned forward and kissed him gently on his lips. It should have ended there, an acknowledgement of his kindness, his generosity, but the moment their lips met, it lit a fuse between them and their arms were around one another, their kisses frantic, their embraces at once familiar and yet new, intoxicating after their years apart. Stephanie could feel tears on her face but whether they were her own or Tim's she had no way of knowing. All she knew was that it felt right to be in his arms and when he stood up, took her hand and led her up the staircase to their old bedroom, it did not occur to her to argue. Once there, he undressed her and made love to her, with a tenderness and compassion that Alex had never once shown her in all their years together.

By morning, they were as much in love as they had ever been.

CHAPTER FORTY-TWO

NEW YORK
June 1985

The heat of the city hit Ella the moment she stepped from the plane at Newark Airport. All the way across the Atlantic she wished she had told Aaron she was coming so that he could have met her. Now, tired and anxious, she would have appreciated his support more than ever, though in her heart of hearts she knew this was the better way. Firstly, she had to find out, or rather confirm, what had gone wrong. She needed to give herself whole-heartedly to the business, and only when she had straightened things out, could she tell Aaron she was back. Without doubt this was the worst crisis of her career, threatening to destroy everything she had achieved to date.

Since the opening of the West London Meyer Centre, Ella had remained in England. She had been dabbling with property in the City of London, enjoying an English spring and the frequent visits from Greg, often accompanied by Belinda. The relationship between herself and Stephanie was still tense, though a little easier. Ella had been genuinely pleased to hear that she and Tim were back together and all she could hope was that as Stephanie's pregnancy advanced, she would mellow a little towards her. It had been a pleasant Spring and early Summer, except for missing Aaron. They had spoken regularly on the telephone and Ella had promised to spend the Summer in New York, for Greg was planning a trip abroad, once he had finished college.

*

This tranquil period had lasted until just a week ago, when the bombshell had struck in the form of a telephone call from Michael Gresham. He had begun without preamble, clearly very angry. 'You have to be the most stubborn woman I've ever met. What's wrong with you, can't you take advice from *anyone*?'

'Michael, I don't know what you're talking about,' Ella had said. 'Can you calm down and start again?'

'I warned you,' he ranted, 'I warned you back at Christmas time to get out while the going was good. When I didn't hear from you I wondered whether Jackie had forgotten to pass on the message but she assured me she did and since then you haven't even bothered to answer my letters. I know I'm only a humble lawyer but I've seen the signs coming way ahead of most people, and if you'd just taken my advice at the time . . .'

'Michael, will you listen to me for a moment? I truly don't know what you're talking about.'

He let out a sigh of irritation. 'Back last Christmas, I came to New York on business. I knew you were in England but I had a long talk with Jackie and explained that I was worried about the oil market in Houston. The price was dropping slowly but steadily, and I had a feeling it was going to have a devastating effect on the City. I asked her to get hold of you urgently. Apparently you weren't at home, you were staying with somebody in the country for Christmas and she promised to contact you as soon as possible in the New Year. This she did, as you well know. What I've been trying to get across to you is the importance of shedding some of your property pretty fast. Back in January the prices were still holding up and you could have got out with all your money intact, whereas now . . .'

'I never received that message,' said Ella, flatly.

'You're kidding,' said Michael, 'I spoke to Jackie from Toronto. I rang her especially – oh, it must have been New Year's Day or the day after – to make sure she'd passed my views on to you, and she said she had.'

'I was in almost daily contact with her around that period,' said Ella. 'We had some lease renewals coming up in New York. Believe me, she never mentioned a thing.'

'Shit.' There was a silence on the other end of the phone for a moment. 'Have you been receiving your mail from New York?'

'Yes, of course,' said Ella, 'Jackie fax's me daily with everything that comes in.'

'Then at least you will have had my letters – why didn't you react to them?'

There was a stunned silence for a moment. 'Michael, there has been no letter from you.'

'God dammit, the little cow. What the shit's she been playing at? She could well have cost you your business, Ella, it's that serious. Don't you read the papers?'

'I know that oil prices have been a bit dodgy recently,' Ella admitted.

'Dodgy! The market's plummetted and as a result this is a sick, sick town, Ella. People are being made redundant, companies are going under, even one or two banks are going.'

'Jack . . . ?' Ella began.

'No, no, he's alright at the moment but he's not having an easy time.'

'Then why hasn't he been in touch with me?'

'Because I told him that I'd already contacted you. I told him there was no need to worry you because I was keeping you abreast with what was going on. We both thought it was odd you hadn't reacted to any of my letters but assumed you were being your usual pig-headed self, choosing to ignore advice, particularly when it comes to the selling of your precious properties. It never occurred to me – Jesus, I see it all now.'

'See what?' There was a long silence on the other end of the phone. 'See what, Michael?' Ella persisted.

'It's my fault,' said Michael. 'At the back end of last year I took Jackie out to dinner one night and somehow ended up in her bed.'

'Oh Michael, not Jackie,' said Ella, 'she can't handle a man like you.'

'Nor I a girl like her it seems,' said Michael. 'I'll admit I was at a loose end at the time. After that, I spent two or three nights with her and then, of course, we speak fairly regularly on the telephone because of your business. When I came up at Christmas time, I took her out a couple more times. When I left New York . . . oh Jesus, what a mess.'

'I don't understand, Michael, what are you saying?'

'Well, I spent Christmas Eve with her. She was kind of upset that I was going back to Houston on Christmas morning but, of course, I had my usual Christmas party. Anyway, I wanted out, so I told her it was probably best if we ended our relationship because you would be coming back to New York shortly.'

'What the hell did I have to do with any of it?' Ella said.

'Shit, Ella, I was looking for an excuse to get out of it all. I know how fond Jackie is of you and so I told her that I thought it was pretty crass of us to carry on an affair in front of your nose. I told her that the trouble in Houston would undoubtedly bring you back from England and for that reason it would be best if we split.'

'Let me get this straight,' said Ella. 'You're saying that Jackie has deliberately avoided telling me about the trouble in Houston, so as to keep me here in England? I can't believe that, Michael, she's so . . . so conscientious.'

'Can you think of another explanation?' Michael asked.

'Not off-hand,' Ella said, after a moment, 'but if you'd already told her that it was over between you . . .'

'Yes,' said Michael, 'but because I'm a coward at heart, I didn't tell her the true reason – that she bored the pants off me. I used you, you and your return to New York, as the sole reason for us parting company. I guess she must have thought that if she kept you out of the country, there might be a chance she and I could get together again.'

'Have you seen her since Christmas,' Ella asked, 'in any capacity?' Her voice was hard as flint.

'No I haven't. I was in Toronto on business until the end of February – a difficult case that dragged on. When I got back to Houston I found the shit had really hit the fan and

I've been here ever since, sorting out my clients' various messes. Oh hell, Ella, I'm so sorry, I should have known.'

'How bad is it?' Ella asked.

'Bad. At a guess I would say your property's worth no more than fifty per cent of its 1984 value.'

'Fifty per cent, so at least it's still holding its own as collateral.'

'Possibly, yes, though I don't know enough about your borrowing arrangements. It can't last, Ella, things are getting worse. How do I get it through to you this is a city under siege, it's in deep, deep trouble.'

'If Jack holds my hand, and he's really got no option but to do so,' Ella reasoned, 'then surely it's just a question of sitting it out?'

'You still need income to pay your interest bill,' said Michael. 'My guess is that soon you'll suffer a lot of defaulting on the part of your lessees. People are dropping like flies, Ella — it's an epidemic, it's frankly terrifying. For me personally, of course, it's good for business, so long as I'm careful to get my fees up front, but I can't say it's causing me any great joy. It's a tragedy.'

'I'll straighten things out over here,' said Ella, 'and I'll be with you as soon as possible. I'll go via New York, talk to Jackie and then I'll fly straight down. I'll let you know which day. Could you tell Jack what's happened?'

'Yes, I will,' said Michael. 'Ella, I'm sorry, really sorry.'

'Jackie of all people, Michael — you must have known she bruises easy. How could you?'

'I guess I can't resist another notch on the belt. You know me, Ella, as well as anyone.'

'Yes, God help me,' said Ella.

On the plane and now in the cab on the way to Lexington Avenue, Ella tried to rehearse and re-rehearse how she was going to handle Jackie Partridge. She had not told anyone she was returning to New York; it seemed better to have surprise on her side. The shock of suddenly seeing her walk through the office door would leave Jackie vulnerable and give her no time to think out an excuse for what had happened. She asked the cab driver to take her round to the back of Gregory Buildings from where she took the service elevator to her apartment. After a shower and a change of clothes, she took the elevator to the ground floor.

'Ella! It's Ella, isn't this just great?' Jessie waddled forward and wrapped Ella in her arms. 'Boy, what a wonderful surprise! Haven't we missed you? Let me look at you.' Jessie held her at arms length. 'You look well, and happy. Old England must suit you, but we sure miss you, don't we Jackie?'

Jackie stood a few paces behind. 'Yes, of course,' she said. 'Hello, Ella ... what a surprise, why didn't you tell us you were coming?' Ella thought she could detect an edge to Jackie's voice, but on the face of it, the girl seemed pleased enough to see her.

'I'll fix you some coffee,' Jessie fussed. 'When did you get in? I bet you're bushed.

'I've only been in about half an hour,' said Ella. 'I've just been up to the apartment to freshen up. Yes, coffee would be wonderful, thanks.' She took her time. She drank the coffee and worked her way through the pile of correspondence which Jackie gave her, made a couple of phone calls and accepted the light lunch Jessie brought to her desk. Only then did she ask to see Jackie. 'Come in and shut the door,' she said. Jackie came in and sat down, apparently unruffled, notepad and pen at the ready. 'I've come back to the States quite specifically to see you and to sort out the mess in Houston. I assume I don't need to say any more than that for you to realize you've been rumbled.'

'I don't know what you mean,' Jackie began.

'Don't let's waste each other's time, Jackie. I know what you did and I also know why you did it. What I don't think you can have realized is the consequences of your actions – you may well have cost me my entire business.'

At her words, Jackie's face crumpled and she burst into great gasping sobs. She began searching, uselessly, for a handkerchief and Ella reached into the drawer of her desk and threw her over a box of tissues.

'I'm so sorry,' Jackie said. 'I knew what I was doing was wrong but I couldn't help myself, I love him so much.'

Ella let out a deep sigh. 'Michael and I have worked out your motives, I'd just like to check them.'

'Michael! Michael knows what I've done?'

'How else do you think I know?' said Ella. 'He rang me in London, in desperation, because of what's happening to the Houston real estate prices.'

'Oh God,' Jackie burst into another fit of crying.

'Stop that,' said Ella. 'As Michael and I understand it, you deliberately suppressed telling me about what was happening in Houston, because you knew that if I was aware of what was going on, I'd abandon my UK projects in favour of sorting out Houston. Michael gave you the impression that the only reason he was breaking up your relationship was because he didn't want to hurt my feelings, so you assumed that by keeping me out of America you stood a chance of maintaining the relationship. Is that right?' Jackie nodded miserably, her head bowed. 'What I can't understand is how the hell you've managed to keep it all from Jessie – Jessie misses nothing.'

Jackie bit her lip. 'It was something that really didn't concern her,' she said. 'I always take the calls from Michael and so far as the letters are concerned, I always do the faxing to you every day.'

'But Jessie opens the post.'

'Yes,' said Jackie, 'but when there was a letter in from Michael, I just told Jessie I was going to fax it right away and then didn't.'

'When Michael first alerted you to the problem in Houston, he reckons I could have got out with all my money intact. Now, he calculates the price of real estate has dropped by fifty per cent. If it drops any more, Jackie, I'll be ruined.'

'Oh, no, oh Ella,' was all Jackie could manage.

Ella was fast losing her temper. 'I was born in Kentucky, with nothing. You may think there's poverty in England, you haven't seen anything compared with the poverty in Kentucky forty years ago. My home was a shack. My mother . . . do you know what my mother did for a living?'

'No,' Jackie wept.

'She was a hooker. I had to crawl my way out of that life, Jackie, dragging my illegitimate son with me. Can you imagine how hard that was?'

'Yes,' said Jackie.

'So how do you think it feels to have come this far only to have my business thrown away by a stupid, lovelorn girl? It's unbelievable — you've been in a position of trust all these years, God knows I've paid you a decent enough salary and looked after you well. In the circumstances, is loyalty too much to ask?'

'I-I've nothing to say,' said Jackie, 'except that I'm terribly sorry and I'll go, right away, of course. I-I think I must have been a little mad. It's just that there was nothing and no one else in my life. I'm just so lonely and when Michael showed an interest in me I couldn't believe it. He's so handsome, successful and, yes, I suppose there was a feeling of triumph that having thrown you over, he was interested in me. When-when he told me there was no future for our relationship, because of you, I could only see you as the enemy.'

The anger left Ella as suddenly as it had come. The bleakness of Jackie's words struck a cord in her understanding. 'Look, Jackie, I'm not trying to say this to be unkind but it's vital you keep a grip on reality. Michael just used me as an excuse. He wouldn't have cared a shit about hurting my feelings if you were the girl he wanted. Michael's a philanderer, a charming, unscrupulous philanderer. He doesn't give a fig about you, or me, or any of the other girls he's bedded. There's no point in loving Michael Gresham, whoever you are.'

'But I do,' Jackie wailed. She began sobbing in earnest, close to hysteria.

With a sudden rush of irritation, Ella leaned forward and slapped her hard across the face. Jackie screamed. 'I'm sorry,' said Ella, 'but you have to stop this nonsense.'

Jessie burst through the door. 'What's going on here, what's happening?'

'Leave us, Jessie, please,' said Ella.

There was no aspect of her life from which Ella had ever excluded Jessie from before. A look of hurt and bewilderment crossed her face. She retreated, shutting the door carefully behind her, but, Ella was sure, staying close enough to see what she could hear through the door.

The shock from the slap had stopped Jackie crying and Jessie's intrusion had calmed the atmosphere. 'Tell me something about your life in New York,' Ella said. 'Do you have girlfriends?'

Jackie shook her head. 'No, not really. There was an English girl I met on the plane coming over. We were quite friendly for a year or so but then she married an American and moved to Philadelphia. She writes, sometimes.'

'So what do you do in the evening?'

'Take work home usually and have a TV supper. Sometimes Jessie asks me round to her house, for dinner with her family. I like that, they're nice people.'

'They are,' Ella agreed.

The bleakness of Jackie's life was all too apparent. To be lonely anywhere was bad, to be lonely in a big city was terrible. Of all the many experiences of Ella's life, loneliness to this extent was unknown to her. She had felt isolated and unsupported on many occasions — particularly during the period she was estranged from Aaron — but never completely alone. There had always been somebody to call on and then, of course, there was Greg. It had been her intention to order Jackie out of the office, there and then, and to threaten her with legal action — to cut her out and cast her off. Now, an odd feeling of compassion made her hesitate. Was she getting soft? She stood up and wandered over to the window. Jackie had done wrong, quite deliberately withholding vital information, but Jackie was not entirely to blame. Ella knew she had been neglecting her business in the States like Greg, the pace of life in England suited her and after her years of struggle, she had enjoyed more leisure in the last few months than she had ever known before. If she had been on the ball, she would have known what was going on in Houston, irrespective of Jackie.

Her decision was so sudden it startled her. She turned from the window. 'I don't want you to leave, Jackie.'

Jackie stared at her. 'W-what?' she managed.

Ella came back and sat down at her desk. 'There are various reasons, the more philanthropic of which is that clearly this job is a major part of your life. While you're in this state of emotional turmoil over Michael, to take away your job and deprive you of Jessie's company is going to be the final straw for you. If I dismiss you for what's happened, then I can't with all consciousness give you a reference and you'll find it difficult to find another job.'

'Ella, I can't believe this . . .' Jackie began.

'I'm not all heart,' Ella said, her voice harsh. 'If I manage to save my business it will be because I've put a lot of effort and thought into the Houston operation. If I dismiss you now, I'm going to have to find someone to take over in New York and whoever I find will have to be trained. Apart from this one very major lapse, you've run this office extremely efficiently and that's what I'd like you to continue to do. Of course, against the advantages of having you here I have to weigh up the fact that I don't know whether I can ever trust you again.'

'You can,' Jackie blurted out, 'you really can, Ella. It was just Michael . . .'

'Enough,' said Ella, 'don't let's go over it again. Let's say I'm prepared to take your assurances. There is however a third element to my decision.,

'What's that?' Jackie asked, nervously.

'I don't think it would do you any harm to see the consequences of your actions. Whatever happens, I'm going to lose a great deal of money, I may even lose everything and I think you should be here to see the end of this particular saga played out to the full. It's a lesson you won't forget in a hurry.'

'Ella, I'll do anything, anything,' Jackie burst out, tears hovering on her eyelids again.

'I want you to go home now for the rest of the day and when you come in tomorrow morning, I want it to be as though this thing never happened between us. I want no tears, no hysterics. There'll be no recriminations from me and I don't want any more stammered apologies from you. It's over, finished. What we now have to do is to try and pick up the pieces and save this business.'

'Will you . . . will you have to tell Jessie?'

'Yes,' said Ella, 'I've never had any secrets from Jessie and I can't start now, but I will tell her you forgot to pass the message on, rather than deliberately failing to do so. I'll say you were so unhappy about your affair with Michael you had a lapse of memory.'

'Thank you,' Jackie muttered, 'thank you for everything. I'm so sorry, I'm . . .'

'Jackie,' Ella said, her voice gentle now. Jackie raised her head. 'The devil you know, right? It's only possible to trust anyone so far. I believe, because of what's happened, you won't ever let me down again. Am I right to have that faith in you?'

'Absolutely,' said Jackie, her eyes shining.

'OK, take off and I'll see you tomorrow. I plan to be in the office tomorrow morning and then fly down to Houston tomorrow afternoon.'

It was after six by the time Ella felt she had done all she could for the day. She had spent long hours on the phone to Houston, which had confirmed that everything Michael had predicted was already coming true. Tessa had a string of lease defaults and by all accounts, on most of them, Michael had not recommended taking legal action because there was no money there to claim. As for re-letting any of the premises, it seemed out of the question, there was far more real estate about than people wanting it.

On the stroke of six, Jessie came in with a bottle of wine and two glasses. 'Cocktail hour,' she said.

Ella grinned. 'I guess I need that.'

'I knew it,' said Jessie, pouring the wine. 'Now, will you tell me what's going on, Honey, or will I have to beat the living daylight out of you, to find out what's happening? You know your Jessie, she likes to know the score.' Briefly, Ella told Jessie the story, the edited version she had agreed with Jackie. When she had finished, Jessie eyed her sceptically. 'I don't reckon she forgot to pass that information through to you, I think she suppressed it deliberately. That's one very nice kid, I'm very fond of her and I'd trust her over anything and everything except men. Where men are concerned that girl's a walking disaster. Why the hell did Michael get mixed up with her anyway?'

'Boredom, I suspect,' said Ella, carefully ignoring Jessie's all-too-accurate assumption.

'Men are shits,' said Jessie. 'So, you're looking for a new member of the team?'

Ella shook her head. 'I'm keeping her on.' Jessie stared at her in silence. 'Well, I felt . . .' Ella began in an effort to justify her decision.

'No need to explain, and I love you for it. Hell, I love you anyway but I really love you for this. You've made the right decision. That Jackie, she'll, sure as hell, never let you down again.'

'That's what I figure,' said Ella.

The joy in Aaron's voice was all Ella needed to drive away her dark forebodings when half an hour later she called his apartment and told him she was in New York. 'How come you didn't tell me?' he said, when he had recovered from his surprise. 'I have the place knee-deep in women and I suppose I'll have to clear them out now you're in town.'

'You certainly will,' said Ella. 'My place or yours?'

'I'll come to you, I should think you're tired out after the journey.'

It was not until several hours later, lying sated in one another's arms, that Ella was able to tell Aaron what had brought her back to the States. Aaron listened in silence. When Ella had finished he let out a sigh. 'I know this is the wrong thing to be thinking but I'm glad you're home, even given the circumstances that brought you back here. For me it's worth it, just to have a sight of you and know that until you've sorted out this mess, you'll be around. I like the way you handled Jackie too – you know something, Ella Kovac, you're an old softie underneath.'

'I *have* changed in the last year,' Ella acknowledged. 'I've tried to work out why, whether it's living in England or just getting old, and I have come to a conclusion.'

'What's that?' Aaron drew her closer to him and kissed her forehead.

'It's your fault,' said Ella, 'you're making me soft, you're making me see that there are other things besides my business and my son. I've started to appreciate leisure in a way I never have before and I spend far too much of my time thinking about you, rather than the next real estate deal.'

'That's as it should be,' said Aaron. 'So, when are you going to marry me?'

'I can't decide anything at the moment, not while all this is going on. You do see that, Aaron, don't you?'

'Not really,' he said, 'I don't see how you and I and the business are connected. Either we're right for each other or we're not.'

'You know we are, but would you please give me a little space just until this is over?' Ella asked.

'I guess so.' The disappointment in Aaron's voice was evident.

They kissed and were interrupted by the telephone. Ella reached out an arm and picked up the receiver. 'Hello,' she said.

'Mom? Mom, it's Greg.'

'Greg! Are you OK?'

He laughed. 'Why is it that whenever I call you unexpectedly, you always assume there's something wrong with me?'

Ella turned over in the bed and shifted herself into a sitting position. 'That's mothers for you.'

'I guess,' said Greg. 'How's New York?'

'Same old city. Where are you?'

'I'm in London, at Holland Park.'

'Alone?' Ella teased.

'Never you mind,' said Greg, with a laugh. 'Actually

Mom, I was ringing for a favour. My exams finish next week and I thought ... well, I thought I might bring Belinda out to the States, just for a week or two, to show her around. Would that be OK?'

'Of course it would be OK,' said Ella, 'and is the next question, please can I have some money, Mom?'

'Something like that,' said Greg, with a laugh.

'OK, I'll transfer some funds to your account first thing tomorrow. When can I expect you two?'

'The middle to end of next week, I think,' said Greg. 'My last exam's on Tuesday morning.'

'You'll call me then, when you've fixed a flight?'

'Yes, of course, that's really great, Mom, thanks.'

'How is he?' Aaron asked, when Ella replaced the phone.

'Fine,' said Ella, 'he's bringing his girlfriend over, I guess to see his roots. I reckon it must be serious.'

'What's he going to do now? He must be finishing college any time?'

'He wants to find a farm manager's job somewhere on a big estate in England.'

'No thoughts then of bringing his qualifications back home?' Aaron's voice was a little wistful.

'No,' said Ella, 'I think he's firmly entrenched in England. Part of it's this love affair with Belinda but it's not as simple as that. He somehow seems to fit over there. I think the trouble is, for him the States means city life.'

'He could always go back to Kentucky. As soon as you've despatched your problems you could set him up with his own place there. Still, in the circumstances, I guess that's not what you want.'

Ella shook her head. 'No, and I think he senses that, too, without understanding the real reason. He has a whole heap of friends in England now and I think he'll make out very well. It'll be good, though, to have him over here, even for just a week or so.'

'I'll call William in the morning,' said Aaron, 'he's coming back home next week too, and so we can have a real family reunion.'

'Will we tell the boys about us?' Ella asked.

Aaron smiled, before he kissed her. 'I don't think we'll have to, do you?'

CHAPTER FORTY-THREE

NEW YORK
June 1985

Across the dining table, Aaron and Ella raised their glasses to one another in a silent toast. Between them, in pools of candle light, sat Greg, Belinda and William. It was proving a wonderful evening. Greg and Belinda had flown into New York the same afternoon and William had returned from college the previous day. It was the first time that the Connors and Kovacs had been together in a very long time.

Greg suddenly rose to his feet. 'I'd like to raise my glass to Mom,' he said, 'for such a great meal.'

'I agree,' said Aaron, 'to the chef.' They drank Ella's health while she beamed at them.

Greg cleared his throat. 'There's another thing.' He glanced at Belinda. 'Belinda and I had something of an ulterior motive in coming to New York. We, er . . . well, we've just got engaged.'

The room exploded around him, there were kisses and congratulations. Ella found herself with her arms around her son, tears streaming down her face. 'I kept wondering,' she admitted, 'but then I guess I thought you guys were perhaps a little too young.' She looked at Belinda and laughed. 'Are you sure you want to take on this great baby?'

Belinda's face creased into a smile, so like her father's. 'Quite sure,' she said.

'We are young, I know that, Mom,' said Greg, 'but where the hell am I going to find another girl like Belinda? If I don't marry her right now, some other guy will get her. She's a one-off, I daren't let her go.'

His words brought fresh tears to Ella's eyes. Aaron came to her side and slipped an arm round her. 'Hey, this is supposed to be a happy occasion.'

'I am happy,' said Ella, 'it's just, well, terrific. William, there's some champagne in the kitchen. It's not awfully cold but let's open it anyway.'

They drank the health of Greg and Belinda, then Aaron made coffee and they went through to the sitting room. 'So, how are you proposing to support this future bride of yours?' Aaron asked, with mock severity. 'As godfather,' he explained to Belinda, 'I have to ask these kind of questions.'

'Well that's the amazing thing,' said Greg. 'To be honest, we hadn't really worked out what was going to happen but when we told Tim about our plans, he straight away suggested that we should take over his old family home, Monkswell Farm. He's been finding it difficult to manage both Wickham and Monkswell since his father died. It's a beautiful house, Mom, the farm has huge potential and Tim's literally giving it to us. It's just unreal, like a dream come true – our own place right from the beginning and a chance to build it ourselves the way we want it.'

His eyes were shining and Ella had never seen her son so happy. Despite his youth, she realized she had no doubts that he was doing the right thing. She knew that Aaron would be thinking, as she was, that Greg settling in England would force upon her a choice as to where she made her main home. However, even the uncertain future of her relationship with Aaron could not eclipse the happiness she felt. For a brief moment her thoughts took her back to the little shack in which she herself had been raised, and to the circumstances of Greg's birth – a fatherless baby, born to a homeless, penniless sixteen year old. Things had turned out differently from how she had expected in many respects, but she had achieved her goal. Greg was marrying a girl in a million, he would have his own place in the country of his choice and a secure and happy future. 'As Tim has been so generous over his old family home, you must let me make a financial contribution to your future,' she said. 'Some money to buy stock, machinery, do over the house, that kind of thing.'

'That's generous of you, Mom, but please don't give us much, it's important we make our own luck. If we work hard we'll be alright.'

Ella gazed at her son with frank admiration. Maybe she hadn't achieved long-term personal happiness for herself, maybe her business was in a mess but she had produced one good thing in her life and she thanked God for him. 'OK,' she said, 'actually things are a little tough at work right now.'

'How come, Ella?' William asked. 'I always boast at college I know the most successful female tycoon in America.'

Ella told the children then of the Houston problems. She had returned the previous day from a trip to Houston which had confirmed beyond doubt that she was in deep trouble. Yet she could not bring herself to believe that things would not work out in the end. New York was still doing well and her dabblings in London were proving lucrative. As the conversation buzzed around her, she thought again of the idea that had been building in her mind during the last two or three days. The whole Houston development was short of cash, the drop in income had seriously undermined her ability to pay interest on her loans and there was no way Jack Smith was going to increase her facilities. If she could sell her interest in the West London Meyer Centre she should be able to raise enough money to keep Houston afloat for some time, hopefully long enough for the market to recover. Her thoughts turned to Stephanie. 'How does your mother feel about your engagement?' she asked Belinda.

'She's really pleased.'

I wonder, thought Ella. She and Stephanie seemed to have drifted so far apart. Clearly, in her mind, Stephanie still saw her as the enemy, as someone who could prove a threat to her marriage with Tim. Somehow they would have to overcome that, now they were to be related by this marriage. Would the sale of her interest in Fulham upset Stephanie? It seemed unlikely that she would be able to afford to put in a bid. It was Joseph Meyer or someone from outside the partnership who would prove the most likely candidate and either way, Ella thought, with a sinking heart, it was not going to endear her to Stephanie.

'Actually, she's very preoccupied with the baby at the moment,' said Belinda, 'it's due next month. Daddy's hoping it will be a boy. It would be nice for him, someone to inherit Wickham.' Clearly from the way Belinda was speaking she had no idea that this child was not her father's and Ella wondered how Tim and Stephanie were going to handle the situation. Would the baby be brought up an Irvine or would the truth of his paternity become common knowledge?' It was not an easy problem to solve.

Later that evening, Ella and Aaron found themselves alone. William had called a girlfriend and arranged to take Greg and Belinda out on the town. 'The stamina of the young,' Aaron said. 'Can you imagine flying in from England and feeling able to stay out all night?'

'Love will find a way,' Ella suggested.

'I hope that's true.' Aaron took her in his arms and kissed her. 'Are you happy about Greg?'

'Very,' said Ella. 'It's not at all what I had planned for him but he's made his own life, the way he wants it, and that's all that matters.'

'She's a wonderful girl,' said Aaron, 'I hope William is as lucky.' He hesitated. 'I nearly said something about us and then I didn't know what to say or how to say it, and I wasn't sure you would be pleased anyway.'

Ella reached out and touched his cheek. 'I think it's a little premature to start making announcements about us, don't you? I just have to get my business sorted out first; in fact I was thinking of flying back to the UK later in the week.'

'Why?' Aaron said. 'The problem's here in Houston.'

'I know, I know, but I think I can raise some money in England.' Ella explained her plan for selling the West London Meyer Centre.

'It sounds kind of drastic,' said Aaron.

'The circumstances are drastic, I really don't have any alternative.'

'Do you think Meyer will play ball?'

'Bound to. He'll know I'm over a barrel and won't be able to resist the chance of a good deal.'

'And then you'll come home?' Aaron queried.

Ella hesitated. 'I've been thinking about that, too. I have to make some money, fast, and at the moment I think I'm more likely to do that in the UK than here in New York. I dare not diversify into yet another area and I am starting to get a feel for the London property scene, particularly round the docklands and in the City. I think there's a killing to be made and I'll need to act fast.' She was carefully avoiding his eyes. 'Then Greg and Belinda say they want to marry this side of Christmas and their wedding will obviously be in England. You see there's not much I can do in Houston that Michael can't handle for me. I'm clearly not going to invest in any new real estate, nor can I sell off what I've got, so it's really just a question of keeping a watching brief on the rents coming in, which is something Michael and his office can do far better than I.' She grinned at Aaron, hoping to relieve the tension that was mounting between them. 'I'm a wheeler-dealer. Detailed administration just isn't really my thing. New York runs like clockwork under Jackie, so it seems – well, sensible to concentrate on the UK market.'

'Sensible!' Aaron spat out the word. 'Does our relationship matter at all to you, Ella?'

'Of course it does. It's just that I can't let my business go down the pan, Aaron, I've put my whole life into it.'

'It's only money.' Aaron released her, walked over to the window and gazed out into the night sky. 'You've always told me that the whole reason for your obsessive involvement in business was to secure Greg's future. Greg's future is secure. You heard him this evening, Ella. Full marks to the boy, he doesn't want your cash, he wants to do it for himself. He's a chip off the old block – he has your independence and God bless him for it. What it means, however, is that whatever steps you take now, Ella, are for yourself, not for your son, and the emphasis you place on the importance of our future opposite your business activities has to be a purely personal one. There's no one else to consider now.'

'You're not being fair,' said Ella. 'How would you feel about it if I asked you to give up your work, give up your patients and come and live in England with me? You wouldn't do it, would you?' She met his eye, challengingly.

'That's a pointless argument,' said Aaron. 'New York is our home, I'm not asking you to leave your home, I'm asking you to come back to it.'

'New York is *your* home,' said Ella, 'I'm not sure it's mine any more. I like England, I like London, I like the way of life.'

'Ella, isn't it time you let go of that boy, now he's made a life of his own?'

'It's nothing to do with Greg —' Ella stopped in mid-sentence recognizing that even to her own ears, what she was saying sounded ludicrous. 'OK, it's something to do with Greg but not everything. Look, Aaron, you're wedded to your work just as much as I am. Surely you can see that after years and years of building something you can't just throw it away?'

'I'm not suggesting you throw it away,' said Aaron, 'it's just that you've made this arbitrary decision to concentrate your efforts in the UK without even consulting me.'

'Why should I consult you?' said Ella, angrily.

Aaron turned away. 'Why indeed. I thought our happiness, our future, was bound together, clearly I'm wrong and that being the case, why indeed should you seek my view on this or anything else? You go your own way, Ella, make your own decisions and don't give me another thought.' He strode towards the front door.

'Aaron, try to understand. Please don't leave me like this, not tonight when everything was so happy with Greg coming home.'

'I've given as much as I can give,' said Aaron. 'I don't want to stay here pretending we have a future together when clearly we have not. You're going your own way, Ella, making your own life. I, clearly, have to do the same. I can't wait around for the next ten or fifteen years, hoping your business decisions will bring you to New York just long enough for us to marry and settle down. In any event, I'm not sure that's what I want any more. How could I ever feel secure in our relationship, knowing that any moment you may take off on some new scheme. I'm used to marriage where decisions are joint, where one partner considers the other's point of view and requirements. I'm not sure I can cope with anything else.'

'You mean what you're used to is Alice acting as doormat, letting you play God and organizing her life entirely round your whims and fancies.'

'Don't you dare criticise Alice,' Aaron's face darkened with anger. 'You have to work out your own emotional problems, it's no good trying to off-load responsibility onto somebody else, never mind poor Alice.'

'I'm sorry, but I don't know what you mean,' said Ella, helplessly intimidated by a building fury in Aaron which she had never seen before.

'I mean that you're afraid to commit yourself to a proper adult relationship, with all the responsibilities which that involves. Your son isn't, your son recognizes his responsibilities to Belinda, you can see that. But as for you, I hate to say this, Ella, but you're an emotional cripple. Over the years I've tried to help you all I can, but my life has taken its own beating of late and I'm simply not prepared to lead some sort of half-life waiting for you. You're right about my dictating the terms, and I'm doing so now. For us to have any future together, we have to be married, we have to live in the same home, in the same city and at the same time. I'm quite happy to tolerate the odd business trip to Houston and, say, a bi-annual trip to the UK to see Greg and Belinda, just as I hope you would tolerate the odd medical conference and lecture tour I have to make, from time-to-time. But that's it – we live together as man and wife or I'm through. So, you go back to the UK, you sort out the sale of the Meyer Centre and if you want us to be together, you come straight home. If you don't, then I'll know the answer.' Without another word, he turned and left the room.

Ella stood where he had left her. She had never felt more miserable in her life.

CHAPTER FORTY-FOUR

LONDON
August 1985

The waiting room at Queen Charlotte's Hospital was hardly an inspiring place. Ella and Joseph Meyer sat beside one another, pretending to read back numbers of *Punch* and *Country Life*. They had arrived independently, within hours of hearing that Stephanie had given birth to a son, and now sat waiting for the opportunity to see her.

In the six weeks since Ella had returned to the UK, she and Joseph had become firm friends. The negotiation for the sale of her shareholding in the West London Meyer Centre had been surprisingly speedy and straightforward. Joseph could have screwed her – they both knew it – but he had made no attempt to do so. As a result, they had met regularly, on the excuse of clarifying an odd point or signing a document, but mostly because they enjoyed one another's company. They were two of a kind, Joseph had pointed out on more than one occasion – tough nuts on the outside, soft centres inside. Ella supposed he was right. Although her success was not in Joseph's league, they had both come from nowhere and in many respects paid a similar price for their success. At this moment, however, the easy companionship they now shared was strained. They sat, waiting for the summons to see Stephanie, both uncertain as to what sort of reception they could expect.

Stephanie had been extremely angry at Ella's decision to sell her shareholding. She had accused Ella of deliberately selling the month before her baby's birth, to preclude her from attempting to raise the money herself. Stephanie saw it as a capitulation to Meyer and was bitterly opposed to finding herself in the position of being the minority shareholder, with Joseph holding the majority. Ella had tried to explain the desperate nature of her business in Houston, which had deteriorated terrifyingly in the preceding month, but Stephanie, already highly emotionally charged, simply would not listen.

The door opened and Tim came into the waiting room. He looked tired and Ella wondered whether the strain of helping Stephanie in recent months had adversely affected his condition – certainly he did not look well. 'Look,' he said, awkwardly, 'I'm terribly sorry but I'm afraid Stephanie won't see either of you. It-it's really kind of you to have come but she just doesn't feel up to it.'

'Is she alright?' said Ella.

'She had a fairly difficult time.' Tim hesitated. 'I have to be honest, though, it's just that she's not terribly ... well disposed towards either of you and she feels she can't cope in the circumstances. I'm so sorry.'

'The baby,' Joseph said, 'is he OK?'

'He's fine,' said Tim. 'We're going to call him Matthew, Matthew Alexander.'

'That's good,' said Joseph, 'very good.'

Tim smiled uncertainly at Joseph. 'Actually ... the baby's in the nursery at the moment. Would you like to come and see him?'

Joseph was out of his seat in seconds. 'That would be kind, so kind.'

Tim smiled. 'Come on then, one sneak preview coming up.'

The baby lay fast asleep in his little perspex cot. Ella had only met Alex Meyer once but even she could see the likeness to his father. She heard Joseph's quick intake of breath beside her and turned to see the old man had tears running down his face. She slipped her hand into his and instantly he gripped it for comfort. 'He – he's so like Alex,' he said, brokenly.

'Yes, I thought that,' said Tim. 'It's strange, Stephanie won't acknowledge the likeness, I don't know why.'

Ella glanced up at him and saw in that instant how much the whole situation was hurting him. Not for the first time, she recognized that Tim Irvine was a very special person. She turned to Joseph. 'Come on, I'm going to take you out to lunch.'

'No.' Joseph shook his head, tears still tumbling down his cheeks.

'Yes,' said Ella, firmly. She looked up at Tim. 'Thank you for showing us the baby, and give Stephanie our love.'

'I will,' said Tim.

'Is your car here?' Ella asked, once they were outside the hospital. Joseph nodded blindly, he was clearly in a state of shock. Ella found the car, told the chauffeur to take them to the Savoy Grill and sat in silence, still holding Joseph's hand, as he sobbed quietly throughout the journey.

At the Savoy he seemed to pull himself together a little, and after a trip to the gents he returned looking pale but dry-eyed. 'I don't know what you must think of me,' he said.

'The same as always,' said Ella, 'that you're just great. Come on, I've fixed a table, we'll go straight in.'

'I couldn't eat anything,' said Joseph.

'You'll do as you're told.'

The ghost of a smile crossed his face. 'Bossy woman.'

In the end, she tempted him to a Dover sole and a bottle of Chablis. He did little more than pick at his food but it kept him occupied. 'It must have been a terrible shock for you, to see how like his father Matthew is,' Ella ventured at last, when she judged Joseph had drunk enough wine to loosen his tongue.

'I didn't know you already realized that Tim was not the father. I thought for a moment I'd betrayed young Irvine's kindness by being very tactless.'

'Yes, I know,' said Ella, 'but I rather think you and I are probably the only two people who do know the true position. I'm not sure how they're going to handle Matthew's future, are you?'

Joseph shook his head. 'I just know that I'm to be no part of it. My only grandchild, my only blood relation bar that poor girl who might just as well be dead, yet I can't even see him.'

'I think you need to give them time,' said Ella. 'Try and see things from their point of view. They have so much pressure on them at the moment. They're trying to rebuild their marriage, they've had to do it against the background of Stephanie carrying another man's child and not just any man but the man who took her away from her husband in the first place. They need to sort themselves out and work on their own relationship before they can give consideration to you and your feelings. It's hard but it's understandable.'

'You're a very wise young woman,' Joseph said, smiling at Ella.

'I'm damn good at sorting out other people's problems,' Ella said, with a wry smile, 'not so hot when it comes to my own.'

'A woman like you shouldn't have problems,' said Joseph. 'Now, if I was thirty years younger . . .' There was a twinkle in his eye and Ella laughed aloud.

'That's better, that's more your style.' He sobered instantly and she regretted her words. Leaning across the table she took his hand once more in both of hers. 'I know how you feel about Matthew. I have a son, remember, who I brought up alone. When I think of anything happening to Greg — well, it feels like there'd be no point in going on living. As for Greg's child, it would be as much a part of me as Greg is himself. I know preaching patience is not an easy thing to expect of you. With all due respect you're not a very patient man, but if you try and play the heavy grandfather now, you'll lose Matthew for good. If you want my advice I believe your biggest ally is Tim. The man has a heart of gold — you saw that for yourself today in the hospital. He couldn't bear to send you away without you having sight of your grandchild. I'm sure he'll work on Stephanie over the next few months. Give him time and I believe he'll see to it that you play a part in Matthew's life.'

'But how long?' Joseph asked desperately. 'I'm not a young man, Ella. Who knows, I may not be here this time next year and babies change so fast. I want to see Matthew grow up, I want to be a part of it.'

'I know it's hard,' said Ella, 'but you have to bide your time. Look, I tell you what, why don't you let me have a word with Tim. I'll see him in the next day or so while Stephanie's still in hospital. At the moment I don't think Stephanie is any more fond of me that she is of you, so I need to see Tim alone. I'll explain to him how you feel, tell him a little about your life and make him realize just how important Matthew is to you.'

'I don't want you making me out to be some pathetic old jerk who can't speak for himself.'

'Oh Joseph, for heaven's sake,' said Ella, 'no one could ever think of you as pathetic, nor old either come to that — you're timeless. It's just that if you talk to Tim you'll go over the top. You'll start screaming and yelling about your rights and then you'll lose your temper and remind Tim that he isn't even a blood relation to the boy. Once you've done that, you'll have blown it completely because that will be something Tim won't forgive. I'm right, aren't I?'

Joseph squeezed the hand he still held. 'Yes, but how come a jumped-up little New York broad knows so much about me?'

'May be because this jumped-up little New York broad happens to be rather fond of you. Now are you going to let me handle this one or are you going to behave like a goddamn idiot.'

'All my life I've been bullied by women . . .'

Joe Allens was already crowded by the time Ella arrived. That was just how she wanted it. She had deliberately chosen to meet Tim in an atmosphere that lacked intimacy and could be guaranteed to be busy and noisy. Joe Allens, in Covent Garden, was perfect. Now, she searched the sea of tables and caught sight of him in a corner, his hand raised, a smile of greeting on his face. She picked her way through the tables towards him. He stood up and kissed her warmly on the cheek. He had already ordered a bottle of wine and poured her a glass.

'Shall we toast Matthew?' Ella suggested.

'Why not?' said Tim, with a smile, 'to Matthew.'

'You must be wondering why I asked to meet you,' Ella said, without preamble. 'You must have thought it was a little odd.'

'I'll tell you what I did think,' said Tim, 'I started wondering when was the last time I saw you entirely alone without the kids, and realized we hadn't been completely on our own once since France, not in all those years.'

Ella toyed with the stem of her wine glass. 'Do you still hate me for how I behaved? It was so childish, so irrational.'

'Of course I don't,' said Tim, 'I understand completely.'

'How can you understand?' Ella burst out. 'If you love someone, what difference should it make that they have . . .' she searched for words, 'an illness you didn't know about. It should just be something you accept as a part of them.'

'It's not just an illness, though, is it?' said Tim. 'It's very distressing, particularly for the onlooker. The mistake was mine, I should have told you about it from the beginning, but somehow our relationship had become so intimate so quickly, that each day it became more difficult to tell you.'

'I can understand that,' said Ella.

'It would have been terribly unkind if you had pretended you could cope with it, when really you couldn't. Then we would have limped on in some sort of half-relationship which could have destroyed us both. You had the courage to tell me how you felt, that was the important thing.'

'Even there you're not being strictly accurate,' said Ella, 'you knew how I felt, I didn't have to tell you, that's what made it so awful.'

'It's true, I did know,' said Tim, 'but it's no good agonizing – it's water under the bridge. There will always be a special place in my thoughts for you, Ella, but there's no pain when I think about us now, I just remember the happiness we shared.'

'I feel the same,' said Ella, 'except for the guilt.'

'Banish the guilt,' said Tim, 'after all, you and I are going to be related very soon and so we have to get along, don't we?' He grinned. 'Are you pleased about Belinda and Greg?'

'That's a silly question to ask,' said Ella, 'you must know I am. You're being very generous to them, I want to talk to you about that.'

For some time they discussed details of their children's future life and the wedding arrangements, for it had been decided that Greg and Belinda would be married on 10th November. They argued amicably enough about who would pay for what and eventually paused long enough to order a meal.

Released from the restraints of guilt which had haunted her for so long, Ella found she slipped naturally into a kind of intimate camaraderie with Tim. They laughed and shared jokes, teased each other and behind it all was the common link of their former intimacy and a future which would be shared by the marriage of their children.

It was only over coffee that at last Ella brought the conversation round to the main reason for their meeting. 'I wanted to talk to you before Stephanie came out of hospital,' Ella began. 'I know she's not feeling very well-disposed towards me at the moment.'

'It's true,' Tim admitted. 'She's angry you sold out to Meyer. I don't know anything about it but I gather you have some kind of financial problem.'

'In Houston, yes,' said Ella, 'my properties have plummeted in value because of the drop in the oil market. Many of them are now unoccupied, my income has dropped drastically and I can't sell them at the moment because I'd never cover my borrowings.'

'That's rough,' said Tim, 'I'm sorry you're having these problems, I had no idea.'

'I did explain it all to Stephanie,' Ella said, a little harshly.

'Yes, I'm sure you did,' said Tim, 'but she's been very preoccupied over the birth of this baby. I think it's thrown her – that and Alex's death. She'll come round in time, it's just that the last thing she wants at the moment is to have Meyer with an even greater hold over her and she felt that the sale of your shareholding was a retrograde step from her point of view.'

'I can see that,' said Ella, 'but I really had no choice.' She hesitated. 'Any way, that's not why I wanted to see you, I wanted to talk to you about Matthew.'

He set down his coffee cup with a look of surprise. 'Matthew?'

'I'm really here as some kind of ambassador, but I haven't been sent – it was my idea to come.'

'Go on,' said Tim, looking apprehensive.

'How much do you know about Joseph Meyer?'

'Not a lot,' said Tim. 'I know he's very rich and powerful. Stephanie sees him as a threat and I can understand why – he's a man used to having his own way. He ruled his son with a rod of iron, he tried to rule Stephanie and she's terrified that he'll get his hands on Matthew. I must say I can't blame her.'

'Can I tell you his story?' Ella asked.

'Yes, of course,' said Tim.

A month or so earlier, Ella and Joseph had shared dinner together and Ella had coaxed his life story from him. He had told her about it in considerably more detail than he had ever told Stephanie, describing the daily life at Treblinka and the appalling effects on his family, his early struggles in the States, the astounding joy of Alex's birth, followed by despair when just a few years later his wife had died.

When Ella had finished, Tim was silent for some long time. 'The daughter... is she still alive?' he asked at last.

'Yes, she's in a home in New York. Joseph pays her a monthly visit but he says she's no idea who he is. It's the one part of the story he couldn't really tell me in detail. I don't exactly know what happened to her, all I do know is that the Nazis in those camps conducted a number of sexual experiments on young girls. Whatever happened to her was so horrific it sent her out of her mind and no amount of psychiatric treatment has been able to put her right.'

'So Matthew is all he has left, is what you're saying,' said Tim.

Ella nodded. 'I-I'm not suggesting, of course, that you should hand the child over to him or that you should make Joseph part of Matthew's every day life. The very best thing that could happen to Matthew, in my view, is that his name should be Matthew Irvine, that he should be brought up as your son and given the same sort of childhood that you gave Millie and Belinda. All I'm asking is that you try not to cut the old man out of the boy's life completely. I don't know whether you've decided to tell Matthew about his true parentage or not. I gather that Belinda assumes he's your baby, at least that's the impression she gave me in New York, and of course all of this is absolutely none of my business. What I am asking is that whether Joseph is admitted into your life as official grandfather, or as an occasional family friend, or godfather or whatever, you let him share some part of Matthew's life. Stephanie worries that Joseph will have a similar suffocating hold on Matthew's life as he did on Alex's but that's absolutely out of the question. Alex, Joseph brought up alone because his wife had died. In Matthew's case, not only does he have you and Stephanie, but long before he's a man, Joseph will be dead. I don't know whether Stephanie's aware of this, but Joseph has had a heart condition for some years. He could die at any time and I suspect that after the years of deprivation he suffered, he won't live to a great age. His mind is as clear and astute as that of a young man, but the flesh is weak.'

'Does Stephanie know about his past?' Tim asked.

'I should imagine so,' said Ella. 'In the early days they had a very good relationship. In any case, after all those years of living with Alex . . .' her voice petered out. 'I'm sorry, Tim, that wasn't very tactful.'

'That's OK,' he replied, 'and I take the point. If Joseph didn't tell her himself, Alex must have done.'

'Can you . . . will you help him?' Ella asked.

'I'll do what I can,' said Tim. 'I agree with you, it's not such a big deal to make an old man happy, but at the same time one has to recognize that Stephanie hates his guts. I don't quite understand the background of her feelings towards him but they are strongly entrenched, and equally, she feels very protective towards her new baby. It's strange actually, she is much more motherly to Matthew than she ever was to Millie and Belinda.'

'Do you mind that?' Ella asked.

'No,' said Tim, 'I'm pleased. Stephanie's lack of involvement in Millie and Belinda's childhood worried me on every level. I minded for her own sake, too — I felt that she was missing out on such a lot. Maybe with Matthew it will be different. I've told her that I will look on him as my own, that I will love him as much as our daughters and it's true — the fact that he isn't mine makes no difference at all. None the less, I think in her mind she feels a greater degree of responsibility towards him than she did to the girls because he isn't mine, and that can only be a good thing.'

Ella smiled. 'So, you're optimistic about your future together, that's wonderful.'

'Yes, I am,' said Tim. 'We're both changed and mellowed and we have so much shared past. I feel, this time, we might be alright.'

'I'm glad,' said Ella, 'very glad.'

Riding home in the taxi, a few minutes later, Ella realized that her words were true. Although she had spent years missing Tim and wishing she could have another chance at their relationship, she found now that she viewed him as nothing more than a dear friend for Aaron occupied all her thoughts. That she and Tim would be linked for ever by the marriage of their children brought a great sense of pleasure and comfort, but nothing more.

Inevitably, her thoughts turned to Aaron. She had not returned to New York after selling her Fulham shareholding. Instead, she had written him a long letter and tried to explain why. Joseph Meyer had been instrumental in introducing her to a number of valuable contacts and she was now heavily involved in the development of the docklands. It was a good, sound project that should bring her a great deal of money, and with Houston temporarily secured by the Fulham money she had been able to deposit with Jack Smith, the answer had to be to stay in London. She knew Aaron would be angry but in her heart she could not but believe he would understand her predicament and give her a few months longer. 'I'll be back in New York for Christmas,' she had promised him. 'I'll just see Greg settled and by December I should be able to leave the docklands project for a month or so at any rate. Please come over for Greg's wedding, we need you to be there.' Aaron had not replied for some weeks. When he had done so, it had been a short, curt note saying that clearly she had not taken seriously his ultimatum and it should be understood that everything between them was now over. He added that he would attend Greg's wedding, since he was Greg's godfather, but only on the understanding that he was coming as a family friend, nothing more.

Ella had been devastated by the letter, yet still she could not quite believe it was true. She had not known how to respond and so she had not replied and as the weeks ticked by, she found herself growing more and more apprehensive about the future of her relationship with Aaron. He was an attractive man. If he was truly finished with her, there would be no shortage of candidates to replace her. She tried to imagine Aaron married again to someone else and the thought horrified, terrified her, yet unaccountably not enough to make her abandon her work. She knew the only way to safeguard the future of her business was to take the course of action she was doing and even the threat of losing Aaron could not divert her now.

When the taxi stopped outside her house, she paid off the driver and wandered inside. It was still her haven and it still brought her comfort, but an increasing sense of loneliness seemed to be seeping into her soul. Greg was so preoccupied and happy, and he and Belinda spent most weekends at their new home now. She had acquired an increasing circle of friends in London, but they were mostly business contacts and as such, she suspected, fair weather friends. Ella realized that but for the genuine warmth and intimacy of her friendship from such an unexpected quarter as Joseph Meyer, her sense of isolation and loneliness would have been complete. It was a high price indeed to pay for business success.

CHAPTER FORTY-FIVE

LONDON
November 1985

It had not been Ella's intention to arrive early for her meeting with Margot — indeed, it had not been Ella's intention to arrive at all. When, at Greg's wedding, Margot had said she needed to see her urgently, Ella's immediate instincts had been to issue a rebuff. They had not met alone since the evening at Margot's home, when Ella had threatened to expose her past. What had stopped Ella from refusing now had been the situation in Houston, which had worsened considerably since the summer. She knew, in normal circumstances, the bank would not have been able to contain the position in which she now found herself. The value of her Houston property now being considerably less than her bank borrowings, her income inadequate to meet the interest and capital repayments and the Fulham money all but gone. It was only the fact that Jack Smith would help himself not at all by foreclosing on her that had so far prevented her business from crashing. Jack had been putting considerable pressure on her of late to pour more money into Houston which Ella was fighting tooth and nail – she simply could not drain her London and New York operations of any more working capital without affecting them. They were healthy in themselves and when she saw how quickly Houston had absorbed the Fulham money, it seemed crazy to throw good money after bad.

It was this position which had her now waiting in the foyer of the bank at Mansion House, for Ella was well aware of Joshkers' shareholding in Sunbelt Industrial Bank. At her most recent meeting with Jack, he had hinted that he was under a considerable obligation to Joshkers who had granted him a loan to keep his operation in business. If there was one thing that Ella had learnt during her years in business, it was that nobody ever did anything for nothing, and she presumed that if Joshkers Bank had bailed out Sunbelt Industrial, it seemed likely they would now be wielding a considerable amount of power down in Houston. Despite her personal feelings, therefore, this was certainly not a moment to cross Margot.

The two women eyed one another across Margot's desk. To Ella, Margot seemed like a dangerous, wild animal, sleek, powerful and predatory. Margot noted the dark circles under Ella's eyes, the pale complexion and the definite lack of normal Kovac bounce. Houston, or something, was certainly taking its toll on Ella. They exchanged perfunctory greetings and paused in conversation while coffee was delivered, giving Ella a chance to look round the room.

Margot's new office was extremely impressive, if somewhat masculine, with wood panelled walls on which hunting prints hung, deep leather armchairs and a spectacular view out across the City of London. Margot noted her scrutiny. 'You're probably thinking it's rather an odd choice of office,' she said. 'It's not mine, actually, it used to belong to our late chairman, Nicholas Goddard. When I inherited it, it seemed sacrilege to alter anything for this room was very much his style, so I've left everything as it was.'

The sentiment surprised Ella but she made no comment. 'So, Margot,' she said, 'you wanted to see me urgently, I gather. I assume it's about Houston?'

Margot shook her head and began her inevitable doodling on the pad in front of her. 'No, not precisely,' she said, 'actually it's about Meyer Hotels' She paused dramatically for a moment, to allow her words to sink in.

Ella frowned. 'I don't follow you.'

'There's a buzz going round the City, a reliable buzz, that Joseph's thinking of selling out.'

'It doesn't surprise me,' said Ella. 'He's old, tired and disappointed. Without Alex, his work has ceased to have much point for him.'

Margot looked up from her doodling. 'I'd heard you two had become friendly. He's an impressive old guy, isn't he?'

'Very,' said Ella, shortly. It irritated her the way Margot always seemed to know everything about everyone. With Fulham long sold, her relationship with Joseph was now entirely personal and no one's business but her own.

'I won't beat about the bush,' said Margot. 'What I want you to do is to put in a bid for the group, before it goes on the open market. I think he would be very susceptible to you taking over the helm – he greatly admires your business achievements and he's clearly fond of you personally. Money, I suspect, will be of secondary consideration to seeing that his baby goes to the right person.'

'Hold it a minute,' said Ella. 'You're saying you want me to bid for Meyer Hotels, the *whole* of Meyer Hotels?'

'That's right,' said Margot.

'You have to be joking!' Ella burst out. 'It has to be worth several hundred million dollars, and even if I could raise that kind of money I'm not a hotelier: real estate is my business.'

'Let me put this another way,' said Margot. 'You're in a mess in Houston, right?'

'At present, certainly,' Ella tempered.

'At present, and probably for some long time into the future. I don't see Texas getting over this problem quickly. The banks are starting to drop like flies and tearing the guts out of the city. It will be some long time before we see any upward turn and there's still some falling yet to do.'

Margot's cool appraisal of the situation sent a chill of fear through Ella but she remained outwardly calm. 'OK, so Houston's not doing so great, but I have my other two operations.'

'You do,' said Margot, 'but they're not big enough or busy enough to cope with the crisis you're facing in Houston. If you acquired Meyer Hotels you could indulge in a little asset-stripping and looked at in the context of your total holding, Houston would then seem small fry. By realizing some of the Meyer assets you could give the Houston operation a much needed shot in the arm, or simply cut your losses and bail out, whichever seemed most appropriate. Either way you could cope.'

'Just supposing I was to go along with such a preposterous suggestion, Margot and I have to say now I will not – your advice seems to be in some conflict. On the one hand you're saying that Joseph Meyer might be prepared to sell to me out of sentiment, because he thinks I'll look after his group. In the next breath, you're saying I should dismember the group in order to get myself out of the shit in Houston.'

Margot let out a sigh of irritation. 'Ella, we're not talking fairy tales here, we're talking about good business sense. What you do with the group once it's yours is up to you. What I'm saying is that I think Joseph would be prepared to do you a very special deal, particularly if part of that deal included a long term commitment to take his grandson into the business, if the boy so wishes.'

Ella's eyes narrowed as she looked at Margot appraisingly. 'So how the hell do you know about his grandson?'

'Does it matter?' said Margot. 'The fact is I do. In normal circumstances, if Stephanie wasn't being so pig-headed, I should imagine Joseph would hand Meyer over to her lock, stock and barrel, if she promised to act as custodian for her son's future. However, since she's not prepared to make that kind of commitment, Joseph, I suspect, is looking round for another way of selling Meyer, while still making sure that Matthew has an entrée into the group if he so wishes. You're the obvious candidate, in my view.'

'Maybe I am,' said Ella, 'but there's no way I'll be a party to this. I can only repeat, I don't want to go into the hotel business, I don't want to find myself heading an operation the size of Meyers and most important of all, I'm certainly not prepared to double-cross Joseph by using Meyer as a bailing out operation. I'm sorry, Margot, the answer is no. I'm surprised you even raised it, you must have known how I would react.'

There was a silence for a moment or two. 'Yes, I suppose I did which is why, although I regret what I'm going to have to say next, it does not surprise me that it's necessary for me to do so.' Ella suddenly felt very cold. There was menace in the air, a sense of foreboding. The image she'd had of Margot, as she had entered the room, now seemed stronger than ever: she felt like a defenceless victim, waiting for Margot to pounce. She forced herself to concentrate as Margot began speaking. 'If you're not prepared to put in a bid for Meyer, then I'm afraid I have no alternative but to advise Jack Smith that he should foreclose on you in Houston.'

'He won't do that,' said Ella, her heart beating so loudly she could barely hear her own words. 'I was talking to him on the phone only this morning. He has made it perfectly clear that he will stick with me for the duration.'

'He's not in a position to make those kind of assurances to you any more,' said Margot. 'He's deeply in debt to Joshkers and as such has agreed to our right of veto on all major decisions. Lexington Kovac is a major decision, so far as a branch of his size is concerned. If we tell him to pull out, he'll have to do just that.'

'Blackmail,' said Ella.

'If you like to call it that,' said Margot, coolly, 'but then you and I are no strangers to the term, are we?'

Her reference to Greg fuelled Ella's anger. 'What I did at the time of your affair with Greg was totally justified and I'm perfectly certain that in hindsight you must recognize that too. This is different. I know my business, I know my limitations and I know my capabilities. I don't want Meyer Hotels and I don't see why the hell you should be trying to force me into it.'

At that moment the telephone rang on Margot's desk, making both women jump. Margot picked up the phone. 'Yes, OK, switch it through to Janet's office and I'll take it there. Sorry,' she stood up, 'a call from a major customer, I'd better take it. Anyway, perhaps a pause is not a bad thing. I'll ask my secretary to send in some more coffee. A few minutes alone will give you a chance to think things out. At the risk of sounding threatening, I can only repeat that I'm very serious in what I say. Bid for Meyer or we pull out of Houston. The choice is yours, of course.' She strode from the office, a tall, elegant figure. Ella stared at her retreating back with hatred. The coffee arrived seconds later.

Left alone again, Ella took her cup and walked over to the window. What puzzled her about the ultimatum Margot had just issued was her motive. On face value it sounded like a crazy deal, taking a sledge hammer to crack a walnut. Why should Margot be so anxious for her to take on Meyer Hotels? OK, so it would mean big banking business but the motives had to go deeper than that, surely? And why threaten to pull out of Houston, it made no sense. It wouldn't just be Lexington Kovac she would be hurting, it would be Joshkers as well. Indeed, the collapse of Lexington Kovac could mean the collapse of Sunbelt Industrial. Maybe that was it, maybe in the world of banking politics this was what Margot wanted to achieve for some reason, though it was hard to see why. It seemed to Ella at that moment that her world was collapsing around her, yet though she knew her mind should be probing the proposition just put to her, she found her concentration ebbing away.

It had been a strange year. However happy she might be about it, the fact was she had lost Greg. He was a married man now and she knew she would have an increasingly small part to play in his future life. Margot was threatening her with the loss of her business and most important of all, it appeared she had lost Aaron Connors. Aaron had come to Greg and Belinda's wedding, as he had promised to do, but he had refused an invitation to stay with Ella, and he had not even allowed her to fix up hotel accommodation for him. He had simply flown in the day before the wedding and flown out again the day after.

The wedding had been a sumptuous affair, with a reception at the House of Lords, to which Belinda was entitled as Stephanie's daughter. The service that had preceded it had been at St. Margaret's, Westminster. To Ella, the whole day had passed in a kind of dream, in which she struggled, mostly successfully, to control her emotions. The little boy, born out of a night of sordid terror, seemed to fit naturally into these surroundings, and thinking of the contrast between how Greg had started out in life and where he was now had Ella close to tears throughout the day. It would have been so much easier to bear if Aaron had been at her side. His skill at avoiding her had been considerable, in that the only time they spoke was when he passed through on the receiving line at the beginning of the reception, giving her a perfunctory kiss on the cheek and mumbling, 'Congratulations.' In desperation, towards the end of the reception, she had swallowed her pride and approached him, but in response to her tentative enquiries as to how long he would be in London and whether it was possible for them to meet, he had dismissed her out of hand and left almost immediately. It had been a stunning blow and one from which she was still reeling.

The sound of the door opening jerked her thoughts back to the present. 'Sorry about that,' said Margot. 'Now, where were we?'

The supercilious smile, the glint of triumph in her eyes, the total confidence that she was already the victor, made any alternative decision in Ella's mind impossible. Suddenly, she did not care about the implications and the ruin it would bring to her. 'I won't do it,' she said, 'you'll just have to make that call to Jack and tell him to go ahead and foreclose. I'm not bidding for Meyers, not under any circumstances.'

'You know,' said Margot, after a pause, 'when anticipating this meeting, it did actually occur to me that you might be just stupid enough to react like this, so it's as well I can force your hand.'

'What the hell do you mean by that?' demanded Ella.

'I can force you to do as I wish over this Meyer bid, Ella, because I own twenty-five per cent of your business.'

CHAPTER FORTY-SIX

NEW YORK
December 1985

Laurie Merman had aged out of all recognition. Ella, angry and preoccupied as she was, was nevertheless startled by his appearance. When last she had seen him, he had been a suave, well-groomed, middle-aged man. Now he was definitely elderly and his appearance, although not untidy, gave the impression that here was a person who no longer cared what he looked like. But as she entered his office, the smile of pleasure at seeing her was genuine, and just for a moment she forgot the reason for the visit and responded to his embrace. 'The rest of us get older, you stay the same. How long is it since you were last here, ten years?'

'Must be, I suppose,' said Ella. She looked around the little office. Laurie didn't believe in squandering money on anywhere the customers didn't see. It was basically a glorified cupboard – scruffy, untidy but oddly endearing.

'Coffee, or something stronger?' Laurie asked.

'What have you got?' said Ella.

'Scotch or some wine in the fridge.'

'Scotch would be nice.'

Laurie raised his eyebrows. 'This is a new side to my girl, Scotch at lunchtime.'

'I still don't normally drink at all at lunchtime,' said Ella, irritated, 'but I think the circumstances warrant it.'

Laurie frowned at her as he poured two hefty measures of whisky and handed one to her. 'What circumstances?' he asked.

'Why did you do it, Laurie, was it out of spite? It can't have been because you needed the money.'

'Do what?' Laurie asked.

'Sell your stock to Margot Haigh, of course.'

At her words, he blanched slightly and tossed back his whisky. 'It certainly wasn't spite,' he said, 'and you're wrong about the second motive too – it *was* money.'

'But how could it have been,' said Ella, 'the Café Colettes are still booming, aren't they?'

'They're on the mend,' said Laurie, 'but I guess you haven't been around New York too much recently. I had to sell some to keep afloat and the business as a whole has been running at a loss for the last three or four years.'

The fact that he had not tried to bullshit her in any way, coupled with the despairing note in his voice, drained much of Ella's anger. 'I don't understand, Laurie, what went wrong?'

'Colette,' he said, after a pause, 'she died.' He reached for the whisky bottle and topped up his glass and Ella's.

'Laurie, I'm so sorry, I had no idea. When?'

'Just over a year ago now.'

'I should have known,' said Ella, 'you should have contacted me.'

Laurie shook his head. 'No reason to do that – you and I went our separate ways. No doubt you've had your ups and downs over the last few years and I haven't been there for you, have I?'

'No,' said Ella, remembering her feeling of resentment at the way he had dropped her after their affair was over.

'Colette died of cancer, throat cancer. It took two years, two very painful years.'

'Oh Laurie,' was all Ella could say.

'We had some fun, though, thanks to you.'

'To me?'

'Yeh, we spent a lot of time in France, at the castle. She, well, just loved it there. Incidentally, I saw on my last visit that you're gutting that little farmhouse of yours.'

'I gave it to Greg and his wife as a wedding present. I only ever went there once and it wasn't a very happy time. Greg and Belinda love it though, so it seemed the right thing to do.'

'Greg, married! I can't believe that.'

'Time passes,' said Ella. 'Sorry, go on, tell me about Colette.'

'When she became ill, really ill, it made me realize how much I depended on her, needed her. It also made me realize how I would have been nothing without her. So, I threw myself into making her last years as happy as possible, which meant, of course, I neglected the business. We had a bad year, money started to get tight and just at a time when I wanted to lavish it on Colette. She's always loved pretty things, clothes, jewellery. We went on crazy shopping trips together. I needed the money, Ella.'

'So why didn't you come to me?'

'I don't know, maybe I would have done, but it was Margot who suggested I sold out to the bank and it seemed like a sensible thing to do. I couldn't see it would do any harm to you, knowing you were in hock to the bank anyway.'

Ella set down her whisky glass. 'Laurie, you *didn't* sell out to the bank, you sold out to *Margot Haigh*.'

'Same thing,' he said.

'No,' Ella thundered, 'it's not the same thing, Margot holds that stock personally.'

'Personally! But why?'

Ella shrugged her shoulders. 'To have some sort of personal hold over me, I suppose.'

'I thought you two were good friends.'

'Were. She had an affair with Greg. Looking back on it, it must have been about the time she acquired your stock. We fell out over it.'

'An affair with Greg! She's practically old enough to be his grandmother. Jesus, Ella, I can see you've had your problems, too.'

'You don't know the half of them,' said Ella. 'What I still don't understand, Laurie, is why you didn't tell me what you intended to do.'

For a moment, Laurie avoided her eyes and played nervously with the tumbler in front of him. 'Because Margot asked me not to. She asked that the stock should remain in my name and that I should not tell you or anyone about the sale. I'm afraid I complied.'

'But you must have thought her motives a little odd,' Ella insisted. 'Didn't you wonder why the bank didn't want to take up the stock in their name in the ordinary way? Good God, Laurie, you must have known no bank would operate in such a way.'

'I guess I did,' Laurie mumbled, 'but at the time I could think of nothing but Colette, the fact that she was dying and that I was running out of cash. If King Kong had offered me the right price for the stock, I'd have handed it over without a qualm. Selling my stake in your business on the open market would not have been easy. Real estate's so volatile and although you have a track record, I wouldn't have known where to begin.'

'You could have tried offering it to me,' Ella said.

'Yeh, I should have done that but somehow I felt awkward getting in touch with you and asking you to help me fund Colette's death. I can't explain it, it just felt wrong, though I guess it's what I would have done if Margot hadn't made the suggestion.' Laurie raised his eyes. 'Ella, I'm real sorry, I behaved like a shit and I know it. If I could just try and get across to you the feeling of panic and hopelessness. I had no one to share my business worries because I had to keep everything from Colette. She was in such pain, and I just didn't know whether I was coming or going. I guess when we're desperate, we all become pretty damned selfish. At that moment, Ella Kovac's business was the last thing on my mind. I'm not proud of it, but that's how I felt. Look would it help you to understand if I said imagine yourself with Greg, in similar circumstances?'

'Don't,' said Ella, 'there's no need to go on, Laurie, I understand, I do, truly. I just wish to God you'd told me about it.' There was a deep, melancholy silence between them. They were both by now a little drunk. 'Supposing we go out and eat something,' said Ella, 'before we both fall over, and I'll tell you the kind of shit I'm in and see if you can come up with any bright ideas.'

The lunch with Laurie was pleasant enough. They found themselves taking a trip down memory lane, talking about old times together, about Greg, as a little boy. Slowly, painfully, like someone removing a bandage from a raw wound, Laurie told Ella about Colette's final months and of his slow but steady attempts to get his life back together since her death.

Ella explained to Laurie in detail the corner into which Margot had pushed her. Margot's revelation about her stock holding in Lexington Kovac had explained her motive for wanting Ella to buy Meyer Hotels – pure greed. The stock would be worth a great deal of money if such a deal could be pulled off. Margot's motive was simple: personal ambition.

Laurie listened politely and asked a few questions, but it was clear to Ella that he was going to be of no use in helping her decide what to do. He had turned in on himself. Without Colette, his confidence and enthusiasm for life had drained away. She had hoped that some aspect of his sale to Margot might have been reversible, perhaps because the stock was still in his name there was some way to get it back, but clearly this was not the case. He held the stock as a nominee only, he had no more power over it than any man in the street.

If she could have been angry with him, it might have helped ease the sense of pressure and stress she was feeling, but while she did not like the way he had so readily given in to Margot's suggestion, she understood only too well how it could have happened. There was no joy in kicking a man when he was down. They were old friends, they had shared a lot of good times, recriminations were out of place.

Back in the office, she dealt with a few queries which Jackie had accumulated and signed the post. Jackie's gratitude at not being sacked was pathetic in its intensity. She couldn't do enough for Ella and this, at least, was a comfort although at times Ella found it a little cloying. Certainly that night she was in no mood for a tête-á-tête with Jackie and as soon as her desk was cleared, she told her to go home.

Jessie lingered though, and as soon as Jackie left the office, she waddled purposefully into Ella's room and sat down. 'Tired?' she asked.

'A little,' said Ella, 'I'm packing up, actually. You go home, too.'

'Not until I've said what I have to.' Ella put down her pen and pushed back her chair, wearily. When Jessie had something on her mind, there was no way you could avoid hearing all about it – her persistence was terrifying. 'It's about this trouble you're in,' said Jessie. As soon as Ella had flown in from London, she had told Jackie and Jessie the full story and clearly Jessie had been brooding on it.

'Yes,' said Ella, wearily.

'You need someone to talk to, someone not involved in this business, someone who knows you well, who can look at your life and come to a decision as to what you should do. I wish I was clever enough to help you but I'm not. The kind of mess you're in at the moment, Ella, you need a friend, a good friend.'

'You're right,' Ella admitted, 'but there's no one right now.'

'There's Dr Connors,' Jessie said.

Ella shook her head vehemently. 'We're not friends any more, Jessie.'

'That's bullshit. You two will always be friends, you go back to when you were kids. OK, you might not be so friendly right now, but friendship like that you can't break altogether. You go and see him, tell him your troubles, he'll sort you out.'

Ella smiled, close to tears. 'It's a nice idea, Jessie, but it isn't practical. Apart from anything else, he'd slam the door in my face.'

'He would not,' said Jessie, 'he cares about you a very great deal, that man.'

'*Did* care,' said Ella.

'*Does* care,' said Jessie. 'I'm not supposed to tell you this –

in fact he'd have my hide so you're not to let on – but he rings me every week to see how you're doing.'

Ella stared at Jessie in astonishment. 'Aaron rings you?'

Jessie nodded, triumphantly. 'Ever since you first started spending so much time in London. It's a kind of habit now, he rings me and I tell him how you're doing. Not business stuff, mind, he's not interested in that. Just how you're sounding, how Greg is – that kind of thing.'

Her words momentarily silenced Ella. Then, almost to herself, she said, 'then why won't he have anything to do with me?'

'Oh Ella, how come you've got so old and you don't know the first thing about men?' Jessie let out one of her gales of laughter. 'You're like a babe in arms at times. Pride, men have pride, it's their guiding light. It's why they need flash cars and all the other crap, just to make them look big, in their own eyes, never mind anyone else's. Your Dr Connors, he's a nice man, a good man but underneath he's just the same as all the rest. He loves you very much but he's not prepared to play number two to your business and since he can't see he'll ever be number one, he's kind of opted out – yet he can't quite, because he loves you so.'

Ella stared at Jessie. 'If you're right, the position is insoluble and it would be better if I didn't get in touch with him, it would be unkind.'

'No relationship is insoluble,' said Jessie. 'You talk a lot of crazy stuff, Ella Kovac. He loves you, you love him, you have all those years and years of past friendship. You're in the shit right now and you need him. Go to him and tell him just that. I lay my life savings, every dollar I've ever earned, on the fact that there'll be no door slamming. Now are you going to do as I say?'

'You're a bully,' said Ella.

Jessie grinned triumphantly. 'That means you'll do it?'

Ella took a deep breath. 'I'll call round on him, like you suggest. If he slams the door in my face, I expect a cheque on my desk by ten o'clock tomorrow morning.'

'You've got it,' said Jessie, with a grin which now split her face in half.

By the time Ella reached Aaron's apartment she was as nervous as a kitten. She gave her name to the concierge, who was new in the block and did not recognize her, and waited with trepidation while he rang up to Aaron's apartment and told him she had come to visit.

'He said to go up,' the concierge said. 'You know the way?'

Ella nodded – first hurdle over, at least he would see her. It looked like she had lost her chance at Jessie's life savings. She stood, nervously, in the elevator which seemed to take an age to reach the twelfth floor. When the doors swung back, Aaron was standing there, a formidable sight, still in his dark suit from work, his face quite inscrutable. 'Hello, Ella,' he said, coolly.

She stepped out of the lift. 'Aaron, I'm sorry to arrive on you unannounced like this but. . . . I need help and you're the only person who . . .' From nowhere came a storm of tears. All the tensions and stress of the last few days burst out. The mask slipped from Aaron's face, he smiled, a beautiful smile, full of love and the sight of it made Ella cry all the harder. He opened his arms and she flew into them.

Inside the apartment, a few minutes later, when Ella was a little calmer, Aaron left her side. 'I'll get you a drink, then you must tell me what's wrong. What would you like?'

'I shouldn't drink anything, really,' said Ella. 'I was knocking back whisky with Laurie all morning.'

'Laurie Merman!' Aaron's voice was suddenly sharp. 'He's a name from the past, isn't he?'

Ella nodded. 'I haven't seen him in years. I went to see him today because . . . well, because he sold his stockholding in my corporation to Margot Haigh.'

Aaron visibly relaxed, clearly having seen Laurie as a rival momentarily, the commercial implications quite lost on him. 'Let me fix you a drink and then you can tell me everything.'

When Ella had finished telling Aaron the whole sorry story, she sat back feeling oddly relaxed and cleansed. It was a very long time since she had taken anybody so completely into her confidence. For years now, she had been operating alone, making her own decisions. Yes, she had a backup team of advisors but nobody with whom she could be entirely frank about every aspect of her life.

She knew, or thought she knew, exactly how Aaron was going to react. There was no way he would want her to become involved with Meyer. It would mean she would lose everything but somehow, sitting in Aaron's familiar apartment, with his arm about her as dusk settled over the city, it did not seem so terrible.

He was silent for a very long time. When at last he spoke, his words astounded her. 'Well, there's not really a choice, is there? You have to go ahead, it's the only possible option.'

'You mean – you think I should buy Meyer?' Ella said, stupidly.

'Of course.'

'But I thought it would be the last thing you would want me to do. It's an enormous group, Aaron. Running it would be a twenty-four-hour job and the headquarters isn't even in America, it's in Geneva. I suppose I could move it back to the States but it's unlikely to be easy, particularly in the early days.' She stared at him incredulously. 'I never thought it would be what you'd recommend.'

'So you wanted me to tell you to let Margot pull the rug, so that you could blame me instead of yourself?'

'No,' said Ella, and then paused, 'at least I don't think so,' she added, truthfully.

'I've thought about that conversation we had in your apartment so much in recent months,' said Aaron.

'Me, too,' said Ella.

'And a lot of what you said was right,' said Aaron. 'It's not making the situation any easier between us, indeed if anything my beginning to understand your point of view makes it more difficult. One thing you said, though, did strike home. You asked me if I would be prepared to give up my career for you. At the time, if you remember, I sidestepped the issue by saying it wasn't relevant because in truth it wasn't. However, I've asked myself that question, Ella, many, many times since. My work is so much a part of me and that's not just since I've been widowed. I guess I do spend a little more time at the hospital than I did when Alice was alive but not that much. The truth is if I gave up my work, I somehow wouldn't be me any longer. What would I think about all day, do all day? I guess I'd find it very difficult to have any confidence in myself if I had no real reason to get up in the morning.' He shrugged his shoulders and smiled sadly at Ella. 'So I guess what I'm saying is that you built this business from scratch, you've put all your life into it, you've seen it flourish and grow and now it's under threat. You can't desert your post now, Ella, you have to fight. If you fight and lose, OK, you've done your best. If you fight and win, wonderful, but not to fight at all . . .'

His unconditional support, Ella knew, should have brought about a surge of confidence and a renewal of hope for the future. Instead, she felt oddly let down. 'So what you're saying is that you're reconciled to the fact that you and I have no future together?'

Aaron removed his arm and turned to face her, taking both her hands in his. 'Yes, I suppose that's what I'm saying,' he said. 'At least I recognize the sort of person you are, Ella, and now I can respect and admire you for it, rather than resent you. Of course you must go for this chance. Who knows, you'll probably make a fine hotelier – you've made a pretty damned fine everything else – and it would be crass of me to stand in your way. Maybe, one day, we can be an old Darby and Joan together, who knows? Maybe we'll find alternative partners that suit our own particular lifestyle, may be not. Either way, any way you look at it, I'll always be here for you, I want you to know that – always have been and always will be. I'm sorry I went off my trolley. I guess I was just looking at one aspect of our relationship, the emotional side, rather than looking at the thing as a whole. Whatever our circumstances, the friendship goes on, right?'

Ella nodded dumbly, close to tears again. She knew his words should have brought comfort but instead she felt a deep sense of desolation. What he was saying was crystal clear. Their relationship was back to where it had been when Alice was alive, and Ella realized, with an awful clarity, that this was not how she wanted things to be. She wanted Aaron to wrap her in his arms, to tell her that he would look after her for ever, to forget her business, Margot and Joseph Meyer, that they could all go to hell. But she had left it too late. He no longer needed her as he had done. He was free of her emotionally in every way except friendship. He was throwing her back out into the jungle again to continue to scrap and struggle to survive. How could she tell him it was no longer what she wanted, no longer what she wanted at all.

CHAPTER FORTY-SEVEN

LONDON
March 1986

Although it was still early March, there was a definite promise of the summer to come. Margot and Ahfaad lounged on the terrace in their dressing gowns, breakfasting on bucks fizz and croissant. It was just after eleven on a Saturday morning. As had become their habit, Margot was spending the weekend with Ahfaad. For once, they had nothing planned – the whole two days stretched ahead uncluttered by business commitments or social occasions. Margot stretched out in the sun, like a sleek cat. Ahfaad eyed her appreciatively. Her auburn hair and creamy skin were perfectly set off by the apricot négligée he had bought her in Paris several weeks ago. It was good to see her out of her inevitable black; the pale, soft colour made her look younger, less austere, almost vulnerable. He smiled to himself that such an adjective could ever be used to describe Margot Haigh.

'What are you smiling at?' she asked.

'Nothing. I was just admiring you – you're a very beautiful woman.'

Margot smiled back. 'Well, I'm wearing a very beautiful négligée.'

'That, too,' said Ahfaad.

They sat in contented silence, the newspapers still unopened on the table. 'What shall we do this weekend?' asked Margot.

'I thought perhaps we might get married,' said Ahfaad.

Margot stared at him. His expression was quite unreadable,

it was impossible to tell whether he was serious or not. 'You're joking!' she said, testing the water.

'I'm not, I've never been more serious in all my life.'

Margot looked positively flustered and her discomforture made Ahfaad smile. 'You see,' she said triumphantly, 'I knew you were joking. What shall we do, seriously?'

'I wasn't joking, Margot,' said Ahfaad. 'I'd like to marry you and there's no better time than the present.'

'I might not want to marry *you*.' Margot suggested.

'Why ever not?' said Ahfaad. 'We're completely right for one another, you know that.'

'If this is a proposal,' said Margot, 'it's not very romantic.'

'We're not romantic people,' said Ahfaad, 'besides which, marriage is a contract and should be regarded in the most business-like manner possible. We have the same interests, we like the same sort of people, we enjoy talking about business, we have a truly wonderful time in bed, we enjoy the same restaurants, we like to travel ... it sounds like the ideal recipe for marriage to me.'

'And love?' Margot asked.

Ahfaad threw back his head and laughed. 'Love! You of all people, Margot. Alright, I love you. Is that good enough?'

Margot looked at him doubtfully. 'What about children? I'm forty-four Ahfaad, I'm too old for children now.'

'I know how old you are,' said Ahfaad, 'and it's of no significance to me.'

'You mean you don't mind not having any children?'

'I have to say I don't somehow see you in the role of a mother,' he smiled, 'and no, I don't mind not having children. The kind of domestic routine they demand would bore me. I loathe other people's children. I suppose it's possible I might become attached to one of my own but it's not a subject on which I feel strongly. If you were twenty-four and made the statement that you did not wish to have children, I would not try to press you. Does that answer the question?'

'Yes.' Margot seemed genuinely ill at ease.

'You don't seem very pleased at my suggestion, Margot. Is it possible that I have misinterpreted our relationship?

'No, it's not that,' said Margot, 'it's just that somehow I never imagined you would ask me to marry you. I thought we suited each other now, but ultimately you would look to a younger woman to provide you with a family. In other words, I did not see us as having a long term future.'

'You under-estimate yourself, My Darling,' said Ahfaad, 'you have made me your slave.' His tone was bantering but the expression in his eyes was warm. He leaned forward and took Margot's hand. 'Come on, open your mind to the prospect. If we were to marry, what conditions would you wish to impose on the relationship?'

'Conditions! None that I can think of,' said Margot, 'I'm very happy with the way we live now. I suppose I would have to give up my house and move in here with you.' She sounded a little doubtful.

'Certainly it is customary for a husband and wife to live under the same roof,' said Ahfaad. Margot tried to ignore the pangs of dread she instantly felt at the thought of leaving her home of so many years. 'No other conditions?' Ahfaad pressed. Margot shook her head. 'I have just one condition for you. I would like you to stop working for Joshkers Bank and come and work for me instead.'

'Complete take-over bid then,' said Margot, 'body, soul and business brain?'

'Something like that,' said Ahfaad. 'I don't know whether it's my Arab or French blood speaking, but I don't like the idea of you working for someone other than myself. In other words, I don't want anyone other than me having a call on your time. I don't think that's unreasonable.'

'I think it's wholly unreasonable,' Margot said. The dazed expression had left her face, she now sat bolt upright in her chair. 'I think it would be positively unhealthy for me to work for you. We'd be in each other's pockets all day and night, and I'd have no sense of independence.'

'Precisely,' said Ahfaad, 'that's the way it should be.'

'You have to be mad!' said Margot. 'You're not talking about marrying some eighteen-year-old straight from school. I'm a woman, almost certainly over half way through my life, and there's no way I'm going to sacrifice my independence to you or any other man. I love my job. If I wasn't so devoted to Joshkers, I wouldn't have stayed with them all these years — there have been plenty of opportunities to leave along the way, God knows. I think there's quite a chance that before I'm much older I might get the chairmanship and I don't mind admitting that's what I'm after. I'll be the first woman to obtain such a position in that male bastion, the banking world. I like the idea.'

'I don't understand why it's so important to you,' said Ahfaad. 'You've nothing to prove, you can compete with any man in a man's world. We have a woman prime minister — as premier of the land she has proved that any position is attainable by a woman. This women's lib. stuff would be understandable if you were an unwashed student but I hardly feel it's either appropriate or necessary to you now.'

'Well, it is and just for the record,' said Margot, with a touch of a smile, 'I was never an unwashed student. I'm tired of having to say I'm no advocator of women's liberation as such. I like men and I enjoy their company a great deal more than I enjoy the company of the average woman. I have no real girlfriends, my closest friends have always been men. I like having doors opened for me, I like somebody helping me on with my coat and I like to be cosseted. The ladies of Greenham Common would certainly not count me among their number. Having said that, I've had to overcome all sorts of prejudice during my working life. Again and again, people have tried to walk over me, dismiss my ideas and sidestep my suggestions, simply because of my sex. You've no idea how irritating and humiliating it can be to work for someone, as I did for Jeremy Colquhoun, knowing that he had the senior job, not because he was talented or clever — he was neither — but simply because he was a man. Largely, now, I've overcome that prejudice. I'm a well-known personality in the banking world, particularly here and in the States. I'm simply Margot Haigh, and whether I'm male or female is of no relevance any more. I have a reputation for being tough, aggressive and ruthless. It is a reputation which

I nurture, because any concessions I make are viewed as weakness or a typical emotional female reaction. I do not socialise with my customers, I don't believe in expense account lunches and any gifts I receive go straight to charity. I've ploughed my own furrow, a disciplined, ordered one, and it's paid off. I'm not about to throw it up, not when the end is in sight.'

'I hear what you say,' said Ahfaad, after a pause, 'and I admire you very much. Nothing you've told me is unknown to me, but Joshkers is a small, not particularly prestigious bank and I think you could do a lot better. Together, you and I could expand and develop my business interests. You have some wonderful contacts, you have a natural commercial flair, you are a prodigious worker the world is our oyster.

'So that's why you want to marry me,' said Margot with a strained smile. 'It's not for me at all, it's for my business acumen.'

'No, God dammit, it isn't.' It was Ahfaad's turn now to feel uncomfortable. 'Look, I'm not used to this, no more than I suspect are you. I can't tell you how many women there have been in my life. I had my first at fourteen, handpicked for me by my grandfather. Since then I've slept with hundreds, dated thousands and lived with a fair number. Women have always been an expendable commodity so far as I am concerned – decorative, nice to have around, a satisfying diversion at the end of a busy day but not to be taken seriously, not part of real life. This attitude has worked very well for me. There have been a few dramas along the way, the odd scandal but nothing I couldn't handle – until now. Now, in you, I know I've met my match. You are not an expendable woman, you are equal to me in every way and for that reason I want you but I want you completely. As you say, a complete take-over bid. I don't think that's asking too much.'

Margot found his small speech oddly affecting and she recognized that in all probability his words were true. It was a daunting thought that she was the first woman to have really had any impact on Ahfaad. She turned over in her mind the thought of marriage to him. It would provide her with the security she had always craved and more personal riches than most women could imagine, and yet to be totally beholden to him for everything was out of the question. Surely if he cared for her as he said he did, he must recognize this. 'I would like to marry you very much,' she said, 'but not at the expense of giving up my job at Joshkers.'

'Then I'm sorry,' said Ahfaad, firmly, 'but I'm afraid I shall have to withdraw my offer.'

The sense of sorrow and loss Margot felt at his words was profound and it shocked her. She just hoped her feelings did not show. 'As you wish,' she said, brusquely. 'So where do we go from here?'

'We go on as we are now.' He stood up. 'What about a ride in Hyde Park, it's a beautiful day. A good idea?'

'Yes,' said Margot.

'Splendid, I'll go and change.'

She watched his long, lean figure as he strode across the patio and back into the house. The subject was clearly well and truly closed. She wondered when, and if, it would ever be raised again.

CHAPTER FORTY-EIGHT

GENEVA
March 1986

It was the first time the three of them had met round a conference table together, in a very long time. They sat now, in Joseph Meyer's elegant office, while his secretary dispensed coffee. Stephanie found herself gazing out across the lake. It was a beautifully sunny day, very reminiscent of that first time she had met the Meyers. She had been so naïve then. It was amazing, looking back on it, that they hadn't screwed her over the Centre des Arts deal. Alex ... she could think of him now without pain, Tim had seen to that. Tim had picked her up, dusted her down and set her back on the right track. It was strange: in all the years that she had known him, she had never before appreciated his strength of character. His easy-going nature she had always mistaken for weakness. Now she knew different.

Stephanie turned her attention to the table. Margot and Ella were sitting glumly next to each other, not speaking. Stephanie was vaguely irritated. With Greg married now it seemed ridiculous that their old feud should continue. Joseph, by contrast, sat at the head of the table, both relaxed and apparently in good humour. He met Stephanie's eyes, briefly. The look was neither hostile nor friendly, just interested. Stephanie was the first to drop her gaze.

Joseph waited until his secretary had withdrawn. When at last he spoke, his tone was measured, friendly and, as usual, he commanded absolute attention. 'You all know why you're here,' he said. 'I've decided, after careful deliberation, that it would be sensible to dispose of the Meyer Group while I still have my faculties. I intend to make public my intention to sell on 5th August of this year. However, in the meantime, I am prepared to entertain a bid, either from you, Stephanie, or from you Ella, with the obvious advantage that should I accept either of your offers, it will be before the group becomes available on the open market. Details of exactly what is involved in the Meyer Hotel Group is contained in these files.' Three identical, bulging files were waiting for them on a side table. 'The group includes restaurants, several catering equipment firms, a large butchery chain in North America, two casinos and an international fast food chain, as well as the hotels with which you are probably more familiar. Contained in the files are accounts for the last ten years. My accountants, and indeed my solicitor, are briefed to accept calls from you at any time, with any queries you may have.'

He turned his attention to Margot. 'Margot is here because she has indicated to me that Joshkers would be prepared to back either one of you in the purchase of the Meyer Group. I have not quoted an asking price because I feel it is better that you make your own assessment as to what it is worth. There are, however, two conditions of purchase. I do not want the group broken up and sold off, putting my staff's future in jeopardy. Many of the personnel I employ go back a long way and for this reason, included with your bid should be a detailed ten year plan as to how you see the group progressing and indeed how you intend to run it.' He hesitated and drank some coffee. 'The other condition is in respect of my grandson, Matthew. Here again, I am not laying down any ground rules, I am simply saying that I would like him to have the option of some involvement in the future of the group should he decide, upon reaching maturity, that the hotel business is for him, and of course,' he looked directly but briefly at Stephanie, 'by some involvement, I am not suggesting he should be given the post of a bell boy in one of the hotels. I am expecting a directorship, a shareholding and a substantial say in the running of the overall group. He is, after all, a Meyer by blood, if not by name.' His voice hardened perceptively. Stephanie felt herself bristling with anger but said nothing. Joseph's gaze swept round the three women. 'Any questions?'

'How and when would you like to receive the bids?' Margot asked.

'I would suggest,' said Joseph, 'that we set a date of 1st August for our next meeting, in New York. In order to give me, and my advisers, time to digest the contents of your proposals, I would ask that you submit bids to me here one week prior to the 1st August. We can then meet and discuss them,' he smiled. 'Shall we say at high noon at the Meyer Headquarters in New York?'

'You're not giving us very much time,' said Stephanie.

'It's as much time as you're getting,' said Joseph, abrasively. 'Most of the commercial world would give their eye teeth for the opportunity I'm giving you. Complaints, I'm not interested in.'

Stephanie remained undaunted. 'What about bidding for part of the group,' she said, 'assuming that only a part interests us?'

Joseph looked at her disdainfully. 'I've already indicated I want a package for the group as a whole, which protects my staff. I presume you're thinking in particular about the European operation. I'm not prepared to sell that separately from the States or the Middle East. Each has its own contribution to make. The European operation is not as profitable as the States but it is more prestigious, the flagship if you like. Of the three, the Middle East has the most potential. The group, as you should know, has been painstakingly built up to provide just this kind of balance. I'm not prepared to entertain a bid for any part of the group – it's all or nothing.' He stood up. 'Are there any more queries, Ladies?' No one spoke. 'Right, if you'll excuse me, I'm a busy man, I'll see you all on the 1st August.' He glanced towards the window. 'It's a pleasant day – why not enjoy Geneva while you're here.'

In the elevator on the way to the ground floor, the women stood silently, each holding their copy of the Meyer file.

'What about lunch?' Margot said, as they came out into the foyer.

'No thanks,' said Stephanie, 'I have to get home, Tim's expecting me. If I hurry I can catch the midday flight.' She smiled a little warily, at the other two. 'See you around.' Ella, who had not spoken once since entering Meyer's office, managed a brief smile in return.

'How about you?' Margot said.

Ella looked at her coolly, 'No thanks.'

'I think we should talk anyway,' said Margot.

'What about?' Ella asked.

'Don't be obtuse, Ella, and don't sulk. You're being given the opportunity of a lifetime, as Joseph Meyer said. You should be well pleased.'

'If I was still my own master, I might be,' said Ella.

Margot chose to ignore her. 'I assume you're staying at the Meyer Hotel?' Ella nodded. 'Let's at least go back there, dump these horrendous-looking files and have a drink.'

In the bar, half an hour later, Ella and Margot sat over two glasses of peach champagne. 'We need to talk strategy,' said Margot.

Ella shook her head. 'No way.'

'Why?' Margot asked.

'If Stephanie puts together the successful bid, you will be backing her, right?' Margot nodded. 'Then in your capacity as her banker it's hardly appropriate for you to be privy to the details of the proposal I'm putting together.'

'I won't let Stephanie out-bid you,' said Margot, 'I've a twenty-five per cent stake riding on this, remember.'

'Precisely,' said Ella, 'so from Stephanie's point of view it would not be ethical for you to be involved in the details of my bid. You could use the information to mess up her chances of success.,

'It won't work, Ella,' Margot said.

'What won't work?'

'Putting in a stupid bid which won't be accepted. If you do that, I'll still pull the plug in Houston. The deal we have is not only that you should bid for the Meyer Group but that you should bid with the intention of winning.'

'I'll do that,' said Ella, 'but I'll do it my way.'

'Without access to the figures you're preparing, I have no way of knowing whether what you say is true.'

'Then you'll just have to trust me, won't you?' said Ella. She leaned back in her chair. 'You're forcing me to bid for the Meyer Group against my will. In order to save my business I'm having to do so, but I would remind you that it is my business – it's my sweat that's gone into Lexington Kovac and it is I, and I alone, who will decide where to pitch the bid. The only figure I will be passing on to you for consideration is the amount of the borrowing I consider necessary in order to fund such a purchase. Your fact file from Joseph will enable you to decide whether the degree of funding is justified by the amount of the collateral. You've put me in the position of having to pitch against Stephanie. If there's going to be a fight, it will be a fair one. The alternative is no fight at all.'

It was not often that Margot Haigh was forced to compromise her views but she had done so on this occasion, she thought ruefully, as she watched from the plane as it circled over London, waiting for an opportunity to land. Ella was one of the few people with whom she dealt who was entirely unpredictable. It was possible, of course, that her motives to see fair play were simply a front, an excuse to exclude her from the calculations of the proposal. Yet despite her suspicions, Margot could not help feeling that this was not the case and that Ella was genuine in her desire to see fair play. Perhaps she and Stephanie were on more friendly terms than they would have her believe, but she doubted it. Tim Irvine still stood between them, she suspected.

It was going to prove an interesting few months in any event and perhaps that was just as well – it would take her mind off Ahfaad.

Since Ahfaad's unexpected proposal of marriage, their relationship had carried on as before. Yet something was different and Margot was not sure whether this difference came from within herself or from him. She found herself going over and over their conversation in her mind, wondering how she could have handled it differently. It was a pointless exercise. She knew she was right not to give up her independence and yet the thought of being Ahfaad's wife was not only attractive, it was rapidly becoming a positive obsession. It had been a very long time since she had belonged anywhere. Her dim, distant childhood, cut short by the bombing raid, was something which seemed to have happened to someone else. Since then, although she'd had help along the way, from the Haighs, from her tutors at Oxford, from Nicholas, she had nonetheless been alone and up until now she had been quite happy for that to be the case. These days, however, she found not only was being with Ahfaad fulfilling, but being without him was not being alone but lonely. The situation disturbed her. No man had ever made her feel so vulnerable before and she knew she must do her best to put him out of her mind. There was a deal to be done and if Lexington Kovac could win the Meyer Group, her own financial future would be secure, with or without Ahfaad.

CHAPTER FORTY-NINE

NEW YORK
31st July 1986

Matthew Irvine enjoyed his first Concorde flight very much indeed. At eleven months old, he showed no desire to walk but was a prodigious talker in a language entirely of his own making. To this end, he entertained the stewardess all the way across the Atlantic and ever conscious of an admiring audience, played to the gallery for all it was worth. Indeed, so little trouble was he, Stephanie found herself wondering whether it had really been necessary to bring Nanny with them.

Their suite at the Meyer Hotel was the epitome of comfort: a room for Nanny and Matthew, with their own bathroom; a large reception room, beyond which lay Tim and Stephanie's bedroom and bathroom. 'More of a flat, really,' Stephanie said, after they had inspected it. 'I wonder if this is significant, it has to be one of the best suites in the hotel.'

'Ah,' said Tim, with a smile, 'but what you have to work out is the nature of the significance. Is Joseph giving us these marvellous rooms as a consolation prize or because he sees you as the future chairman of Meyer Hotels?'

Stephanie looked at him and gave a despairing shrug, 'Who knows?'

'Are you nervous?' Tim asked.

'Very.' She bit her bottom lip, pushing the hair back from her face – a gesture from her girlhood, only now her hair was short and sleek in a fashionable bob. 'It's as though everything I've done to date, so far as my work is concerned, has been leading me towards this point – this is the make or break.'

Tim crossed the room and took her in his arms. 'Not literally make or break. If Meyer sells to Ella instead, you'll still have the franchise and Ella won't screw you.'

'She will, she's bound to,' said Stephanie. 'I've shown you the figures. The franchise is up for renewal in eighteen months time and whoever is the owner of the Meyer Group by then will want a radical re-think on the terms. It was never very commercial, even when I first negotiated it.' She dropped her eyes. 'It was the early days of Alex and me, and amazingly when I think about it now, to some extent he must have let his heart rule his head.'

'Who can blame him,' said Tim.

Stephanie looked at her husband and reaching up to him, kissed him, a long lingering kiss which left them both trembling. 'It's amazing to think,' said Tim, 'that here we are due to be grandparents in just a few months time and you can still set my pulses racing with a single kiss. Not bad for an old married couple, not bad at all.'

Stephanie fingered his lapel. 'Do you think you're right about Ella?'

'I know I'm right about Ella.'

'Even so, she'll want more money for the franchise, she'll *have* to increase the fee.'

'Maybe she will, but she'll recognize you need time to adjust. In my view, the problem lies not with Ella achieving the successful bid but in neither of you doing so. If Joseph is unhappy with what either of you have to offer, then I suppose you could be in for a rocky ride.' He hugged her tight. 'Still, there's no point in crossing that bridge – one step at a time.' He bent forward and began nuzzling her neck, slipping his hands inside her shirt. 'What you need, Mrs Irvine, is an early night.'

'I ought to go over the figures,' Stephanie protested, 'in case he puts me through a third degree.'

'There's a bottle of champagne on the bedside table,' said Tim, 'you go through to the bedroom and open it. I'll tell Nanny we're having supper in bed and don't want disturbing until the morning.'

'I must say goodnight to Matthew,' Stephanie protested.

Tim looked at his watch. 'He'll be flat out for an hour or two yet, I should think. I'll ask Nanny to give us a call when he's awake and had supper.' He grinned. 'You know, you're in serious danger of becoming quite fond of that child.'

'I do love him,' said Stephanie, 'he's made me realize how much I missed out with the other two.'

'They're alright, Steph – they're nice people.'

'I know they are but it's all thanks to you, not me.'

'Bed,' thundered Tim.

'Yes, master,' said Stephanie, with a grin.

Several hours later, Tim brought Matthew to their bed. He was sleepy from a bath and supper, he smelt of talcum powder and baby shampoo. Stephanie took him in her arms and tucked the sheet around him. 'Gorgeous boy,' she murmured.

Tim sat on the bed and watched them. 'The perfect picture of mother and child,' he said.

Stephanie looked up at him, with a sweet smile. 'How come you have this amazing capacity to forgive and forget? However much you love children, by rights you should resent this one and yet you genuinely seem to love him as much as your daughters.'

Tim smiled. 'That's easy. He brought us back together again. If you had not been pregnant, I suppose it's still possible that we might have found some common ground, but you would have been far more brittle and unapproachable. This young man,' Tim reached out and tickled one bare protruding toe, 'has softened you and provided us with the path back to one another. I have a great deal to thank him for.' He grinned. 'Besides which, he just happens to be the most wonderful male child ever born, as an added bonus.'

'Oh Tim.' Stephanie stretched out an arm and he came and lay down beside her, his head on her shoulder. 'So, you can cope with Matthew but why aren't you resenting my bid for Meyer – you seem almost enthusiastic about it?' Stephanie said.

Tim kissed her cheek. 'You really need reassuring tonight, don't you?'

'Yes, I suppose I do,' said Stephanie. 'Why, Tim?' she persisted.

He sighed. 'Because we've both grown and matured and I suppose I'm more tolerant of your business aspirations. I also recognize that this bid gives you an opportunity to cap everything you've achieved to date.' He hesitated. 'And you've changed, too, you're much less obsessional about your business.'

'How do you mean?' Stephanie asked. The baby's head was heavy on her shoulder, his even breathing soft against her face. With Tim beside her, his arm about her, she had never felt more secure and content.

'You have a better sense of balance and appreciate now the importance of family life. You actively want to see something of this one growing up and you seem to appreciate the need for us to spend time on our marriage. Before, the business always came first, now I'm aware that Matthew and me often take precedence. I don't think heading the Meyer Group will alter that attitude. I think that's the main difference.' He shifted his position and raised himself on one elbow so he could look into Stephanie's face. 'It wasn't the amount of time you spent away from us that I objected to, it was that when you were with us, you were always preoccupied and anxious to be off again. It was as though we were a burden to you, a waste of time, a distraction from your real purpose in life. Now when you come home to Matthew and me, it's with evident pleasure and relief. We have a role to fulfil now, to recharge your batteries, to reassure and encourage you and when you're with us, you give us your full attention and your love. OK, it may mean that for a year or two, at any rate, the amount of time you spend with us will be limited, but we'll cope because even when you're away from us, we will know that you would prefer to be with us. That's the difference.'

There were tears in Stephanie's eyes. 'I do love you, Tim.'

'I love you, too.' They kissed.

'So many wasted years,' Stephanie said, stroking his cheek, 'I behaved like an idiot.'

'Not wasted years,' said Tim, 'there's no good looking at it like that. Would we appreciate what we have today if we hadn't lost each other along the way? I doubt it. We've been given a second chance and we're not going to blow this one.'

'There's something I've been meaning to say to you,' said Stephanie. She looked at him, embarrassed, awkward, suddenly so different from her normal self.

'What is it?' said Tim, at once amused and alarmed.

'When this Meyer thing is over, I wondered whether . . . well, I wondered whether we might have a go at having another child.'

A look of joy flared into Tim's face but disappeared as quickly as it had come. 'You don't have to do this,' he said.

'What do you mean?' Stephanie asked.

'You don't owe me a baby, just because Matthew isn't technically mine.'

'I know that,' said Stephanie, 'I just think it would be good for us all. Good for you, good for me and good for Matthew, to have a brother or sister.'

'You're really serious aren't you?' Stephanie nodded. 'Do you think you'll be able to cope with the baby and Meyer?'

'*If* I get it,' she reminded him, 'yes. As you say, we'll make time.' They kissed again.

'I'm going to take this young man away,' said Tim. 'What you need now is your beauty sleep if you're going to wow Joseph in the morning.'

Across town, the atmosphere was not by any means as harmonious. In Aaron's flat overlooking Central Park, Ella, whisky in hand, stood by the window, her expression troubled, the atmosphere tense and agitated. 'Look,' said Aaron, clearly exasperated, 'the die is cast, right? You've put in your bid and it's either acceptable to Meyer or it isn't. At this point in time there is absolutely nothing you can do about it. If he chooses Stephanie Irvine's bid, so be it.'

'How can I make you understand?' said Ella, angrily. 'It's no good saying "so be it". My whole business life is dependent upon this deal. How can I get across to you the importance of my succeeding and the implications of my failing?'

'I have successes and failures in my work, too,' said Aaron.

'Yes, but it's not the same thing at all,' Ella said, dismissively.

'No, I think you're right there,' said Aaron. 'I think mine are a great deal more important.' Ella swung round and stared at him. Aaron met her gaze unrepentant. 'Let me tell you a story,' he said. He stood up and began replenishing his whisky glass. 'In the early hours of this morning, I delivered a woman of twin girls. The woman in question has been married for sixteen years, to a man she loves. They were never able to have children because of my patient's gynaecological problems, but last year I was able to put her up for the AI programme – in other words, her daughters were conceived in a test tube. Everything went well until she went into premature labour. Unfortunately she was away on holiday and took the fatal decision to return here to New York, to me, rather than seek medical advice in Seattle where she was. By the time she reached me, proceeding with labour was inevitable, there was nothing I could do to delay the contractions. I took the decision to let her have the babies normally, rather than by caesarean, because she already had such a well-established labour. The birth was relatively easy and quick because of the small size of the babies but they both died within a few hours of birth. What I haven't told my patient yet is that due to a variety of medical complications with which I will not bore you, I am sure she will be unable to bear another child. She and her husband are now too old to adopt and the combination of their loss and the fact that I can give them no hope for the future, in my experience will probably break up their marriage.' Ella tried to speak but Aaron silenced her. 'So, let us look at where I went wrong. Firstly, I clearly allowed the woman to build up far too much faith in me personally. Her nightmare flight from Seattle to get to me might have been very flattering for my ego but it cost her the lives of her babies. I should have stressed when she went away that should anything go wrong, in view of the precious nature of the pregnancy, she should go straight to a local hospital. Two: was I right not to conduct a Caesarean?

Certainly the operation would have caused less stress to the babies. The problem was that their lungs were quite immature, but who knows, without the trauma of conventional birth they might have stood a better chance of survival. Three: in view of her age, was I even right to suggest the AI route? Nature had not intended her to have children. By playing God, mixing up cocktails of human life, I knowingly and willingly flouted nature. That couple have survived intact for sixteen years without children, they'd have survived another sixteen. Now, however, I doubt it.' He took a hefty slug of whisky and slumped back in his armchair.

'We never talk about your work,' Ella said, in a small voice, after a lengthy silence.

'No, we don't,' said Aaron, 'and normally that's the way I like it. I'm only citing this example because . . .'

'I know why you told me about your patient, Aaron,' Ella said. 'I may be a fool in many respects but I'm not that insensitive. What I'm talking about is the loss of a few million bucks. When compared with the loss of two longed-for children, my aspirations seem pretty insignificant.'

'Not insignificant,' said Aaron, 'I'm just saying that there is life going on outside your business world. Sometimes I think you cling to Lexington Kovac like a kind of life raft to protect you from what's happening to the rest of the human race. OK, so losing this deal might be bad for you, but it really isn't the tragedy you believe it to be.'

'But you wanted me to go after Meyer,' Ella said, exasperated, 'and that's half my problem: you wanted me to do it, Margot's forcing me to do it. The position I'm in at the present is not even of my own making.'

Aaron laughed. 'You can't have it both ways. If you're saying you wouldn't even have put in a bid if it wasn't for Margot and me, then you have no reason to worry about the outcome. If you lose, you'll have won, so to speak.'

'Stop trying to be clever, Aaron.' Ella drained her glass and sat down in the chair opposite him.

Aaron sighed heavily. 'We're going round in circles,' he said, 'I guess the best thing to do is to stop talking about it.

What would you like to do, should we go out to eat, call out for something and stay home – or go to bed?'

Ella stood up. 'Tomorrow's a big day and I'm tired, I guess I'll go home, Aaron.' She saw the expression on his face and softened. 'Look, thanks anyway, it's just that I'm not very good company tonight.'

'I should be able to help you more,' Aaron said.

'Why should you, it's my problem? We all have them as you have so competently illustrated.' She picked up her jacket from the back of the chair and walked to the door.

'When Alice died you were great. You literally saved me from falling into God knows what kind of morass and taking William with me. Yet now, when you need help, there seems little I can do but aggravate the situation.' He put his hands on her shoulders to restrain her from leaving. She stood poised for flight, anxious to go it seemed to Aaron. He let out a sigh, released her and turned away. 'Look, Ella, forget everything that's happened, everything we've said to one another. The truth is I love you and, God help me, I want to spend the rest of my life with you. I don't know whether it's relevant to you right now but that's how I feel.'

'I love you too, I always have ever since I was a kid. Given that fact, don't think I'm not tempted to abandon everything and simply let you take over.' Her expression was defiant but Aaron could see she was close to tears.

'Then why don't you?' Aaron asked.

Ella seemed to consider the question for sometime. 'Because I have to play this final scene alone and give it all I've got. I can't simply give up without a fight.'

'And whether you win or lose, do we have a future together?' Aaron's expression was grim.

Ella met his eye. 'I don't know, Aaron, it depends . . .'

'Depends on what?'

'On whether you'll still have me.' There were no tears now, just an awesome sadness which completely silenced Aaron. There seemed nothing more to be said.

Without another word Ella turned and hurried out of the door. She was already at the elevator before Aaron reached her. She looked at once forlorn, vulnerable and absurdly young and all his instincts were to grab her, drag her back into his apartment and hold her tight all night, to ward off the demons which seemed to be invading her head. Somehow, though, it was not possible. Pride and hurt held them apart, so that they simply gazed at one another helplessly, as the elevator carried her away.

CHAPTER FIFTY

NEW YORK
1st August 1986

Joseph Meyer was clearly enjoying himself. All three women were aware of it and in different ways resented it. Ella was so jumpy that Joseph's almost frivolous attitude to the morning's meeting had her at screaming pitch. Margot, ever the professional, wanted him to cut the small talk and get down to business, and Stephanie, always uncomfortable in his presence these days, simply wanted to be back in her apartment with Tim and Matthew.

After coffee and the exchange of pleasantries which seemed to last for ever, Joseph opened his briefcase and drew out what Stephanie and Ella immediately recognized as being their proposals. He laid them, side by side, in front of him. 'As you can imagine,' he said, 'I have studied these proposals very carefully.' The silence and concentration in the room was awesome. 'Stephanie's bid is a little higher than yours,' he said to Ella. Ella's heart hit the floor, 'but she is not proposing to buy the Meyer Group outright – she is suggesting the slow withdrawal of my interest, over a five-year period. Her reasons for making the proposal are very sound from her own point of view, though I'm not at all sure they are from mine. I'm an old man, I may not be here in five years.'

He turned to Stephanie, who was already planning how she was going to break it to Tim that she had failed. 'Ella is prepared to pay me almost immediately for the acquisition of the group, subject only to verification of the projected figures for the current year. However, her offer is less than yours.' Hope flared in Stephanie. 'Over the question of staff and their future, you have both been extremely woolly so far as reassurances are concerned. I have no doubt that this is because you are not prepared to commit yourself to maintaining my staffing levels and this worries me, because this is one of the main requirements of the sale. There are two reasons for this. Firstly and most importantly, I want to protect those staff that have been loyal to me, but also I want to protect the structure of the group. If you are committed to my staff, then you will be committed to running Meyer as the hotel group it is today. Without that commitment, for all I know you could turn the hotels into ball-bearing factories, thus destroying everything I've built.' Ella shifted uneasily in her seat. She had known that this was the primary weakness in her particular bid. From the sums on which she had worked, it was clear that a degree of decimation of the group structure was necessary in order to shore up the weaknesses in her existing business.

'Then there is the question of Matthew. Predictably, Ella has been far more generous in what she's prepared to do for the boy than his own mother.' He shot Stephanie a none-too-friendly look. 'Against this, of course, I have to temper the fact that while Stephanie's attitude to her son may seem ungenerous compared with Ella's, this may not reflect an accurate picture of the future. In Ella's case, she is entering into a contractual agreement and knowing her as I do, I am confident she will honour that agreement to the letter when Matthew comes of age, if involvement with Meyer is what he wants. However, I have to balance this against the fact that while Stephanie may not be offering him so much at this stage, it is because she wishes to protect him from me and what I stand for. Because the boy is her son, if he shows a very real interest in the business once he has reached maturity, there will be a tendency for Stephanie to be more generous than the terms of her proposed contract would suggest. Indeed, he would be the natural successor to her position as head of Meyer, whereas, Ella, it would not be unreasonable for you to consider your own son as a more appropriate heir.'

There was a lengthy pause during which Stephanie and Ella exchanged a look – it was neither hostile nor competitive, but sympathetic. God, thought Stephanie, I don't know whether we're more terrified of succeeding or failing. The silence persisted for so long that Margot intervened. 'So, Mr Meyer, put us out of our misery. What have you decided to do?'

'Nothing at the moment,' said Joseph.

'You mean you're going to offer it on the open market, after all?' The three women stared at him with ill-disguised hostility.

'No, let me explain,' he said. 'You two are not the only ones to have done your homework in the last few months. I have been looking very thoroughly at both your businesses. Stephanie's is well run, highly profitable and has a great deal to commend it. It is, however, small. Yours, Ella, is far more impressive in terms of size, but while the New York operation runs like clockwork, the UK business is still in its infancy and Houston is clearly a disaster.' It had been ridiculous, Ella thought, to imagine for one moment that a man of Joseph Meyer's stature would not have investigated the extent of her problems in Houston. So that was the end, Stephanie had won. He could not possibly wish to sell out to someone whose financial credibility was in doubt. He was continuing to speak but her mind was reeling away – the thought of bankruptcy and the collapse of her business, suffocating her sensibilities. '... and so,' Joseph was saying, 'bearing in mind that my primary concern is for the future of the Meyer Group, I think it would be sensible to ask you to consider a joint purchase.'

Stephanie and Ella stared at one another in shocked silence, both trying desperately to judge how the other would react. Not removing her gaze from Stephanie's face, Ella said, 'That's ridiculous, it's out of the question.'

'Why?' said Joseph, 'I don't see that at all. Your partnership in Fulham proved highly successful. Now, as well as having established a very satisfactory business relationship, you are also linked by the marriage of your children. Indeed, I'm told there is a grandchild on the way. I'm sure it will have been pointed out to you by Margot — and indeed, it must be obvious to you, yourselves — that you each have qualities which the other lacks. It seems to me to be a perfect arrangement.'

Ella turned to face him. 'You seem to have conveniently forgotten the Centre des Arts. The only reason Meyer became involved in that was because I pulled out. Our relationship may be stable, but its hardly close.' She glanced embarrassed at Stephanie, but pressed on determinedly, 'Indeed, it's not been without its problems one way and another. Maybe, just maybe, it would be worth considering our handling another project together, but when I suggested the idea to Stephanie last year, she was dead against it. Even so, an individual project would be far more appropriate than our permanently joining forces in a business sense, which is what I assume you're suggesting.'

'Obviously it would be the neatest and cleanest way to put together a bid,' said Joseph. 'Since the Meyer Group is so much bigger than either of you, it would seem sensible to pool your resources and operate as one business.' he glanced at Stephanie. 'What do you think?'

'I agree with everything Ella says. We've worked hard to establish our own businesses and our own corporate identity. If either of us had wanted a partner, we would have taken one years ago.'

'I think you're both being very short-sighted,' Margot said, harshly. 'For the reasons I have always wanted you two to work together, putting in a joint bid for Meyer has to make sense, in fact it's the obvious answer.'

'For you, maybe,' said Ella.

'What's that supposed to mean?' Margot said, warningly.

An awkward silence followed, broken at last by Joseph. 'I have to admit I had not expected this kind of reaction to my proposal,' he said, 'in fact I'm disappointed. It seems to me that I'm bending over backwards to help you two and you're not even prepared to meet me half-way. If you don't want the opportunity of a joint bid, fair enough, we'll go public on the sale next week, but I have to say I find your attitude quite extraordinary.'

Stephanie and Ella glanced at one another. 'Am I right in saying,' said Stephanie, 'that you will not consider either of our individual bids, even if we reworked them?'

'That's right,' said Joseph. 'Before this meeting, indeed before I had even received your proposals, I had already decided that neither of you were substantial enough to cope with the Meyer Group.'

'Then why didn't you tell us?' Ella asked.

'Because I wanted to see the nature of your proposals, to see how serious you were. Clearly you have both put a great deal of work and thought into the proposed acquisition which is why I'm prepared to entertain the idea of a joint venture.'

'Well,' said Ella. She glanced at Stephanie and was rewarded by a slight nod. 'I guess we'd better take a look at it. How long are you giving us?'

'Until ten o'clock tomorrow morning,' said Joseph.

'That's ridiculous,' burst out Stephanie.

'We can't do it by then,' said Ella.

'You have to,' said Joseph, 'I'm not prepared to delay any longer, besides which, you've done all the spade work, you know exactly what's involved, it's simply a question of reworking the figures to reflect your slightly different approach as partners. Margot will help you, I'm sure.,

'Yes, of course I will,' said Margot, 'and I must say I think it's an inspired idea.' Stephanie mumbled something incomprehensible under her breath.

'Good,' said Joseph, standing up, 'that's settled then. This room is at your disposal, of course, plus any office facilities you may require. We'll meet here at ten o'clock tomorrow morning.' He smiled, clearly pleased with himself and by the chaos he had created. Ella and Stephanie watched him depart, with undisguised anger.

'I'll order some more coffee,' said Margot. Stephanie and Ella ignored her.

'It's ludicrous,' Ella burst out, 'the whole idea is crazy. Why do *you* want the Meyer Group, Stephanie?'

'To protect my franchise.'

'Precisely. You don't want to head up the whole group for its own sake any more than I do, do you?'

'Not particularly,' Stephanie admitted. 'Five years ago possibly, but today – well I don't know, my priorities have changed somewhat.'

'And I'm in exactly the same position,' said Ella. She saw Margot watching her carefully. Part of the agreement between them had been Ella's undertaking never to disclose to anyone Margot's stockholding in her corporation; she was riding close to the wind. 'As you heard from Joseph himself,' she said carefully, 'I've got trouble, big trouble in Houston. The only reason I want the Meyer Group is because some careful asset-stripping will solve my Houston problem. Jesus, Stephanie, I'm not the kind of partner you want. My business is in a mess right now, my heart isn't in the project as a whole and we have the fiasco of the Centre des Arts still lurking in the shadows to haunt us.'

'Don't worry about that,' said Stephanie, 'Fulham more than cancelled out the Centre des Arts.'

'Alright, if not Centre des Arts, then what about Tim? How do you feel about working, with me, given all the circumstances of the past.'

'Do we have to discuss this in front of Margot?' Stephanie asked, uncomfortably.

Ella shot Margot a look of undisguised loathing. 'Well, she's clearly clinging here like a leech until we've decided what we're doing, so I suppose we have to.'

'I'm not at all worried about Tim affecting our relationship,' said Stephanie. Her expression was unreadable and her words final. Ella realized she'd gone a little too far: it was clearly not a subject Stephanie was prepared to discuss.

The coffee arrived and the three women sat in an explosive silence as it was poured. After the waiter had gone, Margot took charge. 'Joseph is absolutely right when he says you're being given the opportunity of a lifetime. What you have both achieved, to date, is very commendable but it's in a different league from the Meyer Group. Your potential for growth and prosperity by heading up such an organization, is phenomenal and it is frankly a gift from the Gods to be given the opportunity to put in a bid which will be compared to no one else's. Joseph wants you both to have his group. For various reasons he admires you both and he also sees you as the most likely candidates for honouring a commitment to Matthew, which clearly has to be of major concern to him. Given your individual circumstances, I don't really see how you have any grounds for not taking him up on his offer.'

'That's the trouble,' Ella burst out, 'that's what I've been trying to say all along. We're not doing this because we want to, we're doing it because we don't really have any choice.'

'I simply don't believe you have no interest in running Meyer,' said Margot. 'You've always been ambitious, as have you, Stephanie.'

'People change,' Stephanie said.

'Maybe, but not to this extent. Still, I suppose I can't force you.'

Stephanie stood up and wandered over to the window. 'I think we're going to have to go ahead with it, Ella,' she said, at last.

'I agree. It just makes me so mad.'

The three women spent the rest of the day pouring over the figures, and as each new schedule was agreed, it was retyped by a girl they had brought into the conference room for the day. At four o'clock, Margot suddenly said she had an important appointment she must not miss and excused herself. Left alone, Stephanie and Ella ordered fresh coffee and continued working, though now it was simply a question of tidying up the loose ends. Shortly before six, Stephanie said, 'Why don't we take a break? There's only these few figures left to type now. We could take a shower and may be have some dinner together. What do you say?'

Ella, bone-weary and dispirited, was about to refuse when suddenly she realized the suggestion had appeal. 'I'd like that,' she said.

'You can shower in our suite if you wish.'

'No thanks,' said Ella, thinking of Tim. 'I'll go back to my apartment for a change of clothes. Shall we meet in the bar at what, about seven-thirty?'

Several times during the day, Tessa from Houston had tried to contact Ella but she had refused all calls as they worked on the figures. On arriving home at her apartment, she found several messages from Tessa on the answerphone asking her to ring and a message on her hall table from Jackie saying that Tessa needed to contact her urgently. She went to lift up the phone and then hesitated. Whatever it was, it could wait, for undoubtedly it would be bad news. The ever-increasing cash flow problems of Houston were starting to wear her down, and she knew that if she was to make any sense in front of Joseph Meyer tomorrow, she needed to keep her confidence intact. Whatever Tessa's news, it was likely to have the reverse effect.

Ella showered and then collapsed on her bed in a bath towel, still wet. She had promised to telephone Aaron with news as to how the meeting had gone. She dialled his number to be rewarded by his answerphone telling her that he would be working late at the hospital that night. For a moment she toyed with the idea of ringing the hospital and then dismissed it. Her news could wait. She remembered his story of the previous evening and felt humbled by it. Instead she lay back on the pillows, her eyes closed.

Weary and drained as she was, it was tempting to leave the phone when it began ringing – it was probably Tessa again. 'Take the damn call, can't you?' Ella shouted to the answerphone and then she realized that she had not re-set it after listening to her messages. She sat up in bed and reached for the phone. The sudden thought that perhaps it was Aaron made her snatch it up quickly before the caller could ring off.

'Ella?'

'Yes,' she said.

'Ella, it's Laurie.'

'Oh, hi, Laurie.' She could not keep the disappointment from her voice.

'Jesus, you sure know how to make a fella feel wonderful. Am I the very last person in the world you ever want to hear from again, or just the second-to-last?'

'I'm sorry, it's been a rough day,' she said.

'I'm sorry, too, Baby, that's why I'm ringing really. I was wondering if I could help.'

'Help!' said Ella. 'Help in what way?'

'I'm coming to that,' said Laurie. 'I heard you were back in town, so I thought I'd call to see if there was anything I could do, and, well, I have this idea and I . . . I guess I thought you might be interested.'

He sounded better, Ella realized. She knew she should be pleased for him but all she wanted him to do was to get off the telephone and give her a few minutes of much needed peace, before meeting Stephanie. 'What idea?' she asked.

'Before I tell you about it, tell me how are things going with Lexington Kovac?' Ella told him briefly. 'So, tomorrow's a kind of make or break?' Laurie said.

'I guess so,' said Ella.

'Well, let's hope it's make, but if it's break, how about coming into partnership with me?'

Ella laughed aloud, a brittle, tired sound. 'Laurie, you need me like you need a hole in the head. If this deal doesn't work out and Lexington Kovac fails, I'll have nothing more than the clothes I stand up in. Besides which, I know nothing about the restaurant business, you know that.'

'I couldn't agree with you more. It's Uncle Laurie who knows about the restaurant business right? Why should I need a partner to tell me what I already know? Besides, it's not cash I'm after, it's expertise.'

'I don't understand you,' said Ella, irritably, 'you're talking in riddles.'

'Let me spell it out for you,' said Laurie, 'I need a partner who knows about real estate.'

'Real estate?' Ella said, 'you mean you're expanding Café Colette again? But it's only a few months ago you were in trouble.'

'No, I'm not expanding Café Colette. The restaurants I

still have are back in profit and running well. This is a new idea and if you can spare me five minutes, I'll tell you about it.'

'Go on,' said Ella.

'A while back, I had the chance of a lease on a little property in Greenwich Village, just a few blocks from where Colette and I opened the first restaurant. It was a snip – the guy was in trouble and needed out, and I found myself acquiring the lease over a bottle of wine one night, more because I felt sorry for him than for any other reason. It was the drink that got me into it, to be honest – since Colette died I have been drinking way too much.'

'So?' said Ella.

'So, I took over the property and it sat there unoccupied and probably would still be today but for your visit back in March.'

'My visit, I don't understand?' said Ella.

'After we'd had lunch that day and you'd pointed out what a shit I'd been over the Lexington Kovac stock, it kind of made me look at my life and I realized I've done a lot of things I shouldn't be too proud of. I cheated on Colette, I cheated on you, I built my business on the back of my wife's talent and never really gave her recognition for it until it was too late. I also saw myself that day through your eyes. You were shocked by what had happened to me, at the sight of me, how I looked, how I behaved. You won't deny it, will you?'

'No,' said Ella, quietly.

'I realized, I guess, I was heading for being nothing more than a no-good bum. So I decided I needed to achieve something for myself and I had this idea . . . a vegetarian restaurant, Le Jardin Colette I've called it.'

'Vegetarian,' said Ella, 'but that goes against everything the Café Colettes are all about.'

'That's just it,' said Laurie, his voice bubbling over with enthusiasm, 'it doesn't. The Café Colettes are all about French cuisine at its best; we use butter and creamy rich sauces, all the things everyone loves and shouldn't eat.

Vegetarian food by contrast has a reputation for being good for you, but hardly, well, kind of spoiling. At Le Jardin Colette we serve rich, creamy sauces. We make every dish something special, luxurious if you like, if you can apply such a word to food.'

Ella began to see what he was getting at. 'It sounds a good idea,' she said, 'but I don't see what it's got to do with me.'

'I used the lease I acquired to set up the first restaurant. Le Jardin Colette has been running for two months now and it's a runaway success. I've reached an age when I don't really want the hassle of opening new restaurants with all the management and organization that involves, so I've signed up a deal with a marketing guy, to franchise the business. He reckons we can take the idea right across America, from coast to coast. He's confident that he can market the concept, find the staff, all that kind of thing but as we both recognize, the key to a successful restaurant is location. He doesn't have any real estate experience and he's the first to admit it and I, frankly, haven't the time. I thought, well, the three of us could form a new business and split it three ways. Your contribution would be invaluable. It would be a partnership, like old times.' There was a lengthy silence. 'Well, not quite like old times, that's not what I meant, Ella, honest.'

Ella smiled. 'I believe you, you old rogue, though why I should, I can't imagine. It sounds a great idea, Laurie, it really does, but right now I can't think of anything but Lexington Kovac, you must see that.'

'I know that,' said Laurie. 'I may not be the brightest guy on earth but I know my timing is lousy. I just want you to know that there's something to fall back on.'

'You're not creating this job for me, to make up for selling the stock?' Ella asked, suspiciously.

'Come on, when has Laurie Merman ever been a philanthropist?'

'Never,' Ella admitted.

'There you go then. Now you go back to work, like a good girl. Just remember to call me, when you've had time to think about it.'

Ella replaced the receiver, thoughtfully. It *was* a good idea, there was no denying it, but it was not for her, at least not at the moment. Still, it was great to hear Laurie happy and enthusiastic again and above all, it was good to feel valued again in a commercial sense. The last few months of trying to keep her business together had taken its toll. To talk to somebody who wasn't an angry creditor or a discontented bank was a positive novelty.

Stephanie and Ella enjoyed a pleasant dinner. Over coffee, it was Stephanie who raised the question of Tim. 'I'm sorry I cut you short this morning when you mentioned Tim,' she said to Ella, 'only I was damned if I was going to discuss it in front of Margot – it's none of her business.'

'I'm sorry, too,' said Ella, 'it was tactless of me. I guess I just wanted to say how pleased I am that you two are back together again, and that I'd never do anything, *anything* to jeopardise your marriage, even assuming I could, which I doubt.'

'I appreciate your saying that,' said Stephanie, 'and I know it's true.'

'If we are to be working together,' said Ella, 'inevitably the combination of business and the children will throw us all together a great deal. It might be reassuring for you to know that there is someone who I care about very deeply who maybe, just maybe, I'll marry one day, if he'll still have me.'

'Really, that's terrific!' said Stephanie, with genuine warmth. 'Is he English or American?'

'American,' said Ella, 'I've known him all my life. He's a doctor, a gynaecologist. He lives right here in New York. His name's Aaron Connors.'

'So, what's stopping you marrying him?' Stephanie asked.

'Oh, pressure of work and my commitments away from New York.'

'If you love him, don't let that stand in your way,' Stephanie said. 'I learnt that lesson the hard way.'

'I know you're right,' said Ella, 'but it's easier said than done.'

Stephanie smiled, full of understanding. 'Don't I know it. I spent all those years running away from personal commitments and I can't tell you how deeply I regret it now.'

'I'll remember what you said,' said Ella.

'And I'll remember what *you* said,' said Stephanie, 'I don't reckon our working together will be so bad, do you?' Ella shook her head and smiled. 'Look,' said Stephanie, 'you're exhausted – me too. Why don't we meet in the conference room at eight-thirty tomorrow and finish off the figures then?'

'I give in,' said Ella, 'it sounds a wonderful idea.'

Back in her apartment, Ella found that Tessa had rung yet again but it was too late now to return the call. Too tired even to undress and take off her make-up, she collapsed on her bed and in seconds was asleep.

CHAPTER FIFTY-ONE

NEW YORK
2nd August 1986

It had been a long wait. Stephanie and Ella had met at eight-thirty sharp and by five-to-nine, the remaining figures had been typed and checked. Now there was nothing to do but sit around. Both were becoming increasingly nervous, and running hand in glove with this emotion was a feeling of apprehension. The more they had looked at the project, the more they were aware of the enormity of the task which lay ahead of them.

Joseph arrived at exactly ten o'clock. He still had the air of someone well pleased with himself but he stopped short at the sight of Stephanie and Ella seated at the conference table. 'You both look exhausted,' he said, clearly dismayed.

'We are,' said Ella.

The minutes ticked by but there was still no sign of Margot. 'It's not like her to be late,' said Stephanie. 'In fact I don't think I've ever known her not be on time in all the years I've dealt with Joshkers'.'

'Nor me,' said Ella.

'We'll give her until a quarter past,' said Joseph. 'If she's not here by then, we'll start without her.'

They were all reluctant to begin the meeting without Margot Haigh for in a way she represented the catalyst. However, as the time neared the half hour, Joseph, with a sigh of irritation, came and sat down at the table. 'We'll begin,' he said. 'Can I see your proposal?'

Stephanie handed it to him and the two women sat in

silence, watching him as he leafed through the pages: a nod here, a grunt there, a frown and a pencil note elsewhere. It occurred to Ella how strange the circumstances were: here was Joseph, contemplating the disposal of his life's work, without the aid of any adviser, even a lawyer. Yet it was typical of the man and perhaps reasonable enough – after all what adviser would be able to tell Joseph Meyer anything he didn't know himself.

The door suddenly burst open and Margot swept in. She was dressed in black as usual, but there was a difference about her. Her cheeks, normally pale, were flushed and her eyes sparkled. Compared with the weariness of the other two women, she seemed full of vitality. 'I'm so sorry I'm late,' she said, 'but I'm afraid it was absolutely unavoidable. Where have you got to?'

'I'm just looking over the proposal,' said Joseph. 'We waited as long as we could, but without even a call from you, we had no idea whether you were going to bother to turn up or not.'

'I've been sitting in traffic for the last quarter-of-an-hour,' said Margot, 'but I left the bank late and there was a reason for that. Before you go any further with this meeting, I have something to tell you. A number of things, in fact.' So arresting was her sudden appearance that nobody dreamed of arguing with her. She sat down at the far end of the table so she could see them all as she spoke. 'I have just come from Joshkers', where I handed in my resignation – it's that which made me late.' A general gasp went round the table. She looked directly at Joseph. 'My reason for doing so is that I would like to put in a counter-bid to Stephanie and Ella's. My backer is Ahfaad Rochlieu, who you know well, Mr Meyer.'

'I'm sorry, I'm probably reacting a little slowly,' said Joseph, 'you're saying that you and Ahfaad wish to buy the Meyer Group?'

'That's right,' said Margot. 'We're prepared to offer you fifteen million dollars more than the price Stephanie and Ella are suggesting and we are willing to pay the offer price in full, immediately, with no retention. We are also prepared to give ten-year contracts to all of your key personnel, in all areas of the Meyer operation. In addition, so far as Matthew Irvine is concerned, we will gift him an immediate ten per cent stockholding in the group, which will give him a major stake. Thereafter, on 1st January, 2015, we will give him first option to purchase the remaining stock at a substantial discount.'

Stephanie and Ella were so flabbergasted that they were entirely speechless. Joseph, however, rallied immediately. 'I think you may have been a little hasty in terminating your relationship with Joshkers',' he said, coldly. 'Aren't you forgetting the original terms of my proposal? At our meeting in Geneva, I made it plain that I would entertain a bid from either Stephanie or Ella but that if neither of them could come up with a satisfactory bid then I would be offering the group to the open market. A bid from yourself and Ahfaad, however attractive, does not fall within the conditions I laid down at that original meeting.'

'Of course not,' said Margot, 'but to proceed with their offer is no longer possible.' She indicated towards Stephanie and Ella's proposal. 'As for offering the group to the open market, it will require at least another year's lead time to enable potential purchasers to do the same work that Stephanie and Ella have undertaken in recent months. Besides which, even if you did offer the group to the market, I very much doubt if you'd get a better price than the one we're offering.'

'Wait a moment,' said Stephanie. 'What do you mean that our offer's *no longer possible*? It's a legitimate offer, carefully worked out and one with which you entirely agreed up until four o'clock yesterday afternoon.'

Margot swung her chair to face Ella. There was no visible sign of emotion on her face. 'But that was before I knew Jack Smith's bank, Sunbelt Industrial, had gone down.'

'Gone down!' said Ella. 'What are you saying?'

'Sunbelt Industrial Bank went out of business at eleven o'clock yesterday morning. It simply ran out of money and closed the doors. I'm afraid Jack Smith shot himself.'

Ella stared at her and for a moment the picture of amiable, happy-go-lucky Jack came into her mind. It was incomprehensible to imagine him taking his own life. 'Are you sure?' she said, in a faint voice.

'Quite sure,' said Margot. 'What this means, of course, is that you've lost everything so far as Houston is concerned and I'm afraid that one of my last tasks for Joshkers Bank was to advise the Board to foreclose on all your business activities, both here and in the UK. I'm sorry, Ella, it's unfortunate, but the days of Lexington Kovac are over.'

'Unfortunate!' Ella burst out. 'What the hell are you talking about, Margot? You're just telling me my life is in ruins and it's unfortunate! Why didn't I know about Jack Smith?'

'I don't know,' said Margot. 'When I arrived here this morning, I quite expected to find that you had withdrawn your offer. When it was clear you had not, it was equally clear that you had no idea what had happened in Houston. I would have thought your office would have advised you.'

Ella let out a sigh. The endless calls from Tessa yesterday, which she had ignored, were clearly trying to tell her what was going on. Still, what did it matter? She rallied as best she could. 'I did receive a number of calls from my office yesterday, but in view of the importance of getting these figures together for Joseph, I didn't take them. None the less, I would have thought Joshkers must have had some prior knowledge of what was going to happen.'

'Not precisely,' said Margot. 'As you know, we've been extremely concerned about the Houston position for some time, but we had no idea that Jack was sailing so close to the wind. The first we heard about the problem was his clerk ringing to tell us that Jack was lying across his desk in a pool of blood.'

The brutality of the words made Ella flinch. No one spoke and Ella, to her surprise, felt nothing, nothing at all. 'In the circumstances,' Margot continued after a stunned silence, 'the offer from Stephanie and Ella is clearly invalid. As you rightly assessed yesterday, Mr Meyer, Stephanie has not a large enough operation to tackle the acquisition of the Meyer Group alone, and in any event, I sense in both Ella and Stephanie a lack of commitment. They were both making a bid because they felt they had no alternative but to do so. However, in my view, their offer does not stem from a burning ambition to take Meyer Hotels to dizzy heights.'

'When you go for the jugular, you really make a first class job of it, don't you?' said Stephanie, bitterly.

Margot ignored her. 'You don't know me very well,' she continued, addressing Joseph exclusively, 'but you do know Ahfaad. You've dealt with him over many years and you know him to be an excellent hotelier, loved by his staff and slavishly admired by his guests. He has the kind of experience of big hotels lacking in both Stephanie and Ella, in particular. I should tell you that Ahfaad and I were married last week, in Cannes. However, we are both well into our forties, I'm past child-bearing age and if necessary I am very happy to give you a certificate of confirmation from my doctor to this effect. We would like to run Meyer Hotels for the next twenty-five years, but at that stage we'll be more than happy to hand over to your grandson, since we have no children of our own. In fact, both of us would find it extremely appropriate to do so – it seems only right. The discount we are proposing will be generous, and we will be guided by you on this. If Matthew is going to be the kind of man capable of running the Meyer group, it is important that it is not handed to him on a plate. For this reason, Ahfaad and I think he should have to raise the money himself, albeit that the discount should make finding a backer none too difficult. The combination of Matthew's parentage and upbringing should ensure he is the kind of young man you would wish to see heading your business empire. However, if he does turn out very differently from how we all imagine, he will have neither the desire nor the ability to find the necessary funding.'

Joseph let out a sigh and turned to Ella. 'Have you any reason to suppose what Margot has just told us about Houston is untrue?' he asked.

'Of course I haven't been misleading you ...' Margot began.

Joseph raised a hand to silence her. 'Have you, Ella?' he repeated. Ella shook her head miserably. 'And if this fellow, Jack Smith, has run out of cash, can you see any way you can save even some part of your business?'

Ella raised her eyes and met his. The formidable tycoon had vanished – she was looking into the eyes of a caring, anxious elderly man, clearly willing to help her in any way. But there was no way anyone could help her now, it was too late. 'It was the one thing that hadn't occurred to me,' said Ella. 'I was fighting a hard battle down in Houston but I was just about keeping my head above water and I naturally assumed Jack was doing the same. I've been pouring the income from New York and the UK into the Houston operation to keep it afloat. This means, of course, the corporate profits for the last couple of years are pretty much wiped out, and all of the Fulham money has been lost too, but at least I've been coping with the situation. However, the bank going ... I just hadn't reckoned on that. Poor Jack.'

'Yes,' said Joseph, 'and what an idiot thing to do. Losing the people you love may be worth dying for, but losing money ...' He smiled, suddenly. 'Remember that, Ella Kovac. What we're doing here is just playing a game of Monopoly on a grand scale. Today hasn't been a good day for you, but in the scheme of things, in the context of your life and happiness, it's nothing.'

Hot tears gathered at the corners of Ella's eyes. 'I-I think I'll leave now if you'll excuse me.' She stood up hesitantly.

'Yes, of course,' said Joseph.

'Would you like me to come with you?' said Stephanie.

Ella shook her head. 'I'll call you later.'

Stephanie waited until the door was closed and then she turned to Joseph. 'Are you going to accept Margot's offer?'

For the first time in many years, Joseph looked at her without any trace of hostility. 'What would you do in my position, Stephanie?' he asked.

When at last she replied, her voice was entirely without

rancour. 'I'd go with Margot, of course. It's giving you everything you want, with the minimum of hassle. In fact it's an offer you simply cannot refuse.'

'I'm rather afraid you're right,' said Joseph.

CHAPTER FIFTY-TWO

NEW YORK
2nd August 1986

At the sound of Ella's voice, Tessa burst into tears. 'Oh Ella, have you heard?'

'Yes, I've heard and I wish I'd been able to get back to you yesterday. You must have had one hell of a day.'

'I didn't know what to do. What's going to happen now?'

'I'm sorry but I guess you'd better start looking for another job. The bank may employ you for a week or two but no more I would have thought.'

There was a stunned silence. 'Lexington Kovac's really finished then, is it?' Tessa said.

'I'm afraid so. The sooner you find another job, the better.'

'Maybe I'll get married,' said Tessa, brightening a little. 'My boyfriend's always pressing me to do so.'

'There you go, then,' said Ella, with a laugh, 'sounds like your future's all planned.'

'But what about you, Ella?'

'I'll get by. Tessa, I'm surprised I haven't heard from Michael Gresham. I need to get hold of him – is he in the office?'

'No,' said Tessa, 'that was the other problem I had yesterday. He's been out of town for several days on some court case down in Mexico. He hates Mexico, everything always takes so long.' She spoke fondly and Ella found herself wondering whether Tessa was yet another notch on Michael's belt. It wouldn't surprise her. 'I finally contacted him late last night. When he heard the news, he said he'd catch the next plane out. He should be in Houston by now and he said to tell you he'd call you as soon as he got here.'

'Fine,' said Ella. 'I expect I'll be down with you tomorrow. Can you hold on to things until I come? Don't worry about your salary, I'll find that from somewhere.'

'Oh I'm not worried about that,' said Tessa, 'just about you.'

'You can stop worrying about me, I'm fine.' Ella replaced the receiver and then, taking a deep breath, she buzzed down to the office below. For some reason, she couldn't face sitting at her familiar desk, not now it was no longer hers. With Joshkers foreclosing, all the properties would be on the market in a matter of days, even the apartment, too. It still seemed so unreal. Jessie answered the phone. 'Could you and Jackie come upstairs, I need to talk to you,' Ella said. When they arrived, it was obvious that Jessie had been crying and Jackie was close to tears. 'So you know?' said Ella, gently.

'We had a call from the bank this morning, they're sending someone over this afternoon to collect the books,' said Jackie.

'Shit, they don't waste much time, do they?' said Ella. 'Look I'm really sorry but as I told Tessa just now, you two had better start looking for jobs.'

Jessie shook her head. 'No way, not yet. We've already talked about it. We'll stay on with you until the place is sold over our heads. There'll be a stack of work to do, I guess.'

'You can't do that,' said Ella, 'I'm not sure I'll be able to pay you.'

'We've talked about that, too,' said Jessie. 'We'll not accept so much as a dime from you, Ella Kovac. You've looked after us all this time and from now we're going to look after you. Right Jackie?'

'Yes,' said Jackie. 'You can't change our minds, Ella, it's what's going to happen. You're going to need some moral support during the next few weeks.'

For the first time since leaving the conference room, Ella felt close to tears, but she was not going to let them see her break down. 'It's very kind of you,' she said, 'I accept, but you must take off all the time you need to look around for other work.'

'OK,' they agreed.

'Will you have *anything* left?' Jackie asked, tentatively.

Ella thought for a moment. The house in London was in the corporation's name, as was all the UK property. Suddenly she remembered the little farmhouse in Provence, which now had been transferred to Greg and Belinda's name, with the understanding that the whole family could use it. She smiled. 'I have an interest in a tumbled-down farmhouse in the South of France,' she said, 'and I have the clothes I stand up in. That means I'm not much worse off than when I first arrived in New York.' As she spoke the words, she felt a strange sort of exhilaration. She dismissed the feeling: feelings could not be trusted at the moment.

Jessie started to cry, quietly. 'When I think of all you've done, all you've achieved. I remember the first day I came here. Greg was just a baby and . . .'

'Stop it,' said Ella, gently. 'We did our best, Jess, we can't do more than that.'

'You're so calm,' said Jackie.

'I expect it's because it hasn't hit me yet,' Ella looked around helplessly. 'There must be an awful lot to do but I don't know what. I've experienced most of what the commercial world can throw at me, but not going bust – that's a new one.'

'We'll be here,' said Jessie, 'we'll do everything. Now, you should have a rest, you look exhausted, and I guess the bank officials will want to see you this afternoon.,

'I guess they will.'

Both women stood up to go. 'It's all my fault, isn't it? It's just what you said might happen?' Jackie let out a sob.

'No,' said Ella wearily, 'and I'm not prepared to discuss the apportionment of blame. It just happened – a series of circumstances conspired against us. No one's wholly to blame, neither you nor me.'

She sat for some long time, her mind a complete blank, before the idea of ringing Aaron came to her. She knew she should be trying to contact Michael Gresham, but a strange lethargy seemed to have overcome her. When she dialled Aaron's number, she was not surprised when his answerphone cut in and informed her that he was at the hospital. She hesitated and then rang the hospital number. A voice, sounding not quite like her own, informed a series of receptionists and nurses that it was urgently necessary that she speak to Dr Connors. She probably sounded like a woman in labour, she thought, faintly amused. When at last she was actually asked the question as to whether she was a patient, she said she was – it seemed easier. Moments later, she was put through. His voice sounded clipped and efficient. 'Dr Connors, how may I help you?'

'Aaron, it's Ella.'

'Ella! I've been thinking so much about you. How did it go yesterday?'

'It's gone,' said Ella.

'What's gone, you mean you lost the deal?'

'Lost the whole business,' said Ella. 'The Houston bank collapsed and the proprietor, Jack Smith, shot himself. It's the end of the business, Aaron.'

'Jesus! Look, hold it a minute, I can't leave the hospital right now but I'll just transfer you to another room where we can talk in peace.' Minutes later, after a series of clicks, she heard his voice again; it was warmer, more intimate now. 'I'm so very sorry, Darling,' he said. 'How are you feeling, where are you?'

'I'm at home. I'm alright, I guess.'

'What happened, tell me all about it.' Sparing no details, Ella related the events of the last twenty-four hours. 'The bitch!' Aaron burst out, when she had finished.

'Not really,' said Ella, wearily, 'all's fair in love, war and real estate.'

'Hell no, Ella. She and Ahfaad must have been planning this thing for some time.'

'I doubt it,' said Ella, 'I get the feeling it was a snap decision. Up until yesterday, I genuinely believe she was going to back Stephanie and me. OK, she had a vested interest – the shares in my business – but I think she was figuring on going through with it. It was only the collapse of Sunbelt that made her look around for another alternative – that, coupled with Stephanie and my genuine apprehension and lack of enthusiasm about a joint purchase.'

'None the less, I can't believe she couldn't see what was going to happen in Houston. There she was, forcing you to bid for a deal that you didn't even want, her only motive being personal greed, and all that while you could have been using your energies to look for ways of solving the problems in Houston. You've wasted so much time preparing for this bid.'

'I honestly don't think any amount of time I'd have spent on Houston could have saved it. If I'd chosen to realize my properties, the amount of money I'd have lost would have forced the bank to foreclose on me anyway. Hanging around living hand to mouth and waiting for things to improve would have still ended with me being brought down by Jack and his problems.'

'Poor guy,' said Aaron. 'Look, I appreciate that people behave in a kind of strange way in commerce, that the borderline between behaving ethically and like a shit is knife-edged, I just feel that Margot shouldn't get away with it. As you say, she had a vested interest in your business, Ella, one which you didn't even know about. She used that to manipulate you into a position to bid for Meyer when you didn't even want to do so. Then she outbids you by playing her trump card, just when the shit hits the fan so far as you're concerned. I don't reckon Joshkers Bank would like the way she's gone on too much.' There was a long silence. 'Ella! Are you still there?'

'Yes,' said Ella. 'Aaron, I think you may have hit on something. I don't know, maybe I'm clutching at straws.'

'What sort of something?' said Aaron.

'Well ...,' said Ella, slowly, 'Joshkers are going to lose millions of dollars with the collapse of Lexington Kovac. I can't begin to estimate how much – it depends what they realize from the sale of the various properties, but there's going to be a considerable deficiency. Undoubtedly it will be the biggest disaster in their year and there are going to be a lot of questions asked as to the validity of making such large loans available to me. It's going to look kind of odd, too, that up until just a few hours before the Houston bank crashed, Margot was in serious negotiation with me and Meyer, which would have involved her in authorising yet more enormous borrowings on my behalf, and there's her resignation.'

'Yes, yes,' said Aaron, impatiently, 'we know all that but I don't see where it's leading you.'

'It means this,' said Ella, 'she was prepared to allow borrowings to go ahead on a business which she knew was already seriously flawed.'

'Right,' said Aaron.

'And why did she do that?'

There was silence on the other end of the phone for a moment. 'Because – because she had a vested interest in your business,' said Aaron.

'Exactly,' said Ella, triumphantly. 'Surely she had a conflict of interests; her loyalty to the bank opposite her personal greed in wishing to see Lexington Kovac succeed. I'm not sure, but I have a feeling she may have committed a criminal offence.'

'Jesus!' said Aaron. 'In which case you've got her. You might be able to save the business yet.'

'Look, I'll call you back,' said Ella. 'I'll get on to Michael Gresham right away. He's the best person to advise me on this; they don't come much more slippery than Michael.'

Aaron gave a slightly hollow laugh. 'So you've led me to believe over the years.'

'Aaron, thanks.'

'Don't mention it. Look, I should be through here by late afternoon. Shall I come over?'

'Oh, yes please,' said Ella, without hesitation.

She sat for some moments gazing out of the window. From her vantage point on the sofa all she could see was the deep blue of the sky and the corner of the tower block next door. Suddenly, the sun edged round the concrete balustrade at the top of the building, sending a shaft of sunlight piercing through Ella's window, cutting her sitting room in half. The band of golden light seemed like a signal. She lifted the telephone and dialled Michael Gresham's number.

CHAPTER FIFTY-THREE

NEW YORK
2nd August 1986

Joseph followed Stephanie hesitantly into the apartment. Her invitation, so unexpected, made him suspicious and jumpy. At the same time it was irresistible. Without preamble or explanation, she had telephoned him ten minutes before and asked him if he would like to come and see his grandson.

Tim Irvine rose from a chair by the window and came across to shake his hand. He looked from one to the other – they were a charming couple. In different circumstances he knew he would enjoy their company, but clearly there was some sort of trade afoot and he knew he had to be wary. His very strongest emotions were involved, they must know that. Somehow he had to hold on to the fact that this was a business deal. He could not remember feeling more on edge and, yes, nervous. When had he last felt nervous? Thirty years ago, forty perhaps. After Treblinka nothing had really made him nervous again, until now.

Tim spoke. 'Look, Mr Meyer, I know what you're thinking. You imagine we have asked you here to try and change your mind about your decision to sell to Margot Haigh. Even worse, you think we're going to use your grandson to try and twist your arm. I just want to say here and now, before you even see him, that nothing could be further from the truth.' The words were music to Joseph's ears, but still he could not believe them. He blinked, nervously, unable to speak.

Stephanie reached out and laid a hand on his arm. 'What Tim says is true, Joseph. Now you're selling out, it's changed everything. I didn't want you to force Matthew into a mould, to play kingmaker, but you've done the deal and Matthew's a very lucky little boy. He has the opportunity, if he so wishes, to head up the Meyer Group one day, but the decision will be his. So long as you can assure us that you will never apply any pressure on him to take up the Meyer crown, we'd like you to be as much part of his life as you wish.'

Joseph stared from one to the other, there was no doubting their sincerity. 'Thank you,' he murmured.

'Would you like to see him now? He's playing with his toys in the bedroom.' Joseph again tried to speak but nothing happened. Stephanie took his arm and led him to the adjoining room. The child was sitting on the floor. 'I'll leave you two alone,' said Stephanie and giving Joseph a gentle push she retreated and shut the door.

For a moment he felt a sense of panic. It was a long time since he'd had anything to do with small children and this one was little more than a baby. Curiosity got the better of him. 'Hello,' he said, and walking over to the child he sat down beside him on the floor. The sight of Matthew made him gasp aloud. In looks, at first glance, he was entirely Alex's son. The same wild, dark curls, the big blue eyes, the high cheekbones and the startling bone structure already apparent beneath the baby chubbiness. There, however, the similarity ended. The eyes that regarded him now, with interest, were kind and joyful, they twinkled and shone. Joseph smiled and was rewarded by a smile back, a dimple appearing on one cheek. For the first time in his life Joseph admitted to himself what he had always known, that he had never liked his son. Loved him, yes, loved him to distraction, but even as a tiny child, Alex had been discontented and difficult, a scratchy, awkward character who seemed unable to give love due to his own self-absorption. There was no way of knowing why this was so; it might have been the nature with which he was born or the fact that he lost his mother so young. Either way it was obvious that Matthew was very different from his father, very different indeed.

When Stephanie came to join them, twenty minutes later,

they were building bricks – at least Joseph was building them and Matthew was knocking them down, squealing with delight. They were laughing and obviously having a wonderful time. The only difference between them was that Joseph's face was wet with tears.

When Nanny bore away an excited Matthew for his supper, Joseph joined Tim and Stephanie in the sitting room. 'Would you like some tea, coffee or something stronger?' Tim asked.

'Something stronger,' said Joseph.

They opened a bottle of wine and Tim poured three glasses. 'What shall we drink to, the future of the Meyer Group?'

'No,' said Joseph, 'I think we should drink to Matthew Irvine.' He stressed the surname, a point not lost on Stephanie or Tim.

'Matthew Irvine,' they chorused.

'I could insist on some sort of protection for your franchise, as part of the deal,' Joseph said, after a pause.

'No,' said Stephanie, 'Margot has made her offer and it's a fair one – it's the best possible solution for you, for Meyer and for Matthew. I'll just have to take my chances as they come. After all, I've known her a long time and I can't see that she's going to gain a lot by putting me out of business, not if she wants to continue to smell like a rose in the banking world.'

'That's true,' said Joseph, doubtfully.

'Forget it, honestly,' said Stephanie, 'the subject's closed – we didn't ask you here to talk about business.'

'You'll be returning to the UK soon?' Joseph asked.

'Tomorrow, we thought. I have so much catching up to do since I've spent so long on this proposal in the last few months. I want to have everything looking good before Margot's henchmen start poking around.' She smiled, reassuringly at Joseph. 'I hope you will come and see us whenever you feel like it. Where are you planning to be based?'

'In Geneva, I thought. I like it. New York . . . it's no place for an old man. I'll buy myself somewhere on the Lake, so I guess we'll be neighbours, almost.'

Tim and Stephanie smiled. His remark was not intended as any kind of joke. In the world in which Joseph Meyer moved, an hour and a half's flight by private jet qualified as neighbourliness. 'Well, as Stephanie says, you're welcome at Wickham any time,' said Tim, 'any time at all. We'll do the very best we can with Matthew, you know that. As far as I'm concerned, he is my son and I will bring him up as such, in that he will have no less of my time, attention and love than my other children. However, Stephanie and I are both adamant we should not deny him the knowledge of his true parentage, particularly in view of his inheritance. As soon as he is able to grasp a few simple facts, we will explain to him about you and Alex, so that the knowledge becomes part of his growing up, not a sudden shock in later life.'

'You have a very special man there, Stephanie,' Joseph said. What he thought, but did not say, was the difficulty he had in understanding why she had favoured his son in preference to Tim Irvine.

'I know,' said Stephanie.

'You know, the first time I met you, Stephanie,' said Joseph, 'I admired you very much, both for your business acumen and as a woman. I still do and I do so regret the intervening years of difficulty between us.'

'We both did and said things which we should not have done,' said Stephanie, 'but we can put it all behind us now. We have a future and let's look to that future and enjoy it.'

'And you *really* want me to be part of it?' Joseph was close to tears again.

'On one condition,' said Tim, with a grin, 'that when you teach Matthew to play Monopoly, you'll tell him it's as good to invest in houses as it is in hotels.'

Joseph threw back his head and roared with laughter. 'I'll do that,' he said, 'I'll certainly do that.'

After Joseph had left, Stephanie collapsed on the sofa like a rag doll. 'You look ghastly,' said Tim, 'it's bed for you.'

'I couldn't go to bed, I feel too restless. Poor Ella, here's me worrying about the franchise but at least I still have a business, at any rate for the time being. Ella's back to where she started, with nothing.'

'Hardly that,' said Tim, 'she has her experience and her reputation. Ella's a fighter, she'll be alright.'

'I hope so,' said Stephanie, 'she said she'd call me, I hope she will.'

'About the franchise,' said Tim, 'is the picture you paint as bad as all that?'

'I don't know,' said Stephanie, 'all I do know is that Margot is hard as old nails and ruthless as they come and she certainly demonstrated that today. Since she's teamed up with Ahfaad, they're bound to have at their disposal a highly trained, highly skilled bank of senior hotel management. If I was Margot, there's no way I'd hive off the European operation as a franchise. Joseph only did it because he was light on the ground in a management sense. No, if I was Margot, I'd boot me out and run Europe myself.'

'Can she do that?' Tim asked.

'Yes, she can. She has to buy me out, of course, and the price will have to be a fair one based on market value, but I don't have the option to refuse, it's all in the contract.'

'Still,' said Tim, 'you'll have a great deal of capital available, you could start again.'

Stephanie smiled. 'Starting again would involve all the same kind of hassle and pressure as when Millie and Belinda were small, and I don't want that. I have an established business which runs smoothly. It's enough to keep me occupied and interested, it's also familiar and, of course, it's highly profitable. Running my business as it is today is really the extent of my ambitions now, and after the years of struggle, I think I've earned it. Still, it's in the lap of the Gods. We'll just have to see how things go with Margot and Ahfaad.'

'You could have taken Joseph up on his offer.'

Stephanie shook her head, vehemently. 'No way. He'd already shaken hands with Margot and it wasn't fair to put him in a position of having to renegotiate. More important, though, it would have undermined our gesture concerning

Matthew. He would never have been quite sure whether we'd used Matthew as the bait or not.'

'That's true,' said Tim. 'You know, your attitude to Joseph has changed a great deal recently.'

Stephanie slipped an arm round his shoulders. 'I've mellowed, and do you want to know why?'

'Yes, please,' said Tim.

'Because I'm very much in love with my husband and that puts a lot of things into perspective.'

'So it's all definitely my fault again,' Tim said.

'I'm afraid so.'

Their arms were about one another, they were kissing in earnest now. Tim began unbuttoning the front of Stephanie's blouse. The phone rang. 'Damn,' he murmured, 'let's leave it.'

'I can't,' said Stephanie, 'I can never leave phones, I always think it may be something vital.'

'Leave it just this once.'

'No.' She kissed him again and disentangled herself. 'Hello,' she said.

'Stephanie, it's Ella.'

'Ella!' Stephanie caught her breath. 'Ella, how are you? You must feel ghastly.'

'No, I feel fine. Actually I'm ringing because I need us to meet, it's important, something's come up.'

'What sort of thing?'

'I'll tell you when we meet. Can you make it here at my apartment in say, half an hour?'

The thought of crossing town at the end of such an exhausting and emotional day held no appeal for Stephanie but there was no question of her refusing. 'Of course I'll be there,' said Stephanie.

'Good,' said Ella. 'I should perhaps warn you that so will Margot.'

'Margot! Jesus, why?'

'All will be revealed in half an hour,' said Ella. 'See you.' The phone went dead.

CHAPTER FIFTY-FOUR

NEW YORK
2nd August 1986

The door of Ella's apartment was opened by the most handsome man Stephanie had ever encountered in her whole life: his tall, florid good-looks were quite breath-taking, as was the infectious grin and twinkling blue eyes. 'Lady Bonham, I presume,' he said, 'come along in.'

'Are you Aaron?' Stephanie asked, full of curiosity.

He laughed. 'No. My name's Michael Gresham, I'm Ella's lawyer.' Perhaps I could acquire some legal problem in the States, Stephanie wondered, briefly.

Ella stood up as they came into the room. 'Thanks for coming, Stephanie, come and sit down. You've met Michael.'

'I certainly have,' said Stephanie, 'you are a dark horse.'

'He's just my lawyer,' said Ella, primly, but a smile played on her lips.

'More's the pity,' said Michael, sagely.

'This is all very mysterious,' said Stephanie, 'what's going on?'

'We only have about twelve minutes before Margot comes, assuming she's not going to make a habit of being late,' said Ella. 'I want you to listen very carefully to what I have to say, because I want to make sure I'm doing what you want before we proceed with this thing.'

'What thing?' said Stephanie.

The air was electric with excitement when Margot arrived, spot on time. Michael ushered her in and Ella made the introductions. Margot, Stephanie noticed, was not at all at ease. It was the fact that they had a lawyer present which presumably unnerved her, but she put on a good performance of remaining cool. 'I'm sorry if I sound callous,' she said, 'but I really am very busy today. Joseph's only agreed to go ahead with the deal on the condition that I have the whole thing wound up by the end of the month.'

'This won't take long,' said Ella. 'I began doing a little thinking after our meeting and it occurred to me that Joshkers Bank would not be too pleased with you if they knew the true background to this particular scenario.'

'I don't know what you mean,' said Margot.

'I think you do,' said Ella. 'You have not behaved at all ethically so far as the relationship between Lexington Kovac and Joshkers is concerned. You allowed Joshkers to continue supporting me, despite the declining situation in Houston, and you even were prepared to go as far as to recommend the bank make available to me the enormous sums of money involved for the acquisition of my part of the Meyer deal.'

'That is correct,' said Margot. 'I happen to have had a lot of faith in you, Ella. I still do. It was extremely bad luck that Jack Smith's bank went under. But for that I think you would have . . .'

'Cut the crap,' said Ella. 'Looking at it from Joshkers' point of view. I don't think there's any doubt that the way you behaved represents a serious conflict of interest. If Joshkers had known, or indeed were informed now, that you are a twenty-five per cent stockholder in Lexington Kovac, I think they would be very angry indeed about the amount of money that you have let them lose as a result of the collapse of my business.'

'It's all part of the daily banking routine,' said Margot, 'you win some, you lose some.'

'I'm sorry to disagree with you,' said Michael Gresham, 'but without doubt what you have committed is a criminal offence. You know as well as I do that had you admitted your stockholding in Lexington Kovac to the bank at the time you acquired the stock, they would have either asked you to resign or at the very least, moved the account to a different member of the bank. In addition, the idea that Ella should bid for Meyer was clearly ridiculous in the circumstances. It was obvious, and indeed it has been obvious for some time, that Sunbelt Industrial Bank was vulnerable. If I knew that, you must have been even more aware of it, since Joshkers own stock in the bank, and, I understand, made them a substantial loan. From Joshkers' point of view, the whole thing stinks, not least of which because of your hasty resignation. This is not an idle threat, Miss Haigh, I have spent some hours studying the position – Joshkers could throw the book at you for what's happened, and if they ever learn that it is not Laurie Merman but Margot Haigh who in fact holds that stock in Lexington Kovac, I haven't any doubt that they will.'

Margot took a deep breath. 'So, what do you want?' She looked directly at Ella. 'I suppose you're hoping that Ahfaad will put sufficient money into your business to stop it going under. He doesn't have that sort of money to spare, Ella. I should make that point clear before you continue in this ridiculous daydream.'

'No, that's not what I want,' said Ella.

'Oh!' Margot looked surprised.

'I will make sure that your stockholding in Lexington Kovac will never become public knowledge provided that you renew Stephanie's franchise on exactly the same terms as currently, except in fairness to you, from now on, the fee she pays will be index-linked. The fresh contract will run for a ten year period as from today's date and thereafter be subject to renewal. Let me make myself quite clear on what I mean by that: you will have no right to cancel the franchise now or at any time in the future. The franchise goes on for as long as Stephanie wishes. After ten years, it will be assessed at market value by an independent third party and Stephanie can either continue under the new terms or ask to be bought out.'

There was silence in the room. 'Is that it?' said Margot.

'That's it.'

'I don't understand. Assuming your lawyer friend here is right — and I'm certainly not admitting that he is — why aren't you trying to help your own business. Why help Stephanie?'

'Because Stephanie's business is worth saving,' said Ella, 'mine isn't. Because Stephanie's commitment to her business is still intact, again mine isn't. The heart went out of my ambition the day I found out that you were a stockholder in Lexington Kovac. If we did some sort of deal now to save my business, I know you'd insist on being a part of my future. There's no way you would release the stock to me, the business would never really be mine again and I'd resent every last dollar I made for you. I've worked damned hard, I'm tired. I began with nothing, OK, I've got nothing again, I can cope with that, besides which . . .' Laurie Merman's offer came back into her mind as it had several times that day. Le Jardin Colette . . . it was a good idea, no, a *great* idea. She forced her mind back to Margot. 'You see, Margot, the real problem is I simply can't cope with ever having to deal with you again.'

'You sound very bitter and I can understand that,' said Margot, 'but it wasn't my fault, you know. I didn't create the oil crisis, any more than I was responsible for Jack Smith's bank going under.'

'I know that,' said Ella, 'I'm not looking to you as a scapegoat, but you asked me the question and I'm giving you the answer. Stephanie's business is a business worth saving. I doubt you'll be prepared to admit it but neither Stephanie nor I held out much hope of you renewing her franchise unless, shall we say, you have some incentive to do so.'

'I'll need guarantees.'

'So will we,' said Michael, 'which is why I've drawn up two heads of agreement. One is for you to sign, Miss Haigh, guaranteeing the terms and renewal of the European franchise of Meyer Hotels. The other is for you to sign, Ella, guaranteeing silence on the question of the stockholding.'

'Laurie might talk,' said Margot.

'Rubbish,' said Ella, 'Laurie's a strange man but his word is his bond. You know that or you wouldn't have entered into the agreement with him in the first place.'

Margot turned to Stephanie. 'And what do you think of all this? Do you have the same aversion to working for me as Ella clearly does?'

'I won't be working for you,' said Stephanie, 'or even with you. Franchisees work for themselves. I'll be accounting to you with my annual fee and commission on sales and I can assure you that you will be well pleased with the results I achieve. As to the gesture Ella has made, I think it's magnificent and very generous, not only to me but to you.'

'How do you mean?' said Margot.

'You and your banking subsidiary have ruined Ella. You can wrap it up and say you weren't responsible for the oil crisis, but as Michael has indicated, it seems likely that you have known of the imminent collapse of Sunbelt Industrial for some time. Revenge is sweet, and if I was Ella I would be very tempted to drop you in the shit with Joshkers Bank and take great pleasure in watching you being hauled through the courts. Not only is it what I'd be tempted to do, I suspect, so would you, given the same circumstances.'

For once Margot said nothing.

The documents signed, Michael rose, placed them carefully in his briefcase and disappeared into the kitchen, returning moments later with a bottle of champagne and four glasses. 'Some may say that this is hardly the moment for a celebration. We're sitting amongst the ruins of Ella's business and none of you should lose sight of that. On the other hand, all three of you are facing a new beginning in your different ways and being an Irishman, I believe the only way to seal any agreement is with a drink.' He popped the cork, poured the champagne and handed round the glasses. 'Well, Ladies,' he said, 'I would like you to raise your glasses to the deal you've just struck. May it bring you all happiness and fulfilment.'

Just for a moment, despite everything that had happened, the three women smiled at one another, a sense of camaraderie briefly returned. 'To the deal,' they chorused.

EPILOGUE

NEW YORK
2nd August 1986

She stood in the centre of the room in a short, stripey nightshirt, her hair still damp from the shower, a riot of curls around her face which was devoid of all make-up. She looked sixteen, if that. Aaron closed the apartment door quietly and leaned back against it. He studied her in silence and she returned his stare steadily. 'It must be thirty years since I hauled you out of that pile of screaming kids.'

'It is,' said Ella, 'almost to the day.'

'I could do it again, rescue you from a battle zone, set you on your feet and brush you down. This time, though, I'd want guarantees.'

'What kind of guarantees?'

'That if you came under my protection, that's where you'd stay, that we'd plan our future together, not independently, and that you'd become my wife. What do you say?'

Ella looked at him doubtfully. 'I'd still have to work, I'd go insane at home all day. You see I've been offered this deal . . .'

Aaron threw back his head and laughed aloud. 'You're incorrigible — nothing changes. Tell me, will "this deal" take you out of town?'

'Sometimes,' Ella answered.

'Out of North America?'

'No.'

'Certain?' said Aaron. Ella nodded her head. 'In which case, I think you'd better let me marry you. Don't you?'

'Yes . . . yes, please,' said Ella breathlessly as she ran across the room into his arms.